DRAGONCROWN

DRAGONCROWN

Emery Garriott

DRAGONCROWN

iUniverse books may be ordered through booksellers or by contacting:

iUniverse
1663 Liberty Drive
Bloomington, IN 47403
www.iuniverse.com
1-800-Authors (1-800-288-4677)

Because of the dynamic nature of the Internet, any web addresses or links contained in
this book may have changed since publication and may no longer be valid. The views
expressed in this work are solely those of the author and do not necessarily reflect the
views of the publisher, and the publisher hereby disclaims any responsibility for them.

Any people depicted in stock imagery provided by Thinkstock are models,
and such images are being used for illustrative purposes only.
Certain stock imagery © Thinkstock.

ISBN: 978-1-4917-5543-3 (sc)
ISBN: 978-1-4917-5544-0 (hc)
ISBN: 978-1-4917-5542-6 (e)

Library of Congress Control Number: 2014922189

Print information available on the last page.

iUniverse rev. date: 05/19/2015

BOOK I

THE ROD OF COERCION

CHAPTER 1

INTO THE DRAGON'S MOUTH

The highest Green Dragon in the sky that morning saw the sun first. She was the first to speak. From her throat poured a note so low as to be inaudible. It rose in pitch and volume slowly, mournfully, until the sound of it resonated out and down over the entire city.

The first to reply was another Green flying just west of the city over the ocean. The howl of that Dragon climbing its rueful scale added a shudder within the first as she felt the pain of her Sister Dragon's cry. Down below at the docks, a Blue began its rumbling so sonorously and intensely that the water quivered far out into the harbor. Drops spattered the air, making a patrolling Merman instinctively dive for the depths. Beside that one Blue (bound by unbreakable cables to its Dragontailer ship), more Blue Dragons (equally bound) joined the chorus.

All the Dragons - the Greens in the sky, all those on the ground, the Blacks in the Travel Plazas, the Whites in the granaries, and finally within the coin kilns deep beneath the towers of the palace called Blaze, the Red Dragons - all joined with their voices of woe. Because the seventy-seven

Dragons of Isseltrent stayed enthralled to Seldric the Dragonlord through the ancient and unassailable Dragoncrown, every morning, the Dragons mourned their slavery to the Dragonlord. Every morning for centuries and countless generations the Dragon's Lament had awakened the people of Isseltrent.

Jonathon the jeweler awoke to the mournful howling of the Dragon's Lament. He usually hid beneath his covers during the frightful chorus, but that day something was different. Something in the howls or behind the howls shook his bones and jerked him right up in bed as if he had been yanked by a noose. Even though his Warming Blanket slid off the bed with the jerk, his wife, Arlen, lying beside him, snored on. She was far too tired from caring for their seven children to be wakened by a mere seventy-seven Dragons all howling together. The little smile on her plump face was something Jonathon seldom saw while she was awake. In the daytime, she was far too busy with the chores and problems attendant in caring for their children to bother with a relaxed smile.

Jonathon bent to kiss Arlen's cheek but was stopped by a thump out in front of their cottage that rattled the bedroom window. There was a strange thrashing of the bushes, and his pet lark fluttered and chattered about in his cage. Jonathon watched in awe as the ancient oak outside the window majestically rose into the air. The rising was accompanied by the squeaking, groaning and popping of the tree's roots protesting as they were pulled from the ground. The oak tilted slightly and flew with a swish of leaves to land with a splintering thud behind their cottage.

Jonathon felt himself rise as the bed and the whole room lifted briefly just before the roof above him gave way. With a shattering report, one corner slowly lifted up and away. Beams burst. Ceiling plaster crumbled and rained down upon him. One large slab smacked him squarely on his upturned forehead.

Arlen woke with a start. She glanced up, took a look at Jonathon, and yelled, "The children!" She leapt from the bed and made for the children's rooms.

The ceiling gaped between two huge hands that gripped it. They dug into the hard plaster like it was mush. The whole ceiling of the bedroom folded upon itself upward into the morning haze, exposing a huge angry face with wild bloodshot eyes that pinned Jonathon to his bed. Through flabby, snarling lips inside a great hedge of a beard came a voice that sounded like a cross between a bear's growl and a cow passing wind. "Hey, you little rat, gimme my money!"

The Giant who had abruptly unroofed Jonathon's house was none other than Molgannard Fey, the meanest criminal in Isseltrent. And Jonathon owed him money. A lot of money. A whole Glass Command to be exact, more money than Jonathon made in his jewelry shop in an entire year.

If the abrupt entrance and the sight of the Giant hadn't been enough to make Jonathon faint, Molgannard Fey's breath would have done the job. The pungency of sour wine mixed with bile from some poor soul's liver and mule grease slapped Jonathon in the face, making his head swim and his eyes water. Jonathon wondered how many casks of wine Molgannard Fey had guzzled that morning.

Jonathon was far behind on the interest the Giant demanded, but the jeweler's finances were stretched to the limit and at that moment he did not even have enough to pay one Moon's interest. He blurted out, "I don't have it!" before he could think better.

"I don't think you heard me," the Giant said. "Maybe your ears need to be a little closer to your brain." He grabbed Jonathon's head between his thumb and forefinger and began to squeeze. Tremendous pressure built up in Jonathon's head, and he heard things inside his skull cracking.

"No, no, please …" he blubbered. The crying didn't help. The pressure kept building. "I can get it tomorrow," he lied through his tears. At least his crying was true.

"Not good enough," the Giant stated and began to pull up as if to pop Jonathon's head right off.

With a squeal, Jonathon made a desperate grab to catch hold of Molgannard Fey's fingers and save his own neck. He barely caught onto the huge digits. With all his trembling strength, Jonathon just managed to keep his own ample weight from stretching his neck for a few frenzied moments. He felt his sweaty hands slipping. "Good Lord Tundudil, save me."

"You're going to need someone a lot stronger than a god to save you," the Giant snarled.

Jonathon knew Molgannard Fey needed but to give his hand a little twist, and Jonathon would be dead as a chicken dinner. He prayed the

Giant's greed would temper his revenge. "I can give you something special right now!"

The Giant turned the poor jeweler to look into his eyes.

"Yeah, what?" The Giant's breath was so disgusting Jonathon had to breathe deeply through his mouth to keep from throwing up. He didn't want any sudden jerks from the Giant's hand as he dodged Jonathon's vomit.

"Please, can you let me stand?" Jonathon's grip of the Giant's fingers was about to fail.

Molgannard Fey screwed up his lip, looking uglier yet, if that were possible. His nose was mashed to one side, dribbling snot in his anger. One ear was bulbous, and his face was chock full of lumpy scars. Jonathon gave him a quivering, hopeful smile.

"You little inconsequential wimp, what could you possibly have that would stop me from killing you?" He set Jonathon down next to his bed and let go of his head, much to Jonathon's relief. But he couldn't let Jonathon alone. He set the scratchy, rough palm of his hand atop Jonathon's balding scalp.

"Talk, wimp." The Giant increased the pressure enough that Jonathon knew he'd better not move even when he heard movement at the bedroom door.

He looked out the corners of his eyes and saw his twelve-year-old son Theodore gripping their ax tightly in his hands, with Arlen beside him brandishing the Moving Broom.

Jonathon gave a little shake of his head. Arlen restrained Theodore with one hand.

"Go help Judith," she said. Judith, their ten-year-old, would be keeping the other children safe. Jonathon could hear the baby crying and little Luella calling for her father. Theodore looked briefly at his mother. He apparently knew she meant what she said, because he turned and ran back toward the crying.

Molgannard Fey spat a half cup of slimy spittle at Arlen's feet, making her hop back a step. With a grin, he increased the pressure on Jonathon's head by a fifty weight, making Jonathon gurgle as his chin threatened to split his own breastbone.

"You've got to the count of ten to make me happy, or you're going to have to take your shoes off to eat. One … two …"

Jonathon's mind raced, and he looked around his room anxiously. He had only twenty-four Copper Orders, barely a tenth of the interest on the amount he owed the Giant. He needed something to placate the Giant long enough that he could come up with some kind of a plan.

"I've got a Replenishing Pitcher you could have if you give me just one more day."

"Huh? Let's see it." The Giant lifted his hand ever so subtly. Jonathon just stood there and shook.

"Well, go on." Molgannard Fey twitched his head at the white porcelain Replenishing Pitcher, letting Jonathon slide out from under his hand and run to the wash basin so he could pick it up.

Jonathon held it up for the Giant to admire. "Nothing but the best. See the gold filigree incantations on the sides? Turgold the Elder himself made this when he was court artisan to Dragonlord Gojorlingast. This is unmatched. Infinitely finer than the new crude ones they turn out by the boatload. Inlaid gilt, not paint. It has retained its properties for decades. See?" He held it up and turned it slightly. Jonathon was really sweating now, but at least he was alive as long as he could buy time. He heard the back door creak as Theodore and Judith snuck the children out to secrete them in the back shed.

Arlen's worried scowl softened a bit, apparently relieved the children were further away from the crazed Giant. Still, she stayed poised in the doorway, ready to swat Molgannard Fey with the Moving Broom.

"Hrumpf. What does it do?" Molgannard Fey growled.

Jonathon fished a Clay Suggestion out of the leather coin pouch he'd grabbed from the dresser top. Into the empty pitcher he dropped the Suggestion. As soon as the coin clinked onto the bottom of the Replenishing Pitcher, it filled with a gallon of clear water.

"Try it. It's fresh as dew," Jonathon said, handing him the pitcher.

The Giant snatched the pitcher and up-ended it.

"Pah!" he spat. "Water, and hardly a drop." With a flick of his wrist sent the expensive pitcher, the pride of Jonathon's household, shattering against the bedroom wall in a puff of tinkling shards. Jonathon gasped.

"Three, four, five…" The Giant's stretched his arm a bit so it was again over the jeweler like some teetering half-cut oak ready to fall on Jonathon's head.

Jonathon threw up his hands and waved, "Wait, wait! My warming rug." Cringing and grimacing, he motioned to the rug he stood upon. "Believe me, it's a treasure from the far hills of the Commonwealth of Dis, woven by thirty maids over three seasons to make its design peerless. It can warm a room the size of a banquet hall. Please?"

Molgannard Fey screwed up his lip and brought down his hand. Jonathon ducked and clutched his head as if his hands could save him from the falling tree. He felt the rug lift and slide, tossing him onto his back on the bare wooden floor. He opened his eyes to see the rug gathered into a peak, pulled up in the middle of the room by the Giant.

"It's cold as stone!" His head spun around at Jonathon so fast the jeweler had to dodge snot flying from the Giant's flattened nose.

"That's only temporary," Jonathon explained and pointed, "It's just that little spatter of plum brandy obscuring the inscription that interferes. It can be washed off in a trice."

"Six…Seven…," the Giant said, balling his hand into a boulder.

"A Bracelet of Potency!" Jonathon shouted, snatching the item from a pocket in his nightshirt. He was desperate, but he collected his wits when the Giant relaxed his hand and stopped counting. "It's delicate and unobtrusive, a silver armlet made in my shop." He held it up. "I believe it would fit on your finger." Jonathon had had plenty of time to assess the size of Molgannard Fey's hefty digits.

The split roof trembled with the sound of Molgannard Fey's laugh, sending a fresh shower of plaster pattering down around Jonathon. "You're not only a wimp. You're as limp as a noodle."

"Only sometimes," Jonathon said, looking aside briefly, sheepishly at Arlen who looked querulous but remained poised at the door.

When the realization of what Jonathon had said made it through the thick bone of Molgannard Fey's skull, he tightened his shaking fist again so his knuckles whitened with rage. "Are you trying to insult me? You little piece of dirt!"

"No, sir! Heaven forbid! This will just sustain your talents endlessly. That's all."

"Eight…nine." He raised his fist to splatter the jeweler.

"A Mirror Lock. My door. My door!" Jonathon screamed.

"A door?" said the Giant, puzzled.

"Yes, if it pleases you, my front door is a dedicated Mirror Lock, keyed to the reflection of its owner." He gestured toward the parlor at the entrance to his cottage. "A charm has been etched in the mirrors facing both surfaces of my door, conceived by the Court Poet of Dragonlord Hildriberin decades ago and laboriously tooled by Pixits in the bowels of Blaze," Jonathon rattled on, buying precious moments, racking his brain for yet another inducement to stay the Giant's fist. He sincerely hoped the next number Molgannard Fey shouted would be nine and a half and not ten.

"The front door?" the Giant asked, lifting his head out of the bedroom, peering around the front of the cottage, and shifting his bulk, which sent another tremor through the entire house.

"Not the door, Jonathon!" Arlen rasped, but Jonathon waved her silent, pleading with his eyes.

"Allow me to demonstrate, sir," Jonathon said, running through the parlor to the front. When he came to the door, the mirrored surface reflected his robed, fifty-year-old, portly frame. The sparse strands of his white hair were reminiscent of wispy cirrus clouds high in the sky on a bright summer day. His left eyebrow was lowered as if in worry, but anyone familiar with him and his hours using a jeweler's eye held in place by his tight left eyebrow would know different. Even in alarm the twinkle in his eye looked like the sparkle deep within a diamond. As soon as he looked squarely at his eyes in the mirror image, the door swung open to reveal a huge gnarly knot in a newly grown elm tree. No, on second thought, Jonathon realized, that was Molgannard Fey's kneecap.

The Giant bent over and ripped off the door, tearing away hunks of the beam it was attached to. He lifted it to his face and jumped as if he were frightened by his own horrible visage.

"Whoa!" he exclaimed. "Oh. It's a mirror. How does it work, wimp?"

"The Mirror Lock is dedicated to acknowledge all the members of my family by opening for their countenance alone. If this item would suit your needs, I will change its dedication to respond only to your ug... uh... uh... face." Jonathon smiled like a fool blinking sweat out of his eyes.

"Hmmm. I have a box I don't want my wolves looking in. I'll take it. Change the lock." He handed down the door. The weight of it made Jonathon stagger until he propped it up against the outer wall of his cottage.

Jonathon took out a Wooden Request and touched the surface of the mirror which absorbed the magical coin. Being careful to look directly into the mirror, Jonathon said, "The lower inscription cancels out the previous dedication." He read the lower verse etched in the glass: "Gluttonous Sun, Quaff the stars."

The Giant said, "That's it? Will it open for me now?"

"At your leisure, read the top verse aloud after activating it with a Copper Order," Jonathon replied. The top verse read: "Mistress Moon, Scatter your babes."

Molgannard Fey twitched his head toward his monstrous red Flying Carpet, with which the Giant had apparently flown to Jonathon's home that morning. The carpet had mercilessly crushed Jonathon's prized herb garden. The Giant nonchalantly tossed Jonathon's framed glass door onto the carpet where it thumped alarmingly on the dense brocade. Jonathon winced, imagining the mirror cracked and ruined with the Giant's careless abandon. For an instant, he felt his heart stop with the prospect of having to search for one more of his dwindling number of trinkets to dangle before the Giant. With a gasp, he put a hand to his breast but felt the steady beat return when he saw seamless clouds reflected in the mirror indicating it was, indeed, unbroken. Jonathon tensed again as Molgannard's wiggling sausage of a finger took aim at his face.

"You hear this, wimp. If you don't have my money by tomorrow when the lizards bleat, I'll use your head to knock your whole house to kindling. Then I'll to chew you up and spit out your bones to stomp into the dust. The rest of your family out in that shed, I'll take them home for breakfast."

When the huge finger stopped shaking in his face, Jonathon collapsed in a heap. The Giant climbed aboard his virtual acre of a carpet. At a word, it rose quickly into the air and sped off toward the center of Isseltrent.

From the ground, still limp as a boned fowl, Jonathon watched and wished he could hire whoever broke Molgannard Fey's nose to do his bargaining for him the next time he saw the Giant. Jonathon would need many Moons to repair and regrow his devastated herb garden. Of course, that was irrelevant since Jonathon couldn't possibly come up with two hundred Copper Orders' interest in one day. Tomorrow he would probably be part of that very garden.

Jonathon hadn't had time to get up off the ground when Arlen cried, "Jonathon?". Before he could reply, she yelled, "He's dead! The Giant killed my husband! AARHH!"

Jonathon sprang up. "My Sweet! I am alive."

She jumped back a step and grabbed her throat, apparently thinking Jonathon had risen from death to scold her. "Oh! I thought you were dead." She composed herself, thought a bit, and said, "You *are* going to be dead, because I'm going to kill you! Who was that? And how much do you owe him?"

"That was Molgannard Fey. My thankfully-restrained benefactor."

"I've never heard so much drivel. Restrained benefactor? Thank The Three he wasn't your angry benefactor," she sputtered in exasperation until her eyes lit up with a new astonishment. "Molgannard Fey? You're not talking about the Molgannard Fey? Not the money-stealing, animal-slaughtering, skin-splicing, bile-spewing son of Hell Molgannard Fey. Not *that* Molgannard Fey. Surely you're not telling me that you had dealings with the Molgannard Fey that terrorizes half the city by consuming the other half. Tell me he's not *that* Molgannard Fey. Please."

"Yes, Sweetheart, he's the one."

Arlen shook her head, her words quavering with an incredulous chortle of disbelief. "What is wrong with you? Restrained?" She wiggled her hand toward the roof, the door and the garden. "You call that restrained."

He held up a finger to designate his reasoning. "He did not crush me, nor did he tear off my head, although he had every right. I was tardy on our agreement."

"In the name of The Three, what in this world could have made you go to that maniac for money?"

Expenses, Jonathon thought. Dowries for his three daughters, now married and off with their own families. Then came the dozens of children they had adopted through the years, orphans or Royal Bastards, illegitimate children of the Dragonlord, thrown from the court. Someone had to provide for them.

He had no courage to answer before Arlen reiterated her first question, "And just how much do you owe the most evil person in the world?"

Jonathan sighed. "A Glass Command."

"A Glass Command!" she shrieked.

At this, Theodore ran all the way from the shed through the children's bedroom clutching the ax, ready to attack any foe no matter what the size. "I'm coming, Mother!" He skidded to a halt when he saw only his mother and father. Jonathon saw Judith peeking around at the back door jamb, holding back the twins. Luella called from the shed for her mother. A wail came from the baby.

Jonathon reached out to touch Arlen to calm her worries, but she balled her hand into a little fist and poked him in the arm.

He recoiled. "Oohh". She was surprisingly strong for her diminutive stature, probably from the decades of hard work caring for all those children.

Arlen glared at him with those pretty green eyes of hers. But he saw a flash of red in them, probably just a reflection of the red clouds in the east, he thought. "I told you your softness would get you in trouble!"she barked.

"You never told me that."

"Well, I thought it. And you should have known I was thinking it." Arlen's long brown hair undulated in waves as her head trembled with fury. In the daytime she twirled her hair into an efficient bun, but he preferred her freer nighttime hair, even in anger. "You're too generous, Jonathon!"

"Someone has to provide for the welfare of the unfortunates of this city. For lack of pity from the true believers in Isseltrent, you and I have assumed the burden. I am satisfied with our lot. I thought you were as well."

"I'm not talking about that! You're too obliging to your customers. They'd pay twice as much for your jewelry. Why don't you charge more?"

"My loyal customers are dedicated to quality. They stand by my ideal of perfection. You want me to abandon fairness just to match prices with those that raise them at every whim of the economy?"

She just raised her eyes to the heavens beseeching The Three for the thousandth time to grant her husband a particle of sense.

"You pay Bob way too much," she said, referring to his apprentice.

"Bob is a diamond in the slurry. His worth far exceeds his salary. You love him like one of ours, Darling. I'm amazed no other jeweler has snatched him from me."

"He told me they've tried," she admitted, "But he's loyal, and he admires you too much. All right, he deserves what he gets."

"His loyalty and admiration are worth more to me than a few Coppers."

She snorted. "And the Pixets? Why pay them so much?"

"You know Hili is the only one left and, besides, their pay is prearranged by Guild standards. My salaries must adhere to those guidelines."

"So, you're fettered by the standards? Aren't you Master Jeweler and Guild Steward? You're the one who makes those rules. Change them!"

Jonathon pursed his lips and shook his head, flustered. "Manipulating the guidelines for my own self-interest? I'd be no better than Molgannard Fey."

Arlen wasn't about to stop. "Well then, what about all the things you buy your daughters? They're married and have their dowries. You should be done with them. Just last Moon, you gave Laurel six cows. Six! Herkimer will be harvesting his flax in a few Moons. Let him buy his own cows. And Heather doesn't need a Lullaby Crib for little Jacobi. A mother shouldn't let a bed sing to her children. She should do it herself. I do, and there's nothing wrong with my children."

Jonathon just shrugged and looked down, sliding his foot back and forth over the polished oak floor. He knew where all the money went, a hundred Orders for the cows, twenty for the crib, home expenses by the hundreds for their many adopted children, not to mention all the dowries and apprentice fees for the ones who left home. Rent on his shop was an ongoing expense. When all his workers, except Hili and Bob Thumblefoot, had to be let off because Jonathon could no longer pay their wages, he insisted they be paid a Moon's salary each. That was another forty Copper Orders. It all added up, piece by precious piece, to a thousand Copper Orders. They were borrowed here and there from a dozen sources until that idiotic day when he got the idea to get one loan to pay them all back. When he looked for money to borrow, Molgannard Fey was the only one who would accommodate him, as long as he paid the Giant's outlandish interest. Jonathon knew of Molgannard Fey's reputation but rationalized he was just like a guildsman. He fantasized the Giant would treat him fairly, since Jonathon was so well known in the city.

He said, "I thought you agreed we should follow *The Transmigrant* in our everyday lives." As he referred to the holy book of Tundudil, Jonathon looked past her into the house at their well-used copy on the living room mantelpiece.

"Never mind that. We're not Querites, sacrificing our whole lives for the comfort of others because of some crazy interpretation of the scripture. We have to live ourselves to take care of our children." She bit off each word saying, "And, by the way, what gave you the idea of borrowing that much money without even telling me?"

"I didn't want to worry you"

"Worry me?" she said, incredulous. "So I'm not supposed to worry when you're dead?"

He shrugged again. "I guess I'm not very good at these things."

"Huh? That's for sure. Do you owe him all that money by tomorrow?".

"Two hundred Copper Orders."

"Oh. I see. So you don't have to pay him the moon, just a star out of the sky. Real good. And how are you going to do it, may I ask? Borrow more money?"

"I don't know, my Sweet," he said, hanging his head. "There's no possible way. I'm a dead man. Maybe it's for the best. I've made such a mess of things."

She kicked him in the shin, making him hop for a few moments. "Stop it! I don't want to hear that. I'm not having you killed. Go to the constables."

"I tried that, but the captain declared I received everything I deserved as just payment for dealing with Molgannard Fey."

"We pay taxes for that? Go to Rhazburn. He can handle Molgannard Fey."

"I'm not involving my son in trouble that's my own doing."

She stamped her foot and pointed her finger at him. "You go to Rhazburn. I don't want any of your excuses. Rhazburn will be glad to help you." She softened, pleading. "Jonathon. He's going to kill you. You'll be dead. Don't you understand? This is your last chance. If you don't raise the money, we'll all have to leave here and never come back or he'll squash you flat, and probably us too, for good measure. If you can't think of yourself, think of us. Jonathon, please. Talk to Rhazburn. He can help you." Her eyes flooded, tears streaking down her pleasantly-rounded cheeks.

"I will search him out, Honey, but who knows where he hides today? Between the library, his school, the pubs, his bustling hither and yon, it makes me dizzy."

"He's probably at Hell's Breach. Call Smurgen. He'll know."

"More fees? Our meager funds will be gutted by the clever Dwarf."

"So is that worse than what Molgannard Fey will do to you?"

Jonathon gulped. "You have a point."

Jonathon folded her in his arms and kissed the top of her head. "I heartily apologize for this, Dumpling. I'll consult the Dwarf. You're right. He'll know where to find Rhazburn, and Rhazburn can help me, I'm sure." His confidence was all in his words. He wished he had more of it in his heart.

Gently, she pushed him away, wiping her nose on the sleeve of her gown. "Well, get ready then. You'll need a good breakfast. Theodore?" She turned to her son who laid the ax beside the fractured wall and stood at attention, ready for orders. "Light the stove. Judith," she called into the house as she trundled off, "you take care of Luella and the baby." Arlen's orders receded into the house. "Carmella," she said, addressing one of the twins, "it's your turn to boil water. Persephone," the other twin, "cut the fruit." Jonathon knew her instructions would be obeyed. He loved her competence and efficiency.

He went into what was left of the bedroom to get ready. His lark was still twittering, either upset by the commotion or simply demanding his late breakfast. Trying to calm himself, he spent a few moments hissing ineptly through his teeth in a lame attempt to mimic the lark's tune. The lark's tune fascinated him. The bird was especially voluble since the breeding season was in full swing, and he caught glimpses, outside the window, of female larks he wooed fruitlessly. Jonathon was ashamed to keep the lark caged at this time of the year, but he liked the song too much to set him free. With an apologetic pat on the cage, he finally gave into the bird's whistles and sprinkled a handful of seeds through the bars of the cage. The lark pecked up the meal, oblivious to his incarceration, Jonathon hoped.

Caring for the bird was just one of his daily devotions to Tundudil. Finding joy in the care of others, whether a spouse, a child, a friend or a pet was a central tenet in the Faith of The Three. Jonathon tried not to dwell on the paradox of caring for a soul incarcerated in a cage. The cage itself showed disregard for the lark's needs. Could his love and nurturing make up for it? He wondered.

At least, Jonathon was still alive. That was something to be thankful to Tundudil for. He stepped up to the metal asymmetric triangle set in its alcove, took the steel beater, and from the inside, struck all three sides in progression. The left side represented Kris, the Daughter and the Beauty in all things. The lower side of the triangle was Ilsa, the Mother, the unconditional Love one feels when he recognizes that Beauty. Finally, the right side of the Triangle represented Tundudil, the Father, the Care one provides for all he loves, which (if one is devout) includes everything in the world.

"Tundudil." The triangle sang the Three Holy Notes and the name of the triune god also known as The Three. Every time Jonathon rang the Triangle of Faith and said a prayer to The Three, he regretted that the words in *The Transmigrant*, the original holy book of the Faith of The Three, were not always followed by the people of Thuringland. And even though no sane person would join The Querites, the Beholders, or the Choir, the major splinter sects that had developed over the centuries, he still admired their attempt at adherence to the true Faith.

Jonathon dressed quickly and left the bedroom with a little hop over a pile of fallen plaster to get into the dining room. Before he sat down, he did his daily duty. He took a Clay Suggestion from a small dish next to the Timefall and touched it to the Timefall Ball which absorbed the Suggestion. The Timefall Ball he then lifted to the top of the Timefall stand and let go. The Ball settled at Dawn Blessing, the start of the day. The Timefall Ball would slowly fall over the day, tiny Favor by Favor, a hundred Favors in each Blessing, through the seven Blessings of the day: Dawn, Breakfast, Work, Highday, Home, Dinner, and Dusk. The periods of the day were named Blessings because each day was a blessing from The Three, a blessing from The Three filled with their favors. He stood watching it for a whole Favor, just collecting his thoughts about what he must do to save himself and his family. It would not be easy, that was for sure. When he was satisfied he had the beginnings of a plan, he turned, walked to the table, and sat at the head in his favorite oak chair. Old and sturdy, its slick seat had molded itself over the years to the shape of his generous bottom, which was due to Arlen's good cooking.

Luella burst into the room and hopped on his lap, hugging him and whimpering. "Father, I'm scared!" She shivered histrionically and buried her head in his shirt.

"My Little Sweetheart, I wouldn't have you frightened for the world." He pulled her back slightly so he could look into her teary but pleasant eyes. "I'm so proud you stayed with Judith to help the baby. What a big girl you are."

She brightened and smiled, hugging his neck. "I love you, Father. I don't want any more Giants"

"If that Giant comes back here I'll run him off, so we never see him again." Jonathon laughed at the thought, chasing away Molgannard Fey. That was a good dream. A dream with a heroic, powerful Jonathon. Not the real Jonathon, debt ridden, nervous, confused. Young children needed good dreams.

He kissed Luella's forehead and set her down beside the table. "Go help your mother." She ran off, feeling important.

Hullering, the only one of the adopted children still at home that was a Royal Bastard, came to sit beside Jonathon. "Father, can I come with you to see Rhazburn? I want to see Hell's Breach."

Rhazburn, one of his many older brothers and a Royal Bastard like Hullering, was his hero. Hullering obviously felt he deserved a chance to come along.

"I'm awfully sorry, Hullering. I wish I could take you along. Alas, I must concentrate on my business and need time alone with Rhazburn. He may not necessarily be at Hell's Breach today. Besides, even I can't see him at Hell's Breach. No one but Poets are allowed there."

"When I'm a Poet," the eight-year-old said, "I'm going to close Hell's Breach forever." Jonathon smiled at his fantasy, as if that had not been tried a thousand times over the centuries.

Jonathon confided in the boy. "I wish I could close Hell's Breach. I fear for Rhazburn's life every day. And Garrith, too." Garrith was another of his adopted sons, another Poet, another target for the Demons at Hell's Breach.

Hullering bent in his chair, busying himself with his Sprite Slate, writing short poems. Every so often, he would groan, tell the Sprite Slate to erase the words and start over again.

Jonathon picked up a second Replenishing Pitcher and sighed. It was not nearly as beautiful as the one Molgannard had smashed, but it was useful enough and made water just as quickly. From a small pile of coins, he took a Clay Suggestion and dropped it into the pitcher. In a moment, the pitcher was filled with water which he poured into an ebony Vision Bowl. Upon the surface of the water in the bowl he floated a Wooden Request, saying, "Smurgen". When the request quickly dissolved, it was replaced by the face of a Gossip Dwarf. The floating face, bearded and craggy with age and concentration, looked up at Jonathon and said, "Good morning, Master Jeweler. What can I do for you?"

"Greetings, my dear Smurgen. Pressing matters insist I locate my son Rhazburn quickly. I would appreciate it if you could find him so I can contact him immediately. I have no time to rummage the city for him."

The Dwarf looked down past his beard as if he were consulting some notes. "Ah, yes. I see where he is." He looked up, studying Jonathon's face. "Fifty Wooden Requests."

Jonathon groaned. Fifty Wooden Requests was five times Smurgen's usual fee. His few Copper Orders could dribble away quickly while he tried to make more money. "An exorbitant price for a word so simple."

"My fee is higher for hostile jewelers."

"Fine, I'll pay it. I meant no offense, Smurgen." Jonathon took out a Copper Order, dropped it in a Money Changing Box to turn it into Wooden Requests and dumped fifty of them into the water.

From the Dwarf's image, concentric circles of ripples enlarged around the fingers of his hand as Smurgen reached into the water of his own Vision Bowl to extract the fee. After counting the coins twice, he looked again at the jeweler and said, "The Loremaster is at Hell's Breach. He leads the Day Poets today."

"I could have guessed that. You are a thief." He had guessed Rhazburn was at Hell's Breach, just as Arlen had said. He had just hoped he was wrong.

"I will take my leave, Master Jeweler. I have a lot more crimes to commit."

"Smurgen, a moment. I apologize for impugning your character. My mind is in a dither. I've just been threatened."

"By Molgannard Fey," the Dwarf finished his thought.

"Yes, but how did you... ? Of course, all knowledge is at your fingertips. Then you must be aware of the extent of my predicament."

"Master Jeweler, everyone knew how much trouble you were in but yourself."

"I need to consult Rhazburn. When will he be available?"

"Well, the door to Hell's Breach closed at dawn this morning. Once it's closed, the guards have strict orders to kill anyone who tries to force his way into Hell's Breach. I'd say your next opportunity to speak with Loremaster Rhazburn will be at Dusk Blessing tonight."

Jonathon groaned and moved around in his chair. "My problem can't wait the whole day, Smurgen. What do you suggest I do? I'll gladly pay any price for a solution."

"Hmmm. I'll give you this bit for free."

Jonathon perked up. Free advice from a Gossip Dwarf was unimaginable.

"Do you know the bracelets which calm the spirit of the wearer?".

"Yes, yes. I call them Armlets of Tranquility. We make a lot of them. They're very popular with the city folk."

"I suggest you make one and put it on," Smurgen said with a broad smile across his misshapen Dwarf face.

'Never ask advice from a Dwarf' was a saying he had heard since he was young. Shaking with frustration but too polite to swear, Jonathon poured the smart aleck Dwarf back into the pitcher. At least he didn't have to pay for the quip.

Before they all sat down to breakfast, everyone stood in reverent silence while Theodore, the eldest and only child privileged to use the glass beater, chimed the Triangle of The Three hanging over their table. The adults, along with Theodore, closed their eyes in meditation. Judith, holding baby Nathaniel, quietly paid homage to Heaven. Hullering took advantage of the lull by pinching Persephone who squealed, making Luella snicker and Carmella groan in disgust.

Arlen gave the children a sharp look, went to the kitchen and came back with her arms full. She set down a plate of bacon, a pitcher of milk, and warm apple tarts right in front of Jonathon. Theodore, the only child who understood all the implications of the morning's disturbance, gave Jonathon a furtive, worried glance but kept to himself. Judith, preoccupied with family matters, scolded Luella, who was spilling her milk. The twins bustled about helping serve everyone. The help allowed Arlen to relieve Judith and cuddle Nathaniel, nine Moons old and spoiled by all his older siblings.

Jonathon barely smelled the smoky fragrance of the bacon. No one appreciated one of Arlen's good meals more than Jonathon, but today he cogitated mutely on his predicament.

Arlen, who was spooning porridge into Nathaniel, shoveling every dribble and slobber back into his little pursed lips, broke into his thoughts. "Well, did you find out from the Dwarves where Rhazburn is?"

"Yes, my Sweet, I did. He leads the Day Poets at Hell's Breach today."

"Good for him. I feel a lot safer with Rhazburn there. No Demon will get past him into the world. Let them stay in Hell where they belong. We don't need the likes of that awful one in the Dead Lands anymore. I don't know why the Dragonlord doesn't just round the Demon and all his Zombies up and feed them to the Dragons."

Jonathon replied almost unconsciously, "According to Rhazburn, one could more easily fasten a rope around a cloud or put the wind in a cage." She knew as well as he that it was useless to think the Demon could be pried out of his Hellpit and eliminated. Demons could not die.

"Well, go talk with your son. Maybe for once you can take his advice."

"I admit that's a good idea, but the strategy escapes me. They wouldn't open the door to Hell's Breach for the Dragonlord himself once the day has started and the Chamber of Hell's Breach is sealed."

"He's your son, isn't he? They'll let you in. You have to see him today. If you wait until tonight, you can't possibly have enough time to pay back the Giant."

He nodded in silence and chewed his bacon without tasting it.

After breakfast, Jonathon went into the bedroom to pick a Charm for the day. He took advantage of the new skyward exposure, provided by Molgannard Fey, to evaluate the weather. A swath of orange in the east was all that tainted the cloudless sky. It would be another hot, dry spring day. As Arlen came in to clean up the mess, Jonathon picked through a small jewelry box and pinned a Charm of Coolness onto his favorite purple turban. Even with Molgannard Fey's threat hanging over his head, comfort was important to the jeweler. He had a Charm for every kind of weather. There were Charms of Basking, Dryness, and Coolness. This one was a tiny platinum icicle with highlights of diamond, which could be activated by a Clay Suggestion to keep him cool anywhere, even in the desert of the Dead Lands. Like the others, it was made in his shop, so it was, of course, perfect. He had wrought it himself, and Hili, his Pixelle, had engraved the poems of magic upon the diamonds with her tiny tools. The terrifying morning left him flushed with fear so he took out a Clay Suggestion and touched it to the Charm. After the Suggestion was absorbed by the tiny icicle, a pleasant coolness suffused Jonathon, body and soul.

He was interrupted by Arlen, with Nathaniel on her hip. She was arguing with their Moving Broom. "Do you call that clean?" she scolded, pointing to a small drift of dust and plaster in a corner of the bedroom. The old, worn broom hovered in the air before her, slowly sweeping circles as if it were embarrassed. "Go clean it up, and do it right this time." The broom sped to the corner and wiggled its frayed bristles uselessly in the tight angle. The dirt was unmoved, but the broom dutifully lowered its attached dustpan and swept up a non-existent pile. Arlen just shook her head as the broom flew up through the open roof to dump the pan in the yard. The twins cleaned up the kitchen while Judith took Luella outside. Theodore came into the bedroom to see what he could do to repair the roof.

Arlen looked up and saw Jonathon watching her, dawdling, indecisive as usual, and turned to shoo him out the door. "Go on. What are you waiting for? Talk to Rhazburn."

Before he left, he said goodbye to all the children and told them he loved them all. He shoved twenty Copper Orders into his coin purse, leaving three for Arlen and the children.

He shuffled through the demolished door frame but stopped when he saw his pathetic, flattened herb garden, the bent and bruised sprouts and shoots crushed down into the dry clods. He felt sorry for his little plants and decided to give them a sprinkling before he left. From a large canvas bag at the door, he grabbed a handful of Raindust. With a prayer to Tundudil, "Father, please nurture all my verdant children," he cast it into the air, above the garden. Within moments, a dark cloud formed a rod off the ground, and a fine mist began to settle on the flower bed. When the cloud began to shimmer and crackle, Jonathon scurried away with his bottom tucked in protectively. He had been struck in the pants by miniature lightning bolts too many times to take any chances.

Jonathon walked quickly to the Travel Plaza, not wanting to waste any more time. The path wound through a hedge and past a tumbledown, squawkity chicken coop. He tried to sneak past when he saw old miser Gibbel, but the surly man shook a rake at him from behind a rotten picket fence.

"Scare m'chickens, will yuh? What do yuh mean, making all that noise at the crack a'dawn? M'hens won't lay for a fortnight. I'll make yuh pay for it. I will. Cutting trees in the morning and waking a good man up that needs his rest. I'll have the constables on yuh."

"A pleasant morning to you, Master Gibbel. Never was it my intention to waken you. I sympathize with you on this. I, too, was aggravated by the commotion." Jonathon bowed and tried to move politely onward.

"Don't 'pleasant morning' me. Widow Feathertop never scared m'chickens. Sh'was a good neighbor, sh'was."

Jonathon kept walking and smiling affably, but Gibbel kept up his abuse. His insults and complaints faded in the trees as Jonathon started down the hill the two properties stood upon. As he walked through a stand of oak, a doe looked up from her browsing and watched him warily. She could apparently tell by the gentle sway of his hips Jonathon had never harmed a thing in his life and never intended to. As he passed, she resumed her quiet meal.

The oaks cleared past the end of a switchback where Jonathon could hear the distant hooting of a Dragontailer's buglemate. Through a fence of slender birch trees, he caught a glimpse of the slim seagoing vessel. The Dragontailer was being towed by a gigantic Blue Dragon slicing through the waves straight into the wind, leaving the sloops of the fishing fleet far behind in its wake. The Dragontailer's buglemate was blaring his horn furiously, sending musical orders to the Dragon a furlong ahead. The owner of the Dragontailer had to be rich to afford the fees he paid the

Dragonlord to rent the Blue Dragon. He would soon be richer still since his boat would be the first to plunder the rich schools of fish sighted that morning by the similarly paid Knights flying Green Dragons high above the sea.

By the time Jonathon walked into the Travel Plaza, a long line of travelers had already formed. He took his place in queue and waited his turn. Most of the traffic was going from the outskirts toward town as Jonathon was, but the line moved quickly. Jonathon soon came to the waiting gate.

He took a casual glance at the massive Black Dragon sprawled in the plaza and walked up to it. The livid form of the Dragon contrasted sharply with the green of the grass and weeds surrounding it. The enormous chest moved in a slow rhythm, and Jonathon could hear a deep rumbling as the creature breathed. Experts who knew of these things said the sound was similar to the purring of a cat and should reassure the travelers who used the Travel Dragons. It made Jonathon's skin crawl. The Dragon's eyes were, open, but the golden orbs gave no hint of thought or emotion.

Beside a talon of its right forefoot lay a haphazard pile of Copper Orders, silver goblets, golden rings, and other pieces of jewelry. Intermixed among these and scattered about for a rod or so were dented helmets, shattered swords, bits of torn clothing, and assorted human bones, a not-too-subtle warning to anyone interested in helping himself to the Dragon's treasure.

Jonathon took out a Copper Order and nonchalantly flipped it onto the pile. With a disturbing screek of the Dragon's tusk-sized teeth one upon the other, its huge mouth opened. Jonathon steadied himself, holding onto the tips of two teeth, as he squeezed his belly past them and stepped onto the Dragon's soft tongue. As usual, the spongy living carpet moved slightly under his feet, as if the beast was tasting him. Jonathon kept his balance with some difficulty and called out, "City Square Plaza." The maw closed upon him.

Like every other day when he traveled by the Black Dragon, his hair stood on end. After an instant of darkness and panic, the mouth opened with another screek, revealing the clustered shops surrounding the city square before him. He pushed quickly through the teeth, scraping off a button from his jacket in his haste to get out. He hopped onto the ground just before the Dragon's mouth slammed shut with a report like an ancient pine breaking in half.

Jonathon shuddered. Every day it seemed like he barely made it out of the mouth before the jaws crashed together. He sometimes thought the Dragon did it just to see him cringe. Despite the many years he had used the Travel Dragons, he still didn't trust them. He heard too many stories of people entering the Dragons' mouths never to be seen again. The officials warned the travelers these hapless souls had tried to cheat the Dragons, but no one knew for sure. Perhaps the Dragons just wanted occasional snacks.

As Jonathon walked out of City Square Travel Plaza, he turned to look back at the Black Dragon. It looked exactly like the one into whose mouth he had stepped three leagues away. The position of its splayed limbs was different, and the pile of treasure was much larger here in the center of the city, but he could see no real difference. No one could explain how people could travel long distances by stepping into the Dragons' mouths. One theory was that all the Black Dragons were one and the same, a single creature living simultaneously in many places. Thus, stepping into the mouth of one Black Dragon, a person could instantly step out of the same Dragon's mouth many leagues away. But nothing had ever been concluded. Only the Dragonlord knew for sure, and he seemed to relish the mystery surrounding his power. It certainly served to discourage anyone who wanted to challenge that power.

Outside the Travel Plaza, Jonathon was immediately immersed in the city's morning bustle. Coaches clattered past him on the cobblestone streets. Flying carpets swooped over his head. High above the buildings Knights soared, riding slim Green Dragons, as they surveyed the city for commotion. Barkers and hawkers accosted him at every corner. One particularly obnoxious peddler with three Moving Brooms chased him for three blocks.

"Good sir, stop please. These brooms are made by the Sylvets. Yes, it's true. One Clay Suggestion is all it takes to keep one working for a Moon. See how smoothly they move." A broom whirled around Jonathon as he hurried along. He was so angry he almost tripped the broom as it flew past, yet he could not bring himself to take a chance on hurting it. He knew the broom was inanimate and unfeeling, but since it moved, he perceived it as alive and was reluctant to harm it.

To get rid of the peddler, Jonathon stopped a white-haired, wizened woman who walked with an ornately carved cane and introduced her to the peddler. He left her listening with a screwed up face, one hand behind her ear, saying, "What was that? Speak up, young man!" to the peddler's every word.

As he tried to walk quickly away, a line of black-robed Beholders paraded in front of him. As they did every day, they would disperse in the crowds so they might silently behold and worship the beauty in all beings, objects, and places of the world. They were completely concealed within their robes without the tiniest bit of skin visible. They were also forbidden to speak. The Beholders always gave Jonathon the uneasy feeling they were not human. Maybe not even alive. He thought their supposed devotion to Kris, the Beauty aspect of The Three, ignored a central concept of *The Transmigrant* that first one must see the beauty in oneself before he could recognize the beauty in others.

After waiting until they passed, obeying an unwritten law that no one walked through a line of parading Beholders, Jonathon moved onward through the throngs. Sitting in the dust beside a lean-to hovel pitched against a nicely painted Coin Changery, two naked Querites bathed a leper. The two, a man and a woman, immaculately clean but completely nude, washed the leper and carefully combed his hair. The leper, missing an ear and several fingers, gorged on potatoes they had prepared for him. The Querites were too assiduous in their devotion to the role of Tundudil, the Father and the provider, to even wear clothes. Instead, they gave everything they owned and all their time to help others. The reason they were immaculate was because part of their ministrations to others included caring for the others in their cult. In fact, the beggars they cared for frequently joined their ranks, recognizing the benefits of the persuasion. The Querites were intent on caring for others to the exclusion of all else. If their nakedness spurred lust in some criminal's mind and he attacked and raped one of the nude Querite women or men, the Querite stoically accepted the assault and even tried to help the rapist feel less guilty.

Jonathon looked back at the elderly, flabby-chested woman who cleaned the leper's lice off the comb she held by wiping it on her own leg. He felt as little lust for her as if he had accidentally caught his own mother undressed. The Querite woman put down the comb to turn and rub her partner's neck while he in turn gently dabbed a foul sore on the leper's back.

No, Jonathon thought, *I'm not a Querite*. Besides, he knew the woman. She was the one who bought Warming Pendants for her little flock of Querites. Even though they wore no clothes, they were not completely dim. They wanted to live through the winter. She justified the use of the Warming Pendants draped around their naked necks to Jonathon as a means of keeping their caring touch warm to those they served.

Finally, he stepped into Jeweler's Row, a prominent street of small shops frequented only by the richest. His once proud jewelry shop right in the middle of Jeweler's Row languished, his staff trimmed to only Hili, his favorite Pixelle, and Bob Thumblefoot. His debts had even forced him to sell most of his rough gems and precious metal just to pay Molgannard Fey's exorbitant interest, thus undermining any chance he had to make adequate pieces of jewelry to earn enough money to get back on his feet. His pride had not allowed him to accept the offers of money from his children before then, but he realized if he ever got out of this mess, he'd have to depend on his family to help him start his business anew.

Before he stepped up to the door of his shop, the jeweler who owned the shop next door, Harmon Greatflugal sneered, "Master Jeweler, I've a need for more flawed roughs. Business is brisk. I'll give you two Coppers a scruple. A fair price. I understand you still have fifty flawed roughs."

He was bargaining for rough diamonds. Jonathon had ties to the diamond mines of the Cajalathrium States and could get the roughs cheaper than anyone in town, but two Copper Orders a scruple? *Fair price indeed*, Jonathon thought sarcastically. The going price was five a scruple. Harmon was astonishingly correct. Jonathon had just exactly fifty roughs. He had none to spare. Even if he sold all his rough diamonds to Harmon, he'd only net thirty Copper Orders on the deal. His inventory was down to the bare bones.

To shut Harmon up, Jonathon laid upon him a pile of simpering lies. "Harmon, your generosity is balm to my soul. Notwithstanding the attractiveness of your offer, I must demur. Another time, your kindness and patience will be rewarded, I am sure." Harmon was a tough competitor, one of the court favorites. Jonathon distrusted him immensely.

"Well, when you need the money then."

Harmon's flippancy told Jonathon a great deal, that he knew all about Jonathon's financial troubles and was pleased he could exploit them. Every jeweler, especially Harmon, would love to replace Jonathon as the Master Jeweler.

"I saw your brood at Slough Simperdribble's." Harmon thumbed his own satin shirt. "I found this there. I was ashamed to see Simperdribble didn't even give Mrs. Forthright a discount on her linen, seeing Herkimer is one of his suppliers. Pity."

Jonathon's family proudly wore linen while Harmon Greatflugal wore satin. Jonathon did not care how fancy his clothes were, Harmon Greatflugal was a lonely man. Jonathon was the one who pitied him. Jonathon dusted off his splendid linen trousers as if to say he was brushing off that last comment, and with a smile and a nod stepped up to his own shop door.

Before he entered, he noticed a Seer at the corner. Like all the Seers, she was blindfolded by her long hair tied around her eyes. Despite that impediment, she accurately called out the names of people as they passed. One woman stopped and tossed a Wooden Request into the pot at her feet after which the Seer began a steam of pronouncements and predictions. If her statements of the woman's present condition were accurate, she was likely to believe any outlandish prediction the Seer had for her future and would come back with more Wooden Requests. Some of the money the Seer would use to buy another vial of Deathwatch Serum.

If the tales could be believed, the Deathwatch Serum allowed Seers to see and communicate with the countless ghostly spirits hidden from view wandering in the world. Jonathon figured the Seers just made it all up. No one could know the things they professed to be cognizant of about the people who paid for their services. Even the Gossip Dwarves had not the knowledge of people's intimate lives that the Seers professed to know. Few people, Jonathon included, wanted to test Deathwatch Serum themselves. Anyone not trained in the Seers' arts was driven instantly mad if they but tasted the evil brew. Besides, Jonathon didn't believe in Ghosts. Never did. Never would.

How had Harmon known how many roughs Jonathon still owned? Maybe he had used the Seer to spy on him. Jonathon had heard Seers could be used that way but he knew it was impossible. Between the Seers, the Gossip Dwarves, and the Knights flying overhead, no secret seemed sacred in Isseltrent anymore. He shook his head in disgust and reached for door of his shop.

Bob Thumblefoot, his apprentice, swept open the door before Jonathon could touch the latch. "Welcome, master. The shop is swept. The workbench has been repaired. I've fired up the furnace, and I drew a half rod of gold wire." Like every day, Bob had been watching for his master just to open the door for him. Bob's childish face, wedged between tousled brown hair and a sooty smock, beamed at Jonathon like the morning sun. Once again, he had done all the work for the day in Breakfast Blessing before Jonathon had even gotten there.

Bob was merely fourteen years old. Jonathon thought Bob pushed himself too hard and was a little too nervous. But he liked the boy, so Jonathon spent considerable time and effort scrutinizing Bob's drawings of rings and pendants and taught him all he could about minerals and gems. Like a sponge, Bob soaked up all the knowledge Jonathon had gained in his life as a miner, prospector, and jeweler.

"Bob, you astonish me," Jonathon said, ruffling the boy's hair. Bob grinned even wider.

"Do you remember the diamond dust you've been collecting?" Bob nodded his head so vigorously, Jonathon thought he heard the boy's ears rattle. "Do you recollect the name of the person you're saving it for?"

Bob answered in a flash. "Loremaster Rhazburn. To use at Hell's Breach." Bob loved to hear Rhazburn's tales of the battles at Hell's Breach and was proud to collect the diamond dust for his hero.

"Have you had an opportunity to assess its' weight recently?"

"Almost two drams."

"Be so kind as to bring it forth, my good Bob." Bob jogged away before Jonathon could finish.

While he waited, Hili flew up to greet him. Her filmy wings whirred through the air, and she bowed, hovering before his face. "We welcome you, Master Jeweler." Her voice was like a mouse's whisper.

"Pleasant regards to you and the Community, Hili. Even on a beautiful clear morning like today, your presence further brightens my shop." He held out his hand. The Pixelle landed deftly on his forefinger, her dragonfly-like wings retracting into her back to leave two small nubbins. Sitting there, she was as soft and light as a toddler's hand. She wore a satiny gown and had hair to her waist. She was beautiful by either human or Pixet standards, and Jonathon experienced a thrill every time she sat on his hand. He loved her, not like he loved Arlen, but like a distant, inaccessible beauty, a thing of his dreams.

"I regret to say, I cannot attend the shop this morning, Hili. I must leave the shop to Bob's capable hands today."

"We will miss you, Master Jeweler." Pixets always talked in the plural. Each Pixet spoke for all the other Pixets, even when they were separated by space. Jonathon had yet to comprehend how they kept in contact through the distances, but anything one Pixet knew, all seemed to know. By their nature the Pixets experienced much of what the devotees to the Faith of The Three aspired to.

Funny, he thought, the Pixet's pagan religion had nothing to do with the Faith. They had no need for the teachings of The Three. Togetherness was inherent in their daily lives, instinctual. Just as no one needed to teach Jonathon to breathe, no one needed to teach the Pixets to empathize with each other. They thought each others' thoughts and felt each others' emotions.

"I hope to be back by Highday. I have to meet Rhazburn at Hell's Breach."

"Will that not be dangerous, Master Jeweler?"

Before he answered, he thought of the angry Giant. "Not as dangerous as not going, I think."

"Be careful, Master. We don't want to lose you. The Community knows you will soon be making all your beautiful jewelry again soon, and more."

Jonathon nodded, agreeing but disbelieving. Turning toward the door, he saw Bob waiting patiently to give him the diamond dust. He took the small glass vial and examined the sparkling dust inside.

"Ah, yes, Bob, my thanks to you. Rhazburn will be informed of your diligent devotion in gathering this for his use." The boy nodded like a happy puppy.

"An onerous task beckons me," he said, gently tossing Hili into the air. Her wings appeared as she did a neat somersault and stopped still, eye level to Jonathon, fluttering in place.

As he left, Bob said, "I'll await your return, Master. If there are any customers, I'll ask them to wait or return at Home Blessing."

After trying to get into the Chamber of Hell's Breach, those customers may have to wait a long time, like forever, Jonathon thought. He may be killed. Killed if he went or killed if he didn't. Too much for him to worry about. If he could just get to Rhazburn, all would be fine. With that one glimmer of hope, he waved goodbye to Bob and Hili and proceeded through the streets to the chamber that enclosed Hell's Breach.

Like most people in the city, Jonathon knew the way to Hell's Breach but had never gone there before. Only alleyways led the way and they were little traveled. When he saw the massive egg-shaped obsidian block, drops of perspiration began to form around the rim of his turban and not because of the heat. His Charm of Coolness was still actively cooling him.

The seamless black walls were covered with inscriptions, all intended to make the chamber an inviolable prison for any Demons that might escape from Hell's Breach inside. It was impressive but untested. Three centuries before, the crafty Poet Nishbad had formed Hell's Breach to bring forth a single Demon to aid him in his rise to power. Unfortunately, Nishbad, though able to breach the fabric of reality and open a doorway into Hell, was unable to close the breach. Once Nishbad was deposed and killed, his Demon escaped. The Dead Lands now existed as a sign of it. Thanks to the Demonwards, in the centuries since the chamber was constructed to enclose Hell's Breach, not one more Demon had escaped Hell.

Next to the Chamber of Hell's Breach stood a Temple of The Three. A handful of Priests and Priestesses kept up a din on musical triangles of various sizes accompanying their songs. All of the Holy Few, as the Priests and Priestesses were called, had bodies of sculpted muscles and pleasing curves revealed by their scanty vestments. Part of their devotions included fasting and exercise to mold themselves into images of the perfect human body in vogue at the time. Their voices were beautiful as they sang to counter the chaos of Hell. Their singing was completely impotent. The knowledge of the Demonwards was all that held the Demons at bay, not the ineffectual chanting and ranting of the Holy Few. Among the Holy Few strode a Seer, her confident stride amongst the Priests and Priestesses incongruous with the mask of red hair hiding her eyes. Her presence there presumably was to ensure no Demons or lost souls emerged through the door of the Chamber of Hell's Breach. Somehow everyone believed her connection with the departed spirits would allow her to recognize an escapee from Hell. Whether anyone could stop a Demon after it got past the Demonwards remained to be tested. Jonathon figured she was just as useless as the Holy Few.

As he looked up at the black dome, Jonathon felt a bizarre chill and it wasn't from his Charm of Coolness. Nor was it from fear. There was something else. A change he could feel and smell in the wind. Something cool, crisp, dangerous, like a storm just beyond the horizon, beyond his sight. Something ominous he felt but could not see.

To enter the chamber, an iron door had to be passed. In front of the door, a gauntlet of brightly-uniformed sentinels stood at attention, each holding a wickedly-bladed halberd in readiness. Jonathon had to pass through the gauntlet to get to the door. As he walked between the rows of dour guards, he smiled uneasily at each in turn. Before he could touch the door, two stern guards snapped their axes across his chest, barring his way. The barrel-chested leader of the guard, sporting a great wooly beard, bellowed, "Who dares approach the forbidden door to Hell's Breach?"

Deep in the pickets' defile, Jonathon's sweaty neck was in reach of a dozen blades should he say the wrong word or make a false move.

"Uh, Jonathon Forthright, the jeweler," he said, sounding like he questioned his own name.

"The door is barred to all. Move away or your life is forfeit."

Jonathon said nervously, "Here," and clutched at his pocket for the diamond dust.

At his movement, the guards reacted quickly. A razor-sharp blade hissed through the air and stopped, lightly touching his neck.

Jonathon froze, gurgling on his next word. "Diamond dust," he said very slowly. "I have brought diamond dust for the Demonwards." The ax was removed, leaving Jonathon's head in place.

The burly head guard said, "Let's see it."

Jonathon carefully lifted the vial, scanning the tense sentries for their reactions.

The head guard took the vial roughly and shook it before his eyes. He looked at Jonathon. "I wasn't told you were coming."

Jonathon stammered, "The Poets...Loremaster Rhazburn needs it... today...or it will be bad...bad trouble...for all of us. He needs it to fight special Demons coming through Hell's Breach. He's waiting on this very vial of diamond dust. Really. Just ask him. Really. There's not a moment to lose."

The guard hummed a soft growl, thinking slowly, his bushy eyebrows twitching, his grip tightening on his halberd, knuckles whitening. Jonathon realized his attempt to see Rhazburn was hopeless. He began to wonder which manner of death was faster and less painful, being stamped flat by the Giant or being split in two by the guard's finely-honed blade.

CHAPTER 2

HELL'S BREACH

With one foot on the threshold of Hell, the youth pointed into the poisonous mist and cried, "Forms!"

Halfway through a yawn, Rhazburn, Loremaster of the Demonwards, turned his head toward the untried Poet, peering past him through the bulky golden frame of Hell's Breach.

At the cry of Dollop, the young Poet watching the vapors of the nether world, the other Poets leapt past Rhazburn and stopped at their appointed stations. Grunion stopped behind the Silver Dulcimer and tensed, hammers poised above the strings, ready to release a song. Fendrick hefted the Pipes of Power and puffed a bladder to bloating. Meerdrum and Tindal unstopped vials of pearl dust, and Wesfallen, the eldest next to Rhazburn, loosened the strings of the worn leather coin pouch. All were ready for a Demon's emergence from the clouds mingling and rolling behind the Musical Mystical Door, the gate surrounding Hell's Breach. Their job was to stop any being from escaping Hell and entering the mortal world.

To reach the door and aid their sentry, Rhazburn jogged across the ranks of verses inlaid into the floor before the portal. He ran over a mosaic of fire with an Epigram of Fiery Destruction, over a hardwood floor with a parqueted Poem of Sleep, and over the last rank, a marble tiled floor inlaid with a gold foil Verse of Immobilization.

By the time Rhazburn reached the youth, Dollop's finger, stabbing the noxious mist behind the portal, was quivering with tension. "There, Loremaster, down and to the right. It appears as a woman, crying."

This close to Hell's Breach, the acrid vapors burned Rhazburn's nostrils and the infernal heat beyond made him uncomfortably warm. He blew through his teeth. A tortured soul had wandered up to Hell's Breach and was begging to get out of Hell. The spirit, like all the dead, was powerless and could never escape. The Demonwards could possibly aid her, but they dared not interfere with the Wheels of Fate, lest they be ground beneath them.

He said to Dollop, "Just a Lone Weeper. It's a wisp, a wraith, of no consequence. It's not a Demon and will soon be wafted away by an ill wind of the nether world."

Dollop's tremor disturbed Rhazburn. The youth should not be so nervous. Although he had never seen a Lone Weeper, as the tortured souls were called, they were seen frequently by the Demonwards. Lone Weepers were those souls stricken from The List, those still loved but shunned from the company of the believers. They had repeatedly committed one of the three Great Sins: Callousness, Greed, or Violence. The first of the Great Sins was Callousness to the Beauty in all things, the second was Greed, the antithesis of Love, and the third, Violence to life as opposed to the Caring for all things living. Tundudil would not consign one to Hell unless that soul had repeated infractions, but once he was condemned he would forever live with others of his kind. Kitilzgabwed, the Lord of Hell, was the first soul stricken from The List, when eternity for the mortal world began at the whim of Tundudil.

Most of the Demonwards agreed with Rhazburn that the religion practiced in Isseltrent was a sham, useless in a practical sense, recited by uncomprehending adherents. Rhazburn and the Demonwards argued incessantly with the Holy Few about the origin of the Demons. Rhazburn and most of the Demonwards agreed that those souls stricken from The

List of the Blessed, those callous, greedy and violent souls, became worse the longer they stayed in Hell. The eldest, those who had been in Hell for eons, lost all semblance to humanity and became nothing but monstrous predators feeding upon the rampant chaos. Kitilzgabwed was the first, so he was the worst and most powerful. He was the Lord and Ruler of the nether world. Lone Weepers were pitiable but still corrupt. Although they all wanted out of Hell, none stepped toward the threshold. Kitilzgabwed prevented them. The Demonwards never viewed them as a threat, only as a pity.

As Rhazburn's own apprentice, Dollop should have known the spirit was a Lone Weeper and taken the sobbing apparition in stride. Rhazburn turned his head and reassured the others. "A Lone Weeper."

They all relaxed and sauntered back to their resting place, a small cluster of pillows, tables, and chairs a short way from the ranks of inlaid floors.

As he turned again to look at Dollop, Rhazburn had to push back a rebellious shock of his own red hair. Like most of the Royal Bastards, his hair was a memory of a mother who had loved him but left him a score of years before. His eyes were the cool green of his unacknowledged natural father, the Dragonlord. Dollop was a Royal Bastard too. Except for a few Royal Bastards adopted by Jonathon and Arlen Forthright, Dollop was the only one of the fifty-eight half brothers and half sisters, all sired by the Dragonlord, who Rhazburn could call his friend.

Dollop fixed his gaze on the evil mist, as if afraid to look into Rhazburn's eyes. Five Moons before, Dollop had lost his wife and baby in childbirth. In the grief that followed, Rhazburn had feared for his student's life. To Rhazburn's delight, Dollop rallied and returned with a strange urgency, eager to learn. For many Moons, Rhazburn drilled him on the Verses of Power to prepare him for a trial at Hell's Breach. Even though Rhazburn thought the time was too soon for Dollop to become a Demonward, the youth learned the Science of Poetry well, passed all the stringent tests perfectly and pleaded to be given a chance to prove himself.

Rhazburn, like most of his half siblings, needed to think he had a truly close relative. His natural father had disowned him, and his mother had deserted him. Only the kindness and love of Jonathon and Arlen Forthright had saved him from despair after he left the Dragonlord's court when he was eight. At the time, the Forthrights' daughters were all younger than Rhazburn, so he had grown up the eldest of all the Forthrights. He was looked up to by all his many adoptive siblings. His years with Jonathon and Arlen had allowed him to realize his full potential.

Dollop had suffered a similar fate. He had been thrown out of court, like Rhazburn, for some small infraction. Rhazburn first met him eking out a living, whistling for Suggestions in a pub. Since Rhazburn was comfortable with the role of big brother, he vowed to take Dollop on as his apprentice, steep him in the Science of Poetry, build his confidence, and teach him to become the world's greatest Poet. When Dollop passed the tests (and he sorely needed challenging work to keep his mind off the deaths of his wife and child), Rhazburn gave into his pleas. Besides, the Council was forever in need of good Poets. Hell's Breach claimed dozens, slaughtered or crazed, each year.

Hell's Breach was no place for religion or romance. Rhazburn was convinced the Science of Poetry was the only discipline that could hold back the Demons of Hell. Consequently, he was uneasy as he studied Dollop's wistful half smile. Despite Rhazburn's attempt to instill into his apprentice the commitment to practical knowledge as the best defense against the hordes of Hell, Dollop emerged significantly more romantic than his teacher, more romantic than any Poet Rhazburn had ever seen. Rhazburn knew a romantic Poet was a dangerous thing at Hell's Breach.

Rhazburn had no use for romance or religion in his own life. Oh, he had rolled in bed with a few pub wenches, one court lady and one sweet, delectable Choralist, but he had restrained himself from involving a woman in his life to save her the misery of life with a Poet on the edge of death. Besides, only one woman met his standards for a mate. And she would never be available to him. Her history and her life had formed her into an avowed lesbian and hater of men. He tried to quell his fantasies of her whenever they surfaced in his thoughts.

Reinforcing forgotten lessons he had taught Dollop, Rhazburn said, "Heed no wracked spirit pleading in vain, Lest Hell be unleashed, and Life end in pain."

"Marmel's couplet," Dollop said.

"You memorized it, but do you know it?" Rhazburn asked.

Dollop regarded him quizzically. "Remember, all things the Demons say and do are lies. 'A gaze is terror, a word madness, a touch death.' Never forget it, Dollop, never."

"I won't, Master," Dollop replied, his voice trailing off into a distant thought as he turned slowly to contemplate the swirling clouds.

The way Dollop peered into the mist disquieted Rhazburn. The youth searched for more than Demons. "For Three's sake, Dollop, your wife and child are not in Hell. You know that. Quit groping for them."

A wan gaze was his only reply.

"I'm letting Wesfallen relieve you. Hold the pouch for the rest of the morning."

Wesfallen came after a wave from Rhazburn and as ordered, handed Dollop the coin pouch. Rhazburn saw Dollop clutched the pouch much too tightly as if trying to hold fast the values of the world.

Rhazburn believed in Dollop's abilities, but not so much that he would entrust the youth with all the Copper Orders available to the Demonwards. There were about a hundred in the pouch, weighing a couple of pounds all together. Once they were gone, nothing else could power their spells. Rhazburn said, "Dollop, let me have five Orders." Dollop gave him the requested coins. Then, in response to a reassuring nod from Rhazburn, he wandered off among the other Poets. Rhazburn looked up to Wesfallen's groan of displeasure. "What is it, Falli?"

"Rhaz, I don't like it. Next thing you know he'll start chanting from *The Transmigrant*." Briefly, he looked back toward Dollop, turned and shook his head at the mist. "I don't care if he is your pupil. His wife's death has made him a menace. You have to replace him."

"Brilliance can be eccentric. Roses can't flower under a basket. We need him. His memory is immutable as the rings of an oak. I'm his shadow. If he falters, I'll take up the slack until he's had some experience."

Wesfallen sighed. "You're the Loremaster, Rhaz. But, mark my words. That boy's heart is too soft for a Poet. If he doesn't toughen up, he'll die here, I tell you. He'll die here."

Rhazburn was saved from coming up with a response by a call from the inner guard of the entrance to the massive chamber enclosing Hell's Breach. Rhazburn turned to see one of the two inner guards running toward their group. He had left his halberd with the other guard, and

Rhazburn saw they had cleared the great iron door. A poem was etched in the metal of the door which, when activated with a coin, would cause the door to remain strong but appear transparent as glass. It was used so the guards on the outside could make sure all was well within before they opened the door. The iron door was locked from the outside. All that entered were trapped with any Demon that came through Hell's Breach until the next group of Poets came to relieve Rhazburn's. Now that Rhazburn could see through the invisible iron, he recognized Jonathon.

Fifteen years had passed since he left Jonathon and Arlen's house. He had not lost touch with adoptive father since his jewelry was well known in the city, and he was one of the main suppliers for the precious dusts and Gems of Power they used. Rhazburn was glad he could help out some with the needs of the many children. One of them, Garrith, even became a Demonward, capable himself and in charge of the Poets on the night shifts he worked. Rhazburn could not mistake the disturbing change in his father's normally pleasant and cheerful face. Something frightening, something far more terrible in the jeweler's mind than any Demon, drove him to Hell's Breach.

"Loremaster," said the guard as he jogged up to halt at attention. "There is a man at the door who demands to be let in. We told him it was forbidden, but he insists he has something needed by the Demonwards, a vial of diamond dust."

Rhazburn had no idea why Jonathon brought the diamond dust unrequested. Jonathon seldom lied, unless to placate some irascible customer, and even then, it was more to make the other one feel better about himself, but never to take advantage of him. Some powerful and frightening reason had to be motivating Jonathon for him to deceive the guards in such a way. Rhazburn was not going to deny him what he wanted. "Take the vial and thank the good jeweler for me. We can certainly use the diamond dust here. Tell the captain to ask his fee for the diamond dust so the Lord's treasurer may be advised of the purchase."

"We already tried to take the vial as you said, Loremaster, but the jeweler insists on discussing its properties at length with you."

His father wanted to come into the Chamber of Hell's Breach. That was worrisome. Jonathon knew the dangers at Hell's Breach and usually stayed far away. Jonathon was fully as timid as he was honest. For him to want to enter Hell's Breach could only mean something life-threatening was closing in on him. Perhaps it had followed him there. Jonathon could keep little secret from Rhazburn, so he knew of the debt Jonathon owed Molgannard Fey. Rhazburn offered to force Molgannard Fey to give up the debt, but his father was too honest. He insisted on paying his debt himself and forbade Rhazburn to get involved. Rhazburn was very close to disobeying his father. Had he asked Rhazburn before he borrowed the money, the Poet would have steered his father far from the criminal.

"Let the jeweler in."

"We cannot. The Dragonlord forbids it." He doubted these guards knew Jonathon was his father. Rhazburn was well known as a Royal Bastard and few knew the whole history of his life. Rhazburn had little hope that telling them Jonathon was his father would sway their orders. He needed another excuse to get Jonathon in.

"Guard, we need the diamond dust today, and the detailed instructions on its use. If we use it wrong, there well be no Dragonlord because the Demons will destroy me, you, Hell's Breach, Isseltrent, and everything you have ever known. And what's more, even the lucky ones who die will be trapped here in a veritable Hell on the world as we know it. We already saw a Lone Weeper today. The Breach is active. I don't want to face whatever comes out next without that diamond dust."

The young guard was white and sweating. "I'll talk to the captain."

"Tell him Loremaster Rhazburn will take the blame for breaking the proscription. If anyone is punished for this, I demand to be the one."

The guard said no more but ran back to the door of the chamber. Soon the wooden crossbar rasped through iron fittings, and the door swung open. Jonathon sidled in. Before the door was closed, he seemed to listen to something said by one of the guards. The door slammed and Jonathon threw up his hands to his turbaned head. He turned to the door and beat on it as if he now wanted back out in a hurry. The guards ignored him. Shoulders bent, wiping his brow, Jonathon approached the Demonwards.

All the Demonwards except Wesfallen had regrouped at the cluster of tables, chairs, and other oddments that served the Poets' needs while they waited and watched. All the Poets knew Jonathon, if not by acquaintance, at least by reputation. They had all used magical pieces made in his shop. Everyone gathered around Rhazburn who spoke first.

"Master Jeweler, welcome. What can we do for you?" For the last ten years Rhazburn called his father by his title in public. He was the only adopted child of Jonathon's that did. He felt it helped him in his Loremaster position to stay on more formal terms.

"Salutations, Loremaster, Poets," Jonathon said, nodding to them in turn. "I respectfully acknowledge the charity of your offer of help in my plight." All the poets, including Rhazburn looked at him for a moment, blankly. "Rhazburn, I need your help."

"I'm glad to help you, Master Jeweler. I believe I've made my offer clear."

"I don't want that. I'm not a cheat. At this particular juncture, what I require is cash. Quite a bit, actually."

"May I ask how much you need?" Meerdrum asked.

"Two hundred Copper Orders. Or actually one hundred eighty. I have twenty I've saved with me." A few Poets whistled, others laughed. Rhazburn scowled. "How much time do you have?"

Jonathon groaned, "A lot less than when I came here. I had to talk to you, but I didn't know I'd be a prisoner. The guard said I can't leave until Dusk Blessing when the other Poets come. Is that right, Rhazburn?"

"I'm afraid so, Master Jeweler. I put my position on the line just to let you in. They wouldn't let you out before dusk, even if you were dead."

"If he were dead, they certainly wouldn't let him out," Grunion quipped.

Jonathon did not look amused. "If I don't get out of here before dusk and raise the money, I will be dead." Grunion dropped his grin.

"All right, you need ideas," Rhazburn said. "You came to the right place." He looked at the other Poets and gestured toward them with an open hand. They all began fingering their chins or scratching their heads, some with closed eyes, some staring intently.

Tindal was first. "A Reverse Transmuting Box. Take a Wooden Request, drop it in, and instead of a thirty three Clay Suggestions, it makes a thirty three Copper Orders."

"Sounds highly illegal," Jonathon said.

"Well, I suppose it would be, but it probably wouldn't work anyway. Cost too much to make. The one I heard of had to be made from sheets of emerald."

"Sheets of emerald. Does that even exist?" Jonathon shook his head.

"Well, no," Tindal said, "but I think I've come up with a way to transform regular emeralds into flat sheets."

Jonathon just looked blandly at him.

"But you need a ruby the size of a chicken egg," Tindal said.

Jonathon nodded his head slowly and said, "I see. My thanks are extended to you, Poet. And my wish for good fortune in your venture." Jonathon clapped his hand to his eyes and made a faint groaning sound.

Rhazburn knew nothing they could suggest for him to sell or make would get Jonathon out of his plight. He decided to deal with the Giant himself. To offer to fight the Giant here in front of the others would embarrass his father, so he kept the thought to himself. Besides, none of them could leave before the day was over, so he thought to cheer his father, as well as the Demonwards, with a little amusement. "I have a solution, Master Jeweler. Everyone, listen to this poem."

> Atop
> A lonely post
> A hawk spies
> A mouse eye
> Wings wipe wind
> Slide between boughs
> Then the hammer

"Well, Dollop, what do you think?' Rhazburn asked after reciting his new verse.

"Huh? Oh. I wasn't counting. It's prime, I expect."

Rhazburn had singled out the youth because he had again lapsed into a pensive mood.

"Of course, it's prime. Twenty-three syllables with one of surveillance and one of power."

"Have you tested it?" Grunion asked.

"I tried it on a lead box in Grablideck's Granary, but it only caught a cockroach. To catch mice, I figure a small silver cage would work perfectly."

"Silver!" Grunion cried, incredulous. "Silver? Who'd buy a silver mouse trap? For pity's sake, Rhaz, they can get cats for free."

Rhazburn shrugged away Grunion's doubt. "How about a rich merchant or a craftsman? He might buy it as a curiosity." All the Poets turned to Jonathon.

Jonathon blushed beneath their gaze. Grunion asked him, "Master Jeweler, would you buy a silver mousetrap? I'm sure you'd be glad to sell them. But would you pay, say, ten Copper Orders for such a ridiculous bauble?"

Jonathon looked at Rhazburn, as if for guidance.

Rhazburn gave him a cocky smile and said, "You'd buy one, wouldn't you?"

"Uh, sure. Sure I would," Jonathon said, biting his lip.

Rhazburn laughed and said to Grunion, "See, I've sold one already."

Grunion's reply was cut short by a cry from Jonathon. He was hunched over, holding his turban and looking up apprehensively at a blue globe of light that circled above his head and sizzled.

Some of the Demonwards chuckled, but Rhazburn held up his hand and said, "Glitter, stop that."

The globe of light stopped, sputtering as it hung above Jonathon's head.

Jonathon looked at Rhazburn with his eyes wide. "It's alive?"

"Why, of course Glitter is alive," said Rhazburn, amused at Jonathon's surprised look. The globe of Ball Lightning was pure crackling energy, no more alive than a lightning bolt in a thunder storm, but Rhazburn pretended like it was.

"Here, I'll introduce you. Glitter, meet Master Jeweler Jonathon Forthright. Master Jeweler, Glitter." With one hand, he gestured to each in turn, and with his other, he controlled the seemingly animate Ball Lightning. He twitched his finger so the globe bobbed up and down as if it were curtsying. Rhazburn was always the cockiest of Jonathon's many adopted children and prone to pranks even at the expense of his parents.

Jonathon removed his turban and bowed. "Pleased to meet you, Glitter," he said.

"Glitter is one of our many Ball Lightning friends we have here as our allies," Rhazburn explained, waving toward the ceiling of the chamber where a score of multi-colored lightning puffs moved about at random. They seemed to dance and cavort with each other.

"Each has a name," Rhazburn went on. "Fireball," he shouted. A red ball of lightning swooped down from the ceiling and buzzed in place above them, just out of reach. They sounded like huge bees buzzing constantly as they hovered.

Jonathon said, "Hello, Fireball. My name is Jonathon. I'm visiting." He asked Rhazburn, "Is Glitter a lady?"

At that, the Poets burst out laughing and roared until Rhazburn waved them to muffled snickers.

As if he feared he had offended the Ball Lightning, Jonathon said, "Oh, I'm sorry, I didn't mean..."

Before he could finish his apology, Rhazburn said, "Why, yes, Glitter is quite a lady, as Fireball can tell you for sure." He moved his fingers so the lightning balls twirled around each other feverishly.

Jonathon stared, entranced until Rhazburn said, "That's enough of that, you two. Do you want to give our visitor the wrong impression? Now, off you go." He gestured to the back of the chamber, and the two lightning balls sped away in tandem.

Jonathon looked at him seriously.

Rhazburn felt bad deluding his father and said, "I was joking with you. The truth is we make them using verses written in lodestone dust. They're not alive at all."

Jonathon shook his finger at him. "Rhazburn, you're too clever for your own good. Now I really don't believe you. You and all your knowledge of science. Those balls move like they're alive, and I think they understood me. If you ask me, you may have made them, but they really are alive and you can't even tell. I felt it. And if you thought less and felt more, I bet you'd realize it, too."

The snickering stopped, and the Demonwards began to drift away.

Rhazburn knew what his father meant. It was a problem a lot of the Poets had. To work at Hell's Breach, they had to harden their hearts to so much. Even to the deaths of friends and the pleas of lost souls. The successful Poets had to be cold and calculating, unattached even to the other Poets. Rhazburn fit right in. He had fought his way out of his shame as a Royal Bastard. When Jonathon found him dirty and trying to pick his pocket, the jeweler laughed and gave him a warm hug. Instead of turning him over to the authorities, Jonathon took him home for dinner. The next few years with Jonathon and Arlen were the best of Rhazburn's life. At twelve, his ambitions spurred him to leave the Forthrights to apprentice as a Poet. But the values he had learned with the Forthrights stayed with him. Prestige, power, respect - nothing had the effect on him as had those few years with Jonathon and Arlen. Every day, he tried to live up to their high standards of love and respect for all others in the Realm. Every day, he failed at it.

Rhazburn was undisputedly the best Poet now. Loremaster of the Realm with more knowledge than any other Poet in the world. No one had a better memory than he did. He had proven his cleverness with Jonathon. Sadly, it was at Jonathon's expense, the person he respected most in the world. This was how he lost the few friends he had and was the real reason why he never could get married. Jonathon could see it. His cleverness crowded out his feelings and humanity. He had proved himself better than all the court that had spurned him, but he was cold and distant to those he loved.

"Hey, Rhazburn," Jonathon said, "I'm sorry I said that. It was a good joke. I'm just in a bad mood. You know, because of this business with Molgannard Fey. I don't know how I'm going to come up with all that money I owe him." He looked down at the floor and wiggled his head.

"Forms!" Wesfallen cried. "Forms! A Crawler!" Since Wesfallen had as much experience as Rhazburn at Hell's Breach, there was nothing to confirm. A Demon was crawling toward the Door.

The Poets sprang into action, taking their posts as before, except for Dollop and Wesfallen, who had switched places. Dollop began distributing coins of power to all the others. He dropped a Copper Order into the Silver Dulcimer. Another, he slipped in a pocket on the Pipes of Power.

Rhazburn said quickly, "Father, get back to the entrance. They won't open it now. Just stay there in a corner and keep out of the way."

Before he left, Jonathon handed him the vial of diamond dust, "Here, Rhazburn, Bob collected it for his hero." Rhazburn gave him a wink and took the vial.

Jonathon retreated to the door of the huge coffin-shaped room while Rhazburn ran to his charges, shouting "Slam the Door, Grunion."

As the Demon's form thickened in the vapors beyond the Musical Mystical Door, feral eyes blazed at them from a confusion of curling tentacles, grabbing hands, and clicking claws. By the time Dollop had touched a Copper Order to the gold Verse of Exclusion on the Door, Wesfallen had fallen back to aid Meerdrum, and Grunion had begun strumming a magical tune on the dulcimer.

Just as a hideous clawed hand thrust through Hell's Breach into the mortal world, the power of the coin, the golden verse, and the chiming chords of the dulcimer melded. The space enclosed by the Musical Mystical Door burst into a sheet of white shimmers and sparks holding the Demon back with a wall of energy. A tremendous roar from the Demon shook the unbreakable obsidian walls of the chamber and rippled the floor like an earthquake. The strength of this Demon seemed immeasurable in human terms. Sweat poured off Grunion as he tapped out the song. His precise playing was all that stopped the Demon until the Pipes of Power could be played.

At his side, Fendrick's face purpled as he blew into the blowpipe inflating the bagpipes. At last, pumping a swollen bladder with his elbow and fingering the cantor, he wheezed out a harmony to the dulcimer. The sparkling barrier took on a new brilliance and held the Demon in check. Rhazburn watched with satisfaction but slipped his own copper whistle out of its leather cover for a backup should they tire. Shortly, the curtain of light began to wane, and a green tentacle poked through. Dollop, heeding the weakening of the spell, touched another Copper Order to the Musical Mystical Door causing the barrier to brighten again. He whistled the magical tune along with Grunion. Dollop was the only Demonward talented enough to bolster the spell with his whistling alone.

Grunion hammered out the rhythm, and Fendrick tootled the melody without wavering. They could keep it up for two entire Blessings if pressed, but they would tire in the end. Although Dollop had plenty of coins, in less than one Blessing of time his supply would be gone with no more available to the Poets locked in the chamber. So the Poets had to do what they could to banish the Demon far away from the mortal world and Hell's Breach.

Seeing Dollop judge the strength of the Barrier accurately reassured Rhazburn that he had made the right decision about the youth. No one could tell for sure who was right for a Demonward. The tests given the candidates screened out the incompetent. Still, the final decision was up to the Loremaster. Dollop was the best candidate he had ever tested. His memory was flawless and he had musical talent far beyond any of the other Poets. His melodic whistling captivated anyone who listened. In many ways, Dollop was Rhazburn ten years before - young, alone, and driven to achieve. Still, Rhazburn lived with a nagging worry that his love for Dollop had affected his judgment.

Rhazburn tore his gaze from the ongoing musical battle and concentrated on the spells they would need to drive the Demon away.

"Meerdrum, Tindal, a Crawler. Let's try a Poem of Levitation to stop it and a Couplet of Wind to blow it away." They both nodded to their superior.

Wesfallen offered, "How about the third stanza of Wilfonney's Canticle? That worked quite well on the Crawler last autumn."

"Good idea, Falli. I like that one, too." He turned to the younger Poets. "Use the second verse."

"Which is?" Tindal asked impatiently.

> Fervid fingers of sunlight
> Gloved in leaves
> Pluck the dewy strings
> Of a spinning Spider's
> Siren harp
> Beseeching cool mist

Rhazburn turned to Wesfallen. "Falli, help them with the lines."

The three began sprinkling letters in pearl dust on the hardwood rank of the floor. Rhazburn carried all the vials of precious gem dust, but he entrusted them with the pearl dust for this very purpose. The more precious the dust, the stronger the spell. Rhazburn calculated pearl dust would be sufficient for this Demon.

He began going through the various Couplets of Wind in his mind trying to decide which would be the best when he heard a quickening of the cadence played by Fendrick and Grunion. Looking up at the Demon's form softened by the curtain of light, he saw the Demon begin to change. At first, he thought they had won, and the Demon was evaporating back into the poison from which it formed. Instead, the snarling apparition split into several smaller forms. Slowly, the figures molded themselves into six sobbing spirits. From his position two rods away standing on the wood rank, he could just make out the faces of the spirits.

Three, he recognized. One was the departed mother of Grunion. The second was the deceased brother of Wesfallen. The third, however, distressed Rhazburn the most. It appeared to be the dead wife of Dollop. In one arm, she held an infant, and with the other, she reached toward her husband. Rhazburn immediately deduced the Demon's ploy. It was using the Demonward's memories of loved ones passed away to take them off guard. Most of the Poets took a look but, well aware of the deceptions of Demons, ignored them. Grunion didn't miss a note in his magical song. Wesfallen calmly continued to form words in pearl dust on the floor.

When Rhazburn's gaze fell upon Dollop, his heart raced. The youth was frozen, staring at the false image of his dead sweetheart. Rhazburn watched the spirit's lips closely, trying to filter out all the sounds but her voice.

She reached out and cried, "Dollop, oh, Dollop my darling! Save me! I don't belong here. The pain, the fire! I can't stand it! Just touch my hand, and I'll be free!"

Horrified at what he knew would happen to the sensitive youth, Rhazburn burst his lungs yelling, "Dollop, Nooooo!" but he was too late. He ran as fast as he could past the Poets sprinkling pearl dust, even smearing one of the carefully traced words in the process. But Dollop was only two strides from Hell's Breach. The Musical Mystical Door was a barrier to Demons but human flesh could pass. Even with the barrier brilliantly flashing, Dollop could reach through. With a eerie smile and an apologetic tear in one eye, he looked back briefly at his mentor, then turned to touch the spectral hand.

Instantly, he spun around. His scream split the air. With wild and furious eyes, he stared, gnashing his teeth through a bespittled grimace.

Even running at full speed, Rhazburn was so taken aback by the sudden transformation of his gentle student that he skidded to a halt. After assessing the situation a scant moment, Rhazburn lunged at the mad youth. Dollop whirled the heavy coin pouch over his head like an iron morning star, and just as Rhazburn was about to tackle him, he slammed the pouch into Rhazburn's chin. Bright pain shot through Rhazburn's face, and he was thrown onto his back.

A gray world settled upon him. Sounds of scuffling came out of a distant dream. He could hear cries and groans and thought they meant something. As a sharp sulfurous smell of the Hellfire seared Rhazburn's nostrils, he heard a metallic ring far away. He fought his eyes open and struggled to sit up. A light hand touched his shoulder. When he could focus his eyes, he saw Meerdrum looking at him, worried.

Rhazburn came to his senses and sat straight up. He saw Dollop in front of Grunion, who groaned on the floor, clutching his belly. The silver dulcimer lay silent and useless beside him.

Dollop shoved the dulcimer with his foot. The dulcimer spun across the floor, its strings humming. Dollop leapt at Fendrick who was still playing the Pipes of Power.

He tried to push Dollop away with his foot while he kept up the tune on the bagpipes.

Tindal and Wesfallen rushed to help the piper as Rhazburn jumped up to stand.

Dollop, driven to fury, was too fast for any of them. With a flick of his wrist, he grabbed the bagpipe flute and tore it out, ripping apart the bag and breaking Fendrick's arm with a loud crack.

The tune of the bagpipes was replaced by Fendrick's howling in pain as he threw what was left of the Pipes of Power in a silent heap on the floor.

Dollop sensed Wesfallen and Tindal running up behind him, so he turned to swing the coin pouch viciously in their faces.

The barrier of the Musical Mystical Door was faltering, and the Demon had reformed into its original repulsive state. Four clawed hands clamped onto the four sides of the Door as the Demon strained to burst through it.

Rhazburn turned and shouted at Meerdrum, "Get back and finish that verse." Meerdrum fled to complete the poem as the Demon strained to squeeze through the Musical Mystical Door.

As Rhazburn stood up, a toothed claw snaked at his face. He ducked. The claw snapped in the air over his head. Dozens of limbs clutched at him. He danced and dodged while fishing in his vest pocket for Jonathon's vial of diamond dust. A halo of tentacles closed upon him as he flung a cloud of diamond dust in the face of the Demon.

"Portal barred by diamond hard," he rasped. With the last syllable, the tentacles, a touch away from his head, were sucked back beyond the gate. The spell was powerful when activated by diamond dust but would only last a few moments. Rhazburn took out one of the Copper Orders and dropped it on the Verse of Exclusion. From his belt he pulled his copper whistle. Before the barrier flickered out, he touched another Order to the whistle and began to tootle out the magical tune. He pointed the whistle at the barrier and moved it back and forth, strengthening the barrier a little. He wanted to turn around and help the others with Dollop but keeping the Demon behind the Door took precedence. He played the jaunty melody, whistling up and down the scale. If he were in a pub, he'd be doing a little dance.

In the midst of the tune, the scuffling and cries behind him became louder. Rhazburn turned an eye to see Dollop racing toward him. Rhazburn thought that Dollop, crazed by the Demon's touch, in the Demon's power, was about to attack him to silence the whistle. It would be the last obstruction to the Demon's release. He dodged to the side but was shocked when Dollop ran past him without hesitating. Rhazburn suddenly realized Dollop's goal. He stumbled forward, trying to trip the youth, but was too far behind.

Dollop reached the Musical Mystical Door and dove straight through the Shimmering curtain into the infinite abyss, taking the coin pouch and all its magical power with him.

Rhazburn dropped the copper whistle from his mouth and cried, "Dollop!" squeezing the whistle so tight it bent in his hand. As a heavy claw bounced against the barrier of light that faltered without the power of his song, Rhazburn cleared the grief from his head with a shake and a shudder and straightened the bent whistle over his knee. Before the magical curtain disappeared, he jammed the whistle back in his mouth, and ten times louder now, he wailed out the tune to constrain the Demon. In his mind, he cursed himself for his idiocy in allowing Dollop to become a Demonward.

Behind Rhazburn, Wesfallen had righted the dulcimer and retrieved the hammers. The instrument was intact so he began to play the magical tune, backing up Rhazburn's whistle.

When Rhazburn heard the dulcimer, he relaxed and shoved the whistle back in his belt. "Tindal, come here. I have a few Coppers." Tindal ran to him, and Rhazburn gave him the three Copper Orders to fuel Wesfallen's dulcimer and the Verse of Exclusion. Rhazburn ran back to the other Poets.

He saw Fendrick's broken arm and heard the hissing of his breath as the other Poet tried to suppress the pain. "Fendrick, take the first rank," he ordered. "When the tune fails, use the Lightning Balls."

Fendrick nodded shortly, apparently glad to do something to get his mind off his injury. Holding his broken arm tight against his side with his other hand, Fendrick ran to the scintillating Door.

While Meerdrum finished the Verse of Levitation, Rhazburn used the last of the pearl dust to trace the Couplet of Wind. Grunion, still massaging his stomach, shuffled up to Rhazburn's side and volunteered, "Let me help you, Rhaz. What are you writing?"

"Trees wail and bow to Executioner Wind. At a whim, his ax falls." He said it slowly, so Grunion would not mistake his words in the commotion.

The strains of the dulcimer held the Demon at bay until Tindal shouted, "This is the last Order, Rhaz."

"Use it!" Rhazburn shouted. He looked at Meerdrum and Grunion.

They both shrugged. After the last Copper Order was exhausted, the barrier faded fast since they had no more coins to release the magical verses or fuel the tunes.

Rhazburn turned to see the Demon's grasping limbs arching toward Fendrick. The Poet's right arm hung in a sickening twist at his side but with his left, he gestured behind him and cried, "Sparkle!"

A yellow globe of light streaked from the ceiling and struck the Demon full in the face. A concussion shook the chamber as the Ball Lightning burst into a shower of sparks. The force of the explosion pushed the Demon back just beyond the Musical Mystical door.

Rhazburn could wait no longer. If Fendrick had to use all the lightning balls one by one, they would eventually be in darkness, and the Demon would escape, despite all their efforts. Without a word, Rhazburn turned and bolted for the door to the chamber. As he ran, he heard Fendrick yell, "Bolt Button." He saw the green globe fly past him toward Hell's Breach. There were only twenty Ball Lightning globes altogether.

As he ran, all the eyes of the Poets followed him. With a Demon coming through the Gate into Hell's Breach, no guard in his right mind would open the door of the enclosure. As long as the obsidian walls were intact, there was hope a Demon could be contained.

Rhazburn had no time to explain, but he wasn't fleeing. Instead, he made for a dark corner where Jonathon was huddled in terror. When Rhazburn reached the corner, he said, "Father, I need your money."

Jonathon was startled. He was watching the battle, squinting through his fingers, hiding his face like one of his children hiding from imagined Demons in the night shadows. These Demons were real and he wished he were back in his bed. Now Rhazburn wanted his dearly-acquired money. The money that was all that stood between him and the heel of Molgannard Fey's smelly foot. He gripped the leather pouch with its Copper Orders tightly, looking at Rhazburn with confusion and fear.

Rhazburn turned to look at the Gate. Fendrick gestured in the air, and a blue globe sped at the Demon. This time, the Demon parried the lightning ball with a horny claw. It was knocked away, useless, sputtering on the Musical Mystical Door. Fendrick immediately cried, "Glimmer!" and another lightning ball was lost. As Rhazburn turned back to Jonathon, the shouts from Fendrick became quicker and more frantic. "Sunbeam, Fireball, Bright Eye…".

Rhazburn had no time to argue. Giving Jonathon an alarming snarl, he thrust out a rigid hand and growled, "Father… Give… Me… Your… Money."

More afraid of his grown son's wrath than a dozen Giants, Jonathon fumbled the pouch out of his belt and, as if the pouch seared his fingers, popped it into Rhazburn's hand.

Rhazburn softened his gaze slightly and gave a curt nod before he ran back into the thickening gloom of the chamber. The Demon swatted away Ball Lightning after Ball Lightning easily with its many limbs. Six remained to light the chamber. "Firebrow!" yelled Fendrick. Then, only five remained. "Flash!" he yelled, and the chamber dimmed to weak candlelight. "Glare!"

While Rhazburn ran back to the gate, he yelled, "Fendrick, loose the Demon." The Poet sprinted from his post just as the Demon lurched through the gold frame of Hell's Breach. In a moment, Fendrick had joined the other Demonwards who stood in a line on the tile rank. Rhazburn stood in the center of the line, slightly ahead of the others.

Demons were ethereal by nature. The Science of Poetry had determined that, in the ethereal plane of Hell, they appeared and felt solid as any real substance did in the mortal world. Once they passed into the world through Hell's Breach, their ethereal substance became invisible to human sight. It was only by using a Verse of Demon Recognition encircling the Musical Mystical Door that a Demon could be seen by the Demonwards, and then only for a short period of time. Fueled by a Copper Order, that visibility lasted long enough for the Demonwards to dispose of any Demon they had encountered thus far.

As the Demon scrambled on innumerable pads, paws, and hooves into the Chamber of Hell's Breach, a disgusting stench rolled on before it. Rhazburn's head reeled with nausea.

Tentacles and pincers filled the room before him. A knife of cold came from the Demon's eyes and chilled his soul.

As the first mass of limbs touched the wood rank, Rhazburn tossed a Copper Order onto the Poem of Levitation.

Screaming, the Demon rose from the floor, clutches and claws flailing the air. The Demon's screams pierced their ears like ice picks, and several of the Demonwards bowed their heads to cover their ears.

Rhazburn stared coldly back into the lurid red eyes. He thought to himself that nothing is easier than sending a Demon back to Hell. Onto the Couplet of Wind he threw a single Copper Order. One was enough. A cool breath passed Rhazburn's face. A breeze mussed his hair. The wind steadily mounted until his jacket pummeled his sides. On the floor, the Couplet traced in pearl dust was the only thing unmoved by the wind, the power of the coin mixed with the words to make it inviolable for the moment.

The Demon began turning slowly as it waved all its limbs, trying to swim in the air against the magical wind. Slowly, screaming, the Demon passed back through Hell's Breach and was engulfed in the clouds.

No one cheered. Dollop had been lost, and Rhazburn had almost met his match. As the wind slackened, Rhazburn looked away.

Tindal touched his arm. "Rhazburn. The Door."

Rhazburn looked back through the gloom, lit only by three lightning balls. A frail human figure was on the other side of the Door, fighting the wind and grabbing at the frame. When the figure lifted his head, Rhazburn could not mistake even in the twilight that it was Dollop.

"Holy Ilsa's eyes," Tindal said softly.

Dollop shouted, "Master, I've done it! I've come back! The Demon is gone."

No one spoke. They all stared. Rhazburn unclenched his fist and reached in the money pouch.

"Rhazburn, it's me, Dollop. Falli, Tindal, it *is* me. I can prove it. I found the answer. I know how to close Hell's Breach. Just listen to me."

Rhazburn was crying inside. He had no dead parents, wife, or child from the past to sway him and turn his mind against reason. Few people had touched him in the world. His natural father was no closer to him than the Forbidden Mountains. His mother was only a painful memory. Dollop, his half brother, was the closest relative he had known. Dollop, whom he had nurtured through the lore of the Poets and nursed out of mourning. Dollop was one man he could call his friend. Now Dollop was before him. Or was it a false Dollop, spawned by the Demon? He couldn't be sure.

Rhazburn thought that perhaps the Demon affected their minds and each one saw the one most loved, all seeing different people. "Tindal, who do you see and hear?".

"Dollop, Loremaster."

"Wesfallen?"

"Dollop's whom I see."

"Rhazburn, listen, I can recite any poem you name. Here, Gulligan's Missive." Dollop was climbing up onto the frame of Hell's Breach as he began to sing verses of a pub tune Rhazburn had taught him.

> Beset by the bosom of Candiline
> Gulligan lauded bilberry wine
> Arm in arm they tippled a flagon
> He swatted her rump so she rode his Dragon
> Sir Gulligan is cool again
> He's nothing but a fool again

Rhazburn well knew Dollop's voice. It was not quite mature, closer to alto than tenor, a child's voice. Dollop's eyes were frightened, pleading. Singing the ludicrous song, the youth's voice quivered with a suppressed sob.

Rhazburn knew the Demonwards were too far from the Musical Mystical Door to reactivate it. If they could run there, activate the Door and play the Silver Dulcimer, Dollop would have been kept out if he were a Demon. Rhazburn was unsure if the Verse of Demon Recognition would work to highlight a Demon possessing a human body. If the man they saw was Dollop, he still might harbor a Demon within him and it would go unrecognized. There was no time to ponder it further. The situation was a danger to the other Demonwards and all Isseltrent. All the world, for that matter.

"Dollop, stop!" Rhazburn shouted. "If you are Dollop, stop now."

Without looking up or acknowledging Rhazburn's order, Dollop cautiously bent to place his foot on the floor. Rhazburn felt Wesfallen's head snap around at him from the side. Before Wesfallen could say a word, Rhazburn said to himself, "Forgive me, Dollop," and dropped five Copper Orders onto the Couplet of Wind.

Dollop cried, "No, Rhazburn, no!"

A wind built up behind them to gale force and higher and higher in power, whining through the portal like a lost child. The hurricane hit them without mercy, throwing them all on their stomachs. Rhazburn's hair whipped his face. He saw Jonathon's turban sail past him through the door.

Dollop tried to hold onto the frame, yelling, "No, Rhazburn, it's really meee..." His grip was torn away. With his last word, his form shrank into the distance, and his cry died in the wind.

CHAPTER 3

TRALLALAIR

As she sighed a puff of smoke came from Hover's flared nostrils. The Dragonpaddock was barely long enough to accommodate Hover, the Green Dragon of Thunder Brand. Trallalair and her Sinjery Sisters from Thunder Brand surrounded the Dragon. They all had their daggers drawn ready to mete out death.

With a practiced flick of her dagger, Trallalair popped the hand-sized Dragonleech from beneath a scale on Hover's neck. "Wehennah," Trallalair called to the nearest Sinjery Scaler in the Brand. "You've spitted a lot of these nasty suckers already. Mother! There are a lot of them."

"We've been pulling them off all morning," was the Scaler's response. "Most were bloated. I think we just missed them yesterday. These new green ones blend right in until they're fat with blood."

Hover looked fit. A few dozen quarts of blood wouldn't be missed by the Green Dragon. She was all of five rods from snout horn to tail barb, but Trallalair was well aware her own life depended upon a robust Hover. As the Dragonflyer for Thunder Brand, she was the only one of the thirteen

Sisters caring for Hover allowed to ride the Green Dragon. Since Hover was never allowed to fly without Trallalair astride her neck, if Hover, from lack of care, weakened and fell from the sky, Trallalair would fall and die with her. For a Sinjery Dragonflyer it would be a glorious death, but a useless one. She could never deserve to roam the Sky Forests for all Eternity unless she died serving her Sisters in some manner.

Wehennah went on with her complaints. "Sir Dibodel flew by yesterday. Molten was full of fat ones, believe me. And Molten so old. I'm surprised he could open his wings. I wouldn't pay his Scalers two Suggs if I were Dibodel."

Male Knight Dragonflyers used hired Scalers to care for their Dragons. This was a dangerous practice in the eyes of the Sisters, but then, they were men, and men were always brash and careless with their mounts.

The all-female Sinjery Brands used only their Sisters as Scalers. The Sinjery were loyal and fastidious in their care of their treasured friends, the Green Dragons. A Sinjery Scaler could never allow, by the slightest omission of care, any danger for her Sister riding the Dragon.

Hover's scaling proceeded slowly that morning. The Brand was short two Sisters, Kirienesse and Hamrodel. They were two veterans of the Brand who had paid the ultimate price for their Sisters. They had been summoned by Seldric to his chamber years before. The Dragonlord demanded that chosen Sisters share his bed at his whim. If they bore him a child as a consequence it was their problem. No one in the court but the Sinjery Sisters cared what happened to the Royal Bastards from the time they were born. Kirienesse and Hamrodel were absent from the scaling because they were doing their stint that morning in the Sinjery Bough, the nursery for all the young illegitimate children of the Sinjery.

Both Trallalair and Wehennah looked skyward as a shadow passed. What looked like a bird lost in the sun's brilliance, translated below into the shadow of a Dragon with wings spread, rippling through the oaks to the east of the paddock. From behind them came a second Dragon. A rushing of huge wings and a hoarse bellow accompanied an ancient Green Dragon flying just above the oaks. The massive beast soared overhead frightfully close, almost brushing the paddock wall. It was near enough for Hover, with her fierce territoriality, to snap at the fleeing tail. Wind from the Dragon's wings blew Trallalair's long sable hair into her eyes.

She shook her head and blinked it away. The ancient Green was Mace. Atop him was Sir Strumpet in his green armor, holding a lance pennant emblazoned with a silver mace.

Mace ascended quickly to follow the Dragon casting the fleeting shadow. Presently, two more Dragons flew from the hills to rendezvous with them. From behind the golden dome of Blaze, the Dragonlord's Palace, a fifth Dragon erupted. All were Green Dragons, the fastest race of Dragons, and the only type used by the Brands.

Each race of Dragons had their role in society. The Red Dragons had the fires of Hell in their lungs and were the only ones forced to fire the Dragonkilns to produce Glass Commands. The Greens were the lightest and fastest, the mounts for the Brands of the Sinjery Rings and the Lances of Knights. Blue Dragons had no wings nor legs but swam in the sea using their broad tails, guiding themselves with massive flippers. They were used to pull the Dragontailer ships in the Navy of the Dragonlord and the fishing and merchant fleets. White Dragons were used by the Dragonlord for their cold breath to preserve perishable meats from game slaughtered in the far North. The meat was stored in the Ice Palace where more Whites were used to keep the game frozen until the Dragonlord required it for his table or for one of his opulent feasts. The largest and oldest race of Dragons, Black Dragons, possessed within themselves an inexplicable arcane power allowing them to transport people great distances from the mouth of one Black Dragon to another.

Like all Dragonflyers, Trallalair spurned Black Dragon travel. For her, the pleasure of travel was not in getting somewhere instantly but in the traveling itself. Nothing under the sun matched the thrill of flying high in the air astride a Green Dragon.

The flight of Dragons accelerated off into the East. Seldom had so many Dragons been dispatched to any part of the Realm. One Green Dragon alone was as powerful as an army. Some great trouble must have arisen. War was unlikely. No other nation or land, not even the Demon in the Dead Lands, had the power to attack Thuringland as long as the Dragoncrown existed. The Dragons would make short work even of Sverdphthik's army of Zombies and Ghouls.

"Trallalair, my Sister." She turned to the sound of boots crunching the layer of hay over the dirt of the Dragon Paddock. Yllaressa, one of her

Sinjery Sisters and captain of the Dragonlord's personal guards, approached from the Dragonlord's Palace.

"You are beckoned." The Dragonlord's bed awaited. A Knight or a messenger who was not a Sinjery Sister would have been much more formal, saying, "Our Liege commands your presence," or some such rot, but the Sisters had nothing to hide from each other, no pretense to uphold.

Trallalair sighed and smiled wryly at the young warrior. She was clad in crimson armor. This striking red was reserved for the Dragonlord's personal guard, the Inner Ring, and was made up entirely of Seldric's daughters, Royal Bastards all of them. The crimson-clad Sinjery were the only ones who would never be called to share Seldric's bed. He may be lustful, but he was not incestuous. Previous Dragonlords had been much worse.

Trallalair pitied her striking young Sister sweating profusely in the early summer heat. Yllaressa's face glistened alluringly above the steel collar of her armor. The steel was quite a bit hotter than Trallalair's own green leathers and highly inappropriate in peacetime. Trallalair's leather Dragonflyer armor was light, meant only to deflect a spent arrow fired from below. Even though she was required to wear her armor every time she flew Hover, Trallalair was not as flushed as Yllaressa in the full sun of the paddock.

Yllaressa with her beautiful long hair roused a prurient interest in Trallalair, but she deflected the emotion. The Captain of the Guard was far too young for Trallalair and the Dragonflyer was far too loyal to her Soulsister, Saggethrie.

"Get out of this heat, Yllaressa, and pour the sweat out of your boots before you get the foot creep. Why in the world does he have you in full armor on such a hot day?" For spring the sun was too hot, the air too muggy. Despite the clear skies, Trallalair felt the thunderclouds massing just beyond the horizon. If she took Hover up, she knew they'd encounter them.

"You have no idea how snappy he is today. Not telling us though. Even Cithoney hasn't an inkling." Cithoney was the Queen, a Sinjery Sister and source of inside information for them all. "You'll hear first I'll bet. He's just waiting to tell you first. Do you have something to drink?" As the Dragonlord's current concubine, Trallalair was also Seldric's current confidant.

"Apple squash."

"Great."

Trallalair got her a mug of the tart draught which the guard downed without a breath.

"More?" Trallalair filled it again.

This time Yllaressa only drank half, quietly belching and holding the mug, studying the drink as if it held answers to her puzzlement. "You'll see. Blaze is all in a dither because of his ill mood. Like when you're standing there outside his door and you feel like someone is creeping up just around the corner, so you look around it, but nobody's there. Like a Ghost. Creepy. I hope he tells you."

"All right. You better get back inside, so we don't have to give you all our squash to keep you from keeling over. And I better go find out what's up with Seldric."

Yllaressa thankfully gulped the rest of the golden refreshment and nodded herself away to a cooler station inside Blaze.

Trallalair had to change. Even her light armor would prevent the performance of the other chore of the Sinjery, helping the Dragonlord relax by satisfying his lust. The task was as onerous for a Sinjery Sister as was cleaning up a reeking Dragonpile left by another Dragon visiting their paddock. Hover would never foul her own bed with excrement, just like Trallalair would never foul her own bed with a man. Not unless commanded, and then only because the Dragonlord had the power of the Dragons within easy reach of Sinjer to back up his commands.

Trallalair wondered how many times Sinjery maidens that the Dragonlords chose for their bed mates had pleaded with the rulers to use the services of Choralists to satisfy their lust. Hundreds of Choralists stalked the streets and lined the pub walls to satisfy the hedonistic needs of men and women who pretended laying with a Choralist was equivalent to devout worship of The Three. The only purpose of the Choir was to promote the Love of Ilsa through the ecstasy of the physical union of humans. To the cultists of the Choir, Heaven had to be some sort of eternal orgasm. Every time one of the Choir felt that joyful release of love, they praised Ilsa for her blessing and a small taste of the Afterlife. The

Dragonlords with their inexhaustible lust seemed to freely subscribe to the teachings of the Choir.

They were not so naïve, however, these wearers of the Dragoncrown and protectors of the safety of all Thuringland, to allow themselves to be influenced by the substantial wiles of a Choralist. To a Sinjery maiden's mind, a Choralist was nothing more than a whore, and the offerings given to the cult by those they served nothing more than a whore's fees. The Dragonlords had always chosen the loyal and unfailingly-honest Sinjery as their only consorts.

For consolation, Trallalair looked to her mount. Hover's golden eye gave no hint of emotion.

"Hover, you'll get a ram tonight," Trallalair said to her Dragon. The Dragonlord always let Dragonflyers take a treat back to their mounts, as a gift for their service. Hover exhaled, forming transient tornadoes of straw and dust. Trallalair would get no sympathy from Hover.

A soft caress of her cheek from a warm hand calmed Trallalair's discomposure. She leaned her head against the gentle long fingers she knew were Saggethrie's. Another empathetic hand passed through her long black hair, enticing. As usual, Trallalair could not bear to look into Saggethrie's eyes. Every time she went to the Dragonlord, she betrayed her race. She had intercourse with a man, the antithesis of all she believed in, all she had been taught by her loving Sisters. Instead of meeting Saggethrie's gaze, she touched the hand on her cheek and pressed the warmth tightly to her. Clasping her lover's hand in hers, still ashamed to look up, Trallalair led Saggethrie to the barracks where she had to prepare herself for the Dragonlord's huge, rough, disgusting body.

As Saggethrie helped her unlace the taut ties, she passed her hands between the leather and Trallalair's undergarments to pull away the armor. Trallalair pulled away her own linen underclothes soaked with perspiration and lay naked, prone, her folded arms a pillow for her cheek. Saggethrie took out her cruet of cypress oil, rendered from the needles of Mother Cypress that shaded their village in the swamps of Sinjer. When the cruet was brought by the most recent tribute of Sinjery maidens, it had been cushioned in the pack by Anther Flowers, deep red, shaped like hearts impaled by their own pistil.

The heady fragrance of the cypress oil took Trallalair back to their village, to where no one touched her but Saggethrie. Trallalair loved the smell of the oil. For a moment, she was climbing to the top of Mother Cypress, her arms stretched widely, embracing the thousands of birds and butterflies flying above the trees. She could see the churning clouds, feel the wonderful heat. Her skin glistened with sweat as a wall of rain approached to wash her clean of all the grime of the world. Every time she was called to the Dragonlord she had Saggethrie massage the oil into every mound and cleft of her body, not for the pleasure of the Dragonlord, but for the pleasure of her lover's exhilarating touch. Saggethrie supplemented the erotic massage with her lips.

No training exercise of battle quickened her heart like entwining with Saggethrie. The fragrant sheen of cypress oil on her skin remained a memoir of Saggethrie's warmth.

"You give me all the joy in my life. How can I go to him now and let him bore away all the pleasure you have filled me with?" It was a futile question for a concubine.

Saggethrie passed her hand through Trallalair's hair so it, too, blossomed with fragrance. "Let the smell of Mother Cypress link us, a better armor than your leathers. I'll wash his stink away when he is finished."

They would have spent all of Work Blessing together if permitted, but the Dragonlord's command hung over them like spiraling vultures. Saggethrie unfolded Trallalair's blue gown from her footlocker. It was as light as the wind. She smoothed the wrinkles as Trallalair wriggled into it.

The sky blue dress acknowledged Trallalair's willingness to share the Dragonlord's bed. Dragonflyers wore sky blue. Scalers wore green dresses. Fighters in the Rings wore shimmering gold. Apart from their time with the Dragonlord, Sinjery never wore dresses, since no Sinjery maiden ever shared a bed with any other man or cared what men thought of them. Athletic, they preferred clothes that allowed them freedom of movement. Dresses were useless in the hot Sinjery jungle where women leapt from tree branch to bog and mire sucked at their bare feet. Sinjery wore very little in Sinjer, but then again no men were around to leer at them. Trallalair was sure the dress would look better on a soft court lady.

Before she left, Saggethrie blessed her with a kiss on the lips to let the taste of her linger until Trallalair was assailed by the Dragonlord's roughness.

She walked quickly, embarrassment as much as shame spurring her through the sparkling corridors of Blaze. She wanted to pass like a blue wraith to the chamber of the Dragonlord, but her dress instead trumpeted her purpose to all the sniggering courtiers. Of all the men in Isseltrent, only one did she respect. The only one who had a kind word for her. It was not love she felt for him. It was more like awe she felt for him. He was a hero for all Isseltrent. He was competent and confident. And to Trallalair, he was truly considerate.

"Trallalair, my lovely Trallalair." No luck. The voice was Carten's, one of the young court Alchemists and a Royal Bastard. To be polite, she stopped, but made sure it was by an open window so the fresh breeze would dissipate Carten's pungent perfume. He smoothed his hair to get each perfect strand in place, grinned brightly and said, "The light through that radiant portal frames you in an aura, yes, an aura of mystery. The shape of your beautiful figure is only softened, not hidden, by that azure gossamer caressing your skin."

"Carten, I hate wearing this dress."

"Yes, yes, I see. You, no doubt, wish you could rip it off right now, right here."

"I need to go," she said, irritated by the bantering popinjay.

As she walked past, he extended his arm, barring her way. He held a crystal vial filled with sparkling pink fluid. Carten was massive, his arm all muscle. Trallalair never saw him do anything but mix his chemicals and flirt with every woman in court, so she suspected one of his potions gave him his unnatural strength. It was certainly not physical work.

"I have a draught, a sweet elixir here with me for your indulgence. The heavens will rain flowers and your soul will burst forth, ecstatic and free, with just one taste. All the marvels of the world will be yours with a single drop on your luscious tongue."

"Carten, let me pass." He ignored her request, shaking his sickening little vial in her face.

She smiled pleasantly. She waited until his insipid grin degenerated into a insolent smirk. Then Trallalair took great pleasure in turning that smirk into a painful grimace by rapping him sharply at a spot on his extended elbow where a nerve crossed the bone. With a groan, Carten snatched back his hand, dropping the vial, which shattered on the red granite floor. Trallalair sauntered past without a further glance. Furious, towering over her, still Carten backed off. She assumed he knew better than to attempt to best a Sinjery Brandmistress.

As she walked along a marble colonnade on her way to Seldric's chambers, Trallalair passed a small courtyard where the Sinjery Bough, about ten children, all less than five, clustered around Hamrodel and Kirienesse. Hamrodel sang to them while Kirienesse was off to one side, prying apart two girls who were wrestling on the ground. *Typical girls*, Trallalair thought. In a year, they would be off to Sinjer to be nurtured by their mothers in their native land. They would make good warriors and hunters. She noticed the young boys all listened intently to Hamrodel trying to mouth the words with her. None of them would go back to Sinjer with their mothers. They would need all their wits to make a living in Isseltrent. In a few years, they'd be squires to Knights, apprentices to craftsmen, pages in the court or acolytes to the Holy Few.

She passed up the stairs to the chambers of the Dragonlord. Through a window, not much more than a slit, she saw the half-buried obsidian egg that contained Hell's Breach. There she paused a moment with brief regret that the heroic man she knew was not the Dragonlord beyond the doors before her. But if he were the Dragonlord, she doubted he would allow the travesty of subjecting Trallalair and her Sisters to this lascivious slavery. So she would not even be here.

Approaching the Dragonlord's chambers, she passed between the double row of crimson-armored Sinjery guards. Their polite smiles were as brief as their nods. Themselves Royal Bastards, the maidens of the Inner Ring shared her shame every time she passed Seldric's chamber door. The last two in line silently opened Seldric's door for her.

"Took your time, did you, Trallalair?" Seldric said, looking up from his table strewn with documents. The Dragonlord, dressed in a blue robe fringed with red, guzzled a tankard that smelled of ale. Irritated, he nodded his head in the direction of the canopied bed.

Trallalair walked past, feeling cold and dry. "Apologies, your Highness." She would do her duty, but she was not going to run to him like a frightened puppy. "I wanted myself properly prepared for you."

"By the way, that languid wave of yours when Hover flew by was pretty weak. Next time, try to pretend a little enthusiasm."

Get yourself a Choralist if you want enthusiasm, she thought. She nodded in acquiescence, inwardly imagining her fist flattening his nose in response to his rude comment. She had been warned by Sisters long discarded by Seldric that he would often interrupt her daily flights to indulge his whims. Even though she was being displayed like a dessert tart, Trallalair stoically endured his stares whenever Hover was forced to fly by his golden dome. The dome thrust upward within the cluster of Blaze's more diminutive towers like some great gilt erection. Evenly, quelling her rage, she said, "I didn't want to lose my balance."

Seldric harrumphed at her implausible explanation. "If you fall off, I'll have Hover catch you." The Dragonlord's eyes tilted upward toward the Dragoncrown. There it was, a thick black glass coronet within which two white pearls were embedded like eyes staring out from Seldric's forehead. Seldric could do whatever he wanted with Hover. He could make her fly into the sea. He could make her eat rocks. He could do the same with any Dragon in all Thuringland. But Trallalair knew that Seldric was as enslaved to the Dragoncrown as the Dragons were to him. Only for brief moments could it be off his head. Otherwise, the Dragons would be freed. Pain, suffering, and anger from scores of Dragons constantly seethed in his mind. It made him surly and short with everyone around him, even the women who shared his bed.

The Sinjery were unwilling but loyal lovers. They could never allow him to leave the Crown off for a prolonged period. Too many Sinjery lives, especially Dragonflyers and Scalers in the Brands caring for the Dragons, were at stake, not to mention all the male Royal Bastards from courtiers to Knights. All of them Sinjery children. Likewise, the forests and swamps of Sinjer were prime hunting lands for wild Dragons. If the five score Dragons were freed, her entire race would be in danger. The constant threat to all the Sinjery ensured Trallalair's loyalty to Seldric.

Like the Dragonlords before him, Seldric trusted few. Like them, he took advantage of his position toward those who were subjugated by him.

Once every few decades, an anemic rebellion threatened the authority of the Dragonlord. Every uprising was obliterated by the power of the Dragons. The Sinjery Rings and the Knight Lances had little to do but bury the charred and broken bodies of the rebels.

"A Black died today," he said, surprising her with his nonchalance.

"I'm sorry. Was it painful for you?" Since the Dragoncrown allowed the Dragonlord to share the thoughts the Dragons experienced, Seldric must have felt the pangs of distress felt by the Black Dragon. Yet he was outwardly calm. He looked unaffected.

"No, no, that's not it. The Black was killed."

Trallalair jerked her head back in disbelief. "Impossible. Nothing in the world can kill a Black Dragon."

"Nonetheless."

Her mind groped for an explanation. Logically, only one explanation was possible. "The Demon?" she gasped.

"Yes, so I believe."

She thought back to the unusual congregation of Knights flying east. "The Knights. Five of them. That's where they were going. Was the Black killed near the Dead Lands?"

He nodded again. "Inside Sylvanward." Sylvanward was the land of the Sylvets. It encompassed the Forbidden Mountains, a granite wall protecting Thuringland from the Dead Lands, and was the farthest the Dragoncrown reached. Only a few token Black Dragons were tolerated there by the Sylvets. Knight Dragonflyers flew over Sylvanward regularly, but they were proscribed from landing. Of the all Tributary States, Sylvanward was the most obscure. No one was allowed in but the Sylvets themselves. In the past three centuries, the only people who dared to enter the Forbidden Mountains were never seen again. Since then, the mountains were off limits and pronounced forbidden to all. Most assumed the danger existed for the inhabitants of the Dead Lands as well. Nothing was ever reported passing through Sylvanward into the Realm. No one in Thuringland understood the arcane power of the Sylvets, but that power had been unquestioned since the Demon destroyed ancient Verdilon east of the Forbidden Mountains and formed the Dead Lands. As Sinjer was inhospitable to men, Sylvanward was inhospitable to any but the Sylvets.

The Forbidden Mountains acted like a buffer between the Dead Lands of the Demon and the Realm of the Dragonlord.

The Eastern Muster of Knights had seven Lances each with its own Brand. The Lances were named for aspects of their Dragons. Their names were Eye, Ear, Mind, Fang, Horn, Scale and Claw. All those Lances and Brands constantly scoured the foothills to the west for anything sneaking through Sylvanward into the Commonwealth of Dis.

Trallalair was still in shock. "I can't believe the Demon could kill a Black in Sylvanward. The Sylvets would never permit it." It was a widely-held belief, but few Sylvet emissaries had been seen in Seldric's lifetime. They were exceedingly rare. No one really knew what the Sylvets would or would not permit to pass through their land.

Seldric shrugged. "I believe the Demon took the Black by surprise. I doubt the Sylvets even knew. If they did, I probably won't hear about it for a decade." Any news of changes in Sylvanward had a way of lingering there for many years before it came to attention of Isseltrent. Another mystery none could explain.

"Could the Demon have traveled here by the Black?"

"That would be foolish. I'd just destroy his stolen body, or better, have the Demonwards toss him back into Hell. He will never dare come to Isseltrent as long as I wear the Dragoncrown."

Trallalair thought Seldric rather overconfident. Sverdphthik was fully as powerful in his demesne as the Dragonlord was in Thuringland. For three centuries, the Demon had resisted any attempts to destroy him or his followers. It was common knowledge that he collected dead things, using them as walking but dead servants, building up an army over the years. The longer the Demon waited, the stronger his army became. She doubted whatever power existed in Sylvanward could exclude the Demon's army from Thuringland forever.

"You are not worried at all? The Demon has never dared kill a Dragon before. Maybe he is testing his strength against you. I think he means to come here. Maybe he wants to assassinate you and take the Dragoncrown."

Seldric guffawed. "Let him try. No, the Demon will go back to his Hellpit. I am sure. Prattlers of doom surround me, expecting me to quiver in fear at a single Demon when we vanquish scores a year at Hell's Breach. There is no danger. I sent more Knights to the near side of

Sylvanward to destroy his body as he leaves the mountains. I have never feared Sverdphthik, but he has a lot to fear from me." He laughed at her discomfiture.

For once, his laugh, intending to be callous, seemed nervous. Seldric was frightened. Still, she could tell he would never admit it. She sensed he wanted her concern, even though he refused to acknowledge it. All men were born to be frail. She shielded her thoughts. Someone must protect the Realm from the Demon, even if Seldric's pride refused to let him guard himself properly. The lives of her Sisters were at stake as well.

"Right now I need a break from all this seething Dragonbanter in my skull. Come, Trallalair. Say no more. Relax."

Seldric's command to relax started a reflex tension throughout her body. Only by fantasizing about her lover, Saggethrie, did she have any hope of hiding her disgust. Trallalair had never become pregnant by the Dragonlord, but since she was his current favorite, called for at least every other day, it was only a matter of time before she was with child. A girl child she could take back to Sinjer to be trained as a warrior and come back to serve the Dragonlord. But a boy... a boy she would abandon to the court nurseries and schools when she returned to her homeland. No boy could survive the Curse of Sinjer. The Prayer of the Curse had been uttered by the First Sisters, and Mother Earth had answered their prayer. No man who entered their land of Sinjer, for all the generations since, ever survived. The Curse was their bastion against the onslaught of men and all their cruelty. The sons of the Sinjery Sisters suffered as a consequence. None of them knew their mothers past the time they were tutored by them in the Sinjery Bough.

Seldric stroked Trallalair's hair, bringing it close and inhaling deeply. She was well aware that passion dominated his life. He held the rage and agony of a hundred Dragons in his mind every Favor and Blessing of the day. Still, he could think and emote as if woe did not suffuse his soul constantly. All the troubles of the Realm and the Dragons were mundane duties to him.

She knew making love quelled the thoughts for a short span. She was ready to do her duty. She just hoped he was ready, so the tedious intimacy did not take too long. She was still sore from his last rigorous assault.

She sighed and smiled, acting her part. No Sinjery had lust for a man. They had been trained from childhood to see men as irrational bulls. Seldric held her hand with the tips of his fingers as he led her to his canopied bed. She quickly pulled her gown over her head and tossed it onto the plush chair. Her small breasts over her powerful chest muscles were firm and still. They were certainly not like the court ladies' voluptuous breasts, jiggling with their laughter, barely concealed by silken gowns which were as insubstantial as the whispers they spoke into the ears of Knights.

Breathing heavily, Seldric tore off his cloak. She held his Crown as he lifted her up. He was as powerful as he was passionate, more than a head taller than Trallalair. He held her easily as he kissed her again and again. He pressed her lips so hard his beard scratched her chin. Sometimes she went to her bunk with an abrasion on her chin that lasted for days. Another brand of her role.

Abruptly, he parted the thick canopy and lay her on the bed, dropping her, too fast, as he slipped on the fringe of the canopy in his haste. He didn't apologize for his weight crushing her into his featherbed.

She felt his passion as he peaked and growled in spasms. She held him tightly, steadying the Dragoncrown as he exhausted himself. No matter how violent his upheavals, she knew the Crown would never fall off. Part of its power was to remain tight on the bearer's head regardless of what happened - sleep, battle, or dalliance. Still, it was almost an instinct. So many of her Sister's lives depended upon his control over the Dragons.

Seldric held her for a long time. Finally, he rose. The act of sex seemed a compulsion with the Dragonlords, each one trying to outdo the last in numbers of liaisons. Only the constant flow of Sinjery maidens could accommodate him. His wife, Cithoney, had been worn out years ago. Her chamber was now, to her relief, separate. Cithoney had put on a valiant effort. After all, she was one of them, chosen from among the Sinjery Rings when he was a youth sampling their flesh. Of all the Sinjery, the Queen was the only one allowed to stay in Thuringland past her five years' tribute. The Sinjery warriors depended upon her to provide care for all Seldric's children, legitimate or not. She had organized the Sinjery Bough. All other Sinjery Sisters were prohibited from staying past their time or ever returning. The price they paid in Seldric's service was too high. They all needed the solace of Sinjer forever after.

As Seldric left, Trallalair saw his eyes briefly fill again with the woes of the Dragons and the Realm. Just before the door thumped shut, she saw him harden back into his irascible, inconsiderate demeanor. He barked to his guards, "Summon Gashgrieve to the throne room." She was left alone in his chamber to reassemble herself. She used the Dragonlord's bath cubicle for cleansing, but she would not feel truly clean until Saggethrie gave her another exquisite massage.

That afternoon, she awoke from her reverie under Saggethrie's soft touch. In the ecstatic pleasure she experienced in Saggethrie's hands, Trallalair forgot all about Demons and dead things.

"Your muscles are like knots. What is it? Something you heard?" Saggethrie said.

"Your fingers don't lie. But it's not something I heard. It's something he didn't say. A worry I felt in him. I think the Dragonlord wants me to disobey him." She had told her lover all about her brief conversation with the Dragonlord and how he was overly confident the Demon was too weak to challenge his power. "I think he's too proud to admit it, but I have a feeling he is asking me to guard his back from the Demon while he puts on a facade of contempt for the Demon's abilities."

"You know Seldric's devious and a fool, to treat you such. It doesn't surprise me he'd do such a thing."

"We'd all be foolish to think the Demon will never try to enter Thuringland or attack the Realm. Really, what has he to lose? He can't be destroyed, even by Dragonfire. All he will lose is a stolen body he could replace in an instant.

"What if he begins attacking the Realm? He could sacrifice his Zombie hordes, retreat and go build them up again. It would be all the same to him. And if he succeeded in battling his way into Isseltrent, all the way to Hell's Breach, he could release any number of Demons. One is bad enough. What if there were a hundred?"

"You know what would happen. Nothing would survive."

"You see the reality. Seldric does not," Trallalair said.

"You should talk with Cithoney. Together you could convince him to mobilize the Knights."

"You have good thought, but I'm not sure we have time and I don't think he would agree. He thinks he is above all that. He expects us to guard him. He knows how much we have to lose." Trallalair was not one for procrastinating. "We must mobilize the Brands on the pretext of looking for Skin Splicers. We will monitor every one passing through the Commonwealth of Dis and entering Isseltrent for a fortnight." As Trallalair spoke, she was already donning her leathers. The sun was high in the sky. They still had all of Home Blessing and Dinner Blessing left before sunset and Dusk Blessing.

A low grunt and flash of fire alongside the barracks signaled Hover's rousing from her deep Dragonsleep. The Green raised her head, stretching her prodigious neck to its fullest. She scanned the sky and sniffed the air. A gale through the trees was the sound of Hover's wings opening.

Trallalair knew Hover had sensed the Dragonflyer's approach. The Brandmistress immediately ran up and motioned the Brand to assemble. A coolness now stirred the air. Trallalair could feel the thunderclouds just beyond their sight. She spoke to the group.

"Sisters, you feel the change in the air as I do. After my conversation with Seldric today, I am convinced the Demon may be headed this way." All the Sisters knew the Demon's capabilities. Dead bodies were his vessels. He could inhabit and control a living person briefly, but the resistance of life to death was too strong. After a short stay, the theory was, he would be cast out. It was only a dead body that could not resist his intrusion. If he came to Isseltrent, the Demon would be walking the land hidden in an abomination. Trallalair felt he could not disguise himself against a concerted search. Inside or outside Isseltrent, any dead body could be used by him as a vessel for his evil being. On the plains outside Isseltrent, they could see every creature that moved. The Dragons missed little. Outside Isseltrent was the Sisters' best hope for finding the Demon.

She told them, "All Sinjery Brands must be alerted to patrol the perimeter of Isseltrent and arrest the people entering the city to question them." Finding all the dead in the city was impossible, but there was one place in Isseltrent where dead people went unnoticed for long periods. The Jungle. "All the untended dead in the Jungle must be taken outside the city and burned. No corpse must be left for the Demon to steal."

Relaquy was the first to question her. "You're taking on a lot, Trallalair. Is this the Dragonlord's command?"

"You're concerned I may compromise my position. True, it is all my idea, but I believe Seldric expects we will guard him, however we can."

"You're acting in his behalf, but what if he doesn't agree?"

"Can you take a message to him that we are patrolling for Skin Splicers entering the city again? I believe he'll understand our real purpose and won't pretend to object." The Dragoncrown let the Dragonlord know constantly what every Dragon was doing in the Realm. They could never hide the actions of Hover or any of the Dragons from him. They could only make excuses for their actions. The Sinjery Guards had a lot of freedom to guard Isseltrent and Blaze as they saw fit, unless directly commanded by the Dragonlord.

Many of the Sisters laughed at Trallalair's mention of the Dragonlord's pride. But Relaquy was not amused, nor was she convinced by Trallalair's thinking. She said, "You told him your fears and he laughed at you."

"You know that haughty laugh he has? It doesn't ring true for me. I think he was commanding me without words to protect his skin."

Wehennah and Laramee, two scalers who had had turns as his concubines, laughed knowingly. Mens' emotional disguises were so easy to see past. Seldric's apparent disregard of the Sinjerys' cares was typical. Still, he expected them do their duty to the Realm. Someone had to be responsible. That was why the Dragonlords named the men of his army Knights, but the Sisters he named Guards. For the moment, Trallalair was the closest person to Seldric within the realm. They would have to defer to her judgment as to Seldric's response to their mildly-seditious actions.

Wehennah said, "You have more to tell us and worse, I think."

"You are correct, Wehennah, the Demon already killed a Black."

"Killed a Black?" Wehennah exclaimed, incredulous. "Impossible."

"Your thought was exactly mine. He informed me it was true. He claims the Demon would not have tried to use the Black for fear of the power of the Dragoncrown. But I feel Seldric is mistakenly cocksure. I think the Demon tried to travel by the Black but somehow killed the Dragon instead by the very action of using its power.

"Seldric says he does not fear the Demon. Were you there, you'd see that all his aggrandizement was just more of his bluster. I sensed the fear in him."

Wehennah said, "You know, arresting innocent travelers and burning the dead isn't going to stop the Demon if he wants to come here. But what else do we have?"

Trallalair nodded soberly. They had to try. If Seldric insisted on ignoring the threat, they, his Sinjery Guards, would have to protect the integrity of their land and their own Sisters. After Thuringland was invaded by the Demon and his Zombie hordes, Sinjer, just to the south, would be next. Trallalair would not allow that, whatever price she had to pay.

Ultimately, they all depended on Trallalair's judgment. As the Dragonflyer, she was the leader of the Brand. She allowed them to discuss her orders, but in the end, they would do as she requested.

She agreed with Wehennah. What else did they have? Hover was already active, stomping and extending her wings with quick thrusts and a blizzard of straw. "Relaquy, will you go to Seldric?"

Relaquy nodded her consent.

"Wehennah and Saggethrie, can you alert the other Brands? All thirteen should be in the air within thirty Favors. We'll still have plenty of time before sundown. Three can patrol the Jungle while the rest of us circle the city."

The two Sisters nodded and, splitting apart to make better time, jogged off to the other Brands scattered about the city.

Two of the Sinjery Scalers sang to Hover to calm her. Only the women of her Brand could approach the Green Dragon or speak to her. Any others she regarded as a snack. For the safety of Hover Brand, the Dragonlord restrained the Green from killing her personal Brandmistresses, but for security, he allowed Hover to kill anyone else who approached her.

Bright afternoon sun sparkled on the walls and highlighted every dust mote floating above the paddock. Trallalair was ready to fly. Her Sinjery Blade was sheathed at her waist. Her bow and quiver crisscrossed her back. "Hover, regard."

With a crackling of scales, the Green raised her head high above them. A spout of fire another two rods into the sky was her equivalent of a good stretch. She whipped her massive neck, stopping just in front of the gathered Brand. There it was. The threat of her immense power. Veiled, but always there, restrained only by the influence of the Dragoncrown.

Trallalair nodded to the rest of her Brand. They all scurried back away from Hover's dangerous wings. Trallalair took two loping strides and leaped, planting her right foot precisely on Hover's flexed elbow. She gripped the ridges of the roughly-textured scales with her flexible boots. From there, she jumped up to catch the Green's shoulder with her left foot, then up again, flipping and vaulting to land heavily but precisely in the scant space between two of Hover's rapier sharp spines. She came to rest straddling the Dragon's broad neck. Not a twitch came from the massive Dragon as Trallalair's weight hit her.

Trallalair tightened her knees and felt a pleasing warmth surge through her as the Dragon raised her neck between Trallalair's legs. All the Dragonflyers shared the secret of this pleasure. Saggethrie always chuckled when she talked about it. Trallalair's pleasure in it made her all the more alluring to her Soulsister. Everyone else understood the exhilaration of flying high in the sky, and that was enough for them.

The rest of the Brand backed off to a safe distance. Hover would flap her tremendous wings when ready. If a scaler was beneath who would be crushed by their first movement, too bad. When dealing with a Dragon, the Sisters had to watch out for their own safety. Although the Brand cared for Hover with love, Hover mostly ignored the warm-blooded things she broke and trampled... unless she ate them.

Hover hopped the stand of oaks beside the Brand's enclosure, caught the wind in her wings, and lifted herself up into the gathering clouds. Guided by Trallalair's knees tightening on her neck or pushing this way or that, Hover ascended higher and higher until Trallalair could see the entire city spread beneath her.

On the north side, Blaze dominated the city, tower upon tower rising high above all else. Just south of the palace lay the huge financial district of Isseltrent with its guild shops, warehouses, and markets. Its narrow streets were always packed with people. Flying carpets flitted about the financial district like flies above a meat stew. To the south and east, gradually-thinning residential areas extended into small towns which had been engulfed by Isseltrent. Now, only the richest lived in these enclaves. To the west, wharves rimmed the harbor. A few idle sailing ships and Dragontailers dotted the wharves. The half-submerged heads of the Dragontailers' resting Blues gave a mere hint of their huge shadowy forms. Most of Isseltrent's Dragontailers, fishing sloops and merchant ships were still out to sea. Between the busy financial district and the quiet wharves crawled a festering labyrinth full of criminals and their victims, imprisoned by poverty and fear. It was aptly named the Jungle. In the middle of the city, the arcane dome of Hell's Breach squatted. It reminded some of the shiny back of a poisonous spider skulking in a web, still as a stone, just waiting.

Trallalair looked down again. At the edge of the Jungle, near the wharves, close to the few ships probably filled with contraband, was an ancient dilapidated tower where lurked the king of the Jungle. Molgannard Fey. Before Trallalair became a Dragonflyer, she had spent many days with her Ring rounding up his Skin Splicers to jail or execute them. She always wondered why the full force of her Ring was always held back, only rendering token dragnets for Molgannard Fey's criminals.

Now Trallalair looked far to the distant north. There, on a mountain above the clouds, was Molgannard Fey's palace. Another blight they were forbidden to eradicate. His wife, Ludmilla, and her servants resided there. Trallalair had long ago decided Ludmilla must have been the real intelligence behind Molgannard Fey's operations. The Giant seemed too slow of wit to coordinate his Skin Splicer operations and all his other organized crimes.

Trallalair had asked Seldric once why he was so easy on the Giant and the Giantess, but she received only evasive excuses. It was as if they had insidious connections in court and the Dragonlord feared repercussions leading to foment in Blaze. She wished Seldric would just burn the Jungle to the ground and be done with it. In fact, she was about ready to tell him outright what she thought would be good for the Realm. Why not? The worst that could happen would be a fall out of favor with him. That could lead to a break from his attentions. More likely, he'd just use her more roughly. Besides, a break from his attentions for her only meant the same disgrace for another of her Sisters. By putting up with his attentions for as long as she could, she saved one of her Sisters from the degradation of his lust for a while.

Farther still in the distance beyond the horizon was the North Wall and the Cajalathrium States imbedded within it. Beyond that was the Plateau of the Giants, too far for the Dragoncrown to reach. The race of Giants was held back from invading Thuringland and its Tributary States only by the force of the Dragons. An occasional Giant was hired in town as a laborer. Rarely, an especially aggressive one like Molgannard Fey infiltrated the Isseltrent business market. His business hadn't stayed legitimate for very long after he came to Isseltrent fifty years before. Now he seemed too entrenched in the various markets of the city and the underpinnings of the court for the Dragonlord to pry loose.

Above the Jungle, two Green Dragons, Wind and Moon, were already patrolling. Trallalair was glad to see that the other Brands had trusted her judgment.

She squeezed Hover with her feet, signaling the Dragon to dive. Trallalair loved the inner titillation she felt as Hover plummeted toward the ground. She had calculated right. The dive took them just past the eastern edge of the city, right to the area she was to patrol. Beneath her, a Black sprawled just outside the city limits. A line of people waited near the beast to enter the city.

She guided Hover to land next to the Black Dragon. Dust filled the air as she landed, and the queued people scattered in terror. She shouted, "All you people! Stop in the name of the Dragonlord." None that heard her disobeyed. A Dragonflyer was not to be questioned.

One man out of range of her voice continued to sprint away. Trallalair could have flown Hover to catch him, but instead she said in a quiet voice, "Speak."

Hover lifted her head and opened her fanged jaws. A deep sonorous bellow emerged. It was so loud that pebbles bounced on the ground beneath her. The cowering people nearby covered their ears and fell to the ground. As the bellow stopped, the sprinter slowed to a halt. When he turned to see Trallalair and the Dragon regarding him maliciously, he fainted in a heap.

"All of you will wait here beside the Black Dragon until we come back to question you. If you move, the Black will eat you." She wanted time to question them. No man could possibly fail to notice an unclean dead thing walking on Mother Earth. They certainly would not have been calmly waiting in line for the Black if they had seen such a thing. But maybe they had seen something suspicious. Besides, by stopping anyone from using the Black, she would help insure the Demon did not slip by them.

She pointed to a couple of young, strong men and said, "You two will carry the one who ran." She pointed toward the unconscious bolter. "Bring him back here and tell him the order when he awakens."

With no time to escort these people back to the palace dungeons, Trallalair depended on their fear of the Black to keep them in place. Of course, she had no control over the Black. She just hoped, if the Demon tried to use a Black again, the Dragonlord would take notice of the Demon in the Black's mouth and destroy his enemy, at least the body he had stolen. Hover was the only Dragon that obeyed Trallalair, and that was only at the bidding of the Dragonlord.

Far south, a Green Dragon wheeled through the clouds. By its playful expansive flight, Trallalair could tell it was a young Green, younger than Hover. She figured it must be Pinion, flown by Mebarethy. The youngest of the Greens with the youngest of the Sinjery Dragonflyers. Constantly trying to prove herself, Mebarethy flew dangerously. Even for a Sinjery. She was the only Sinjery Trallalair knew of who had actually fallen off her mount and survived.

At Trallalair's cue, Hover leapt into the air, unfurling her wings with a crack that made the prisoners below cringe and cry out. Soaring with wings outstretched, she struck her feet down into a passing hill, pushing herself even higher where the rising currents were sufficient to balloon her wings to their fullest. Her wings beat slowly, hugely, taking her up where Trallalair could spy anyone walking toward the city. Luckily, Trallalair's side of the city was mostly plains and meadows with a few bushes and isolated stands of trees. Off to the west, above the vast ocean, thunderheads signaled the storm brewing, which she had sensed earlier. The weather was changing for the worse. The rain was still far away, but soon the storm would quash all hope of intercepting the Demon.

Off to the east, a massive flock of geese flew toward the sea. Their V formations passed like waves. Trallalair recognized each goose was in the slipstream of the one in front, easing the flight for the long journey they faced. Dragons flew the same when in a group. These Vs seemed somewhat ragged. Trallalair thought they must be tired, too many leagues without food today. She thought it odd they came from the east and flew west instead of north for the summer. She wondered how they had avoided the Dead Lands directly to the east. Odd.

She stowed the question in the back of her mind for further consideration. Below her was a more immediate concern. Trallalair flew Hover in a wide arc first. Then, in tighter and tighter arcs, she spiraled down to check a lonely stand of poplars. She hoped to flush out any lurkers. A herd of deer scattered, and Hover swooped to snap up the largest. The buck was impaled on Hover's fangs and made a few useless kicks before Hover crushed out its life. Just a quick flip of Hover's head sent the buck up in an arc that kept pace with Hover's flight, so when it fell, Hover's open maw devoured it in one gulp. Nothing else dared run from the trees.

One more tight circuit around the treetops told Trallalair no one was hiding there. As they completed the circuit, Trallalair again felt the pleasing rush of warmth starting from her thighs and coursing throughout her body. She loved flying.

Rising again, Trallalair was surprised to see the flock of geese flying steadfastly toward the city. Even more surprising, the geese seemed of different varieties. Snow Geese, Gray Bards, White Ringed Black Backs, even, inexplicably, Trumpeter Swans. Never in her years in the swamps of Sinjer had she witnessed so many different varieties of geese flying together.

Trallalair wheeled Hover around to intercept them. Enjoying the pleasure of riding Hover, she had foolishly ignored the geese until they were nearing Isseltrent. The flock of geese were the real threat, not the dead in the Jungle, not the travelers taking the Black. No natural explanation could account for the phenomenon she saw, many different birds in the same flock. The Demon must be at work there somehow. The Demon that Seldric boasted would never attack Isseltrent had slipped past all the Sinjery Brands looking downward for intruders. Slipped past even Trallalair. Just innocent geese flying. Trallalair cursed herself. Alone, even with Hover, she knew she did not have time enough to burn them all from the sky before some of the geese flew into Isseltrent. She needed the help of any Dragonflyers she could gather together.

"Hover, fire!" she exclaimed. An explosion of flame erupted from Hover's throat. The fireball barely dissipated before Trallalair flew through it. Trallalair meant it as a signal for all the other Sinjery Dragonflyers, hoping they would fly to her assistance.

As she twisted her head around, Trallalair saw only one Dragon respond to her flame. Pinion's serrated wings grew from an answering cloud of flame as the dragon rushed toward her.

A half league or so ahead, the multicolored flock of geese flew erratically, starting to descend toward the city. Any one of them could be possessed by the Demon. Or all of them. Trallalair cursed herself again. She could see that destroying them all would be almost impossible, even if she had all the Dragons at her side.

With her feet, Trallalair spurred Hover to plummet, hoping they could get under the flock and burn the geese from below. But the flock was huge, huge and fragmented. Too many targets.

Still, Trallalair had a Dragon to fight with. Hover was much faster than the flock and was beneath them within moments, just before the geese had gained the city limits.

"Hover, fire!"

But before Hover could open her mouth and immolate a part of the flock, the geese scattered, some of them flying away and some attacking Trallalair. They acted more like eagles than geese. They mobbed Hover, who struck back at them, catching and consuming scores. Trallalair drew her Sword. She chopped at the menacing birds as they flapped about her, pecking her as they passed. Up close, the geese were piebald and wasted as if they had been dead a fortnight. Some had wings so bereft of feathers it was a wonder they even flew. Clearly, they were dead birds that the Demon had animated into flight.

As she slashed at the Zombie birds, cleaving many in two, Trallalair could feel the blade of her Sword striking hard chunks within the birds. It was as if they were filled with gravel. When one exploded apart at her slash, glittering pebbles rained down upon the city below.

But no, not pebbles, Trallalair thought. Before she could identify the glittering contents of the goose, one of the pecking beaks struck her on the temple. Trallalair's head filled with shooting stars. It was all she could do to grip Hover's neck with her knees to keep from falling.

When Trallalair finally shook her head clear, she grabbed one Zombie bird from the air with her left hand and holding it by the neck like a flail, smashed it down upon the spines on Hover's back. Between the unbreakable scales and the sharp spines, the dead bird was disemboweled and beaten into a disgusting pulp. Even with its entrails hanging loose, the Zombie bird struggled in her grip.

Eventually, it stopped writhing. Trallalair hung onto it even though it stank. Putrid oils oozed between her fingers. After Hover had cleared the air of the birds mobbing her and Trallalair, the Dragon exhaled a stream of flame into the scattering flock ahead. The flame caught a few. There were still hundreds left. Over her shoulder, Trallalair could see Mebarethy on Pinion careening, burning scores of geese. Two other Greens approached from high above.

Hover darted back and forth, crushing geese with her claws, swallowing dozens whole, and disintegrating many more with her fire. When the two reinforcing Dragons joined the fray, what they could still see of the flock was wiped out in short order. However, Trallalair knew that in the confusion, many of the Zombie geese could have flown down to the city, or they could have fallen. They were already dead. Falling to the ground made no difference to the Zombie birds. They could not get any deader.

She still held her loathsome trophy, the goose she had grabbed from the air. After stabilizing Hover's flight, she sheathed her Sword and palpated the goose's gut. Like the others she had cut with her Sword, it was filled with pebbles. Trallalair used the spine between her legs on Hover's neck to rip open the stomach. Glass Commands by the dozen, more than she had ever seen, poured out. As Hover leaned into a swoop, the coins skittered over her scales and rattled off. They joined thousands more coins released from the other burning and exploding geese, twinkling below her, as they fell into the city. Sweeping her hand deftly through the scattering coins, Tralallair came up with three she slipped in a pouch hanging from a belt on her leathers. They were evidence for the Dragonlord.

She realized that if the Demon was among the geese that were falling to the city streets, he could have already inhabited some poor soul's corpse missed by the Sinjery searching the city. The Glass Commands were payment and power to accomplish whatever foul deed he meant to accomplish. And she, Trallalair, veteran Dragonflyer, Guard of the Realm, had let him pass.

She waved her hand, holding the gutted bird as Mebarethy passed. Pinion raised a wing and spun around to bring the younger Sinjery within calling distance. "Mebarethy, you have saved my life, but the geese were all dead!"

"Yes, my Sister, you led us to kill them all!"

"You thought as I did that they were living geese, but they were dead before we burned them. They were controlled by the Demon. They were filled with Glass Commands!"

"Mother Earth! What does it mean?" Mebarethy shouted. "What vile purpose empowers them?"

"You know that nothing in this land has power over death. The Demon wrought this." Trallalair cried out in despair, "I have failed, you!"

Pinion's wings tipped upward and filled, slowing his bulk to Hover's speed. Mebarethy called back, "You have prepared and warned us. We need now vigilance, not remorse."

Trallalair knew she was right. With the chaos of the battle, one or more of the Zombie geese had probably landed and delivered the Demon in the city, but no plan could have prevented it. They needed to redouble their efforts, scour the city, and find the fiend before he brought chaos to them all.

For a moment, Trallalair thought she would have to report to the Dragonlord her failure to protect the city, but she knew better. She knew the Dragonlord had seen it all through the eyes of the Dragons and was cognizant of all that had transpired in the battle. That she was correct became perfectly clear as Hover and the rest of the Sinjery Dragons stopped obeying the Sisters' commands and began to fly back to Isseltrent on their own. They were now obeying the internal commands of the Dragonlord. Trallalair knew he could no longer ignore the threat that a Demon was in the city. She just hoped Seldric had his own plans to thwart this new threat, now that hers had failed.

The Demon had to be found. Trallalair felt Hover turning in the direction of Blaze under Seldric's control. She called out to Mebarethy whose Dragon was moving away from her toward the heart of the city. "Patrol the city. Alert the Rings. Search for the Demon."

She knew Mebarethy and her Sisters would comb every part of the city. At the same time, she saw the futility of it. Judging from the flock of geese they had just fought, Trallalair realized the Demon could inhabit anything, living or dead, human, horse, dog or rat. Maybe even a Dragon. She could see little hope in any attempt to stop it. She felt Seldric wearing the Dragoncrown was the Demon's target.

As Hover flew toward Blaze, Trallalair felt a strange fervor, almost eagerness, in the Dragon as she approached the palace. It was as if the fear of the Demon had been transmogrified into lust. Seldric wanted her for something other than information about her discoveries. He wasn't even waiting for her to put on her blue dress. He wanted her now. He probably wanted her to jump off Hover as she passed his balcony and hop right into his bed. With danger at hand. How could he be so foolish? Trallalair shook her head.

How his mind must be twisted by the Dragoncrown, she thought, to allow the bloodlust the Dragons felt during the battle with the Zombie birds to grow into his own erotic desire. She knew his mind was filled with emotions, mostly the rage of the Dragons at being enslaved. How could anyone hold it within himself? All the thoughts, the sights, maybe sounds, smells and tastes of a hundred Dragons at once. What it could do to a soul was something Trallalair would never know. She only knew her Sisters suffered from the result. She again told herself she was saving another Sister from the disgrace by her submission to the Dragonlord.

Below her, the city looked calm enough, but above, the two remaining Green Dragons of the Isseltrent Muster flew slowly as the five hundred Knights of their Lances fanned out below them searching. At least Seldric was cured of his feigned complacency. She only hoped it wasn't too late.

The thunderheads would be over Isseltrent before sundown. Trallalair prayed to Mother Earth that the Demon would be found before the storm hit. She hoped Seldric's lust permitted him to remember to protect the Chamber of Hell's Breach. If she were the Demon, that was where she would go. Only another Demon would aid one so evil and cruel.

CHAPTER 4

FORTY-ONE COMMANDS

At the end of Dinner Blessing, Rhazburn and Jonathon emerged from Hell's Breach. A strange flurry of activity was about. Many more Green Dragons than usual filled the sky. Jonathon thought they flew in patterns crossing the sky from north to south and east to west as if they were searching for someone. A cool wind presaged a storm. It made Jonathon intent on getting back to his shop as quickly as possible. In the distance, people ran through the streets and cried out in cheers. Just down the street, a great mob fought among themselves, heedless of a Lance of Knights in tight columns approaching with swords drawn. Jonathon could not imagine what all the commotion was about. People were scrabbling and pushing each other away from whatever they were picking up. Jonathon wanted no part of it.

With the sky threatening rain as Jonathon and Rhazburn left the double row of guards, Rhazburn turned toward the obsidian chamber and said, "I'm not leaving Dollop to that fate."

Jonathon questioned his son with his eyes. Rhazburn returning his gaze. "I'm going to find a way to release him from Hell." Rhazburn was obviously preoccupied with his thoughts and his new, hopeless quest. Jonathon saw his son took little notice of the odd intensity in the sky or the commotion in the streets. Sweeps of Isseltrent by Lances of Knights were common enough. The Knights' actions were futile, however. The Skin Splicing trade continued, and most people simply avoided the Knights.

Jonathon whispered, hoping the guards would not hear him, "The Dragonlord's law precludes such action, Rhazburn. Even saying such a thing must be tantamount to treason."

Rhazburn didn't lower his voice. "Father. I know the law. I enforce it myself at Hell's Breach, but law or no, damnation or no, I'm going to get Dollop out. It may take me ten years and my life, but I'm responsible for his loss. I'm his only hope. Even a honeybee will sacrifice itself to defend its friends. Surely I can muster the courage of an insect."

Never had Jonathon heard Rhazburn talk about himself in such deprecating terms. He clearly felt he had failed his friend. Pluck his friend from Hell? Only Rhazburn could be so bold as to even imagine it was possible. Even when Rhazburn had been in Jonathon's house, he was headstrong and made his own decisions. Once he had made up his mind, Jonathon had never been able to dissuade him. Still, when the Demon turned his student and friend into a raving maniac, Rhazburn's power at Hell's Breach had been defied more sorely than ever before. Jonathon knew there was doubt in his son on how to obtain that goal. Even Rhazburn had limits, though he would never admit them.

Jonathon could not give up and condone his son's impossible task. Dollop was already dead. Did Rhazburn think people could be brought back from the dead? Even if the lad could be brought out of Hell, Dollop would be a Zombie, no better off than those in the Dead Lands. What possible purpose would it serve for Rhazburn to sacrifice himself for that? Jonathon was about to play upon his son's glimmer of doubt when he felt a tug at his sleeve.

"Master," Bob Thumblefoot said from his side.

Jonathon looked at him, surprised. "My dear Bob, what brings you here?"

"I just got here. A man came to the shop just a short time ago and said he would wait for your return. He gave me this." Bob handed him a folded sheet of expensive parchment. On it were the words, "I am a messenger from the Dragonlord with an urgent message."

"The Dragonlord?" Jonathon exclaimed.

Rhazburn said, "Who?" and looked at the message.

Jonathon clutched his face. "It's too late. They've come to arrest me for my dealings with Molgannard Fey," he groaned miserably. He knew the Dragonflyers in the sky and the Lance of Knights were looking for him to take him to the dungeons beneath Blaze.

Bob said, "He's not a constable, Master. He looks like a Beholder. He must be a Beholder. Wouldn't even talk to me."

Rhazburn said, "Calm down, Father. This doesn't look like a summons." At that, he looked upward as if wondering at the increased activity in the sky for a moment. He shook his head, as if clearing his brain of useless information, and concentrated again on Jonathon's newest problem.

"Would that it were a summons," Jonathon said. "Starving in a dungeon is surely preferable to gazing again on the face of Molgannard Fey, a moment before he squashes me." But then he thought of his family in the hands of Molgannard Fey and wiggled his head again, lost as to what he could do to stop his doom. Jonathon prayed that if he let the Giant crush him or eat him or whatever Fey had in store, maybe he'd spare Jonathon's family. Still, Jonathon had a feeling that mercy was not a concept the Giant was aware of.

"Come on, Father. We have lots of time. You don't have to be afraid of that Giant. Get me a vial of ruby dust and I'll write a poem that will chase him so far, he won't even be a bad dream."

Jonathon shook his head. "I conducted business with him at my own foolish presumption that I was capable of paying him back. I'll only receive my deserts. I'll not be a dishonest cheat. He'll have his due one way or another. But I can't let Arlen and the children suffer for my mistake."

"Master, should I tell the man to leave?" Bob asked.

"No, no, Bob. I'll see him. Perhaps he's a scribe of the court." He queried Rhazburn, "Seldric employed a Beholder as a scribe once, didn't he? He could pen my will while I can still move my tongue."

"Father, quit your silliness. The court doesn't care about your problems. You're not important enough for the Dragonlord to take notice of anything you will ever do. He'll never even know your name. He probably had one of his lackeys find a jeweler to make him a bracelet of potency so he can sire more like me. The lackey chanced upon you because your shop is prominent. I'll go with you. Between Molgannard Fey and the court, you act like you're between a falling tree and a boulder. I can deal with both of them. Don't tell me you don't want my help now. When you came to Hell's Breach, you cleaved the emerald. Now make a jewel of it."

Through Rhazburn's calculating eyes, Jonathon saw the seriousness of Molgannard Fey's threat. Maybe he should let Rhazburn deal with the Giant. He had no doubt his son could handle him, but first, the stranger in his shop.

"All right, my good Bob, lead on. By the way, what's all this hurly-burly?"

"I have no idea, Master. I've been in the shop all day. I saw all the ruckus and went another way, so I could be here when you came out."

"Strange," Jonathon pondered aloud as they skirted the riot.

On the way back to his shop, another thought came to him, something he had wanted to ask his son many a time. "Enlighten me, Rhazburn. For what reason does Hell's Breach still open to the nether world? A method to close it exists. Admit it." He thought that in the hundreds of years and at least as many Poets since Hell's Breach had been opened, methods surely had been theorized or attempted.

"Oh, I know a way. A glass door made from two hundred thousand Glass Commands studded with a thousand diamonds of everlasting would close it up tight."

"All right, I'll be quiet," Jonathon said. To make that many Glass Commands would be impossible. The Commands were formed by a laborious process using Dragonfire and alchemy in the Dragonkilns deep beneath Blaze. From the Glass Commands formed, all the other magical coins were produced, nine hundred ninety-nine Copper Orders from each Command, one hundred eleven Wooden Requests from each Order, and thirty-three Clay Suggestions from each Request. There were only thirteen Dragonkilns, each fired by a Red Dragon. Each furnace could produce ten Glass Commands a day, all inscribed with verses by Pixets. At that rate, two full years would be needed to make Rhazburn's door.

That is, if the Realm were to stand still while they were produced, since no Commands would be available for the thousands of magical spells used daily by the people. The prosperity and peace of the Realm was tied to the Red Dragons and the Commands they produced. If the flow of the Glass Commands were ever lost for even one Moon, much less two years, society as they knew it would slow to a halt and degenerate into confusion. He wasn't sure if even the power of the Dragons would hold society together if the flow of the magical money the Realm depended upon was ever to cease. So, since the Dragonlord would never permit the prosperity of the Realm to slow down, Hell's Breach would forever stay open, and therefore, thought Jonathon, Rhazburn's role in the land would be assured for as long as he wanted to remain the Loremaster. One could argue that Rhazburn's actions, by not cajoling the court into making the seal for Hell's Breach, was self-serving. Jonathon refused to believe that of his son.

At the shop, Hili greeted them in the air. "Welcome back, Master. Loremaster, We are glad to see you again." She drew their eyes with a gesture to a black-robed figure sitting at a small pine table. Jonathon heard her whir to Bob's shoulder and settle there.

Jonathon looked at the man, expecting him to rise out of courtesy, but he did not move, not even a rustle. Jonathon could not see his face in the shadow of the cowl he wore. His hands were gloved in black. Not a patch of skin could be seen, and nothing human was visible on his figure. He could have been a mannequin sitting there dressed like a holy man. He certainly looked and acted like a Beholder. A Beholder concentrated solely on his own experience of the Beauty of the world and his own ruminations upon that experience. This man seemed rude and heedless of what others thought of him, typical for a Beholder.

Jonathon felt a peculiar dread just looking at the man. He walked over and stood before the figure, but he did not hold out his hand. The figure was haughtier than the worst of Jonathon's customers, and the jeweler had had plenty of experience placating haughty customers. This Beholder acted like the Dragonlord himself. Just because Beholders served The Three, they expected everyone else to afford them some special homage. Still, Jonathon did not want to inadvertently insult the Dragonlord.

"Loyalty and praise to our liege the Dragonlord. We are at your command, your service, your pleasure." He expected no reply. He had given the normal greeting expected by an envoy from the Dragonlord, but Beholders were bound by their vows to never speak. Some, who felt themselves weakening in their resolve, had their tongues cut out to ensure obedience to their vows. Jonathon had never directly dealt with a Beholder. They always kept to themselves, even growing their own food on monastery grounds. The monasteries, purchased and built entirely through donations to their sect, were shrouded, dark and secret like the inhabitants. Many people donated to them, but only because the altars they produced had the most alluring representations of Kris imaginable. Kris was usually depicted in their paintings and statues as voluptuous with long hair cascading down around bare breasts, her arms raised above her head in an enticing dance. Men would toss small coins in the dish, always guarded by a vigilant Beholder, just on the chance they might behold Kris in a dream that night. Women would drop coins in the dish with the hope that visions of Kris would satisfy their husbands' roving eyes and their lusts, allowing their wives a break but keeping the men home, away from the Choralists. Few women wanted their men to spend their donations on Choralists.

The figure raised his head slightly, as if he had just realized they were there. His visage remained obscured by his cowl. Without answering, he reached into the wide sleeve of his robe and extracted a small box. Its mirrored surfaces reflected the decor of the shop. Jonathon recognized it as a Message Box like the ones he used for transactions at a distance. The messenger laid the box on the table and opened it.

A man's voice came from the box. "I am the Dragonlord." Jonathon felt a few drops of sweat roll down the inside of his arms. He had heard the Dragonlord's voice before but only at a distance. The voice commanded attention and obeisance. Jonathon had an urge to fall on the floor kneeling. "This man, a devout Beholder, is deaf and the only one I will entrust with this message," the voice from the box continued. The Beholder was still again, hardly breathing to Jonathon's eye. "I have recently discovered that many of the nobles and courtiers have become proud and ambitious in our present prosperity. They plot to assassinate me and take the Dragoncrown for their own purposes. They care nothing for the evil that will befall the Realm."

Jonathon's ears began to buzz. If the Dragonlord lost the Dragoncrown, all the Dragons on which the land depended for their work and the Glass

Commands they forged with their fiery breath would be in the control of renegades. They could do as they pleased, taking all for their own, like a thousand Molgannard Feys run amuck. Jonathon knew his fate was sealed because of his debt with the Giant, but he feared even more for his wife and children if traitors stole the Dragoncrown. Why had he always believed that was impossible?

"They have many allies around me in the court. I am taking a chance enlisting your aid, but I have no choice. I trust you are far enough removed from the court to be untainted by their intrigues. I know of your work. It is said you are the most skilled jeweler in all Isseltrent. I depend upon your honor to keep the purpose of my message a secret. If you reveal it to any, the conspirators will take action earlier."

Jonathon was loyal enough, but he had been a citizen of the Cajalathrium States decades before and was no more fervent in his love for the Dragonlord than any emigrant from the tributary lands. He certainly did not want to get involved in some squabble among the powers of state. Still, the Dragonlord losing the Dragoncrown? Jonathon could not comprehend all the possible implications.

"Master Jeweler, hold out your hand to my messenger."

Jonathon extended his hand cautiously as if he were going to pick up a snake which may or may not be dead. The deaf Beholder apparently picked up the visual cue and pulled a leather pouch bulging with coins from his sleeve. He opened it, spilling the contents on the table.

When Jonathon saw the coins, he reeled. Rhazburn grabbed his arm tightly so he could regain his composure. The pouch was filled with Glass Commands, dozens of them, more money than Jonathon had ever seen. A lord's treasure for sure.

"These will be your pay. You may take them now as a sign of my need. If your help aids me in this, an even greater reward will be yours."

A fly flew into Jonathon's open mouth, making him cough and spit.

"Some of the money will be needed to fulfill my commission."

Jonathon looked at Rhazburn, who stood fingering his lips. He did not look at the money as Jonathon did, but was staring at the robed figure.

The box went on, "I need a rod of power that will act to change the will of my enemies. Spare no expense. Its power and effect must be dependable and fitting the Dragonlord. It must be light enough to carry but affect all within its range, be they quick, simple, deaf, or sleeping. It must never fail me. In this way, with your skill, the Realm will be preserved."

Jonathon had no idea if such a thing could be made. He had never heard of a like object. Even so, could a thing so powerful be entrusted to any mortal, even the Dragonlord?

He looked at the large pile of Glass Commands. One alone would save his life. He looked again at Rhazburn. The Poet's gaze of the messenger was hard and cold.

The voice continued. "The Seers warn me of a terrible doom that awaits on the day of the Dragonegg Festival, seven days away. Their words are cryptic, and I trust them little, but the end of the Realm approaches. My power is great toward foes outside the Realm, but against foes within the court, I have only the Sinjery Guard at my side and some of them may be the enemy. If you accept the commission, take the box and my messenger will return on the evening before the Dragonegg Festival. But, if you cannot or will not aid me in this, then give him back the box and may The Three have mercy upon us all." No more words came from the box. The monk stayed still as death.

Jonathon was mesmerized by the pile of Glass Commands. They were his salvation. Whatever the Dragonlord wanted, he would make by the dozen to pay off Molgannard Fey. His eyes sparkled with greed as he reached to take the box and the Dragonlord's commission.

Rhazburn's hand caught Jonathon's, gently restraining him. "Father, don't do it."

"Rhazburn, I don't understand you," Jonathon said. "This is perfect. I can pay my debt. We'll have all the money we'll want for years. We can help the Dragonlord. You can show the court again that you are the Master Poet and deserve to be the Loremaster, and we'll all be famous heroes."

"I can't imagine you believed that bizarre story. That is the craziest proposition I have ever heard. A man we can neither talk to or even see wants you to make an object with powers that should never be given to anybody."

Jonathon threw a hand back at the hooded figure and blurted, "He's a Beholder. Can't you see that?"

"He may be a monk, I'll grant you that, but why wouldn't Seldric just summon you to his presence, send everyone from the room or take you to a tower top where no one can listen to walls, and talk to you? Then if you refused he could summon a Dragon and have it eat you to keep you quiet. I doubt this Beholder is even deaf."

"How can you say that?"

"If he were deaf, he'd be looking at us more. He could not rely on our conversation to know what we were doing and the sounds about him to let him know where we were."

That made Jonathon pause. Rhazburn had a point, as he always did when Jonathon tried to argue with him.

"Here, Father, face me. Turn so he can't see your mouth." The jeweler turned and glared at his son. It wasn't that his arguments were not logical, as all of Rhazburn's arguments were. Still, it prickled Jonathon that his son wouldn't let him just scoop up the money and save himself despite some slight ambiguities in the proposition. That was typical of Rhazburn. Even as a child when he was friendless and dependent on the charity of Jonathon and his wife, he took nothing at face value. Rhazburn always looked for hidden reasons.

Speaking slowly, emphasizing his words, Rhazburn said, "Now say in a loud voice, 'Messenger, bring me the box.'" Jonathon fumed but did so. Rhazburn hummed a note and watched with two fingers on his chin.

"Well, did he move?" Jonathon said after a moment of silence.

"Not a twitch."

"So it's proven. The proposition is legitimate. Do you agree now?"

"Huh-uh. I'm even more worried. That man must be highly intelligent. To hear that and not move a muscle takes a lot of discipline."

"Maybe he didn't hear it."

"Oh, he heard it all right. He's just trying to outsmart us. But he hasn't outsmarted me." Rhazburn stared so intently at the robed figure, Jonathon thought his eyes would peer right through the rough wool, right down to the flesh.

"Look at all those Glass Commands. They're fresh out of Blaze's kilns or I'm a horse."

"Careful how you curse yourself, Father."

"Who but the Dragonlord would have so many commands?"

"A thief or a traitor."

For his next repartee, Jonathon made a few profound grunts and smacks as he swallowed an answer. He rallied his wherewithal by puffing his cheeks and said, "But the voice from the message box, I know it's the Dragonlord's. I've heard him at the Dragonegg Festival many times, and that's his voice. You know his voice better than I do. You must agree it's his."

"The voice is clear and sounds just like Seldric."

"There. You see."

"Father, it's obviously a fake. No one talks that carefully unless they are trying to mimic someone's voice."

"But what if he is the Dragonlord?"

"That would be worse. I know that despot can't be trusted. If he is from the Dragonlord, I'd stay even further away from that deal."

"You can't be vengeful, Rhaz. Not you. How can you be jealous of those sycophants that Seldric chose as his heirs? If he thinks they will make good rulers, then it seems to me it's a privilege not to be chosen."

"I wouldn't have accepted an inheritance like that. The whole dynasty is corrupt and Seldric along with it. No one who has that many mistresses can be trusted."

"It's tradition. The Dragonlord needs a lot of children to pick the best for his heir."

"Well, it didn't work, did it?"

"Uh, well, no," Jonathon stammered, having again just argued himself into a corner. The best would have been Rhazburn, but he was thrown from the court and now worked with all the other common Poets. Jonathon knew he could never outmaneuver Rhazburn in an argument, but he wanted to set things right in his life and for his family by taking the commission. The pile of Glass Commands possessed him like a Demon, like the Demon had possessed Dollop, but this was different, Jonathon thought. This was good. He could not pass them up. The proposition was strange but he had a deep feeling the threat to the Dragonlord was real and he alone could save the land. He clenched his fists and set his lips tight, trying to look determined.

"Rhazburn, I'm going to take the box."

"Don't be a fool. Nothing but trouble will come of it."

"Will you help me?"

"I will, Father. I'll get Molgannard Fey out of your life."

"No. I'll not have it that way. Hili, what would the Community do if I took the commission?" He looked with undisguised hope at his tiny business partner.

She sat on Bob's shoulder, leaning back with her arms straight, looking at her feet which she kicked playfully, oblivious to the argument. She looked up and smiled. "The Community trusts the Master Jeweler's judgment in this. We are citizens of Isseltrent for the time being, but the workings of the ruler mean little to our race. No evil can approach that from which we fled centuries ago. When the Demon Sverdphthik invaded Verdilon, we tried to save the flowers and the animals, but we lost it all. Here, we do what we can to survive in the human society. We leave the decision to you, Master Jeweler."

Jonathon turned his head smartly to Rhazburn and gave a short nod for emphasis. Rhazburn looked at Bob and asked, "Bob, what do you think?"

Bob twitched, apparently startled to be asked his opinion. He smiled at Rhazburn, obviously proud to be addressed on an equal footing by the Loremaster. Then he seemed to think better of it. He turned hesitantly toward Jonathon and blushed at the jeweler's stern gaze. "I obey my master," he said quietly, cowed by Jonathon. As Rhazburn turned again toward the boy, Bob regained some pluck and added, "But that monk scares me. I was glad to come and get you. I wanted to get away from him as fast as I could. I would never trust him if my Master didn't tell me to."

Jonathon did not care if his apprentice supported his decision, but he admired the boy for his spunk, speaking up as he did against his master's opinions. To reassure the nervous boy, Jonathon gave him a pat on the shoulder and wiggled a nod of his head. But Bob's opinion still did little to dissuade Jonathon. He turned again, pleading to his son and most trusted counselor, "Rhazburn, this comes just when I need it the most. I can't pass up the chance."

"If nothing else, that by itself should convince you to shun this deal like it's a pack of wolves. It's pretty coincidental this messenger comes when your need is greatest. This whole deal sounds treacherous to me. You just can't agree to make something that powerful for a stranger. It's all too complicated. Things don't happen like this."

Still unconvinced, Jonathon studied his son. He could tell the Loremaster was not going to help him in this commission and all his reasons were, of course, valid. Rhazburn was Rhazburn and never made mistakes, but Jonathon was the one who was to be killed by the next morning, and treachery or not, those Commands were his only salvation. He could worry about the consequences later, which was something he couldn't do if he didn't take the money. There would be no later. He said, "I'm taking the money. Are you with me?"

"No. I'll not be a part of it, and without me, you cannot fulfill the commission."

"I'll hire a dozen Poets to help me. There's more than enough to pay them."

Rhazburn smirked and shook his head. "Go ahead. Get a dozen. Get a hundred. All of them together won't figure out the verses for this one. Even if they could, they certainly won't take the risks necessary to finish it."

"But you could do it, couldn't you, Rhazburn?'"

"I'm not saying."

"Well, if you could do it, then it must be possible. I'll do it myself."

"You don't know the verses."

"I'll go to the Wishing Drop and find out the prescription myself," he said, closing his lips and eyes and sticking his nose in the air. He wasn't about to listen to any more of Rhazburn's arguments. They were too good, and Jonathon's resolve was wavering. He wanted the Glass Commands, no matter the cost to himself. This way, he had a chance to save himself honestly, doing the craft he knew best, jewelry.

He strode to the table where the robed figure sat. Behind him, Rhazburn said, "If you go to the Wishing Drop, you'll die as surely as if Molgannard Fey sits on you. Don't do it, Father." He raised his hands as if to restrain him, but he did not. After all, Jonathon was still his father.

Jonathon had to use his utmost willpower to keep from being dissuaded by his son's arguments. He suppressed all his thoughts and grabbed the Message Box before he could think better of it. Once he picked it up, he smiled broadly. He felt the cloud of evil and terror around his soul disappear. The Glass Commands were his. He was safe. He was rich. He never had to worry again.

As soon as Jonathon picked up the box, the Beholder stood up, his head slightly bowed so Jonathon still saw nothing of his face. He smelled funny as well, kind of musty. Jonathon suspected they never bathed. He was probably filthy and ugly. The figure turned, opened the door and walked silently out.

As he left, Rhazburn followed him through the door and shouted, "Tell whoever sent you they are dealing with Loremaster Rhazburn. This thing we make will work for no one but the Dragonlord. I promise you that." The messenger walked steadily away without missing a step. Rhazburn scowled and shook a taut fist in the air.

When he turned, Jonathon was looking at him. "You'll help me, then?"

Irritated, Rhazburn ran his hand through his hair, clutching it as if to strangle it. "Father, I'll help you on two conditions."

"Yes?" Jonathon replied.

"I make the inscription so no one but the Dragonlord can use the rod. And our mysterious messenger reveals his identity before we give the rod to him. I need to look into his face. I don't care if his beliefs forbid it. Furthermore, I am certainly not giving anything to him - not the rod, not anything. We will personally deliver this thing to the Dragonlord himself. Agreed?"

"Agreed," Jonathon said as he began to count the Glass Commands, his eyes wide with awe.

As Rhazburn watched Jonathon, he pitied his father. The money was so important to him he set aside good judgment. Rhazburn knew it was Jonathon's generosity that had gotten him in this position in the first place. Now their course was set. Rhazburn doubted the messenger was real or the commission was legitimate. But he would make sure no one took advantage of his father. Jonathon's talk about going to the Wishing Drop worried Rhazburn the most of all the things he had said. Wishes at the Wishing Drop brought visions only. Dozens of people, distrusting the pronouncements of the Seers, insisted on taking the journey to the Wishing Drop for a vision of the future or to find some precious person or thing. Only one out of ten people who tried to get a vision at the Wishing drop came out alive. Rhazburn had no way to help his father if he went there, and Jonathon was just foolish enough to do it.

Jonathon looked up from the sparkling pile of Glass Commands with an avaricious gleam in his eye. "Forty-one Commands."

Bob whistled.

"And it's all mine," Jonathon cackled with glee before he caught the sadness in Rhazburn's eyes. "Oh, we'll split it, of course. Three ways. You, the Community and me." He rubbed his hands.

Rhazburn said, coldly, "Keep my share. I don't want a Suggestion. Someone else's pain and suffering is etched on every one of those coins."

"Rhazburn, I thought you were with me on this."

"I'll help you so you can pay Molgannard Fey. If we save the Realm, so much the better. You made the deal, not I. You keep the money." In the back of his mind, Rhazburn was trying to suppress a seditious thought. If they made the rod and it was really for the traitors the box had spoken of and not for the Dragonlord, it would be nothing but justice meted out by a forgotten son.

"Why don't you put your treasure away and start figuring out how to make this rod the Dragonlord wants. And I use that term, Dragonlord, loosely. I still don't know who is behind this proposition. Not the Dragonlord, I think."

At least Jonathon's debt could be paid. Rhazburn would deal with the Beholder impostor another time. Another thought supplanted the seditious one. If he were to make this rod of power over men's minds and they presented it to the Dragonlord, perhaps his influence in the court would be enhanced and he could finally try to mollify some of the Dragonlord's excesses. Then again, commissioning a device of such tremendous power would be typical of Seldric's excesses and probably only serve to enhance them. If the Demon could be controlled with it and eliminated from the world, maybe the need for Seldric's excesses would disappear. Rhazburn had an ominous feeling. Thunder rumbled in the distance. He could feel a tingling in the air, charged with lightning. More than the weather was changing. He had to help his father, but he was being swept into something boding ill for all of them. Just as he did at Hell's Breach, he had to watch for signs of trouble and fend them off in time. Every time he walked through the iron doors into the Chamber of Hell's Breach, he had confidence in his resources. He had yet to be challenged beyond his capabilities. Then he thought again, *Today was different, losing Dollop.* He had utterly failed that challenge. Would this also be beyond his skill? For the first time, Rhazburn felt doubt in what he was capable of. Yet the path seemed set, for good or ill.

Jonathon didn't seem to hear Rhazburn's last comment. Jonathon apparently had no doubts. "Right, Rhazburn. Do you have any ideas? I thought you said a hundred Poets couldn't make it."

Rhazburn smiled.

Jonathon continued, "But Rhazburn can do anything."

"Not exactly. We have found that anything we can imagine can be made, if we have the right verses and the right materials. The verses are fairly simple for the most part. The materials needed for the spells are usually the limiting factor. I know how we could make a rod that will coerce others to do the will of the holder. I fear it won't be easy, and may not even be possible, because we lack the most important item."

"What's that?"

"The horn of a Unicorn."

When he said the word Unicorn, Hili popped into the air off Bob's shoulder where she had been lounging. She looked horrified into Rhazburn's eyes. "There are no more Unicorns. The Demon killed them all when it stole Verdilon. Even if any were alive, We would not permit you to kill one just to steal its horn."

"I'm sorry, Hili. I meant no offense to the Community, but a Unicorn Horn is needed for an effect this powerful."

"Maybe we could get a Horn from a Unicorn already dead," Jonathon said.

"The last one died three centuries ago. We have a song about him. His death, like all the deaths of our hoofed friends, was a tragedy for all the world. Now that the Unicorns have fled the mortal world, we owe it to them to leave them undisturbed. Using the Horn of a dead Unicorn would still be immoral."

"Maybe something else would work." Jonathon glanced at the Poet.

"No. I'm sorry."

"We cannot condone it," Hili said.

Jonathon replied, "Hili, you said the Community trusted my judgment. I say if a Unicorn Horn is needed for this work, then we are committed, I to the Dragonlord, and you to me."

"Master Jeweler, you have never before taken advantage of Us, but this would be against all We hold to be true and dear. Find another way, We beg you."

"Hili, I need your help."

"If We do this, We will never work for you again," the Community said through Hili.

Jonathon's magical jewelry depended on the work of the Pixets, who etched the tiny poems on the jewels. His relationship with the Pixet community had always been beyond reproach, but now he saw his tie with them undermined by his need to pay the criminal. He could never again make a magical jewel without their help. Then again, with all the money he had now, he would never need to work again, and without the money, he would die and his family would die with him. If the choice was between his family and his livelihood, his life-long work must end. But he was rich, so what of it?

"Then it must be so," he said finally, but blinked a few times in disbelief at what he had just done. The Glass Commands, the debt to the Giant, this Beholder, all of it was changing him, and he was not totally sure it was for the better.

Hili, eyes downcast, said, "We require five Commands as Our fee, since We feel the commission is immoral. As a last service to you, Master Jeweler, in appreciation of all the years you have generously supported Us, We will do this for you. We will aid you in making a magical weapon out of a Unicorn Horn, if you can find one. There is no one in the world We would do this for but you. After We carve the verses on the gems for the object you propose to assemble, We will sever Ourselves from anything you will ever do again. We will send a party to pick up the fee." Without raising her eyes or looking Jonathon in the face, Hili flew away.

Jonathon was feeling worse with every turn of events. He thought all his problems would be solved if he repaid Molgannard Fey, but now he understood how dealing with a criminal could undermine his very morality. He wanted to be rid of his debt, finish the project for the Dragonlord, and be done with it all.

As if he shared Jonathon's mind, Rhazburn said, "I'll send the Glass Command to the Giant with a note." Jonathon shook his head anxiously. He knew Rhazburn would have some choice comments for Molgannard Fey and was afraid of angering the criminal.

"Father, if my hands are occupied wrestling with Molgannard Fey, I can't very well write the verses you need for the scepter. If that Giant is breathing down our necks while we are trying to put it together, we'll never get it done in time."

Jonathon fanned the air with his hands. "Oh, all right." He clamped his eyes shut for emphasis. "But just don't offend him, please."

"I'll be sweet as honey," Rhazburn said. Jonathon shuddered at his sarcasm.

Rhazburn fetched his personal Flying Carpet from his room over Tell Borgamuffin's candle shop. Jonathon supplied one of his Message Boxes, not nearly as flashy as the Dragonlord's but adequate for the job. From the thirty-six Glass Commands left after the Pixets' fee was set aside, Rhazburn selected one to put in the box. So the Command itself wouldn't be used by the box to activate its magical properties, he wrapped it in a small piece of leather. He placed the box on the carpet and dropped in a Copper Order he still carried from the Chamber of Hell's Breach. The bag of coins Dollop had taken with him into Hell had been replaced with two bags of two hundred Copper Orders for the Night Poets to avoid a similar disaster.

Rhazburn dictated his message into the open box. "This message is for Molgannard Fey. Open for no one else. Take this message: Molgannard Fey, I am Rhazburn, Loremaster of the Demonwards. I am speaking for Jonathon Forthright, whom you have cheated long enough. In this box is a Glass Command, payment in full for his loan from you. I intended to deal with you myself to avenge my friend's honor, but he prevented me. It was because of his honesty, even in dealing with a scoundrel like you, that he insisted on paying you back. So the debt is paid, and I agreed to be generous and let you live your seamy life for a while longer. But hear this. If you or any of your ruffians come near Jonathon Forthright again, I will rid this land of you forever."

Jonathon hid his face almost in tears. "I'm glad you didn't insult him, Rhazburn."

"Don't worry. You won't hear from him again. He knows I can back up my words."

Rhazburn slipped another Copper Order in a pocket on the Flying Carpet and said, "Carpet, take this box to Molgannard Fey. Then return here." The carpet lifted off the floor.

"You'll never see your carpet again," Jonathon said.

"Would you like to wager on that? I sewed a special Poem of Persistence into the fabric with silver braid. It will come back. Wait and see."

After a time that Jonathon estimated was no more than thirty Favors, the carpet came back to hover like an obedient pet before Rhazburn. On its surface was a splotch of blood and what looked like a dog's tooth with a bloody root stuck in the fabric.

Rhazburn looked over at Jonathon and said, "They made the mistake of trying to stop it from coming back. It would have quite a tale to tell if it could speak."

"Thank you, Rhazburn. Now we have to find a Unicorn Horn."

"No problem. If one exists, I'll find it."

Jonathon jumped to his feet. "Rhazburn, you aren't thinking what I think you are thinking."

"Of course. The Wishing Drop." Jonathon's heart began to pound. When he had mentioned the Wishing Drop, he never intended to send his son there.

"Rhazburn, I won't let you."

The Loremaster waved his hand as if to dismiss his fear. "Relax. It's me. I can handle this."

Rhazburn seemed full of bravado, but Jonathon could hear a hint of uncertainty in his son's words. He remembered that same tone when Rhazburn spoke of saving Dollop from Hell.

CHAPTER 5

COMMUNITY

At the instant Jonathon Forthright had asked the Community to inscribe Gems of Power to set in a Unicorn Horn, the Community had decided to follow the cloaked priest from the Master Jeweler's shop. It was easy. Flying, the Pixets made no sound. They could fly unobserved, working through their melded minds, each one watching for a turn of the quarry's head, communicating to one another so each in turn could flit away unseen. One Pixelle, Faith, watched him from above. All the Pixet Community watched through her eyes. The cloaked man walked straight down the center of the streets, intent on his purpose, turning neither this way or that. People avoided him, somehow sensing some evil purpose.

As the figure walked steadily onward, the Community saw his goal was the Jungle. He passed the end of Guild Way and turned to walk down a narrow, dismal road. It was overshadowed by tawdry buildings filled with feral, increasingly evil characters. First, Faith saw diviners, then what the Community recognized as gamblers, then whores, next burglars, and then thieves, mobsters, kidnappers and murderers. Finally, she saw the worst of all the criminal group, the Skin Splicers.

It was almost overwhelming for Faith to follow the cloaked man. The Community siphoned off as much misery as they could. As she followed him closer to the evil center of the Jungle, Molgannard Fey's tower, the whole Community staggered. Rarely did they encounter an abode so evil.

Faith swam through the air against a current of hate coming from that tower. The cloaked figure marched right up to it. The tower was monstrous, ramshackle gray, nearly windowless like a burned stump. The Community made her stop when the stench of thousands of animal skins reached her. The cloaked figure never hesitated, but Faith could no longer follow. It was too painful for the Community. All that needless death for someone's pleasure? Faith fled.

Aside from the distress which the death of so many animals caused for the Community, a new threat appeared. They could see a blackness in the sky above the harbor. Where floral hues of a pleasing sunset should have been, gray shadows cloaked the horizon. Scores of Pixet eyes around Isseltrent recognized the approach of a thunderstorm. Faith flew back to Skysweeper, the Community's tree, before the storm dashed her from the sky.

The entire Pixet Community was agitated with exasperation at what the Master Jeweler had asked them to do. Jonathon Forthright had suddenly changed from a kind and generous human, something rare in Isseltrent, to one insensitive and greedy. He seemed possessed. The Community always nurtured and cared for all living things they came in contact with, even human beings. How uncharacteristic for the Master Jeweler to betray their trust and ask them to do something utterly immoral, turn a thing of natural beauty and power, the horn of a beloved Unicorn, into a spangled bauble.

As the Community reflected on this and Hili felt all their thoughts wafting through her mind, she flew through town high enough so she would miss pedestrians but low enough so Flying Carpets would miss her. She was famished, looking for food. As always, the smells of the city nauseated her. Flowers were what she sought and few flowers grew in Isseltrent.

In Verdilon where the Pixets had lived centuries before, the seas of grass were dotted with wildflowers. Unicorns had roamed free there. The memories of the beautiful land, long destroyed by the Demon Sverdphthik, could never fade in the Community as long as any Pixet lived. Hili knew where all the best flowers had been in Verdilon, but that would help her little in Isseltrent.

Pixets shared much more than thoughts and beauty. When a baby Pixie was born, all the Community felt the boundless joy of new parents, and when any two made love, all the Community shared in the ecstasy. Sounds, tastes and smells of all were immediately shared, energizing the entire Community.

Pain too was shared, but instead of augmenting, as mutual joy did, the shared pain lessened as each Pixet accepted his or her share of the burden and drew off some of the pain, soothing the one injured.

Sharing their thoughts constantly meant each Pixet's memories stayed clear and accurate, the good ones treasured, the bad ones suppressed, but still available at need. Everything each Pixet saw, heard, tasted and felt from all the centuries past were as real to Hili as her own memories of her life in Isseltrent. There were so many memories. Each Pixet lived ten years or so. Even so, Hili was comforted that she would live on in the thoughts of Pixets forever. Not just her thoughts but her unique essence would mingle with the goodness of world and forever after give sustenance to all the wonderful growing beings within the Natural Presence.

Hili recalled seeing sweet orchids on a tree through the eyes of Pixelle Reweese who had found them the day before. Hili had smelled their fragrance at the moment Reweese did. Tired as she was from her dealings with Master Forthright, the Community let her mind seek the orchids and sweet satisfaction.

Little time remained before darkness fell and the approaching storm drove the entire Community back to its haven, Skysweeper. As she flew, Hili felt the rhythm and heard the melody in her mind as Pixets danced in the air around Skysweeper, the huge elm where the Community slept at night.

She passed a statue of a long dead Dragonlord, Mabarani, on his favorite horse. Mabarani and his horse were well remembered by the Community. The statue was a mockery of their beauty. The building of

Isseltrent had hushed the natural streams and waterfalls on the land and changed them into culverts and water tanks within the city. Hili flew over a fake waterfall the humans prized and called a fountain. The original it replaced was much prettier and its splashing far sweeter. Pictures of trees were plastered to building facades. There were no birds, no bees, no lovely small life in these flat images. It was a poor substitute for the original.

No, there was little natural splendor in Isseltrent. Humans spent their time collecting and hoarding artifacts of the wild world. Destroyed forests, animals and rivers were mocked by paintings, statues and fountains. The Community was ashamed they had been forced to help the humans mock the pinnacle of natural beauty, a Unicorn Horn.

Hili felt Pixelle Dael fly to a still-dewy leaf hidden in a cool fern grotto, just to find a pure drop of water she could share with a moth. At the same time, Hili passed a human laboring to earn a Wooden Request just to drop in a replenishing pitcher on a washstand for a cup of water to wash away the city dust he breathed all day long during his work.

Suddenly, a black net engulfed her. Hili curled in a ball, but her wings did not retract. Quickly, she changed and spread wide her arms and legs, flying on through the net.

It was Theth, many city streets away, who was enclosed. Every Pixet in the city knew what had just happened. They saw and felt it just as did Hili. Some evil man had surprised Theth and was extracting him from the net, only to thrust him into a stinking bag. The canvas bag was slimy with oil from animal skins. The man had to be a Skin Splicer. He probably thought he could extort ransom from the Community. Poor misguided fool.

The man with the bag ran down Guild Way in the general direction of the Jungle. Hili, on the other side of town, saw and heard it all through other Pixets' senses. From Pixelle Dorma's viewpoint, who was twenty flutters behind the man, Hili saw him run down the broad thoroughfare. He shoved others from his path, even an old woman he threw to the ground. She screamed in pain, holding her thigh, unable to get up again.

He dashed around a corner out of Dorma's view, but Hili saw him approaching head on from Pixet Joac's eyes at the end of Guild Way. Then she heard his clattering footsteps to her right through Rheem's ears, lounging behind a barrel past which the man sprinted. While Hili sped to the scene, she saw the Skin Splicer from increasingly numerous vantage points. From above, compliments of Pixet Trumm. From the left, through Pixelle Weena pacing him. And when he passed Edwin Presmack's textile shop, Hili caught a glimpse of him as Pixet Faer watched through the window. The Pixets calculated the man's speed, judged his fatigue, estimated his strength and appraised his fear, doing it all together as one mind manifested in tiny points spread throughout the city

The man had surprised Theth, all alone, but he had no conception of the impossible task of taking advantage of two hundred twenty-one Pixets, who were simultaneously intent on saving their comrade. They all knew, moment by moment, which direction the man looked, and from which direction he could be approached, unseen.

As the man reached the end of the cobblestone street, the roadway fell away from him, and he suddenly floated up into the air. A hundred tiny wings raised him up, lifting him high above the pavement. His clothes were gripped by a hundred tiny hands. He froze, quailing to beat off the Pixets lest they drop him headfirst forty flutters down to the street.

The bag dropped, released in silent surrender. It was caught by a squad of five Pixets and untied in the air. Two Pixets held Theth safe until his senses recovered.

The Skin Splicer was flown to the Dragonlord's Palace and dropped before three Knights who had been informed by Pixelle Gwere of the man's crime. With a cuff on the ear and a kick in the ribs, the three Knights hauled him to the dungeon.

It had been a rare crime by a desperate man naive of the power of the Pixet Community. Most of the population of Isseltrent knew that any attempt to cheat or harm one of the Community was bound to fail. Again, Hili thought sadly, the Master Jeweler's betrayal was most unusual. If any human knew the Community's resolve to do right by all nature's creatures living or dead, Jonathon Forthright did. She and the other Pixets turned their attention to soothing Theth. In a short time, his sense of horror and discomfort were alleviated.

On the other end of town, in a wealthy ship owner's garden, Twill pulled the vane of a feather from his Morning Glory Tendril Belt and dipped it in a lupine. Sticky sweet nectar clung to the tiny bit of a feather. Twill licked it off and slipped the vane back in the lupine for more. A hundred lupine flowers in the garden brimmed with nectar. Twill shared the flower feast with a line of coordinated bees traveling between the garden and their hive. Some nectar was left for other Pixets but not much. Those most hungry, including Hili, a pregnant Pixelle and a few Pixies the size of Dragonflies flew to the garden. The others looked elsewhere. All agreed in their communal mind who should eat first.

Sipping nectar lasted most of the late evening for Hili and the other Pixets. The young ones were light enough to sit astride their flowers, relaxed, while they dipped and sipped. Hili and the pregnant Tarn had to hover as they drew off the nectar a few drops at a time.

While Hili enjoyed the fragrant fluid, a biting gnat landed on her arm. She shook it off before it jabbed her with its proboscis, but the black gnat was persistent, swirling for another attack. A bite from the gnat would make her arm swell for days. Tarn was watching a cornflower by the lupine straddled by a Pixie. A bright yellow crab spider on the cornflower awaited prey smaller than the Pixie. Tarn was watching to see it did not threaten the Pixie, only a year old. Hili saw all this through Tarn.

Annoyed by the gyrations of the gnat, Hili straight-armed it in midspin and held it tightly by the neck as it vibrated in her hand. She flew to the crab spider and offered the gnat. The spider raised its forelegs slightly higher, ready. She tossed the gnat toward the patient arachnid. In a wink, the spider clutched the gnat, gave it a paralyzing bite and threw a few sticky threads of silk around it, fouling its wings. Hili knew how strong spider silk was. Her dress was made of it.

Hili was ready to return to her meal, but two bees chased little Ceepee through a cluster of daisies. Twill was gone, having left long before, sated. Hili could not expect Tarn, big with child, to confront angry bees. Hili was Ceepee's only hope. Hili flew her fastest to intercept the bees who were gaining on the frightened Pixie. As Hili passed the leading bee, she slapped it to get its attention. Both bees charged her with their stings tucked forward glistening with poison. A bee sting was quickly fatal for a Pixet, so Hili had to dance.

Just out of reach of their deadly stingers, Hili twisted and turned in the air tracing complicated patterns. Learned centuries before by Pixets in Verdilon, none forgot 'Peaceful Bees', the dance used to calm bees with which Pixets flew constantly in their search for food. These bees began to move with her rhythm, retracting their weapons. Hili also knew the dance that would tell the bees about the orchids seen by Pixet Reweese the day before. As soon as the bees were calm, she danced 'Sweet Orchids', adding to her dance movements to give them directions to the tree where they grew. Bees loved orchid nectar, and these bees were satisfied, whirling away to dance the news for the rest of their colony.

Far away by the wharf, Pixet Inzle felt the first mist heralding the rain. To the northwest just beyond Landprow cliff, dark clouds slashed the sea with whips of rain. A pattering of droplets moved through town and soon soaked all the Pixets in the garden. A much harder downpour approached, so Hili, Tarn, Ceepee and the other Pixets left their meal to seek the protection of the broad elm leaves of Skysweeper. A little rain was welcome to the Pixets, but a gale with torrents would disable their wings. High winds would tear them from perches and bash them against buildings. On the ground, they would be safer from the wind, but they would be easy prey for dogs, cats, or humans. Most times, the risk of an occasional gale was worth the security.

By the time they reached Skysweeper, most of the Community was there hastily repairing their bivouacs. Hili flew to her own leaf tent. With the touch of the elm leaves surrounding the open doorway, her wings retracted. The early gentle rain drummed on her tent, quivering the leaf walls. First, she carefully prodded her pet spider, Spinner, down between chinks in the bark. Next, she inspected the ant-silk lashings that held her tent to the tree limb. They were firm but would not hold up to gale-force winds. Spinner had sucked Hili's ant grub dry. Her thought turned to Dorma, only a flutter away. Dorma had several grubs she was finished with and was willing to give one to Hili. Hili popped out of her tent and flew past Dorma's who had her arm out the door holding the grub for Hili to grab. Hili picked it up and looped back to her own tent. Inside, she concentrated on the weakest connections to the branch, holding the grub in one hand and tickling it with the other to make it release threads of sticky silk which Hili used to glue her tent more firmly to the branch.

Other Pixets were reinforcing their own bivouacs and many needed help. Joac was rapidly binding leaves, reinforcing a tent for a group of Pixies on one of the safest branches while the Pixies huddled around a twig. A few weak elders were carried to the safety of an abandoned woodpecker hole. The canopy of the tree branches and leaves would partially protect the twenty strongest Pixets and Pixelles who had remained outside, braving the downpour. When the wind flurried and the rain tore through Skysweeper, they were ready and watching for bivouacs torn apart by the wind so they could help the inhabitants.

With the first gust, Fleble, a youth of one year, was torn from her perch. Hili spun around a branch, dodged tumbling leaves, and caught Fleble around her tiny waist. Fleble was laughing with the fun of being blown by the wind and hugged Hili. Her glee was cut short when a big drop slammed into her face. Her tears were soon lost in the deluge. Hili's wings were hit by too many leaden drops, and she struggled to land under a sprig in a crotch between two branches. She wedged Treble in the crotch, the sprig making a rude umbrella. Hili made sure Treble gripped the ridged and wrinkled bark and felt secure. Then Hili picked her way up the branch.

She felt Caene, one of the watchers, hit by a gust that took him tumbling off a branch above her. To catch him, she had to fly out into the wind herself. As soon as she left the protection of the sprig, she was pelted by the torrent. It was much stronger than she had expected. Her wings retracted reflexively and Hili herself plummeted. Two other Pixets dove from above to help her. They too were hit by the torrent, and their wings retracted by instinct. All four Pixets were now falling. Caene hit a rock and was killed instantly. There was no doubt in their collective mind he was dead. Even if one of them was stunned unconscious, a glimmer of thought could still be felt by the Community. But with Caene, nothing was felt. Nothing but his memories, which they would cherish for as long as one of them survived.

Hili abandoned any attempt to help her fellows and stretched toward Skysweeper's bark. She stuck herself spider-like to the furrows and cracks. Quaid recovered before he hit the ground and flew up to catch Flynn, still tumbling. Since they knew nothing could be done for Caene, the Community chose to let his lifeless form lie until the storm ceased lest they lose more members to the gale. Through the night, the storm wailed, punishing Skysweeper with lashing gusts and flailing cataracts. Most of the bivouacs held tight, and no more Pixets were lost.

In the morning, as soon as the rain pattered away, two Pixets flew to retrieve Caene and take his body to a nearby woods to let his essence mingle with the goodness of the soil and the trees. His small body was gone. All they found was a man's footprint, like a rude Pixet grave, dug into the mud beside the dim outline of Caene's body. The Pixets attempted to follow the tracks but they were lost in the mire of Isseltrent.

CHAPTER 6

THE WISHING DROP

Rhazburn picked up a stone as big as his head and knocked again on the splintering oaken door that was the delivery entrance for Blaze. The stone thudded against the door so hard it cut deep gouges in the wood, and particles of cement dribbled down from between the limestone blocks that made up the castle walls.

"Open up," he shouted. "I have brought the ale for the larder-master's men." He heard a rushing about behind the door, then a crash in the storeroom. Rhazburn pictured a storeroom custodian scrambling to get the proffered ale, tripping over a cask support in his haste, spilling its contents. Rusty bolts were thrown with screeches and snaps, and the door swung wide before a skinny, pockmarked face. Rhazburn got a whiff of the vinegar that had been spilled in the man's haste to get the ale.

"Where's the ale?" the man said, looking over Rhazburn's shoulder.

"Since you dawdled all day to answer the door, the brewer left in disgust. But here's a Copper if you let me in. I have business with Honor

Gashgrieve." He held up a Copper Order close enough for the man to see clearly but far enough so he could not grab it without letting Rhazburn in.

"No visitors. The cook'd have me hide."

"All right, then. Point me to the carriage entrance. I'll see if the horse groom has need for this." He flipped the coin in a tight spin and caught it fast in his hand.

"Wait. Not so fast there." The man touched a bony finger to his pursed lips as he looked at Rhazburn past a blotchy beak. Twisting his neck further than any human should have been able, he inspected the storeroom behind him for listeners. He let his body follow his neck, twisting around, and with a glance to either side, he went in, waving Rhazburn in behind him.

"The hallway to the kitchen is up the stairs and to the right," he said, motioning ahead with the back of his hand. As Rhazburn passed, the man's arm came down like a tollgate, palm upward.

Rhazburn gripped the coin tightly. "Let me have that basket of apples so the cook won't ask any questions." The old garrulous cook of his youth was long dead. Rhazburn was unconcerned he would be recognized by the present staff of the Dragonlord's kitchen, but he wanted no needless delays.

The skinny man pressed his lips together in exasperation. Muttering some oath, he twirled around and grabbed the open-mesh basket of apples, shoving it at Rhazburn who traded the Copper Order for it. With the basket balanced on his shoulder, Rhazburn jogged up the stairs into the dark hallway.

In the kitchen to one side, a cook's helper stood at a table and beat out a rhythm with a spoon on a copper pot. On a cutting board in front of him, two cleavers danced on their own in time to his rhythm. As the cleavers clomped along the board, they chopped up a pile of onions and radishes. In a corner of the kitchen, another man watched darting shadows in a large ball of water suspended in the air. Suddenly, he whooped, thrusting his hand deep into the floating water. His hand emerged holding a flopping fish. Several others were equally intent on their assorted jobs. Rhazburn sauntered in like he belonged there. A portly cook with a gravy-smudged smock sharpened a butcher knife and gave him a glare. Rhazburn didn't stop to explain but walked through briskly, balancing the basket of apples on one hand while he waved a bumptious goodbye. A rude grunt came from the cook's direction, but Rhazburn was out before the cook could say a word.

Out of the kitchen, Rhazburn entered the maze of halls surrounding Seldric's throne room and the main living areas of the palace. These were all familiar to him from his youth, and he wound his way easily through the labyrinth to the stately, wood-paneled corridor that led to the chambers of the Dragonlord. The intricately-carved wainscoting and moldings of the corridor told the story of the creation of the Dragoncrown, the crowning of the first Dragonlord, the binding of the Dragons, and the expulsion of Sverdphthik from the territories of the Realm. Inlaid in the multi-colored wood floor of the corridor were representations of the Demon, its Zombie hordes, the Sinjery armies with bows and quivers crossing their backs, the Lord of the Sea and his Mermen riding fantastic fish, and all the other foes of the Dragonlord. The images faced the door of his chambers and prostrated themselves in abject humility. He could walk on their backs to his rest every day. Like everything that appealed to Seldric and his forbears, the floor was pompous and insolent.

Rhazburn wanted to stride right to the Dragonlord's door to confront him as to whether he had sent the mysterious messenger, but five braces of dour crimson-clad Sinjery Guards protected the approach. They were Rhazburn's half sisters, Royal Bastards too, but fiercely loyal to their father and under strict orders to kill anyone not allowed down the corridor or accompanied by the Chamberlain, Honor Gashgrieve. A fly could not get into Seldric's chamber unannounced. The Sinjery who were not his daughters were frequently his concubines and one, Cithoney, was his Queen. The Sinjery cared too much about each other and their homeland to allow any danger around the Dragonlord.

Rhazburn had arranged with the other Poets for time away from Hell's Breach to help Jonathon. Loreadept Kimberlain could lead the day Poets for a few days. With Wesfallen in the group, he would have little trouble. Rhazburn's adoptive father was worried that seven days was much too short a time to find the Unicorn Horn and fashion the staff paid for by the messenger, but Rhazburn was not worried about the staff itself. He was more worried about the validity of the commission altogether. He gave little credence to the mysterious messenger that seduced his father. His real purpose in coming to Blaze was not to take the journey to the Wishing

Drop. It was to confront the Dragonlord, question him face to face, and prove the messenger false. He knew expecting to speak with Seldric without permission was impossible. He had to go through Gashgrieve, who screened all of Seldric's audiences.

Gashgrieve's chambers were down a short flight of dismal stairs lit by glowing crimson crystals. A snarling, rampant male lion in bronze relief bloodied by the glow stared at him from the door to the Chamberlain's suite. There was no human guard, which to Rhazburn boded ill. The door was unfamiliar. It had been made since he had left the court when he was eight. Snarling lions weren't cast in bronze just for the beauty of it. Rhazburn took it to mean, 'Do not disturb. Go away.' No one in their right mind would touch such a door.

Through the door, Rhazburn heard high-pitched screams of laughter. Gashgrieve, married and with two children, was wenching again. Probably one of the court Choralists. Just a few days before, Rhazburn had run into him with his arm around a lusty red-haired Choralist. She fondled the official gold pendant of the Dragonlord's Chamberlain around Gashgrieve's neck while he fondled her ample breasts. A typical trade-off for the Chamberlain.

The floor in front of the door was covered with some soft wood. It wasn't oak, so it was probably soft enough for his purposes. Rhazburn set down the basket of apples. He took off his belt buckle and used it to scratch a poem into the floor before the door.

> Brazen eyed beast, born of metal
> Remember your feast, yawn and settle

He had written better poems, but it fulfilled all the criteria for a magical effect when a coin was used.

He stood back and pulled two apples out of the basket he had carried. With both apples in his right hand, he took a Wooden Request out of his pocket with his left and dropped it on the verse. At the same time, he tossed one apple at the door. The lion came to life with a roar and leapt out of the door onto the floor of the hall right at Rhazburn. But instead of slashing Rhazburn to bleeding shreds, the lion stopped and shook his head, sending ripples through his thick golden mane. He blinked. He yawned. He settled down on the floor, going to sleep in a moment. Rhazburn took a bite out of the other apple and reached down to pet the dozing feline. The door opened a crack and out peeked a slim blond man hastily tying a thick green robe. Rhazburn heard blankets rustling on the bed behind him.

"Rhazburn!" he exclaimed. Narrow critical eyes surveyed the scene before him. "I thought they found something more useful for you to do than play tricks on the court pets."

"I've heard better, Gashgrieve." He pointed to the pendant of his office undoffed for his tryst. "Even that hunk of gold around your neck hasn't improved your insults."

"What do you want, half-stranger? I didn't get my position listening to fools' drivel." Gashgrieve was a Royal Bastard, too. Few of them had the same mothers, since Seldric invariably discarded any Sinjery concubines who became pregnant.

"I have a serious problem from Hell's Breach to tell Seldric. So impress that sweet thing in your bed and announce me."

"That's 'His Highness' to you. Give me your message. He can't be bothered."

"The message is: 'There's a way to close Hell's Breach, but it can only be accomplished using the Dragoncrown. If anyone but the Dragonlord and me learn of the method, the Demons will find out, and we will lose our chance forever.'" The whole message was false, but Gashgrieve was not a Poet. Rhazburn had little respect for his ability to judge the validity of such a statement.

"Tell me the method. I will see if it warrants the attention of the Dragonlord."

"I cannot. Such a confidence would ensure the method's failure. The Dragonlord is protected from releasing the information to the Demons by the power of the Dragoncrown, and I am guarded by powers that check any intrusion into my mind. These spells are useful only to myself and are too esoteric to explain to anyone not trained in the Knowledge." Only Rhazburn could make such an outlandish assertion and hope to get away with it.

"The Dragonlord is away," the Chamberlain said, peevish.

"Away?" Rhazburn raised an eyebrow in disbelief. "Then why all the guards down the hall? A couple of guards would be sufficient if they were watching an empty room. No need for ten."

"Yes, away. So go away yourself. Your scheme will have to wait on our Lord's pleasure." He waved at Rhazburn with the back of his hand as if he were shooing away a bothersome dog.

Rhazburn dismissed his gesture with a sneer and looked him hard in the eye. "Where can I find the Dragonlord? My message cannot wait."

"You, Poet, cannot find the Dragonlord anywhere, because only the privileged of the court are allowed to know His Highness's whereabouts. Come back begging on the eve of the Dragonegg Festival. Then will I reconsider your request." He kicked the sleeping lion, who woke with a snarl and a snap, nearly taking off the Chamberlain's leg. Rhazburn's spell from the single Request was already exhausted. Gashgrieve pointed to the now-smooth bronze door and yelled, "Mauler, back in your cage!" throwing a Glass Command pulled from a robe pocket at the door. The lion, constrained by the spell on the door, leapt back into the bronze of the door which softened to receive him. Of course he was still a feral beast. He turned, roared, raised up to pounce upon them again, but solidified into an angry carving.

"The fate of the world bides your petulance, Gashgrieve."

The Chamberlain slammed the door.

"Sometime you'll come out with an empty pocket!" Rhazburn yelled at the door. *What a useless nabob*, he thought.

Something was amiss in Blaze. As the Loremaster, Rhazburn should have been allowed access to the Dragonlord. Maybe the crazy claim of the Beholder's message box was true. Maybe the Dragonlord did need them and their help. Rhazburn regarded the door a while, trying to think of ways to force the Chamberlain to take him to the Dragonlord. Thinking of none, he retreated back up the stairs to the Dragonlord's corridor, gazing at the distant iron door to the Dragonlord's chambers in frustration. He needed a Cloak of Invisibility. Too bad Cloaks of Invisibility were illegal. Highly illegal; punishable by death. He finally gave up and, taking another bite of his apple, started on his way to the Wishing Drop to find a Unicorn Horn. He had already decided to ask the Wishing Drop another more important question: Was the message from the Dragonlord real?

The Wishing Drop was really the only place to get the information he needed. The Gossip Dwarves might know a Unicorn Horn existed somewhere in the Dead Lands, but it was highly unlikely they would know its exact whereabouts. He knew Jonathon could in no way survive a trip to the Wishing Drop. Rhazburn had never tried the Wishing Drop himself, but he was confident he could drink from the Drop, have his visions of the location of a Unicorn Horn, discover the validity or falsity of the commission they were to fulfill, and leave without incident. One out of ten made it, and in Rhazburn's mind, he was one out of a million.

His memory of the scores of chambers and halls in Blaze that led up into the tower sanctum of the court Alchemist, Rulupunerswan, was flawless. A black glass stairway led to Augury Hall. Augury Hall was a place of dreams and disappointments. He passed all the gawkers looking into the multiple reflections of the Mirrors of Portents on opposing walls which reflected each other. Because of the mirrors opposing each other, images were multiplied again and again, so the myriad images of any person standing between them, each offset by a small degree, faded off into an infinite distance. For one Wooden Request, the images of the onlooker, each one farther away by the width of the corridor, would change in a progression of natural aging, allowing one to view himself off in the distance as he would appear in the future as an old man. But there was a risk. If the onlooker was to die soon, the images stopped much too quickly. Many people, aghast at what they saw in their future, left in shock. That day, three of the gawkers he saw were crying inconsolably. Another one he passed gasped. Never before in the years he had visited Blaze had he seen so many people unsettled by what they saw in the mirrors. Unusual that so many apparently found they had little time left to live on that day. Just a coincidence? Once again, he pondered whether some rebellion in Isseltrent were truly in the making.

Rhazburn had never looked at his own images previously. He knew his images would be cut off long before he reached middle age. After all, he did work at Hell's Breach. From rumors he had heard, the images one saw were not the caliber of those visions seen in the Wishing Drop. The future one could see in the Mirrors of Portents was vague, incomprehensible to most of the onlookers.

Rhazburn thought, *why not?* At the moment, he was interested in the future, especially related to the magical item his father and he were about to make. Maybe looking into his future in the mirrors would help him make up his mind.

He took out a Request and touched it to the mirror. The substance of the mirror turned fluid as it sucked in the Request, rippling out until his image wavered and changed. He had expected his reflections to stop long before middle age, but he was unprepared for the reality he saw. His image stopped just beyond the one which reflected the present. It just disappeared for a space. Then, the reflections began again, but none were Rhazburn. There were animals, birds and fish, followed by skeletons. Far off in the depths of the mirror, some dark-skinned, red-bearded, nearly-naked savage covered with tattoos took his place. Rhazburn shook his head in puzzlement, and so did all the others. The animals, the dead skeletal bones, the savage man, they all shook their heads. It was almost as if Rhazburn was seeing himself die very soon to be reincarnated as a variety of different beings. He would die again as a human, his flesh rotting off his bones. Finally he was to be reincarnated as a savage in the woods.

Rhazburn pondered the situation. Who cared how he was reincarnated? His death was imminent. That should stop him from pushing his luck in the Wishing Drop. Its threat of death would stop any careful person. Maybe he would die even if he turned away from his purpose. No, that would not save him. He used his reasoning. The risk of death had never kept him away from Hell's Breach. Why should it stop him now? How long did he have be for he died? He tried counting the multiple receding images, dividing by the number of years in a normal lifetime, to figure the time between images in the mirror. It was less than reassuring. He came up with less than one Moon, maybe just a fortnight. Just long enough to make the staff with his father, or maybe not even that. Rhazburn stepped away.

Beyond the Hall of Mirrors, he descended another short flight of marble steps and entered a colonnade that opened upon one of the many courtyards in Blaze. In the colonnade, walking resolutely in his direction, was a slight woman dressed in a blue gown that clung to her taut athletic figure. She was apparently on her way to the Dragonlord's chamber. Rhazburn felt a warmth in his chest, and his breathing deepened. This woman he admired not just for her beauty, which was far beyond that of the vapid court ladies. He admired her for so much more. Her bravery. Her tenacity. Her physical prowess. And her loyalty. On his rare days off from Hell's Breach, he had surreptitiously watched her fly her Green Dragon. She rode the beast with a facile grace unknown to the burly Knight Dragonflyers. Rhazburn remembered seeing her on her first visit to the Dragonlord's chamber. He remembered the way she had walked and held herself, proud but unpretentious. He had been smitten. That first day, his greeting was met with only a pleasant nod, but her eyes connected with his soul in a way few people would understand. Distrust of men was there behind the veneer. But in her glance there was also a warm feeling of relief that he was polite to her. He felt she had no attraction for him, but there was an alluring energy in her that he knew the Dragonlord felt. He suspected the lust *she* felt was only for her female Sinjery lover. No doubt their passion was intense.

Rhazburn tripped on an uneven brick. Chuckling at his clumsiness, he watched her lithe and supple form emerge from the darkness at the end of the colonnade. On the first day he saw her, he had asked a courtier her name and was told 'Trallalair'. Her blue gown, worn for the Dragonlord's pleasure, signified her as a Dragonflyer. The fact she was the concubine of the Dragonlord only appealed to him more. She was a forbidden fruit, luscious and tempting. Finding where her Brand's Dragonpaddock was located had taken him only a day. Since then, he had spent much of his free time sitting on a bench outside a nearby pub as he read tomes of poetry, listening for Hover to stretch her wings, hoping to glimpse Trallalair rise up into the air astride her winged beast.

Rhazburn was fascinated by Trallalair's acrobatics and her total disregard of death. When she stood between Hover's wings high in the air and leaped into a flip, she landed precisely balanced, even when the Dragon banked or changed direction. Trallalair's affinity with the Dragon's rhythms was remarkable. After that first day, Rhazburn's greetings to her evoked a slight nod that he hoped was appreciative. If the Mirror spoke truly, this may be the last chance he would ever have to tell he what he thought of her.

Obviously Gashgrieve had prevaricated about Seldric being away. Away from his duties caring for the safety of the Realm was more like it. Rhazburn knew if there were a plot to steal the Dragoncrown, Trallalair would not be part of it. His instinct told him she was too honorable. Still, the Sinjery had the greatest grievance with the Dragonlord and his policies. Their land was subjugated by men whom they had hated for centuries. They were forced to pay the tribute of maidens to guard the Dragonlord and the Realm. Despite their service and loyalty, they were constantly debased by the Dragonlord's degradation of their proud womanhood.

Rhazburn was tempted to use his tenuous friendship with her to get to Seldric, but he knew he would only be adding another insult to her morals by turning her into an agent for his use. If he believed the Mirrors of Portents, he had little time left. His father's promise to the Dragonlord would come first, but if he had less than a single Moon to live, he resolved to spend the rest of his short life helping Trallalair and her Sisters make themselves a better life.

As she approached the man in the corridor, Trallalair recognized Rhazburn and loosened her tight stride. He had introduced himself once briefly, so she knew he was the Loremaster of the Demonwards. She could not help but admire him for his prowess. She, like everyone in Isseltrent, had heard often of battles at Hell's Breach. Rhazburn's pleasantness, unlike the disrespect most of the courtiers showed her, lessened her sense of shame.

"Hello, Brandmistress. I hope you are well and have a pleasant day."

"Regards, Loremaster. I pray for your successes at Hell's Breach."

She looked up into his eyes, then turned her head, questioning, sensing something behind his casual greeting. "Loremaster, you look unsettled."

"It is of no consequence, Brandmistress Trallalair."

She smiled, knowing that with the evil forces he battled daily, everything he did was of consequence. But, like herself, he spoke little of his deeds. "As you wish. I must go." She turned to continue to her appointment.

Rhazburn touched her arm, lightly, to stop her before she left. "Trallalair," he said making her start with mild astonishment. Never before had he acted so familiarly as to address her without her title 'Brandmistress.'

For once, she was suspicious of Rhazburn. He was, after all, a man.

He said, "I just wanted to tell you, I admire you above all others. I wish I could change things for you and your Sisters. I believe you deserve better."

She did not know what to say. No man had ever said such things. Her suspicion melted away. His touch was disturbingly pleasant. Inwardly, she shielded herself. Saggethrie was her love.

He went on. "If I can, I will help you and your Sisters. I promise you. I have something I need to do first. If I survive, I will use all my energies to better your life."

She felt honored. But she and her Sisters needed no help from any man. Trying to quench the unnatural passion for Rhazburn she felt smoldering within her, she politely bur formally said, "Loremaster, the Sinjery have no need of any sacrifice of your time. We care for ourselves." She meant that two ways and hoped he caught the gist of it.

He nodded, smiling, "I will do as you wish, Brandmistress."

She passed by without another word, intent on her duties, trying to suppress any need she had for a man's touch. Certainly she had no need of Seldric's.

As always, Rhazburn's gaze lingered on her receding body barely hidden by the tight shimmering gown. He thought of her riding her Dragon. How different she looked in her armor, but alluring all the same. He thought he would never see her again with or without her armor. He had tried but failed to tell her the extent of his admiration and lust. For a moment, he had felt it within her, too. He was glad she was content with her female lover. Why tell Trallalair he loved her when he would die soon? What could be more cruel for both of them?

Tearing himself away from his lovesick thoughts, he proceeded outside the colonnade and made for a tower that brooded over the adjacent courtyard. It was one tower few people entered because of the reputation of Rulupunerswan.

Rhazburn's reputation made him most unpopular with all his jealous half siblings in the court. He had left the court and become successful without dependency on the leavings of the Dragonlord. He seldom hid his pride or his loathing of the fawning courtiers. Though Gashgrieve was at odds with Rhazburn, Rulupunerswan hated him and would just as soon see him dead. Rhazburn was looking forward to solving the problem of the Wishing Drop which was in the Alchemist's control. It was like a game to him, foiling Rulupunerswan. He had no choice, regardless. There was no record of any Unicorn Horn still in existence, so the only way to find one was to make a wish for a vision at the Wishing Drop.

A spiral stone staircase wound around the inside of the tower to the top where Rulupunerswan and the Wishing Drop resided. The red granite portal to the chamber needed no door. Only a tattered woolen curtain stood in Rhazburn's way.

"Enter if you dare, Rhazburn," came a nasal, rasping voice. Rulupunerswan had not seen the Poet but apparently knew he was coming. Rhazburn swept aside the curtain to see the back of a bent figure covered in a black robe trimmed on the sleeves and collar with mangy fur. He stooped over a cauldron that emitted green steam. Rhazburn was not impressed.

"Is this how you entertain the Children of the Court? I'm not here for a show. I'm going to drink from the Wishing Drop."

The Alchemist spun around and hissed, "You act so bold, Rhazburn, but you won't escape the curse of the Wishing Drop. None of your tricks will work in here."

"And how would you know, Rulupunerswan? I hear you never took the journey yourself, though you guard the Drop." Rhazburn folded his arms and looked at the Alchemist with undisguised contempt.

"I have better ways to learn all I need to know. The Drop is not a source of infinite knowledge. The Drop, like all in the land, serves the Lord. Few return from entering it. And why? Because it can sense an evil scheme in the mind of a half-wit. The Drop itself culls the dolts and dullards who come here looking for riches to be stolen somewhere in the world. You'll join the rest. I can tell from your eyes and your simpering whine. You come searching for some treasure to steal that cannot be found, just like the others."

Rhazburn hid his surprise at the accuracy of the Alchemist's suspicions with an attack. "Twenty years ago, when you took this charge, the Drop was the Wishing Well with wishes for all. It was accessible and held no danger to the wisher. If you knew your art, you would have replenished the well instead of letting it dry up to what is left today."

"This power is not for every scalawag to use as he will. I knew its benefit for the Realm lay in granting wishes to only the select. In my wisdom, I chose to regulate it better than the faker before me." He tried to lift his head, but the hump behind his head stopped his haughty gesture. He grimaced instead.

Rhazburn knew Rulupunerswan's words were all lies, but he did not want to waste any more breath on the bitter man. "Lead me to the Drop."

"You haven't the price to use the Drop. So leave or I'll have the Guard test your skill as a Poet by throwing you out yon window." He pointed into the rear of the room where a cleft in the stone looked upon the city far below.

Rhazburn took out two Glass Commands and said, "I have the price. Show me the way."

"No Poet makes enough to save two Commands. That gives me proof you are a criminal. You're probably the one all the Guard is looking for at this very moment. Let's see what the Chamberlain and the Guard have to say about a thieving Poet." With a flourish, he snatched a vial from a nearby stand and lifted it over his head.

"You will look a fool if you have to explain your mistake to the Chamberlain."

Rulupunerswan hesitated.

"Contact Jonathon Forthright, the jeweler, and ask him if he hired me to come to the Wishing Drop on his behalf." Rhazburn bet that Rulupunerswan, sequestered in his tower, had not heard of Jonathon's poor fortune.

"You lie," the Alchemist spat, pointing a crooked finger at Rhazburn.

"Contact the jeweler. If it is a lie, have me arrested."

Rulupunerswan cackled and replaced the vial carefully on the warped top of the wooden stand. "I have no need for that. You will die within a single Blessing in the Chamber of the Drop, so why bother myself? What message should I give the jeweler after you die?"

"Tell him you are a fool."

Rulupunerswan hissed, "Give me the Commands!" He thrust out a hand like a claw.

Rhazburn stepped up to him and looked down at him. He dropped the Glass Commands in the outstretched hand a little off center, so

Rulupunerswan had to jerk to catch them and keep them from breaking on the stone floor. The Alchemist stabbed him with his eyes and bent his head to look at the coins, turning them over and over in his hand like a rat examining scraps. With tremulous fingers, he slowly opened a faded brocade pouch and dropped them in. The same tremor shook the hand he extended toward the back of the room to point out the Chamber of the Wishing Drop. He never took his filmy eyes off Rhazburn, leering at him as the Poet squinted to see into the shadows.

Heavy, black curtains kept the sun out of Rulupunerswan's chamber as if he feared the daylight. There, on a black painted table, its top even with the window sill, was a translucent stone. The stone glowed in the light of a single large candle that dripped milky wax onto the peeling tabletop. The stone was almost perfectly round with a slightly knobby surface. A tiny wooden wedge led like a ramp to a hole no bigger than Rhazburn's thumb that pierced the surface of the stone. After walking up to the stone, Rhazburn saw it was a geode, round outside but holding a crystal-lined chamber within. Although the stone was small enough to be lifted, Rhazburn did not touch it.

"Well, learned Poet," the Alchemist scoffed, "have you no spells to take you within the chamber?"

"I need none. The Glass Commands I gave you purchased my way into the chamber. You fear I will solve the riddles within, which you dare not attempt, and so you hesitate to tell me the way in. I understand."

"Don't mock me, Poet. Once you are in the chamber, you may realize I am the only friend that is near."

"So show me the way, 'Friend,'" Rhazburn jeered.

Rulupunerswan shuffled to a wooden trunk with a broken brass clasp and lifted the lid. He pulled out a dirty rose-colored suit that looked like it had been made as an undergarment. The suit would cover Rhazburn completely, from a hood for his head to stockings for his feet and gloves for his hands. It was all of one fabric, a kind Rhazburn had never seen before. It caught the light and shimmered slightly. The Alchemist threw it over his shoulder and walked to the cauldron over which he had been standing when Rhazburn first walked in the room. With a grunt and a lurch, Rulupunerswan heaved the cauldron over, dumping its contents through a grate in the floor. He righted it and poured in yellow fluid from a tall dusty crystal decanter. From a burning brazier, he took two glowing rocks with a pair of iron tongs and dropped them in the cauldron. A handful of blue powder followed, then one of Rhazburn's Glass Commands. While the fluid was still bubbling, the Alchemist stuffed the suit into the cauldron and beat it down with his staff. After a moment, he used the staff to pull the suit out of the cauldron. It made a loud sucking sound as it came. He tossed it with a splat, steaming, onto the floor.

"Pick it up and put it on, Poet," he said, pushing it toward Rhazburn with the staff.

Rhazburn picked it up, gritting his teeth against the scalding fabric, and waved it in the air to let it cool. Rulupunerswan laughed at him. "You must don the suit before it dries."

Rhazburn inspected the suit. A line of buttons down the front were undone. He tried to step into the suit, but stopped at a guffaw from the Alchemist. "Take off your clothes, Flea-wit. All of your clothes. You can take nothing into the chamber except your puny body and that suit. The power of the chamber will allow no magic but its own."

Rhazburn took off his clothes quickly, unashamed before the Alchemist. His body was hardly puny compared to the Alchemist's. The priests of The Three exhorted that all people in loving themselves should keep good care of their own bodies and exercise to keep their bodies close to the new ideal of beauty. Rhazburn disdained their drivel. He exercised daily, but it was to keep himself trim and strong for trouble at Hell's Breach. The suit fit loosely. After all, it had to fit all comers. Its moist heat quickly washed away the chill of the tower air on Rhazburn's naked skin.

With an irritated wave of his hand toward the geode, Rulupunerswan hurried Rhazburn to step up to the black table. "Place a gloved finger in the entryway to the Chamber of the Wishing Drop." He waited a moment while Rhazburn studied the tiny hole. "That is, unless your valor has suddenly fled. I'm sure you could lie to your benefactor. Tell him you really entered the chamber. Make up a story of the visions you saw. You should be good at that."

Rhazburn paid no attention to the taunt. He slowly inserted a finger into the hole in the rock. Almost instantly, he felt the previously loose garment tighten around his entire body. He let out a groan as the suit squeezed him mercilessly. He felt his face pumped full of blood, ready to explode. Tears ran from his eyes.

Rulupunerswan laughed. "Are you in pain, Poet? Try some of your proud bluster now. Perhaps it will ease your discomfort."

The pressure built up steadily, trying to crush him all at once, head to toe. For an instant, he thought the Alchemist had tricked him and was killing him with the suit rather than letting him into the Chamber of the Drop.

Suddenly, something gave way within him. The room around him and the rock before him began enlarging noticeably. He had a hard time keeping his finger in the hole and had to keep shifting his stance to keep close enough as he shrunk steadily. Soon he was shorter than Rulupunerswan, who glared down at him with hate. When Rhazburn had to reach upward to keep his hand in the hole, he used his free hand to climb up on the table. He looked over his shoulder at the swollen figure of Rulupunerswan, who stood three times as tall as Rhazburn and was growing constantly. He felt extremely vulnerable to the hostile Alchemist, who towered over him with his heavy staff still tightly clutched in his hands.

The Alchemist continued to grow as tall as a tree and taller. The rock before him expanded to a boulder, then a monolith as Rhazburn shrank. He then had to reach up to the hole while he stood on the table top. He found he could actually step onto the small wedge of wood and was forced to walk up it progressively.

The Alchemist bent to look down at him. His face, as big as a house, loomed above Rhazburn. "What stops the shrinking?" Rhazburn yelled.

"Cowardice!" boomed the Alchemist's thunderous voice. "If you cower and skulk away from the Chamber of the Drop, the shrinking stops and you will regain your height. Or if, in your fear, you take off the suit, your shrinking will stop. Of course, if you take it off inside the chamber, the suit will still shrink, and you will stay a flea forever, since you need the suit to regain your height. But that is your calling, I believe - to be a flea. Now you have your wish."

He let out a few roars of laughter. "You might like it in there. Stay as long as you like. Keep shrinking and shrinking until you are a nit or a mote of dust. Go to oblivion with the rest."

The hole into the chamber looked as vast as a cave, and Rhazburn had walked up to the lip at the end of the ramp. With his last word, Rulupunerswan took in a breath and blew at Rhazburn. The breath was like a gale, and Rhazburn was thrown, somersaulting, into the cavernous mouth of the Chamber of the Drop.

CHAPTER 7

PRISONERS OF THE DROP

Rhazburn awoke from his daze face down on a bed of nails, or so it seemed to him. He pushed up, his hands stuck by dozens of sharp points. A diffuse wavering light moved about the chamber around him. He thought back to his life in another world and realized the light was the single candle on Rulupunerswan's table which shone through the translucent rock.

When Rhazburn could finally focus his eyes, he saw a wonderland of white, yellow, and purple crystals. They were everywhere. Jutting out of the rock from every surface, he saw a forest of twinkling needles, spikes, spears, and pillars. They were mostly small, no longer than his finger, but they covered everything. The rock bulged in lumps and waves, but the crystalline surface followed all the contours. The tips of the crystals pointed toward an axis in some places and fanned out from a central knob in others.

As Rhazburn gazed, enthralled, he noticed the majority of the crystals had grown to the size of his hand. Shaking his head, he came out of his trance and surveyed the marvelous landscape to look for the object of his quest, the Wishing Drop. He was still shrinking and would continue to shrink until he disappeared if he didn't find the Wishing Drop, get the information he needed, and escape in time. Looking up over the arching inner surface of the geode, he found the tallest part of the chamber. Below it on the floor, a small body of clear water nestled in a bramble of crystals. It might be a drop, or more accurately, a spoonful of water to the outside world, but to Rhazburn, it looked like a small pond. At his size, it appeared no more than three rods away. That only applied for an instant, since he continually shrank. The next instant, it would seem three and a half rods.

At that moment, looking at the small body of water, Rhazburn realized the problem of the Wishing Drop and the incredible danger of the chamber. As long as he was in the chamber with the suit on, he would shrink smaller and smaller. To take the suit off was suicide, since the suit would continue to shrink and he could never again put it on. Only with the suit on could he regain his height outside the chamber. The chamber grew constantly in relation to his size. At that moment, the crystals on the floor were merely an inconvenient rocky road, the distance only a few relative rods. In a short while, when his height was divided by ten, the road back would be a maze of boulders many rods long. If he dawdled again as long, he would shrink to one hundredth of his present height, and the path would be a league of crystal hills. Another bit of time would make the distance thirty leagues of mountains. The longer he stayed, the more difficult the trek outward became. Like some spider web spun of deceit, the trek itself kept him in the chamber longer and longer by adding more and more length and difficulty to his journey back, moment by moment. He could, all too quickly, come to a point where no matter how fast he traveled, the relative expansion of the distance to the door and freedom would outdistance him. He imagined his predecessors in this quest, the nine of every ten who were never seen again realizing this all too late and ripping off their shrinking suits to stop the boulders before them from becoming mountains. To be charmed by the beauty of the cavern or fascinated by whatever vision the Wishing Drop provided was certain death. Rhazburn had to move fast.

He stretched his leg out and stepped on the shimmering crystal floor. The points stuck through the flimsy material of his suit and dug into his feet painfully. He gritted his teeth and walked forward gingerly, hoping if he placed his feet slowly, the sharp points would not hurt. It was no use. Each step was torment. Resolving to get the agony over as quickly as possible, he sped to a saunter, then faster, to a loping jog. Every time his feet hit the floor, the crystals stabbed him. He knew the crystals were gouging and slashing his feet, but he had to endure. Jonathon depended on him. And he wanted to foil Rulupunerswan.

At what to his size seemed one rod from the Wishing Drop, Rhazburn slipped on a loose piece of quartz. He almost went down but caught himself by waving his arms over his head for balance. When he stopped, his feet were on fire. First, he tested his ankle to make sure he had not sprained it when he slipped. A sprain there could be fatal. The ankle was still strong, but when he looked at his feet one at a time, he saw splotches of blood covering the soles and soaking through the fabric. Bandages would have to wait. He stood back on the wicked carpet and stretched for the final few strides.

Before he took a step, the sound of a high-pitched crying stopped him. It was like a sobbing sparrow. He looked around at the confusion of crystals. About six steps to his right, atop a crystal slightly taller than the rest, crouched a naked human, no bigger than Rhazburn's throbbing foot. It was a tiny woman. Not a Pixelle. Rhazburn was already smaller than a Pixet's thumb. The long ermine white hair and the abundant curves beneath the olive skin were unmistakable, even at Rhazburn's distance. He took two giant steps to get closer.

"Madam let me help you? I am Rhazburn, Loremaster of the Demonwards." he offered.

The woman looked up, startled, and immediately slid from her perch.

"Wait!" Rhazburn called as she disappeared with a twist around a clump of crystals. For a few precious moments, Rhazburn searched in and around the local cluster of crystals, calling out, "Come back. I can help you get out of here. I want to help." No response. The woman remained hidden. Clearly to Rhazburn, the woman was one of the prior wishers trapped by the paradox of the chamber and the suit. He expected to find more of them, but to help them would only trap himself.

The Wishing Drop lay only a few steps away. Because of the crystal bed, its shape was very unpondlike. Instead of being rounded and symmetric, it molded around, over and through clumps of crystals. It heaped up against gleaming facets and meandered out into the forest of glassy pillars.

Rhazburn's feet had slipped down between the jagged spikes because he had shrunk to the point at which most of the crystals came up above his ankles. Walking the last small distance to the Wishing drop was much less painful, but took a different kind of effort. He had to walk on the sides of his feet jammed down between the facets of the crystals.

Finally, he stopped before the Wishing Drop, his feet squeezed down uncomfortably in a crevice. His anger at the terrain burst out of him, and he tore at the crystals around him, breaking them off by the handfuls and tossing them into the water before him. When he threw them, he noticed something he had not expected. Many of the smaller crystals bounced on the water and never even penetrated, making the surface of the water jiggle like a mass of quivering flesh.

After he had cleared away a small space bare of crystals around him, he knelt. The water was perfectly clear, and more facets like a mass of diamonds carpeted the pond bottom. The water's edge was bizarre, not flat but rounded, a lip he could grasp.

Trying to touch it, Rhazburn felt the water to be as thick as molasses. As he had shrunk, the water had become thicker and thicker relative to his size. Time was running out. He picked up a drop that rounded between his fingers and fell in huge gobbets that rolled like balls back to the rest of the water. A small portion he crammed in his mouth and swallowed. It felt like a raw egg going down, but when it had passed his throat, he felt a rush of power expanding from his chest into his head. For a moment, all knowledge was his. He felt as omniscient as The Three.

His first duty was to Jonathon's problem, so he concentrated on the whereabouts of a Unicorn's horn. As he closed his eyes, hundreds of Unicorn Horns appeared before him, all of them in the Dead Lands, ruled by the Demon Sverdphthik. None existed outside. They were all inaccessible. To enter the Dead Lands was certain death. The Dead Lands were proscribed territory for the citizens of Isseltrent and all of Thuringland. If the Demon and its fell thralls did not kill him, the law of the Dragonlord would. That is, if the courts learned about his journey.

He concentrated closely on each Unicorn Horn in turn. Most were carried by dead Unicorns which walked in the Dead Lands as Zombies under the power of the Demon. To see the proud beasts so hideously enslaved offended Rhazburn as it would offend the Pixets who had fled

Verdilon. It had been their land, the land which Sverdphthik stole. He had killed everything in the beautiful country, including the noble Unicorns. They had been nurtured for millennia by the Pixets. They had also been friends. Rhazburn vowed to keep this hideous vision a secret from Hili.

At last, he came upon a Unicorn Horn which had been severed from its animal centuries before. This one lay nearer to Isseltrent than any other. Although it lay within the confines of the Dead Lands, it was close to the border. Rhazburn could see through the lands between as if they were as transparent as the crystals about him. He peered deep within a mountain, through a cave wall into a room hewn from the granite, to the bottom of a pile of treasure. Here there lay coins, gold, jewels, silver, and silk. At the very bottom lay a milky spiral. The Unicorn Horn. The mountain was named Devil's Fang. It was known as Grimtooth by the Sylvets who guarded the Forbidden Mountains. Devil's Fang was the southernmost mountain of that range and the only one beyond their control. It was a source of blight for the surrounding territory. On the border of the Dead Lands, Devil's Fang spread the Demon's evil and filth into the land of men. A Zombie lord dwelt within, and a tribe of humans who lived in the caverns of Devil's Fang worshipped him and carried out his will. They brought humans alive or dead to him as sacrifice. All this Rhazburn knew with the knowledge of the Wishing Drop.

Too bad he could not just wish he had the Unicorn Horn and it would appear in his hand. Unfortunately, that was not the nature of the Wishing Drop. Answers to his questions were the only things that were allowed by the present Science. If the Alchemists could come up with a fluid that would grant more than visions, allow one to change reality, they could just wish away the Demon and Hell's Breach. They could even change all water in the world to the fluid that grants wishes and allow everyone to become gods. Power like that could change reality at a whim. Rhazburn knew that could never be. Everyone gods? Everyone as powerful as Sverdphthik or the Dragonlord? The world would surely end. Rhazburn knew that too much power in one hand was not a good thing. And yet, here he was, accomplishing the very thing he knew was wrong, even if it was to save his father.

Rhazburn was distressed by the horrors he saw in his vision and withdrew his mind from the scene. As he pulled away and came out of the trance he had fallen into, he felt the power of the Wishing Drop leave him. He looked around to see the crystals had continued their steady growth and were now half his height. If he didn't start back soon, he would be trapped for sure. But whatever the danger, he refused to leave before he found out if Jonathon's deal was legitimate or not.

Big as his knee, the rounded edge of the water felt thick as tar. He clawed at it to break off a hunk. It came out perfectly round like a glass globe used by the some of the Seers. Although to the outside world it would be only a droplet of mist, to Rhazburn it could fill a tankard. He bit off a chunk and forced it down, looking into the globe to see his vision of the future that awaited Jonathon and himself if they completed the scepter.

A golden Dragonegg filled his mind. Then, around it, he saw the Dragonegg Festival in the central court of the Dragonlord's palace. Clouds of Pixets were flying everywhere, twirling, looping, and diving in an airborne ballet. The sound of drum dancers hopping about on their table-sized drums reverberated through the courtyard. At the end of the courtyard filled with humans and Dwarves, Seldric's Red Dragon towered above the Dragonlord on his throne. Seldric talked to Queen Cithoney sitting beside him. Rhazburn could just barely see the Dragonlord's head because of the semicircle of Sinjery guards in sparkling crimson mail that surrounded him. Suddenly, the drumming eased. The courtiers and the Dragonlord turned to look at something. That was the last Rhazburn saw.

His head exploded with an impact that pushed his face into the thick water. Something sat on his head and pinned his arms and legs. He couldn't breathe because his face was against the resilient surface of the water. He felt tight thin bands around his limbs. It was as if he was being held by a pack of spiders. The one on his right leg was just above his knee. Rhazburn bent his knee and kicked, tossing that one off with a squeak. Even though there were a lot of them, they were light. With a great effort, he pushed himself up on straight arms, bounced once, and spun around to dislodge as many spiders as he could. As he threw his arm around and fell on his back, he saw them.

They were men. Wildly different sizes, and all naked as a bunch of Querites. The only difference was that Querites would be sacrificing their own comfort, carrying him on their shoulders or rubbing healing balm on his feet, rather than trying to kill him. The one that had been on his right arm, and about as long as his arm, had been thrown off by Rhazburn's twist. He sailed to ricochet off the surface of the water just as the small crystals had done. The one on Rhazburn's head was now under it. Rhazburn thrust his head back again and again, slamming the little man into the crystals, until the small arms relaxed unconscious. The one on his left arm hung on like a bulldog. He was half Rhazburn's height and glared at the Poet in defiance. Rhazburn punched him square in his angry little face, spread-eagling him off to the side. The last little man, about the length of Rhazburn's thigh and about as fat, let go his arms encircling Rhazburn's waist and backed off without a struggle. As Rhazburn watched them all scatter, he complimented himself for just beating up a gang of babies.

When he saw them looking up, he followed their gaze. There, at least three times Rhazburn's height, stood another angry naked man. This virtual Giant looked down on Rhazburn. In his hands above his head, the man held a crystal as big as a coffin, ready to drop on Rhazburn. Just as the Giant inhaled, tensing to throw the crystal on Rhazburn and crush him, a small blur with long white hair jumped from the top of a standing crystal and lunged at the Giant's face. Rhazburn saw the figure of a naked woman, the same he had seen before, make a precise kick to the Giant's eye. She was tiny compared to the Giant, but the kick had its effect. The Giant wailed and grabbed his eye with one hand, letting go of the massive crystal. The crystal rotated on his other hand and smashed into his own head. It felled him like a tree. The woman landed on the ground like a cat.

Rhazburn knew she had to be one of the Sinjery Guard to move like that. She looked old, but she was more than a match for any man her size in a fight. The other men didn't attack her directly but retreated a few paces and began to pick up broken crystals to pelt her.

Rhazburn leaped to his feet and ran to the Sinjery woman as the first few rocks hit her. The men hid behind other crystals but kept up a withering rain of rocks. There were about a dozen of the others, and even though small, they could no doubt handle Rhazburn and the woman in a prolonged battle. They stood between Rhazburn and the path out. The woman dodged the rocks skillfully at first, but as they increased in number, filling the air about her, she took a hit on the temple. She fell and curled up as more rocks struck her.

Rhazburn picked her up by the waist and turned to protect her from the rocks with his body. Since he was five times her height, he shielded her quite well. That made the back of his head their target now, and stone after stone slammed into his scalp. He had to escape them, but the only path open was away from his freedom. Right now, he was taller than them all, except the fallen Giant who was beginning to stir, but since he still had the suit on, he would shrink until he would be easy prey. He started around a long bay of the pond, scrambling over the crystals, using one hand to steady himself and carrying the unconscious woman in his other. The small men's aim worsened as he got ahead of them, but they all followed as soon as they were reassured the Giant was rousing himself and could back them up.

In his arm Rhazburn felt the woman struggling. He said, "You are safe for the moment. Let me carry you until we get away. My name is Rhazburn. Thank you for saving my life."

She relaxed and said, "And thank you, Rhazburn. I am Jiminic, Sinjery. Let me climb on your back so you have your hands free." Rhazburn stopped a moment, and she hopped up to be carried like a child, grasping his shoulders and wrapping her legs around his waist. He continued scrambling away from their pursuers.

When she saw the direction they headed, she cried, "Go the other way, you fool! Don't you know you can never get out if you shrink much more?"

"I know, but I want to get away from those men. Why did they attack me?"

"They are desperate. They want your suit. We are all trapped in here without the suit. Most of them could not get out in time and took off their suits only to lose them."

"And you? One of the Sinjery would not let herself be trapped."

"One of them stole my suit as they would steal yours. You must get back before it is too late, or you will become one of them."

"If you can hang on, I think I can lose them."

She only grunted. What did the grunt mean? Yes, since she was Sinjery, of course she could hang on? Or no, you can't lose them? Rhazburn didn't ask.

As they rounded the end of the bay, Rhazburn looked back to see the Giant man towering above the crystals, carrying the dozen smaller men, some in his arms and some on his shoulders. He strode easily through the crystals and quickly caught up to Rhazburn and Jiminic. Rhazburn's back was to the pond, now a lake in Rhazburn's frame of reference. The Giant carefully set down his friends who spread out and began picking up crystal fragments to stone them again.

Rhazburn climbed a crystal and said to Jiminic, "Hang on."

When the first rocks began to fly and the Giant bent to pick up a long crystal cudgel, Rhazburn turned, took two long strides and made a shallow dive at the lake. He hit on all fours but his hands and feet did not pierce the surface. Like a pond spider skating on the surface of the water in the real world, Rhazburn slid across the water. He had pushed off his perch with enough force so he and his rider slipped across the small bay and landed on the opposite shore. Before he stood up, he scuttled, like a crab, up and into the forest of crystals. When he stood, he held Jiminic's hands fast to his shoulders so she would not fall. Behind them across the lake, their pursuers were arguing and scratching their heads.

"What is the fastest way back to the entrance?" Rhazburn asked.

"That way." She pointed past his head toward a pathway cleared of crystals. "I've walked it a hundred times, like a caged beast pacing. The prisoners cleared the path from the lake to the entrance."

Rhazburn started jogging up the path. The crystals about them were growing ever larger, many taller than Rhazburn's head already. He had no idea whether or not the other men were still chasing them, but he knew his own pace was slowing. When he had been fighting and fleeing, he had ignored the pain in his feet, but now it hit him again. The pain of the cuts and punctures chewed away at his remaining strength. Since he was shrinking but Jiminic was not, she was becoming heavier with each moment that passed. Still, he slogged onward.

Soon, the trail began sloping upward to the entrance of the chamber. Rhazburn slowed to a crawl, grunting and straining with his load.

As Rhazburn began to tire Jiminic pushed herself off, saying, "You must go on alone from here, Rhazburn." She pointed again up the cleared trail that was now as wide as a road. "The path leads straight to the entrance. Hurry now. You haven't much time."

Rhazburn looked at her closely for the first time. She was still two heads shorter than he. He judged her to be around fifty years old, but the lines carved in her face were seventy years deep. "Sinjery, you are no stranger to sorrow. I want to help you."

"I cried today, but I am resigned to my fate. Now go. Waste no more time."

"I think you were not crying for yourself."

"I cry for my son. He was a Knight who died in war with the Demon and his minions. I came here against the law of Sinjer and the Dragonlord to ask of the Drop his whereabouts. I cry because his spirit will never rest. He is a slave of the Demon." She spoke looking downward, her voice insecure. Rhazburn felt she lied. Lying was unheard of with the Sinjery Guard. That was why the Dragonlord trusted them, they always told the truth. "Go. They will catch you."

Instead of running away, Rhazburn quickly took off the suit. She looked at him startled but not at his nakedness.

"Are you mad? You have doomed yourself."

"I am not mad. Put the suit on fast. It is already too small for me. But you can still fit in it and escape."

"Your charity is wasted on me," she said as she slipped into the suit.

"You saved my life. I am only repaying you." As he looked on the Sinjery woman, he saw his mother who would be about her age. He wished his mother had loved him enough to come looking for him.

"You are a brave and foolish man, Rhazburn. You know I will die anyway."

"Why? You will grow to your normal size. You can return to Sinjer."

She shook her head. "The Alchemist recognized I was Sinjery and had broken the exile we all face after our five years of service to the Dragonlord. When I entered the rock, he told me so and said I would be given up to justice if I did not die within the chamber."

"What punishment could be prescribed for merely coming back to the land you protected in your youth?"

"Death."

Rhazburn was shocked. "I lived in the court as a child. That is not the Dragonlord's law." He had almost given himself away as a child of a Sinjery Guard. Few boys but Royal Bastards and the Heirs of Seldric lived in the court.

She looked at him with pity. "It is not a law of the Dragonlord. It is a Sinjery Law."

He sputtered.

"Do not question it, Rhazburn, Sinjery son." She had guessed the truth. "Yes, I can see my Sisters in your eyes and your heart. Some day you may know more of the Sinjery Spirit. What is the name of your mother?"

He felt ashamed before her. Ashamed for his mother having left him in his youth. He cared not that his mother had no choice. Here was a woman who risked certain death just to find her son. Rhazburn knew his mother would never have done the same. He wanted to say he had no mother, but instead, he said with a slight stutter, "I never knew her name. She left or was killed before I was old enough to ask. When I was old enough, I was afraid to ask about her." Of course, he knew her name: Bresmarion. Her laughter and gentleness he knew as a child would never leave him. The emptiness of its loss had not left him either until Jonathon Forthright had given him his first hug. It wasn't something he would share with many.

The pity in her eyes deepened. She clearly knew he lied. "I knew your name, Loremaster, long ago when you were less than four. I taught you ballads in the Bough. You learned the songs quicker than any other child, but you constantly changed the words of the songs to suit your mood. Very rebellious you were."

Rhazburn did not remember her, but he tried to forget much of that time in his life.

"I remember your mother, too. Bresmarion. And I remember the way she cried and the way you cried when she left."

"I don't remember anything of it," he said, but of course he remembered every painful moment. He was able to suppress his tears from many years of practice.

He needed not ask her what happened to his birth mother. She volunteered, "I was there when she died. Like many of the Sinjery forced to leave their children, she suffered the Pains as we call them. None of the Sisters could console her. I too suffered the Pains until I decided to make my final journey looking for my son. He was little younger than you were."

"I can only remember my brothers who stayed in Isseltrent and became Poets. The others disappeared in my memory like so much smoke a few years after I was thrown out of the court," he said.

"No Sinjery chooses to leave her child. No male has ever survived the Curse of Sinjer. For centuries the curse protected us from those we hated. We never imagined it would tear us from those we loved."

Rhazburn had known deep in his heart his mother was dead. Hearing how she died made it only more painful. "You must go. I will help you. If I could, I would end the suffering of the Sinjery Sisters. Unfortunately I am clutched in Rulupunerswan's claw. I can no longer help anyone."

"Loremaster, you have sacrificed your life for me. I must die, but I vow to aid you in whatever way I can, before I walk the Sky Forests."

She began to walk reluctantly back to the entrance, and he followed, glancing behind to see if the men of assorted sizes had ended their argument and were pursuing them. Perhaps they realized the suit was too small for any of them to use and had given up the chase. She had already shrunk to half his height again.

"You must get out and away from Rulupunerswan, for my sake," he said, keeping up the pace and urging her on.

"Tell me what I can do for you. You are trapped like the others, but I will take on any task you wish."

"I need you to give a message to Jonathon Forthright, a jeweler in the center of Isseltrent."

"If I am not immediately arrested, I will take your message gladly and tell him of your fate."

"Tell him this poem.

> Between the sun and Sylvanward
> Grimtooth gores a cloud
> Therein is laid a stallion's sword
> That bitter fates enshroud
>
> Fell servants of a Zombie lord
> In caverns deep and cold
> Sing his praise with knife and cord
> And guard his treasure trove

Under the heap
Deeper than deep
The horn is asleep
While Unicorns weep."

Rhazburn wanted Jonathon to get directions to the location of the Unicorn Horn he had seen in the vision from the Drop. He knew his father could figure out the riddle. The jeweler knew the name Grimtooth Mountain as well as Rhazburn. By getting the information, he had fulfilled his pledge to Jonathon. He didn't expect his father would go after the horn in the Dead Lands, especially after hearing Rhazburn's poem. That was what Rhazburn wanted. He still didn't trust the deal and hoped Jonathon would not go through with it. Without Rhazburn, he would not have the right verses for the scepter, regardless of whether he could make it or not. Rhazburn had another reason for giving Jiminic the message. He hoped she would save herself if she had a mission rather than let herself be arrested because of her pride in the "Sinjery Spirit."

Jiminic repeated the poem as they walked on. "I can remember the poem, Rhazburn, but I will still be caught by the Alchemist." At her height, even growing steadily after she left the geode, her tiny steps at the great speed of a Sinjery Guard would still be no match for a Giant Rulupunerswan with strides a relative league to her finger's breadth.

She was shorter than his lower leg now and had to lope along just to keep up with his slow walk. "Here," he said, motioning for her to climb again on his shoulder. "I can carry you easily now." She grabbed his hand and flipped herself up to his shoulder with the ease of an acrobat. She held his thumb with her hand to steady herself.

He tried to walk faster, despite the aching of his feet. The trail sloped ever upward.

"I know a way you can elude the Alchemist. Only a Sinjery could escape this way because it requires fearlessness."

"Courage is all I have left, Rhazburn."

"Do you know the tower window beside the table on which the rock of the Wishing Drop sets?"

"Yes, but if I try to climb down at this size, it would be like descending a tall mountain. I would surely fall." He felt her shake her head.

"I want you to fall," he said. She squeezed his thumb, in surprise, he thought, not in fear. "In fact, I want you to jump. Jump from the tower window." She said nothing, obviously believing he was truly mad.

He continued, "Have you ever seen a leaf fall?"

"Once or twice in my fifty years," she said condescendingly.

"No leaf ever broke in half, no matter how far it fell. Small things like leaves and insects fall as far as they want without injury. You will be not much larger than a baby mouse."

Her feet didn't even reach his collar bone by that time. Her voice squeaked in his ear. "I see, Rhazburn. I will take the leap and hope the wind does not blow me out to sea."

The entrance to the chamber came into full view. The size astonished Rhazburn. The top of the finger-sized hole was so high as to be almost out of view.

By the time they reached the entrance, Jiminic was like a mouse he had to cradle in one hand. He realized that, had he tried to walk back in the shrinking suit, he would have never made it.

From his hand, Jiminic pointed toward the left. "Rhazburn, look at that." He saw a yellow globe covered with studs and holes, crammed between two facets. "That is your food here in the crystal chamber. You must eat those whenever you find them."

"What is it?" he asked.

"A grain of pollen. Eat the inside."

With a couple steps to the side, he was close enough to break open the globe with a kick. A thick, egg like substance spilled out. It tasted no better than a raw egg but would be nourishing enough if he decided to prolong his imprisonment. Shrugging, he walked the few strides to the opening of the chamber.

He stopped at the opening and set her outside. He could barely hear her voice as she shouted, "Before I go, I must tell you I lied. I was not crying for my son's fate. The tears from that had dried up many days ago. I was crying for you. I had tasted the Drop again and asked if I would ever escape. I saw you and your deed and saw in you the image of my son. I knew you would doom yourself today for my sake, and I was ashamed to cause your death."

Without another word, she turned and fled.

CHAPTER 8

JIMINIC

The next morning, Knights of the Dragonlord were prowling the streets. Nobody that Jonathon asked knew what for. The day before, when Rhazburn left, they noticed more Dragons in the sky. Jonathon had wondered about it even before they heard the Dragonlord's message and he suspected that all the heightened security in the city had something to do with the Dragonlord's request of him. Trouble was brewing in the land, and Jonathon Forthright could be the Dragonlord's only hope. More than ever, he was convinced of the validity of the hooded messenger's claim.

Jonathon told himself throughout the night that Rhazburn could take care of himself and didn't need any interference from a bumbling old man. That was enough to let him sleep, even though his son had not come back. When Rhazburn did not meet him at his shop the next morning as he had promised, Jonathon imagined something horrible. Rhazburn always kept his word.

"Bob, fashion a morsel for my pocket. I've no time for breakfast. Rhazburn needs me."

The boy piped, "No, Master! You mustn't risk it. Rhazburn is the greatest Poet. If he met with some disaster in the Wishing Drop, there's not a man living who could fight whatever has befallen him. Please hire another Poet, or better, three Poets to find him."

"Bob, desist." His apprentice cast down his gaze, as if ashamed to question his master. "Not because you shouldn't contend with me, but because you may win and twist my head away from my responsibility. When you have children, Bob, you'll understand. I'm petrified, but, well, you know, I'm accountable for whatever mire Rhazburn has waded into." He remembered Rhazburn's vow to walk into Hell to find Dollop. Jonathon could never be that brave, but he could try to follow Rhazburn's example. Rhazburn's courage certainly didn't come from his teen years with Jonathon. Rhazburn's courage had been part of him long before Jonathon met him.

Bob started to rush off to do his master's bidding when a knock at the door made him stop in his tracks. They both looked at each other with hope. Rhazburn was back.

Bob ran to the door and yanked it open. There stood a tall white-haired woman dressed in a soiled and torn rose-colored garment covering her from head to toe. Her hair was mussed and she was sweating profusely. From what she had apparently been through, she should have been ready to drop, but there was a strength in her Jonathon had seldom seen.

"Admit the lady, Bob." He waved her to a purple padded chair meant only for the richest customers.

She sat down heavily and asked in a terse tone, "Jonathon Forthright?"

"I am honored you know my name."

"My name is Jiminic. I have a message for you from Rhazburn."

"Is Rhazburn all right?" Jonathon exclaimed.

"When I left him last night he was still alive. But hear his message, please." Jonathon was unsettled but beckoned her to get on with it, listening fretfully.

She recited the poem just as Rhazburn had dictated it. "Do you know what it means?" she asked after she finished.

"The meaning is self-evident. Rhazburn is in trouble and needs my help."

"I do not think you can help him. Not unless you can change the properties of the Wishing Drop."

Not change the properties of the Wishing Drop? Jonathon was not convinced. If the toughest substance in the world, a diamond, could be shaped and changed, anything could be. Rhazburn had often said that Poetry allowed anything imaginable to be done with the proper verses and ingredients. "Indulge me, I beg you, fair lady. Explain your understanding of these properties of the Wishing Drop. How their immutable qualities are relevant to Rhazburn's condition. How you are yourself immune to them. How you made your escape, despite their presence."

She told about herself, why she had entered the Chamber of the Drop, how her shrinking suit had been stolen, how she had seen her rescue in a vision from the Drop, and how Rhazburn's charity to her had doomed him. She went on to tell of her escape.

"After I walked out of the Chamber of the Drop, I began to grow instantly. The window I had agreed to leap out of was so far away for my initial size. You see, when I wore the shrinking suit in the chamber, distances got larger the more time I spent there. Once I was free of the chamber, the distances shrank as I grew taller. With this encouragement in mind, I started out on a seemingly endless trek to the distant window. After a few Favors, I was only a small distance from the entrance to the chamber, but I had grown to half the size of a baby mouse. I could begin to make better time. It was then my jungle sense told me I was being watched.

"A cat, no doubt supplied by Rulupunerswan, was watching my movements from across the room. I was easy prey for a cat, and since the stone of the drop was closer than the window, I ran back. The distance by that time took me only a single Favor since I was steadily growing. I watched the cat at first slowly stalk me, then suddenly it ran. I barely got inside the Chamber of the Drop just before the cat leapt up onto the table. Luckily, Rhazburn was lounging near the entrance. I had grown to be many times his height, and I nearly crushed him as I threw myself into the chamber.

"'I was waiting for my feet to heal,' he shouted at me. 'Nothing better to do.' He could see my plight easily since the cat was clawing at the entrance and would periodically place a gigantic eye to the entrance.

"'Gather the largest crystals you can,' Rhazburn shouted at me. 'The next time his eye fills the chamber entrance, throw them in.' He tried to help, but his size prevented him. I collected a double handful of the sharpest crystals I could find. When the cat's eye appeared again, the target was so huge I hit it easily. The cat jerked back with a screech and fell off the table. I dared not spare time to thank Rhazburn. I ran for the window.

"Rulupunerswan looked up from his desk and, without seeing me at that distance, said, 'Ha, Rhazburn. There you are. I knew the cook's cat would find you. Too bad he's as stupid as the cook. I hoped you would make him a tasty morsel.' He rose to find me himself. Obviously, he thought I was Rhazburn. I don't think he expected me to run behind the stone to the window because he spent a lot of time searching the table in front of the stone and the floor around it. When he finally found me, I was already to the sill. He reached for me just as I leaped. All the way down, I could hear his shrill voice, 'Die, Rhazburn, die.'

"From the wind passing me, I felt like I was falling fast, but I could see the city floating around below me for ages as the air currents blew me about. Finally, I hit the ground. I concentrated for the last few moments on keeping my feet pointed to Mother Earth, so I struck feet first. Despite what Rhazburn had said, I hit with such force that, had I come down any other way, I would have surely broken my back.

"On the ground, my adventure had just begun. I fought my way here street by street. I was potential prey for lizards, crows, and street dogs. I was nearly crushed by a hundred people before I grew big enough to protect myself. I hid in alleyways to avoid people seeing me half the size of an adult. When I had finally grown to my normal size, I asked around the city for directions to your shop. I came here at last close to midnight and slept outside overnight, waiting for you open this morning. Your work is well known, Jeweler. Many men know of you."

Jonathon's head was filled with pictures of shrinking men, giant cats, and dives out of high towers. All in a day's work for one of the Sinjery, but it frightened Jonathon even more as he faced saving his son.

He squinted to clear his head of all the thoughts that would dissuade him from going. "Mistress Jiminic, resourcefulness shines from you like sunlight. I thank you for the part you played in saving Rhazburn. Now

I must proceed and do what I can to extricate him from that rock. All I lack are your prowess, your strength, your courage and your quick wit."

He could use a resourceful Sinjery at his side, but she had risked death many times already to save his son and bring back his message. Even though he knew he had little chance of freeing Rhazburn alone, Jonathon would not directly ask more of her. "Rest here as my guest. Bob, if you please, accommodate the courageous Guard as best you can. Mistress Jiminic, can you but tell me the way to the wishing Drop?"

"I will do anything to save the one that gave his freedom for me. You will need me. I know a way into the Dragonlord's Palace little remembered these days."

"Mistress Jiminic, you have exhausted your strength and your luck today. Please, I beg you, rest yourself."

Jiminic stood up strong and true, "I am rested, Master Jeweler. Please. I, too, must repay the Loremaster."

She already risked her life while tiny in a hostile world just to bring back a message, Jonathon thought. Going back full-sized would add little to the dangers she had overcome scurrying through the city.

"Very well, my kind and brave lady. I accept your generous offer, and am humbled by you." He bowed low.

"No one has ever bowed to me before, Master Jeweler. I will remember the way you honor me and my Sisters."

"Thank you. Now, my dear Mistress Jiminic, by what agency can we pry my son from that rock and enlarge him back to human size?"

"He is your son? I thought he was a son of Seldric and Sister Bresmarion."

"I found him as a child wandering the streets. To my wife and I, he was a orphan. We took him in."

"Again, I will remember your kindness to the Sinjery and to their children. Now I wish I had looked beyond the instant that Rhazburn took my place in the Chamber of the Drop. I could not bear to look further, lest I witness his slow death there. Had I looked beyond that moment, I may have foreseen what we must do."

She set her lips tightly in resolve. "I may have seen that we fail. Since I did not, there is still a chance, but I admit the solution is presently beyond me. There is no way to free someone from the Chamber of the Drop without sacrificing another in his place. Anyone who enters the chamber in a suit must take the suit out with him to grow back to a normal height. I could give him the suit as he did me, but I know he would not allow it. I have seen my death in another vision from the Drop, and it does not lie within the chamber."

"Sacrificing you for Rhazburn would not be acceptable to me, Mistress Jiminic," Jonathon said. "If his intention was to save your life, I'll not be the one to thwart his efforts. Even though Rhazburn feels justified sacrificing himself for you, I don't intend to let him die. There is a means by which he can be released. Anything is possible with the right spell. Rhazburn himself said so."

Jiminic said, "After seeing what the Loremaster accomplished in the Chamber of the Drop with no magic at all, I can believe that for him, that may be true."

Bob only shrugged and shook his head.

Jonathon mulled on what the Sinjery Mistress said and tried to imagine what she had not. He looked at Jiminic and the pink suit. He remembered her description of how the suit was made to shrink, by placing one finger in the entrance to the geode. The suit was much too large for Jiminic, the tips of the gloves flattened fabric empty of her short fingers.

He snapped his fingers. "Take off the suit."

She gave him a startled look.

"No, no. Forgive me, Mistress Jiminic, my words raced ahead of my thoughts. The suit," he said. "Who says a human must be in the suit for it to shrink?"

"Rulupunerswan said as much to one of the other prisoners in the chamber. I have had long conversations with them about all possible means of escape."

Jonathon pointed at her, meaning to point at her statement. "But that's it. Rulupunerswan's word is worthless. Prevarication is as integral to Rulupunerswan as are his bones. Rhazburn implied it, and Rhazburn never lies."

"Don't be too sure of that. Anyone will lie at the right moment." Jiminic's comment produced a puzzled look from Jonathon. "Anyway, we need a fortune to have a suit activated, even if it can be done without a person inside."

Jonathon pulled the leather pouch out of his pocket and opened it to show her the thirty-three Glass Commands still left. "Will this be sufficient?" he asked.

Jiminic's eyes widened. She looked at him suspiciously. "Even a jeweler does not make that much money. Are you a thief?"

"I'm not sure. I hope not." Jonathon thought of the agreement he had made with the messenger, presumably from the Dragonlord. He was confidant the proposition was from the Dragonlord, but Rhazburn's suspicions gnawed at his resolve.

She gave him a peculiar look, then shook it off and said, "Do you have any clothes? Once I took my clothes off inside Rulupunerswan's chamber, but I'll never expose myself to that vulgar villain again."

He had Bob fetch her a long white smock into which she changed behind an inlaid screen Jonathon had saved from the other items auctioned to pay the interest to Molgannard Fey. Of course, that was before Jonathon became a fabulously-rich man.

After changing, Jiminic said, "And now I need a sword. I fear we will have trouble with the Alchemist. He seems to hate Rhazburn."

Jonathon rummaged through a drawer and gave her a small rod with a smaller blade affixed to its tip.

"Is this what you call a sword?" Incredulous, she turned it over in her hand, studying the meager weapon.

"It's a jewelry knife. Very sharp. Be careful."

She laughed as she slipped it up her sleeve. "I'll try not to scratch myself."

After Jonathon told Bob to keep the shop open until they returned, he carried the shrinking suit as he followed Jiminic to Blaze.

Unaccountably, the great portcullis into Blaze was shut. Crimson-armored Sinjery Guards lined the entrance outside and in. No one could get into Blaze that way. Jiminic did not even attempt it. Jonathon was unsure why she would not at least go talk with her Sisters. He noticed that many people were leaving by a well-guarded side door, but none were entering.

In the days before the Dragoncrown, the palace was an impregnable castle filled with Knights of the Realm. But since the Dragons were tamed and the Dragonflyers ruled the air, the castle was usually less well-guarded. Something had surely changed. Jonathon felt that whatever he accomplished in the next few days would be pivotal in the existence of Seldric's reign. Jiminic led him to one entrance she remembered that could still be open.

She approached the northeast corner of the palace where a slow-moving stream issued from the palace springs under a grating.

Jiminic said, "I knew the attendant who polished and oiled the grating. He had been at his post thirty years ago when I was a Ringmistress in the Guard. He was old when I first came here, but I have a feeling he may still be here at his post."

They ducked under a culvert, their eyes slowly accommodating to the dimness within a rock-walled tunnel.

A man leaned on a well-used wooden staff, looking at them with bright and cheerful eyes. All but his eyes had withered with age. He had shrunk as if he were sinking, year by year, into his grave rather than going all at once.

"Ah, Mistress Jiminic," he said, looking at her white hair, squinting with eyes unclouded by age. "Pretty as when I saw you last. What beautiful hair you girls have." Thirty years seemed to hinder neither his vision nor his memory.

"I'm glad to see no one will ever replace you at your post, Turble." She laid a gentle hand on his shoulder. "This is my friend in need, Master Jeweler Forthright. I must help him find his son."

The old man nodded to Jonathon. "I've heard of you, Master Jeweler. Any man one of these lasses calls a friend must be a good man indeed."

"Master Turble," Jonathon asked, "what is all the frenzied activity about these last two days?"

"I have no idea," the old man answered. "I'm afraid they tell me little these days. I think they forget I'm even here. But no one would take the time like I do, keeping this grate clean. It has to be done right. I tried to train some of these young louts, and they just didn't care to do a good job. I told the Chamberlain 'I'm never leaving my post.' I vowed not to die as long as this grate was around." He unlocked and raised the grate, letting them pass through without a question. They paid him with smiles and a wave.

After they passed the spring, ringed by a brick wall with one large opening through which the clear water tumbled into the tunnel leading to the grate, Jiminic led Jonathon through the corridors and up the spiraling stairs to a dark chamber. Its doorway was shrouded by a filthy curtain. They met no Sinjery, and the few courtiers about were too young to remember Jiminic. It seemed most of the Guards were outside the corridors patrolling the perimeter of Blaze. Jonathon had never before been to Rulupunerswan's Alchemical Laboratory, but he trusted that Jiminic knew the way. As the Sinjery woman pulled away the curtain and motioned Jonathon inside, any doubts that this abode was that of the Alchemist were erased by a confusion of unearthly odors, some sharp, some rancid, some exotic, some that brought tears to the jeweler's eyes.

The Alchemist looked up and feigned a smile. He apparently saw in Jonathon a rich customer and addressed him alone, ignoring Jonathon's shabbily-dressed companion as if she were a servant. "Good day, sir. You look to be a man of means with a purpose. What is your request for the Court Alchemist?"

"Help me release the Poet, Rhazburn, from the Chamber of the Wishing Drop. I have money and will pay for your assistance."

Rulupunerswan turned his head so as to look at Jonathon out of the corners of his eyes. He rubbed his chin and squinted, then opened a hand toward Jonathon. "You are Jonathon Forthright, a jeweler. Is that not so?"

"I am. How do you know my name?"

"Your friend, Rhazburn, told me your name before he went to his death."

"You know him to be dead."

The Alchemist smiled and said, "Alas, I do. I saw him fall..." Before he could finish, he glanced at Jiminic. Instantly, his smile dropped and he leaned away from the Sinjery. She was carrying the rose suit over her arm. His eyes froze on her face, and he nodded. "*You* are the one." His quivering finger pointed at her. "You survived the fall. You are the Sinjery exile who flaunts the law of your own people. You stole the suit from the Poet. Another felony on your head. The Guard will be interested to hear of your crimes. I'm sure your Sisters will oblige you with a swift sword." He made for the wooden stand with its lone vial.

Jiminic intercepted him with a leap and gripped his collar, stopping him short. Instantly, the jeweler's knife was in her hand and at his throat. "That must wait. We have come for Rhazburn. You must release him."

Rulupunerswan tried to push himself away but was held tight. "The Poet has met his fate. No one can change that."

With a motion almost too quick to be seen, she let go of his collar then yanked on his sleeve and flicked the knife. Half the sleeve was sliced cleanly away. Jiminic held up the severed piece of sleeve and dropped it auspiciously onto the floor at his feet. Rulupunerswan poked his hand through the remnant of his sleeve and looked at his fingers, moving them back and forth as if to reassure himself they were all there. His head jerked back as she again yanked his collar, pointing the knife to his throat.

"He will die, no matter what you do to me," the Alchemist spat. "It will only go worse for you. I will see you both become Dragon fodder before the day is out."

"You will die first, if you do not aid us," Jiminic said through clenched teeth.

He laughed. "Do you think you can kill me? Many have tried. My power is greater than you can imagine. Even if I can change the Poet's fate, there is nothing you can do to me that could force me to interfere with the nature of the Wishing Drop. The Drop carries out the will of the Dragonlord. I am only its keeper."

Jiminic looked puzzled at first, but her face brightened as she gazed at the far wall of Rulupunerswan's room. There, leaning against the wall, was a jumble of boxes, shelves, and cabinets filled with the vials of Rulupunerswan's reagents. It was an Alchemist's library, an Alchemist's treasury.

Jiminic motioned with her head for Jonathon to move to the stacks. "There on that middle shelf, where the fancy bottles are. Pick one up."

A group of ten containers were more carefully arranged than all the others. Each of the bottles was made of expensive colored glass, Some had magical verses fused into their substance. He selected a red vial with a Dragon painted on it.

"Don't touch those. I warn you," Rulupunerswan said, this time pointing with a finger that was stiff and still.

"Drop it," Jiminic said. With a sly smile, Jonathon dashed the precious vial to the floor. Rulupunerswan cringed and covered his face.

"You fools! Do you know what you're doing? The Realm depends on the power in those potions."

Jonathon picked up another, an opaque green flask. Rulupunerswan shouted, "Stop it now!" Jonathon released it casually. It hit the stone floor and burst. The potion inside began eating into the floor and released small clouds of vile green fumes. Jonathon stepped away from it.

The Alchemist said, "You will pay for this, Jeweler."

Jonathon gave him his angriest look, not very frightening on his cherubic face. He had gone too far to turn back and was determined to free his son, one way or another. He snatched a blue decanter from the shelf and raised it over his head.

Rulupunerswan screamed, "No, no! Not that one! Stop! I'll do whatever you say."

Jonathon smiled broadly and nodded to Jiminic, who winked back at him.

"Put it down carefully. Please." The Alchemist held his gnarled hands in the air as if he could catch the decanter.

With a swagger, Jonathon slipped it in a large pocket of his coat and said, "I'll just keep this convenient until Rhazburn is safely restored."

The Alchemist seethed but said, "Give me the suit. The effect requires a Glass Command." With a smirk he added, "A second Glass Command is the Dragonlord's fee for this service." The smirk became haughty. "Or is this mere extortion?"

Jonathon gave him two Commands, keeping a hand on the decanter.

Rulupunerswan went through the ritual of preparing the garment and threw it on the floor. "Which one of you thieves will wear the gown?" He looked expectantly at Jiminic, the obvious choice. He would love to have the Sinjer gone and be alone with Jonathon. "Whoever goes will have to give the Poet the suit and stay in his place. Since both of you are to be executed when the Guards come, it makes little difference."

Jiminic kept the knife on him, and Jonathon picked up the suit, which was still steaming. "Neither of us will wear the suit."

He carried the suit to stand a stride in front of the geode and called, "Rhazburn! If you can hear me, this is Jonathon. I am going to stuff the suit into the hole in the chamber. When it shrinks to the right size, put it on and join us back out here where you belong."

Rulupunerswan said, "That will never work. A human must wear the suit for it to shrink."

Jonathon ignored him and stuffed a finger of the suit into the hole in the rock. Immediately, the suit began to shrink. Jonathon looked back at Rulupunerswan and smiled again.

"You are upsetting the balance of the Wishing Drop. Grave consequences will befall you and your friends."

Jonathon waved at him to be silent, and Jiminic tightened her grip on his collar, choking off his next argument. The suit continued to shrink until Jonathon could push it through the small hole. Then, they waited. Almost all of Highday Blessing passed. Jonathon watched Rulupunerswan's old and filthy Timefall anxiously. Favor after Favor passed, ever so slowly. Jonathon had pulled up a chair to watch the entrance to the geode, but he was losing hope. If Rhazburn did not hear his speech, he may have wandered off without finding the shrinking suit in time.

Just as Jonathon's spirit was failing, he saw a tiny figure hardly a mote of dust stride out of the chamber. Jonathon cheered and said, "Rhazburn! Welcome back!"

They had more waiting as the suited figure grew to a recognizable size. When the man was tall enough for his face to be clear, Jonathon became distressed. The expanding man had a beard. Rhazburn had been clean-shaven. One day could not grow the beard the tiny figure sported. This one could not be his son.

Shortly after Jonathon realized the figure was not Rhazburn, a triumphant Rulupunerswan cried with glee. "See! You cannot twist the Wishing Drop to your schemes. The Poet is dead."

"No, he is not," said the growing figure.

Jiminic said, "I recognize that voice. It is the Duke of Brione."

"Yes, Ringmistress Jiminic. It is I. I, your fellow prisoner, equal in fate but not in courage. I stand ashamed I tried many times to steal the suits from others that I might be free. Even the Loremaster, who has saved me in a most magnanimous gesture, was my intended victim. When he knew your plan, he called all of the prisoners together and promised to wait until all of us were free before escaping himself." The Duke was growing ever larger as he spoke.

Rulupunerswan fawned, "Your Grace, never did I suspect you could have survived within the Chamber of the Drop. Had I but known..."

The Duke harrumphed, "I'll take my clothes now, Alchemist." Jonathon noticed the Duke did not bother with Rulupunerswan's title.

Smiling, simpering, Rulupunerswan motioned to a rough pile of discarded clothes, cob-webbed and dust-ridden in a corner of his chamber. "Your clothes are safely stored, Your Grace."

The Duke walked to the pile and cast the Alchemist, who was busy making them all turn around to give him a little privacy, a withering look. The discarded rose suit landing at Rulupunerswan's feet signaled to them that he was dressed and they could turn back.

Jonathon had a sinking feeling. If Rhazburn would not come out until the others were saved, he would have to spend more of his fortune to release the others. Obviously, Rhazburn thought this was the only way he could get his father to agree to financing the others' release. "How many more unfortunate ones are there within?" he asked the Duke.

"Thirteen, including the Loremaster." Jonathon groaned. Twenty-six more Glass Commands. That would leave only five by the time they were finished. The Pixets had already retrieved their payment.

Jiminic pushed the Alchemist toward his cauldron and barked, "Get to work. We will be here a long time."

The Alchemist grumbled, "If you must go through with this insane plan, let us finish quickly. I have more suits, and I can treat more than one at a time." Jonathon's eyes lit up. He expected to save some money. "Each suit will still require a Glass Command. No one has that much money."

'I do," Jonathon said with a sigh.

Rulupunerswan had three extra suits. By treating them all at once and stuffing them in the geode at the same time, all the prisoners were released and brought to their normal height by the end of Dinner Blessing. As the westering sun's rays bore straight through the tower window, Rhazburn, the last, came out alone. When he came out, Jonathon forgot his loss of the money. With tears streaking his round cheeks, he hugged Rhazburn. All the others shook the Poet's hand and thanked him again and again. Jiminic relaxed her vigil on the Alchemist to hug the Poet herself.

As she was distracted, Rhazburn peered over her shoulder and shouted, "Jonathon, the vial. Don't let him break it!"

He was too late. Rulupunerswan rushed to the stand near his cauldron and threw the vial that rested on top to the floor. Jonathon barely took a step before the vial shattered, leaving a small puddle of a silvery fluid on the floor. The fluid began to move on its own power toward the door. Jonathon, frightened, hopped away.

"Don't let it leave the tower!" Rhazburn yelled.

Jiminic tried to step on the liquid, but it sloshed around her foot. Jonathon stepped over to it and stuck out a foot to block it, but the fluid rolled up over his foot like a living thing. Jonathon squealed in disgust as it passed him by and dribbled out the door.

Rulupunerswan laughed at them all. "Now we will have justice."

Jiminic stepped before him and said, "I'll give you justice." She leaned over the table and picked up the geode Chamber of the Drop. With all her Sinjery strength she threw it to the floor, smashing it to pieces.

Rulupunerswan wailed in disbelief and fell to his knees like he had been struck by a sword.

Rhazburn said to Jonathon and Jiminic, "Quickly, we must leave! He has called the Guard."

Jonathon followed them down the spiral stone stairs. He hadn't planned on being a fugitive from the court guards, but he wasn't about to argue.

Emerging beneath reddening skies onto the stone staircase where it left the tower and descended into the main courtyard, they all stopped. There, below them, were thirty Sinjery Guards, their longbows strung with arrows aimed at Jonathon and his friends. Jonathon did not move a muscle. He had heard many tales of how the Sinjery could hit anything within range of their bows, even a sparrow on the wing. They surely would have no trouble hitting his rotund self close up.

From behind them, Rulupunerswan said in a haughty voice, "Kill them. They are all traitors to the Dragonlord. The Sinjery woman destroyed the priceless Chamber of the Drop."

Rhazburn threw up his hand. "No, it is Rulupunerswan that is the traitor to the Dragonlord and the Realm. Ringmistress Jiminic rightly destroyed a lethal trap that the Alchemist has used to improperly trap souls until they starved to death."

One of the Sinjery, their leader, relaxed her bow and said, "We know the Alchemist. Who are you?"

"I am Rhazburn, Loremaster of the Demonwards, and I tell you he lies to protect himself."

Jonathon looked up at Rulupunerswan. Behind him were the prisoners of the Wishing Drop they had saved. The Duke of Brione was in front. Jonathon said to them, "I thought you were Rhazburn's friends. Why are you doing this to him?"

As the Duke conferred with the other former prisoners, Rulupunerswan pre-empted him, shouting to the Guard, "Take them away, if you do not trust me. Let the Dragonlord deal with them in his own good time."

The Sinjery Ringmistresses started up the stair to arrest them, looking puzzled as if she knew not how to proceed with all the conflicting claims. Jonathon hoped she was unwilling to execute them without the proper procedure.

The Duke called out to Rulupunerswan, "Yes, take us all to the Dragonlord so he can hear how the Alchemist keeps men trapped to die in the Chamber of the Wishing Drop. He even says he does it in the Dragonlord's name."

At this, the captain of the Sinjery stopped, and with a hand sign she told the Sinjery Sisters to halt. "We know you, Sire. All of us recognize the Duke of Brione." Then, with another motion, she ordered one of the Sinjery to go, saying, "Bring the Chamberlain. There are too many accusations here for us to decide alone."

Shortly thereafter, Jonathon heard a movement below them on the steps. The Chamberlain of the Dragonlord was pushing his way through the Sinjery Guard. He stopped directly in front of Rhazburn, complaining, "What trouble have you caused now, Rhazburn? You should not even still be here. None but the Court are allowed inside Blaze today."

"No trouble, I never left since I saw you yesterday," Rhazburn replied. "The good Alchemist is overtired from his efforts in releasing these men from the curse of the Drop and has made a slight mistake. Unfortunately, the Chamber of the Drop was damaged accidentally."

Rulupunerswan looked between the Chamberlain and the Duke. The Chamberlain suddenly recognized the Duke of Brione and bowed. "Your Grace. You are saved. We had all thought you were dead by the curse."

"No, I am alive, thanks to Rhazburn and his friends."

The Chamberlain regarded Rhazburn and said, "And just why were you at the Wishing Drop?"

"I'm still looking for the Dragonlord. Had you told me where he is, all of this would have been avoided."

One of the Sinjery said to the Chamberlain, "The Alchemist has accused the Loremaster of treason."

Gashgrieve shot a glance at Rulupunerswan and said, "Is this true?"

The Alchemist bit his lip but prevaricated, "No, no. I was tired from my labors, as the Poet has said. I had fallen asleep and had a strange dream that seemed real. Now I know it to be only a nightmare. The Poet is not a traitor." When he finished he looked quite ill, ready to vomit.

Rhazburn gently pushed Gashgrieve aside with the back of his hand and said, "Then we will take our leave." The Sinjery started to part but were obviously watching Jiminic.

As they walked down to the squad of archers, Rulupunerswan spoke up again. "As a true citizen of Thuringland, I must tell you that the woman with the Poet is one of the Sinjery in breach of her exile."

"Your Honor," said the Captain of the Sinjery guard, "you need not tell us that which is already known. Our Sisters are familiar to us all."

The Sinjery made no move. Neither did Jiminic. Rhazburn said, "Wait. Her efforts have saved all these men." He turned to Jiminic. "I can help you. I have connections in the court that will help save you from this fate."

Jiminic put a hand on his shoulder. "No, Rhazburn, Sinjery son. Stop thinking like your father, the Dragonlord, and consider your mother's thoughts. Death is the solution for us here, not the problem. Some of us can be degraded by our time here and still live free. Those with Soulsisters are the safest in this regard. I have no Soulsister. My son is dead. My life has no purpose. I chose my course when I came to Isseltrent. I am not afraid. I welcome death. All Sinjery know the Sisters who make the journey back wish to die honorably with their Sisters and by their hands. I go willingly. I long for the Sky Forests. Go in peace with your friend."

Rhazburn looked deeply into her eyes and saw her unshakable resolve. In the back of his mind, he began hatching a plot to set her free and convince her to live, even though he knew she would not accept it. Perhaps he could talk to Trallalair. "How long before the sentence is carried out?"

"I will make my peace with Mother Earth and my Sisters over five days. Then I will fly to the Sky Forests."

Five days. He might be dead before then. He needed time to aid both his father and Jiminic. What if he saved her only to fail his father? If the Dragoncrown was really at risk, many more could suffer. He doubted he could successfully intervene in an affair of the Sinjery. While bending their morals for the sake of their race, allowing themselves to be concubines of the Dragonlord, they still clung to their rigid codes of conduct like cats to a tree. Quickly, he calculated the time he needed to find the Unicorn Horn and get back to Isseltrent. With luck, he could do it in three days. There were five days left until the Dragonegg Festival, plenty of time. The Unicorn Horn and his father had to come first. He turned and said, "Father, let us leave this place of joy and woe and go home."

Jonathon gave the blue decanter back to the glowering Alchemist, who cradled it in his hands like an infant. They turned to walk through the crowd of Sinjery women on the stairs who parted to let them by. Neither looked behind them as they were taken under guard through a side door of the palace and back to Jonathon's shop.

CHAPTER 9

THE BLACK COACH

A hot wind blew dust devils along the deserted road until, at a lonely crossroad, the tiny clouds whirled themselves to oblivion against the immovable flank of an ancient Black Dragon. The Dragon took no notice of their feeble energies but lay still as the red sandstone around him. He didn't even move his massive head when his two attendants, clothed in home-stretched leather, slowly coaxed three blindfolded cows to their appointed duty.

When the cows were close enough to the Black, the men walked away much faster than they had approached. They didn't bother to look back. There was no doubt in their minds what would happen next.

The vertical slits in the golden eyes of the Black Dragon dilated sharply at the mournful lowing of the cows. With a rustle of scales that startled the cows, he slowly raised his head. Before the blindfolded cows could decide which way to run they heard a gust of wind which were the Dragon's rough scales rushing through the air as a huge clawed foot slammed down on two of the cows, flattening them into the dust. The third cow heard a terminal gust as the Dragon's head struck, huge fangs puncturing its chest. With a bleat, the cow's life was crushed out. One at a time, the Black Dragon swallowed them whole.

A few moments after he had settled down to digest his meal, a wisp of smoke came from his nostrils. His jaws opened again, and Rhazburn hopped out onto the road. He wore a sturdy wool jacket and breeches, his personal Flying Carpet rolled and strapped to his back. It had taken a Glass Command to take the Black Dragon from Isseltrent, but it could not be helped. Almost half the time they had been given was gone. Depending more on his wits than equipment, he carried no other magical objects except for a little Firedust to kindle fires for cooking, two more Commands, and a score of Coppers. Despite all of the increased security in Isseltrent, the Black Dragons were still allowed to transport people. The Dragonlord had little need to stop Black Dragon traffic since he could use the Black Dragons themselves to screen travelers. Every person could be heard, seen, smelled and tasted by the Dragonlord through the Black Dragons. The only thing the Blacks could not do was read minds.

The night before, Rhazburn had told Jonathon the whereabouts of the Unicorn Horn. Jonathon had despaired. He was planning a trip to the Dead Lands to fulfill his commission and he did not want to involve his son anymore. Jonathon was more afraid of the Zombies he would find there than he had been of Molgannard Fey. Still, he was a man of honor. Certain death was not a thing he would rush into, but his staunch principles would start him creeping in the direction of Devil's Fang, regardless of his fear. When Jonathon started making a list of his possessions and instructions for Bob Thumblefoot to portion them out between his wife and children, Rhazburn stepped in.

"Father, the Dead Lands are the abode of the only Demon yet to set foot in the world. Now, just which one of us has more experience in dealing with Demons?"

Jonathon shrugged, obviously agreeing Rhazburn was the one. Bob said to Rhazburn, "You are the Loremaster and Bane of Demons."

"Right, Bob. You can't drive a nail with a gold ring."

"But, Loremaster, is it not illegal to go to the Dead Lands?" Bob asked.

"Our friend, the Dragonlord, should pardon us, since we are doing this to save his neck. Don't you agree, Father?"

"Pardon us when we flaunt the law? I fear your confidence eludes me, despite your wisdom, my Son."

"Don't worry. To Seldric we're hounds sent after a rabbit. As long as we bring back the rabbit, he could care less how we catch it."

Jonathon looked up, no less worried. "I never intended for you to imperil even one red hair on your head for me. This all possesses some terrible momentum of its own, like some horse I spooked and drove mad so it's galloping headlong at my entire family. Unstoppable."

"What do you know of horses? I know 'whoa'."

"Right, you know whoa, but I don't want you to know woe from this." Pun aside, Jonathon was still dubious and worried about Rhazburn's errand.

"It will take most of the money you have left," Rhazburn said.

Jonathon regarded the five Commands left in his pouch. "Only the Pixets got their share, and the Giant, of course."

"You are a savior to twelve men and one woman."

"Oh, I don't begrudge them their freedom, but you never got your share."

Rhazburn said, "I already refused any of that money, although I guess it was used mostly for my purposes, saving those men from the Chamber of the Drop."

"Fine. Take it," Jonathon said, pushing the pouch across the table to Rhazburn. There was little else he could do to help his son. On the journey Rhazburn proposed, Jonathon could only be a burden. What could a fat, timorous little man do on such a fantastic adventure? Devil's Fang indeed. Just the thought of it made him shiver. If he even laid his eyes on something as horrible as a Zombie, he'd surely die of fright.

"I'll need three Glass Commands and a little extra. It will take one to go by Black Dragon to the border of the Dead Lands in the Commonwealth of Dis. It will take one to get back, and I'll need one to purchase the Unicorn Horn. I want to make a strong bid so I don't waste any of our time."

"Bob, have one of the Commands changed. Be quick," Jonathon ordered. The boy was off in a blink. He sighed, thinking, *A little more than one Glass Command remaining from a fortune. Tundudil's justice for my profligate ways.*

Hili was staying away until her services were needed for the engraving of the jewels for the scepter. She was true to her word that she and the other Pixets would have nothing else to do with Jonathon after his moral betrayal of the Community. Rhazburn used the opportunity to speak privately to Jonathon.

"I may not return from this venture."

Jonathon was slowly pulling at the silk sash around his middle as if it were the last thing he would ever see in the world. He looked up. "You know, I never expect anything could get the better of you, Rhazburn. But me?" he shrugged, "Everything seems to get the better of me."

"You're not that hopeless, Father, and I'm not that powerful. For now, humor me. I want to make sure if you try to make this without me - and I know you will - that you do it right. It must be made so no human but the Dragonlord alone could possibly use it. I can design it so it would be absolutely useless in anyone else's hands. I can dictate to Bob all the poems for the scepter and the jewels on it. I don't have to be here for that. One thing must be transmitted by you alone. When the messenger comes, you have to take the scepter to the Dragonlord personally. You must whisper in Seldric's ear a poem that he needs to speak out loud or merely think in his mind to activate the scepter."

"I see. Without the poem, the scepter is useless, even if activated with a coin."

"Exactly. Here is the poem. You must memorize it and not write it down.

> Through ears, hearts, minds I call
> Obey my will, one and all."

"That's it?" Jonathon asked.
"That's the whole thing."
"It's memorized. Now tell me just how to make the scepter."

Even though Rhazburn knew his plan for the scepter was foolproof, he wanted to be there himself when the messenger came so he could unmask the messenger and prove him a fake. But, if Jonathon ended up making the scepter by himself and had to confront the supposed messenger, and if that charlatan somehow stole the Unicorn Horn for his own use, Rhazburn had made the verses for the object to be responsive to the Dragonlord alone. The Unicorn Horn device would not exert control over anyone if used by any other person. The poem was just a way to further ensure that the scepter would be unusable in the wrong hands. His plan was foolproof.

The peak of Devil's Fang soared into the sky before Rhazburn. At its base was a cavern he had to find. A few towns of hardy frontiersmen and women dotted the scrub land at the foot of Devil's Fang. On the other side of the mountain, the Dead Lands began. There, no living thing set foot untainted and nothing escaped.

Rhazburn heard a whining to his right like wind off a heavy object falling from a cliff. In the sky, he saw a Green Dragon with wings outstretched soaring toward him faster than any bird could fly. He ducked as it passed overhead. The wind from its wings lashed at his clothes. On the Dragon's back, scrutinizing Rhazburn, was a green armored Knight of the Dragonlord.

Rhazburn waved to appear as if he had nothing to hide. The Dragonflyer sailed off toward a flat-topped pinnacle far in the distance. This close to the Dead Lands, the territory was watched closely. Anyone entering or leaving the Dead Lands was killed and incinerated without question or hesitation.

Rhazburn spent the rest of the day walking along the road in the general direction of Devil's Fang, looking for a small town where he could make inquiries. He walked rather than rode his carpet. He did not want to reveal his Flying Carpet to the watchers of the Dead Lands too soon, lest they become suspicious of his intentions. That evening, through the distant sunset haze, he sighted a cluster of meager dwellings. Exhausted from the day's trek, Rhazburn decided to set up camp and have a meal to refresh himself. He made a fire of branches gleaned from the scraggy brush around him. The absolute devastation of the Dead Lands had not reached this far, but the plants looked sickly and twisted. He expected the people looked the same.

Long after sunset Rhazburn fell asleep, leaning against a boulder of granite, his Flying Carpet thrown over his lap for a bit of warmth. He was awakened by a rustling in the bushes nearby. The fire was only glowing embers by then, but his eyes had adjusted to light of the feeble waning moon. Peering into the dark, he sensed what appeared to be a pile of rags approaching the fire. The monstrosity whimpered.

It whimpered, "Kind sir. Have you a morsel to save a poor soul feeble of limb?" Coming closer, the monstrosity of rags sprouted a cowered head and frail arms. At least there were only two arms. One hand leaned upon a bent and quivering staff, the other extended toward Rhazburn in supplication.

"I have some dried beef you are welcome to share, my good fellow," Rhazburn said.

"Oh, thank you, kind sir," the man replied.

"My name is Rhazburn."

"And mine, Gruber." With the few teeth left to Gruber, he gnawed at the beef Rhazburn gave him and hungrily eyed what was left. Rhazburn gave it all to him. What Gruber didn't worry away with his mouth, he crammed somewhere inside his filthy rags. Rhazburn hoped the lice and fleas left some for Gruber's next meal.

Gruber was not about to leave and started to warm his hands on the remains of the fire. "Seems the fire needs to be stoked."

Rhazburn tossed a few dry branches on the fire, which smoked for a few moments, then burst into flames. "Seems the village yonder would be more hospitable for the night."

"I agree, sir, and it's to that village that I be going. At least, for the time of the Last Knife Moon. It should be safe." Rhazburn looked up at the quarter moon. It did look a lot like a curved blade.

"Safe from what?"

"Ah, a stranger ye be to these parts then. Well, I'll give you some advice for the food you've given me. Stay in that village for the next few days, then leave."

"Why leave? I plan to gather stories of the land to take back to the court. I'm a singer for the Dragonlord."

Gruber studied him for a moment, and apparently decided to believe Rhazburn's lie. "Well, in the time of the First Knife Moon, you'd better be elsewhere. Or strong. Not like a crippled beggar. I make the rounds to keep my miserable life my own. You could follow me for a share at your fire. I could keep you out of trouble and tell you plenty of tales to sing."

"Tell me what you're running from."

"Why, the Black Coach, of course. It's what everyone is frightened of in these parts." He gave Rhazburn a quizzical look. "Have they not heard of the Black Coach in the Dragonlord's Court?"

Rhazburn slowly shook his head.

A twig cracked, and Gruber jumped to his feet, ready to bolt. After staring with wide eyes into the gloom for a prolonged moment, he apparently reassured himself they were alone and sat down again, this time much closer to Rhazburn. When Gruber's stench hit him, Rhazburn had an instinctual urge to sidle away lest he contract some dread disease. It took all his will to suppress the gorge rising in his throat and listen politely to his pathetic guest.

"Ghouls. Ghouls it is that drive the coach. They take the dead to the King of the Zombies in the Dead Lands."

"You mean to the Demon."

"No, I don't think so. Call it his lieutenant, if you like. The Ghouls do his bidding. They terrorize the land."

"Why don't the Knights of the Dragonlord stop them?"

"You're from the court. You ask them. They don't care what happens to us. If they burn up a few Zombies that try to leave the Dead Lands, they report all is well to the Dragonlord. They are up in the sky on that rock." He pointed toward the distant pinnacle Rhazburn had seen earlier. "We down here on the ground have to deal with the Black Coach."

"Why don't the people band together to stop them?"

"You can't fight Zombies. You can't kill them. They're already dead. The Ghouls take the dead as their tribute for letting the rest of us live. If they don't get their dead body when they come around, they raise one from the grave. Have you ever seen a man come out of his grave and walk big as you please?"

"Can't say I have," Rhazburn said as he stirred the fire with a stick. His face remained a mask, hiding his many years of dealing with spirits and Demons at Hell's Breach.

"You make light of it, but it's true. No one wants to see that happen. So, if a crippled beggar happens to be in the way when the Black Coach comes around, well, he might find himself having an accident, like getting hit on the head with a club. Now, there's a song for your court ladies."

"So where is it I should not go tonight?"

"A town called Paradise straight east from your fire. Believe me, I know just where not to be. Take it from an expert at the art of running and hiding. Go anywhere tonight but Paradise."

Ominous tidings of evil were just the thing to invigorate Rhazburn and banish his exhaustion. Rhazburn bade the refugee a safe escape, unrolled his carpet, and in the face of Gruber's astonishment, flew directly toward Paradise.

The town Rhazburn saw was hardly his idea of Paradise. A few crumbling brick structures crowded a score of hastily-constructed lean-tos and shacks. Everything seemed deserted except one brick building in the middle of them all. It was a pub called Angels' Rest. The sides were black, save for thin cracks of light squeezed between tight shutters.

When Rhazburn entered, arguments and murmurs ceased. Everyone turned to study him. The center of the pub was filled with benched communal tables at which were a score of drinkers. The owner's table with three kegs of ale filled the far wall. In front, quaffing a tankard, an astonishingly-fat man in cook's clothes filled most of a bench. Small tables with clusters of chairs occupied by gamers and drunkards animated all the other walls. A few brightly-dressed women with lusty eyes leaned against or sat on the laps of the biggest and strongest men. At one table, a man snored loudly, his face laying comfortably in a puddle of spilled ale. A boy, not more than ten, limped around, cuffed and laughed at by the men as he sang bawdy tunes for a few tossed Suggestions.

They quickly lost interest in Rhazburn and returned to their more important business of drinking. He proceeded to the sturdy, rough-hewn owner's table, bought himself a tankard of ale, sat in the small space left on the cook's bench, and leaned back against the table to watch and listen.

From one bench, Rhazburn heard a fist hit the table. The burly man attached to the fist shook his tankard at the door. "They'll not take my wife. Not while I still breathe." He downed the contents of his tankard.

At another table, a thin sweaty man, breathing hard and gripping a long knife at this knees, scowled at the others like he was eager to cut the throat of the first man to cross him.

Rhazburn turned to the fat cook. "Busy night for you."

"I know when to stock up. They all come this time of the Moon. Safety in numbers, you know. Like a herd of cows or a flock of scared pigeons."

"Is everyone always this angry when they're out for a drink?"

The fat man laughed. "Hang around. You'll see how angry they can get."

Rhazburn did just that. He bought a meal of a cheap stew too spicy to eat without the more expensive ale to cool off his mouth. Moving to one of the benches at a long communal table, he sat and ate slowly, spitting out as many of the dead cockroaches as he could recognize with his tongue. To quench the fire in his mouth, he ordered more ale, listening all the time to the talk around him.

A thick-muscled man with two fingers missing on one hand pointed the two that were left at his companion, a scrawny white-haired wretch who sat leaning against the table, cradling his ale. "I sends my wife to Grisenbourne for these times. When the consumption takes her one of these days, I wants her out of the reach of the Ghouls. When she sees the Death Moon, she knows it's safe and brings our wagon and the children back with her. Oh, I hauls nothin' while she's gone, but what's I to do if the Ghouls takes her?"

In one corner, the talk was building to a crescendo. A grimy man with a paunch yelled at a small knot of men, "Where's the body, they'll ask. What are you going to say? Take mine? Is that what you'll say?"

An old bent man shook a cane and snarled. "Let anyone tell them Tand Hingwhistle is ready for a ride in their coach, and they'll feel my cane on their ear."

A very thin and very evil-looking man spat on the floor to get the attention of the rest. He waved a hand at the sweaty man with the drawn knife Rhazburn had noticed earlier. "Wolder has the fever. It's no loss to the rest of us."

Wolder stood up, hearing the threat, and walked with an unsteady gait toward the group. He pointed the knife at the thin man. "I'll see them eat you before I die."

The thin man stumbled back a couple of steps and pointed at the crippled child. "Give them the boy. He has no family. He should have died when he was born. We're only finishing what fate began."

The group and all the people in the pub turned to the crippled boy. He was deep in their midst and could not possibly flee. A tremble shook his twisted limbs, and his eyes were wild with fear. The men in the pub pushed back their benches with scrapes and thumps as some benches fell over in their haste getting up. They moved as one in the boy's direction.

Without hesitation, Rhazburn ran to the boy's side and picked him up by the arms. Wild with fright, the boy beat Rhazburn's head with skinny fists, but Rhazburn held him tight and leaped upon the tables, jumping from one to another until he was in front of a barred window. He put down the boy, who cringed, whimpering, under the window sill. None of the others had tried to stop him. Rhazburn hoped they thought he was helping them to dispatch the boy. Rhazburn stood with his back to the boy and the window, then threw his carpet on the floor directly before him. It had been activated with a Copper Order and would do his bidding for fully seven days. He said, "Leave the boy alone. Fight among yourselves if you need a body for the Black Coach."

A voice shouted, "Kill them both, and save one for next Moon's tribute!" The men surged forward, one with a big scowl and oily muscles bulging from torn sleeves taking the lead.

Rhazburn held out his hands and said, "Stay back. I am a Poet and will not allow this young one to be harmed."

The closest five men dashed at him. As the man with rippling muscles stepped on the carpet, Rhazburn said, "Carpet, up table height." The carpet snapped into the air, throwing the angry man back onto the others, bowling them over into a pile of tangled limbs and curses.

Rhazburn did not wait for them to rearrange themselves but picked up a chair and smashed the wood bars on the window. With a single motion, he picked up the boy by his shirt and swung him onto the carpet, shouting, "Carpet, take him home, then return to me."

The carpet with the boy on top slid through the window and into the night. Rhazburn followed it out, dogged by the hoots of the ruffians in the pub. They did not follow to attack him, however. Rhazburn well knew they would look for an easier victim.

After his carpet came back to him, he rolled it up and tied it to his back. Then he hid in the shadows outside and watched the pub. In a few Favors of time, a limp body was tossed out the door of the pub. The man's throat had been cut, and his eyes stared vacantly at the stars. Rhazburn recognized the clothes and the man as the drunk who had been sleeping when the Poet entered the pub.

No one left the pub for the rest of the night. In the early morning twilight of Dawn Blessing, a ragged woman walked slowly up to the pub. When she saw the dead man, she screamed, "Will! Ah, my Will. Nooooo!"

Wailing loudly, she knelt down and held his flaccid body in her arms. After a while, she quieted some and began looking about anxiously. Then she got up and, groaning and sobbing, started to drag the body away. She had not gotten one rod distant when a horse-driven coach could be heard coming down the road. When she heard the coach, she began pulling frantically on the body and looked up every few moments with cries and spasms of fear contorting her face.

A huge black coach drawn by four sable horses rolled to a stop beside her. Two men robed in black looked down at her, one saying, "This one is not of your realm but of ours. Stand aside." Their faces, powdered white with shadowed eyes, looked like naked skulls.

She stood up and positioned herself between them and the body. "Get away, you fiends. My husband was wretched in his life, but he's no Ghoul. I won't let you take him."

"He comes of his own choice," the man said, holding up a black medallion on a gold chain. "Rise and come to your master."

The woman looked back in horror as the dead body pushed itself up on its arms and stood. "No, Will!" she cried.

The dead body lurched forward. When it approached her she reached out for it, but it raised an arm and slapped her aside. She fell weeping in the dust. The body walked to the coach, opened the door, and got in. With a whip from the driver, the black horses whinnied and sprang off into the twilight.

Rhazburn unrolled his carpet and, being careful to keep low and out of their sight, followed them to the cavern in Devil's Fang.

CHAPTER 10

THE CLAN OF THE
LAUGHING SKULL

Rhazburn followed the galloping horses of the Black Coach throughout the rest of the early morning before Breakfast Blessing. The stars slowly disappeared above him. His eyes had long become accustomed to the black shadows, so he was aware when the greater blackness of Devil's Fang slowly blotted out the heavens ahead of them, signaling their approach to the Ghoul's hideout. When they finally reached the foot of the mountain, the first light of sunrise glimmered in the East, allowing Rhazburn to discern the entrance of the cave far ahead. An overhang of rock thrust out above two holes bored into the cliff. Right below the holes was a gaping portal. The whole arrangement resembled a granite skull with its jaws gaping to engulf anything coming its way. Two robed men with white-powdered faces and long-bladed spears guarded the entrance. They both jumped aside so the horses need not slow their pace as the Black Coach raced into the cavern. The sound of the clattering wheels echoed far down into the depths.

While the guards were occupied and watching the coach, Rhazburn stopped the carpet, rolled it, and strapped it in its place on his back. Before the guards saw him he crouched hiding behind dense, bizarrely-twisted undergrowth. There he could face the entrance, study the guards, and wait for full sunrise. As the twilight shadows crept back into the cliffs and the boulders, he heard a reedy whistling accompanied by harsh bells approaching from the road. Soon a procession of men and women hooded in brown, all with red painted hands, walked in lugubrious pomp up to the maw of the death's head.

From within the cavern, a group of white-faced people wearing black robes emerged as if they were expecting the delegation. One held up a gnarled staff topped by a human skull. Its loose jaw clapped with each gesture as he waved it on high and spoke in a sonorous chant. "Die. Die. Die."

The leader of the red-handed band echoed, "Die. Die. Die."

"Split my skull and spill my brains," the white faces sang.

"Slice my neck and drain my blood," the red hands returned.

"Rip my chest and crush my heart," the white faces chanted.

"Chop my limbs and rip my skin," the red hands replied.

In unison they all chanted, "Flesh to nourish the Eternal Order, Souls to nourish our Lords."

"Die soon," all the white faces chanted together.

"Die soon and serve our Lord," the red hands added.

"We welcome the Clan of the Slashing Claw and bid you everlasting death," the leader of the white faces said.

"May a plague strike the land of the Laughing Skulls, and bring you a host of dead," came back the leader of the red hands.

Their weird pleasantries now complete, the two groups mingled and embraced each other, then retired into the cave. Rhazburn waited a few moments, digesting the character of the people he was about to deal with. They seemed more eager to deal out death than any group he had ever encountered before. With that disturbing thought in mind, he sauntered up to the guards.

They swung their spears in his direction. He walked up until the spear tips were at his throat. "Hail, brethren of the Laughing Skull," he said, raising his hand in a salute.

"What is he?" the smaller of the two said.

"Ain't a Slashing Claw," said the taller, looking at Rhazburn's unpainted hand.

"What Clan be ye of?" the tall one asked.

"No Clan of yours," Rhazburn replied.

They both gaped. One of them barked, "An outsider, Coulom! Kill him!" They tensed for the lunge.

Rhazburn shouted, "Stop!" as he threw up his hands, pushing away both spears at once. "I have come with a message for your Zombie Lord. Kill me and my spirit will take the message you hinder. Your lord will be very displeased with you."

His gambit worked. They hesitated, then whispered together, watching him out of the corners of their eyes. The short one ran off, leaving Coulom to watch Rhazburn. A long time later, the short man came back followed by two more guards. He said to Coulom, ignoring Rhazburn, "The Council of Servants will hear the renegade before they pass judgment."

The new guards goaded Rhazburn down into their cave with their spears. The opening led to a long tunnel carved out of the rock, passing at an angle into the base of the mountain. After what seemed a half league of torch-lit tunnel, they came to a dead end where the carriage stood and the horses ate from nose bags. Huge piles of stinking skins were scattered haphazardly about. These Ghouls not only dealt in dead humans but in all manner of dead creatures harvested from the territory adjacent to the Dead Lands. They had the look of skins destined for Molgannard Fey and his Skin Splicer trade in Isseltrent. At the rate they were slaughtering animals, soon none would remain alive in the surrounding land. Rhazburn was sure their 'Zombie Lord' would approve of that.

The guards looked up through a hole far, far above in the ceiling. To Rhazburn, that ascending chimney looked black as death.

One of the guards called, "Tagneth, we return with the renegade." He stepped aside as a rope ladder unrolled from above and cascaded, rung after rung. Finally the last few rungs plopped onto the floor. With his spear, the nearest guard motioned for Rhazburn to climb. They did not follow him, but remained below. Rhazburn climbed upward alone, rung after swinging rung, onward and onward until his legs ached and his hands were blistered. Three times on the way up he had to rest, holding the ropes twisted around his elbows as he blew on his hands and shook life back into them. Still farther he climbed, counting more than three hundred rungs before he surfaced.

He peered into a small, dimly-lit, crowded chamber with a massive circular stone resting against one wall. Ten more men were inside the chamber. They were white-faced like the others, but they had doffed their black robes and were dressed in the most garish clothing Rhazburn had ever seen. They affronted all convention and fashion, piling on the most expensive articles, no matter how discordant they looked. One man had on a pink silk dress over green brocade pants with gold embroidered shoes and a feathered hat. Gold earrings by the fistful hung from multiple punctures in his ears, and his hands were so full of rings, Rhazburn was surprised he could use his fingers. When he sneered at Rhazburn, his sneer was ragged with teeth that had been filed to points. All the men had pointed teeth, and all were dressed as distastefully.

Without a word, they pulled up the rope ladder, reverently stacking it in an alcove which looked carved specifically to accommodate the complex pile. To Rhazburn, it seemed this could be the one and only entrance to their lair, ensconced deep within the mountain of Devil's Fang. Obviously, care of the rope ladder was key to the Ghouls' survival. After the center of the room surrounding the entrance was clear of the rope ladder, all ten Ghouls, grunting and groaning, tilted the immense round slab of rock off the wall it leaned upon and heaved it over. It slammed down on the opening, sealing all of them, Rhazburn included, inside the bowels of the mountain. It had taken all ten men to move the stone so as to drop it onto the hole in the floor. Rhazburn tried to picture his escape from the Ghoul's demesne, but was having a hard time of it.

Where the slab had been propped prior to being moved, a door was now revealed leading into a rough corridor. Armed with curved daggers, still silent, the ten escorted him to a side chamber where another seven, all fat and dressed as gaudily as the others, sat behind a long stone table. On the table were heavy golden pitchers and all manner of expensive drinking vessels, silver goblets, crystal chalices, and porcelain mugs. They were filled with a dark red wine. The man in the middle, obviously the leader, held a human thighbone he used as a gavel. Rhazburn assumed these men were the promised Council of Servants. *Servants of what*, he wondered. Probably servants of the Zombie Lord he saw in his vision.

The leader of the Council of Servants remained seated, saying, "A heretic returns to the Law. What are your words before we assist you back to the Eternal Order?"

Rhazburn had an idea what the Eternal Order meant - death and service to the Zombie Lord and the Demon. All he wanted to do was to find the Unicorn Horn by any means and get away with it as fast as he could. If it meant tricking the Ghouls to get it, he was more than happy to oblige them.

"I am Maconeel, a Poet, and can serve your lord. He will have use for the things I can make." Even though Rhazburn knew he was safe from discovery by the court of the Dragonlord, he wouldn't take the chance of giving his own name.

The leader turned his head slowly to his right and said, "A legend speaks." The others laughed. Addressing Rhazburn he said, "There are no Poets, except in renegade lies." Renegades? Apparently renegades were anyone not belonging to one of the clans of Ghouls.

"I can prove it. I can change that wine into blood. Can a legend do that?" He pointed to a crystal chalice setting before the leader.

The leader pushed forward the chalice and said, "Proceed, Poet. Amuse us." They all laughed again. "A little blood would taste good right now."

That made Rhazburn hesitate a moment. He had suspected all the Ghouls lived up to their names and actually ate human dead, but being confronted with the perversion was another matter. Maybe dealing with grave robbers, murderers and cannibals was not such a good idea after all, no matter what Rhazburn's intention was.

Too far in to back out, he went through with it. He requested a diamond ring from one of the council, and after emptying the chalice, he used the ring to scratch a verse on its glass surface. Carefully concealing his action from the council, he touched the inner surface of the chalice with a Copper Order, then filled it with wine. Into the chalice, he dipped two fingers, wiping blood on his sleeve. "There, you have your legend. I can do much more for your Lord."

"Let me see that," said the leader, taking the chalice. He took a long drink, smacking his lips and revealing his pointed teeth, now covered in blood. "It's blood all right," he said, passing the chalice to the others in the council. They all followed his example, and talked among themselves quietly.

After a lot of nodding and murmuring of the council, the leader stood and gave the stone slab a sharp crack with the thighbone. "The Council speaks. This renegade will be taken living to our Master for his pleasure. He must not see the way, and must never leave our refuge alive." The stone slab received three more cracks with the thighbone, and the Council stood to wander away.

Three guards collared Rhazburn, blindfolding him. Around his neck, they tied a hemp noose and tether, leaving his hands free. He soon realized why. The path to the Zombie Lord's chamber would have been impossible for him had he not the use of his hands.

First, they descended a steep slope over a well-worn path. At the bottom, his guards turned him around several times to disorient him before they dragged him through a series of chilly, winding tunnels. Often, Rhazburn could feel the walls of the cavern on either side, and at times, the guards pushed his head down to lead him in a crouch through rocky tubes. Twice, they crawled in the dirt through tight crevices. At one point, he heard a splashing in front of him, and the next moment, his feet plunged into cold water. The water rose up to his knees as he tried to maneuver over a slick bottom without seeing where he went. Long, soft things brushed against his legs and nipped his pants. Further on, the water began to move and soon hastened, becoming such a torrent that the guards led him to a bank where frigid mud tried to steal his ankle boots, filling them with muck and gluing them to the stream bed. The noise of a tremendous waterfall came closer and closer until the guards clapped his hands on a thin rope and nudged him along a narrow ledge. Hanging on to the rope, he felt his way along the ledge with the waterfall before him, spray and wind from the cascade dragging at him to pull him into the chute. He came off the ledge soaked, shivering, and cold to the bone, but the guards prodded him onward.

A few strides down the next tunnel, Rhazburn felt a wave of dread pass over him. As they proceeded, the horrible feeling increased progressively. Even blindfolded, Rhazburn knew they had passed out of the land of the living and into the Dead Lands. Despair hung about them like a pall.

Behind him, one of the Ghouls breathed deep and sighed with pleasure, as if he enjoyed every depressing pang. Nothing could live for long in this grim atmosphere. Everything, from human to toadstool, died in the Dead Lands, the place where the Demon defiled the land.

With Rhazburn's spirit strangled by deep depression, the trip seemed to take much longer than the reality of it. Finally, they stopped, clumped together in a shallow pit, while one of the guards ran ahead. Rhazburn felt the weight of all the world's ills on his shoulders as he waited to confront the Lord of the Ghouls. At last, a whistle from the scout summoned them, and the guards pushed him the last few steps.

Holding his arms securely at his sides with a knife to his throat, the guards took off Rhazburn's blindfold. The chamber was as big as a cottage. The roof was domed, easily two rods high. Iron hooks for chains and sconces, some with lit torches, dotted the walls. At the far end, a pile of treasure was heaped as high as a man's head. Gold vessels, chains, sword hilts, some with shiny blades, rolls of silk, intricate rugs, piles of coins, silver plates, and jewels were there. There were more riches piled in one place than Rhazburn had ever seen. Somewhere beneath the pile was a Unicorn Horn, and he had to get it, one way or another. Around the pile littering the floor, a dozen complete human skeletons smiled sardonically into eternity. Behind the pile was an archway to a tunnel which, Rhazburn surmised, led on to the plains of the Dead Lands beyond Devil's Fang. On a gold-plated throne beside the pile, the Zombie Lord sat, watching Rhazburn.

Rhazburn silently cursed the Demon for animating the unfortunate soul's dead body. It sat upright with its neck bent to one side, the head leaning unsteadily against an upraised shoulder. The skin resembled battered parchment and the eyes, white round stones. When it moved, a loud cracking and grinding of ancient joints accompanied every gesture. Its jaws moved beneath rigid lips. "What have you brought me today?" it croaked. The voice mimicked a man's dying breath.

There was a knife at Rhazburn's neck, but he took a chance and spoke up. "I am a Poet and..." Before he could finish, the guard pulled back his head and dug the edge of the knife deeper into his skin, cutting off his next breath. His own warm blood trickled down his neck. He took the advice of the knife and shut his mouth.

"A Poet. Let him speak," the Zombie rasped, lifting a creaking arm. The knife eased off.

"I can aid you in your conquest of man."

"Why would an outsider want to aid me?"

"The Dragonlord is my father, but he made another his heir. I will have my vengeance on the culprit and his brat." Even saying such words made Rhazburn uneasy. He hoped he could stop before actually helping the servants of the Demon. "I can fashion an invincible sword that will do your bidding and kill at a distance. No power in the world can stop it."

"I will test it on you."

"Go ahead. Once the sword is made, my revenge will be served. I must live until I have the materials and make the object. I know it may take a while for your servants to find the most important thing I need. A Unicorn Horn."

"I will allow your service," the Zombie said imperiously. "To prove your faith to me, you must first bring me the head of a human you have killed yourself." He waved them off, and Rhazburn was dragged away. Blindfolded again, he was shoved back through the caverns, the waterfall, the stream, the mud, and the rocky tubes to the cluster of rooms belonging to the Clan of the Laughing Skull.

The guards brought him before the council again. The members had a heated discussion over the matter. He must bring back the head of a human, but he must not be allowed to leave the refuge lest they be discovered. Since their lord and master apparently had use for his services, they proposed to bring back a live human for him to kill so he needn't use any of their group.

Rhazburn said, "Before you bring the human, I must first gather materials and devise poems for the spell."

The leader said, "You have a single day. After that, we will hasten your work with a few slashes of tempered steel. Take him away."

Two armed guards flanked and goaded him wherever he went. They took him to a cell with a single door guarded within and without.

The older of the two guards, Nukkle, explained, "Anything you do is on our heads. If your hand touches a weapon, I will cut off that hand. If you try to escape, your flesh will nourish the Clan, and you will serve our Master all the sooner as one of the Eternal Ones."

That evening the guards took him from the cell. He asked, "Where are you taking me?"

Nukkle replied, "To the feasting hall. Elders want to see you again. I think your strange ways amuse them. Never before has the Lord wanted a renegade to serve him alive."

They led him, this time without a blindfold, to a spacious cavern, loud with chatter. His seat was a cold granite boulder with a flattened top behind which stood Nukkle and his young assistant. They both nervously clutched their curved daggers, seemingly in readiness for their prisoner's first false move.

Rhazburn saw many white-powdered faces of the Laughing Skull Clan mingling with others who had red-painted hands, members of the Slashing Claw Clan Rhazburn had seen earlier.

On the table were small bowls of root vegetables, cups of soup, large pitchers of wine and, prominent in the center, loomed a large pile of raw meat which the Clans were grabbing and arguing over. One of the pieces was a skinless human arm.

The leader of the council caught his attention and held up the chalice Rhazburn had altered. "Poet, why does this glass no longer turn my wine to blood? It was a trick. Admit it."

"No," Rhazburn said, morose from the spiritual depression lingering in his soul from his trip into the cavern of the Zombie Lord, "It was no trick. Another power is needed to complete the effect and extend it indefinitely." The leader scowled, unconvinced.

Rhazburn picked up a piece of some kind of cooked root. He smelled it and inspected it for blood from the meat. Finding it clean of odious fluids or flesh, he started to eat it slowly. A man to his left wore a green shirt so tight it had been cut down the middle, the halves hanging down over his shoulders like useless dead skin. He shook a piece of meat in front of Rhazburn's face. "Here Poet, take some nourishment."

"What kind of meat is it?"

"Hmm. Back I think." He barked at a tiny man across the table, "Flail, what is this? Back?"

Flail pulled back a tall brown collar so he could see better. "Nah, calf, you fool. See this? That has to be the heel cord." He pointed to his own heel cord.

Past their heads Rhazburn saw a woman with the severed human arm grasping the hand like she was shaking hands with its owner. She waved it to make a point in her conversation with her friend, then she peeled meat off the bone with her teeth. She chewed thoughtfully for a few moments before she spat out the gristle.

"I'll have some more of this," Rhazburn said, holding up the root vegetable, willing himself not to retch.

A filthy and angry woman dressed in sparse rags crouched on the floor. She had neither a white face nor red hands. She was chained to the wall by a locked leather collar encircling her neck. When she snarled at the others, Rhazburn saw her teeth were filed like the rest of the Clan's.

"What was her crime?" Rhazburn asked the man who had offered him the meat.

"Life," he sneered.

Many of the Clan taunted her and spat in her face. Some used ornately-beaded belts to whip her as they passed. She dodged the thrashings by moving around a table leg, glaring defiantly at her persecutors, and grabbing at their makeshift whips.

Rhazburn could not stand to see anyone, even one of the Ghouls, mistreated in such a way. From his pocket, he secreted a Glass Command in his hand. He stood and walked to the leader of the council, his guards shadowing him.

He pointed to the woman. "I wish to buy her freedom."

"She is no concern of yours, Poet. Her punishment is well-deserved."

"Nonetheless, I will pay for her release."

"You have nothing we desire but your own death. Kill yourself and I will release her."

Rhazburn gestured to the chalice in the leader's hand. "The goblet. I can make it change wine to blood forever."

The leader regarded the chalice, then smiled. "Show me."

Rhazburn gestured with one hand over the chalice, holding it in both hands while he blew on it. At the same time, he touched the inside with the Glass Command, which evaporated and activated the chalice. He poured in wine and poured out blood on the floor, again and again, to the amusement of all the Ghouls. He knew the spell would not really last forever but long enough, hopefully, for him to accomplish his task.

The leader took the chalice and tried it himself. He did not spill the blood on the floor but drank it, glass after glass. After many glasses of blood, he finally stopped and belched loudly.

Rhazburn suppressed his nausea and said, "The woman?"

"Take her." The Ghoul spat in her direction. "Screela, you are shunned from the Clans and barred from the Eternal Order. Go with the renegade." He motioned to a man sitting near him. "Release her. May she live in the worms that feed upon her corpse."

With her release, the woman looked up at Rhazburn for the first time. Her hair was dark, but her skin beneath the filth was ivory-white as if she had never looked upon the sun. The rags of her dress hung loosely on a wasted body which she tried to move in an alluring way as she approached Rhazburn. He pitied her, a starved temptress, all her assets lost.

She said nothing as she came to his side, eyeing his food. He took another hefty root from the table and gave it to her. She threw it on the floor and went for the meat. Before she made it to the table, one of Rhazburn's guards jumped in her way and threatened her with his dagger. The leader said to Rhazburn, "She is no longer of the Order."

"How about the roots?" Rhazburn asked.

"She may eat of the plant food, but she may not partake of the True Nourishment."

If she did not eat that meat, it was fine with Rhazburn. "Let's take the food we can eat and go," he said. They pocketed a few pieces and left. The guards followed.

"My name is Maconeel." She looked at him suspiciously. He turned and eyed the guards. The youngest snickered at him, obviously thinking Rhazburn wanted the woman for carnal entertainment in his lonely cell.

"I will take you to a place we can be together," he said, playing along with their thoughts. She took his arm, feeling his muscle in a disturbing manner, more like a predator than a lover.

At the door to his cell, he bowed to let her in. After Rhazburn followed her in, the older guard stepped inside. Rhazburn faced him and gave him a sly smile. "How about leaving us alone for a while? I can't go anywhere with you outside."

Phlegmatic, the guard said, "You have no time to waste. You must prepare for your service as you told the Counsel. Otherwise, there is no reason for your life."

"I will begin when I am brought the materials I need. A handful of gold thread like that I have seen on many shoes your comrades wear, rags, and red and gray face paint. All these are needed for the spell to make the sword for your Master. Bring them to me if you wish to fulfill your duty to your Counsel."

The elder guard ordered the younger to find the materials. Then he turned to Rhazburn and said, "I will stand outside the door until he is back. You may have your sport with the shunned woman. She deserves to be degraded."

When the door was closed, Screela sneered at him, daring him to force her to his pleasure. Rhazburn had the feeling she wanted him to take advantage of her, defiant as she seemed.

He only asked her, "Why do they torture you so?"

At first, she was astonished he did not want to take her to bed. Then, she looked at him, puzzled. Finally, she clenched her fists and spat out, "I hate them all, but they were right to beat me. I have broken the Law."

"What Law?"

"I caused life unsanctioned."

Rhazburn cocked his head to see her expression better. "You mean, you bore a child?"

She nodded with her eyes closed.

"Where is the child now?" He wasn't sure he wanted to hear her answer.

"He came from me, and by the Law, I had to take him back."

Rhazburn was chilled to the heart. "You ate your baby?"

She gave him a strange look of righteousness. "It is the way."

Suppressing a shudder, he shook his head. "Well, now you are free. You may leave this place forever."

"They will never let me leave. I will rot in here." She looked at the locked door. "They hate me. I am shunned. Did you hear what they said? Their Master will shun me for all eternity. I will die the death of a renegade. There is nothing for me here. I must leave. I want to die with my own Clan. Not here, where I am hated. I cannot stand the pain of separation from my Master, and now, I am barred from sustenance. I am starving." Crying, she took out one of the cold, cooked roots and threw it down as hard as she could. She wept and fell against Rhazburn, clutching at him and sobbing against his shoulder. Her body was warm as he held her, but he could only think of her dead child. No physical warmth could mask her cold heart.

Still, she was a woman in need and helpless in the company of the Laughing Skull Clan. "I will be able to get out," he said, not wholly undaunted by the solid stone encasing them both. "When I leave, I will take you with me," he told her.

She looked incredulous at his statement. "You cannot leave without permission."

With his gaze looking straight into her tear-blurred eyes, he asserted, "I will leave when I want."

"If you leave, I want to come with you."

As if on cue, her sobbing stopped and she held him closer, nuzzling his neck. A sharp pain sliced through his ear lobe. He jerked back and touched the spot, feeling a wet notch. Blood covered the tips of his fingers. Screela licked blood from her lips.

"Why did you do that?" he said.

She smiled, baring her filed teeth, looking a lot like a stalking cat. "You do not nibble the ears of loved ones where you come from?"

"Not with sharpened teeth, we don't."

"It is the custom in all the Clans. At least, it is in mine and the Clan of the Laughing Skull."

"What is your Clan?" he asked.

"The Clan of the Angry Eye. They could use your talents. Our Master would reward you."

"Your Clan? Your Master? How many Clans and Masters are there?"

"I do not know. I know of ten Clans, each with their Master, but I have never been north of the mountains. I am sure there are more. One day, I will serve the Great Master. Then, I will know everything."

"I can help you escape when I can get out myself. To do that, I need your help. But, I warn you, it will mean playing a trick on the Master of the Laughing Skulls." She would only be trustworthy if she was desperate enough.

She laughed a single note and said, "I am cast out. I have no allegiance to any of the Laughing Skulls or their Master. I will help you if I can escape. What do you want of me?"

"Your head," he said.

He wasn't prepared for her reaction. She threw back her head, baring her neck and throwing out her wasted bosom at the same time. "Go ahead. Take it."

The door opened, and the old guard came in. He saw her compromised posture and the tear on Rhazburn's ear. "So renegades do have lust. I have heard you were all castrates."

Rhazburn took the thread, rags, and paint the guard had brought and said, "I will work faster if my lust is satisfied. Leave us for a single Blessing, and I will be ready to speak to your Counsel."

The guard screwed up his face. "A blessing? Why would we give a renegade like you a blessing?"

Rhazburn realized the Ghoul had no idea what a Blessing or a Favor was. He probably had never even seen a proper Timefall. The Ghouls had been so divorced from anything civilized that they knew nothing of the conventions of normal society, including the measurement of time. Underground, day was no different than night. What clues did they even have about the passage of time, and what did they care of it? They planted no crops, opened no shops. They probably ate when they were hungry, slept when tired, and got up when commanded.

"No, no. That is not what I meant," Rhazburn corrected his request. "Give us how long it takes to prepare a meal and eat it."

The guard thought on it a long time. He finally said, "You mean a Butch', you need a whole Butch' to lay with the outcast."

"Is that the amount of time it takes to fix and eat a meal?"

"Well, yes, one Butchery, of course. Everyone knows that, even the smallest child can tell time."

Rhazburn knew what it was they butchered. It was obviously the only thing important to them. They even told time by it. The thought made him queasy. "Fine. Can we have one Butchery? To ourselves?"

"One Butch' is all I will give you, Renegade. Then, you will give us results, or we will give the Master your head."

After which, Rhazburn thought, they would take a Butch' with him, the renegade.

CHAPTER 11

THE UNICORN HORN

Screela's vacant, unmoving eyes stared from an ashen face above a bloody stump of a neck. Her tongue protruded out one side of her still lips.

"Perfect," Rhazburn said.

Screela smiled. "I like being a corpse."

"Don't take your role too seriously," he chided her.

They had spent all the time they were allotted preparing for their charade. Rhazburn had used the gold thread to stitch a verse in the black woolen blanket in his cell. The verse read:

> Clear as glass
> Whisper of air
> Heedless eye passes
> With a vacant stare

With the verse in the wool, a Copper Order transformed the blanket into a Garment of Invisibility, something forbidden for use by anyone in the Realm of the Dragonlord or the Tributary States. Rhazburn was not planning to tell the court he had broken the Dragonlord's law. The now-magical cape tested out perfectly. Screela had it around her neck, hiding the rest of her body, which was now cloaked in invisibility. The cadaverous appearance of her face and the artificial blood around her neck had been painted by Rhazburn. The effect was to make her head appear dead and decapitated, floating in the air. Rhazburn braided her hair in a loop so he could pretend to hold her head up with his hand.

Although he had not as yet confided to Screela the existence of his Flying Carpet, he planned to have her stand floating upon it, to further enhance the illusion of him returning with her head as required by the Zombie. Screela had told him she knew the way to the Zombie's lair, so she could lead Rhazburn to his appointment. Rhazburn only wanted to get his hands on the Unicorn Horn and escape on his carpet with Screela.

He knew Screela was not to be trusted. She was full of bizarre Ghoulish nurturing, in which even motherly love was subjugated to perverse beliefs. Her banishment from the Clan of the Laughing Skull and her hate of its members took the edge off Rhazburn's suspicion. Nevertheless, he had little choice in confederates at the moment.

When the Butch' had ended and the guards strode into the room, Rhazburn and Screela were gone, hidden by the cape in a corner by the door. The guards pushed over the table, tore apart the bed, and rapped on all the walls, looking for their means of escape.

"Gone!" cried the elder guard. He turned to his inferior and slapped him with the back of his hand as if to vent his anger on something, anything. "How could they have gotten past us? We must find them, you lout! Tell no one what has happened. We must split up or the others will wonder where the renegade is. If anyone asks you, tell them he is with me. When you find them, kill them both. Do not talk to the renegade. He is treacherous. Kill him first."

Rhazburn and Screela, wrapped in the the blanket of invisibility, tiptoed out through the open door and down the stone passageway while the older guard railed at the younger.

After the guards left the room, locking the door behind them, the older guard rushed down the tunnel away from them while the younger jogged toward them making them sidle to the wall.

Rhazburn whispered, "You must lead me to the chamber of the Lord of the Laughing Skull Clan. Your freedom depends on it. You do know the way?"

"Of course. Everyone knows the way to the Master."

Rhazburn heard a little too much respect and awe in the way she said 'Master' for his comfort level. Still, at least Screela expressed no overt intent to kill him.

She led him, skulking, through the abode of the Laughing Skull. Most of the time they held the cape around them, quietly passing unseen as they skirted by crowds and hugged the walls. Rhazburn purloined a brand to light their way when they came to unlit, unoccupied passageways. They shunned halls filled with the sound of revelers and dashed past lighted doorways. After far too long sneaking through the tunnels, negotiating a sharp bend around an onyx pillar, the turn brought them into a sparkling stone corridor lit by torches in iron sconces. The tunnel ascended over a small rise. No one was about, so they dropped the cape. Rhazburn threw it over his shoulder. Screela gave him an odd look. Rhazburn looked at his shoulder where the cape lay. A large chunk of his body was missing. He had to feel the cape to make sure it was there.

She pointed over the rise. Softly she spoke, "Beyond that crest stands the guard to the Way of Truth. That is the pathway to the Master."

Again Rhazburn didn't like the tone she used when she said "the Master", and he began to have serious reservations about his plan. He gripped Screela's arm and looked into her painted face of death. "Can you betray this Master, Screela?"

She turned her head away to sneer down the hallway. "He is not my Master but that of these puppets." She looked back and met his gaze unflinchingly. "I long to serve the Great Master, it is true, but my place is with my people. The Clan of the Laughing Skull cast me out, and I sever myself from them and their Master." She ran her finger deftly across her painted neck as if she were slashing her own throat in some Ghoul sign of allegiance to Rhazburn.

"Then we must pass the guard," he said. The power of the cape was good for two Blessings, but precious Favors were falling away. They walked quietly over the rise, holding the cape before them. They could see through the cape from their side, but the guards lounging on a glistening stone shelf could not see them. Two guards were before them. One guard was white-faced, heavily-muscled, and young. To keep warm in the chilly cavern, he was stuffed into three gaudy jackets. The outer one, inappropriately the smallest, had sleeves that came only to his elbows. Rhazburn did not think he was trying to look comical. One of his hands unconsciously fingered a thick gold ring piercing his nose. His other hand caressed a feathered spear propped beside him, as if the feel gave him confidence. He talked to a second guard, the old one from Rhazburn's cell. He was pretending to make idle conversation with the other, all the time scanning the tunnel for his quarry.

They passed within one stride of them. As they passed, the old guard sensed their presence by sound or smell and turned around, searching the corridor. The other guard roused himself at the elder's actions, rubbing his eyes and waving a torch around to send light over all the cracks and crevices.

"What is it, Nukkle? What do you hear?" He looked Rhazburn straight in the eye but saw nothing.

"I hear movement... and... breathing," the old guard replied. Rhazburn and Screela stopped cold. They tried to stop breathing.

"I see nothing. Could it be one of the Master's servants? One of the Eternal Ones?"

"I think not," Nukkle said, taking out his curved knife. He reached toward them with the knife and waved it before him, cutting through the air a few inches from Rhazburn's chest. Rhazburn feared Screela would panic and give them away. But she only gripped his arm quietly and stayed still beside him.

Nukkle said, "Give me that torch," grabbing it roughly from the young guard. "I could swear someone is standing before us." He peered at them for a long time, listening. At last, sighing, he said, "The labyrinth plays tricks on the ears and the mind sometimes. Especially on the fearful." He gave the torch back, sliced the air in front of Rhazburn's throat one more time, and sheathed his knife. "I've been standing here too long for my own good. I must get back to my prisoner," he lied. He walked away, and the young guard settled back on his rocky lounge.

Very slowly and carefully, Rhazburn and Screela backed further down the tunnel, always holding the cape between them and the guard. Screela seemed to read his mind, stepping in rhythm as carefully as he did until they were far down the passage and around two corners. When, blind in the darkness of the unlit cave, Rhazburn barked his shin on a stalagmite, he surrendered to in-caution and tossed a pinch of Firedust on the torch he carried. The torch sputtered and burst into flame and lit their way onward. Past that last guard, Rhazburn assumed they were beyond the inhabited tunnels, inhabited by the living anyway.

They remained silent for most of the journey. At first, they sauntered down a wide hallway hewn from the rock by human or previously-human hands. When Screela began to lead him down into the blackness by a steep stone stairway, Rhazburn stopped her. He could remember all the details he had felt during his previous blindfolded march to the Zombie, and he knew he had not descended a stairway. "Are you quite sure this is the way to the Master's chamber? I don't recall any stairs."

She gave him a quizzical look, then said in sudden realization, "They tricked you, leading you all through the caverns to confuse you. I doubt they wanted you to come back to the Master alone."

Her explanation seemed reasonable, but he was surprised that the Ghouls had such foresight. Her reassurance only magnified his qualms. He wondered who led him astray, the Ghouls before or Screela now?

They descended the staircase into the gloom below. It was not so much a stairway as a slightly tilted cliff, the steps being so narrow he had to walk sideways, holding onto a step above him for balance. Screela seemed to have no fear of the pitch they descended but negotiated the stairs facing forward and confidant, as if she would welcome a lethal tumble into the darkness that yawned like a starving gullet beneath them.

After a few dozen stairs, Screela inhaled deeply with a sensual sigh and stretched her chest while squeezing her breasts. When Rhazburn descended to her level, he understood what she had felt, a the resurgence of the oppressive fear he had experienced before. They had crossed into the Dead Lands. His soul felt stifled even more than before when he had been prodded to the Zombie's chamber by the Ghouls. Since he was approaching the Zombie by his own efforts this time, the tainted atmosphere of the Dead Lands had a much greater effect upon him. Despondency lay like a pool of mire before him. He could barely muster the will to take another step. Screela obviously thrived on the melancholy and hurried down the stairs gleefully.

All the worst memories of Rhazburn's life whirled around him, flogging him with whips of regret. The ignominy of his father's neglect, the pain of his mother's desertion, the guilt of his blunder with Dollop's life, indeed, anything he had ever done wrong and any pang of loneliness he had ever felt grated his spirit. The feeling intensified as he proceeded.

Surrounded by all the cares of his life, Rhazburn's head spun with a physical vertigo that made him miss a step and slip on the steep stairway. As his boots skipped uselessly over damp stone, he leaned into the stairs and dug his fingers into the rock. His hands fought a losing battle with the implacable granite which scraped his skin raw and tore his nails off painfully. Finally, he had to thrust his face into the passing fists of stone steps, taking a dozen blows on his chin before he stopped his fall.

Far below him, Screela held the torch he had dropped and waited impatiently. She evidenced no concern for his trouble and offered him neither a sympathetic word nor a helping hand.

With tears of pain in his eyes, Rhazburn straightened himself on the decline, and holding onto the step above his head, clenched his teeth and waved his stinging hand with the bleeding fingernails. The waving did little for the pain. He knew he needed to move on and try to ignore the misery. Anxious to avoid further slips and scrapes, he carefully negotiating the remaining stairs using both his hands, literally crawling backwards down the incline. Screela remained impassive at the bottom. She ignored his accusing scowl and turned to lead onward. Before he moved a step, he stopped her with a hand on her shoulder and whispered, "How far is it to the Master's throne room?"

"Not far. Down the hall and a short way to the right."

"We must make our preparations now," Rhazburn said. "Before we are within earshot.'"

Screela consented reluctantly, seeming irritated with their planned theatrics. He trusted her even less now, but he knew that as long as his Flying Carpet was near, he could always escape if things took a turn for the worse. He amended that thought. *When* things took a turn for the worse.

Around her neck, Rhazburn wrapped the cape and erased her body from sight. Only Screela's head, with its eerie cast, could be seen. He rearranged the cape so her red painted neck peeked into sight above the cape, appearing at a distance like a bloody stump. Close up, it would fool no one, not even a Zombie. All Rhazburn needed was a few precious moments to get the Unicorn Horn out of the treasure heap. From his vision at the Wishing Drop, he could picture exactly where the horn was in the pile. He knew he could go right to it when the time came.

The next thing Rhazburn did surprised Screela. He unrolled his Flying Carpet, folded it into a shape she could stand on, and made sure it was hidden by the Cloak of Invisibility when she stepped upon it. Then he slipped a Copper Order into its pocket and bade the Carpet to rise up a hand span.

Unprepared to be airborne, she threw out her arms to balance herself, grabbing his shoulder. "Mother of Hell!" she gasped.

"Steady. You will not be harmed but will float along beside me. I will hold your hair as if I am keeping your head suspended. It will help you stand." She calmed a little at his words and carefully lowered her arms, shifting herself to regain a stable center of gravity.

"I never expected you had such power," she said with awe.

"Come," he commanded, grabbing her braid. "We must be quiet. Do not speak again until we leave his chamber. I will tell you when it is safe. Close your eyes, and let your tongue hang out as you did before. Do not move. Carpet, hover beside me until I release her hair. Then stay still."

Down the hallway he forced himself into the thickening sense of depression and doom with Screela's head seeming to float beside him. Rhazburn's dread became so great as he approached the door to the Zombie's chamber that the entire scene seemed a delusion. Was this maybe a nightmare, a nightmare in which he had actually killed Screela and was in the power of the Zombie?

When Rhazburn turned the corner into the chamber, the Zombie sat in exactly the same position as before. Rhazburn didn't know why he had expected the Zombie to move. After all, he was dead. This time, the Zombie looked even more dead than before. His head was tipped back, and his mouth was open in what looked like a last gasp.

"I have brought the human's head, Master," Rhazburn said, addressing the Zombie.

The Zombie's head flopped forward so the decayed eyes pointed approximately in Rhazburn's direction. Rhazburn made a motion with Screela's head as if to hang her on a chain-bedecked iron hook driven into the cave wall. The carpet floated her into place. The illusion was so good, Rhazburn shivered. He hoped the Zombie would not ask to inspect her head closely.

The Zombie lifted a limp and blackened hand, gesturing toward the mound of treasure. "I had a Unicorn slaughtered for you," he lied. "Its horn has been placed at the bottom of this pile of useless trash. Fetch it here for me, then kiss my foot, slave."

Rhazburn planned to be gone before the foot-kissing stage. He stepped over one of the dozen human skeletons cast about on all sides of the pile. Out of the corner of his eye, he thought he saw one of them stir, but when he glanced at it, only a jumble of bones lay there, still as a cord of wood. He had to climb to the top of the pile to dig for the Unicorn Horn. Goblets and pendants, jewels and coins shifted about and slipped under his feet. Nothing he tried to grab gave him support. After working up quite a sweat, he made it to the top and thrust his hand down into the gold and silver toward the precise point at which he had seen the Unicorn Horn in his vision at the Wishing Drop. His arm wasn't long enough, so he started to move treasures aside to lower himself into the middle of it. He felt as if he were bathing in wealth. Glass commands and copper orders were there by the hundreds. He slipped a couple of Commands with some rubies and sapphires into his pocket while he was burrowing into the riches. He wanted all the treasure but shook that foolishness out of his head.

While he strained again, reaching for the horn and forcing his face into the treasure, he heard a grunt and a scream. He looked up at Screela, who had torn off the garment of invisibility and thrown it onto the ground.

"Master, he is a fraud. He will not serve you but only wants to steal your treasure," she yelled. At the same time, she hopped off the carpet, grabbed it, and impaled it on the iron hook, ripping through the carpet's weave. She wrapped the chain around it tightly, hemming in every fold.

Rhazburn yelled, "Carpet, come here." He was too late. The carpet wriggled on the hook like a trapped animal, but it could not extricate itself.

Rhazburn heard the Zombie say, "I am not the one deceived. He is. Slash, Snuffle, Mince, my Eternal Ones, kill him and bring me his soul."

Within moments, all the skeletons surrounding the treasure stood up on their own power and poised to rush Rhazburn. Frantically, he shoved his hand down deeper into the treasure. He could hear the animated skeletons clattering up the sides of the treasure mound while his hand groped around cold chains, candelabras, and jeweled scabbards. At last, he gripped a smooth, warm helix. Looking up, he saw upraised, skeletal arms and a leering skull leap at him.

The Unicorn Horn, gripped in his hand, sent a surge of strength through every limb of his body. He felt a tingling vigor spread into his chest, up into his head and out to every hair on his scalp. The feeling of dread caused by the fetid atmosphere in the Dead Lands was dispelled in a rush of potency. He felt as powerful now as he had felt omniscient in the spell of the Wishing Drop.

With a cry, Rhazburn wrenched the Unicorn Horn out of its precious bed, scattering treasure, and with the Unicorn Horn gripped in both hands like a God-sent Holy Club, he swiped at the onrushing skeleton. When the Unicorn Horn hit the skeleton, the bones were torn apart and scattered.

Rhazburn was still half-buried in the treasure, and he found his eyes were hip-high to the next skeleton attacking him. He swept the Unicorn Horn across its knees, felling it like some ancient, crisp tree. The arms were still animate, though, and clutched at him. He clubbed what was left of the skeleton to shambles and turned just in time to smash two more skeletons behind him. Before the others could reach him, he tucked in his head, slammed the Unicorn Horn down before him with all his strength, and somersaulted out of the hole. Rhazburn surprised himself with his newfound agility. His body felt lithe and supple, stronger than ever before.

He had little time to enjoy the pleasant sensation as two bony hands dug pencil-hard fingers into his arm. He used the horn in his other hand to beat them off, bruising his own arm with the blows. The skeleton's skull was not stopped, however, and it shot at his face. Rhazburn met its mouth with the butt of the Unicorn Horn, knocking the skull off the neck. He stood up into another pair of charging skeletons which he raked across the ribs, chopping them in half. Totally unconcerned at their mutilation, the legs and hips kept coming, piling into him with their momentum, pushing him backward onto the shifting pile of treasure. Catching himself, he picked up one set of hips and legs with his free hand hurled them against a wall. The other he cracked the apart with the horn.

Rhazburn had a scant moment to glance toward Screela. She stood, cringing, beside his useless carpet. In that moment, the rest of the skeletons grouped into a grimacing horde between him and his carpet. They seemed to know that his only means of escape was the trapped carpet. He should have given up in desperation, but the Unicorn Horn imbued him with a strength and confidence he had never known before. Fury built up within him until he no longer needed to think about his actions. He let his rage control his blows. Although he slipped and careened on the slippery slope of riches, he ran down, diving through the skeletons and whirling the horn over his head. They all shattered with his wild swings, sharp backhands, and bludgeoning thrusts until only a field of disarticulated bones lay around him.

Rhazburn did not stop but sprinted at Screela with the horn upraised. She fled from the hook where his struggling Flying Carpet hung. Rhazburn slid to a halt before it, unwrapped the chains, and threw them to the floor of the cave. The carpet pulled itself free from the hook like a sentient creature. It hovered in front of Rhazburn.

The Zombie Lord had positioned himself in Rhazburn's path and in front of the exit which led to the rooms of the Laughing Skull Clan. The Zombie would be a much harder foe than the flimsy skeletons.

Screela ran to the Zombie and prostrated herself, holding his ankles. "Master, I came only to serve you and bring you the renegade. Save me, I beg you." Bones floated through the air. Bits and pieces of dead humans moved or rather flew slowly as if carried by an ill wind. They all hovered briefly at the exit Rhazburn needed to pass. Then they lined themselves up to assemble like bars across the opening. Rhazburn was locked within the Chamber of the Zombie Lord. Some of the arm bones still had hands attached, ready to clutch at him if he tried to force his way through.

Rhazburn had little time to think of the best escape. He stabbed the carpet with the Unicorn Horn so it was stuck in the fabric. Simultaneously, he yelled, "Carpet, hold onto this horn! Fly to Isseltrent and Jonathon Forthright."

When the carpet began to fly toward the barrier of bones, Rhazburn grabbed onto the sides of it, hoping to trail himself behind it in the air, keeping a low profile in order to fly above the Zombie and through any crevices the carpet might pick. As the carpet accelerated toward the exit, Rhazburn was caught from behind. Bony fingers as tight as steel bands throttled Rhazburn's neck. He was dragged, choking, from the carpet which flew on, whirling past and evading the Zombie, then crashing through the barrier of bones. Rhazburn could not breathe, let alone call out for the carpet to stop.

He fell heavily onto his back and wrestled with the skeletal fingers around his throat. He felt he was about to lose consciousness. With a great effort, he pried them away and turned. Fear and horror burned throughout his body. Without the power of the Unicorn Horn, the awful oppression of the Dead Lands crushed his spirit again with redoubled force. Even without the oppressive feeling, he would have feared what he saw before him.

The jumbled human bones had reformed themselves into all manner of frightening shapes. None was in the least human-like. The hands that throttled him were attached to a half-dozen arms, end on end, to form two extremely long limbs protruding from a headless torso. Another set of ribs had two legs with five arms at odd angles, each holding a snapping skull. Six other legs had clustered about a pelvis skittering about as if it were the insides of a human spider. Another snarling skull was on the end of a hundred vertebrae strung together like a huge snake. There were other monstrosities even worse. Skeletal hands fished in the treasure mound, extracting gleaming swords with bejeweled pommels and golden-hafted spears. All the apparitions turned at once and came at Rhazburn.

He was trapped in a stone tomb, weaponless, and beset by fears from within and without. The only thing that could help him, the Unicorn Horn, was too far away to be recalled. There he lay, alone in a nightmare, with no way to wake up.

CHAPTER 12

THE ROD OF COERCION

Jonathon turned the deep-purple amethyst over in his hand so the sun glinted off a facet. The poems inscribed by Hili were perfect. Every surface was covered by verse. When he let the reflected light rest upon the wall, he scried the verse backwards upon the plaster. The previous evening he had finished the last setting as prescribed by Rhazburn. Every stone that was needed had been engraved by Hili during the time Rhazburn had been gone to the Dead Lands. Now, all the silver settings were finished, too.

Still, Jonathon felt that nothing was accomplished. Without the Unicorn Horn, his work was useless. Furthermore, without his son, Rhazburn, at his side, all his efforts seemed a self-serving lie. If Rhazburn had been killed by Jonathon's actions, the jeweler's work through the years, his sacred morals, his whole life was a sham. Rhazburn had warned him about this commission, but Jonathon had been both deaf and blind, worse than the Dragonlord's messenger. His foolishness with his money had led to the fatal deal with Molgannard Fey, and his cowardice in the face of the Giant had led to his greedy acceptance of the Dragonlord's proposition.

Hang loyalty to the Crown. Jonathon was no more patriotic than any other immigrant from the Tributary Lands. Did he ever really think he was capable of opposing any revolution against the Crown? Not hardly. He knew he was impotent to do so. He had no control over his own destiny, much less that of the entire Realm.

Less than a day remained before the Dragonegg Festival. The day the world would end. If the revolt took place, as Jonathon knew in his heart it would, the Dragons would be loosed. Isseltrent, and all he knew in the world, would burn. His shop. His apprentice. His family. Jonathon had always hoped to spend the last day of his life with Arlen. Dying with his hand in Arlen's and all his children around him seemed a fitting end to a long and happy life. Instead, he was stuck in his shop. His end would be lonely indeed, Jonathon thought gloomily. Because of the heightened security in the streets, even travel in the streets was restricted. Commerce was curbed, limited to only those having business related to the Dragonegg Festival and of course, religious matters. Of course, the Beholder from the Dragonlord on the Court's official business would have no trouble coming to his appointment. Jonathon had no idea how he was going to tell a deaf mute what had happened. Perhaps, empty hands would be proof enough of Jonathon's failure.

"Master, your morning tea."

Jonathon looked up from his ruminations into Bob Thumblefoot's empathic eyes. "I'll have the brandy this morning, Bob."

Bob lowered his gaze and ducked away, carrying the wooden tea tray deftly balanced on the fingers of one hand. Before Jonathon could finish his next sigh, the boy had the brandy bottle and a half-filled cordial on a silver tray in front of the Master Jeweler's nose.

Jonathon looked up and smiled. "Half a glass? To blazes with my gout, Bob. Fill it up. I don't want to feel the rope, or the Dragonfire, or whatever execution the Dragonlord will have for me when he finds out I've betrayed his trust and spent all his money. Even if Rhazburn came back this instant with the Unicorn Horn, I couldn't possibly get it done in time." Bob filled the glass to the rim, and Jonathon quaffed it, only to present it to his apprentice for another round.

"What am I to do?" he asked himself. "I've killed Rhazburn by my greed. Killed my son. I know it as sure as..." Pausing to guzzle another glass, he puckered his lips. "As sure as this brandy is sour."

Once again, he raised his glass to Bob, who filled it while giving Jonathon a worried look. Jonathon met Bob's concern with a feigned attempt at drunken apathy. "Here's to justice for the greedy," he said, raising his cordial to clink the half-empty bottle.

An explosion of glass from the window behind him made him throw his hands over his head and shut his eyes tight. Flung by his jerk, his cordial hit the wall, adding to the shower of shards. Jonathon knew Molgannard Fey was back, angry at Rhazburn's curt message and ready for revenge. "Run, Bob. Save yourself. It's me he wants."

Bob juggled the brandy on its tray until he caught his balance. Jonathon uncovered his head to see Bob staring wide-eyed to his right. There, Rhazburn's carpet hung in the air with a white spiral horn thrust through the fabric. Grasping the thickest part of the Unicorn Horn above the carpet was a chalky skeleton hand with dried bits of black flesh hanging from the frozen joints.

"Loremaster!" Bob cried suddenly, dropping the tray and shattering the brandy bottle. He covered his eyes and wept.

Jonathon went to Bob's side and held his shoulders, squeezing tightly. As the jeweler looked longer at the skeleton hand, he relaxed. "That's not Rhazburn's hand," he asserted. "It's old, years old. Bob, look. It's Rhazburn's carpet, but that's not his hand. He sent the Unicorn Horn to us."

Bob turned his head up to sniffle. "But where is the Loremaster? And what is that?" he said pointing to the hideous bones.

Jonathon remembered the poem that Rhazburn had sent to Jonathon through Jiminic the first time the Poet had ever needed Jonathon's help. He knew where Grimtooth was and had a pretty clear picture in his mind what Rhazburn was up against. He had heard stories, late at night around pub fires. Stories that were calculated to frighten but which were all in fun for Jonathon, as long as he was not in the middle of them.

"I think I know where he is, and it's not a place I really want to go." He knew, however, that he had to go. He had to search for Rhazburn.

He certainly wasn't going to tell the boy where Rhazburn was. Bob was impulsive and loyal enough to follow him.

"A real Unicorn Horn," Jonathon said, contemplating its flawless beauty. "Quite unfortunate I haven't the time to finish the scepter before the Dragonegg Festival. By my weakness, the Realm is doomed."

"Master," Bob said.

Tired with all the worries and fuzzy with brandy, Jonathon regarded his student with a baleful eye.

"Have I been a fair apprentice?" Bob asked.

Jonathon was shocked. "My dear boy. I have always asserted you are the best. I humbly admit I am the one person most qualified to make that statement."

"I could help, if you would only give me a chance!" the boy exclaimed. Jonathon's drunkenness drained away as if Bob had dumped him through the thin ice of a winter pond.

"Bob, you've never even lifted a jeweler's eye. Another year must pass before you're allowed to touch a gem. Speak no more of it." But Jonathon thought to himself, Bob's help could save the Realm. Perhaps save all their lives.

For the first time in his apprenticeship, Bob disobeyed his master and pressed on. "I have made some tools myself, Master. I have been practicing on my own at home, using garnets and bits of tin."

Jonathon tightened his brow, pretending displeasure. The youth was molded from his master's example. Jonathon had done the same thing behind the back of his own master thirty years before. He was proud to have taught Bob such dedication. Still, he had a responsibility to the regulations of his trade. "I would have to abrogate your vow of service."

Bob was not swayed by indiscriminate rules. "Master, I can make the settings. I know I can. Give me a chance. For the Loremaster's sake, if not for the Realm."

Jonathon knew he could not finish the project alone, and there was no one else he trusted. Bob was good with his hands, probably as good as Jonathon, and he learned things in a flash. He would be as good an assistant as Jonathon could find. "For this, only perfection will be tolerated," he said, giving the boy his hardest stare.

"It will be perfect. I promise."

"The tiniest mistake could destroy the Realm."

"There will be no mistake, Master," the youth said, solid as a diamond.

Jonathon wished he was as sure of himself as was his own apprentice. He turned to the patiently-hovering carpet. "All right, let's get the horn and go to work."

Bob was gone when Jonathon twisted his head toward the boy. Bob came back holding a broom. "For the hand, Master," he said, pointing to the bony claw.

Jonathon took the broom, and with a squeamish grimace, tapped the hand. It fell apart, clattering onto the floor, making Jonathon dance around it. He swept it into a corner.

Next, he grasped the Unicorn Horn and tugged. It didn't budge. He pulled with all his might but had to stop, moaning, when he got a cramp in his groin. "I can't do it alone, Bob. Give me a hand."

Together, they wrestled with the horn. The carpet hung onto it like a mastiff with a bone.

Panting, nearly exhausted, Jonathon said, "One last try, Bob. This time on three. One, two, three." They both cried out with a burst of strength and yanked the Unicorn Horn free, ripping the carpet apart with their effort. Rhazburn's Flying Carpet fell in two pieces, dead, to the floor.

Virtually paralyzed with the beauty of the Unicorn Horn, Jonathon stood staring as he reverently held it in his hands. Although Jonathon knew the horn had to be centuries old, the rich whiteness of its helical surface was unmarred. It felt light as it imbued Jonathon a strange power, foreign to a middle-aged jeweler. It was warm, as if it still crowned the legendary equine with the stallion's hot blood coursing within it.

Bob intruded into his awe. "It is destroyed, Master. It will never fly again." He was kneeling, holding Rhazburn's carpet in his hands like a dead child.

"It must fly. That is the only carpet that can find Rhazburn."

After feeling around in his pocket, Bob took a Clay Suggestion out, found the slit sewn in the fabric for coins and inserted the Suggestion. "Carpet, rise up," he ordered. The torn pieces of fabric remained lifeless on the floor. Bob looked up at Jonathon and shook his head.

Jonathon thought of the long walk to Devil's Fang to look for Rhazburn. He had one Glass Command left for a Black Dragon. That would take him one way only, and he had no other means of rapid travel. If he were the Unicorn whose horn he now held, he could run there like a summer breeze, but that was just a foolish fantasy. Unicorns were gone from the world and would never run again. Thinking of Rhazburn trapped somewhere, surrounded by men without flesh on their bones, made him too weak to stand. He reeled toward his plush chair so he could fall into something soft. Bob steadied him as he landed heavily. Dust flew up and made him sneeze. He was overcome by the enormity of a trip to the Dead Lands, searching in caves filled with monsters, deep beneath the Forbidden Mountains from which no human had ever come back, for a son he wasn't even sure was still alive.

And what about the rest of his family, Jonathon thought miserably. None of his other children, not even Arlen, had any idea what he and Rhazburn were up to. Jonathon had told Arlen he was working straight through, trying to make money to pay back Molgannard Fey. He warned her to stay away and keep the children safely distant from his shop, in case the Giant paid him another visit. Arlen had already chided him, twice, from his shop Vision Bowl. She complained that he needed to keep her better informed, so she did not have to send Constable Pickery to look for him.

So many problems. Every time one was supposedly solved, a dozen others reared their ugly heads. Rhazburn had sent the Unicorn Horn, but their time was almost up, the poor Flying Carpet was a lifeless heap, and Rhazburn... what of Rhazburn himself? Jonathon felt so inadequate. He broke out in a sweat just imagining trying to come up with an excuse for tromping off to the Forbidden Mountains without admitting he had gotten Rhazburn lost. Bob was so frightened of Jonathon's appearance, he fetched him a cool dry towel.

Such a small act of kindness. Yet Jonathon lived for these acts. He wiped the sweat from his face slowly and thoughtfully. He was a jeweler. A Master Jeweler. And a Master Jeweler could at least do what he was good at. He had the Unicorn Horn. He had the verses Bob had taken down from Rhazburn's dictation. There was only one Glass Command left, but they had bought the materials they needed and still had hundreds of Copper Orders left in change. He had Bob's new-found courage and skill. Lastly, he remembered all the times Rhazburn had extricated himself from adversities.

The Unicorn Horn lay shimmering with an energy Jonathon found irresistible. Even if Rhazburn were not at his side at the moment, he and Bob had things to work with. And work they would. Jonathon gave Bob a grateful smile. He set down the towel, stood up, and said with new determination in his voice, "Bob, let's get started."

Bob took Rhazburn's carpet to a small table under a window. He folded it neatly, laying the torn pieces to rest. At Jonathon's work bench, the boy carefully prepared the surface and arranged the tools they would need to work on the Unicorn Horn.

Jonathon took charge of the engraving, carving the poems from the Loremaster that Bob had faithfully transcribed. A verse of bondage was on one side of the spiraling surface. On the other surface was a poem Rhazburn had not explained. It dealt with powers of the mind unknown to common folk.

Bob's role was to drill holes in the horn and place the completed gem settings in proper relation to the engravings. This task gave Bob responsibility, but it was not nearly as exacting as carving the poems themselves. For the settings, the inscriptions in the jewels already chiseled by Hili's tiny hands were the critical step in their production. Still, Bob worked carefully and very slowly in the beginning, taking a full Blessing for the first setting. The second took him half as long, the third even less. By Dinner Blessing, Jonathon had completed his part and assisted Bob with the finishing touches.

The snow-white spiral of the Unicorn Horn was now covered with the magical verses. It was studded with seven Diamonds of Lasting and five Rubies of Hypnosis. The base of the horn would act as the top, and capping this was an Amethyst of Kingly Power in a platinum setting, resembling a crown. A slot beneath the amethyst could accept coins to activate the device.

They set the finished horn on a velvet pillow and admired their work. "We gaze upon perfection, Bob. Thanks to you." Jonathon patted him on the back. "And yet, like a lord among jewels, it requires a title." The boy looked uncertain.

"Hmmm," Jonathon hummed as he fingered his chin. "If Rhazburn were here, he'd have a name for it." He thought again out loud. "It's a scepter or staff or rod that coerces people to obey the will of the bearer." He nodded making up his mind. "How about the Unicorn Scepter of Coercion?"

Bob repeated it quickly a few times. "Unicorn Scepter of Coercion, Unicorn Scepter of Coercion, Unisord Sceptem of Curshion." He shook his head. "It is something you must say with respect and slowly, Master."

"Ridiculously complicated, you think?"

The boy nodded gravely.

Jonathon played with it a bit. "The Unicorn Scepter? No. Scepter of Unicorn Coercion. That's even more ridiculous. The Unicorn's Rod. Oh, no, no, no." He shook his head, flustered. Bob snickered.

"All right. How about the Rod of Coercion?"

His apprentice whispered it several times to himself and nodded. "I like it."

"Me, too," Jonathon said. "The Rod of Coercion it is. A good name."

Jonathon was about to comment on its beauty when a knock at the door made them turn together. "The Dragonlord's messenger," Jonathon said, gripping Bob's shoulder so hard the boy winced. Bob ran to the door and opened it.

There, instead of the Dragonlord's messenger, stood Rhazburn, panting, his woolen shirt torn, the knees of his trousers worn through. Deep gouges scored his neck, his chin, and his left ear. When he collapsed in exhaustion, Bob was barely able to hold him up. Jonathon rushed to Rhazburn's side and helped Bob half-drag Rhazburn to the soft chair. He said, "My son, you are alive. I thank The Three!", and he clasp his son's hand warmly reassuring himself Rhazburn was really there.

The Poet was panting. "Am I too late? Has the messenger come?"

"No, my son. We have just finished. See, the Rod of Coercion is complete. And still here."

Rhazburn gazed upon his father's, Hili's and Bob's masterpiece. His eyes widened. He stood up, suddenly reinvigorated, and strode to the Unicorn Horn. He picked it up, tenderly, and let out a gasp. "You did it!" There was a pause. "Oh this frightens me... more than all I've been through." Rhazburn corrected himself. "All *we've* been through."

He gave his father with a wry smile. "Rod of Coercion?"

His father shrugged.

"I like it. The name. Well, and the marvelous thing itself. Amazing. I didn't really think there would be time. You do amaze me, Father. The perfection of it." He held it so the light glinted from the jewels as he slowly turned it, reading every verse on every stone.

"Bob helped."

Rhazburn winked at Bob, making the boy beam with pride.

"Have you tested it?"

"No. We just finished it."

"Good. I'm glad you have not tried it before I arrived. Believe me, I had a lot of doubts I'd even be here." Rhazburn's eyes returned momentarily to the exhaustion they held when he entered, and Jonathon moved closer to him. Rhazburn gazed again at the Unicorn Horn and collected himself. "I'm glad I got here before the messenger. When the messenger comes, I will look into his eyes and know the truth of his claims before we follow him with the scepter. I'll give it to no one but the Dragonlord himself. Once we give Seldric the scepter, let the traitors revolt. He will quench any revolution. I do have my doubts he is worthy of this power. But then, the alternative could be much worse, knowing what I do of many of the tainted souls in his court. I could imagine any of them, or all of them together if they could stop squabbling among themselves, festering a plot for their own pathetic power. None of them, I am sure, are as qualified or as capable as Seldric is to control five score dragons."

"But Rhazburn," his father broke into his lecture, lifting a torn flap of the Poet's shirt to look at his bruised arm, "are you all right? What evil you must have endured there in Devil's Fang! The horn came to us with the hand of a dead man holding onto it. You must have wrested it from the Demon itself."

"Not quite, but nearly. I'll tell you the tale while we await our deaf acquaintance." He did not try to hide his dubiousness at the deafness of the messenger.

Without being asked, Bob made tea and came back with a cup for Rhazburn. The boy offered it to him with a plate of bread and cheese.

Just a thank you from Rhazburn lit up Bob's face anew. They all settled down while Rhazburn told them the entire tale of his adventures in the Dead Lands. He finally came to the point at which the carpet flew away to Isseltrent, leaving him alone with the Zombie and his monsters.

"You should be dead, Rhazburn. I truly feared you were. How did you escape?" Jonathon asked.

"I came very close to death there. The Zombie's chamber was a black hole of despondency. Even a league from that dread hole, I nearly died of the despair alone. In some ways, I feel I did die there and have come back from Hell." He stared into his tea for a while, thinking of Dollop again. "No forget that. No one can get out of Hell."

The others said nothing. Rhazburn shook his head and blew through his teeth. That was another problem yet to solve. "Thank The Three we don't have to go into the Demon's Hellpit. After being probably twenty leagues from it, I am convinced that no living being could travel to the Demon's Hellpit and survive."

Rhazburn finally shrugged. "I used the only tool available to me. The Cloak of Invisibility I had made. I didn't know what force animated the skeletons or whether they could see past the disguise of the cloak, but I had no other way out. I was too weary to fight without the Unicorn Horn in my hand, and not just from physical fatigue, the oppressive atmosphere of the Dead Lands was far worse. Even though I suspected Screela would betray me, I hoped to win her over from her perversions. When she ran to the Zombie and groveled before him, I saw the worst aspect of mankind.

"The cloak was on the floor. I could spot it easily because a hole was in the floor where none should have been. The skeletons had me surrounded, but I dove and rolled to the cloak, covering myself and getting up as fast as I could.

"I was in luck. I knew from their movements that I was hidden. The Zombie and all his creatures looked around, confused. Screela shouted, 'The cloak! He wears the cloak! Don't let him slip away. He is merely invisible. He can still be killed!'

"They all gathered with the Zombie and Screela at the exit to the chambers of the Laughing Skull Clan. I knew if I tried to break through them, I would be discovered and killed, so I took the route they did not expect, through the other exit I could see. Beyond the pile of treasure was a tunnel which I thought led straight into the Dead Lands.

"Unfortunately, as I escaped, I disturbed some of the treasure on the floor. Screela pointed straight at me and shouted, 'There he is!' The Zombie ordered the skeletons after me. I slipped and stumbled over the mound, sliding across layers of precious plates and coins. The skeletons followed me. Luckily, they were ungainly and slow enough that I could avoid them if I kept my wits about me. Still, they were frenzied, whipped by the Zombie, and they nearly caught my cloak and unveiled me with swipes of their claws. Once I made it through the archway and out of the Zombie's throne room, I flattened myself against the wall. The skeletons rattled past me down the tunnel, chasing nothing. I stayed there because I didn't want to leave Screela without one more attempt to save her.

"It was a foolhardy gesture. I quietly crept back into the Zombie's chamber. Screela was still there, kneeling before the moving corpse. Her hands were clasped, and she pleaded with him. 'Master, I long to serve you for all eternity. Take me into your flock, I beg you.' The Zombie seemed to grow stronger before her, a devouring evil looming over her.

"Before I could rescue her, she shouted, 'Do it now, Master. Take me!' She threw back her head and arms. Fast as a striking viper, the Zombie pounced, clutching her offered neck in his sepulchral hands. She choked out a final cry as he strangled her and gnawed her neck with his sulfurous teeth. I could stand no more of the despair I felt watching that spectacle. I fled.

"The image of her pleading to be killed further leeched my strength, and the evil atmosphere intensified the effect. I was still in the black cavern, but it was leading me farther into the Dead Lands. I seemed to be in darkness for days, though I'm sure it was only a few Blessings. Horrors passed by me and seemed to pass through me as if hopeless wraiths, whipped by fear, entered my mind looking for solace. I could offer none, and they floated away in misery.

"At long last, I came upon light, the tunnel exit to the plains of the Dead Lands. At that opening, all the skeletal monsters watched motionless, as if they could guard the caverns of Devil's Fang for a century without bending a bony joint. I made sure the Cloak of Invisibility continued to hide me by using one of the Commands I had slipped in my pocket. To avoid the dead things, I climbed to a high ledge and crawled out over their heads. They never twitched. I'll bet they'll be laying in wait there, like that, for years.

"In daylight, under the hot sun, without shade or water, I skirted the base of Devil's Fang. I was near exhaustion, but I refused to stop until I broke out of that dismal air. Finally, I came upon the merest sprig of a desert plant. It was the first sign I was free of the Dead Lands and the horrible depression and despair I had felt faded as well, quickly thereafter.

"I still had to hide from the Dragonflyers patrolling the border of the Dead Lands, so I left the Cloak around me for a while. When I was well within the living desert, I buried the Cloak of Invisibility deep within a stand of scrub where no one will ever find it. I didn't dare bring it back with me, but I couldn't bear to destroy it since it had saved my life. It took me a whole day to walk back to the Black Dragon. I used one more Glass Command, one of the ones I stole from the Zombie's hoard, to get back to Isseltrent. Then I ran to your shop so I could be here when the hooded man returned." Rhazburn gazed at Jonathon with concern. "I don't want you to face him alone, Father."

His father slapped his head. "The messenger. He will be here any moment. I don't even know if it will work."

Rhazburn knew he had to stay to unmask the mysterious messenger before he took the Unicorn Horn scepter. Only afterwards could he go look for Trallalair to attempt to save Jiminic from execution. A whole day had been wasted finding his way back from the dead lands. He would barely have time. Rhazburn mastered his trepidation and said as calmly as he could, "Did you follow my prescription?"

"To the letter."

"If you made it as I envisioned it, the scepter will achieve the desired effect."

"We must test it before he gets here."

Rhazburn gave his father an enigmatic smirk, handing him the Rod of Coercion.

"Go ahead. Try it out. A Suggestion will bring about an effect for just an instant. A Request is good for about two Favors. A Copper Order will last a whole Blessing, and a Glass Command should extend the effect to an entire day."

"The power of forcing someone to abide by my will frightens me. What if I accidentally tell someone to do something and he hurts himself?"

"The scepter cannot cause anyone to do anything directly harmful to himself. For instance, if you say to someone, 'Kill yourself,' he will not obey. But, to tell you the truth, I do not know myself what other bounds are on its power. If you were to say to someone, 'Walk twenty paces north,' and there was a cliff at ten paces, he might just walk over the edge."

Jonathon said, "Horrible. Pity we have no one here to test it on."

Bob stepped up. "Test the rod on me, Master. I am not afraid."

Jonathon looked at his son, who nodded. The jeweler took out a wooden request and slipped it into the platinum slot beneath the amethyst at the top of the scepter. He held the Unicorn Horn in the air, and after a short hesitation, said, "Bob, sleep."

Still standing, the boy squinted his eyes shut and clenched his fists. Jonathon looked at the Poet, who wore an enigmatic smile. Bob stayed awake. In his son's expression, Jonathon saw a hint of what was wrong. He had not thought or said the poem that Rhazburn insisted must be used by the Dragonlord for the full effect. Jonathon gave him a knowing smile and nod and said aloud:

> Through ears, hearts, minds I call
> Obey my will, one and all.

Then, with a grandiose wave of the Rod of coercion, he said, "Sleep, Bob."

The boy remained standing. "Bob?"

"I feel a little sleepy, Master. I think I will fall asleep soon." He shut his eyes even tighter.

Incredulous that the scepter should not work after Rhazburn had composed the verses for it, Jonathon spun around crying, "Rhazburn, the Rod of Coercion is useless! It does nothing!"

"No, Father, the rod works as it should."

Bob opened his eyes. "I did feel a little sleepy, Master."

"It did not work!" Jonathon was livid, shaking the scepter at his son.

"The scepter is not intended to work in your hands, Father. No human being will ever use it but the Dragonlord. I made sure of that. I wasn't about to make such a power for any purpose but the one I intended for it. Only one possessing extraordinary mental powers may wield this tool. The Dragoncrown itself will allow the Dragonlord to utilize the Rod of Coercion. For all other men, the rod will be nothing more than a beautiful club. This I promise."

Jonathon was perplexed. "Then, why the poem? If no one but the Dragonlord will ever be able to use the rod, why make a poem that must be thought to make it function?"

"Another safeguard. I'm taking no chances. Besides, only the Dragonlord will touch this rod after it leaves our hands. I'll not give it to that messenger, even if he is authentic. Which I doubt. He's probably not even a Beholder. We'll see what happens when we ask him to accompany us to the Dragonlord's castle."

As if in answer to his statement, they heard a heavy-handed and insistent thumping at the door. Bob started toward the door but Rhazburn grabbed his arm, stopping him. "Bob, we don't need your assistance."

Rhazburn glanced to Jonathon, who understood his thought. The Poet did not want to expose the boy to any altercation that might occur if the messenger was not what he professed to be.

Jonathon patted the boy on his back. "Go on, Bob. Leave by the back. Go home. Enjoy the festival tomorrow. And if I find you came here to clean up on your day off, you'll get two more days off as punishment."

Bob looked disappointed that he could not be a part of his master's triumph, especially after the boy had worked so hard at the Master Jeweler's side to complete the Rod of Coercion. Still, Jonathon didn't want to dash the boy's spirit. "You did an excellent job, Bob. After tomorrow, I plan to put my shop back together. I may need a junior partner sooner than I had expected." Bob brightened up considerably.

"We'll see you at the festival, Bob. Save us a good seat in the courtyard for the Egg Cracking." Bob ran off through the back door so as not to interfere any longer with their dealing with the Dragonlord's messenger.

After a second, louder knock, Jonathon set the Rod of Coercion back down on the velvet pillow and went to answer the door.

Rhazburn picked the Unicorn Horn up off the pillow and followed him. Rhazburn wanted to be in control of the Rod of Coercion. When the door was opened by Jonathon, the hooded figure stood before them, as dark and secretive as before. The twilight shadows, quivering with the candlelight that flickered, only added to the obscurity of their guest.

Jonathon shuddered, involuntarily chilled by something other than the balmy air of the evening. Jonathon sensed something he had missed when the Dragonlord's messenger had first appeared. A coldness that hung about him that seemed nourished by the encroaching darkness. Jonathon was also newly aware of a stink that clung to the messenger's robes. It was a stench far different from that of dirt and sweat. A certain reek was expected from a beholder. Beholders thought bathing beneath them. They were meant for greater things, spending all their lives observing the beauty of the world, savoring it but not really participating. But this smell was something beyond that. It was more like the robes were hand-me-downs from someone who had died of some nauseating plague. He almost held his nose as he showed the messenger to the soft chair, then pulled up a small round table and two hard-backed oak chairs. They would have to write their conversations with the messenger since he could not hear them.

Rhazburn came forward as Jonathon was about to sit. "Father, take the rod and do not under any circumstances give it to this man." Rhazburn wanted the Rod of Coercion away from the messenger's grasping fingers just in case he grabbed for it. And Rhazburn needed both hands free for what he was about to do.

Obedient to his son's command, Jonathon took the rod.

Rhazburn watched the figure for any signs of recognition but saw none. Something was wrong. Rhazburn felt strangely apprehensive. The man in the robes was slight as before, but his gait was different. Before, the small but able figure had walked well. This time, the figure seemed to have shrunken slightly, and he walked with a shuffling limp. Rhazburn doubted the messenger was even the same person. The most disturbing thing was his reek of death. After his recent sojourn in the Dead Lands, he was very familiar with the smell of death. Rhazburn was not going to let him near the Rod of Coercion.

He spoke outright to the man. "Messenger, we refuse to deal further with you until you show yourself and tell us your name. You disguise yourself as a Beholder, but you are not one of them. Of that I am sure. This charade has gone far enough. You cannot take this rod, and it would do you no good. Only the Dragonlord can use it." Rhazburn was fully confident the Rod of Coercion would be safely inert in any other hands.

Nauseated at the smell that came from the messenger and anxious to be done with the proceedings, Jonathon said quietly, out of the corner of his mouth, "Rhazburn, the messenger is deaf. Stop plaguing him with these accusations."

Rhazburn answered aloud, "He is not deaf but plays us for bumpkins. He will find out I am not deceived by his impersonation. Now he will be brought to justice." Quickly, he stepped to the messenger, and with a flick of his wrist, he threw back the man's hood.

When he saw the face under the hood, Rhazburn's heart pumped fear through his body instead of blood. The face was that of a corpse. Translucent, waxy skin puckered around orbless eye sockets and a tongueless mouth. Rhazburn knew this was no mere Zombie like the one that nearly killed him a few days before. He knew no Zombie could walk so far from the Dead Lands with the animating force of the Demon. The horror facing them could be none other than Sverdphthik, the Demon itself. How could Rhazburn have been so foolish? The robes. The trumped up story of being a deaf mute and working surreptitiously for Seldric. The limp. And the smell.

It was as clear as the scream from a Poet killed at Hell's Breach. No *man* but the Dragonlord could use the Rod of Coercion that Rhazburn had so cleverly conceived, but the Demon was another matter. Its ability to control the mind would easily allow it access to the rod's dreadful power. Rhazburn had, unwittingly, egotistically, egregiously provided that power for the Demon.

Rhazburn had to stop the Demon before it went any further. He lunged at it, pinning the dead limbs against the arms of the chair. He needed a poem to paralyze the Demon. If he could hold it long enough for Jonathon to find some gem dust, they may have a chance. "Father, it is the Demon. Quick! Get pearl dust and a Copper Order," he shouted, gripping as hard as he could, waiting for the Demon-controlled Zombie to struggle free. He never imagined he would be fighting Zombies again so soon after his fateful trip to the Ghoul's den.

"I'll tell you the words to trace." The Zombie did not move. Neither did Jonathon. Still pinning the Zombie's arms to the chair, Rhazburn craned his head around.

Rhazburn had moved too fast for Jonathon to react. When the Poet pulled back the hood of the messenger and pinned him to the chair, Jonathon could not believe what he saw. Instead of a filthy but human Beholder, he saw a man long dead who had walked into his shop and had been dealing with them all. When Rhazburn declared the man to be the Demon, the very one that had been the Scourge of Verdilon and the embodiment of all that was evil in the world, Jonathon could not move. He was glued to the floor by his terror, as surely as if Molgannard Fey stood on his feet. He could not even use the Rod of Coercion in his hand. He could only stand there dumbly, wanting to run far away but loathe to abandon his son.

Paralysis turned to disaster. The smell of the Zombie alone choked Jonathon nearly to death. Laughter came at him from all sides, a harsh, strident laughter that seemed to drain him of any courage he had left. His fear was so great he fled deep within himself to huddle in a distant corner of his mind, leaving his physical body standing still. In fact, he barely perceived that his body was moving without his volition. His own spirit had not precisely fled. It had been pushed or rather slapped aside by some incomparable evil present within himself. This thing was all of knives and needles too harmful to touch, full of unnatural utterances too horrible to speak and steeped in feelings of sadistic pleasure at others' distress which were too cruel to imagine. From a tiny recess tucked away in the last refuge in Jonathon's mind and soul, command of his own limbs was relinquished to the ravening Demon that had invaded his body.

Too late, Rhazburn realized the Demon's foul spirit had transferred itself to possess Jonathon as quick as a thought. The dead limbs he held fast to the arms of the chair were no more dangerous than the chair itself. Jonathon had been transformed into his enemy. Rhazburn saw his gentle father with an abhorrent look of hate on his face. Jonathon held the scepter high above him, ready to pound it down upon Rhazburn's head. Rhazburn could not both dodge and hold the Demon tight at the same time. When he saw the Unicorn Horn racing to strike his temple, he only had time enough to turn his head so the it would hit him on his tougher forehead right between his eyes. Everything seemed to slow down as he tried to raise his arms from the chair to fend off the blow. It was as if he was in a dream in which he tried to run but was incapable of mounting any speed. Rhazburn's arms crept upward while the Rod of Coercion, spurred by the Demon's vicious will, flew at him with the speed of lightning. The Rod of Coercion had been his triumph. Now it was his failure and death. It was, in fact, the instrument of the death foretold by his ill-advised gaze into his future in Augury Hall. It was his failure to his father, betrayed by his incompetence. It was his failure to the Dragonlord, who would surely lose the Dragoncrown to the Demon. His failure to Jiminic, doomed to die, and his failure to Trallalair, whom he loved but whom he had cursed by his actions. Rhazburn had failed all of Isseltrent. After one bright flash and a crack of thunder within his skull, only darkness followed.

Jonathon had watched, helpless, as his own hand lifted the Unicorn Horn and slammed it into Rhazburn's skull. Rhazburn gasped and fell, blood puddling around his head. Jonathon knew he was dead. He knew he had killed his son. In grief and panic, he fled deeper into his mind.

That was when the real nightmare began for Jonathon. The raving, grotesque beast within him clawed at his soul. Talons of remorse and dismay slashed and rifled his thoughts until the beast found what it was after, the poem needed to activate the Rod of Coercion. It plucked the memory like a ripe apple from Jonathon's brain, then left him unable to feel his own limbs and afraid to think.

When Jonathon crept back into the reality of his own bones, he saw his hand extended to the foul creature before him, offering it the rod. Before Jonathon could think to close his fist on the rod, it was gone. The Zombie held it.

Jonathon shuddered at all he had witnessed and felt. He looked at Rhazburn's still, pathetic body. "Rhazburn!"

Hearing the end of Rhazburn's verse for the Rod of Coercion brought Jonathon's gaze back to the dead thing. As he heard the Zombie's hollow voice finishing, "Obey my will, one and all," Jonathon noticed its gloved hand, obviously twisted with rigor mortis, withdrawing after tucking a Glass Command beneath the amethyst in the scepter. As the Glass Command disappeared, Jonathon remembered Rhazburn saying that no human in the world but the Dragonlord could use the Rod of Coercion. But Rhazburn never imagined the Demon would hold it in its claws.

The Demon said, "Remain still and speak not."

Jonathon was turned into a statue of flesh by the spell. The Demon's shrill laugh was the last thing Jonathon heard as his vision dimmed. Why had he ever doubted the rod would work? Rhazburn knew his craft. Jonathon's last thought were Rhazburn's words, "a Glass Command will extend the effect to an entire day." Even as his consciousness left him, the Demon controlled every muscle in Jonathon's body. The Demon had commanded him to remain still. He fainted standing up.

BOOK II
THE KNIFE OF LIFE

CHAPTER 13

THE DRAGONEGG FESTIVAL

Trallalair slid her sword from its sheath so slowly that no sound was made. Male Knights named their swords and spoke of them as if they were trusted friends. But a Sinjery warmaiden would no more name her sword than she would name her own hand. When she wore the sword, it was part of her flesh.

As she bent to place her sword at the feet of Jiminic, Trallalair looked up at the older Sinjery's face. It was as calm and obscure as the dark water beneath the roots of a tupelo in the Sinjery Swamp. Trallalair smelled no fear, nor did she hear any sighs from the woman. She placed her Sinjery Sword on the ground with its hilt next to and pointing toward Jiminic. It completed the Honor Ring of Swords, one hundred thirty-four swords in a ring, all the hilts pointing toward Jiminic. The Honor Ring of Swords was comprised of all one hundred twenty-one Sinjery Swords of Thunder Ring with the thirteen swords of its attached Brand, Thunder Brand. All the Sinjery of the Ring knew Jiminic. She had been a Ringmistress in Thunder Ring many years before. She lived in a different village in Sinjer than did Trallalair and Saggethrie, but since she had returned from the Sinjery's self-imposed exile after these many years, her Ring of old had the honor to send her to the Sky Forests. Many of them, including Trallalair, had never met Jiminic, but all Sinjery were Sisters.

Jiminic was dressed in a white surcoat reaching her knees, white stockings, and no boots. White clothes to clearly reveal the slashes.

Like all the other Sinjery Guards, after placing her sword lovingly at the feet of her Sister, Trallalair said what she felt. They were the last words she could ever say to her Sister. "You honor us, Sister. You will join all the Sisters who have gone before you. May you find your son in the Sky Forests." She stepped half-way around Jiminic and turned to walk back to the encircling Sinjery who stood facing Jiminic at fifty paces. Just as her back was turned, she felt as if Jiminic had turned her head to speak in her direction. Trallalair heard Jiminic's last request.

"Trallalair, let none of the Sinjery forget Rhazburn and Jonathon Forthright."

Trallalair stopped. She wanted to ask why but thought it rude to question the last request of her Sister. She turned her head slightly so Jiminic could see her gesture, nodded gravely, and walked to the Sinjery Ring. Rhazburn, the Loremaster, what had he done? He was kind and intelligent, unusual for a man. Whatever Jiminic referred to, likely it was something brave and altruistic. Trallalair knew she never would forget Rhazburn. No one else had ever offered to help the Sinjery out of their plight. Who was Jonathon Forthright? Not a courtier that she recalled.

Jiminic waited until the ring was complete. Then she took a deep breath, raised her arms and, smiling with her eyes closed in ecstasy, shouted, "Sinjer!" A moment later every voice in Thunder Ring echoed, "Sinjer!" At that shout, all the swords called by their mistresses flew to their hands, every sword passing through the flesh of Jiminic.

Her spirit was freed to fly to the Sky Forests, and her flesh, reduced by Dragonfire to ashes, was sent to be spilled into the waters of the Sinjery Swamp. The Ring spoke together of her bravery and none cried.

Skyweaving is what the Sinjery called it, but it was more like dancing, Dragon dancing. Dragons did the dancing ridden by the Sinjery high in the sky. They circled and swooped, rising and careening, passing each other by as little as Trallalair's standing height. Sinjery Dragonflyers tossed huge, fluttering banners to one another through the air as they passed. The Dragon dance was all the more difficult since it was black of night and overcast with no moon. Dragonfire in bursts lit the sky for instants at a time, showing the positions of the thirteen Sinjery Dragons, briefly. On the ground, people saw brilliant flames lighting Dragons first here, then there, magnificent wings spread, weaving complicated patterns just beneath the clouds. The clouds reflected the flames like heat lightning. The thunder of the bursting flames just reached the ground and the astonished crowds.

From Atherraine on her dragon Breeze, a furlong ahead of and a dozen rods above Trallalair, an oak-emblazoned banner fell. Slowed by the air currents, the banner, which was as big as a blanket, wafted back and forth as its spear staff dragged it downward.

Trallalair squeezed her thighs tight against Hover's neck, signaling her to accelerate. As she squeezed harder and harder, the Dragon's wings pumped faster and faster. Reports like deep drumbeats came with each wing beat as the loose leathery skin ballooned taut, trapping cartloads of air to keep the Dragon and Trallalair aloft. Hover accelerated, while the falling flag, caught by an updraft, slowed slightly. It was slightly too high for Trallalair to grab as she passed.

As the banner disappeared again in the gloom between Dragonflames, Trallalair released her thighs and grabbed the top of the spine on Hover's neck in front of her. Then she bent her knees and pushed her feet into Hover's shoulders, crouching slightly. After a few beats of Hover's wings, with a sudden whoop, Trallalair stood up, balancing on the flying Dragon's shoulders, leaning forward, her toes in her leather boots gripping Hover's scales so she stayed in place despite the gale from Hover's rapid soaring. If she fell forward or backward she would be impaled on the Dragon's rapier sharp spines. She had to balance precisely.

From the Dragon's shoulders, Trallalair leaped straight up, caught the banner, and summersaulted to land, balancing again on Hover's shoulders for an instant before sliding deftly to straddle the neck between the spines.

The occasion was the Dragonegg festival. All Isseltrent was there. Puppetmasters on temporary stages made children squeal with laughter. Sweaty men shouted rude remarks at gyrating Choralists. The smells of hot savory dishes and sweet spicy rolls from rows of open Keepers made the mouths of passersby water until they dug into their pouches for coins to purchase their stomachs' desires. One Green Dragon in a corner, coached by his Dragonflyer Knight, exhaled bursts of flame at the back end of a huge brick oven, while cooks with long handles pulled out simmering steaks and roasting legs of lamb they sniffed and poked, flipping some onto huge trays and shoving others back in to be broiled longer.

Some Choralists atop table-sized drums danced to their own music, tapping it out rhythmically with their feet on the tight drum skins. Their bouncing breasts entranced scores of men who jostled and fought each other to be first in line when the Choralists finished. Other Choralists slithered through the crowds, luring men and women into an orgy of uninhibited dance. The rapt and envious crowds watched every move. Clouds of Pixets and Pixelles, Hili among them, wove their own patterns in the air, flying in dances even more complicated than the Dragons high above or the revelers below. Lining the walls, a grim row of Beholders only watched and listened. They were saving their participation in any hedonistic frenzy for the Afterlife. In groups of seventeen-man Blades, Knights stood watching for trouble. Trallalair had alerted them to her suspicion so they were alert for any intruder that could be linked to the Demon. Two Sinjery Rings were present, clustered like the Knights in small groups. Almost all the Brandmistresses were there, since their Dragons were performing. Far below her, Trallalair saw a knot of green-clad Sinjery wave her way. She waved back, trying to pick out Saggethrie from the group who were, most likely, her own Sisters in Thunder Brand. From that distance, she could only recognize the green surcoat, breeches and mantle uniform of the Brands. Like the other Brands, only the Dragonflyers like Trallalair were armed. The Scalers were not. Although they owned Sinjery Swords and bows and kept them in their barracks, they seldom had need to use them. Their duties were to care for Hover, not to fight. Trallalair imagined one of them beamed a bigger smile at her and hoped it was her lover Saggethrie. She would have preferred sharing the night with her to celebrate the Dragonegg Cracking, rather than make Hover perform like a trained dog for the inane festivities. But she had no choice. Seldric had commanded all thirteen Sinjery Dragons to participate in the Skyweaving that night.

After Trallalair caught the flag, she flew Hover back to the palace wall where the other Dragons were already stationed. The other Sinjery flyers had landed their mounts on separate walls and towers so as not to concentrate too much weight on any one wall. Trallalair was part of the entertainment, but like her sister Dragonflyers and the Inner Ring, she was also guarding the Dragonlord against danger.

The Dragonegg Festival had been allowed to proceed like every year. Trallalair had advised Seldric to postpone it until the Demon was found, but he said there was no need. He believed that Trallalair had destroyed the Demon when the Sinjery destroyed the flock of dead geese. He said that the Zombie birds were only a feint to test the strength of his forces, and thanks to Trallalair, the feint had been repelled. He said he had seen it all through the eyes of the Dragons involved in the fray. He said he knew for a fact that the Demon still squatted in his Hellpit. After all, he saw through the eyes of the Dragons guarding the Dead Lands that the movement of the Zombies within the Demon's domain continued unabated. This, he said, in itself proved the Demon still sat in his stronghold. Though several Seers had told him the Spirits were restless, terrified of something hideous, he discounted even their advice. Lastly, he was convinced by the Chamberlain that the city had been scoured and no trace of the Demon found. Seldric claimed there was nothing to fear.

Trallalair had none of his confidence. She had been there and had seen all the confusion with the Zombie birds. She still had a deep sense that one of the Demon's minions or the Demon himself prowled the city. She had advised the Inner Ring, the other Ringmistresses and the Lances to be alert. Despite all her fears and protests, the Dragonegg Festival proceeded as usual. To her relief and astonishment, none of the omens had materialized after all. Nothing untoward had occurred, and the forces of the Demon were not heard of again.

The courtyard of the palace was filled with revelers, Guards and Knights. At the end, just in front of the main tower, Cataclysm, a gigantic Red Dragon, Seldric's personal Dragon, sat on its haunches with broad, outstretched wings extending nearly to the courtyard walls. Cradled in one forefoot, he held a dozen of the court children high above the mass of people.

Beneath the Red's smoldering head with its feral eyes, the Dragonlord sat on his throne. Cithoney, his Queen, sat beside him. She was dressed in a long blue gown, decked with necklaces and studded with gems that sparkled with each burst of Dragonfire. A red-gold circlet, holding her hair tight, was in the shape of a sinuous Red with glowing eyes. It was her protection in the eyes of all mortals.

Besides the Dragoncrown, Seldric wore a bright white surcoat, and around his neck, a long shimmering blue cape of Dragon skin. The skin had been thinned and softened and was covered with a verse of power, the purpose of which only the Dragonlord knew. The golden talons of a Red Dragon clasped the cape at his neck. One side was fashioned into a Dragon's head, its jaws wide, while the other side was the shape of the world. When clasped, the jaws engulfed the world, just as Seldric's control engulfed much of the known world. Trallalair wryly thought that, for Seldric, the whole world would have been preferable. But the range of the Dragoncrown only encompassed Thuringland and the Tributary States.

Thanks to Trallalair's suggestion, the Inner Ring of crimson-caparisoned Sinjery shielded Seldric and Cataclysm. With their bows in hand, they formed a picket line in a half-circle thirty paces away from the Royal Family and their protective Red Dragon. No one was allowed alive within their guard unless the Dragonlord commanded it. A mere four strides separated one Sinjery warmaiden from the other. They could raise their Sinjery Swords and touch the tips together in the space between. The area they guarded was much greater, however, since the Sinjery never missed a target within range of their bows. The Dragonlord was also protected by the Knight Blades in the crowds, the Dragons of the Sinjery Brands which were perched on the walls of Blaze, and the watchful presence of Cataclysm, the most powerful Dragon of all. Nothing in the entire city could harm Seldric.

The Dragonlord looked up at the Red Dragon behind him. With a casual motion of his hand, he silently bade the Red to lower the royal children to the ground just inside the Sinjery Ring.

"Let the children come to me," Seldric commanded. His children, and these were, of course, the legitimate ones, piled onto him, laughing. He kissed and hugged the girls and patted the boys on the back or roughly tousled their hair. Cithoney smiled and clapped her hands, accepting the attention of the children when the Dragonlord had finished.

Within the Ring of Sinjery in front of the throne was a pit of sand. In the center of the pit rested a golden Dragonegg, two strides long. It was the focal point of the festivities. At midnight, the Dragonlord would command the Dragon within to break free. No one but the Dragonlord knew what type of Dragon would emerge: a Green, the best of flyers, a White, with breath of ice, a wingless Blue with paddles for feet and a tail like a fish, a Red with the fire of Hell in his belly, or the largest, a Black possessing unfathomable, arcane powers. At Midnight, many a wager would be lost on the identity of the Dragon.

Trallalair watched intently as the crowd hushed and opened a path for a lone-robed figure, one of the Beholders, oddly walking into the midst of the proceedings toward Seldric. Stranger still, the Beholder carried a gleaming white staff, the details of which which Trallalair at her distance could not make out. Beholders never wore jewelry or carried possessions. Perhaps it was a gift the Beholder would present to the Dragonlord.

No one ever expected a Beholder to speak, much less scream. But this one raised the staff and screamed so loudly that the dancers slowed. The singers hesitated in the middle of their songs. All the revelers sober enough to take notice turned toward him. "Through ears, hearts, minds I call, obey my will, one and all! No one touch me, injure me or stop me! Seldric, stay where you are."

Trallalair could hear his words much more clearly than she should have, but the acoustics of the courtyard had played tricks on her before. The words meant nothing to her, but she knew they meant danger for the Dragonlord. Loyal to her duty, she sat up to spur Hover to attack him. To her bewilderment, her limbs would not move. She could not speak. Hover stayed still as the cloaked figure advanced on the Dragonlord. Her Sisters on their Dragons all startled, but like reflections of her, none made a move. Like crimson statues, the Inner Ring of Sinjery Guard stood still, barely moving to regard the figure. He walked straight through the cordoned area and walked confidently up to the Dragonlord. More than a score of Sinjery arrows should have skewered him, but the Inner Ring stood like mannequins.

Seldric shouted at his children to run to the palace with the queen. Cithoney scurried with the children under the Red Dragon's wing and through an oak door into the main tower of the palace.

With a slow agonizing movement, Seldric grasped his jeweled sword as the figure advanced. Like everyone else, he could not even draw his sword.

Trallalair wondered why he failed to have his Red burn the cloaked man. Obedient, patient, oblivious, the Red sat unmoving.

A few strides from the Dragonlord, the figure flipped back his black hood and revealed a cadaverous rotting face. The face was so misshapen, Trallalair could see the deformity from her post sitting on Hover's neck atop the palace wall. This was no Beholder, as everyone at the celebration had apparently believed. She knew without a doubt, that the being possessing this pitiful man's dead, corrupted body was the foul Demon, Sverdphthik and he was there because she had failed.

Even in the face of the worst threat to the Dragonlord and the Realm she could imagine, Trallalair was virtually paralyzed from acting. She could move on Hover's neck, use her limbs, turn and breathe, but when she had the slightest thought of intervening in the spectacle below, her arms refused to do her bidding and her voice was cut off. She could not call out to Hover to attack the Demon or even to shout stop.

Obedient to their last command, all the Dragons, including the Dragonlord's huge Red, remained passive at their posts. Apparently the spell was so strong that the Dragonlord himself was unable to muster up the thought of a command for Cataclysm to incinerate the Demon. The magic stopped anyone from touching the Demon, but it did not stop people from screaming in terror or scrambling away. The crowd turned into a foaming sea roiling through colonnades, leaving in its wake bloody residues and a twitching, twisted flotsam of bodies.

The Dragonlord stood transfixed as the Demon walked toward him, made another gesture with the staff he held, then roughly yanked the Dragoncrown from the Dragonlord's head. He smiled as he fixed it to his own head. No one could remove the Dragoncrown from the bearer's head without the bearer agreeing to release it. Even that small resistance was impossible for the Dragonlord.

Holding the staff high, the Demon screamed, "Jonathon Forthright and Rhazburn made this rod with which I command all!" With cackling laughter, he swung the rod with a backhand slash across Seldric's face. Seldric was knocked to the ground to lie in a pool of blood. Then Cataclysm bent his neck, allowing the Demon to climb up as if he were a Dragonflyer.

Trallalair could not believe what she heard. Jonathon Forthright and Rhazburn, as Jiminic had warned her with her last breath, were not to be remembered because they had done good but because they had aided the Demon. They were the traitors that had brought the Demon to the city and given him that power. What had stopped Jiminic from telling them the whole tale? Perhaps she had had no proof but had seen something through the Wishing Drop that the two men needed watching. Trallalair had misconstrued her words, allowing them to complete their plans and produce whatever magical tool the Demon now had in his hand. Trallalair knew, if she lived, she would not rest until she found them both and saw them die. She had misjudged Rhazburn. He seemed so kind and generous when he spoke to her, noble beyond the bounds of heredity or station. She had certainly been fooled. Never again would she trust a man.

Trallalair could do nothing to help the Dragonlord. She also realized that with the Dragoncrown on the Demon's head, Hover herself was in the Demon's control. She leaped from Hover's neck, hitting the ground running, heading for the nearest merlon where she dove behind it, crouching down. She just had time to spy the other Sinjery flyers doing the same along the wall and towers when the flame from Hover hit the merlon. Only her left foot was exposed to the flame. Her boot caught on fire instantly, giving her unbearable pain until she could rip the boot off.

All the Dragons gained the air. Even Cataclysm whipped the courtyard with his wing beats as he lifted off, now bearing the Demon who wore the Dragoncrown and still held that hideous staff. Trallalair watched as the Red, ridden by the Demon, inhaled to bathe the Dragonlord in flame. At the last moment, one of the Sinjery Guards ran to Seldric's prone figure and, ripping the cloak from around his neck, threw it over him. She whirled and raised her shield just as half of the Sinjery Inner Ring gathered to form a wall of bodies in front of the prostrate Dragonlord. They held their shields in a useless but courageous barrier high above their heads. The flames covered them. Without uttering a cry, all the crimson-armored Sinjery died, immolated by the curling flames of the Red's breath.

Leaving only a withering pyre where Seldric and his Guard had stood, the Demon released a shriek that pierced Trallalair's soul. On the Dragonlord's Red, he rose into the air where thirty other Dragons awaited, hovering with slow, heavy wing beats.

Without bothering to personally attack the courtyard again, the Demon flew the Dragonlord's Red to the East in the direction of the Dead

Lands. Only his laugh lingered as the other Dragons began to destroy Isseltrent. Trallalair realized that they had a new Dragonlord, Sverdphthik the Demon. Every Dragonlord was a curse for Sinjer, but the Demon was a curse on the entire world. Nothing would survive.

Trallalair took the respite provided by Hover's rendezvous with the other Dragons to sprint as best she could, hobbled by a seared and blistered foot, to the closest tower portal. At each agonizing step, she bit back cries as her burnt foot hit the flagstones of the walkway. Before her, pirouetting around the corner and disappearing down the spiral stair in the tower, Dirmissilig, the eldest Brandmistress, raced to the courtyard. The other Sisters were faster than Trallalair, appearing below in the courtyard before Trallalair even entered the tower. Luckily, none of them had been injured as she had been. She stopped to catch her stuttering breath just outside the tower portal and surveyed the scene in the courtyard below.

Already, two full Rings of Sinjery Guards had assembled from the throng and were arrayed in killing arcs, bows taut with arrows, prepared for the first Dragon to descend. Just as she was turning to enter the portal to the spiral staircase inside the tower, Trallalair was buffeted by the gale of a Green's wings as the Dragon whirled about the tower, shearing off the banderole atop the roof. The wind pushed her back against the closest merlon on the wall. Flames of the Dragons filled the sky, lighting the courtyard with a scintillating brilliance long enough that she beheld the activity in the courtyard below. When the first flashes subsided, the flames of burning structures and burning people were enough to cast the courtyard in a ghastly red glow.

The lone male she saw rushing through the ranks of the Sinjery, handing out golden-tipped arrows, was Julian, Blaze Poet. As each Sinjer received an arrow, she replaced the one in her bow. Nowhere but in the Dragonlord's Palace were the golden Dragonscale-Piercing Arrowheads allowed. Trallalair had a sense that these gold-tipped arrows must have been made for this very emergency.

While all the Dragons in the air split up to cover the city, one Dragon, Hover, fell toward the courtyard. Trallalair screamed, "Hover, up! Up! UP!"

Unheeding, Hover flew straight at the twenty dozen Sinjer. At a shout from Neskagel the Ringleader, one Ring fired their arrows. The second Ring kept their magic arrows in reserve. One hundred twenty-one gold-tipped arrows flew to meet Hover. Every arrow hit its mark. Hover's eyes were blinded, her wings torn to shreds, her throat nailed shut, and her heart punctured a dozen times.

Trailing fountains of blood, she crashed through the wall behind the Sinjery, throwing blocks of stone in all directions. The half-ton blocks thrown by Hover flew like pebbles kicked by a child, but when they hit Hover's attackers watching the sky, the golden Sinjery armor they wore was crushed, along with the Sisters wearing it. More than a score of Guards died this way.

Hover thrashed pitifully among the rubble, wings broken, blood pumping from numerous wounds. Finally, with a gurgle of blood from her nostrils, she died.

Trallalair was stunned, and tears, the first in her adult life, came to her eyes. Her mount and friend lay slaughtered by her own Sisters, who now were desperately tearing the golden arrows from Hover's hide, desecrating the Dragon she loved. Trallalair wanted to shout at them to stop but merely fell, sobbing, to the cold stone of the tower entrance. She knew she should get up, must get up, but she was too weak with the horror and pity she felt.

Slowly she breathed, stuttering, deeper and deeper breaths, trying to find her Sinjery Spirit. More screams, cries, and Dragon roars brought her back to her senses. With a shake of her sable tresses clearing her head of the last vestige of pity, Trallalair dove through the tower portal and leaped down the stairs five at a time, caroming off the encircling walls, ignoring the pain in her foot. Her own bow was in her hand with an arrow notched by the time she burst into the dark courtyard.

Hover was there, an inert, bloody mass, but Trallalair suppressed her grief. Another blast of heat coming from her left made Trallalair spin and, by reflex, fire an arrow at a swooping Green. Her target was a precise spot at the base of the wing, a critical joint that would drop the Dragon like a stone if it were disabled. Her non-magical arrow deflected off the tough scales. Twenty Sinjery archers holding their ground had been incinerated by that last pass, but the Green Dragon sprouted dozens of gold-tipped arrows as he flew past.

There was precious little time for the defenders until the Green Dragon wheeled above the towers, banking tightly to dive again. The remaining Sinjery archers, including Trallalair, Dirmissilig, Atherraine, Mebarethy, and the other Brandmistresses searched Hover's now-still corpse for gold-tipped arrows. Each Dragon was tough enough that fifty to a hundred magic arrows would be needed to kill it. Their limited supply of the Dragonscale-Piercing Arrows was dwindling fast. Trallalair knew the Sinjery were fighting a losing battle. They needed another weapon.

Trallalair tugged at an arrow in Hover's hide. Her first pull failed to dislodge it from the rocklike scale. She concentrated all the strength in her forearm, and with a cry, she tore out the arrow, spraying Hover's blood over her clustered Sisters. Spinning with the momentum from tearing out the arrow, she turned toward the fray. All her Sinjery reflexes made the turn one fluid coalescence as she notched the arrow in her bowstring, aimed at the open maw of a diving Green, and let the magical arrow fly into its throat. Two dozen arrows flew together at the Green's mouth to silence it before the Green could spit fire again. They were an instant too late. The golden arrows, the last of their meager arsenal, were met by a ball of flame and consumed. Since the flame was spent on the arrows, the Sinjery archers were only singed by the backlash. But as the Green rose again to clear the wall behind them, its tail dragged through their ranks, smashing and crushing many. Young, bold Mebarethy drew her sword as the huge tail raced at her. Even the tough Sinjery Sword was broken, along with her body. Trallalair dove and rolled so as to be hit by only a glancing blow. A Dragon scale ignored her leather armor and slashed her thigh, slicing deep into her flesh. Her now-useless bow was whacked from her hand as the Dragon's tail slashed her. Her rage quelled the pain in her foot and the pain she should have felt from her cut thigh. As long as she could move, she would fight.

Even before Trallalair could roll completely out of the way, the wall behind her erupted with two monstrous Reds from the palace Dragonkilns. They had been driven into a frenzy and were battling each other, tearing apart the palace wall in their struggle. Blocks of stone rained upon the Sinjery Ringmistresses. One fell on Atherraine, crushing her leg and making her wince with pain as cups of blood seeped from beneath the marble block. She pushed at the massive stone but could not move it. Trallalair dodged the flailing wings, legs, and tails of the fighting Reds as she ran to her injured Sister.

At her side, Saggethrie and another Brandmistress ran up to help. By the time they reached her, Atherraine's eyes fluttered with the weakness of blood loss. As Trallalair leaned her weight against the marble block, her feet slipped on the sanguine mud around Atherraine. Trallalair's own blood oozing from her leg only made it worse.

"Together!" Trallalair shouted. The three Sisters regarded each other with silent intuition of the others' tensing muscles, and as one together, they slammed their shoulders into the stone. Through the block, Trallalair could feel stone scraping the bone of Atherraine's maimed leg. Trallalair threw off her leather doublet. She quickly ripped away a handful of cloth from her shirt sleeve and staunched Atherraine's wounded leg, while Saggethrie and the other Brandmistress lifted her and carried her in their arms. They ran for a corner of the courtyard, where they all lay Atherraine on some soft dirt. With Atherraine finally safe, they collapsed, exhausted.

There were eleven other Red Dragons in the Dragonkilns, and the entire palace was quaking with their struggles below. Trallalair lay farthest from the wall and Atherraine. Saggethrie carefully bandaged Atherraine's leg, but as soon as her Sister's leg was dressed, Saggethrie eased up from where Atherraine had fallen, doffed her mantle, and came to tend Trallalair.

The horror they all felt twisted Trallalair's face as Saggethrie pried apart the sliced leather breeches wet with Trallalair's blood. Ripping off a corner of her own mantle, Saggethrie stuffed it beneath the leather as a crude pressure bandage. With another rip, she tore off a long strip and tied it around Trallalair's stuffed pants leg. Trallalair only had time to crack a smile and touch Saggethrie's sweating cheek in thanks. Able to stand with slightly less pain in her leg, Trallalair got to her feet. As their only remaining Guard with a weapon protecting Atherraine, she drew her sword against the ravening Dragons.

A clawed forefoot rose from the ground only a single rod before them, then another. Dirt and rocks sprayed Trallalair as a Red Dragon's head emerged from the depths and looked into her eyes. It opened its jaws to roast them.

Instead of flinching away from the blast, Trallalair cried out, "Sinjer!" and with her teeth clenched against the pain of the fire she knew was coming, she charged her foe, meaning to strike out its eyes with her Sinjery Sword. It was one of the few weapons able to pierce Dragonscales.

The Red was not prepared for one so meager as a human leaping at its face and, by instinct, it recoiled, clapping shut its jaws. The Dragon's recoil extended its neck two rods up in the air, far from her reach.

With only his two front legs and his head and neck out of the ground, the Red inhaled deeply through his nostrils. Trallalair knew nothing on Mother Earth could withstand the direct, concentrated blast of a Red Dragon's fiery breath. In a final ineffectual gesture, she turned and dove to cover Atherraine with her body. "Run, Saggethrie!" she cried out.

Neither Saggethrie nor the other Brandmistress ran. Instead, true to their Sisters, they copied Trallalair and dove to cover helpless Atherraine. All would die for their Sister. With Hover gone, the Dragonlord dead, and all the lands around at the mercy of the Dragons and the Demon, Trallalair had nothing better to die for. The world would be a living Hell. Best to die serving a friend. Lying there with all her Sisters, she could hear the Red Dragon building up a tremendous breath to roast them all. She gritted her teeth, tightening every muscle in her body for the blast. She felt Saggethrie's strong fingers grip her arm, tightly tensing against the expected searing pain, and her lover's long unbound hair caress her face as it had a thousand times when they lay together in love. She had always dreamed of dying with her lover.

Just as the Red was at the peak of his inhalation and ready to spit fire, a smoldering and bloody white-garbed figure stepped in front of the Red Dragon. It spread a cloth shield before them so Trallalair could not see the Dragon's head. The flames hit with the force of a hurricane, throwing the white figure back against them. The cloth he held covered them all. The force of the breath still slid them all back and Trallalair slammed into the blocks in the corner. She felt the skin seared off her right arm and lost her grip on Atherraine's thigh. Blood poured again from her macerated flesh. Sulfurous fumes burned her nostrils, and she heard the other Sinjery grunting, trying to extricate themselves from tangled limbs.

To her amazement, they were all alive. Nothing could withstand Dragonfire, or so she had thought.

By the time Trallalair, their white savior, and the other Sinjery were able to lift the cloth shield and stand in the smoldering ground, the Red had pulled himself up from the ground, sprayed the other side of the courtyard with death, spread his magnificent wings, and lifted into the air to fly away.

Trallalair turned to see her savior was Seldric, the Dragonlord. His Dragonhide Cloak, apparently the one thing in existence immune to Dragonfire, had been their shield. Seldric had not been killed by the blow from the Demon's rod but only stunned, and he had a purple, freshly-bleeding lump on his head to show for it. His Guard in their last heroic service to him had spread his invulnerable cloak over his prostrate, unconscious body to protect him from the Dragonfire that killed them all. They had probably thought him dead, but instead of protecting themselves, they chose to save the Dragonlord the indignity of immolation by his own Red Dragon. In his turn, he had endangered himself to save Trallalair and her Sisters from the Red Dragon blast. It was only because the Sisters had tried to protect their injured Sister Atherraine in a pile of faithful, sacrificial flesh that the small robe had been adequate to protect them all. Had they tried to save themselves and run, they would have all died.

With a glance at Atherraine's bleeding wound, Seldric took over the task of bandaging her leg. Trallalair sweated with the searing pain of her burned arm and foot and her lacerated leg. Steadfast and, for the first time, thankful for his presence, she asked, "What would you have us do, Your Highness?"

The screams of the burned and wounded in the courtyard added to the crash of stones and the thud of dirt fountains accompanying more Red Dragons as they exhumed themselves from the Dragonkilns below. All this ruckus tried to drown Seldric's shout. "Look to the center. All the Sinjery must huddle around the Dragonegg."

Trallalair followed his gaze and saw fires and blasted ground everywhere in the courtyard except in the center, where the Dragonegg still lay. For a small distance around it, the ground was untouched. It was as though the Dragonegg had a protective ring around it. Somehow, even the Red Dragons rising up out of the ground avoided the egg, as if they sensed its presence and dug their way to freedom away from the precious egg.

"They won't harm the egg. Not even the Dragoncrown can make a Dragon harm a Dragonegg. The instinct of preservation of their race is too great within them. If the Guards surround the egg, they will be unharmed."

Trallalair's voice was clear with her youthful vigor, stronger than Seldric's, and could pierce the din around them. She called out to the Guards, "Knights, Sisters, gather around the Dragonegg! No Dragon will harm you there."

As if they had practiced the maneuver their entire lives, the Sinjery Guards and Knights that were still standing clustered around the egg in two small but orderly rings. They all drew their swords and waited. All the gold-tipped arrows had been used and lost. Just as Seldric had said, the Dragons ignored their little knot of defiance and busied themselves incinerating everything else.

For a bare moment, Trallalair and her companions by the wall had been spared the wrath of the Dragons, but they were far from the Dragonegg sanctuary and would soon be targeted.

Obviously heartsick, Seldric said, "All the Dragons must be killed. Can you walk, Trallalair?"

She nodded curtly.

"You must find the way." Then in a rare display of honesty, he said, "You were right, Trallalair. The Seers, too." His eyes turned to where many of the Inner Ring had fallen. Although he had never shown them love, all of the Inner Ring were his daughters.

Trallalair wasn't sure whether the tears brimming his eyes came from the sting of smoke or from the loss of most of the Inner Ring. Callous as he was, she felt he still had a heart that could bleed.

Drenched in sweat from heat and pain, shaking little rivulets away from her own eyes which already watered profusely, she and Saggethrie hustled the party into a postern door at the base of a tower so they would be freer from the depredations of the Dragons. She gritted her teeth against the urge to limp, walking into the outer halls of the palace, all the way helping support Atherraine, who was so weak from blood loss she was dead weight. Trallalair noticed Knights of the Isseltrent Muster and Court Poets gathering together all the weapons, magical and non-magical, they could find. On Flying Carpets, a group of Knights, holding lances, sailed past to engage a Green assailing a smaller courtyard. The lances were too flimsy to pierce a Dragon's hide, but the Knights would die trying. They took Atherraine to a room filled with wounded Knights and Sinjery, where

Alchemists led by Honor Rulupunerswan worked doggedly preparing potions to heal them.

With Saggethrie's tight cloth tied around her left leg wound and another wrapped around her burnt left foot, Trallalair could walk after a fashion. She still didn't think she would run very fast. Her right arm, weeping from the large macerated burn, she left open to the air. The flesh was fine, only the surface of the skin was gone. Just trying to clench her fist made her cry out, despite her Sinjery training in pain control. If she concentrated and used that power of will over emotion, she could still use her sword, if need required. Beyond that, her wounds would have to wait. Many others had worse injuries and needed the potions the Alchemists produced.

Saggethrie and the other Brandmistress were ready to aid her. "You are our leader, Trallalair," Saggethrie said. Instead of preoccupying her, the pain now piqued her thoughts, clearing her mind of detritus and allowing her to rapidly consider, then discard, many possible courses of action. In the space of one pass of a Dragon reverberating through the wall beside them, she reviewed all possibilities and made a decision.

"Your presence quells my pain. We must be quick. We need large Flying Carpets and as many Sisters as we can find."

Within a space of thirty Favors, they gathered together twenty-five Sinjery and four Flying Carpets and, at her lead, ran as best they could through the corridors to the west wall of the palace. Trallalair had little trouble keeping up with most of her Sisters. They each had their own injuries which hobbled them. The injured Sinjery Sisters seldom grimaced or groaned in pain, but they all had that look of concentration. They took the intensity of the throbbing flesh and turned it to their own purpose, the protection of Isseltrent and their remaining Sisters.

Two Sisters Trallalair saw were unscathed. They had purposely kept themselves apart from the raging battle, having a more important role. Hamrodel and Kirienesse had split apart from the mass of revelers when the Demon loosed the Dragons. They had found the children of the Sinjery Bough and took them deep within the walls of Blaze to a place of safety. Trallalair had seen them as she passed a room off the main corridor. Kirienesse was comforting the children while Hamrodel, with a borrowed sword, guarded the door against panicky people who could injure the children in their crazed flight. They also tried to protect the children from witnessing the worst of the horrors that abounded.

Trallalair and her company needed lances like the ones the Knights had, but gigantic lances for gigantic foes. Beyond the main formal courtyard of the palace, hidden behind curtain walls, there were other courtyards. Hopefully some had been spared the depredations of the Dragons. By the far western wall, the main repair and storage courtyard was the one she ran for now.

"We need a Poet!" she shouted to her Sisters.

Yolochine, a Sister from Thunder Ring, shouted back. "You have not been yet told. Julian is dead." Julian had been Blaze Poet, the one best able to come up with the verses to power all the magic needed to stem the tide of the Dragons. Now, in their time of greatest need, he, too, was unavailable to them. Yolochine volunteered, "When a Red broke up through the floor of the Nursery Hall, Julian was called. Julian used Sprite Shovels to undermine the pillars supporting the ceiling above the Red. While everyone else ran, he stayed, instructing the shovels. He was crushed as the ceiling collapsed."

"You may depend upon me, my sweet Sister," Saggethrie said.

"You must be careful but quick," Trallalair said, fearing for Saggethrie's safety. But she could not protect Saggethrie from every danger. There was none she trusted more with any task than Saggethrie. "We need a Poet and adzes. Meet us by the stores of wood."

Saggethrie nodded, looking both ways down the corridor. Up one corridor, Knights with halberds were hacking at the legs of a Red Dragon forcing itself through a wall. Down another, a continuous line of courtiers carried injured people on makeshift stretchers. Saggethrie made her decision and sprinted off into the fray.

The noise was incredible. Shouting was accentuated by the barking of choking throngs coughing on smoke from the many fires in the halls that sheltered them. Through the palace walls could be heard Dragon roars, human screams, and crashing walls of stone. Everywhere was the sound of boots running. And calls. Calls for weapons here. For more Knights there. Underground rumbling signified Red Dragons still clawing their way up through clay and stone. Every so often came the crash of another wall crumbling or another floor collapsing, as the raging beasts below shattered their supports.

The storage courtyard was thankfully spared destruction for the moment. There, men ran up to the lumber piles and carried away timbers to use as supporting beams for the falling ceilings within Blaze.

Trallalair led her party to the stack of untouched logs, where she helped her Sisters roll whole logs onto the huge Flying Carpets they had brought. It took several tries to get them balanced right when the Carpets were activated and hovered in the air.

Soon, Saggethrie literally pushed the Poet Canntrixel into the courtyard. As he was absorbing Trallalair's plan and composing the poems needed, Saggethrie disappeared again, only to reappear within a few Favors with five Sprite Adzes, two crowbars, and a set of chisels. She organized the Sisters to trim the front ends of the logs using the Sprite Adzes, sharpening them to tapering points, turning them into the equivalent of gigantic log lances. After Canntrixel composed the verses to harden the points to the strength of steel, he etched the verses into the lance-heads using the chisels. Copper Orders were used to complete the process. The Log Lances were ready.

Trallalair leaped astride one of the logs as did three other Sisters, one Dragonflyer and two Ringmistresses, on the three similar logs. They ordered the carpets up high above the ramparts of the palace and down into the main courtyard where the two Dragons still fought. Between bursts of Dragon fire the early morning sky was black as death. Hundreds of fires below gave new credence to the name the first Dragonlord had chosen for his palace, Blaze. For their part, Trallalair and her companions astride the log lances could use the light of the fires to find their foes.

One Dragon, the older one in the main courtyard battle, was tiring slowly from fighting another Red Dragon as well as all the insignificant people. By the time Trallalair's squad of Log Lances on Flying Carpets descended into the spacious square of the main courtyard, the older Dragon had tried to flee, failed, and fell dead from a fatal bite to the neck from a younger, stronger Red Dragon. The triumphant Red, in a frenzy, tore mouthfuls of flesh from his dead adversary, gulping them whole.

While the Red was occupied with eating to strengthen himself, Trallalair lined up her squad broadside to the Dragon's flank and, on a hand signal, flew with the other three toward his side. The four log lances slammed into the Dragon's side, punctured the Dragonscales easily due to their sheer mass and momentum, and penetrated deeply between the Red's ribs. It was a deadly blow.

Trallalair expected to be thrown against the Dragon's side when her log lance hit, and she was. She had her hands on the log and let herself flip, pushing herself with her hands so when she struck the hide of the Dragon, she hit with her feet instead of her head. She bent her knees as she hit and, despite all her injuries and a shock of pain as she hit, Trallalair was able to spring off to land on the ground in front of the Red's left forefoot. With the effort, her leg wound broke open and blood soaked through the bandage again.

The other Dragonflyer in the squad had the same idea and survived landing beside the Dragon's hind leg, only to be torn apart by his death throes.

In a heartbeat, Trallalair drew her sword, just in time to impale the Red's clawed forefoot as it swept toward her in a final defiant lunge to kill his assailant. She was thrown on her back, but sensing death closing in quickly, she let go of her precious sword and rolled away. the Red closed the talons of his forefoot to crush her but crushed smoky air instead. His forefoot opened as he died. Trallalair cried, "Sinjer," calling her nearly unbreakable sword which ripped out of the Dragon's forefoot in a cloud of blood and flew to her hand with a resounding, moist slap.

One Ringmistress, encumbered by her heavy gold armor, had been unable to leap off as her log lance struck. Her neck shattered as she was thrown headfirst into the Dragon's side. The last Ringmistress, similarly encumbered, held onto her lance like a cat digging its claws into a branch, but she was inundated by fiery vapor exploding from the Dragon's lungs. She died painfully but quickly.

Trallalair had no time to mourn her fallen Sisters. She ran to gather more carpets and make more log lances for the Knights and the Sinjery Sisters to fight off the Dragon horde. This time she would instruct the riders how to avoid further deaths. Saggethrie was there helping her and her Sisters. As she ran, checking on the progress of small groups of Poets, Knights and Sinjery, Trallalair thanked Mother Earth because Saggethrie had survived the first onslaught of the Dragons. No one could tell if any of them would survive to see the morning.

CHAPTER 14

THE STRANGLING OF
THE COMMUNITY

With all the other Pixets, Hili had been flying the dance Breeze Rustling Thistles for the Dragonlord when the cloaked figure walked up and screamed for none to interfere. When the Community recognized the messenger holding the defiled Unicorn Horn to be the same as had been in Jonathon Forthright's shop, the Community fled in anger and fear to Skysweeper in the Dragonlord's garden two courtyards distant. They thought Skysweeper would be the safest place for them in Isseltrent. They wanted to be nowhere near the desecrated Unicorn Horn with its unimaginable power over minds. Majestic, fully-leafed Skysweeper could hide them all. They expected trouble but nothing like what they experienced next. Screams came from the main courtyard, and they soon saw all the Dragons, free of their Dragonflyers, leap into the air. The magnitude of the disaster was unbelievable but true. All the chaos was caused by the corruption of the Unicorn Horn. In that instant, the Community knew they were to blame. Had they simply refused to mar the

Unicorn Horn and not given in to the Master Jeweler's anxious pleas, none of this would have happened. Loremaster Rhazburn devised the verses and Jonathon Forthright altered the form of the Unicorn Horn, but in the end, it was the Pixets who gave it its power by inscribing the gems.

When they saw some Dragons descend back into the courtyard blowing fire, the Community knew their precious Skysweeper was negligible protection. They realized that if the Community remained clustered together, one blast of Dragonfire could kill them all. They dispersed, flying in different directions to find corners and holes in Blaze and Isseltrent best protected from the coming firestorm.

Hili, in mute agreement with the Community's decision, flew through the castle's corridors to watch the main courtyard and observe what disaster had happened. As she approached the exit of the corridor to the courtyard, she had to stay tight against the ceiling. Hundreds of courtiers, townsfolk, and Knights pressed through the door in panic, many falling to be trampled. It was a lot to bear. The scattering Pixets of the Community were all preoccupied so they could salve very little of her terror. She had to press on with her tiny resolve alone. She stopped at the door to the outside and watched, trying to decide when to fly out. The other Pixets were far away by now, and none looked upon the courtyard to aid her timing.

After the door was bathed in flame and she heard the roar of a Green Dragon passing, Hili made her breakout from the corridor. She synchronized it perfectly with the instant the Dragon was flying away from Blaze. She flew just above the heads of the mindless rout so as to pass through the door as far as possible from the burning threshold. As she entered the courtyard, smoke burned her throat, and the heat of many fires pushed her toward a spared tower. Her filmy wings fought torrid updrafts as she strained her eyes to see through the haze of smoke. Finally, almost too late, Hili was able to breathe a whiff of clean air. Her vision cleared and she glimpsed a Green Dragon soar in an arc, coming back to sear anything left in the courtyard. Sinjery Guards stood their ground, firing arrows at the Dragon. One Green Dragon lay twitching in the throes of death behind them, its hide pierced by dozens of arrows, blood pumping into the sand.

Hili barely made it to the cool tower as the Dragon assailed the courtyard again. The cloaked figure that held the Unicorn Horn was nowhere to be seen. To the dismay of the Community, the Unicorn Horn was gone. The Community vowed to take back the Unicorn Horn in whatever way they could. Obviously, the object had not been given to the Dragonlord as was Jonathon Forthright's plan. Hili spotted the Dragonlord stumbling toward a Red Dragon that had cornered several Sinjery. He jumped in front of the Red and spread his Dragonhide cape to protect the band of Sinjery and himself just as the Red Dragon exhaled a torrent of flame at them. Through her, the Community saw the Dragonlord had no Dragoncrown on his head. Someone, probably the cloaked man, had stolen it.

A piercing shriek drew her eyes skyward to see the man in the cloak riding a huge Red Dragon. It was not the cry of a man, but that of some malevolent creature, cold and heartless. In the early morning darkness punctuated by flashes of red from Dragonfire, she could make out few details. From the tower, she flew as fast and high as she could to try and catch up with the creature. She had to see him close up for the Community to try and determine a way to get the Unicorn Horn from his grasp. Dragons could fly leagues higher, faster and farther than Hili could. But she had to try.

The hooded man flew the great Red high into the starry sky in an easterly direction. Hili beat her filmy wings furiously to try catch up, but the Red Dragon was nearly to the clouds already. The Red had been going straight east, so Hili took a chance and flew directly east, hoping to intercept the dragon if it descended from the sky. Soon, not far ahead, the Red dipped beneath the clouds and circled around, apparently looking for something. Presently, it was joined by ten other Dragons, two Reds and eight Greens. As they circled together, Hili had a chance to fly toward the oncoming Red. None of the other Dragons had riders and none of them even noticed one so tiny and inconsequential as Hili.

Undetected, Hili was able to fly up within a few flutters of the hooded creature. A horror beyond belief slapped her backwards. All the Community reeled along with her discovery. Beneath the hood was a rotting corpse wearing the Dragoncrown and clutching the Rod of Coercion. At that instant, the Community knew they and all Thuringland were betrayed. Not only had they helped to fashion a powerful magical object from the treasured Unicorn Horn, but it had been given to the Demon, the very being who had destroyed their precious Verdilon, doomed all the Unicorns, and driven the entire Community into exile.

As he flew past, the monster turned toward her, regarded Hili briefly with its rotted eyes, and reached into a pouch at its waist. Its hand clutched a tiny decayed being, like a doll image of itself, but which Hili could see had once been a Pixet.

Only one Pixet in the Community was unaccounted for at that moment. Caene. Lost to the knowledge of the Community the night of the storm. The monster quickly brought up Caene's body to stick its tiny head into the Demon's corrupt mouth.

Along with every Pixet in the Community, Hili felt a horrible strangling come over her. She choked on blackest despair filling her mind, and her wings retracted in fright as she recognized the Bane of Unicorns and Scourge of Verdilon within her. Through Caene's lifeless body, the Demon Sverdphthik was attacking the mind of the Community. They were all helpless, gripped simultaneously by talons of fear and horror. Even in death, Caene's substance was tied to the Community, opening a portal into the center of their consciousness.

Hili fell from the sky, as did every flying Pixet in the Community. As she fell, she felt Torley crumple and tumble into a bonfire. The pain of his burning flesh and his awful screams filled her head. Through Dorma's eyes, she looked up too late to see an unavoidable tree. Hili felt every bone in Dorma's body shatter with the impact, then felt an awful blackness as the flame of Dorma's spirit was snuffed. They felt a Pixie fall before a crow which pecked and killed her. The Community shared her guardian adults helplessness to save her as she writhed with pain and fear. All actions were impossible. None could help any other and they all suffered.

Hili forced her eyes open as she fell. Trees below rushed up. With her mind ripped by claws of ice, she held her head in her hands to no avail. The terror was too powerful to fight. Before she hit the ground, however, she began to feel something else. It was anger. Anger at the destruction of Verdilon. Anger at the loss of the Unicorns centuries before. Anger at the deception of the Community and Jonathon Forthright. Anger at the defilement of the Unicorn Horn. Anger at the Demon's evil use of poor dead Caene. And even anger at her own rapidly-approaching death. All the anger built up so she strained against the paralysis imposed by her fear.

Her own immense anger reached out to all the other Pixets and imbued them with enough power to rally their spirits and resist the Demon's hate. The Community passed back to her a burst of will that empowered her to take control of her limbs and wings. In the last moments before she hit the ground, she expanded her wings a bare wingspan from a rock. She stopped herself, grimacing and hovering, screaming at the Demon with her tiny voice. Other Pixets, who had boosted Hili's strength, now had their own spirits bolstered with Hili's defiance and saved themselves.

The Demon was foiled, at least temporarily. It could not kill them all as it had intended. As a last insult, it seeded their consciousness with the inconceivable truth that it could enter their minds at its whim. Then, leaving their minds raw, the Demon's feral spirit inexplicably disappeared. All the pride and complacency of the Community had been scraped away forever.

They were to be the whipped thralls of the Demon. Anytime, anytime at all, the Demon could use Caene's corpse to enter their most precious possession, their collective consciousness. It could see and hear everything the entire Community saw, heard, did, and thought. Every thought the Community had for all their history was laid naked before it, to scourge and rape as it pleased. Only the death of every Pixet in the world could save them now.

CHAPTER 15

THE SUNDERED REALM

Even though the smell of smoke and the sound of screaming from the street outside his shop greeted Jonathon after he was fully aroused, it was the pain that first awakened him from his prolonged faint. He was frozen by the Demon's order into the most uncomfortable position imaginable - standing, bent forward at the waist, with his arms half-raised and his mouth wide open. He could just make out Rhazburn's body a little to his right. Of course, the spell from the Rod of Coercion prevented him from moving even a hand's breadth. It was like one of his distressing dreams right after falling asleep in which he felt paralyzed but was still able to hear the sound of Arlen breathing beside him and still able to feel the slippery silkiness of the Warming Blanket on his lap. In that dream, he only needed to move a muscle in his little finger to break free of that awful paralysis. But this was no dream. Nothing would free him before the effect of an entire Glass Command wore off.

At least he had done something right, Jonathon thought sadly. He had no more doubt that the rod would work. Hopefully Rhazburn had estimated the period of effect correctly. Rhazburn had said a single day was the limit, even with the use of a Glass Command. The pain of his stance was already unbearable to Jonathon. The only part of his body not aching was the top of his bald head. If he stood there a second day, he would die for sure.

Smoke curling into his shop via the little crack beneath his door stung his eyes. He heard the crackling of fires, the running of people in panic, and the crashing of buildings. The whole city sounded full of unbridled chaos. Jonathon knew that the Dragoncrown had been stolen from the Dragonlord. What else could cause such devastation? The very thing he wanted to prevent by making the Rod of Coercion had come to pass because of what he had done. The Demon ruled the Dragons, and Jonathon was to blame. He hoped the flames would consume him and his shop as a punishment for what he had done to the world. No failure could have been worse than this triumph of his workmanship. He wanted to die, hoped to die, knew he would die if he had to stand there much longer.

Arlen's voice outside his shop brought him out of his self-pity. "Back away, if you don't want this broom atop your skull. Be off, I say." Then the door of his shop burst open, their moving broom was tossed onto the floor, and Arlen twisted around the door, slamming it shut with a single motion. Her hair was wild, her dress torn half off, and soot smudged her pretty cheeks. She did not even seem to see Jonathon but quickly turned and slapped the brass bolt, locking the door. Then she turned to dive at a heavy bench, trying to drag it in front of the door, only to grunt and lurch in place ineffectually.

When she saw Jonathon out of the corner of her eye, she snapped, "Don't just stand there, you lug. Help me! They're *crazy* out there."

When he didn't move, she turned, facing him, and said, "Jonathon, I don't have time to play games. Quit making silly faces and help me." Getting no response, she put her fists on her hips and demanded, "Come here! Are you possessed?"

At last, she realized something was not right. "Jonathon?" she said, stepping toward him. Before she took two steps, she suddenly dropped out of sight with a thud. He heard her say, "Rhazburn get up from there. Are you dead? You're stiff as a board. What's this? Blood on the floor.

Hmmmmm. You're still warm." She pushed herself to her feet and squared off in front of Jonathon. "*What* is going on here?"

Arlen stood there herself a moment. Then, with a comprehending gleam in her eye, she exclaimed, "A spell! That's it. You're both in the power of a spell." Her eye squinted angry. "What have you been drinking?" She waved a hand before his face, scowled, then said, "Can you hear me?" Jonathon could not even blink in response. She put her lips against his ear and screamed, "Can you hear me?!" The pain in his ear made tears roll down his cheeks. His wife saw them and started. "Oh. Sorry, dear. I guess you *can* hear me."

Arlen got more determined. She searched his pockets. She found a few coins and his Bracelet of Potency. He had always kept it a secret from her. Even though he had offered it to Molgannard Fey, he doubted she realized what she held. She turned it over a few times, inspecting it, then put it on his wrist.

After she touched a Wooden Request to the bracelet, Jonathon forgot all about his pain and had a sudden urge to tear off her clothes and make love to her. Lucky for Arlen, he could not move. Of course, she saw nothing of this and pulled off the bracelet in disappointment, tossing it over her shoulder. Jonathon's pain came back twofold, searing him to the bone.

Arlen disappeared to the back of his shop. He heard her rummaging through the gems and finished pieces of jewelry. Not many were left, since he had sold almost everything to pay Molgannard Fey. She came back with a few pieces. Jonathon doubted she had any idea what they were or what they could do.

First, she took a Buckle of Levitation, which was one of the many Jonathon had made for the Rockskippers of the Cajalathrium States. She removed his own belt buckle and replaced it. Then she pulled out a request and touched the buckle. Jonathon quickly rose to the ceiling, rapping his head sharply on a rafter. Startled, Arlen clutched at his trousers, but she could not pull him down. She held on to him and shuffled her feet to a heavy chair, using its weight as well as hers. After more than a few grunts of effort, pulling hand over hand, she finally managed to pull him to the floor. While she fumbled to get the buckle off, she lost control of him twice. Each time, he floated again to the ceiling and hit his head. Now every part of his body hurt, including the top of his head.

The Buckle came off and flew up to rest above them. Arlen was still game. This time, she pulled out a pendant made of smokey quartz in the shape of a garlic clove. It was a Wolf-Bane Pendant made for a hunter. As Arlen touched it with a request, the pendant radiated a terrifically bad odor, guaranteed to keep wolves at a safe distance. Grimacing, she held her nose as she removed the pendant with the tips of her fingers. She ran to the back window to throw it out of the shop, but he knew the shutters were closed and latched. He could not see what she was doing, but he heard her take a breath so she could release her nose, flip the latch, shove open the shutter, and toss the smelly pendant unceremoniously out the window. Jonathon heard retching, then desperate running footsteps outside the window, then a thump followed by groans, as if someone, fleeing the horrible odor, not watching where he was running, had run into the side of Shamus Blinkendorfer's candle shop across the alley and lay stunned and in pain on the ground. Jonathon heard Arlen slowly close the shutter, as if she wanted to go help the person but could not. Not with the chaos and the smell outside the shop and Jonathon frozen within.

What he could see of her expression when she came back was one of disgust. She passed Jonathon, more statue than human, and sat on the bench. Arlen took more care with the other pieces, frowning at one, shaking her head at another. She surprised Jonathon with a snap of her fingers, saying, "Bob... I'll get Bob. He'll know what to do. He's probably trying to protect his mother from the ruffians." She got up and unbolted the door.

As she left, Arlen held out a hand to Jonathon. "I'll be right back, dear. Don't move. Or, no... *do* move, if you can. Ohhh, you know what I mean," she stuttered, then bustled out the door.

Jonathon had a lot of time to relish his pain and think about how bad a mistake he had really made. He felt the day was well into Work Blessing before the door opened and Bob came in with Arlen. After one look at Jonathon and Rhazburn, Bob said, "Something terrible has happened here to my Master and the Loremaster. I knew better than to leave them. I should have stayed. But they insisted."

Arlen said gently, "Your mother needed you, Bob. Whatever happened, if Rhazburn couldn't prevent it, you would have been stiff right there with them. Stiff, or dead. Now, at least you can help them."

"I guess you're right," he said. "The Master looks well enough."
Jonathon did not feel well enough.

"Maybe the Loremaster is only paralyzed as well. The Loremaster said a Glass Command would make the effect last a whole day. Since I left the shop at the End of Dinner Blessing when the messenger came, the spell should last at least until then."

The lad fished in his pocket like he was getting a Clay Suggestion out. He was out of Jonathon's sight but was probably over by the Timefall.

"Hmmm," Bob hummed. "It will be a few Blessings, two maybe, no, make that three, yes, at least three Blessings yet before it wears off."

Jonathon wished he could have groaned. Three more Blessings! How could he survive in his ridiculous position for even one more Blessing, much less three?

With Arlen at his side, Bob looked at Rhazburn. He felt his chest, listened to his lips. Then, lifting his lids, Bob gazed into Rhazburn's eyes.

"I think he's alive but unconscious from a blow on his head and paralyzed by the spell of the Rod of Coercion. He needs care. I hope he will wake up. My uncle was hit by a brick when he was younger than me, and he woke up, but it took five days and he could never smile on the right side of his face again. The Loremaster has lost a lot of blood, too. I don't know what to do, but my Mother will. I need to get him to my Mother."

"I can stay with Jonathon until he wakes up. I would rather be here alone with him when that happens. He has a lot of explaining to do," Arlen replied.

Jonathon knew what she meant. He had never even hinted to her that he was involved in making a magical object for the Dragonlord. He had implied that Molgannard Fey had given him an extension on his debt. He wanted it to be a nice surprise, all that money. Now all that money was gone. Not spent for something good, but twisted into harm, great harm of everything and everybody. He had been greedy, unthinking, his wits gone in a swirl of money-lust. Jonathon tried to shake his head, but it stayed rigid on his neck. Rhazburn had warned him, but he had not listened. Rhazburn and everyone in the Realm were now paying for Jonathon's mistake.

While Jonathon was trying to figure out what to say to Arlen, Bob pulled a push cart up to the door. Bob and Arlen used a charred board to lever the stiff body of Rhazburn into the cart. Arlen gave Bob a number of coins she found in the shop, saying, "Whatever money you don't need for the leech, use for yourself and your mother."

The boy trundled Rhazburn away.

While they waited for the spell to wear off, Arlen organized a small meal from provisions Jonathon always kept in his shop. One thing he was never far from was good food. Not if he could help it.

The end of the spell came all at once. Jonathon fell, groaning, to the floor.

Arlen rushed to him, cradling his head.

Every movement hurt, and he winced at her touch.

"Maybe you'd rather stay on the hard floor," she said, sounding even more annoyed, if that was possible.

A long time and a lot of moaning passed before he could talk. "Thank you for taking care of Rhazburn, Dumpling." The effort of speaking made him grab his jaw muscles in misery. After rubbing them for a few moments, he was able to get out, "Are the children all right?"

"Theodore has them in the cellar. When I left, nothing had been touched on our hill, but we have to get back and check. I say we go to Herkimer's. We can live off their vegetable garden and blackberry patch, if anything is left."

"I agree. Let's get out of here, but I have to freshen up first. I've been waiting for a whole day to relieve myself. If you please, make me some tea, and I'll tell you the whole story, Honey."

This seemed to mollify Arlen. She helped him stumble to the back room where he could take care of his long-overdue bodily needs. On the way, she began her own tale, "You have no idea what I went through just to get here. I couldn't take the Black Dragon. I'm sure it flew away with the rest. I probably would have been swallowed if I had tried. We could see the burning of the city from our house. Dozens of Dragons were flying about. It would have taken a fool not to know something was wrong. Theodore wanted to come to get you, like he's a big man all at once, but I knew he also liked being in charge of the children. He can boss everyone around till we get back. I looked back toward the hill a while ago. No smoke from the hill yet."

Jonathon closed the back room door while she continued. "You know, Farmer Gibbel said the Dragoncrown has been stolen by some treachery. I knew better than to go to the Travel Plaza. I almost got killed half a dozen times coming here to see if you were still alive."

"I suspect that Master Gibbel should be able fend off a few measly Dragons from his chickens," he interjected.

"He was outside when I left, shaking his rake at the sky. I would have run here, but I would never had made it, so I ordered our Broom to fly here, and I just held on. It's a wonder I'm still alive. If it wasn't dragging me over the ground, it would suddenly bound up into the trees and there we'd go, swish-swash, right through the leaves. I could be wrapped around a branch right now clinging on by my fingernails, for Three's sake. Only the grace of Tundudil protected me. I hope he protects our children too."

Arlen's banter floated on and on through the door. As Jonathon was finishing washing up, he noticed that Arlen had ceased her monologue. That was quite unusual for her. Arlen seldom stopped talking if she had an audience. He dried off, adjusted his shirt, and opened the door to find out what had happened.

An arrow pointed at Jonathon's nose, not a hand span from his face. Attached to the arrow was a black bow held by a beautiful, dark-skinned woman covered in sooty and dented golden armor. She was one of the Sinjery Guard. Behind her were a score more of the grim female warriors. One held Arlen's hands behind her back. Arlen's mouth was gagged with a black cloth, and her eyes bulged with anger.

One of the women said, "Are you the traitor Jonathon Forthright?"

Jonathon tipped his head to the side to get out of the way of the arrow. The arrow moved with him. "I am Jonathon Forthright." He was more worried about Arlen than himself. "Please, I beg you, kind Ringmistress, release my wife. She was totally unaware of anything that occurred here."

The Sinjery said to the other Guards, "Mark what the traitor says. He admits his guilt."

"My wife is innocent as a baby of this!" Jonathon insisted.

"Silence him. By the Dragonlord's law, the wife of a traitor is as guilty as he. Tie him and let us leave." Thin but very strong hands bound his wrists behind his back and stuffed a cloth in his mouth. After confiscating the box of coins and jewelry open on his workbench, they shoved Jonathon and Arlen into the street.

A man carrying sacks out of a wrecked shop took one look at the Sinjery and ran, dropping his loot on the ground. Before he could take three steps, an arrow pierced his neck, dropping him in mid-stride.

Leaving a guard at Jonathon's shop door and without another glance at the dead looter, the Sinjery prodded Jonathon and Arlen to move on through the streets. Jonathon feared their cold precision and pattered before them, encouraged to be nimble by a sharp sword tip lightly poking his rump. Once, Jonathon saw Arlen try to kick one of the guards, but the woman parried her foot with an easy slap of her sword. Arlen glowered at the Sinjery but followed Jonathon.

A few fires still burned in the city. Most were quenched by a heavy rain pouring down in some areas of the city while other areas without fires were relatively dry. The rain looked most unnatural, sporadic, and concentrated in the worst burning areas. Jonathon surmised it must have been formed by Raindust dropped from Flying Carpets.

Soon, their procession came within sight of Blaze. High above the castle, a thin Green Dragon flew erratically, harried by Knights swarming around it on Flying Carpets. Every so often, the Dragon would stretch its neck and spit fire toward the flock of Carpets. Several Carpets would burst into flame, falling to the ground with their hapless screaming riders. Again and again this happened, but the Knights that were left persisted in their mobbing of the Dragon until it flew off toward the distant mountains.

Blaze smoldered with the rest of the city. The walls were ragged with smashed stonework. Turrets and towers bristled with the readied spears of a thousand Knights probably called from their duties elsewhere to guard the Ruler of the Realm.

As they were passed through the gate then into the main courtyard of Blaze, Jonathon saw the crumpled body of a small green Dragon. So many arrows pierced its hide, it looked like a hedgehog. Knights and Sinjery were harvesting missiles from its carcass.

They avoided the front stairway and skirted the main enclosure of the castle. One of the Sinjery called out to clear a path. "Make way for Jonathon Forthright, Traitor of Isseltrent." A few working men paused to sneer at Jonathon and spit on him. The guards kept anyone from actually attacking Jonathon or Arlen. They took them to a gloomy yard filled with stocks, dunking pools, chopping blocks, and gallows. In the middle of all, a heavy iron grate lay flush with the ground. At a word from the Sinjery, two male Giants, dressed in black leather, used all their strength and a groaning oily winch to pull up one end of the grate. Jonathon and Arlen were pushed down into the Dragonlord's dungeon. At the bottom of a slippery, spiral stone staircase, they were prodded along a narrow passage that reeked of human offal. Torches lit their way through dank stone corridors. The walls were featureless except for dripping water and occasional patches of a colorful but vile-appearing mold that crept from crevices, looking for something to putrefy.

Locked doors of iron were seen at times in the torch light. Behind some of the doors, Jonathon heard muffled moans or plaintive singing by inmates awaiting the swift ax or the slow rot to end their suffering. At one, he heard a hideous scrabbling, as if some crazed wretch frantically tried to scratch his way through the bolted door to flee some nameless terror.

Arlen and Jonathon cringed at every sound, while the silent Sinjery guards walked stolid and heedless. Finally, at a barred enclosure where a few tables were strewn with cups and bowls of half-eaten food, the guards stopped Jonathon and Arlen. The couple were made to strip and don scratchy woolen cloaks tied with rope. Jonathon wished they had given him shoes when he saw a gray rat skittering toward a hole in a corner. A moment later, it was neatly skewered to the floor by a precise arrow from one of the Sinjery Guard. The Guard left it there, apparently as a warning to other vermin, Jonathon included.

The Guards took Arlen down one tunnel and Jonathon down another. They pushed him into a small cell with a floor of straw and a single smoky lamp smudging the ceiling. A waste hole adorned one corner. One of the guards untied his hands with a flick of her wrist and clanged the door shut, leaving the cover of a small peephole open. He tore off his gag and shouted out the peephole, "Suffer my wife to stay with me, please!". They slammed the cover in his face.

After they left, Jonathon sat on the dismal floor and brooded over his plight for a long time. The time he spent there with his misery was immeasurable. He knew not how many days passed. In that dark, fetid cell, the sun and any indication of the time was far, far away. His sleep was fitful. He startled and woke at the chittering of rats in the shadows. Later, he thought toward dawn of another dismal day, jangling keys at his door woke him up. The silhouette of a woman tossed him a moldy bread brick ringed with nibble marks, as if the rats had rejected it. Then she poured him a cup of cold broth thinner than tears.

As the woman left, he stood up and demanded, "Tell me how my wife is."

The cell door shut, but he pounded on it and shouted, "You can't keep her like this. She is innocent!" Silence was the response. He hit the door again, hurting his hand, and sobbed at the thought of Arlen wasting away, dazed at her imprisonment.

And the children. Jonathon knew that his older children, the ones from the city, would be checking on the younger ones at their home as soon as the chaos abated. That is, if any of the older ones had survived. Theodore was clever and brave. Jonathon just hoped he was circumspect enough to avoid looking for Jonathon and Arlen, that he would keep the little ones safe until some of the other adults of the family could aid them. Whether Rhazburn was even alive after he, himself, possessed and controlled by the Demon, had struck him down, still plagued Jonathon's thoughts.

It wasn't fair for Arlen. He was to blame for all of her trouble, but she was made to suffer. He thought of trying to scrape through the stone walls to find her, but the only thing hard enough to do the job in his cell was the bread he was supposed to eat.

Jonathon languished still for an unknown length of time, tedious and uncomfortable, until the door was opened once more. Again he was tied, this time without a gag, to be led out of the dungeon. Arlen was nowhere to be seen.

"What have you done with my wife?" he asked, angry and frightened.

With a chisel-cold stare, a Guard answered, "Another word from you unbidden, and we will gag you again." Jonathon was afraid that further protests would make Arlen's predicament worse, so he walked, passive, among nine Sinjery Guards. They took him out the same way they had entered, down the long tunnels lined with locked doors, up the stairs, and out under the iron grate held unsteadily by the Giants. The Grate looked like the jaw of a Black Dragon ready to crush the life out of him.

The Guards gave a password at a side door to the central enclosure of the Dragonlord's castle. The door was opened by another Sinjery, this one dressed in a tailored mail shirt and greaves of a reddish metal. They entered a wide and lofty chamber, pillared and lit with shimmering crimson. It was the throne room of the Dragonlord. The group stopped, and the leader walked around a stone pillar. They had entered far from the end of the chamber behind one of the pillars. Darkness in the shadows from the pillar surrounded them. In more shadows behind more pillars, Jonathon could discern whispering clumps of people and numerous Guards at attention. Like the sentry that let them in, all the Sinjery Guards in the Chamber were armored in red mail. The sanguine light of the throne room glinted off their armor and added to the color. The Sinjery glowed as if they were red-hot. They held tall spears with voluptuously-molded blades that could slice off a limb with the ease of swatting a fly.

The leader returned at a half-trot, and Jonathon was pushed into the center of the great hall to stumble toward a blaze of light at the far end. He found himself flanked by the huge stone pillars standing only a dozen steps apart, which explained the deep shadows behind them. The corridor between them was certainly bright enough. Each pillar was encircled by a long snakelike Dragon carved in relief that wound its way slowly to the top. At each top, the Dragon head, made of iron, snarled forth a plume of flame. Its faceted glass eyes were transparent, and the fire glowed through them like hot coals. The flames and the light from the Dragon-eyes illuminated the central promenade of the hall. Jonathon and his captors now faced a much larger fire. One so bright, Jonathon could barely see the shapes of the figures just in front of it because of the glare.

The red tiles they walked on to the throne dais were in the shape of scales. The central promenade was like the hide of a gigantic red Dragon, the tail at the entrance to the hall and the head a monstrosity of carved stone thrust upward behind the dais. The open jaws spewed forth a great flame a rod high into the air. As Jonathon approached the dais, the details became clearer. On a throne of black marble upon the Dragon's neck, his bare head raised up, level with the Dragon's great forehead, sat the Dragonlord. The back of the throne flared out to protect the Dragonlord from the flame. Jonathon cowered before the heat and brilliance of that flame which seemed to rise from Hell itself.

The Sinjery Guards stopped Jonathon just out of roasting distance from the flame. "Fall on your knees before His Highness, Cur," came a woman's snarl from his shoulder. Too lightheaded to continue standing, he obeyed. The tile scales of the Red Dragon walkway bit with a vengeance into his already aching knees.

Jonathon raised an eye to look at the Dragonlord. No Dragoncrown was on his head, and the Dragonlord did not hold the Rod of Coercion. The Rod of Coercion was surely to blame for all the destruction and chaos he had witnessed, and he, fool that he was, had made it.

There on his knees, scrutinized by the Dragonlord's angry scowl, Jonathon began to put all the pieces together. Molgannard Fey was in league with the Demon. There could be no other conclusion. Rhazburn had described the piles of animal skins within the Ghouls' cavern destined for Fey's Skin Splicer trade. Jonathon did not doubt the Giant to be in business with the Demon and its minions. It would be typical of Molgannard Fey.

The Demon had probably heard about Jonathon's skills from the Giant. It probably even knew that Rhazburn was his son. Not much was hidden from the criminal's underground sources in Isseltrent. The Giant, in collusion with the Demon, set everything up for the plot, knowing that there were none in all Thuringland who could accomplish such a feat except Jonathon and Rhazburn. He must have been watching for the right moment. When Jonathon was short on cash, he must have made sure the jeweler heard about him as a good source for money. He had been duped by the two of them long before Molgannard Fey ripped off Jonathon's roof.

All of this was the result. Rhazburn was seriously injured, if not dead. Arlen starved in the dungeon. Maybe many of his children were dead in the city, too. Not to mention the distress and destruction caused by the loosed Dragons, or the economic shambles the Realm would be in once the lack of Glass Commands from the idle Dragonkilns caught up with the people of Thuringland and the Tributary States. All of it was due to the knowledge of Rhazburn and the skill of Jonathon Forthright, Traitor of Isseltrent, in making the Rod of Coercion. Jonathon did not expect to live much longer, there in the midst of so much well-deserved hate. He just hoped he would be spared torture before the Dragonlord had him executed.

Chapter 16

The Dragonlord

The great hall was silent. Even though Jonathon could sense a throng of courtiers to his sides, none of them spoke while the Dragonlord inspected him. Jonathon's skin prickled under the hateful stares he felt from all around.

On either side of the Dragonlord were his closest advisors. To Seldric's left, Rhazburn's friend and fellow Demonward Wesfallen stood, obviously in place of the Court Poet who was unaccountably absent. To Wesfallen's side, a tall Sinjery woman, dressed in golden scale armor with a gold-tasseled helmet, tightly gripped the hilt of her sheathed sword. Anger suffused her striking face. Beside her, Rulupunerswan gazed at Jonathon with haughty contempt. To the right of the Dragonlord stood Pavnoreth, the highest priest in the Realm next to the Dragonlord. Pavnoreth was known as the Second for The Three. Too old and too important to bother with the Rule which demanded physical beauty of the Holy Few, the Second did as he pleased. With a pitying gaze for Jonathon, Pavnoreth had an ethereal countenance, his fat head upraised and floating on a cloud of pleated robes that covered his holy rotundity. Beside him, Chamberlain Honor Gashgrieve looked impatient to have Jonathon beheaded and be done with it. On the end of the group, Katherine Ribald, Seer to the Dragonlord, stood. Her red hair was tied about her face, and her eyeless gaze uncannily assessed Jonathon as he kneeled quietly, too afraid to even whimper at the pain in his knees thrust against the hard tiles. All the advisors sweated profusely in the heat of the showy fire.

Dragonlord Seldric studied Jonathon with weary eyes. He did not have the appearance of a broken man, but rather that of a man whose spirit had been weighed by decades of carrying the Dragoncrown. He wore no jewelry, and his robe, though fine, was plain. A beautiful jeweled sword lay unsheathed across his knees, the only official sign of his authority. Jonathon saw a livid bruise and crusted cut on his right forehead. He imagined the bruise to be the shape of the crown atop the Rod of Coercion. Apparently the Demon had paid the same compliment to Seldric as he had to Rhazburn.

Seldric cocked a thumb at the fire behind him, addressing Rulupunerswan. "Quench that infernal flame. By The Three, I'll keep control over one Dragon."

Rulupunerswan produced a powdery pouch from his robe and flung it into the marble Dragon's mouth. After mushrooming in a final blast, the flame was gone, and the throne room darkened considerably. Jonathon's eyes, half-blinded by the flame, slowly adjusted to the dimness.

Before another word could be spoken, a male Knight, wearing blackened armor and holding a helmet with its tassel singed off, walked in. Metallic ringing from his armored boots accompanied his precise steps. He stopped beside the Chamberlain, whispering into is ear.

At a nod from Seldric, Gashgrieve raised his official staff and chanted, "By the might of His Highness Seldric Gojorson, Dynast of Thuringland, Grand Admiral of the Fleet of the Realm, Supreme Commander of the Guard, Chief Brandmaster, Protector of the Cajalathrium States, the Commonwealth of Dis, the Hundred Isles, Sylvanward, Sinjer and the Sea, Vanguard against Hell, First for The Three, and Dragonlord, by his might in battle, all fugitive Dragons have been driven from Isseltrent. All hale our Lord." A weak cheer rose from the ranks of the disgruntled courtiers.

After a kick to his leg from one of the guards, Jonathon croaked out, "Hooray".

Seldric ignored the formality, sneering at Jonathon's forced cheer.

Gashgrieve stepped forward, only to be waved back by Seldric.

The Dragonlord commanded, "I will question the jeweler myself." He pursed his lips, leaned back into his throne, and pressed the tips of his fingers together. "Jeweler, did you bejewel a rod that has the power to mesmerize?"

"Yes, Your Highness, but..."

"He admits his guilt!" Rulupunerswan interjected.

The Dragonlord silenced him with a sharp glance, then turned back. "Jonathon Forthright, you admit to this treachery?"

"Sire, I made the rod for you and the good of the Realm." Jonathon flinched at the incongruity of his assertion and looked desperately from one hostile face to another. Whatever had come from his making the rod, it had certainly not been "the good of the Realm". The Dragoncrown was on a Demon's head, and the land was in a state of war as the unconstrained Dragons slaughtered and burned everything made by man. Now that the Dragonkilns were idle, the few Glass Commands still left in the Realm would soon be used up, and all the magical items that kept the Realm in motion would be useless. Besides, when the coins ran out, Hell's Breach would be an open portal to all the horrors of Hell. No one could live through that.

The Dragonlord sighed. He acted like he had no time to waste on paradoxes. He said, half to himself, "I would have the truth from this man."

Jonathon's next breath caught in his throat. Torture. That must be what the Dragonlord meant.

Instead of calling for whips and thumbscrews, Seldric nodded to Katherine Ribald. She bowed to his nod. Jonathon still couldn't imagine how she saw through her thick hair. He thought maybe it was a trick and she had it combed so she could see through the strands. She stepped easily over the neck of the tile Dragon without tripping. Too easily not to be watching her feet, he thought. She walked up to him and stopped, exhaling audibly as if releasing some humor within her.

Jonathon felt a presence within him. Not as evil and harsh as that of the Demon who had plucked the verse of activation for the Rod of

Coercion from his mind, but an extraneous presence never the less. It was as if he was filled with the mind of a man, not that of a woman like Katherine Ribald. This one, one who wanted to please Katherine Ribald and delve for the truth within Jonathon's soul, but the presence fell away quickly and Katherine Ribald staggered back in horror.

She cried out, "The Demon resided within this traitor recently! The residual taint is too great for us. We cannot endure the pain of it." She turned sightless toward Seldric. "I am sorry, Your Highness. We had only a glimpse. I cannot be certain of his guilt but he shared his body with the Demon! There is a memory that this traitor gave the Demon the device... the weapon. Also we know the jeweler named the weapon 'The Rod of Coercion'."

From the feeling of another being briefly within him, something he was familiar with, thanks to the Demon, Jonathon surmised some ethereal creature accompanied the Seer wherever she went. It felt like the spirit of some man severed from his own body as if by death. Maybe Jonathon could believe in Ghosts, after all. He certainly believed in Demons.

Seldric fumed, apparently peeved at not having his way with Jonathon. He shifted uncomfortably in his very comfortable-looking throne and said, "Alchemist?"

The Alchemist's eyes glowed with revenge, as if he could finally pay Jonathon back for foiling his attempt to keep Rhazburn captive. He looked like would enjoy torturing Jonathon. Rulupunerswan ran off as he said, "I must prepare the potion, Your Highness."

Jonathon knelt on the marble floor with its sharp scales for so long, he might just as well have been kneeling on steel blades. He wanted to move, but the tense blade of a Sinjery Sword at the back of his neck dissuaded him.

While they waited, the Dragonlord quietly consulted with the Knight on the dais. Rulupunerswan came back much too quickly to have prepared any potion. Jonathon suspected he just pulled it off his shelf. The Alchemist walked to Jonathon and motioned to have the guards let him stand. By then, the pain in his knees was lessening because they had become totally numb. Jonathon stood, and the numbness of his legs soon turned into an unbearable tingling, making him fidget in place. Rulupunerswan sneered at his discomfort, then held aloft a cruet of a vile green liquid, saying to Seldric, "The Potion of Truth is ready, Your Highness."

"I desire the truth," said the Dragonlord.

Jonathon had heard about Truth Potion. It was basically an extremely powerful poison. Theoretically, if Jonathon drank the potion, it would remain harmless in his stomach unless he lied. If he uttered the tiniest mistruth, he would suffer a quick but agonizing death.

Rulupunerswan turned and held the unstopped cruet in front of the jeweler. "Drink this, Traitor."

Jonathon picked it up lightly, expecting a firm grasp would drive the poison through the skin of his fingers. Raising it slowly to his nose, he sniffed the potion. That was a mistake. The smell alone could have killed a horse.

Rulupunerswan snarled, "Drink it, now. Quit wasting the Court's time." Jonathon again felt a slight pressure of the blade against his neck emphasizing Rulupunerswan's order.

Jonathon gagged as he forced down a swig of the foul liquid. He retched for a long time, while the Alchemist watched with glee and the Chamberlain tapped his foot impatiently. Teetering with faintness, Jonathon tried to fix his gaze on the Dragonlord.

"The truth, Jeweler," the Dragonlord said.

First, Jonathon blurted, "My wife knew nothing of the deal with the Demon. She had no part in making the Rod of Coercion." Since he did not die, they must believe him. Or so he hoped.

"Get on with your confession," the Chamberlain said churlishly.

Jonathon thought for a few moments before he spoke so he could tell the story and give the impression he had done it all himself. He certainly did not want to implicate Rhazburn, Hili, or Bob. He left out a lot of details to avoid lying and, consequently, no one was fooled.

Wesfallen was the first to catch the deception. "Jeweler, who wrote the verses for the Rod of Coercion? Who engraved the stones, and how did you acquire the horn of a Unicorn?"

It was bound to happen. To keep his friends out of the story, Jonathon had to lie. So his time had come. He was doomed from the day he made his deal with Molgannard Fey. He had betrayed the trust of his wife, the Pixets, and Rhazburn. If he did not put his friends' heads on the chopping block with his own, he would die of the poison in his stomach from the lie. Die alone or take them with him. The choice was easy. He refused to betray his friends again. He had to say that no one had helped him, even though no one would be fooled, since he would curl up screaming and expire.

Jonathon opened his mouth to lie and die. Just as he formed the first word, a commotion from among the courtiers drew everyone's attention to the side of the throne room between the pillars. Jonathon was so surprised, he shut his mouth.

A man in a gray cloak pushed through the front row and shouted, "Say no more, Master Forthright!" Rhazburn pulled back his hood, revealing a black welt on his forehead much like the one on the Dragonlord. The Demon, using the dead muscles of the body he possessed to strike them down, must not have had the strength to kill with one blow. Lucky for Rhazburn and Seldric.

"I, Rhazburn, gave the jeweler the Unicorn Horn. I took it from a Zombie in the Dead Lands."

A gasp went up from the onlookers, and the hall was filled with murmuring. Jonathon just stood there. His own death could not save Rhazburn now. His son had admitted a capital crime. Sinjery guards ran to Rhazburn, encircling him with leveled halberds.

Rulupunerswan seized the opportunity. "The insolence! Your Highness, allow me the honor to carry out your law and have this brash rebel executed immediately."

Seldric regarded the Alchemist as he would a toad sitting in his food. "Silence! Remember, it is *my* law."

Jonathon tried to catch the Dragonlord's attention. "Your Highness. Your Highness."

Seldric's eyes bored into him like awls.

Jonathon spoke anyway. "Your Highness. The Loremaster warned me against the deal I made and refused to be a part of it. I forced him into helping me." Jonathon's stomach gurgled. He broke out in a sweat, thinking he had spoken a slight inaccuracy and would expire with his next breath.

The Dragonlord watched him for a while. When the jeweler stayed erect, Seldric turned and said, "Rhazburn?"

The Alchemist held the cruet of truth potion, shaking it in the air, so Seldric could see it.

The Dragonlord waved the idea away like a bothersome gnat.

Letting his gaze linger on the Alchemist, Rhazburn said, "I do not fear the truth, like some do."

To an astounded audience, he related his part of the drama, leaving out details unimportant to the course of things, like Bob Thumblefoot's part and the depressing role of Screela. He had to fill in part of Jonathon's story of how Hili engraved the stones. "But, Your Highness, you know the Pixets as well as I, and none of them would have had any part in this venture if they thought the Demon was involved. They long refused to engrave the gems because they knew the gems were to be set on the Unicorn Horn. Only as a final favor to Jonathon, who they knew to be true and loyal to His Highness, did they agree to let Hili engrave the stones. They should be the first to be absolved of their role."

"That is for me to decide," the Dragonlord said.

A handful of Guards left the hall hastily.

Rhazburn knew they had been dispatched to arrest the Pixets. Out of the side of his vision, he saw Rulupunerswan looking at his face, intent on some detail.

The Alchemist asked, "May I speak, Your Highness?".

"Yes, Alchemist. What is your opinion of the Poet's tale?"

"Your Highness. This man lies. He is in league with your enemies, and I can prove it."

"What proof do you have?"

Full of smarmy arrogance, Rulupunerswan said, "We have, over the years, had the opportunity to question some of the man-eating chattel of the Demon. They have peculiar habits, like eating small pieces of their...". He gestured with his hand, as if he could not come up with a socially acceptable word for use in the throne room, then said with a sneer, "wooers."

Very proud of himself, the Alchemist walked to Rhazburn's side. With his actions backed up by Sinjery halberds, he didn't hesitate but grabbed the top of Rhazburn's head with one hand, turning it sharply with his other hand.

There, in Rhazburn's ear for all to see, was a triangular bloody tear. Triumphant, he cried, "This man has a Ghoul for a lover!" A gasp came from the crowd.

Rhazburn shook himself free from Rulupunerswan's grasp. "I can explain that."

"With more lies?" the Alchemist jeered.

Seldric looked disappointed, as if he had truly hoped his bastard son, Rhazburn, would have been innocent of the crime.

Jonathon could not stand to see his son treated so cruelly. "Your Highness, punish me but spare Rhazburn." He raised a finger, thinking about his next statement. He almost said, "The Realm needs the Loremaster at Hell's Breach," but he decided that Rhazburn might not be indispensable there. Since he needed to continue living, at least for a short while, to make his point, Jonathon hedged and said, "The Loremaster could be useful at Hell's Breach."

The Dragonlord saw the conflict in his eyes and chuckled. "Cleverly said, Jeweler." Then he made the barest sign to the Chamberlain, waving them away.

"Take them away," Gashgrieve said. The Sinjery guards hustled them toward the side door.

Rhazburn knew they would not have another chance to plead their case. Before they were out of earshot, he shouted, "I know how to defeat the Demon." He hardly got out the shout before the guard looped leather restraints around his wrists and muffled his cries with a cloth over his mouth. Amidst his fruitless struggling, he did not even hear the Dragonlord's response, but the guards led him back to the dais.

"Remove the gag," the Dragonlord said. "Alchemist, your potion."

Rulupunerswan cackled, "Your servant, Your Highness," then produced the cruet and thrust it at Rhazburn. Rhazburn inspected it to make sure the Alchemist had not substituted another container of unadulterated poison and, without further hesitation, downed what was left in the cruet.

Rhazburn had a theory about the Demon and how to defeat it, but he was not sure if all he would say was true. He believed it all and, to him, it all fit together. He had no idea whether the potion of poison would act on a wrong supposition, or only if he knew his theory to be untrue and spoke it to deceive. He was about to find out.

"I ask you, why has the Demon fled Isseltrent in its day of triumph? It has the power to sit now upon the throne of the Dragonlord."

Gashgrieve raised his staff as if to strike Rhazburn dead for his blasphemy.

Rhazburn quickly added, "The power of the Dragoncrown and the Rod of Coercion make it almost invincible."

For the first time, the stately Sinjery woman standing beside the Dragonlord spoke. "The Guard has driven the Demon away."

Rhazburn stretched out a hand, and one of the guards prepared to cut it off. "Believe that if you like. But consider this. The Dragoncrown requires many days, perhaps many Moons, for its full power to be realized, even by the rightful owner. Our Lord can attest to that fact." Seldric said nothing, but Rhazburn had the strength of the Potion of Truth on his side. Rulupunerswan, by giving him the potion, had verified his words.

"The Demon controls only a few Dragons at once and sporadically. In time, it will know how to coordinate their efforts." That was a true statement, easy to deduce. His next was supposition. "Once the Demon learns how to control all the Dragons together, I believe it will level Isseltrent and kill all the inhabitants. I believe the reason it will do this and the reason it fled your armies are one and the same. I believe it fears something in Isseltrent." Rhazburn hoped they missed that he had said nothing at all. He had only stated he believed what he said to be true, not that what he said was actually true. Since he did not insist it really corresponded to facts, he was safe from lying.

Rhazburn paused, and Rulupunerswan put in a jab. "I suppose what the Demon fears is Rhazburn." He laughed, looking at the court to muster support. Few laughed with him.

"No, Alchemist, it fears the Jewel of Nishbad." That was Rhazburn's biggest gamble. He awaited the judgment of the poison. Nothing happened.

Therefore, he had possibly guessed right at that one supposition. Or maybe the potion only had the power to recognize what Rhazburn knew to be untrue.

The Dragonlord glanced at Wesfallen, who could only shrug. "Rhazburn never told me of this."

A few people in the throne room knew what the Jewel of Nishbad was. Jonathon, of course, Wesfallen, Gashgrieve, the Dragonlord, and probably Rulupunerswan, although he pretended not to hear. Rhazburn explained to the rest of the group. "Nishbad was the ancient evil courtier and student of the then new Science of Poetry who had opened Hell's Breach and let Sverdphthik into the world. He had done it for his own designs, but then with the Demon's help, Nishbad assassinated the rulers of his time and claimed the Realm for his own. Fifty years later, when his life was waning, Nishbad was finally overthrown by the first Poets who had secretly conceived and made the Dragoncrown, then used its power to depose him. Nishbad was executed, but the Poets could not harm Sverdphthik and he escaped to Verdilon to corrupt it into the Dead Lands. The legends told of a huge star sapphire which was found on a chain around Nishbad's neck. The poets reckoned it had the power to entrap the Demon if touched by him. In this way, Nishbad had protected himself from his ally. The poets planned to use the gem against the Sverdphthik, but it was stolen for its beauty one night and never seen again."

After waiting for his last statement to have its full effect, Rhazburn said, "Many thought Sverdphthik had it stolen, but I know different. I alone in these three hundred years have seen and recognized the Jewel of Nishbad."

This time, Gashgrieve spoke up. "You have condemned yourself with those words. Who but one in league with the Demon would hide that fact from the Court or his fellow Poets?"

Rhazburn answered, pointing his finger at the Dragonlord's advisors and holding his voice steady. "Who, you ask? One more loyal to the land than most of you in this room. As Loremaster, my duty was to protect the Realm, not for one day, but for all eternity. The Court Poet will tell you that Demons are not blundering monstrosities but crafty beyond conception. At Hell's Breach, we must change our tactics constantly. They learn both from our mistakes and from our victories. Many years ago, I used the Demon-Trapping Gem. It was a huge star sapphire covered with verses I memorized. When I was a young, ambitious Demonward, I constantly scoured the shops for items to use at Hell's Breach. I chanced upon the gem in a shop of precious antiques. The seller had no idea of its value, and it was easy for me to barter my talent for the stone. I tried to trace how it had come to him, but I had no success. The verses upon it told me it could be none other than the Jewel of Nishbad."

Rhazburn continued, "I showed the stone to no one but kept the secret to myself. Many of you have heard the tale of the day I was left alone to face a Demon when all the other Demonwards were killed at Hell's Breach. As the Demon emerged through the Musical Mystical Door and attacked me, I took out the gem and activated it with a Copper Order. When the Demon touched the Gem as it tried to destroy me, it was pulled within the substance of the Gem. Once the Demon was inside the Gem, the crystal glowed with an arcane energy. I threw the Gem and the Demon back into Hell."

Gashgrieve interjected, "The tale you told made you seem much more resourceful. Had we known of the Gem, you would have never been made Loremaster. But this you knew, so you never told the truth until now, when you are forced to by the potion. You will never be a legend, Rhazburn."

Rhazburn retorted, "I said I was ambitious, but I didn't keep it a secret solely because of ambition. I confided in no one else for another reason. Fear. The object is as powerful as the Dragoncrown or the Rod of Coercion. I imagined dozens of Demon-Trapping Gems being made, whatever the cost. All of them could be used and thrown back to Hell. Does anyone believe that no scheming or planning exists in Hell or its denizens? There in Hell, the other Demons not trapped within the Gems could possibly inspect them, discover their secret, read the verses, and learn a lot about how we turn them back from the Gate. I imagined they could find a way to foil the Demon-Trapping Gems or use them against us, throwing them through Hell's Breech by the handfuls to break open and release the Demons held inside. Or they might find ways to use the whole system of Poetry for their own purposes, perhaps opening many Demon Gates. That was my dilemma. I held the fate of the world in my hand. I couldn't take the chance anyone else would learn the verses. The temptation to make many Demon-Trapping Gems would be too great.

So, I kept silent all these years, reserving the knowledge for the worst of catastrophes. This may not be the worst, but the need is at hand."

"Ha!" Rulupunerswan had his arms crossed, angry. "So you are the keeper and judge of all the Realm." He quieted when the Dragonlord leaned forward.

"Tell the court poets the verses on the Jewel of Nishbad. We will prepare your Gem."

Rhazburn said, "You all think I am disloyal to the Realm. In all respect, Your Highness, I am loyal to the people of the Realm, despite what you think." They watched. He did not die, confirming for all the validity of his statement.

"When I devised the Rod of Coercion, I composed the verses so no human but the Dragonlord could use it. But I, Loremaster, was duped by the Demon. I fight Demons day after day in Hell's Breech, but I could not recognize one standing two strides in front of me. A tragic blunder, but not disloyalty to the Realm. There is only one person in all the Realm I will trust with the knowledge of the verses on the Jewel of Nishbad. He is also the only one I know of that can make the Gem flawless enough for the verses to exert their true power. That man is Jonathon Forthright, Master Jeweler of Isseltrent!"

No one looked impressed. Rulupunerswan was first to say, "There, Your Highness. By his own words he condemns himself. Such brazen disregard of your laws must be punished. May I give the order to have these two traitors beheaded?"

Seldric seemed to be thoughtfully calculating, realizing that the two before him had skills worth exploiting but impossible to control. "Take them away. I will decide the manner of their death."

As five Sinjery guards leveled their halberds at him, Rhazburn shouted, "I can protect Isseltrent from the Dragons!" The truth of his claim was reinforced by his ability to stand unaffected by the Potion of Truth. But it meant little to the implacable maidens. Too many of their Sisters had been lost by his actions.

Three of them expertly restrained and bound his wrists, then one pressed a tender bone at the angle of his jaw so he gasped just long enough to have a rag stuffed in his mouth. She tied a second rag around his face, muffling any further protestations. With the tips of five halberds at his ears and neck, Rhazburn was prodded toward the dungeon.

Jonathon only had time enough to groan at Rhazburn's indignity before he was similarly trussed and prodded away.

CHAPTER 17

DEATH VERSUS LIFE

Languid and peaceful, Trallalair gazed into Saggethrie's gentle eyes. Purely naked, they lay together one last time before the Rings, Brands and Lances assembled for an all-out attack on Sverdphthik and his Zombie host. Neither of them knew whether they would live through the coming confrontation with evil. Like all the other Sisters left alive who still had lovers, they had sought the warmth that bound them to each other and sealed their love. After a desperate, passionate Blessing in which their mutual cries of love were echoed by many other couples in the barracks, Trallalair's head lay across Saggethrie's naked breasts so she could hear her lover's relaxed and steady heart beat and feel her chest rise beneath her with Saggethrie's every sensual breath. Saggethrie thrilled Trallalair with each soft stroke of her hair and each circle her fingers traced on Trallalair's responsive nipples. They knew their desire was not yet sated, but the sun would soon peek through the window. At its rising, they would have to take up the weapons laid out on their footlocker and join their Sisters in the host to be assembled. Trallalair slid her fingers into Saggethrie's auburn hair and pressed her trembling mouth to her lover's. She cried through her kiss at the beauty of the moment and let it last a long time. Another might never come.

Trallalair's burns had been treated with a salve that banished the pain and began the healing process so as to leave no scars. The burns were still angrily-crusted but would not disable her. Further healed by Saggethrie's ministrations, Trallalair thought herself as ready as she could be for what was to come.

The host assembled in the sky high above Blaze. Four tiers of the largest Flying Carpets available carried a thousand souls. The long tresses of one hundred five Brandmistresses from the the destroyed Brands and three hundred thirty Ringmistresses waved in the wind. Their streaming hair was joined by the waving tassels crowning the helmets of five hundred Knights of the Realm, as many as could be collected from the Isseltrent Muster. Sufficient Knights had returned from the Northern Muster and the Eastern Muster to protect the city while the host attacked Sverdphthik in his Hellpit.

Saggethrie stood beside Trallalair along with seven other Scalers of Thunder Brand. When members of the same Brand or the same Ring fought together, their total strength was much greater than the sum of the individuals. The bonds of love between members augmented their determination to protect each other, making them almost fanatically strong opponents when any one of them was in danger. Saggethrie, like many of the Scalers, wore the armor of a Ringmistress who had been seriously injured. The Ringmistress was convalescing in her barracks, cared for assiduously by one of her Sisters. Many had been injured and many more Sisters stayed behind to nurse them. The Dragons were still loose and other battles for the city might have to be fought. Even Seldric realized the need to heal as many injured Sinjery as possible. Every Sinjery Guard brought back into fighting trim would increase Isseltrent's chance for survival.

Trallalair still felt foolish that she had believed Rhazburn wanted to help the Sinjery Sisters. How she could have become enamored of a man was beyond belief. Saggethrie was the only lover she would ever crave. Saggethrie stood there beside Trallalair stuffed into the golden breast plate of the absent Ringmistress. The small hard metal breasts on the surface of the breast plate may have fit the woman for whom it was molded, but they were a poor reflexion of Saggethrie's ample bosom. Trallalair tried to keep her mind on the war tactics at hand. All the Sinjery with Soulsisters had their lovers close by these days. In any danger, Trallalair wanted Saggethrie nearby so she could protect her. She would die to protect Saggethrie and any of her Sisters if it came to that. But the force that had been gathered was so powerful, few doubted it could fail. Almost a thousand Knights and Sinjery stood shoulder to shoulder on nearly one hundred of the largest and finest Flying Carpets in the Realm. The finest Alchemists and Poets had supplied them with thousands of newly-forged gold tipped Dragonscale-Piercing Arrows and Log Lances. They were also responsible for Verses of Nullification stitched into the carpets and etched on the fighters' helmets to counteract the effect of the notorious staff - the staff made by the Traitors Jonathon Forthright and Rhazburn. The staff which could ensorcel the unsuspecting and make them obey the bearer's will. They would not have a repeat of the fiasco which lost the Dragoncrown in the first place.

The Dragonflyers and the other Sinjery Brandmistresses were responsible for thirty-nine Log Lances with unbreakable tips shimmering with verses to split the gut of any Dragon rash enough to fly near the host. The remaining fighters had learned hard lessons from the disaster the night of the Dragonegg Festival and the way the Sisters died astride the Log Lances. They had all practiced the maneuvers needed to successfully drive the Lances into living Dragons and survive themselves. None of the Brandmistresses looked forward to killing Dragons, many of whom they may have cared for. But the protection of the Sisters left in Isseltrent and those in Sinjer, well within the reach of the Dragon horde, was paramount in their thoughts and intentions. They were prepared to destroy their beloved charges for the protection of their Sisters.

Honor Pavnoreth with Honor Gashgrieve at his side tried to remain calm and stolid as they stood on a smaller Flying Carpet floating at the level of the lower tiers of the host. However, they were unsuccessful. Many of the Knights tried to hide their muffled snickers as the two men frequently waved their arms off balance, not because the hovering carpet was unstable, but because the sight of so many others flying into formation gave them the illusion of movement high above Blaze. No Sinjery warmaiden laughed.

Honor Pavnoreth had a fair-sized triangle he could barely hold aloft as he struck the Three Holy Notes invoking the blessing of The Three. His words of prayer were lost in the spring breeze. The Sinjery needed no prayers. Mother Earth watched over them in life and death. Every action they took, every day, was done in reverence to Mother Earth.

Up from the main tower of Blaze rose one huge ornate carpet with a single figure standing calmly upon it. The Dragonlord, balanced as agilely as the Knights and Sinjery, raised his arms above his head as he ascended. He spoke in his deep stentorian voice which they all heard easily, even with the spring breeze whining between them. "Never has a greater or more powerful host risen from the flames of chaos to save the Realm. Nothing can stand in your way that you cannot swat aside. Follow the horrid Demon to the ends of the world if you must, as it will surely fly from you in fear of your strength. Nothing more must delay the restoration of the Realm. With the Dragoncrown back in our hands, we will have vengeance for this perfidious attack. All the souls of those killed by the Demon will rest in peace again. Within a fortnight, we will celebrate your triumph."

All those assembled shared the Dragonlord's confidence and fervor. They all had friends to avenge, and they let out a cheer that reverberated for ecstatic moments between the walls of Blaze below and the massed carpets above. The resounding cheer itself further invigorated the exultant host.

Before he left them, Seldric picked up a cloak from the carpet. It was the Dragonhide Cloak he had worn the day the Dragoncrown was lost, the very same cloak he used to save the lives of Trallalair and her Sisters. "Use this cloak to aid in your quest." He flew to the nearest carpet and presented it to Dirmissilig. She was the eldest Brandmistress and Sinjery Dragonflyer, and Seldric had named her leader of the host. The Sinjery had always been the Dragonlord's most reliable guards, protecting the Dragoncrown from all threats. Now they had the charge to bring it back to him.

"Fare well, protectors of Thuringland, the Tributary States and Sinjer." For once, Seldric separated out Sinjer from the rest of the Tributary States, presumably in deference to Dirmissilig and all the Sinjery Sisters in the host.

Trallalair could not see how they could fail. Scouts had followed Cataclysm with the Demon on his neck for scores of leagues right back to the Dead Lands and his Hellpit. The host could fly to the Dead Lands within two days. Their tactics had been worked out and practiced constantly for the few days prior to their assemblage. The Knights and Ringmistresses would engage the Dragons with their Dragonscale-Piercing Arrows while the Brands killed them with their flying Log Lances. None of the Zombies Sverdphthik controlled could do the host any harm, since they would be flying high above them. If the Demon brought out some of the dead birds like Trallalair had fought when the Demon came to Isseltrent, she was confident they could crush them by their very numbers.

With his final words, Seldric on his ornate carpet, in tandem with Gashgrieve and Pavnoreth on their smaller one, descended out of the way toward the towers of Blaze beneath them.

At a hand signal from Dirmissilig, the entire host sped forward. All carpets flew in unison, thanks to Poems of Convergence sewn into the carpets. Tier upon tier flew, sunlight glinting off the golden armor of the Ringmistresses and the silver armor of the Knights, newly burnished, so they shone brightly. The carpets flew with a speed that nearly matched that of the fastest Green Dragon alive. Altogether, the carpet assembly sounded like some deadly whirlwind as they cut through the sky, tattering clouds as they passed.

On the first day, they flew over the smoldering fields of the Commonwealth of Dis, newly charred by wild Dragons. Farmers who had worked for a Moon or two planting and nurturing their crops had lost them all in one day of terror. Trallalair pitied the farmers, understanding some of the terror they must have felt from the battle she fought with the Dragons when they were first released. It must have been much worse for the farmers, few of whom survived, since they had no Knights or Guards to protect them and no Dragonscale-Piercing Arrows to defend themselves against the onslaught of the Dragons. Trallalair and the host rode proud in the heavens, tasting the mists of the clouds, confident their force would prevail.

No Dragons challenged their force that first day. At night, Dirmissilig set sentries above them on circling carpets while the rest of the host slept. To light the land and sky around them so no Dragon could fly out of the gloom and surprise them, Dirmissilig had the Demonwards on loan from Hell's Breach produce huge brilliant Ball Lightnings. More than a hundred coursed through the skies around them, lighting the land for a good distance in all directions to the brightness of daylight. If an attack came, the Poets could produce more of the sizzling globes to use in battle against the Dragons and the Demon. Except for the sentries, they all slept soundly that night.

The next day, long before they even approached the Forbidden Mountains, they spied the first Dragons. Three of them approached warily from the front of the host, one White Dragon in the lead, followed by a Red and a Green. The Knights thought the Green Dragon might be Shudder, the mount of Ganwellan Cree, a Knight Dragonflyer who, like many of the Knight Dragonflyers, had been killed by his Dragon the moment the Dragoncrown was stolen.

Trallalair pitied the Dragons attacking their tight array of death. Golden-tipped arrows hobbled both wings of the White Dragon before he was close enough to attack them with his freezing breath. He fell to the ground and died with a broken neck.

The Red Dragon tried to pull up and avoid their arrows but was blinded by accurate shots from the Sinjery Ringmistresses. Trallalair and seven of her Brand, including Saggethrie, were aboard a large carpet upon which rested a Log Lance. Since the Log Lances were Trallalair's idea and she was the only one left alive who had ridden one of the huge lances, her group, Thunder Brand, was meant to be the vanguard of the other Log Lance carpets. Trallalair spurred her carpet to the attack. Two other groups of Sisters aboard Log Lance carpets flew on either side of her. This time, none of the Sisters rode upon the lances but they all stood beside them on the carpets. Thunder Brand's log, all of two rods long, stuck out a half rod from the end of the carpet. Its tip was hardened by verses to allow it to pierce through Dragonscales like they were made of paper. She ordered the carpet to dip down and come up slightly beneath the Red. The Red was blinded and hovered, confused, while more golden-tipped arrows found their marks in his throat, disabling his most fearsome weapon, his breath of fire.

Trallalair heard him grunt with the pain of the arrows in his throat moments before all three of the log lances struck his broad flank. Trallalair and her Sisters had practiced the maneuver for days. Just before the log lances struck home, they all stopped their carpets and sped backwards a rod. The momentum of the log lances carried them off the Carpets and through the Red Dragon's scales and flesh, their tips puncturing his heart and lungs. Fire spewed forth as it had when they tried the log lances for the first time, but Trallalair and her Sisters were by then far from harm's way. The Red, growling in pain and fright, plummeted from the sky to his death. Tears burned Trallalair's eyes once more. Watching the magnificent beast die, she relived Hover's death in the main courtyard of Blaze. The Sinjery flew the empty carpets safely away from the last oncoming Dragon, Shudder. All the log lances and gold-tipped arrows would be recovered after the Dragons were defeated.

Much to the surprise of Trallalair, Shudder did not attack the host but flew east toward the Dead Lands as if he was afraid to engage the Knights and Sinjery. Trallalair had never imagined a Dragon could be afraid of anything.

Dirmissilig ordered them all to stand fast and recover their weapons. She said she did not want a headlong pursuit of one Dragon to draw them into a trap.

Trallalair suspected the Demon had sacrificed the two other Dragons only as a test of the strength of the Isseltrent host. She knew the next encounter would not be so easy.

For the rest of the day, they sailed through the cool mists above the Forbidden Mountains. They saw no more Dragons. Trallalair had an uneasy feeling, as if she could sense the Demon's cold lifeless spirit plotting their demise. She said nothing to Saggethrie close beside her, but she felt her own confidence fading away. When the host flew past the Forbidden Mountains and entered the Demon's demesne, she could sense the confidence fade from the rest of the host, whether Knight, Sinjery, Poet, or Alchemist.

It was the Curse of the Demon on the Dead Lands. The cool mist of the Forbidden Mountains evaporated in the heat of the Dead Lands. Every thought of courage evaporated from the host as well. The intensity of the Demon's hate was such that even the Sinjery quailed in fright and terror when the host entered the Dead Lands.

Even though Dinner Blessing and Dusk Blessing remained, for the sake of their spirits, Dirmissilig had them all land just within the border of the Dead Lands. They would set a perimeter for the night and send up the Lightning Balls. They could all concentrate on their tactics and have the security of the Lightning Balls to bolster their spirits. Hopefully, by morning their courage and confidence would return.

Saggethrie tried to appear staunch but Trallalair felt her trembling. She was as skillful with bow and sword as was Trallalair. All the Sinjery were expert bow-women since their daily lives depended on their skill in the hunt in the Sinjer forests. None of the Sisters were sent as tribute to the Dragonlord unless they could wield their Sinjery Swords with consummate ability. Still, Saggethrie trembled.

Trallalair, for her own part, tried to suppress the unnatural loathing she felt entering the Dead Lands. She knew the Curse of Sverdphthik on the atmosphere of the land could bleed the life out of any creature who stayed in that land for very long. More than that, the Curse even drained the life out of the plants. Their only hope was to fly to the dreaded center and defeat the Demon as quickly as possible, before the Curse could wither them all.

The night passed uneventfully though dreadfully. Early in the morning, Trallalair and Saggethrie were awakened for their own stint as sentries. They were stationed aboard a Carpet patrolling the eastern side of the encampment. With the light of the Ball Lightnings, Trallalair and Saggethrie could easily survey the gravel plain surrounding their camp. There were no trees or even tall grass to hide their foes. More sentries patrolled the sky on other flanks and pickets, fifty Knights on the west and fifty Sinjery on the east watched the shadows from below.

Trallalair had noticed a rather large boulder only six rods from the camp. It looked out of place, almost as if it had been put there to hide something. She flew the carpet over it several times to make sure no one was hiding behind it.

Saggethrie watched it, too, when Trallalair scanned the sky. Trallalair had begun to think her fear of the boulder was more of the uncanny apprehension stimulated by Sverdphthik's Curse upon the Dead Lands when Saggethrie gripped her arm. "You were right to watch that rock. Look, it moves."

Flying high above the boulder, Trallalair could barely make out the movement below. The boulder itself was slowly rolling over. Underneath, a black hole was revealed, like a doorway into some loathsome tunnel. By the early morning light, she could see two men in garish dress slip up from the hole and head for the camp.

With one voice Trallalair and Saggethrie yelled, "Sinjer!" It was a warning to all sentries around them and below them. Trallalair's sword slid from her sheath and slapped into her hand as did Saggethrie's. Saggethrie sheathed her sword and raised her bow. Her own sword raised in a salute of defiance, Trallalair swooped the carpet down toward the sneaking men while Saggethrie notched an arrow. The pickets below quickly saw the danger and many converged on the boulder. More men erupted from the tunnel and spread out to attack the camp. Trallalair heard yells from the western side of the camp. Whoever attacked the camp had coordinated two attacks at once. Trallalair watched Saggethrie's deadly shot hit one of the first men in the back. He sprawled on the ground, inert.

All the Sisters used their bows. None of the assailants had bows or even spears. A few assailants threw inaccurate rocks. The attack was pathetic. Only a handful of poorly-armed men attacking a thousand well-armed, armored, trained warriors. All the assailants were slaughtered in short order. Only one Knight on the western side was killed by sheer bad luck, when a heavy rock hurled in desperation by one of the assailants hit the Knight's head. His head stayed protected by his helmet, but the weight of the rock broke his neck.

After the dead assailants were inspected by the Poets and Knights. They pronounced the men Ghouls who were known to live on the border of the the Dead Lands with the Forbidden Mountains. They were known by their garish clothes and their sharply-filed teeth which aided them in chewing the gristly human flesh they cannibalized in their abominable habit.

The Knight's body was laid out in honor by one of his friends on a Carpet. The body would be carried securely until it could be taken back to Isseltrent. His sword and bow were laid across his chest where his hands would clasp them when the Death Rigor took him. The dead Ghouls were left to rot in the open, not even given the respect of a funeral pyre, and the tunnels through which the Ghouls had come were filled with dirt, capped by the boulders, and locked in place by verses chiseled into the boulders. None of host would fear the Ghouls.

As the sun chased the shadows away and the Lightning Balls were extinguished, some of the pall of the Demon's Curse was lifted by the ease of the host's victory over the Ghouls. The Knights even began joking about their foes. The Sinjery never joked about battle.

Trallalair was sitting with Saggethrie and most of the the Sinjery. Relieved of her shift of duty, she able to eat a leisurely breakfast with her lover. They were all sitting down to ale, sausage and bread. Many of them, like Trallalair, had their helmets off to eat. Trallalair was watching the Knights clustered around the dead Knight several rods away away. She was pleased that the Knights showed such reverence for their friend. The young Knight who had laid him to rest was sitting beside him, no doubt his long-time friend.

Trallalair was as astonished as the young Knight when his dead friend suddenly sat bolt upright. The young Knight dropped his food but didn't seem to know what to do next.

Trallalair almost choked, trying to yell, "Run, away from him, you fool!" She was too late, or the young Knight too startled. The dead Knight quickly lifted his bow, notched an arrow and fired it into his friend's face, killing him outright. The other Knights around him drew their swords, but two more fell to his arrows before they could pile into him. They were swinging their swords, madly hacking away as the dead Knight beat at them with whatever he could, bow, quiver, even the stumps of severed arms.

Trallalair was on her feet in a instant. "Saggethrie, Wehennah, gather the Brand. Arm yourselves."

She looked toward the boulder which had hidden the tunnel but saw no movement there. What she did see was movement among the dead Ghouls. The were all stirring, rising up, covered with blood from the arrows that had killed them and been retrieved by the Sinjery. Some of the rising dead still held the rude clubs and hatchets they had brought with them. No one had thought it necessary to remove them from the dead men's hands.

She heard more cries and glanced at the Knights. The three Knights killed by the one dead Knight were standing, all of them hideous with arrows protruding from their faces. They had drawn their swords and were hacking down their previous companions. Many more Knights charged into the fray, chopping and hacking the walking dead. As more Knights fell, they too rose up to kill more of their companions. It was like an avalanche of death sweeping through the ranks of the Knights. Very quickly fifty dead Knights fought with the four hundred fifty live ones. Moments later, a hundred dead stood mixed in a chaotic melee with those alive. Trallalair could see the confusion as the living mistook the dead for their allies and were cut down to join them. Men refusing to strike their dead but animate friends were killed along with those who resisted.

Saggethrie, Wehennah, and all the hundreds of Sinjery Sisters Stood together facing the oncoming thirty or so stumbling dead Ghouls coming from the east. Trallalair no longer thought the attack of the Ghouls to be pathetic. Instead, the defense of the live Knights against the dead among them was turning out to be horrendous. Every Knight dead was another enemy which had to be literally cut to pieces to be stilled. Mutilated Knights hideously fought on against the living. The dead Knights fighting were growing in numbers while the live Knights were being rapidly depleted. Beyond the camp, she could hear cries as if the dead Ghouls to the west also attacked the Knights in their own picket line.

All the Sinjery fired at a signal from Dirmissilig. Hundreds of arrows hit the oncoming Ghouls, causing them to stumble or fall. Every one of the Ghouls got back up and kept coming, waving their clubs and hatchets.

"Sinjer!" Dirmissilig cried out. All the Sisters shouldered their bows and echoed, "Sinjer!" Their swords leaped to their hands. They advanced together and cut down the Ghouls, chopping them to pieces. Trallalair was at the head of her Brand. She lopped off the head of a Ghoul, but headless, he still swung a spiked club at her, so she had to step back to avoid the blow. Saggethrie slashed off the Ghoul's arm. Wehennah took off a leg and Trallalair cut his torso in half. Soon all the Ghouls were piles of disgusting dead meat.

The roar of the fighting amongst screams and cries of terror coming from the beleaguered Knights behind them was deafening. The Knights were faring very poorly. The entire troop was in chaos fighting each other. Trallalair could only estimate that half of the five hundred Knights were already dead. How could she really tell? Most of the Knights, whether alive or dead, were up and fighting. The ones that fell got back up unless they were hacked to pieces. A friend guarding the back of a Knight would be killed and, in the next moment, instead of guarding his friend, he would turn and stab him in the back. Dirmissilig called the Sisters to turn and aid the Knights. "Stand together, Sisters. Advance together slowly and let no one come between us."

They advanced in three ranks. Above the battle, Trallalair could see the flying sentries still patrolling for Dragons. Trallalair realized that if even a few Dragons attacked while they were battling the dead, all would be lost. Their proud, invincible host had become disorganized and vulnerable in an inconceivably-short time.

Before the Sisters could close with the fighting Knights, a score of the dead ones took up bows and arrows and began firing into the Sinjery ranks. Trallalair ducked as she saw a golden-tipped arrow come at her face. She heard a cry and a gurgle behind her and turned. Saggethrie had an arrow in her throat and was gurgling on bright red blood that poured from her mouth. Trallalair gasped, almost dropping her own sword. She remembered to sheathe it before she knelt to comfort her lover, who had fallen to the ground in a growing pool of blood. Trallalair knew the wound was fatal. Saggethrie's frightened eyes told her she knew it as well. If Trallalair tried to remove the arrow, Saggethrie would only die faster. There was nothing Trallalair could do to save Saggethrie. Nothing. All she could do now was cradle her friend and lover in her arms. Trallalair tried to stifle her sobbing. She said softly, miserably, "I love you, my sweet Sister. I will always love you."

Far in the distance, somewhere in another land or in a dream that Trallalair heard and observed but had no part in, Dirmissilig shouted, "Charge them! Silence the bows first." Trallalair knew the end was coming. Off to her right, she thought she heard screaming coming from a group of Sinjery. Sinjery never screamed. She looked up from Saggethrie's sweaty, fading face and saw Sinjery Swords rising and falling with gouts of blood filling the air. Limbs were tumbling to the ground like leaves blown from dying trees. Some of the fallen limbs were still trying to swing swords to cause even more mayhem. Bloodied, dead Sisters, some headless, were crawling and clutching at their screaming live Sisters who chopped them to pieces. The infection had hit the Sinjery.

Trallalair knew they would all die.

She was watching all the horror around her, her spirit stunned and dazed, when she felt a blow to her temple and saw bright lights explode in her vision. She fell back and dropped Saggethrie. With a shake of her head to clear it from the mist beclouding her thoughts, she looked up. Saggethrie, her Soulsister, the arrow still in her throat and the glazed look of death in her eyes, lifted up her Sinjery Sword to strike Trallalair. She had hit Trallalair with the pommel to disable her so she could stand up for a killing blow. Her Soulsister was one of the walking dead, and soon so would be Trallalair. As much as she loved Saggethrie, Trallalair could not let that happen. The imminent approach of death was the only thing that could awaken her spirit. She was much quicker than the dead woman and rolled out of the way as the sword struck the gravel beside her head.

She leaped to her feet crying "Sinjer!". Her sword was in her hand in an instant and she cut off Saggethrie's sword arm in the next. Saggethrie, staring at her from somewhere beyond death, somewhere beyond meaning, stumbled forward and raised her other hand. With a cry of grief, Trallalair cut off that arm as well. The arms that had soothed her many a night, massaging away all her own tiredness and distaste for her role as concubine to Seldric, the arms that had held the ugliness of the world at bay, Trallalair had cut them both off. Saggethrie opened her mouth in a feral snarl to bite her and came running, armless, at her. Trallalair could take no more of it and fled into the mass of Sinjery still battling the dead.

"Dirmissilig!" she shouted to her Sister when she came into earshot. Dirmissilig was covered in blood. "You cannot win. You must leave while any of us still live."

Dirmissilig looked behind her at the groups of Sinjery fighting their dead Sisters. She looked at the Knights ahead of her in a melee of chopping, hacking, falling. She nodded. "You are right, we cannot prevail." At the top of her lungs, she shouted, "Sinjery Sisters, Knights of the Realm, Poets and Alchemists, anyone still alive, take to the air while we still can!"

Trallalair found Wehennah and, with Dirmissilig, looked for a Carpet still serviceable. Many had been sabotaged by the dead. Clearly, there was an intelligence motivating them. They were not simply mindless abominations. Dirmissilig found a carpet which she activated with a

Copper Order. Trallalair stood guard behind her, slashing at an oncoming press of rampaging dead Knights and Sinjery.

She pushed Wehennah toward the Carpet. "Wehennah, go! I will stand here until you are aloft!" Five other Sinjery and two Knights fought their way to the carpet. One of the Sinjery had a desperately bleeding sword cut to the abdomen. Another, obviously dead, lurched at them from the side away from Trallalair.

Dirmissilig hacked at the dead thing and kicked it away from the Carpet. "Trallalair, we are leaving. Get on the carpet, now!" Trallalair wanted to stay and fight, protecting her Sisters, but she knew Dirmissilig would only leave if Trallalair boarded the Carpet. She leaped onto the Carpet just before a swung sword and two arrows passed through the air where she had stood an instant before.

As they rose into the air, the bleeding Sinjery died. They rolled her off the carpet before she could stand up dead and attack them as well. Twenty Carpets were all that made it into the air. Less than two hundred of the host survived. Fighting continued below them but Dirmissilig shouted. "We cannot go back. Some of them below may still survive, but we cannot help them."

It was then that Trallalair noticed the sentries in the air were gone. Surely they had not fled. The morning mists still clouded the Forbidden mountains to the west. Trallalair saw dark shadows looming from the mists. For a moment she hoped they were the sentries who were missing. When the shadows took shape, she saw they were all Dragons flying from the west.

Dirmissilig tried to lead them away from the Dragons, but that meant flying deeper into the Dead Lands into what Trallalair saw as Sverdphthik's trap. With the horror of the lost battle tormenting their thoughts, the evil pall over the Dead Lands suffused their souls with a renewed depression that literally crushed Trallalair's companions to the Carpet. Only Trallalair and Dirmissilig had the strength to stay standing. The rest fell to the Carpet, men and Sinjery, crying in grief. Even Dirmissilig and Trallalair cried, but they stayed alert. The Dragons were closing on them as they flew toward a large group of rocks, some almost monoliths, that stood out from the plains of stark gravel.

Dirmissilig guided their Carpet toward the rocky outcropping. All the other Carpets followed her lead. "Our only hope is to get to those rocks and hide from the Dragons in the cracks and fissures until nightfall," she said to Trallalair.

Trallalair nodded but thought the hope of hiding from so many Dragons a slim one. Few creatures had better eyes than a Dragon. What choice did they have? No one had the wherewithal to take a log lance into the sky after flying from the dead things. They had all left weapons behind them in the chaos of the battle. Trallalair took inventory of what little they had left: three swords, two bows (one broken) and a total of five arrows, with only one golden-tipped Dragonscale-Piercing Arrow. Their only hope was to take refuge in the rocks ahead of them, where they might or might not be able to hide from the Dragons. Not a promising prospect.

Trallalair and Dirmissilig were watching the Dragons behind them as they flew over the rocks to gauge how to land. Neither of them saw the Dragons who came up from the rocks below where they had hidden until the right moment. Almost simultaneously, all the carpets went up in flame. Trallalair felt her leather become searing hot and felt her hair sizzle. The carpet dissolved beneath her feet and she fell toward the rocks below with all the others. Dirmissilig only had time to shout as they fell, "The last Sister alive, go to Isseltrent, even if you must CRAWL!" Trallalair heard Dirmissilig's shout cut short with a thud. That was the last thing Trallalair heard or knew.

CHAPTER 18

THE DOOM OF JONATHON
FORTHRIGHT

A fortnight later and twenty pounds thinner, Jonathon Forthright, Dungeon Inmate of Isseltrent, was bitten on the thumb by his pet rat. Jonathon jumped to his feet, whining and shaking his hand while the rat made off with his dinner and dragged it down a rat hole.

It was just as well. Jonathon did not like the variety of mold on the bread that day. The best molds, to Jonathon's palate, were the reds and yellows. The blues he did not care for, and the greens were absolutely awful. That day they gave him green bread.

A scuffling sound in the tunnel outside his cell made him forget his misery. He stumbled to his cell door, planting his ear against it. Any sound he could hear relieved his loneliness. The softest footfall was a pleasure to his ear and heartened him because it could be the footsteps of Arlen.

A man shouted, "You won't stop the Dragons this time. Your army is like a pack of mice to them!" His scream was stifled by a gag as they dragged him away, probably to his death. Having had a similar experience,

Jonathon could almost taste the poor wretch's gag, somewhat tastier than Jonathon's supper had been.

Two good things had come of all this business. By being guests in the dungeon, he and, probably Arlen, were undoubtedly in the safest place in Isseltrent with marauding Dragons about. Moreover, he was now a completely honest man, since he had no way to know if the Potion of Truth had, or ever would, wear off. So, he just wouldn't lie unless he wanted to commit suicide. In his present state, imprisoned and awaiting execution or torture, even that might come in handy sometime. All he would have to do is say something crazy like, "I am the Dragonlord," and the potion would put a swift end to his misery. He just wished he could get news of his children, not that he could do much about their plight.

Marching, jangling boots approached and a key rattled the lock. Jonathon was puzzled. Couldn't be dinner, he already had his, or at least the rat had his. There were no second helpings.

Three Sinjery maidens, their golden armor gleaming in the light of a torch carried by a shirtless prison guard, glared at him. "Traitor Jonathon Forthright, come with us," one barked. His hands were bound behind his back with tight rawhide strips, and he was prodded down the dark tunnel and up through the opening for the heavy trap door. The trap door had been torn off and thrown aside, the Giants gone. The palace execution yard had been commandeered by the Palace Guard. Knights and Sinjery together repaired an onager and tested a giant crossbow. A row of thirty Sinjery in variously colored armor, all with readied bows, lined the walls above. Trumpet calls and shouts echoed through the palace.

Before they entered the Dragonlord's Palace, a Green Dragon soared overhead accompanied by the crash of some engine of war toppled from the battlements. The Sinjery archers fired arrows, all hitting their marks. Most of the arrows bounced off, clattering on the palace roof. However, the archers achieved their goal, several hitting vital or soft spots and convincing the Green to fly off to some less bellicose target.

The path the Sinjery pushed him through in the confines of the courtyard was short, their goal the central golden-domed tower of Blaze. The golden dome, the tallest in the palace, was still unbroken, protected by verses traced in glittering tile around its circumference. Once inside the palace, the guards took him through seemingly interminable hallways twisting this way and that, going up several short stairs, past locked doors, and finally up a spiral staircase like the one to Rulupunerswan's laboratory.

At the top of the stairs, a brace of Sinjery Guards came to attention at a heavy wooden door. One stooped to lift a brass bird cage. After she opened the wooden door, she called, "Traitor Pixelle Hili, come here." Hili flew up and flitted through the cage door but with none of the precision she had always shown. She hit the door and literally fell into the cage. Her beautiful hair was unkempt, and her spider-silk gown was covered with dust, turning it into fluttering cobwebs. She gave Jonathon a sullen look and lay there, powerless to rise or simply too depressed to even get up. Jonathon thought he understood. *Why should she bother, if she could not fly?* Heartbroken, Jonathon looked away.

Before the door to the room was closed, Jonathon glimpsed dozens of Pixets huddled in groups on the floor and on the rough furniture in the room. A wire screen blocking the only window was watched by a Sinjery Ringmistress in the room. Although the Pixets were usually a cheerful folk, constantly flying and singing throughout the city, all Jonathon saw through the door was shivering. All he heard was weeping. Many were prostrate, languishing for the open air. None had brought their pets, and inside the castle, there lived very few of the orb-weaving spiders they used to make their clothes. They looked like Hili, unkempt and tattered.

Unable to control his revulsion at their plight, Jonathon cried, "You're killing them. All of them. Do you want to slaughter their entire race?"

One of the guards growled, "Hold your tongue, Traitor. The Dragonlord has been lenient with them and holds them close to the open air until he passes judgment."

This was intolerable. The Pixet Community had been steadfastly loyal to the Dragonlord. They had traded their ability to etch verses in Glass Commands to give the coins their power for the privilege of staying in Isseltrent. For them to be treated like criminals? Jonathon was appalled. "But not one of them is guilty of any..." His protest was cut off by the tip of the Sinjery's sword at his throat. His words were muffled with a familiar, stinking rag she pulled from her belt and tied with a knot in his mouth.

"His Highness knows of their close affinity in any venture in which one of them is engaged. Thus, if this one assisted you to aid the Demon," she pointed to Hili, "they all had a part." Hili sat miserably in silent agreement in her cage.

With cage in hand and Jonathon silenced and spurred on before them, the Sinjery Guards marched to the suite of Honor Gashgrieve. Four Sinjery stood before his door, somewhat more informally, one petting the mane of a powerful male lion. Jonathon was pushed toward the door. He sidled past the lion, watching for movement in case he had to get away quickly. When Jonathon was within a claw length, the lion bared a finger-long fang, twitching his tail. Jonathon leaped into the room unceremoniously, scurrying out of paws' reach. Safe inside, Jonathon stopped, panting in fear. The Sinjery, snorting in disgust, grabbed the rawhide around his wrists, menacing a twist of his arms so he stood still. What was he waiting for? He had no idea.

The room was paneled with greenish wood and lined by shelves packed with scrolls, sprite-penned books, elegant bottles of wine, and presumably magical items. There were few which Jonathon even recognized. On a broad and heavy wooden table, a map of the known world in mild relief lay studied by three Sinjery, five Knights, and Gashgrieve. At a position on the map far to the east of Isseltrent, a red spot glowed. Hundreds of tiny figures, armored men and Dragons, moved slowly about the surface of the map as if they were alive.

One of the Sinjery in fire-blackened green leather armor, one sleeve missing, dominated the conversation, but her back was turned to him. When Honor Gashgrieve finally looked up at Jonathon, they all regarded him, and the Sinjery in scorched armor turned as well.

When he saw her face, Jonathon jerked, unable to hide his alarm. Her face was a fright. A mass of crusted blisters hid a red swollen face, and she peered at him with puffy eyes which were mere slits. Singed stubble covered her scalp where hair once grew. A bloody bandage encased her left arm, replacing the leather armor which had been cut away. Her right hand, white with anger, clenched the pommel of her sheathed sword. Even through her scalded features, the look of hate she wore so frightened Jonathon that he choked and retched on the rag in his mouth.

Viewing Jonathon with utter contempt, Gashgrieve said to the Sinjery, "The Traitor, Jonathon Forthright," not even deigning to address him directly. To Jonathon's guards, Gashgrieve asked, "What new treachery has he admitted?"

"He inferred he forced the Pixets to inscribe the Unicorn Horn against their will."

Unsure whether the truth poison was still in his veins, Jonathon hesitated to acknowledge the Sinjery's statement. What she said was virtually true. He *had* forced them to inscribe the Unicorn Horn, using the power of their social debt to him from the years he had employed them. He nodded slowly at first, then with more vigor, expecting any moment to fall in agonizing death. He wanted to absolve the Pixets from the crime, even if it meant his death, but nothing happened.

Gashgrieve dismissed Jonathon's admission of his culpability with a wave of his hand. "Keep him gagged. Nothing he could say interests me." Then he took the injured Sinjery aside and whispered to her. She stood rooted, laconic, but her manner expressed tremendous rage. She nodded to his whispers.

They turned and approached. Honor Gashgrieve said, "Jonathon Forthright, Traitor of Isseltrent, this brave woman has been injured a thousand times by you. Her name is Brandmistress Trallalair. You will only address her as Brandmistress. She will be your guard for the rest of your miserable life."

The look in her eyes told Jonathon his life would be very short indeed once he was alone with her.

"Brandmistress, he is yours. Tell him what he has wrought."

Jonathon tried to look apologetic with the filthy gag clenched in his teeth.

"See Brandmistress," Gashgrieve said. "He begs for his life. You can see it in his eyes."

Trallalair opened her eyes the best she could, cracking the burned skin of her cheeks, making fluid run from blisters. Irritated, she wiped it off, oblivious to the pain she caused as she brushed her seared skin. She had refused the healing salve she had been offered. Little of it remained in the kingdom, and little more could be made with the coins rapidly being depleted. Besides, no more coins could ever to be produced, since the Dragons had been lost. Others had burns more serious than hers and deserved it more than she did. She pointed a finger at Jonathon and said, "Traitor, my Sister Jiminic warned me cryptically of your treachery with her dying breath. If I had had the foresight to question her about her meaning, I might have been able to stop you by finding you in the act and executing you before all this evil befell the land.

"No one but the Dragonlord has heard the full tale of our journey to the Dead Lands, not even Honor Gashgrieve. I will tell it now to him. Listen, if you dare to hear the horrors your deeds have caused."

The running blisters wept fluid-like tears from her eyes, but she was not crying. She had cried out all her tears long before. She was finished with grief. Only vengeance filled her thoughts now. Vengeance on the Demon. Vengeance on Jonathon Forthright. Definitely vengeance on Rhazburn. Even vengeance on Seldric for forcing her Sisters to lie and die for him.

"After your treachery lost the Dragoncrown and freed the Dragons, Isseltrent's chaos lasted many days before the combined powers of all the Rings and the Lances called from the Tributary Lands, with all the Poets, Alchemists and Seers, using up half of the Dragonlord's treasury, finally drove off the Dragon hordes. His Highness said the Dragons would not have stopped if the Demon had full control of the Dragoncrown, and the Seers divined the Demon had to return to his Hellpit to strengthen himself and learn the Dragoncrown's full power.

"Time was running out. We knew we had to attack with all possible force to wrest the Dragoncrown from the Demon's head before he realized its full potential. We were told if he were to gain full control of the Dragons, all would be destroyed." She laughed sarcastically, then crinkled her ruined face to sneer. Sneer at the traitor. Sneer at Seldric's delusion that they could fight the Demon's hordes. Sneer at the absurdity of it all. Gashgrieve gave her a disturbed look, as if he detected her disguised criticism of the Dragonlord.

Trallalair felt that she, too, was to blame for the deaths of all the host. She had fought the flying dead birds that had flown from the Dead Lands long before even one person had died in the harrowing of Isseltrent by the Demon. If she had only remembered the way the dead birds fought her and her Sister Dragonflyers, she would have realized that the Ghouls would rise up as dead things and attack them. If she had had the foresight to have the Ghouls burned, her Sisters and her Saggethrie might have been saved. Still, after what she had seen and experienced in the Dead Lands, Trallalair realized deep within herself that the host was doomed the moment they entered that perfidious territory cursed by the Demon.

"By the time the Dragonlord held council on the matter, all the trade routes were severed, the navy and all the merchant ships were sunk, and the year's crop was burned long before fruition. Even if all were to be set right at this time, famine and pestilence will still ravage the Realm for many Moons, if not years, all because of you!" Trallalair wanted nothing more than to kill the maggot before her, but Honor Gashgrieve had ordered her to stay her hand until the Dragoncrown was back on the Seldric's head.

Even the Dragonlord, when he saw her after she returned from the dead and told her tale, commanded her to protect the jeweler and force him to make amends by attempting to recover the Dragoncrown. Seldric had told her of his bizarre notion that Jonathon Forthright, since he had fashioned the Rod of Coercion, might be able to produce something to somehow counteract its hideous power. She knew Seldric well enough to recognize he saw the vengeance in her eyes, but all he wanted was his power back. Of course that included his power over the Sinjery. So, Trallalair must keep from harm the one she hated the most, to try and give Seldric that power back. She wondered if the Dragonlord could distinguish the difference between the vengeance she wanted to inflict upon the jeweler and the vengeance she wanted to inflict upon Seldric for his despicable treatment of the Sinjery. For now, vengeance upon the Demon and his minions, one of whom stood right before her within her reach, was first.

"Traitor, doubt not that I despise you. Were it not for the proscription of the Dragonlord, I would throttle you here and now and rid the world of you." The traitor stumbled back a couple of steps in fear, tripping over a chink in the floor to fall squarely on his rump. The gag fell further back into his mouth, making him gag and causing his eyes to water. Trallalair hoped he choked to death, but then she could not fulfill her mission to take back the Dragoncrown. Even though Seldric was a blight upon her Sisters, at least he let Sinjer exist, whereas the Demon would destroy everything within his power and then his power would grow apace. Eventually that power would reach and destroy Sinjer and all her Sisters. She knew from her brief time in the Dead Lands that death aided the Demon just as life aided the living. Sverdphthik's power was growing with every death inflicted. With every death, the Realm's power diminished.

She had nothing else to die for now. She should have died with her sweet Sister, but her own self-preservation and reflexes honed by decades of training had saved her. Out of all her Sisters and the whole host, the host that, in their ignorance, they all believed was invincible, there had been only one survivor. Herself. Trallalair had not been able to save Saggethrie nor even one of her Sisters that rode with her in the host. But if there was any way to save the rest of her Sisters that still remained in Isseltrent and Sinjer from the evil that befell her companions, she must try.

Trallalair conjured up an even bigger fantasy. She wondered if she could somehow save her Sisters from the degradation of the tribute they owed Seldric. With the Dragons gone, every Sinjery wondered if they still owed him tribute. If she were the one successful in taking back the Dragoncrown, she would probably re-establish that obligation for the Sinjery. Neither Seldric nor any man deserved that hold over her Sisters. Trallalair gritted her teeth. For the moment, the Demon and his unstoppable horde of death was the bigger threat. None of Sinjery wanted the terror of the destroyed host to come to Isseltrent or, Mother forbid, to Sinjer.

The closest Sinjery guard yanked the traitor to his feet and pushed him hard into a bare wooden chair, making him squeak like a rat when he hit.

Even Trallalair's voice had changed. A fortnight before, her voice and songs could warm the heart of anyone, even the hard heart of the Dragonlord. Now she growled like a beast, her voice parched by smoke and hoarse from shouting during battle.

She continued her tale. "It seems years, but after counting the days with Honor Gashgrieve, it was little more than a fortnight ago that the Dragoncrown was stolen. In this short time, I have seen the horrors of a hundred lifetimes. I would have gladly gone to the Sky Forests with the others, but our Captain, Dirmissilig, shouted as she died, 'The last Sister alive, go to Isseltrent even if you must crawl!'

"To my sorrow, I am that one. The last of the thousand Sisters and Knights who flew to bring back the Dragoncrown." At that, the jeweler drooped noticeably in his chair, abashed. Trallalair sniffed and shook her head at her pathetic charge.

"Yes, a thousand of us, gathered together by the Dragonlord. A thousand of us, charged with finding the Demon in his Hellpit and tearing the Dragoncrown from his head, while there was still time, while our forces had any strength at all."

As she recounted every heart-rending moment in the disastrous flight of the Isseltrent host she no longer mourned. All she felt there in Gashgrieve's office was anger and a need for vengeance. Those feelings suffused her with such agitation that she had to restrain herself lest she slaughter everyone in the office. She had to stop and collect her own sanity before the end of her tale. She took a deep breath, gripped her sword tighter yet and went on.

"When my Sister, Saggethrie, whom I loved the most, was struck down, I comforted her until she died." Trallalair burned with renewed hate for the traitor. "My Sister rose up and struck me. Had I not recognized that her dead body was now possessed by the Demon, I would never have struck back at her. Those hands that had soothed me with their touch many nights, I hacked from her body. And still, armless, with eyes cold as stone, she came at me. I backed off. I could not force myself to strike her again. I was ready to die.

"Finally, a few of us still alive realized the danger and strove to take all the living into the air and leave the walking dead things below. Dirmissilig shouted for us to push those from the Carpets who had just bled to death. We did so, then rose up together. Out of one hundred Carpets, few made it into the air. A pitiful fraction of our proud host were able to pull themselves from the fray below.

"We fled in terror. I never would have imagined we could be defeated so quickly. All we could do was run and hide. Even that was impossible.

"In the air, our Carpets were burned from the air by Dragons we no longer had any power to resist. We all fell. I was dashed unconscious, my fall cushioned only by the dead bodies of my Sisters who had fallen below me. When I awoke, it was blackest night, and the bodies I lay upon were still. Why all of them did not rise up, I have no idea. I too would have undoubtedly died if the Demon had not thought us all dead and let the

Dragons fly away. Mother Earth must have other plans for me. I alone came back, crawling like a cockroach."

As Brandmistress Trallalair finished her tale, Jonathon saw the grief within her and was amazed she did not weep. Nor did she acknowledge Jonathon's tears. He knew in his soul he was to die, had to die to pay for what he had done. He just hoped they'd spare the Pixets and Rhazburn. And, of course, Arlen. He couldn't meet Gashgrieve's withering gaze, but sat forlorn, studying his knees.

"Traitor, here is your doom," Honor Gashgrieve pronounced. Jonathon was jerked to his feet. "You must take back the Dragoncrown from the Demon you have aided and return it to Isseltrent to place upon the Dragonlord's head." Jonathon looked him straight in the eyes. A fortnight before, he would have fainted to hear those words, since they were a death knell. Since then, he had been through so much and had caused so much sorrow, he knew it was right. He would die trying to bring back the Dragoncrown. Yet, a thousand Knights and Sinjery failed to accomplish that deed. How did they expect one chubby little man, frightened as a rabbit, to succeed? Besides, after all of this, how could they trust him ever again? Why would they simply let him go and trust he'd go to the Dead Lands?

"Pixelle Hili," Gashgrieve said, "You must go with Brandmistress Trallalair and the Traitor Jonathon Forthright to the Dead Lands and be our eyes and ears through the Community so we will be informed continually of your progress. If the Dragoncrown is returned, the Pixet Community will be pardoned and allowed to stay in Isseltrent.

"Traitor, since you are evil through and through, in league with the Demon and all Hell, we trust you'll do everything in your power to keep the Dragoncrown on the Demon's head, so we have some inducements. Rhazburn will stay in prison for one fortnight, time enough for you to succeed or die trying. Then he will be cast into Hell through Hell's Breach, where he belongs. His Highness has given me the discretion to carry out his sentence sooner if I deem it prudent. The Pixets will be held in prison until the Dragoncrown is back. As a further inducement for you, we have something else. Ringmistress Cippion, bring Honor Rulupunerswan here with the seeds." She nodded and left, stroking the lion on her way past.

They waited half a Blessing. Trallalair conferred again in hushed tones with Gashgrieve and a Knight sporting fire-blasted armor and missing an arm. Furtive glances Jonathon's way told him they were discussing how to force him to help them. If they just took away his gag, he would have begged to help, even without their inducements. After all, he was virtually a dead man. And rightly so. If the Dragonlord had been able to get the Dragoncrown back already, Jonathon was well aware that his unseeing eyes would be staring at the wrong side of a coffin lid.

At long last, the sneering Alchemist was ushered into Gashgrieve's room. "Do you have the seeds, Honor Rulupunerswan?"

The Alchemist reached in his filthy cloak and brought out a filthier cloth bag. Just looking at the bag, for some strange reason, gave Jonathon a chill, as if something beautiful was within the bag struggling to get out. Rulupunerswan with his evil eyes, clutching it in his sepulchral hand, could just crush it, like a butterfly damned in the hand of Evil.

"Untie his hands." Gashgrieve waved at Jonathon, and a Sinjery cut the cords. Jonathon massaged his hands for a long time before the numbness subsided.

"Here is your family, Traitor," Gashgrieve said, casually. Rulupunerswan snatched Jonathon's hand and poured some seeds into his right palm. There were eight. Jonathon recognized most of them. A Blue-Eyed Kaitlin seed with a wisp of a green bud, two Sweet Peas, a Foxglove, one tiny Baby's Breath, a Dandelion, and two others he didn't recognize.

Jonathon looked up and hummed "Hmm?" through the rag.

"Your family, Traitor. Honor Rulupunerswan transformed them all with a potion into seeds." Gashgrieve took a disinterested look at Jonathon's hand. "As I recall, the Blue-Eyed Kaitlin flower seed is your wife, the others your children."

Jonathon still didn't understand and shook his head.

"All these plants, including the Blue-Eyed Kaitlin flower, live one season. They will all germinate this summer. By the end of this summer, these plants, your wife and children, will have flowered and died."

Jonathon's eyes became wild with fear. He mumbled and gurgled on the rag, nodding his head, pleading to speak.

Jonathon looked again at the seeds in his hand. They were warm. He could almost feel love emanating from them. Trembling with fear, he looked up, pointing with his left hand to the gag. Beseeching them with his eyes to let him speak.

"Brandmistress?" Gashgrieve said.

Trallalair gave a curt nod.

They removed the rag, and he spat filthy bits that fowled his mouth. "So you killed my wife and children, who had nothing to do with any of this!" he croaked, shaken, quivering.

"Yes, they are all there. But they are not dead yet," Gashgrieve retorted.

Jonathon shook uncontrollably. "What kind of people are you? Innocent children and a woman who has only love in her heart? My family," he sobbed. "How could have you have done this to my poor family?"

Gashgrieve's eyes turned to steel. "How could *you* have done what you did to *our* families? What of all the children that have died this last fortnight, Traitor? My entire family is dead, Traitor. And Knight Thackery's, here by my side, and hundreds of Knights, and Sinjery, and countless others. And still the deaths go on. By your will, and your Demon!"

Jonathon shook so that he cried aloud with great shuddering breaths. To his horror, one of the shudders blew the Dandelion seed from his hand. One of his children. He clutched for it but only succeeded in dropping more from his hand so they tumbled to the floor among the feet.

He shrieked and grasped the other seeds firmly, so as not to lose more. With the utmost care, he knelt, his wild eyes frantically searching for the tiny seeds on the floor. There was the Blue-Eyed Kaitlin, the tiny shoot thankfully unbroken, the Foxglove. He found one of the Sweet peas but not the second, so he panicked, until he realized the other Sweet Pea was still in his hand with the Baby's Breath and all the others except the Dandelion. At last, perilously close to the mailed boot of the Knight, he saw the Dandelion seed with its downy umbrella susceptible to be blown away by the least breath. With utmost care, he lifted it from the danger of the Knight's foot.

Now he was cowed and anxious to keep the seeds safe. "Honor Rulupunerswan, please, may I make a request?"

Rulupunerswan peered down at him imperiously.

Jonathon pleaded, "I am at your mercy. I implore you. May I borrow your pouch to protect my precious family?"

The Alchemist clutched his grimy bag like it was finest silk, not to be given up to one so vile as Jonathon Forthright.

Gashgrieve's hard eyes had no hint of pity. He said nothing but motioned with his head at Rulupunerswan. The Alchemist reluctantly gave the bag to Jonathon. With trembling fingers, the jeweler gingerly dropped the seeds back into it, unsure whether his family would fester and rot within the filthy purse. But what choice did he have?

Jonathon slowly shook his head. If his wife were to die irrevocably and his children were forfeit anyway, how was this to induce him to go on with the mission with any fervor? Why not just lay down and die himself?

Gashgrieve anticipated his question, an obvious one. "There is a potion that will transform them back to normal, Traitor," Gashgrieve said.

Jonathon snapped his head up, expectant.

"However, the potion needs something to activate it. Something that will never be, unless the Dragoncrown is returned. Dragonfire. Only with Dragonfire will the potion be activated and your family be made whole again. We promise this: though your own life is forfeit, no matter what happens, your wife and your children may still live, if you return with the Dragoncrown."

Return the Dragoncrown? Fight the Demon? Go to the Dead Lands? Jonathon looked at them flabbergasted. Were they all mad? Did they really expect him to just saunter up to the Demon past all the Ghouls, Zombies, Dragons, and Tundudil knows what, knock the Demon on the head, and stroll back to Isseltrent alive with the Dragoncrown? He always knew Rulupunerswan was mad, but the rest of them? They all just expected him to die. Why didn't they just chop off his head and be done with it? Of course, he'd try to get back the Dragoncrown if it was the only way to save his family. He was going to die either way. He might as well die trying to set things right and bring his family back, although he felt a nice quiet suicide would be a lot simpler.

"Fine. I'll do whatever it takes. But my family, if I bring it back, are they absolved of any crime?"

Gashgrieve huffed as if it were a moot point, since Jonathon's quest was hopeless. "I suppose, if you live through your trip to the Dead Lands, if you defeat the Demon and all its minions, if you bring back the Dragoncrown in time so that your family still is alive, if there is still a Dragon left to transform your family, if the potion works, AND if the Dragonlord is in a charitable mood, I suppose they may be be allowed to live."

"Fine."

"Of course, you must die."

"I know, I know." He could only die once, and there were so many deaths awaiting him, one more wasn't much of a threat.

Clutching his family's pouch warmly, he said, "I must plant my family and water them."

Rulupunerswan, Gashgrieve and Trallalair looked one to each other and shrugged. Gashgrieve said, "Brandmistress Trallalair is your guard and guide to the Dead Lands. It is up to her."

Jonathon regarded the fierce Brandmistress. This woman who hated him was to guide and help him? She looked as if all she wanted was to slit his throat as soon as they were alone. She softened not a whit but said, "You may plant your family, but make haste. We must be on our way to the Dead Lands quickly before the Demon gains even more strength."

Jonathon was amazed. She talked as if he was going to succeed where a thousand better people, all trained warriors, had failed.

Gashgrieve dismissed them with a wave of his hand, as if he had wasted enough of his valuable time.

The Brandmistress Trallalair clutched Jonathon's arm in a grip of iron, leading him from the room.

The thought of another he had led astray and disappointed came to him. "Wait!" Jonathon called before he cleared the door, "I need Loremaster Rhazburn to aid me. With his help, I have a chance to get back the Dragoncrown. Without it, I have no chance."

Rulupunerswan screwed up his face, obviously astonished that Jonathon would ask such a favor. Gashgrieve shook his head. "Rhazburn will stay in prison and be thrown to Hell in one fortnight. We don't fear you in the control of the Brandmistress, but Rhazburn, we know what he is capable of. It was he that entered the Dead Lands, made a pact with the Demon, brought back the Unicorn Horn, and devised the verses to give the Demon its power. Nothing could convince us that he will do anything but plot the downfall of his father the Dragonlord. He wants the throne himself. He was probably promised the throne by the Demon."

Jonathon was shocked that they could believe such things of Rhazburn who had protected Thuringland for a decade fighting at Hell's Breach. He needed his son's knowledge and bravery. At the very least, he needed to figure out a way to release him, so he could talk with Rhazburn to get ideas from a Poet's perspective.

"You are wrong about Rhazburn. He would never have helped me if he thought evil was behind the plan. He, too, thought he was aiding the Dragonlord. He is a Demonward. We need his knowledge to fight the Demon."

Gashgrieve slowly shook his head.

Rulupunerswan lashed out, "He fights for the Ghouls. He has one as a lover!"

Jonathon had an urge to insult the prattling fool, but he knew he had to coddle them all to get what he needed. "Honor Rulupunerswan, you are perceptive."

The Alchemist looked triumphant.

"But in this you are mistaken. The Loremaster was held captive by the Ghouls and faked friendship to aid in his escape."

Gashgrieve looked unconvinced.

"Can I just talk with him, with the Brandmistress listening, of course?"

"Brandmistress?" Gashgrieve deferred to her. "He is in your power. You may decide his every move. Just watch for his treachery. If he falters in his quest, you have the Dragonlord's permission to kill him, instantly. No one will question your judgment in this, Brandmistress."

Trallalair gazed at Jonathon through her blistered and swollen eyes. She sighed. She felt tired beyond thought. Pampering this wretch was too wearisome to be believed, after all her tribulations. Still, a nagging doubt of the Loremaster's role in all of this tarried in her mind, so she said, "Agreed. I want to hear how a man such as the Poet could have been twisted into complicity in this odious plot. But only words may pass between you."

She truly regretted that Rhazburn, who had briefly befriended her in a selfless and kind way, and whom she had thought above selfishness, had dealt with the Demon. Had she not heard the Demon speak of it, she would have doubted the truth. Perhaps the Demon lied, but Saggethrie and many of her Sisters were dead. Those responsible must be justly punished. She could not think of a more fitting punishment than taking the criminals to the Demon's Hellpit. If they could steal the Dragoncrown back, all the better. If they failed, she felt certain that the friends of the Demon would be tortured just like the rest. It would serve them right. As for herself, she would gladly die to be with her beloved, wherever she was.

"All right then," Gashgrieve said, "take the Pixelle Hili with you."

Rulupunerswan looked aghast. "Words, you say? Only words may pass between them? Are you deranged, or merely simple? Words are a Poet's weapons! Words facilitate all the spells. Do you really believe the Poet Rhazburn cannot harm you or the rest of us with just words? Was it not words on the scepter that facilitated the Demon stealing the Dragoncrown?"

Trallalair was not concerned. She had fought Dragons and Zombies. "I do not fear the Poet as you do, Honor Rulupunerswan."

"His words will only cause more grief. He must die now for his part in the treachery before he has an opportunity to formulate more *words* to break out of the dungeon and fly to his master Demon. The Dragonlord has said nothing to allow him any freedom."

He turned a haughty eye on Trallalair. "Do you really think you are immune to his wiles? A Poet's tongue is coated with honey. If he can argue with Demons at Hell's Breach and win, do you think he cannot taint any person's soul or twist anyone's mind? If you have ever spoken with him as I have, you would realize he can lie in a most pleasing manner."

She looked at the Alchemist with swollen, rueful eyes. What he said was very close to the truth. She had been seduced by his manner into feeling he was kind and thoughtful. It could have been a ruse. Each time she had been on her way to the Dragonlord's bed, ashamed and accosted by callous courtiers, she had been vulnerable to his charms. Maybe he had enchanted her and meant to use his power over her for his own nefarious purposes. His ploy had accomplished his end.

"Reconsider, Brandmistress. I have no doubt that you can slay him, but even you may be fooled by his charms. Honor Gashgrieve and even the Duke of Brione were fooled. Now the Duke is dead because of Rhazburn's perfidy. Even I, the Alchemist of the Dragonlord, was tricked by him as he left the Chamber of the Wishing Drop. Had we arrested him and executed him then and there as I knew we should, none of this would have ever happened."

Gashgrieve seemed swayed as well. He said, "Yes, perhaps Honor Rulupunerswan is correct in this."

Trallalair could easily imagine Rhazburn to be inherently evil. Were not all men self-serving and cruel? She said nothing to alter the course the counselors of the Dragonlord were taking.

Gashgrieve thought only a moment more. The decision seemed to please him for reasons beyond those espoused by Rulupunerswan. Apparently little love passed between the Chamberlain and the Loremaster. "Yes, I believe the Dragonlord's Alchemist is correct. Rhazburn is dangerous."

Turning to Cippion again, he said, "Have the Poet thrown into Hell forthwith."

Trallalair felt the sentence to be just for the duplicity she recognized in the Poet's words to her.

Jonathon, horrified, mouthed words that he could hardly form. His attempt to influence them into letting Rhazburn help him had worked in the opposite manner. He had just eliminated the last meager fortnight his son had to live in the world.

"No, please, Honor Gashgrieve. My son is innocent!" In his grief, he foolishly revealed that Rhazburn was his son.

"Ha!" Rulupunerswan said. "He is your son. All is clear. Innocent, is he? A son obeys his evil father out of loyalty, and you expect us to believe he is innocent? Now we know the truth. Execute the Poet!"

"I agree," the Chamberlain said.

"Brandmistress? Please. My son." Jonathon cried. "My son."

She said nothing. The decision was out of her hands. Rhazburn was the only man who she ever felt merited her respect, and now he had betrayed her trust as well, causing the destruction of the Realm, the slaughter of her Sisters and the hideous death of her Soulsister, Saggethrie. Death was too good for him. He needed to suffer as Saggethrie had. As Trallalair had.

"Gag him." Rulupunerswan ordered. The gag was shoved back in Jonathon's mouth, his hands were tied in front of him, and Jonathon, pushed by the angry Sinjery, stumbled off, totally defeated.

CHAPTER 19

RHAZBURN, DUNGEON MASTER OF ISSELTRENT

The absolute blackness of Rhazburn's cell threatened to darken his soul. Only a fortnight before, he knew he, Rhazburn, Loremaster and Bane of Demons, could do anything, compose any poem, make any magical item, defeat any foe. Then Dollop believed a Demon instead of Rhazburn. Then Jiminic chose death, after he saved her. Then Screela betrayed him to die and join a Zombie lord. Then the Demon tricked him. Then the Rod of Coercion, that he devised, caused the death and destruction of his friends and of the very people he wanted to serve. Even the magnificent Trallalair, for whom he would have done anything, was probably dead because of his pride. He had been determined to prove his ability against all odds. He had done it, and failed everyone around him. He had even failed his father whom he should have protected from Molgannard Fey to begin with and the Demon to end with. The very pride and abilities which had caused all the grief, that was all he had left.

Rhazburn was still determined to be the master of his own destiny. His cleverness would see him through. If he could free himself, not all could be set right. He knew that. Never could all the damage be undone. But they needed him more than ever with the Dragons loose and the Demon possessing almost limitless power. However, nobody but Rhazburn knew that he was indispensable.

In the blackness, Rhazburn held out his hand. His pet rat dropped a Copper Order into his palm. Rhazburn felt in his pocket for a piece of hard bread and held it so the rat could smell it. Rhazburn let the morsel fall when he heard the faint sniffing of the rat, so it wouldn't nip his finger to make him drop the bread. The sound of rapid chewing was the rat holding the bread between his paws, gnawing it. Rhazburn could depend on the rat staying for a while within reach of more bread, should Rhazburn be so inclined. Soon, however, the rat would give up and scurry off to search for more little discs as it was taught to do. Rhazburn had trained the rat to bring him little discs by making a little disc of mud he had scraped from the cell wall and dried. Then he trained the rat to fetch it. Now the rat brought him little discs he found in nooks and crannies all over the palace. Many of the discs were coins. Plenty of coins lay around in the chaos and destruction. Rhazburn's rat had brought him eight Clay Suggestions, five Wooden Requests, and two Copper Orders.

Rhazburn had wasted one Copper Order inscribing a Poem of Release on his prison lock. The second Copper Order would provide the power to unlock it. Splad, his surly and hurried dungeon keeper, never bothered to look at the lock. Rhazburn could get out whenever he wanted. The door was left unguarded most of the time, since the dungeon keepers were using a skeleton crew. Rhazburn was not even worried about the three more locked doors remaining between him and the courtyard above, because he had already figured out a way to train the rat to bring him keys.

Rhazburn was quite a bit thinner, but he had kept up his strength by straining his muscles against the walls of his cell. Filth caked his clothes. Before the oil in his lamp had given out, he had fashioned a rude needle out of the handle of his metal water cup. He had dyed string harvested from his clothes with pigments made from the molds of his breads. This allowed him to sew verses of power into his clothes - a Verse of Hardening in his tunic and a Couplet of Flying in his breeches, similar to that on a

Flying Carpet. He even had a small ruby and one Glass Command stolen from the Zombie Lord's treasure trove and kept hidden through all the searches he endured on his way to the dungeon. All he needed was a Pixet with his tiny tools to make a Gem of Power. He doubted he could train the rat to do that.

Rhazburn had plenty of time in the dungeon to contemplate the enormity of his blunder. Hundreds had died, if not thousands. If the Sinjery Brandmistresses had been riding their Dragons when the Demon took the Dragoncrown, they were probably all dead. He hated to think he had caused the death of Trallalair. Even if she hated men, he felt she had admired him. The fantasy that he could change her Sinjery ways and make her accept him as a friend had been bound to fail, and he had proved her suspicions of all men by unknowingly aiding the Demon to destroy the world. He did not doubt he deserved to be punished for what he did, but no one else in the world was as qualified as he was to set things right and protect the Realm from the new threat. Already, he was formulating a plan to counteract the Rod of Coercion and the Dragoncrown.

Slow, ringing steps of feet in armor approached in the corridor, interrupting Rhazburn's thoughts. The warriors were either tired or accompanied by someone walking slowly, someone weak, someone old. Rulupunerswan's abrasive voice proved it was also someone haughty and cruel. "Three of you, draw your bows. I expect you will have to kill him. there is no one more treacherous than the traitor Rhazburn."

Rhazburn took out his undamaged Copper Order and his Glass Command. He knew that if he was to help defeat the Demon Sverdphthik, this would be his only chance for escape. It sounded like Sinjery Ringmistresses accompanied the Alchemist. Although he hoped Trallalair survived, he hoped she was not among the group approaching. She was the last one he wanted to fight.

The lock clicked and torch light flooded the cell, hurting his eyes. "Bind his hands! Gag him!" croaked Rulupunerswan. Splad entered first, followed by two shapely armored Sinjery with bows readied. They were both too tall to be Trallalair. One Sinjery he could not see stayed outside with Rulupunerswan.

Rhazburn touched the Glass Command to his Shirt of Hardness and the Copper Order to his Flying Breeches. "Breeches, fly to the entrance."

His pants strained at his crotch lifting him above their heads, then sent him through the door, surprising even the Sinjery. They still managed to fire their arrows at his heart. All three hit his chest over his heart, and all were stopped by his magically-hardened shirt. As he passed, he batted the torch out of the hand of Splad and kicked the closest Sinjery, knocking her into a second. The tunnel darkened as the torch sputtered in a puddle. He ignored Rulupunerswan.

That was Rhazburn's last mistake. He saw a glint of a crystal vial tumble past his head. His ears were slapped by a concussion that filled the corridor with fire, smoke, dirt, and flying blocks of stone. The sound rang his ears, deafening him, the dirt filled his eyes, blinding him, the smoke seared his throat, choking him, the blast shocked his skin, numbing him, the stones pummeled his skull, dazing him. His flying pants ripped asunder, slamming him against the tunnel floor where he was buried by heaps of stone and clay.

Rhazburn lay coughing, covering his ears and blinking his watering eyes. He lay heedless of the hands that stripped his body of clothes, tied his limbs with cords, and restrained his tongue with a knotted rag. They didn't bother lifting him but dragged him deaf, mute, blind, and naked through the corridors, courtyards, streets and alleys, all the way to their destination, Hell's Breach.

The last voice he heard on the mortal side of Hell's Breach was Rulupunerswan's cackle, "And now, Rhazburn, Goremaster, you may join your friends, the Demons!"

The three Sinjery swung him in rhythm. From his knowledge of the Chamber of Hell's Breach, Rhazburn sensed he was headed in the direction of the Musical Mystical Door. In silent agreement on the third swing, the Sinjery released him. Wearing only the taut cords that bound his arms and legs and a bloody rag clenched in his teeth, he soared through the Musical Mystical Door into Hell.

He sailed. He flew. His eyes, nose, and throat burned. He vomited sour stomach fluid, coughing it around the gag, making the rag taste putrid. The infernal heat felt like molten lead poured upon him, so every strain against his bonds made him burst out in sweat. Helplessly falling in a bottomless abyss, he lost his urine and stool by the sheer fright.

With nothing but mist and more mist as points of reference, Rhazburn did not know whether he fell, flew, or spun in circles. However, something was there with him, something irritating and vile. Something that kept pace with him, or it filled all of Hell. Around him, inside his ears and his heart, a sustained hiss. A sibilance that built up, level upon level, until the sound excluded all thoughts from Rhazburn's mind. The hissing became his whole universe, infiltrating his soul, so he could not have moved on his own volition, even if he were released from his fetters. It was as if the Ruler of Hell, the Devil Kitilzgabwed, squeezed him in his horny fist.

It was then that the real horror came. The sound. It was not the Devil. The unbreakable, unchangeable susurration was the sound of millions of voices crying out in fear, all at once, all blurred into one constant hiss. When a thousand voices stopped in exhaustion, ten thousand more took up the cry, so the sound was seamless, without end or structure, neither rising nor falling, all one note or all notes, all voices together, a constant noise, hopeless and immutable for all eternity. And to Rhazburn's terror, his scream was among them.

CHAPTER 20

A SLIGHT DELAY

On the way out of Honor Gashgrieve's chamber, Trallalair took the traitor and the cage with the Pixelle Hili. Stumbling ahead of her, the jeweler sobbed.

The Pixelle lay inert, like a toy a child had discarded. "Stop, Traitor," Trallalair said. The traitor stood still, crying, his rounded shoulders convulsing in spasms. "Do not make me chase you," she warned, expecting him to bolt at the first opportunity.

She gently placed the tarnished brass cage on the wood flooring of the corridor. With the jeweler at the corner of her vision, she knelt and unlocked the cage. The Pixelle did not stir. Trallalair reached in the cage and touched the tiny body. Hili's head turned and looked at her with baleful eyes. Trallalair offered her hand. The Pixelle moved slowly, like the world was too much to bear, as she slid onto Trallalair's hand. She was warm, warmer than a human, and light as Peep, the pet mouse Trallalair had loved as a child in Sinjer.

"Can you sit on my shoulder?"

A miniscule nod was Hili's only response. Trallalair had only wisps of singed hair left, but she pulled it to her left shoulder and set the Pixelle there. "Hold my hair to steady yourself."

The traitor Jonathon Forthright's muffled whimpering and constant gagging annoyed Trallalair so much she took the rag out of his mouth. In gratitude for her generosity, he whined about the tight cords around his hands. She drew her sword and raised it above her head just to see him cringe. She felt Hili tighten her grip on her hair. When she sliced downward, only his bonds were cut, making him giggle, quavering. She wanted to slice him in two as neatly, but duty came before revenge. Usually.

"Come, Traitor, you are dawdling. We must go."

"My family, Brandmistress? I need to plant them."

They were dead, she thought, *Why bother?* "It is useless."

"Please." She thought he looked genuinely concerned about his family. Strange for one so evil.

"We have little time."

"I will be able to help you better if I know they are safe."

Safe, she thought. *Nobody is safe these days.* "All right. Where must you go?"

"To get a pot. How about the kitchen?"

Silent, she grabbed his arm and started toward Blaze's main cook room, jerking him along at her pace. The Pixelle bounced slightly on her shoulder.

Humoring the traitor and allowing him to satisfy his dire need seemed a much more efficient use of her time than arguing with him or dealing with his peevishness. Reluctantly, she led him to the cook's pantry to get a pot for the seeds.

Trallalair knew that the frantic head cook, working with a skeleton crew, had to feed hundreds of extra Knights recruited from the Tributary States to protect the city. Between absent workers, those injured or frightened away, and rapidly diminishing and irreplaceable supplies, she knew he was sorely pressed to keep up with the demands. That made him surly and reticent to surrender anything he could use himself. When Trallalair told him that the existence of the Realm hung by a thread and the Dragonlord had assigned the traitor to bring back the Dragons, he burst out in a laugh but froze at Trallalair's icy gaze. After grumbling about how was he supposed to carry out his own duties to the Dragonlord, he tossed the traitor a crockery pot which was fumbled and dropped. Trallalair twisted and swooped it out of the air a hand span from the ground.

Feeling Hili's slight touch disappear, Trallalair looked up to see the Pixet hovering with her filmy wings fanning the air. Trallalair offered her hand but Hili shook her tiny head and said, "Even in the deplorable condition of our Community, We are strong enough to sustain flight."

The traitor took the pot and hugged it like an infant. In the main courtyard, he filled it with dirt, carefully inserted the seeds with his thumb, and sprinkled it with water from a well.

Since he was done with his silly planting, Trallalair said, "Let us leave, Traitor. Your doom awaits."

"Noo."

"No?"

"I mean, I can't take this with me. It will be destroyed."

"So?" She refused to be taken in by his fantasy that he would succeed in this quest. Of course it would be destroyed, as would he. Surely, he could see that all of this was useless. She just wanted it over as soon as possible. If she did not long for one last chance to destroy the Demon, she would just execute the traitor, here on the spot, to finish his treacherous life. Despite her longing, she knew nothing could kill the Demon. This journey was as doomed as that of the host of Sinjery and Knights of the Realm.

"Let me talk with the Pixets," he said.

"I don't think they want to talk with you, Traitor."

Hili flew up a hand span in front of Trallalair's face. "We will hear the Master Jeweler's request."

"Please take me."

She could see what he was doing. More procrastination. Anything to stall. "This is *absolutely* the last detour we will take."

"Agreed."

Hili flew ahead a few paces, obviously pleased to get back to the Community's bosom, even for a brief visit. She led them quickly back to the Pixets' room. Trallalair realized that the Pixets' real love was nature, particularly the land that the Demon had stolen from them centuries before. She never thought they really cared what happened to the humans. Still, she pitied them, wasting, laying languid like lizards on a hot day.

They should be free spirits flying, bathed in the crisp air of the sky. The same feeling of loss weighed down her own soul. With Hover dead, she would never feel the joy of flight again.

Trallalair's Sister Guards let them pass through the door into the Pixets' cell. Hili flew into the center of the room and turned to watch the traitor. She said not a word but, of course, the Pixets never needed words between each other. Very few of the tiny beings even bothered to look up. Trallalair reasoned they did not need to look. They probably saw through Hili's eyes and heard through her ears.

The traitor seemed on the verge of tears. His voice cracked with the strain of holding them back. "My dear Community. I beg you to listen to my pledge. I pledge to do everything I can to undo the chaos I have caused. I was wrong to use a Unicorn Horn to try and save the Realm, and it turned against me. I, too, have suffered. My son Rhazburn is dead, and my family soon will be."

The Community seemed to take an interest in the traitor's last statement. Many sat up. Some even took to the air. Like the Sinjery Sisters, Pixets understood the importance of belonging to a group.

He held out the flower pot. "Here is my family, turned into seeds by Honor Rulupunerswan. I planted them just now."

Several Pixets and Pixelles flew up and peered at the soil. One placed a hand on the soil as if to test the moistness. Another sniffed. "This soil will nurture them, Master Jeweler," one of them said.

"Please help me. This has nothing to do with engraving jewels. Just help these seeds grow and live while I am away. Save my family. Once they flower and die they will be gone forever. I have so little time... so little time."

Pixets always answered quickly. As if their communal mind took scant moments to make a decision. "They will grow well here in the window." Ten Pixets formed a nimbus around the pot. It rose from Jonathon's grasp and floated, carried by their fluttering wings, to the window, where it settled on the sill, reverently in the sunniest spot.

Trallalair was surprised that the Pixets gave in to the evil traitor's pleas. She never had the feeling Pixets were evil, just interested in the affairs of their Community at the expense of others.

The traitor seemed satisfied with the Pixets' enthusiasm in caring for his plants. "Now I have to get some supplies at my shop. Come, Hili." The Pixelle flew up, but not too close to the traitor.

At this idea of more delays, Trallalair became furious. "Traitor, enough trifling. You will do your duty now, or you will die right here." Trallalair just placed her hand on the pommel of her sword as a reminder of who was in charge.

The traitor cringed, but then he stood straight up and declared, "Brandmistress, you can kill me whenever you like, but that won't bring back the Dragoncrown."

Now, she thought, *his true, haughty, petty self comes through.* "Traitor, I have had a vision, and in my vision, I kill you. I can see it in my mind as clearly as I see your face right now. I had this vision the night we all died in the Dead Lands. It was as if I stepped over into a different land. A land of the mind, or an existence beyond the death and destruction of this world. Into a place where all things are revealed. It was as if, for a short while, because of all the terror and pain I held within me, Mother Earth allowed me to walk in the Sky Forests with my Sisters who have departed from this world. For a few moments, I had all the knowledge of Mother Earth." The jeweler backed away with his eyes wide.

"Yes, you heard me right. I died, too, that day, and as I was lying on my Sisters' bodies, many thoughts passed through my mind. I could see the past and the future. Much of what I saw was evil and hurt my soul. One thing alone felt good to me and let me rouse myself from the dead around me. The vision of me firing an arrow toward your evil heart. I knew it was right, I knew it was for the good of the Realm, and I knew it would come to pass. In my reverie, I felt as if I were aiming my arrow at the most evil being in the world, like you were the Demon himself. For this, and for this alone, did I return." She gripped his shirt and looked into his eyes.

Hili flew up close as if to observe for the Community. Trallalair turned at the movement, her eyes intensifying in recognition. "A Pixet... yes, a Pixet was there as well. You? Was it you? Yes, I believe you were there as well, and somehow had a part in it all. Like a dream, the details blur."

Trallalair turned back to study the fear in the traitor's eyes. "Your eyes tell me much, Traitor. You know I speak truly. You, too, can feel it in the center of your evil heart."

Trallalair knew she looked frightening with her swollen and crusted face. She pulled his face close, enjoying the sight of him turning away in fear and disgust. What a weakling, she thought. How could a man like him deal with the Demon? His eyes told her he was an easy man to cow. Many would use him for their purposes. "I will be your executioner, Traitor."

Even though Jonathon was tight with fear, he relaxed, boneless as a jellyfish washed up on Sinjer's shore. She released him.

Limp and insipid, he said, "Brandmistress, I'm sure I deserve to be killed by you. If you would permit me to be of assistance to you first, I vow to try my utmost to purloin the Dragoncrown from the Demon."

Vows? What did he know of Vows?

"You expect me to believe that vow? You will go with me because you must. You have no choice, Traitor."

He whined, "I want to follow you, but my jewelry... I have strong magical jewelry that can aid us. Aid you. I want to help you."

"Your magic disgusts me. More tricks to cause more deaths? All I need is my Sinjery Sword." Again she gripped the gold pommel of her sword.

"Anything that can help us is worth the time of a few Favors, surely. My shop is on the way out of town." He pointed in the direction of the East Gate.

"A dozen Poets and all the magic they had to fight with failed to defeat the Demon. Why do you think your tiny little trinkets will bother him at all? And why should I trust you?"

"I know I have neither the skill nor the strength to confront the Demon. I know I will die. My only object is to present to you the magical objects we have available for you to chose from at my shop. Even after my demise, you may still defeat him if we find something that can protect you a little. Like the Jewel of Nishbad." He shook his head and said, "Alas, that power is lost to us with Rhazburn gone. He was the only one who knew the verses."

"He was lying about it to save himself. Thankfully for the Realm, that ploy was ill received. No one was fooled." She would never be fooled by Rhazburn again. Of that she was doubly thankful. Seeing that she could not be swayed, the traitor gave up his nagging about the Jewel of Nishbad.

Trallalair knew the jeweler had nothing in his shop powerful enough that the Demon or a Dragon would take the slightest notice. Still, she respected the power of Poets. Poets had devised the verses on her Sinjery Sword, and she knew what power it held. There might be something, some weapon of legends that would have the power to destroy the Demon. Obviously it would not be in the traitor's shop, but he might have a clue. As she held that thought, she softened a bit and said, "We need supplies before we leave. We must walk to the Dead Lands, and the journey will take a good fortnight. So you may stop at your shop to look for supplies. But be warned. I will tolerate no treachery. The moment I sense you are at odds with my purpose and the charge of the Dragonlord, that moment will be your last."

Trallalair had the power to be charitable. Finally, some power over someone. After so many failures, this was her last chance to do things right. Although she trusted her sword more than anything they could find, maybe a little magic on their side was not a bad idea. She had received her last command and would perform one last duty to the Dragonlord. Take back the Dragoncrown or die trying. No one but the traitor and the Pixelle would go with her to the Dead Lands. For good or ill, all the decisions were hers from now on.

The traitor and the Pixelle followed Trallalair meekly back through the halls and courtyards, out the main portcullis of Blaze, and onto the ravaged streets of Isseltrent. She planned to get some supplies in what was left of the city. They needed food for a long enough trip to get to the Dead Lands. They wouldn't need rations for a return trip. She had her Sinjery Sword in her scabbard. Across her back, she slung a new bow and quiver given to her by the few Sinjery Guards still living in Blaze. They had given her nineteen arrows, three of them golden-tipped Dragonscale-Piercing Arrows. The Pixelle, she noted, had a small pouch tied at her waist. It bulged with her tiny tools, in case the Community's skills in engraving gems to make magical devices was needed.

As they entered the smoldering streets, they walked past some areas charred and unrecognizable, while others were virtually intact. Like a lottery, some shops had been lucky in the holocaust and some hadn't. In Jeweler's Row, the traitor's shop had been lucky, almost untouched by the destruction, more evidence that he was in league with the Demon. Few people remained in the city and certainly none needed jewelry, when most had neither food nor shelter. His shop was guarded by a single Sinjery, Atherraine. She had barely survived her crushed leg. All the Healers and Poets had been able to do was reverse the damage partially. She still wore a bloody splint, and her crutch was propped against the wall.

Trallalair said, "You are in agony. I admire your courage."

Atherraine's eyes spoke a multitude of thoughts and feelings to Trallalair. Thanks for saving Atherraine's life, as well as recrimination for letting her live when so many Sisters perished. In those eyes, Trallalair also saw determination to carry on with her duties despite her pain and disability, grief for all those killed, as well as empathy for Trallalair's burns. More empathy was there for Trallalair and her burden, hauling the foul baggage of the traitor back to the Dead Lands. The command Trallalair received from the Dragonlord was well known to all the Sinjery. All were ready to aid her in any way they could.

Atherraine said, "Your injuries grieve me. You must know I suggested we burn this shop. You may want to hold your nose. The stink of the Demon taints it all. Honor Gashgrieve refused to let us burn the shop or take away any of his artifacts lest they be cursed, but he left it all as a lure for the Demon."

She gazed harshly at the traitor Jonathon Forthright. "You bring back the traitor who owns this shop, the one in league with the Demon? Could he lure the Demon back here for us?" She leaned menacingly toward him, making him step back in fear. She added, "Don't you think he will lure the Demon back even better if he is dead? The Demon is drawn to dead things."

Trallalair answered, "You are correct and have every right to hasten his death, but rest assured I will personally see to his execution. Of that you may be certain. You may tell all our Sisters that I have seen it in a vision granted me by Mother Earth when I lay unconscious upon our beloved Sisters who died in the battle with the Demon's minions. For a moment, their spirits carried me along with them to the Sky Forests. There I saw it as plainly as I see your face."

Atherraine nodded in respect for Trallalair's sincerity. No one could look at her fire-blasted face and deny she had experienced misery.

"You know I have been given a mission, to take the traitor back to the Dead Lands in one last attempt to take back the Dragoncrown. You won't see us again, after we take whatever might aid us in this quest."

Atherraine gave a curt nod. To Trallalair, she needed no words to say she wished to go with her, spend what was left of her life in homage to her Sisters. If it were not for Atherraine's shattered leg, Trallalair knew her sister would gladly go with her. Without saying more, Atherraine unlocked the door.

Trallalair stayed at the door with Atherraine. They watched the traitor bustle about his shop. Hili sat on a bench and dangled her legs weakly, her dusty gossamer dress barely concealing her skin. The traitor rummaged through drawers and unlocked or broke open boxes and chests as he collected pendants, pins, bracelets, jewels, chains, and coins.

With Trallalair and Atherraine following and watching closely, he circled the outside of his shop and picked up a piece of jewelry in the alley behind. All of it he stuffed in a small plain strongbox. In a small silk pouch, he put a few of the precious coins. With the Dragonkilns stilled, these were among the last in the world.

They all left the shop when the traitor declared nothing of value remained. "Ringmistress," he said, addressing Atherraine, "I will not be coming back to my shop. Maybe others wanting shelter could use it."

Atherraine ignored the traitor's statement, but looked to Trallalair who said, "You may burn this accused place now."

"Your duty to the Dragonlord is complete, but I must first report to Honor Gashgrieve," Atherraine said and turned toward Blaze to leave.

"Ringmistress, Honor Gashgrieve already knows. Pixet Thesbe is constantly reporting our progress," Hili said, flying up to within one human stride from the Sinjery Guard.

"I understand you. Nonetheless, you realize that by my duty, I must report." She nodded and started off at limp.

Immediately after Atherraine left toward Blaze, Trallalair began to plan the supplies the three of them would need and where to buy them. Her thoughts naturally wandered to weapons. Her sword and arrows were useless against the Demon. She knew that from experience. She was trying to imagine what powerful, legendary weapon she could use when a glimmer of a conversation with the Dragonlord about just such a weapon formed in her mind. She remembered a weapon... powerful... feared even by the Dragonlords. Something they would not touch.

"Traitor," she said, suddenly making Jonathon cringe as if she was going to strike him.

"I remember a story of something. A legend. A knife, I believe. Powerful against dead things."

"Yes, Brandmistress, I know the legend. The Knife of Life."

"I heard the story from the Dragonlord himself." She now spoke easily of her close association with the Dragonlord. Her experience in the Dead Lands had made the shame of her role as his concubine insignificant.

"Yes, he told me this story. A hundred years ago, the the great-grandfather of the Dragonlord, Kavakum, died a natural death. No legitimate son of his lived, and the Dragoncrown was placed on the head of one of the Royal Bastards, a man who had little strength of mind and soon pleaded to be released from his duty.

"It was a time in which a dozen brilliant court Poets thought themselves capable of anything. They were much like Loremaster Rhazburn in their foolish pride. Together, they devised a device to bring Kavakum back from the dead. They molded a dagger of such power, and called it the Knife of Life. After testing it on a dead duck, they exhumed the Dragonlord's body and stabbed it with the Knife of Life. To their amazement and joy, the Dragonlord was resurrected on the spot. When Kavakum awoke from death to life, he was enraged at having been stolen from the arms of his Queen who had preceded him in death.

"When he saw what the poets had done, that they had presumed to have the wisdom of Tundudil and had wielded the power to interfere with his eternal happiness, he cursed the Poets and had them all fed to the Dragons. To insure no similar mistake was ever made, that no person content in the rewards of the Afterlife could be brought back to misery, he announced that he would dispose of the Knife of Life and wipe all knowledge of its making from the world. No one, not even his descendants, know what happened to it. He kept his decision a secret."

Trallalair looked straight at the traitor. "The Dragonlord believes that the Knife was not destroyed as Kavakum had intended. Instead, he thinks it was merely hidden and still exists. He thinks that if it had been destroyed, Kavakum would have made a spectacle of it and many would have known of it."

"That is the weapon I need," the traitor replied.

She knitted her brow in response. She hadn't meant to supply the traitor with a weapon.

He quickly corrected himself. "I mean that you need. For you, Brandmistress, for you to fight the Demon."

"Yes, but it is lost. If the Dragonlord does not know of its whereabouts, no one in court will. Besides, the Poets who made the Knife of Life were cursed by Kavakum. How can we presume to look for something no Dragonlord has ever wanted to find?"

Within moments, Hili flew up before them and said, "Thesbe confirms from Honor Gashgrieve that no one in court knows the resting place of the Knife of Life. They will spare none of the Knights protecting the Dragonlord to look for it, but if we vow to bring the Knife back to Isseltrent along with the Dragoncrown, we may pursue it now to aid us."

"Maybe someone outside of the court would know of it?" the traitor asked.

"Highly unlikely," Trallalair mused.

"Would you consider an attempt to try and find it? I have a vision bowl at home. At your indulgence, we could talk to the Gossip Dwarves. They are capable of locating almost anything."

"It is probably a waste of time, Traitor. Besides, I doubt that any of the Gossip Dwarves still exist. Thanks to you, they are all dead or fled from Isseltrent."

"But we can try. At my house, I have stores to supply us with food and clothes for our journey. We could consolidate several of the chores we have to prepare ourselves."

They did need supplies. Just picking them up at the traitor's lair would save some of the time they would need if they wanted to look for this legend.

"My house is an excellent starting point. It rests on a hill on the outskirts of the city. From the top we can see for a league to see if we will be safe."

She had to make a decision. She grunted and nodded in agreement. The traitor beamed, obviously pleased with himself. Trallalair was offended by his complacency because she knew she would never smile again. "Only I shall touch the Knife of Life if we find it."

He flinched. "Of course, Brandmistress."

He pointed to the south beyond the limits of the city. "There is the hill my house rests on, if my house still exists after all this."

Her eyes followed his finger to a prominent patch of green oddly spared from Dragonfire. Like his shop, it was one of the few hills surrounding the city that was still untouched. The hill was off in the distance south of the financial district, about one league by Dragonflight. She could just barely see a house on top.

"I see your house was not burned, just like your shop. More benefits of friendship with the Demon, I presume."

He squinted. "You think my house is still there? I'll bet the Dragons just didn't want to tangle with Farmer Gibbel."

When she looked quizzical, he explained, "He's my neighbor and he is a tough one. When it comes to protecting his chickens, I don't believe there's a thing he'd be afraid of. I saw him swing his rake and send a fox flying right over a maple tree."

She snorted at the ludicrous idea. It was the first thing she'd found funny in a long time. This traitor was odd.

"You'll see," he went on. "I can help. I have some contacts in the city. Many of my children can help us find what we need."

"How many children do you have, Traitor?"

"Uhh, thirty-one. As I recollect."

She looked at his portly frame, no doubt thinned from dungeon life, but still with a double chin and that pasty kind of skin from too easy a life. He didn't look like he could have sired thirty-one children. "How many wives have you had?"

"Just one. Oh, oh. No, no they aren't all mine. Just two. Two girls. The others we adopted."

Trallalair thought, why would an evil man adopt so many children? Some kind of profit no doubt. Money probably. A fat man like him was surely a money grubber, only interested in filling his house with baubles. "I imagine there is some profit in so many children. Did someone pay you a lot to care for them?"

"I wish someone had. No, I'm afraid that's what started all this. I borrowed too much for all the debts from so many. Still, I'd do it again. Adopt them, I mean. But not borrow the money."

What prattle. All this terror and destruction because he needed money? She just shook her head. What a pathetic human he was. He had no money but wanted all those children. When he couldn't pay for their keep, he got himself into unconscionable debt. "So what are you saying? You sold the Rod of Coercion to the Demon to pay off your debts?" She was getting madder by the moment.

"I didn't know he was the Demon. He disguised himself and said he was from the Dragonlord."

What a preposterous story. "You'll have to come up with a better story than that, Traitor. Even assuming you were only a fool, the crime is still yours."

"I know."

She said no more, wanting no more inane lies. They walked through the charred remains of the city. A few people recognized the traitor Jonathon Forthright and knew the rumors. Some spat at him. One man pulled a knife and advanced on them with murder in his eyes, but he backed off when he saw Trallalair's drawn sword. Trallalair was content that few people remained in town, most having fled to the country. There were too few to make a mob that her sword could not dissuade. Hili flew high enough, so she was safe from the unruly townsfolk.

Around sunset, they climbed the hill through a stand of oaks that were intact. Sure enough, as they passed a chicken farm, they saw the owner, a thin, intense man, wielding a rake like it was a halberd. He took a look at them and raised his rake higher. Then he seemed to recognize her burnt and torn armor as that of a Sinjery Dragonflyer and Jonathon as his neighbor. He said, "I thought you two were more of those three forsaken looters after my chickens. You owe me, Jeweler. Many thieves would have ransacked your house had they gotten past my farm."

"Thank you, Master Gibbel. I am in your debt."

When they came within sight of his house, she saw the roof and front door torn off, the garden smashed, and a huge oak uprooted. One Sinjery Guard slept in a blanket beneath a tree in the garden. Another, Vailisk, stood by the front door frame. She thought the traitor would be shocked at the damage. Instead, he was pleased. "You were right, Brandmistress. My house is fine."

Vailisk, too, had been seriously injured, keeping her out of the host that had died in the Dead Lands. She had a dent in her skull and a wooden brace around her neck. She called, "Prisoners, you may come out."

To their astonishment, nine people emerged from the ruined house, five adults and four children. With tears in his eyes, the traitor hugged them all and talked about what had happened. When he told them about his wife and children, the other adults cried as well. The young children looked in astonishment and kept asking where the other children were. Vailisk watched them closely. The sleeping Sinjery, Quintella, woke up, strapped on her sword, bow and quiver, and came up for support.

Trallalair soon found out that all the damage had been done by the Giant Molgannard Fey shortly before the Dragons were released. Jonathon's family members had come looking for their mother and siblings, so they were detained as hostile enemies of the Realm.

The traitor claimed the reason his house was spared was because any Dragon seeing the ruined house thought it had already been pillaged and flew elsewhere.

Trallalair knew his family had been spared because of his deal with the Demon. This was just further proof. More to justify her execution of the jeweler.

The young ones were the traitor's grandchildren. The mother, Laurel, was one of his natural children and was there with her husband, Herkimer. Another natural daughter, Heather, had come for a short time, leaving her children with her husband, but ended up there for the duration. Apparently, she had gotten a message to her family and warned them to stay away.

The other two adults were two of the traitor's adopted children. Patrick was twenty-four, a bachelor in the rug trade. He had brought food and some money, expecting to find Arlen and the children. Like the others, he had found incarceration instead. The food was used for all of them, even the Sinjery Guards. The last was Will, tall and strong. He wanted to repair the roof, but the Sinjery forbade it despite his constant, annoying pleadings. They had not come prepared to fight off prowling Dragons that might be attracted by the activity.

Patrick sounded adamant. "Father, they can't believe you're in league with the Demon. What is wrong with them? Look at us. If we had come to visit you in the dungeon, we'd be there ourselves. I heard them talking about it. They're tired of watching us here. Maybe they'll just chop off our heads."

The traitor tried to shush him, like the Sisters had never considered that before he mentioned it. Quintella and Vailisk disregarded his ignorance. Trallalair spoke with her two Sisters about her idea of the Knife of Life. Quintella had heard the story as well when she had serviced the Dragonlord a year before. To Quintella's delight, he had tired of her when he became familiar with Trallalair. Quintella had confided her relief while expressing her pity for Trallalair's position.

Apparently to change the subject, the traitor said, "And what about you, Will? Thinking of repairing the roof? I concur with the brave Ringmistresses. Since when are you immune to Dragonfire?"

The big man said, "I haven't any family, Father. No wife or little ones to suffer if I die."

"Forget it, Will. What you repair today, the Dragons may smash tomorrow. Desist until the Dragons are tamed again."

"Most people think that will be never."

"My thoughts exactly," the traitor said.

Will was unhappy, but agreed to stop bothering the Sinjery for a while, until things were clearer.

When the traitor went inside, he looked in a cage similar to the one which held the Pixet. In this one, only a dead lark lay on the floor. Oddly, he started crying again.

Laurel said to him, "He was already dead when I got here, Father."

"I should have freed him when I had the chance. Now, like everything else, it's too late." He sniffled and stuttered for a long time. The traitor apparently had compassion for pets. Why not for humans? At least his two natural daughters seemed somewhat normal.

After taking the dead bird to the garden and burying it, he conferred with his family and pronounced, "Brandmistress, we must acquire food elsewhere. The day I left home, ample stores of food remained in our larder, most of it dried. More provisions yet Arlen had cooked a fortnight before and preserved in the Keeper. I am loathe to report that the majority has been consumed by my family and the Ringmistresses. I abjectly apologize to you, Brandmistress."

The main object of their visit was the Knife of Life. Trallalair said, "Stop your dawdling, Traitor. Find your Vision Bowl and contact the Dwarf."

The traitor did as he was told. He placed his Vision Bowl on a kitchen table and filled it from his replenishing pitcher. While Trallalair watched his every move and noted his every word, he floated a Wooden Request on its rippling surface and said, "Smurgen".

A Gossip Dwarf appeared, the image of his head wiggling about on the unsettled water. A purple bruise marred his left eye.

"Smurgen, you're still alive," the traitor said.

"One of the few, Master Jeweler." The feeling of hate he put in his words was unmistakable to Trallalair. She could certainly empathize with the Dwarf.

"From your tone, you accuse me of causing their demise," the traitor said.

Smurgen said, "It was your fault."

The traitor hung his head. "True in a sense. But it was through foolishness, not design. But I'm committed to make it right. Or die in the attempt."

"Make it right or die? I think you'll die, Master Jeweler. So what do you want from me?"

"I need to find the Knife of Life."

"I know of it, but I can tell you nothing."

"Why is that? The Dragonlord won't let you? But I work for the Dragonlord now."

"No. His Lordship Molgannard Fey won't let me."

"Huh?"

"I am here with his Lordship Molgannard Fey." He flinched and looked to his side as if expecting to be struck. "Lord Fey in his wisdom protects many people from the Dragons now."

"You are there of your own free will, I suppose."

"Of course," Smurgen said.

Trallalair knew the hapless Dwarf had been kidnapped. Molgannard Fey was taking every opportunity to profit from the Dragonlord's loss.

"So how can I get the information I seek?"

"Lord Fey will allow you to purchase the answer to that question alone for two hundred Copper Orders. You must bring it yourself and place it in his hand. I believe that is rather generous of Lord Fey," he said, looking again to the side with a questioning look, obviously trying to please the Giant.

The traitor turned, looking quite despondent, and told Trallalair, "This is where I started."

Turning back to the Vision Bowl, he said, "The Brandmistress Trallalair is my kind custodian. She determines my every move and accompanies me at the Dragonlord's command."

Smurgen turned again to listen to someone off to the side, presumably the Giant. "The Lord Fey grants that you may bring her. But no weapons. You may bring no weapons."

"Agreed," Jonathon said.

"Then we are done," the Dwarf said. "Goodbye," he said with one last pleading look to them. The Dwarf disappeared. Trallalair dumped the water out to cancel the connection from their end. She did not want the Giant listening in on their conversations unbeknownst to them.

About the condition of going weaponless, Trallalair had not agreed. She had no intention of going to Molgannard Fey's Skin-Splicing den unarmed, but she said nothing. She knew why Molgannard Fey allowed her to bring the traitor. She was well known to the Giant from her years in the Ring of Guards, and she knew he had a special reason to allow her to come to his fortress.

A small voice from behind said, "The Demon is friends with Molgannard Fey." Trallalair and the traitor turned to see Hili in the air at a level even with his head. While they concentrated on the conversation with Smurgen, they had forgotten Hili was with them.

Trallalair said as she turned, "Is that true, Traitor?" He should know all the dealings of the Demon.

Again damning himself in the eyes of the Brandmistress, the traitor replied, "Yes, I'm sure that's true. I'm sure that's how he got into the city, found a dead body, collected Glass Commands, and found me. How else would he know to single me out and offer me the money I was in desperate need of? How would he know that I was the one person in all of Isseltrent who could get the assistance of Rhazburn and the Pixets to make the Rod of Coercion, unless Molgannard Fey had told him? No one could have made the Rod of Coercion but me."

Hili piped up, "When the Demon left the Master Jeweler's shop, we knew something was amiss and we followed the cowled man, not knowing he was possessed by the Demon. We followed him all the way to Molgannard Fey's tower, but we had to flee. The stench and the sight of so much death was too much to bear."

Trallalair's verdict was that the traitor Jonathon Forthright had purposefully helped the Demon. Why anyone would aid a Demon was too unbelievable to be born. "So it should be easy for us to deal with the Giant. You, the Demon, the Giant, you're all a family."

Incomprehension filled the traitor's face as if she were speaking Sinjery, the language of Sinjer which was never shared with any outsiders.

The traitor seemed aghast. "Molgannard Fey is not my family. Haven't you heard me? I owed him money. See this?" He pointed to his ripped-off roof. "Does a member of your family do that? He was going to kill me. That's how this all started."

"Preposterous." Trallalair had enough of his lies. "We must get some sleep."

The traitor acted like he wanted to talk more about it, but she waved him silent.

He stood with his knees together like he needed to relieve himself or was frightened his fear would loosen his bladder.

"What is it, Traitor? Be brief."

"I haven't enough money to ransom the Dwarf."

"Ha!" she said, not laughing. "You are a fool. If he is not your friend but inimical as you propose, do you really think that criminal will make a deal with you for money?"

"Well, yes. I've dealt with him before."

"And?"

"He was going to kill me."

"I prove my point. After he takes our money he will kill us. Or maybe kill us first and then take our money. Why bother bringing any money at all?"

"But, but... then why are we going?"

"We'll have to deal with Molgannard Fey in the only way he understands. Fight our way in, take the Dwarf, if the Giant has not already killed him, and fight our way out. Have your dealings with him taught you nothing?"

Looking weak as a kitten, the traitor sighed and implored, "Please, Brandmistress, let me try the ransom first. The Giant is a thief, but he is a tradesman first."

"We will go tomorrow morning with whatever funds we can carry. I'll not waste another day getting money together."

"Can my family help me gather money?"

So he plotted again. Her brow felt tight as a bowstring. Exasperated, she said, "You want them freed?"

He nodded much like a little bird nodded its head while it strutted about searching for seeds and bugs. "They can help us. My family left in the city still has some resources."

She took out her sword, peering at the side, holding it so she could see only his head above the horizontal blade as if she had chopped his head off. "You see this blade? This blade is all we need to ransom your friend."

"Please?" he whimpered.

Just one Moon before, she had felt confident she could take on Molgannard Fey and all his Skin-Splicer cronies. But now, after burns, gashes and bruises, after the loss of much of her physical prowess, losing the love of her life and having her spirit all but crushed, she reluctantly relented. "Oh, very well. I am in charge of you and your family. We will allow one of your children to go tonight if he can find money, but he must be back before morning. And with food."

In the small strongbox the traitor had brought from his shop, he had all his inventory. It wasn't much. First of all, they needed two hundred Copper Orders. Between what he had in his box and what he could scrounge from around his home, he had accumulated a total of 15 Copper Orders, a far cry from the exorbitant fee to ask Smurgen a single question. The traitor would have to take money from his children.

She watched and listened while the traitor, anxious as always, approached his son Patrick first. His rug trade sounded lucrative enough to gain some profit his father could use. "Patrick, I need a favor."

"Father?" His son sounded surprised. "I'm sorry, Father. I'll do anything I can to help you."

"I need two hundred Copper Orders."

Patrick choked. Even for a rug merchant, two hundred Copper Orders was a lot of money. "With the scarcity of money these days, that's a lot. I have half that in my shop, or what's left of it, but I don't expect to make much more. The rug trade is rather slow. Flying Carpets don't last long in the sky with the Dragon's about. Most people are afraid to fly at all these days."

She almost felt sorry for the rich man until he admitted, "Of course, with so many buildings gone, Warming Rugs are selling very well. In a few Moons when it gets colder, we'll sell them all."

In order to bring his son back to the subject, the traitor said, "I need the money today, Paddy. Now. Tonight."

His son crooked a thumb at the Sinjery. "I don't think they'll let me go, Father."

"I have the Brandmistress's permission," the traitor said.

Trallalair nodded to Patrick's questioning look.

"I'll go get it right now, Father. I'll ask Herkimer how much he can spare."

By midnight, several sons and daughters had contributed a total of three hundred Copper Orders, fifty-eight Wooden Requests, and hundreds of Clay Suggestions. Patrick had flown back on a huge Flying Carpet full of provisions for the travelers, the Sinjery Ringmistresses and family. It consisted of a bushel of dried beans, ten bags of flour, three wheels of cheese, and an aromatic dried sausage that made Trallalair's mouth water. Many days had passed since she saw such food. Nowhere in the crippled city could anyone find that much food altogether. Trallalair's suspicions were piqued again.

The traitor gave twenty Copper Orders to Trallalair. Two hundred, the ransom, went in his strong box. A few dozen Wooden Requests and ten Copper Orders stayed in a silk pouch at his belt. The rest he left on a tall chest ostensibly for Arlen and the children. Just in case he was killed but the return of the Dragoncrown allowed Arlen and his family to be transformed back into human beings. Small chance. He seemed to want to burden Trallalair with bringing his family back to life. As if she didn't have burdens enough.

When the traitor seemed content with his preparations, Hili went to the garden to sip some nectar and found a perch to rest for what was left of the night. Trallalair escorted the traitor finally as he went to his bedroom, moldy from the weather and littered with leaves and petals that had entered through the still-open roof.

As always, when not at her barracks, Trallalair slept outside. If the jeweler tried to escape, she knew she would awaken easily. The slightest sound, vibration from the ground on which she slept, or even an unusual smell, like the sweaty smell of a fearful traitor skulking about, could awaken her. After years of Sinjery training, her acute senses filtered out those clues irrelevant to her needs like the smell of flowers or animals rustling the bushes. On that next day, Molgannard Fey's career would end if she had her choice. Not bring her sword? How ridiculous.

She could see why the traitor chose this hill for his cottage. After all the fire and death in the city, the crickets there still sang and leaves sighed in the breeze. As she drifted off, lying on her back, the twinkling stars in the Sky Forests appeared as did the glimmerbugs in the Sinjery swamp. She was so very weary of fighting and terror and loss. The relative quiet was like some soporific, and for the first time in many days, she slept dreamless, peaceful.

CHAPTER 21

THE JUNGLE

When Jonathon awoke, tired from little sleep, the world was strangely quiet. No Dragon's Lament. Until that morning, he never realized how accustomed he was to Dragons controlling his life. Their howls had awakened him every morning, the coins they produced had governed what he could and could not do, the Black Dragons he used for travel had frightened him every day, and the Dragonflyers surveying the city from high above and spying on everyone had annoyed him. All of that was gone. Maybe losing the Dragons' presence was not so bad.

Of course, enjoying the absence of Dragons would have to wait until the Dragons flying about burning and killing, unfettered by Seldric, were similarly gone. He looked out his bedroom window over the city and saw one lonely Green Dragon flying erratically, mobbed by a small flock of Flying Carpets studded with Knights. Isseltrent was in sunshine and relatively peaceful for once, quiet as a cemetery.

The thought of confronting Molgannard Fey sent a shudder from his prickly spine up to his sweaty brow then down to his clammy hands and his icy toes. Jonathon could still feel the Giant's hand on his head threatening to squash him like he would squash a bug. It had been merely one Moon before. Even remembrance of the smell of nasty, rotten bread he had tried to eat for a good fortnight hadn't erased the reek of the Giant's wine-tainted breath in Jonathon's nostrils. Why worry about the Demon? Molgannard Fey would probably kill him as soon as he was within reach. There was no use thinking about it.

He had an inkling that the Knife of Life was an ideal weapon and, thanks to Smurgen's statement, Jonathon suspected that it still existed. Maybe it had been buried somewhere nearby in the ground a century before and all they had to do was dig it up. It might be that easy. But fate had decreed that before they could even find out where to start looking for it, they had to attempt to talk to Smurgen. Besides, the Brandmistress seemed determined, despite impossible odds, to wrest Smurgen from the clutches of the Giant.

Jonathon took a few moments to spend time with his family. With them all gathered around him, wiping the tears from their eyes, Jonathon gave his grandchildren little pins from his shop. He told them all how the charms would protect them from everything bad if they obeyed their parents and learned everything their parents taught them. Hili seemed healthier, and she flew around entertaining the children by dancing in the air. She had gorged on nectar from Jonathon's garden, since she desperately needed food, and lots of it, to heal the wounds of her incarceration.

His adult daughters cried piteously over their father sauntering into the murderer's den. Even the men, trying to be strong before the children, had moist eyes when Jonathon told them what he had to do to save the family. None of them expected him to come back, and no one tried to stop him.

Trallalair took her time sharpening her sword. Bored with the sight of women crying and Jonathon fawning over his grandchildren, she watched them casually. She was anxious to move along and deal with Molgannard Fey. Still, she knew she needed patience to accomplish anything in this life. As she burnished her own blade, she thought about swords and knives and all manner of sharp weaponry. The idea of the Knife of Life intrigued her. If it existed, it would be no ordinary blade. And if it was even half as powerful as they said, it would hold a temptation unlike any she had ever felt. A temptation to change all the events of the last fortnight. All her Sisters, dead and corrupted, could they be saved and brought back to life? Even her sweet Saggethrie? Unbelievable. Too much to absorb. Would she feel guilty using it to steal them back from the Sky Forests where they now wandered in bliss? In decades past, a previous Dragonlord had been so angry at those who brought him back to life that he had them all executed. Perhaps her Sisters too did not want to come back to the trials of the world. Even so, the Knife of Life would be a powerful weapon in a land where everything was dead and the weapons that killed were useless. She had more experience than she ever wanted with the futility of weapons in the Dead Lands. A life-restoring weapon, however, that would be devastating. In a parallel move, when her foes had multiplied their numbers as her friends were killed, this time her allies could increase with each dead person resurrected. That is, if what she had heard in legend was indeed true.

Trallalair just hoped that these moral considerations did not stay her hand when she was confronted again with the horror of animated, dead friends in the Dead Lands. What if Saggethrie was brought miraculously back by the Knife of Life. Would she still be maimed, a body without arms? Just to think of it nauseated Trallalair. She shook the idea from her thoughts. Meddling with Death was not something for mere humans. Only Mother Earth had that right.

After the traitor's family ceased their histrionics, Trallalair got up, sheathing her sword. She was more than ready to get moving to Molgannard Fey's tower. "Let us leave, Traitor. We should get back before dark."

"Wait."

"No, Traitor, we will not wait."

"I mean, let me bring some jewelry to help us."

"I never wear jewelry."

"No.. no, not just to wear. I suggest we carry a few items I brought from my shop which may assist us."

Trallalair fumed. "Very well, but get them quickly and tell me the properties of all those magical items you want to bring. I'll not have any treachery this time."

Jonathon needed to carry the strong box, but he considered each piece of jewelry and picked a few pieces. First, he showed her the Buckle of Levitation. "Brandmistress, this buckle was made for the Rockskippers in the Cajalathrium States. It allows one to float up light as a feather."

"Does it allow you to fly?"

"Alas, no."

"How far up will you float?"

"It was made for inside the Rockskippers' tunnels, where the ceilings would stop them. I don't know if you'd ever stop if you were outside. I suppose you would when the effect of the coin wore off, but then you'd fall down to the ground."

"Doesn't sound of much help."

"You could wear it in case the Giant throws you out a window," he said.

"He will never throw *me* out a window, but you, maybe. Demonstrate it for me."

Jonathon attached the buckle to the belt around his waist and fastened it securely. He walked over to a large oak, looking above him for small branches he could grab onto, trying to avoid getting whacked by a big one. Even though he had been paralyzed by the Rod of Coercion, he remembered whacking his head on a beam in his shop when Arlen tried the buckle out on him. With a Clay Suggestion, he touched the Buckle of Levitation and instantly began to rise.

Trallalair grabbed his pants leg, trying to restrain him, but she was pulled up as well. Vailisk came to their rescue, grabbing onto her Sister's leggings. The combined weight of the three allowed them to sink back down to the ground, but very slowly. Apparently the buckle could lift two people but not three. Vailisk held them down until the effect wore off after a few Favors.

When she asked him, the traitor was not sure whether a stronger coin would make the effect only last longer or whether it would be stronger as well, allowing more than one person to be pulled aloft.

"It may be useful, Traitor," Trallalair admitted. "Do not use it unless I give you permission. If you do and you fall, I won't catch you. You'll dash yourself to pieces."

The traitor said he would wear it to give him more confidence, not that he planned to really use it.

Next he presented a Ring of Light to her. She had seen them before and knew their use. Again, she let him wear it in case they did not make it back before nightfall. She was not anxious to walk through the Jungle in the pitch black of night. He slid it on his left middle finger where it seemed to fit the best.

The next trinket in the traitor's bag of tricks was an Armlet of Tranquility. He explained that he could use it to calm his shaking knees. She fully realized how his fear was likely to interfere with her purpose in the Jungle, and allowed him to wear it on his arm.

The last object was the one he had fetched from behind his shop. It was a Wolf-Bane Pendant. She had heard of them, but thought they were for cowards. *Appropriate for the traitor*, she thought. Probably useful for a coward in the Jungle where forest animals, albeit Skin-Splicers, prowled the city streets just as they did in the wild. She, on the other hand, needed nothing but her Sinjery Sword to ward off predators in any jungle. Not many wolves roamed the Sinjery Swamp, but leopards and tigers were aplenty.

Trallalair said, "Enough. Bring the ransom money and let us go."

The traitor picked up the small strong box and walked up to her. She shook her head. "Traitor, take the money but leave the box."

"I always carry my valuables in this box."

"Not in the Jungle, you don't. My sword will protect us from a lot, but not from every Skin-Splicer, thief, and murderer in the city."

After the grumbling traitor put the money in a silk purse and tied it to his belt, he was ready. When he saw the sword still at Trallalair's belt, he said, "Brandmistress, we are supposed to go unarmed."

"I did not agree to that ludicrous condition." She left her bow and arrows she had with Vailisk. No Skin Splicer was a worthy enough foe to warrant wasting an arrow. She decided to save them for the Dead Lands and the Dragons.

"I gave my word," the traitor insisted.

His word indeed. Trallalair expected all the traitor's words held duplicity. He pretended to scheme with her to find the Knife of Life, but it all could be a trap with Molgannard Fey a spider in his web waiting for her to blunder in. She had an opportunity to uncover the details of the plot, bringing the traitor back for the Giant to question, but she would not go weaponless.

"If you gave him your word, then you shall bring no weapons," She said. "I have not given mine."

That was an easy condition for him, thought Jonathon, since he had never owned a weapon and would never have known how to use one even if he brought one. He thought back on the conversation. 'You may bring no weapons' the Dwarf had said, perhaps hoping Molgannard Fey would think he meant that restriction to be for both Jonathon and the Brandmistress. At the same time, the Dwarf might be hoping the Brandmistress would not accept the agreement to be binding upon her. Smurgen probably knew she would not come unarmed. Jonathon had a feeling that Smurgen expected the Brandmistress's honor would make her attempt to save him from the Giant.

Further, Jonathon thought, a gossip Dwarf with his almost-limitless access to knowledge was a powerful tool that the Giant could use in all his nefarious dealings. Jonathon thought that the Brandmistress would not allow Molgannard Fey to have that power if she could prevent it.

Jonathon still hoped he could just buy the information from the Giant controlling Smurgen and be gone. It went against his own basic principles to leave Smurgen in Molgannard Fey's ugly hands. Still, he had to consider the greater good, his quest to take the Dragoncrown back from the Demon. Jonathon wiggled his head once more in silent doubt. Compromising his morals for what he thought was the greater good had ruined him once. Now he faced more puzzles. What *was* the right course of action? Jonathon wished with all his heart that Rhazburn were here to talk things over with.

In answer to his ruminations, the Brandmistress said, "My sword is our only protection. Without it, what's to stop the Giant and his thugs from just killing us and stealing the ransom?" As she spoke, she took one of the Copper Orders in her pouch and touched it to the pommel of her sword. The Order dissolved, and the powers of her sword were renewed.

He knew the powers of the famed Sinjery Sword. A Poem of Strengthening made the steel almost unbreakable, able to cleave any other metal as easily as if it were a rotten branch. A Verse of Sharpening kept its edge keen enough to cut through a silk neckerchief floating down through the air. Most important was the Word of Recall. It allowed her to call the sword back to her hand. All Sinjery Swords were made the same and personalized for the bearer. Like everything in Thuringland and the Tributary States, the power of the Sinjery Swords would be lost if the Dragons were not brought back under the rule of Seldric, since there would be no more coins to activate their amazing powers.

Jonathon suspected the Brandmistress might have a point. Molgannard Fey might not even let them negotiate for Smurgen's service. He might just kill them first and keep both the money and Smurgen's services as well. He was unused to thinking in terms of treachery, but for Molgannard Fey, it came as natural as breathing his foul breaths. Jonathon knew the Brandmistress was wise to bring her sword. He didn't want to make the Giant any madder than he already was, but he had an omen that her sword would be needed before the day was out.

Before they could even confront the Giant, he and the Brandmistress had to walk through the city and run the gauntlet of the citizens full of hate for Jonathon and what he had done. Luckily, the few people who remained in town were still asleep at that time of day, or had more pressing problems than accosting the traitor Jonathon Forthright.

After passing through a few districts of the city, Jonathon was already tiring. His legs, unaccustomed as they were to long hikes, were weaker yet from his fortnight in the dungeon. Also, he felt a peculiar dread which seemed to sap his strength, and got more intense with each step he took closer to the Jungle. It was his dread of Molgannard Fey. In Jonathon's mind, the misshapen face of Molgannard Fey loomed. Its huge, ugly grin made him cringe as they walked. He imagined his feet straining for the ground as the Giant held him up, his hideous broken nose a hand span from Jonathon's face.

"What is it, Traitor? All is quiet here. The Jungle is still far ahead."

"I wish we had some help. Like the fellow that broke Molgannard Fey's nose."

"I broke his nose," she said.

At that, Jonathon stopped and stood surveying the Sinjery maiden's small frame, shorter than his by a head. She was small, but muscled with steel cords. The crusts on her face were softening, and the swelling of her cheeks receded. She had fought Dragons and Zombies. Why should a mere Giant frighten her?

"Why do you think he wants me to come with you? He knows me and wants revenge. Well, he's not going to get it," Trallalair said with a self-assured smirk.

Jonathon wished he could feel as confident, but his fear did ease a bit. Between the prowess of her sword arm and his money, maybe they did have a chance to survive.

After twenty street crossings, the charred remains of the city faded into unburned but equally miserable buildings. They had entered the Jungle, where no one had repaired a building in two centuries. The Dragons could hardly make the area more wretched. Buildings, once proud brick, were flaked and crumbled into drunken wastrels, while previously brightly-painted wooden ladies, now termite-tattered and gray, creaked in the breeze. A surprising number of ragged people sat languid and bored in the dirt, leaning against the weakened walls. Others reeled about, drunken and vomiting. A few leering men were drunk enough to make lewd remarks to the Sinjery maiden. Her look said it all. If she were not so intent on her purpose of finding the Knife of Life and killing Molgannard Fey, she would have answered them with a swift sword through their guts, ending their misery.

Hovels sprawled on either side, a few filled with raucous laughter and angry shouts. Outside one gloomy, dilapidated tavern, a rotting, bodiless head lay face down in a puddle of offal. As they passed, a stumbling inebriate tripped over the head a few steps away and fell like a rag doll, giggling in the mud.

At another corner stood a shack with an open door and a crude drawing of a woman with her legs spread. It stood as the sentinel to a street full of scantily-dressed women and men. They looked tired, filthy, older than their years. Many recognized Jonathon for a tradesman and called out, beckoning him to spend his money on them.

Trallalair could barely look at them, wondering if she was of their ilk. From her years in the Ring of Guards policing the Jungle, she recognized the street as Choir's Strut. Like everyone who entered the Jungle, these once-beautiful, alluring Choralists of Isseltrent proper had degenerated into dirty, maltreated, forgotten women and men. They still plied their trade but never again hoped to emulate Ilsa of The Three.

Everything in the Jungle was run-down or falling down, but clearly nothing in the Jungle had been destroyed by the Dragons.

"Traitor, your friend's district has been spared, just like your shop and your house. Proof enough for me that he is in league with the Demon and must be expunged like you."

"Yes, I agree," Jonathon said, trembling. He meant he agreed that the Giant was in league with the Demon and that made him even more frightening than Jonathon thought him before. Also, he realized he must pay for his crime, inadvertent as it was. Resigned as he was to his just punishment, he still feared death and always would.

Jonathon looked about at the dirty denizens of the jungle. They were all human. Strange. Where were all the Skin-Splicers? He expected to see them by the dozen as soon as they entered the Jungle.

As they passed a small windowless shack, dark as death, the answer to his question came from the shadows. A deep growling warned them not to approach. It had been a whore's hovel, but that within sounded like a huge predatory beast. Hopefully it was sated. Certainly it was not to be disturbed. Jonathon wondered what happened to the poor wretched woman that had lived and worked there. He shuddered at a black trickle of old blood that peaked from the doorway. Had she been the predator's victim, or was she the beast and her catch of the day her meal too?

Trallalair drew her sword and pushed Jonathon behind her as she faced the door, watching and listening. Moving sideways she stepped past it, calm but taut, ready for an instant lunge. She knew how to deal with beasts. She motioned the traitor to precede her as she protected them both.

Even though Trallalair sheathed her sword after they passed the predator's den, she periodically glanced behind them as they made their way down the Choir's Strut, watching for a stalking great cat. She was well aware how quietly and quickly a big forest cat could stalk its prey.

Jonathon was now visibly shaking. Skin-Splicers frightened him even more than murdering Giants. They were so unnatural to human reason. Skin-Splicers spent money to turn themselves into specific animals so they could release all their repressed instincts and passions. Those passions surfaced and solidified into the raw instincts of the animals they became. And like many activities that involve passion, the skin-splicing became an addiction for those who indulged.

Over his shoulder, a small bat flew spasmodically. It fell in the mud three strides ahead of them, making the Brandmistress lay a hand on her sword hilt again. Her sword would get a lot of use that day.

The form of the bat softened, expanded, and took on the image of a human. Slowly, it coalesced into a sobbing woman who beat the mud with her fist. A Skin-Splicer. The first one Jonathon had ever seen.

He had heard the skins were costly. He realized that this woman had paid a dear price of money, probably stolen or earned by selling her body, for the skin of a bat treated with an arcane brew. With more money, most likely a whole Copper Order, the bat skin on her shoulders transformed her into a bat. She could fly and maybe drink blood for a night, until the spell wore off. During that time, she was spliced with the skin of the bat and lost her human identity. She was freed of the cares of the human world.

She had the power of flight and movement in the dark. She shared all the appetites and lusts of the animal. Maybe she had found a male bat, had brutishly mated, and longed to get back to his claws. She would whore and steal to do it again and again. But for now, she was lost, back in the Jungle without a Suggestion, starving, friendless.

Jonathon wondered just how much of her human self still remained when she had become a bat. It could not have been much, or she would be horrified as to what she had become. Being in that state, losing one's self in the mind of a beast, must be a terrible thing. To want that, again and again? To what end? It was too much for Jonathon's conventional mind. He thanked The Three that he never had to be in that predicament.

Trallalair let go of her sword but walked past quickly, feeling their goal approaching.

Above the battered rooftops, Molgannard Fey's sturdy edifice peeked. On its roof, a barely-visible handful of figures walked. Trallalair thought she perceived crossbows in their hands.

From the alley ahead and to their right, they heard a wheezing grunt, as if a huge animal was blowing its nose. Trallalair hesitated, watching the alley carefully as they walked past. When they were even with the alley's entrance, a piercing trumpeting preceded a full-grown elephant that charged them. Beneath its pounding, tree-sized limbs, the ground trembled.

Trallalair knew her sword was useless, so she left it sheathed and shoved the traitor to the left where he tumbled into a pile of shattered boards. Her familiarity with the beasts in the lands south of Sinjer told her that elephants had better hearing than sight, so she yelled and waved her hands to attract it away from the traitor. The towering beast came straight at her much faster than she could run. She waited until she was almost in reach of its powerful trunk, then she dove to the right and rolled, landing against the wall of a deserted clothing store.

The elephant's momentum made it lumber past her and the traitor and on toward a building. Dust flew and a few boards shook off the wall Trallalair lay against. The powerful creature charged right at what looked to be a bakery, one of the few still in business in the Jungle. Seemingly, the elephant was not interested in them at all. It looked like the bakery was its intended target.

Pushed aside by the Brandmistress, Jonathon fell painfully against a pile of boards. When he looked up, a monstrous beast, big enough to squash a house, roared past like a living avalanche. Jonathon was thankful for the abrupt shove of the Brandmistress. She had probably saved his life.

A skinny, grim mercenary guarded the door to the bakery. When the scrawny man looked up and saw the charging monstrosity, he threw down his useless spear, ran for cover, tripped over his feet, and scrambled away on all fours. The beast smashed through the front wall, thrashing about for a few moments as it tore down shelves lined with loaves. When the dust settled, Jonathon saw the beast, oblivious to the shouts of the owner, picking up whole loaves with its long dribbling proboscis, shoving them into its flabby mouth, and then defecating on the counter.

Jonathon no longer wondered where all the Skin-Splicers were. He never wanted to see another one.

Only a short walk away, the Giant's gray tower loomed above the shacks and was framed by the harbor beyond. To Trallalair's surprise, a grove of trees stood in the middle of the narrow street a hundred paces ahead. Many shapes and shades of green leaves waved in the warm spring breeze, because every tree was different. A pine, cedar, oak, hickory, and many more, all together, all out of place. They were undoubtedly Skin-Splicers who had used tree-bark cloaks to turn themselves into trees. As trees, they had no more pain, obsessions or fears. Their thoughts were as still as wood for a few Blessings or days.

Hanging from the hickory, a black and white monkey sampled nuts. Skin-Splicer itself, the monkey seemed undazzled by the phenomenon of trees filling the street.

At a birch sapling, a heavyset man with a cleaver hacked a branch. As they passed, the man turned his head and said, "The bastard stole my ring. When he wakes up, he won't have a hand to wear it on!"

Trallalair thought he was no threat to them, but glanced back after they passed to be sure.

As Trallalair led the traitor around the last corner, a disgusting stench hit them both. A tall pile of animal skins leaned against the tower of Molgannard Fey, staining it with blood and ooze. There were huge hides like the elephant they had just seen, medium-sized ones like horses and lions, and very small ones like rabbits and rats. The hides were rotten, dribbling fetid oils, but beyond that, there was a stink of something acrid that lanced their nostrils and watered their eyes. It was the chemical odor of the brew made by Molgannard Fey's Alchemists to treat the skins and give them the power to turn men into animals.

Dozens of tough men with wolf hides tied around their necks strutted around, bullying trembling wastrels who bought smelly Skins and then fled, clutching them compulsively. Most of the toughs were armed with clubs and daggers. Some had crossbows they had cocked and aimed at Trallalair. Obviously, they did not consider the traitor a threat. He was probably their confederate.

Trallalair held up her empty hands, shouting, "We come at the behest of Molgannard Fey. This is Jonathon Forthright the jeweler with a fee for information from the Dwarf Smurgen."

The thug with the coldest visage said, "Aren't you an ugly one. And that's His Lordship Molgannard Fey to you, Strumpet! Yes, I know all you Sinjery women are Seldric's whores." He baited her with his words and his eyes. He was bold enough with dozens of men clustered around and ten crossbows aimed at her chest. She stayed cool and stood her ground. She would deal with these ruffians later.

With a gruff order, the thug dispatched a lackey who approached the locked door of the tower. Giving a word of recognition, he was ushered in after many bolts were thrown. A long delay preceded the lackey appearing again. He was accompanied by six more wolf-garbed thugs. They were the tallest and heaviest she had yet seen. Their hairy, oily arms rippled with tension as they gripped maces and axes, holding them up for Trallalair to see. She had to keep herself from laughing outright at their pretentiousness. They would go down like wheat under her Sinjery Sword.

After a word with the lackey, the cold-eyed thug said, "Give me your sword, Bitch."

Jonathon thought the Brandmistress would attack him right there, even with all the other gang members at his back, but she drew her sword slowly and handed it to him by the hilt, the tip pointing to the sky. "I'm warning you. Do not touch the blade."

With a smirk, he took it from her and purposely grasped it by the blade, laying it over his shoulder. "Now you may go bow before his Lordship and do his bidding."

The Sinjery Brandmistress looked at him with utter calm. Jonathon recognized the hate in her eyes, having seen it many times when she looked at him.

The taunting ruffian led them into the tower. Snickers and catcalls dogged them as they walked through the unruly mob. Jonathon thought any one of the loathsome men would gladly brain him with a club and steal his money, but apparently, they were constrained by Molgannard Fey.

The heavy wooden doors creaked open for the thug at a word they could not hear. Inside the tower of Molgannard Fey, the stench of the close air was strong enough to make Jonathon retch. Many more of the animal skins were piled against the inner walls. There seemed to be no end to the animals slaughtered for this abuse. How anyone could don one of the filthy, putrid skins for some kind of visceral pleasure, Jonathon would never comprehend. The Sinjery maiden didn't flinch.

Through cracks in the floor, Jonathon saw movement of more men in a basement, and he heard the laughs and shrieks of women, there for the mob's pleasure. A reek of chemicals used to transform the skins into magical cloaks came from below. Barrels of wine at the walls were constantly tapped by wavering revelers. Most of the activity was below or on the ground floor. The wide cylinder of the tower rose at least six rods tall to his estimation, seemingly empty. Only faint glimmers in the shadows suggested movement high above them. At the far wall, a single rickety stairway led up into the dimness.

There was only one other pathway leading upward, and it was to this they were pushed. It was a Flying Carpet, many rods long but only a stride wide. It spiraled like a staircase progressively up into the gloom, hanging in the air, floating but stable. When they approached it, they saw it was colored mostly green and covered with verses and pictures of forest animals being slaughtered and eaten by snarling wolves and angry men.

The ruffians poked spears at them to goad them onward up the green carpet. The cold-eyed man holding the Sinjery Sword snarled, "To kneel before His Lordship Fey, you must first walk the Path of Fear." He jerked a pointing finger at the green carpet for emphasis. His voice echoed from above.

The Brandmistress nudged Jonathon to take the lead since they had to walk single file.

Jonathon looked up at the climb with tears in his eyes, quivering like a frightened child.

"Well, Traitor, ascend!" she barked at him.

He turned and said through shaky lips. "I'm petrified of heights. I have never ridden a Flying Carpet in my life."

"I don't want to hear that now. I will walk behind you and steady you. Now ascend!"

The first step was the hardest for Jonathon. He almost threw up and had to stop to retch for a few moments while the thugs laughed at him. He took another step, and the carpet swayed slightly, making him shudder and cry out. The Brandmistress had to hold his belt to steady him. His footing on the narrow strip was precarious, and nothing would stop his foot from slipping off the edge if he faltered. The higher he walked, the more tremulous his knees became, and at times, they buckled. He caught himself by grabbing the edges of the carpet with his sweaty hands.

Behind the traitor, Trallalair half-expected a crossbow bolt in her back, but she refused to even turn her head and look at the churlish men. None of the thugs followed them.

Half-way up, the traitor was shaking too much to go on. Tears flooded his eyes, and he sobbed, "I can't do it. I'm too dizzy. You go on."

"We cannot stop now, Traitor. The fear you feel here is nothing like that you will find in the land of the Demon. Move on!"

He seemed to force himself to trudge onward, one step, then another. At one point, he wobbled and tottered so much Trallalair had to hold his collar in one hand and his belt with the other. She used all her strength, lifting and pushing him up the climbing carpet ahead of her. Even her Sinjery stamina would be barely enough.

One rod distance from the top, she saw their goal, a huge Flying carpet filling more than half the tower's interior, blocking meager sunlight from shuttered windows at the top.

Trallalair let go of the traitor's shirt. "Crawl if you must, Traitor. I need my hands free."

Jonathon collapsed to the narrow carpet and began to crawl. He decided he liked crawling. All four limbs on the surface of the carpet was much better. If he slipped off, he could hold on to the tasseled edge for a moment or two, maybe long enough to scream once before he fell.

Whimpering, he looked over the side. That was a mistake. Drunken thugs far below were the only thing to break his fall. His limbs froze in place. He stared at the carpet, making sure it didn't move beneath him. He had an irrational idea the carpet could simply flip him off into space, like a dog shaking water off its back.

"Move along, Traitor!" the Brandmistress yelled.

"I cannot."

"You must!"

"I need help."

"Then give me the bag of coins. I will deal with the Giant."

The bag of coins. That was it. Right then, he remembered the jewelry he brought. "I have the Buckle of Levitation, Brandmistress."

"Use it then if it will help you walk up this carpet."

"No, no. It's only for a crisis, like a fall. If I use it, I'll float up to the ceiling instead of falling to the floor."

"What about when the spell wears off? Won't you still fall to the floor?"

He hadn't thought of that. His hands and legs took root on the carpet. "Please help me. If I can just hold a Copper Order in my hand, I think I'll be able to move."

"So hold one."

"I can't move my hands. Can you reach in my bag and take out a few coins please?"

"All right, if it will loosen your limbs and tighten your lips." The Brandmistress had to lean around him over the side of the carpet, but she knew how to balance her slight weight perfectly and looked as steady as if she were standing on the ground. She opened the pouch deftly and extracted a fistful of coins, laying several next to his right hand. She kept the rest.

Jonathon slowly twisted his hand, straining against the paralysis of his fear. With tense fingers, he raked a few coins into his palm. They were a balm to his quavering spirit. The distance to the floor was no different, but he could now kneel on the carpet.

With his eyes on the coins, he noticed the Armlet of Tranquility on his wrist. If ever he needed it, this was the time. He took a Copper Order and touched the Armlet of Tranquility.

All the weariness and fear melted away. The carpet beneath him felt like a mountain of stone. With no more tremors he stood up on his own, turned, and smiled at the Brandmistress. To Demonstrate his new-found confidence, he bowed slightly and spun about to face the climb ahead. His overconfident turn was a little too fast and much too sloppy. His right foot missed the edge of the carpet, and he lurched off the side.

Trallalair cursed, "Mother!" and caught him by the shirt as he fell. She had to squat and hold the opposite edge of the carpet to avoid being pulled off by his weight. Gnashing her teeth at the strain, not to mention the anger she felt toward this clumsy oaf, she used the leverage of her hold on the carpet and every bit of her strength to slowly pull him back onto the carpet.

"Whoa, that was wild," he said in a silly tone. "A little giddy, I guess."

"Traitor, get a hold of yourself. Go back to crawling."

It was like he was drunk.

"I'm fine. I'm fine." He said, standing up at attention. "Brandmistress, follow me." He stepped smartly to the center and climbed the carpet all the way to the top. In this point, it stopped in mid-air, a full rod from the monstrous red carpet set in the air about two rods below the ceiling of the tower.

In the gloom from the shuttered windows, Trallalair's eyes adjusted slowly. At the far side of the carpet, at least four rods distant, Molgannard Fey lounged on a hundred pillows. He held a broiled cow leg in one hand and a barrel of wine in the other.

At first, Trallalair thought he wore a scarf, but the scarf moved and raised its head. It was a thickly-muscled, glistening snake draped around his neck, its mouth crammed with a wriggling rabbit which it slowly swallowed. Across his knee, a black jaguar licked a raw side of beef. On his right shoulder, a carrion bird fanned its broad black wings to balance itself, while it stretched its naked pink neck and pecked pieces from the Giant's huge drumstick.

To the side, the rickety wooden stairway stopped a long stride from the edge of the Giant's carpet. At the top on a platform stood five thugs, three with iron maces, one with a drawn crossbow, and one, the foul-mouthed butcher who held Trallalair's sword by the blade over his shoulder. Trallalair would have to leap the gap to get to the Giant. Sitting off to the left side, cradling a gleaming silver Vision Bowl in his lap, Smurgen, Chief of the Gossip Dwarves, cowered. In addition to the snake, there was something else tied around the Giant's monstrous neck. It appeared to be a thick stiff gray hide of some massive beast.

"The wimp and the strumpet." Molgannard Fey addressed Trallalair and the traitor. "I thought Death here would have a meal," he said, dropping the huge drumstick and stroking the carrion bird which folded its wings and glared at the traitor. "This is Night," he patted the jaguar. "And Murder." He held his arm before the constrictor snake, which flowed over it like water over a log in a river. "You met Grip." The butcher still gripped her sword by the blade. "And my hearties." He put down his cask and gestured below with both hands. "Of course, you know my guest, the good Dwarf." He reached back and almost smacked Smurgen in the face.

The sullen Dwarf ducked out of the way. He already had one black eye.

Since the Armlet of Tranquility still clouded Jonathon's judgment, he thought the Giant's pets were cute, and despite Smurgen's black eye and terrified, trembling cringe, the Dwarf looked well fed.

The Brandmistress spoke first. "Giant, we have brought your price. We want to question the Dwarf."

"I prefer to deal with the jeweler, not a court whore."

The Sinjery Brandmistress seethed beside him, but kept quiet. Jonathon smiled and nodded to her pleasantly, appreciative of her restraint.

"Jeweler, we've done business before. To buy the Dwarf's information, one question that is, which is all I will allow," he stipulated, "I require two hundred Copper Orders. If you don't have it, begone." He waved his hand at them like he was brushing away fleas. After a long swig from his barrel came an equally-long, sonorous belch.

"I have it, my dear Lord Fey." With a flourish, Jonathon held up the the bag of coins. His mind was still quite tranquil.

"Here, Jeweler. Send it to me so I can count it." The Giant picked up a small roll and touched it with a coin. The roll snapped open. It was a small yellow Flying Carpet floating steady before Molgannard Fey. "Yellow carpet to the jeweler." It sped to hover before Jonathon's eyes. He had to move a little to see past the small carpet, but it stayed with him, floating a few inches from his face.

Jonathon opened his silk pouch and slowly, lovingly, counted out two hundred Copper Orders onto the small carpet, closing the pouch and replacing it at his belt. "Here is your fee, Fey." He giggled at his joke. "Or should I say, here is you money, Honey." He giggled again. "Or maybe, your ransom, Handsome." To this one he guffawed, while Trallalair cursed quietly.

The Giant said, "You find this funny, Jeweler. I'll make sure we are all amused." He called back his carpet, counted the money, and said, "All is in order, Jeweler. Smurgen you may answer their question as soon as the Jeweler has paid his debt to me."

"What debt?" Jonathon queried.

"The Glass Command you owe me," the Giant replied.

"I paid that," Jonathon insisted.

"Now pay me the interest," Molgannard Fey demanded.

"So how much is that?" Jonathon questioned.

"Another Glass Command from all the interest on the interest you never paid and a lot more because I didn't kill you like I was gonna. You're buying your life back, wimp, if you got the money."

Jonathon tranquilly realized he was about to die. Lances of sunlight streaming through the shutters accentuated mist or smoke rising above him in the fetid quarters. It was like fulfilled souls ascending to the heavens. '*Soon,*' he thought, wistfully, '*I'll be insubstantial as that mist.*' Wistful mist.

Trallalair heard the Giant's threatening voice and prepared herself for something much different than death. She still squeezed the handful of coins she had taken from the traitor's pouch on the Path of Fear. The traitor was in front, and beyond him, a gap of only one rod separated their green carpet staircase from Molgannard Fey's red carpet lounge.

The Giant saw her tense and said, "I tire of this, Jeweler. You have had all the chances I care to give. Green carpet..."

Trallalair took her cue. She reached around the traitor's belly and slapped his Buckle of Levitation with all the coins in her hand, gripping the belt as they started to rise.

"... Drop." As Molgannard Fey finished his command, the whole green carpet collapsed, crashing down upon howling, cursing ruffians below.

Bug-eyed, flying upward into the fog, hanging below the ceiling, the traitor waved his arms wildly. Trallalair saw his pants slipping down with her weight and hitched herself up, climbing to his shoulders. When their initial inertia slowed, she felt them leveling off well within the range of the crossbow held by the thug at the top of the stairs. The thug seemed astonished that they were flying in the air and hadn't the wherewithal to act. She took the brief respite to leap from the traitor's shoulders toward the Giant's carpet. With the momentum of falling from a full rod above, the leap across the gap was easy, and she landed like a cat on the near edge of the huge red carpet three rods from Molgannard Fey.

Since the Sinjery maiden's weight was lost, the Buckle of Levitation was more than adequate to pull Jonathon upward again. He sprang up to the ceiling, striking and cutting his head on a beam. Ever tranquil, he marveled at the view. Floating in air was like a dream. He didn't even notice the pain in his head or the blood dribbling from his scalp into his ear.

When she hit the carpet, Trallalair yelled, "Sinjer!" calling her sword. The foolish leering Grip still held her sword by the blade. The Sinjery steel slid cleanly through his fist. Half his hand fell away. Where the blade touched his neck, blood spurted from a severed vessel. He choked and staggered off the stairway, taking two more luckless lackeys with him. They all fell, screaming, to the floor far below. Trallalair's sword flew precisely to her hand.

"Death, get her sword," shouted Molgannard Fey. 'Night, Murder, kill the bitch." The carrion bird flapped its wings and took off. The snake still had a bulge in its throat where the rabbit was being consumed. Even so, the thick constrictor obeyed, flowing to the carpet, and slithered surprisingly fast at Trallalair. The jaguar stalked forward, looking for a weakness in its prey.

On the rickety stairway, the thug with the crossbow fired desperately, missing Trallalair by an arm's length. Ignoring the beasts, Trallalair pinned the thug with her eyes. She ran at him as he fumbled with another bolt, trying to load it. While racing, she estimated the distance and threw her sword end over end. The blade buried itself in his chest, the impact splitting his breastbone. Blood pumped from his chest over his stomach. He coughed up tankards more blood and crumpled. The last thug sprinted down the stairs, away from swords that killed at a distance on their own.

Before Trallalair could call her sword again, the black carrion bird dove for the hilt and grasped it firmly.

"Sinjer," came her cry but too late. The sword, hobbled by the bird, wobbled in the air, jerking a hand span at a time toward its mistress. The bird flew up beyond the height Trallalair could leap. Trallalair watched her only weapon fly away. At her feet, the snake bit her ankle, making her flinch and grab its neck just above the rabbit's bulge. Faster than she could fend them off, its rippling coils wrapped around her legs, her chest, and her neck. As the coils of the constrictor reached her neck, Trallalair realized she had only one hope left to her. Traitor to the Realm. Fat, out of shape, a schemer, not a fighter, and half-asleep, floating in the rafters above her. With her last breath, she yelled, "Mother Earth, Jonathon Forthright, wake up!"

High above, with his head scraping the splintering beams, Jonathon saw the fight and knew he was somehow involved in all this. In his altered state of mind, tranquil to a fault, he didn't care much about what happened. They would all die, and then they would all would be at peace. Being at peace was the only really important consideration.

When Jonathon heard her call, he realized he was was responsible for the young woman's predicament. Her life or death was in his hands. He might be relaxed, but, like any good father, he knew duty when it called.

Still levitating up against the ceiling, he regarded the Armlet of Tranquility. How beautiful it was, and how very effective. He hadn't felt this relaxed in many Moons. But the world beckoned him. He reached down, slid it off his arm, and put it in his pocket.

The spell was instantly broken. Horror, death, and madness greeted him.

At one end of the red carpet, Molgannard Fey, wearing his stiff gray skin, had risen from his pillow couch and called for his troops to come up from below. To make room, he kicked the bloody crossbowman off the stairway.

Below Jonathon, the carrion bird flapped its wings, fighting the jerking Sinjery Sword in its talons. Clearly, the bird was tiring.

To Jonathon's right, the great cat watched the Brandmistress being crushed and strangled by the massive snake. The great cat was apparently more afraid of the tightening coils of the snake than of the Sinjery Brandmistress.

Jonathon had to make fast decisions. He reached in his pouch and fished out a Copper Order, touching the Wolf-Bane pendant with it.

The foul odor of the piles of skins were nothing compared to the reek that filled his head. It was like a skunk was suddenly shoved up his nose, one that had bathed in a putrid swamp and had vomited blood. He couldn't rip it off fast enough. He wanted it away from him as quickly as possible, but he held his breath for a moment to aim at the cat and threw it hitting the great cat by sheer luck squarely in the face. The cat shook its head, sneezed, turned tail and ran past the Giant down the stairs. Molgannard Fey tried to cuff the cat in disgust as it ran. Shouts of consternation from the ruffians that had been ascending the stairs at the Giant's call came from below as the great cat fell among them.

The carrion bird was below Jonathon and only a rod away. Jonathon was plastered against the ceiling, so he held onto a beam and raised his legs with difficulty trying to get a purchase on the rough wood. With his arms and legs both raised over his head, he was tiring quickly. He managed to crawl like a fly along the ceiling several body lengths until he was directly over the bird. When he was right above the carrion bird he thankfully let his feet and arms drop back down and looked between his legs at the flapping bird still seizing the Sinjery Sword beneath him. The bird was still in the air above the Giant's huge Flying Carpet.

Jonathon clutched at his pouch of coins with his right hand and he unclasped the Buckle of Levitation with his left, pulling his belt free of his pants. First, his pants fell off his spindly legs and flopped onto the carrion bird's back. The belt flew up toward the ceiling, and Jonathon fell like a stone, dropping on top of his pants and the bird. As he fell, his weight drove the bird to the carpet in a flapping, screeching pile.

The sword was forgotten and released to fly up free again to answer the Word of Recall, traveling in a narrow arc to the Sinjery's waiting hand. However, she was too encumbered and weakened by the constrictor to even use her sword.

Under Jonathon, the struggling bird turned its head and pecked his face, barely missing his eye. That took away the last of Jonathon's tranquility. Driven and strengthened by rage, he found its skinny neck and grabbed it with both hands. With a few hard twists accompanied by popping bones, he wrung its head right off, then squealed at the bloody mess in his hands.

Trallalair's face was purpling with the choking coil around her neck and her eyes began to glaze over.

Jonathon looked up from the dead carrion bird and toward the Giant to see what he was doing.

Molgannard Fey took a coin from the tiny yellow carpet and touched the gray animal skin he wore. His form shimmered and began to change.

Jonathon tore his eyes away and looked at the Brandmistress, limp in the grasp of the snake. He tried to get up but fell back down from pain in his legs. His fall on the bird had bruised and twisted his knees. He tried once more, but his knees felt like they would break apart. They buckled again, throwing him back down to the carpet.

He was only a short creep away from the Brandmistress, so he crawled on his hands and knees as fast as he could, still wincing in pain.

She was covered in a twisting, tightening serpentine mass.

Jonathon grabbed a coil and pulled himself up.

The Brandmistress barely breathed.

He searched for the end of the snake and found it, a taut but twitching tail.

Jonathon decided the snake was much too tense. He took the Armlet of Tranquility from his pocket and fell onto the tail, clutching it as it wriggled and shook. He dropped the Armlet twice trying to slip it over the flapping end of the snake. When he looked up to see Molgannard Fey's form solidifying into a huge thick-legged beast, Jonathon let out a howl of frustration and brought his face down to chomp on the tail with his teeth. Holding it with hand and teeth, he was finally able to slip on the Armlet of Tranquility. He slid it up until it was tight, and for good measure, he took out another Copper Order and touched it to the Armlet.

As the spell took effect, the writhing coils of the boa relaxed visibly and drooped down a bit.

The Sinjery maiden breathed easier but remained limp.

Jonathon looked toward Molgannard Fey whose form had become a four-legged thick-skinned beast with a sturdy but sharp horn sprouting from its snout. The beast was at least as massive as the Giant but looked meaner. The horn looked big enough to put a hole the size of a fist through Jonathon, and it was aimed at his heart.

Jonathon had little time. He wrestled with the slack coils around the Brandmistress, loosening those around her neck and those around her chest, slipping them over her head. The snake had already released its grip with its teeth and seemed to be sleeping.

The Sinjery maiden looked to be in no condition to confront the beast that Molgannard Fey had become. She was still limp with her eyes fluttering. Her sword lay useless on the carpet.

The beast was snorting now and pawing the carpet, looking their way. Molgannard Fey was bound to kill Jonathon one way or another, but Jonathon wasn't going to let the Brandmistress be gored while she was half-awake.

All he had was his tired, hurting body, a few coins, and the Ring of Light he had on his left middle finger. He looked at the Brandmistress's sword but knew better than to pick it up. If he tried to stick a sword in that beast, he would really make it mad. Inside the tower, the sunlight barely filtered through the shutters and gloom still shrouded the details on the carpet. The Ring of Light was his only weapon.

When he touched a Copper Order to the Ring of Light, he knew enough to look away. Sharp shadows stood out on the carpet below as the brilliant point of light burned like a miniature sun on his hand.

The tiny eyes of the heavy beast were dazzled, and for a few moments it stopped its pawing, disoriented. After it reoriented on Jonathon, it bellowed and charged.

Jonathon just wanted to keep the beast away from the Brandmistress, so he held his brilliant middle finger high over his head and stood up, his eyes tearing with the pain from his knees as he faced the charging, transformed Giant. He yelled, "Come get me, Molgannard Fey," shaking his raised middle finger at him in defiance. "You want to kill me, Molgannard Fey?" he asked as he started walking painfully to the right, away from the now coughing and gasping Sinjery.

Jonathon tried to jog while he taunted Molgannard Fey. "I spit in your face, Fey!" He made for the side of the carpet where the green carpet had been floating, but the charging beast was too fast.

When Molgannard Fey was only a single rod away, Jonathon realized that the beast wanted to put the point of his horn through the Ring of Light. He yanked the ring off his finger as he stumbled toward the edge of the carpet. With the beast two strides away, Jonathon held his arm out stretched, and the animal, bedazzled by the light so he could not see Jonathon to the side, swerved toward it.

At the last moment, Jonathon threw the ring at the edge of the carpet and fell, exhausted, barely to the side of the beast's charge. Sure enough, Molgannard Fey galloped past, his heavy tread bouncing Jonathon on the carpet nearby, one sledgehammer foot barely missing his head.

The ring rolled off the edge, and the brilliance was gone. No longer blinded by the ring and almost too late, Molgannard Fey in his beast form swerved and stopped, teetering on the edge.

Jonathon had had enough of Molgannard Fey. "Oh no you don't, Molgannard Fey!" He ran at the Giant's back flank, away from his deadly horn, and pushed with all his might. The Giant teetered more but held. He was far too massive for Jonathon to even budge. Jonathon had almost given up when he saw a graceful figure fly through the air over his shoulder.

The Sinjery Brandmistress had leaped and slammed both her feet against the beast's side. With her Sinjery Sword in hand, she drove its point deep into the beast's hip. As she pushed herself off, leaping away, leaving her sword in his flesh, the thrust of her legs pushed Molgannard Fey just enough. His two right feet slipped over the carpet's edge, and he rolled, squealing like a giant pig, falling all the way to the floor of the tower and on through the flooring. His massive weight threw his men hither and thither among flying boards, dust, and splattering wine.

"Sinjer!" The Brandmistress cried. Her sword rose from the dust, leaping for joy to the Sinjery's hand.

Jonathon fell on his back, groaning.

"Master Jeweler, save me."

Behind them, the thugs were hauling the Dwarf down the wooden stairs.

"I will deal with those fiends," the Brandmistress said, running after them.

Jonathon could barely sit up, much less keep up with Trallalair's sprint. He thought it useless to try to dissuade her, though he knew the odds were still too great against her, even with the Giant gone.

Crossbow bolts fired from below erupted through the carpet all around them. The archers could not see them, so they were depending on luck to hit them. Nevertheless, an unlucky bolt through a foot could easily disable one of them.

The Brandmistress leaped across the gap from the carpet and met the first two thugs on the top platform of the rickety stairway. She slashed their arms off before they could raise their clubs. The next one had a shield and was stronger, parrying her blows expertly.

No one but Jonathon was left on the red carpet. Everyone knew how Flying Carpets worked. Only the one activating the carpet with a coin in a special pocket could control it. He lurched like a cripple across the carpet. Searching quickly, he found the small embroidered pocket near Molgannard Fey's stack of pillows. After taking a handful of the Copper Orders from the tiny yellow carpet still hovering by the pillows, he selected one and slipped it in the pocket. Then he shouted, "Brandmistress, get on the carpet." She glanced at him. Recognizing that he finally showed some confidence, she hopped back off the rickety stairway on to the carpet and ran to him.

"Jeweler, the Dwarf," she said, pointing to the stairs below them. He noticed she had said 'Jeweler', not 'Traitor'.

"I know. I know."

Thugs from the stairway began crowding up to go for them again, but the one with Smurgen continued on downward.

The thugs were rightfully hesitant to jump onto the carpet and confront the Brandmistress. Their armless comrades lying in pools of blood were a testimony to her ferocity. They waited until there were three of them abreast on the top platform of the rickety stairs.

As they got ready to leap onto the carpet, Jonathon said, "Carpet, up one rod."

He had timed it just right. The carpet rose. The thugs, overbalanced with their aborted leap and nothing in front of them, waved their arms uselessly, trying to regain their balance. It was to no avail. The carpet was too high for them to grab onto, and they all fell, still waving their arms, as if they were trying to fly. A few sickening thuds echoed from below.

"Carpet, down two rods," Jonathon said. He and Trallalair descended quickly and surprised the thug on the staircase holding Smurgen. The Brandmistress stepped up and decapitated him, deftly dodging the blood squirting from his neck. She grabbed Smurgen's arm and pulled him onto the carpet. They still had to get out of the tower.

"Carpet, down to a hand span from the floor." Again the carpet descended quickly, crushing many of the ruffians that had been firing crossbows at them. Two dozen more of the snarling men brandishing axes, knives, and spears poured onto the carpet, slashing at its woven words until the verses were ruined. The red carpet fell dead to the floor, covering the hole through which Molgannard Fey had fallen.

The Brandmistress waded into the middle of the thugs. Her sword whirled about her as she sliced and slaughtered them by twos and threes. "Jeweler, take Smurgen and run," she cried.

All of Jonathon's joints ached, and he knew he could not run fast enough to elude a tortoise, much less Molgannard Fey's furious mob. He could see that they had bolted the heavy wooden door from within. The bolt was a ponderous wooden beam, much too heavy for him to remove. They were still trapped and he was helpless.

He looked at the Sinjery Brandmistress, covered in blood, surrounded by thugs, but sweeping them away. She was sorely pressed. He knew the mob would eventually engulf her. He looked at the pile of stinking skins by the door. He looked at Smurgen, the person they needed to find the Knife of Life, if only they could get out.

"Smurgen, can you ride a horse?"

"I have never ridden a horse, but if it will save me, I will learn quickly."

Five thugs had broken off and were coming at Jonathon. He spotted a horse skin on the pile and forced his agonizing legs to carry him toward it. The skin was heavier than he had expected. He leaned back, using his weight to drag it from the pile. Behind him, the thugs picked up the Dwarf in triumph. With his last ounce of strength, Jonathon threw the foul horse skin over his shoulder. He pulled the boneless muzzle over his scalp and let the front legs dangle to the floor in front of him. The skin was so heavy that his knees faltered again as he crashed to the floor. Like all the others, it had that weird alchemical smell about it, as if it was prepared for a Skin-Splicer to use. The thugs holding the Dwarf started his way.

Jonathon had no choices left to him. There was only one course he could take, vile as it was. It was a course unknown and unappealing. He had no knowledge of how Skin-Splicing worked, and he feared it nearly as much as he feared Molgannard Fey. But it was all he had. He had to take it. Taking one last breath of the foul, stinking robe he had put on, he touched the nose of the horse's skin with a Copper Order.

The world clouded over like the end of a dream or the end of a life.

This dream, however, was very real. His flesh burned like it was on fire, and he yelped as the horse skin fused to his body. He watched his own fingers and toes coalesce weirdly into hooves. His face was yanked into a snorting muzzle. His vision in the dimness was much better. Sounds were much louder and more distinct. The horrible stench was intensified, but now it meant something much different to him. Instead of horrifying him, he was picking out the scent of living beings. He saw clearly ahead of him the thugs that meant him harm, and the smell of them enraged him.

Despite all the other bizarre changes, it was Jonathon's muscles that were transformed the most. His muscles took on a strength he had never known. Not even as a young vigorous man mining for a living had he been as powerful. He felt his back could hold a ton. His flying hooves could shatter trees. He could run all day without tiring. All his pains, his uncertainty, his weakness, they faded into things of the past.

Infuriated at these small, annoying creatures threatening him, he snorted and leaped at the thugs, scattering them like leaves.

Smurgen was dropped. Jonathon gave a slight hop and sailed well over the cringing Dwarf, knowing in his animal brain that the female human fighting his foes was his friend and his hope.

In a moment, he was beside the Brandmistress, rearing up, half a rod tall on his hind legs. When his hooves came down, a thug's skull was crushed, and ten others backed away. He lashed out with his strong neck and another thug was thrown aside.

Smurgen came up next to Trallalair as she backed away from the angry horse. The Brandmistress was ready to defend herself from this new threat, but she hesitated as the horse did not attack her.

Smurgen said, "Brandmistress, help me up. This horse is the Master Jeweler."

She was in no condition to question any bizarre statement at that point. Without slowing her slashing against the now returning thugs, she grabbed the Dwarf's collar with her free arm and lifted, helping him to scramble up onto the horse's back.

With a parting swipe of her sword in the ruffian's faces, Trallalair leaped onto the horse's back. Straddling the horse was far easier than straddling an immense flying Dragon. She saw two crossbowmen fire at them. One bolt missed, the other bolt she knocked away with her sword. She bent and said in the jeweler's ear, "The door, Jeweler."

Even with his thoughts clouded by equine instincts, Jonathon again noticed that she had addressed him as 'Jeweler', not 'Traitor'. Perhaps she was changing from hateful to grateful, at least for the moment.

Immediately, he turned and charged the door, rearing up and pounding it with his hooves. On his back he perceived that Trallalair used her left arm to hold onto his mane and cradle the Dwarf. Her right arm wielded her sword which sang through the air, lopping off heads right and left.

When the battered door began to give way, the remaining thugs, about ten in all, backed off. Jonathon could see partially behind him with his horse's eyes that looked more to the side and behind than human eyes.

Clustering together around their leader, the ruffians still wore their wolf skins. At a word from their chief, they all touched coins to their skins. The thugs dissolved and in a few moments, a pack of angry wolves appeared in their place.

The sight of the snarling wolves further motivated Jonathon to kick the door down, but his strength now came from instinctual fear. The fear of a ravening pack of wolves. With one last powerful kick and a resounding neigh, he burst through the door, leaped over the splintered wood, and galloped away from Molgannard Fey's awful tower. Trallalair and Smurgen hung on desperately to his mane. No horse in any race could have outdistanced him as he raced through the squat Jungle and smoldering city with a howling pack at his hooves.

He was much faster than the wolves and soon left them behind. The howling followed. Like a wild horse on the plains, Jonathon knew the wolves could follow him forever at their own slower, loping pace. They could follow his scent and the sound of his hoof beats, then take turns running so as to tire him out. When he was finally exhausted and could run no more, they would surround him, disable him with a few bites to his legs, then kill him and eat him. Fueled by these fears, he ran on and on through the city and up the hill on which his house stood.

The commotion he made as he galloped past Farmer Gibbel's woke the old man. The miser came out with his rake, cursing horse riders that trampled people and barnyard fowl.

Jonathon thundered into his yard where Vailisk and Quintella already sighted bows at them. Apparently, they recognized the Brandmistress because they quickly redirected their aim beyond them toward the howling that chased them.

Despite his animal mind and demeanor, Jonathon recognized his home and pounded to a halt at his door, where the Brandmistress and Smurgen dismounted. The Sinjery drew her sword, preparing to fight off any of the wolf pack that made it past her Sisters' arrows.

The howling approached, progressing ominously up the hill. Unlucky for the wolves, before the pack was in sight of Jonathon's farm, they had to pass Farmer Gibbel's.

Jonathon heard the miser's voice. "Wolves is it? We'll just see about that. You're not getting <u>my</u> chickens!" Above the bushes they saw his rake rise and fall like he was swatting flies. Whimpers and yelps of injured wolves filled Gibbel's yard. They only saw two of the Skin-Splicers get away alive, fleeing back to the Jungle with their tails between their legs.

CHAPTER 22

LIQUOR OF SUSTENANCE

The next morning, Jonathon woke standing up. He looked down at hooves where his feet should have been. When he tried to yell, "What in the name of The Three?'" all that came out was a whinny. That made him whinny more until the Brandmistress came to him and lay a warm, gentle hand on his muzzle.

She fed him a beet from her hand. With her hand on his mane, she led him slowly to a patch of grass at which he could graze.

Jonathon's weak horse memory slowly pieced together the previous day's events.

Smurgen was there, studying the water in Jonathon's Vision Bowl. He muttered continuously about the poor craftsmanship and how long he had to wait to make connections in his network of Gossip Dwarves.

Trallalair left the jeweler who had become a horse to his grazing and walked over to Smurgen. From behind the Dwarf, she peered over his shoulder. Hili flew about and watched the proceedings.

Smurgen said to the Dwarf in the bowl, "Connect me to Grisbarth, if he's been in touch with the Mermen." The Dwarf's image split into spicules of light that swirled around for a long time while Smurgen grumbled again. His own silver vision bowl that he had lost at Molgannard Fey's was apparently much faster. Finally, the spicules re-formed into another Dwarf, red-bearded, scrawny, and nervous.

"Grisbarth."

"Smurgen? I heard you were residing at Fat Fey's Fort and a whole Lance of Knights attacked to save you and cleaned up his whole mob. It didn't take the Skin-Splicers long to learn that no one was guarding the precious hides. Free Skins for everyone."

"I saw the whole thing. They were beset by assailants more fearsome than a Lance of Knights. I'll give you details later, but first, I'm looking for the true location of the Knife of Life. I know it was thrown into the sea, but that's the closest I can get."

"Yes, the sea is rather large. I can narrow it down a little."

"How much."

"Ten O."

Smurgen looked up at Trallalair. "We need ten Orders, Brandmistress."

She still had the nineteen the jeweler had given her the day before in her girdle pouch. Ten of them she counted into his hand. They went into the bowl, disappearing.

The image of Grisbarth's hand reached toward them. The image twisted with distortion as it passed through the surface of the water in his Vision Bowl. When the quivering ripples settled again, he was inspecting the coins one by one.

"Landprow Cliff," he said. "It was hurled into the sea from Landprow Cliff."

"Can you be any more specific? Where did it land? Do the Mermen know of it?"

"Oh they know of it all right. The Lord of the Sea brought his wife back to life with it. The Knife of Life is a hallowed object for them."

"Then the magic of the Knife may be undiminished despite the fall into the sea. We need it to fight the Demon," Trallalair said.

The stiffly-haired brows fringing Grisbarth's eyes rose, questioning. "To fight the Demon? With all the Sinjery recently killed?"

Trallalair tried to ignore Grisbarth's intimation that she wanted the knife to bring back all her Sisters. No use denying that the thought had crossed her mind. Who wouldn't consider bringing loved ones back to life with such a powerful item, if given the chance? The Lord of the Sea knew its worth.

The Dwarf went on. "I don't think they're going to give it to you."

Hili flew up to Trallalair and said, "We can speak with the Mermet Community. We talked with them a century ago. They will help us." A century, to the Pixets, apparently was like yesterday in their collective memory.

Trallalair said, "Will they go get it for us?"

"We'll ask."

A voice came from behind them. "I'll bet we have to go find it ourselves." All three of them, even Trallalair, jumped. The jeweler was behind them, a man again. He looked haggard. There was a bloody crust on his face where the condor had pecked him, and more dried blood from his cut scalp. His dirty, rumpled shirt had a rich horsehide scent, as if he has been sleeping in a stable, and his pants were missing. They'd been left back at Molgannard Fey's tower.

Trallalair said, "Jeweler. So the Giant wasn't your friend, after all. How is it, then, that you are a friend of the Demon?"

Jonathon snorted and shook his head. He wanted something to eat like, like... newly sprouted grass? No... bread. "I could use some food and some pants. I feel like I just ran more than a league."

"You did, Jeweler. With me and the Dwarf on your back. You were quite agile."

"Oh, right. The memory is indelible, yet incomprehensible." Jonathon looked briefly at the vision bowl with Grisbarth's face. He knew most of the Gossip Dwarves. "Salutations, Grisbarth."

"Hello, Master Jeweler. So now you are a Skin-Splicer, too?"

"True, my worthy sage. I fear I now warrant that dubious distinction." His mind was still dazed from the confusion of the day before. The walk through the Jungle, the climb up the Path of Fear, the apathy from the Armlet of Tranquility, the levitation up hitting the ceiling, the fight with the carrion bird, the gigantic snake, the gray thundering beast, and the horse's hide.

The horse's hide. The power of his four legs. Jonathon looked at his hands. He balled his fists. Not much like hooves. He looked at his bare skinny legs. Where were all those muscles he had last night? He wished he had that power again. No hesitancy. He had jumped, kicked and run like the wind. All he needed was another horse's hide. He shook the idea out of his mind. For him to be a horse for a day, a real horse had to die forever. But there was another way. "Brandmistress?"

"Jeweler?"

"Do you think we could go back to Molgannard Fey's and see if there are any horse skins left?"

The Brandmistress gave him a look to chill his bones. Hili shook her head. From the vision bowl, Grisbarth piped up. "See? He is a Skin-Splicer, just like I said."

Trallalair grasped the hilt of her sword. Even though she had been exhausted the night before, after they finally decided the wolves were gone and they were out of danger, she had cared for her sword. She had carefully cleaned off all the blood that clouded the Verses of Power. The sword now shone, mirroring the sun as she drew it. The steel moved so fast that the jeweler tensed suddenly as she touched the tip lightly to his throat. Her face was still cherry-red and swollen, almost cherubic, but anger emanated through her flaking skin. "Jeweler, you will end your craving for the Skins and help us obtain the Knife of Life. We have a Realm to save. And the Demon to destroy."

In another time of his life, Jonathon would have fainted dead away to have a sword at his throat. But now, after the initial surprise, it was only an annoyance. Didn't she realize he could be more help if he were a horse? The Brandmistress and Hili could ride him to the Dead Lands, and she could fight from horseback against the Zombie host. In his mind, he saw her riding with regrown, long hair flying in the wind, the Knife of Life resurrecting people by droves.

He thought back to his family in the pot of dirt and his family still in the city. The Knife of Life had to come first. He would have to squelch his craving for the sake of others. Regarding the Brandmistress in a detached manner, he nodded. She peered into his eyes intently, still uncertain of his sincerity. The sword withdrew and she fluidly slid it back into its sheath.

"Smurgen?" Jonathon said.

"Yes, Master Jeweler."

"If it's in the sea and the Mermets can't get it for us, how can we find it?"

"Hmmmm. I was thinking about that very problem myself. The truth is as inescapable as a Giant's fist." He turned around and regarded Jonathon and Trallalair. "You can't get it." He paused for an appropriate pregnant interval. "Unless you have some jewelry to allow you three to walk on the sea floor and live?"

Jonathon shook his head. If Rhazburn were alive, he could devise something, but none of the other Poets possessed the knowledge, or the all-consuming drive, to create such a device.

Smurgen continued the thought. "The answer must be a potion. I'll consult the Alchemists, if any remain uneaten." He waited a moment, then said, "Vision Bowl, Alchemists." More spicules of light, more waiting. Smurgen twiddled his thumbs.

Jonathon found another pair of pants, then went back to watch and wait with the others. Jonathon found he did not mind standing as he waited. A few days before, he would have preferred to sit in a comfortable chair, but his legs since leaving Molgannard Fey's lair seemed much more suited to standing for long periods.

Hili had to go out to the yard and find flowers to sip nectar from.

Smurgen asked for ale and venison, but settled for water and sausage.

359

The sun passed over their heads, shadows disappeared, then began lengthening.

Jonathon watched a slug crawl down the garden pathway toward what was left of his herb garden. Smurgen would call out the name of an Alchemist and wait a while, repeating the name several times, to see if any responded. He had had little luck so far, and it was a tedious process. After ten or so tries, even Smurgen himself dozed off waiting for one of them to respond, his bearded chin slumping to his chest.

Watching the slug he could barely see at the end of the garden path, Jonathon worried that it would eat the green leaves he so wanted to munch on. Like the strength in his legs, his peripheral vision seemed better as well, because from the corner of his eye he saw movement in the Vision Bowl water. He turned and whooped, "Smurgen! Smurgen, wake up."

The scene in the water was one of neat shelves filled with books and bottles of reagents. From his vivid memory, Jonathon could tell it was not Rulupunerswan's chamber and was thankful of that. He didn't feel like arguing with that evil wretch again, and he could harbor nothing but hate for the Alchemist after what Rulupunerswan did to his family. But then he thought back to Rulupunerswan's chamber and remembered that he had no vision bowl in his chamber. He thanked The Three for that, being saved from trying to negotiate with Rulupunerswan.

Smurgen woke, shook his head to clear the cobwebs, and stated, "This is Binthwang's shop." He looked back at them. "A Royal Bastard, but reasonable."

"Binthwang! Binthwang!" Nothing. The Dwarf shrugged. "His cat, perhaps."

"Binthwang? My son Wally apprenticed for him a few years ago," Jonathon said. "He'll remember Wally. He let him skip his last Moon's fee to allow him to purchase his own shop." Jonathon stopped and slapped his head. "Wally... I never thought of Wally. We can always inquire of Wally. I've always found him a fountain of facts about potions."

"Vision Bowl, Wally Forthright," Smurgen said into the Vision Bowl. It was fast this time. After a few moments, all they saw was the bottom of the bowl. "Hmm. No Bowl, Master Jeweler."

"I donated one to his own shop when he signed the lease. Of course, we never went down Alchemist's Row on our way back here. His shop may have been incinerated for all I know. He's all right though, Patrick told me so. But I never asked about his shop."

"Vision Bowl, any other Alchemists." Bottom of the bowl again. "Looks like it's Binthwang, and no one else. At least you maybe saw something move there." Smurgen said, "Bring me some food. I'll stay in Vision for a while more."

Jonathon had no meals in the Keeper. All the meals that Arlen had baked and kept safe before the day of the Dragonegg Festival had been eaten by his family. Heather drifted around nearby. She had baked some bread and brought what was left of the sausage Patrick had found, setting it on the dining room table.

Jonathon got a plate of bread for the Brandmistress which she ate quickly. For himself, he found some dried apples and early lettuce from what was left of his vegetable garden. Meat had lost its appeal. Carnivores - disgusting. He ate standing up.

Hili had eaten early in the morning. She was anxious to look for the Mermets and ask for help to take the Knife of Life from the sea. She had spoken confidently that the Community could enlist the aid of the Mermets, but the last time they had dealt with them had been almost one hundred years previously. At that time, the Mermets came to them out of the sea to meet them in the harbor near Isseltrent. Isseltrent may have seemed daunting to an aquatic folk, but the city was relatively small compared to the vastness of the sea, and the harbor was easy for the Mermets to find, since ships emanated from the harbor to plunder the sea. The meeting had been arranged by emissaries of the Dragonlord speaking to ambassadors of the Lord of the Sea. This gave the Community an idea where to start. Once the Mermets were found, their friendship of old could be drawn upon for help. Still, the task was anything but certain. After obtaining permission from the Sinjery Brandmistress, with a promise secured by the life of the Community to return if she lived through the search, Hili flew away toward the sea, a place as hostile to Pixets as the Dead Lands.

Contemplating a walk through water to find the Knife of Life, Jonathon looked over his magical jewelry. He was certainly glad he had taken some with him to Molgannard Fey's. This time, Trallalair did not say a word to him. There wasn't much left that could be useful in the sea. A tiny shimmering topaz in a gold, radiant sun setting he pinned to his vest. It was a Charm of Dryness. He took out a turban he could tie to his head and pinned on it a jeweled, silver dung beetle with multi-colored iridescent wings. It was one of his most beautiful Charms of Luck. Why dung beetles were lucky, he never knew, but the Charms of Luck had certainly been lucky for his jewelry business. He charged a lot for them.

"Binthwang. Binthwang! Wait. Come back," Jonathon heard Smurgen exclaim, trying to get the attention of the Alchemist. "Binthwang."

"Smurgen? I thought you were dead. They told me you were at Molgannard Fey's hide-out. I figured you got killed with the rest of his mob. They say three hundred Knights and Sinjery stormed the place and slaughtered his whole gang, including the Giant himself. Only two beggars got away to tell the tale."

"I know the entire tale and you may have it for a paltry fifty Woodies." Smurgen was drifting back into his Gossip Dwarf mode. Binthwang was not interested. He'd get the tale for free if he waited long enough. Smurgen went on, "Listen, I need a potion to allow the Brandmistress Trallalair, Pixelle Hili, and Master Jeweler Jonathon Forthright to go under the sea. They have business with the Lord of the Sea."

"What? They want to talk with the Lord of the Sea? I hear the Mermen are having their own problems with the Blue Dragons. I think they'd rather the traitor drowns, like most of us do."

"He has been commanded with the Brandmistress and the Pixet to find and bring back the Dragoncrown. They need something that is at the bottom of the sea to fight the Demon. Can you help them?"

"I've made similar potions for the Seawalkers to use in their abalone trade. I still have a few draughts left, but it isn't cheap these days. I can't make any more. No suppliers and no coins. Twenty Coppers a draught."

Smurgen said, "That's outrageous. If they defeat the Demon, your profit as one of the few Alchemists left in Isseltrent will be fantastic. You should give it to them for nothing."

"They probably won't even return from the sea. And the Dead Lands? When the Thousand Warriors Host was decimated? Don't be stupid. I'm getting my profit now. These will probably be the last Coppers I'll ever see."

"How much of it do you have?"

"Enough for the three. Each draught lasts one Blessing. Or one of them could go down for three Blessings."

Smurgen tossed his head back and looked at the Brandmistress leaning over him. He waited for her decision.

She was in charge. She nodded. They would have to take most of the money Jonathon had intended to leave for his family. "Jeweler, get sixty Copper Orders."

He did so swiftly, from the stash he had left for his family, and dropped the sixty Coppers into the Vision Bowl, where they were soon replaced by three small, stoppered vials containing blue elixir.

"The Liquor of Sustenance. I guarantee it will allow you to live under water as if you were walking in a pleasant rain shower."

Trallalair slid her hand into the water of the Vision Bowl, retrieving the vials and asked, "What if it doesn't work and we all drown?"

"Well." He looked offended, as if the very idea was unthinkable. "If you drown, you or your survivors may have all your money back."

Unamused, she unstopped a vial and sniffed the liquid. Sweet, like honey. She replaced the stopper tightly and placed them all securely in the pouch at her girdle.

Smurgen thanked the Alchemist whose image disappeared. Fully awake again, the Dwarf said, "I think I'll look around for a while and catch up." He requested and received for his service a small pouch of Wooden requests to fuel the Bowl. Setting it beside him, he settled in, eating his dinner and calling out visions, cursing again the torpid response of the bowl and the lackluster colors of the images.

Trallalair said to the jeweler, "We must get some rest while the Pixet is gone." She did not wait for his reply, but lay her blanket outside the front door of his cottage and quickly fell asleep.

Jonathon went to the small grassy sward out by his woodpile. Again forgetting he was no longer a horse, he stood there in the morning sun and fell asleep.

CHAPTER 23

THE LORD OF THE SEA

Hili could scarcely concentrate on the search for the Mermets because the Community was preoccupied with the hideous link they had with the Demon. To end the link and free the Community, they had to go to the Dead Lands and take Caene's desecrated body back to be properly consecrated and given back to the Natural Presence. Only by resting as part of the hallowed soil could Caene nurture bushes or trees with all the goodness of his body. In time, he would live again, beautifully, as the flowers that he nourished. Perhaps he'd rejoin the Community through the nectar of flowers the Pixets fed upon. If they were unable to bring him back, they were determined to all go back to the soil from which they came. They would rather nurture plants with the goodness of their bodies than be slaves of Sverdphthik.

Until they reached the Demon and wrested Caene from it, they could tell no one. They were at the Demon's beck and call. Whenever it wanted to enter their mind, it could do so and prey upon the Community. The Demon could possess them, but it would never control them. For the

Demon just to reside within the Community mind, though, was still a way of using them against their will. Once it had entered the Community mind, it could see what they saw, hear what they heard, and know all their thoughts and plans. All the secret plans of the Brandmistress and the Master Jeweler would be revealed for the Demon to thwart.

Despite all that, the Pixets had to help the quest for the Dragoncrown while the Community still had some strength left. Aiding the Brandmistress was their only hope for salvation from the Demon's hold, and they would use what little resources still remaining to them for that end. Incarceration in Blaze constantly leeched the Community's strength. They needed fresh flowers and clean, sunlit air, not bread crumbs and darkness, to thrive. Despite their sapped powers, the Pixets constantly prepared themselves to fight the Demon if it entered their minds again. In their cheerless cell, little else remained to occupy them. Most of the time, they lay still and thought together, strengthening their will to resist. The Demon could have access to all they had ever known, taking what it pleased from them, but together they would stiffen their mental defenses. If they could stay rational while Sverdphthik used them, maybe they could reverse the purpose of the Demon's enthrallment. Just maybe they could use the Demon's own eyes to disclose its location and use the knowledge of its whereabouts to aid Hili, the Master Jeweler, and the Brandmistress.

The Community knew exactly where to start searching for the Mermets. The harbor a hundred years earlier had been smaller. At the Southern docks, an outcrop of granite peeked above the plashing waves. It was a hazard for ships, so a Diamond Beacon on a pole had been erected. It stood gleaming in the sun and sparkling beneath the moon. Since the Dragons were freed and the ships of the merchant and fishing fleets had been destroyed, the beacon stood lonely, abandoned, and was dark at night. Skeletal timbers of the burned ships rocked in the swells like the gnawed carcasses of frightful sea beasts. There, above the granite outcropping, one hundred years before, two Pixets and a Pixelle had spoken with a Mermet at the behest of the Dragonlord. They had warned the Lord of the Sea to desist retributions against the fishing fleet, or the Dragonlord would hunt him and his family down with Blue Dragons. The Lord of the Sea never responded, but the attacks from sea creatures such as whales, sharks, and giant squid had ceased the next day.

Hili flew over the water. The murk and sunlit sheen on the surface allied to hide anything more than a wing span below the surface. The harbor wall, built two hundred years before, shielded the docks from the crashing surf on the other side. Isseltrent's natural harbor was a line of rocks normally covered with barking seals. Now empty and silent, the rocks extended southward from Landprow Cliff, a hundred flutter tall buttress of granite tapering to a leading edge that mimicked the prow of a ship slicing through the waves. From that promontory, the Knife of Life had been hurled into the sea by an ancestor of Seldric.

According to Grisbarth, the Knife had been found by the Mermen, used by the Lord of the Sea, and then hidden in a place of reverence, possibly much farther out to sea. The Community had no idea how to approach Mermen. After all, they were relatives of humans, and fully as large and unpredictable. They were ruled by the Lord of the Sea and would not aid the Community, Jonathon Forthright, or the Brandmistress Trallalair unless their Lord approved, but the Mermets were another matter.

Distantly related to Pixets and Sylvets, the Mermets were another one of the races of tiny beings inhabiting the world. Each of these races was separate and distinct. They were all about the same scale as Pixets, and all intensely tied to the natural world which nurtured and protected them. Like the Pixets, who had cared for the meadow life of Verdilon until those meadows were razed by Sverdphthik, the Mermets still cared for the creatures of the sea. As all things in the ocean, they were ultimately ruled by the Lord of the Sea, just as the Pixets in Isseltrent were ruled by the Dragonlord. Still, the Mermets, unlike the Mermen, were independent in most of their dealings with other creatures, at least those dealings which did not impinge upon the Lord of the Sea's concerns. They constituted a group with which the Community could negotiate for the location of the Knife of Life. That is, if the Mermets could even be found in the vastness of the ocean, Hili thought sadly as she flew.

The murky waves sped by beneath her as she scanned them for flashes of light that would signal a school of fish or Mermets. There by the shore, the water was filled with silt from the land. After HIli spent all of one Blessing studying the surf, she knew further searching was hopeless so close to land. Farther out to sea, the visibility beneath the waves would be considerably better. The Community agreed. Hili would search the open ocean. They all understood the risks. None of them had ever been that far from land. If she tired, there would be no perches, and Pixets could not swim. They all agreed, Hili had to take the risk. The trade winds were in her favor, so she rode the air currents, unconcerned as to which direction she was taken. Anywhere at sea was a good place to start the search.

Somewhat later, she saw a group of sea-going Blue Dragons plying the surface, Some arched in great leaps, hardly splashing as their streamlined serpentine bodies slid back beneath the glittering waves. When Hili flew closer, she clearly saw shimmering schools of fish over indigo fathoms. At times, the teeming clouds of fish were split by massive sharks. As she watched the spectacle, spellbound, one of the sharks was itself swallowed whole by a Blue Dragon that suddenly rose from the depths, jaws agape. The Community knew that Hili was much too small to be noticed by a Blue Dragon, much less pursued as a snack.

Hili flew as close to the water as she dared, close enough see a short way beneath the surface but not so near as to be easy prey for a jumping fish.

The sun had long before reaching its zenith. Now it dipped toward the distant sparkle on the horizon, and Hili still had no idea where the Mermets were. The Community knew she had but one choice, something frightening for a Pixet. She had to dip her head under water. To do that, she had to fly back to the rocky shore.

More time was wasted flying back the way she had come. This time a breeze fought her, costing her precious Favors. When she finally made landfall, the surf crashing on fractured boulders between the piers sent fountains high into the air. Just one splash of spume could leaden her filmy wings and suck her into a watery grave. She had to pick her seat carefully.

In a small bay, the pounding waves constantly ground down the screening rocks. What was left of their force became a swirling pool, busy with yellow and pink fish that nibbled bits and darted into crevices. In this bay lay a slab of granite. Half of it was slippery with seaweed where it faced the sea. But on its other side, toward the land where the tide had not yet reached, it stayed dry. Hili sat herself carefully on the slab and warily watched the frightening, moving surface. Her reflection was twisted and torn apart repeatedly by ripples and whirlpools, suggesting it could, as easily, tear her apart. She needed all the strength of the Community's thoughts to summon the courage to take a breath and dip her face into the water.

She hesitated far longer than the short time before sunset allowed. She finally felt enough confidence, and before she could argue herself out of the dangerous act, she shoved her face into the brine and opened her eyes. Her eyes stung so much she barely kept her wits to stop her urge to pull her head back out. Something else, something even more frightening, made her want to lift her head. The thoughts of the Community disappeared, but they were replaced by another presence in her mind, the strange thoughts of the Mermets.

The alien thoughts and sensations were there, all around her in the water. They came at her from all directions, just like the mind of the Community did above water. Smells and tastes seemed to dominate the Mermets' minds, but there was much more. Sounds penetrated their entire bodies like a chorus of drumming, clicks, whistles, and moans. The sounds were nothing like the everyday sounds Hili experienced above the water. Even the sound of the surf was remarkably lessened underwater. Here, it sounded less like thunder and more like wind. She could stand it for bare moments, and rose up to rub the stinging water from her eyes.

The second time she dunked her head, she tried to organize the Mermets' perceptions to understand better. Some of the Mermets could see far into the crystal-clear water filled with fishes, while others swam in water too cloudy to even see their own bodies. These Mermets relied on sound, smell and other senses. Their sense of touch was bizarre, almost painful, and there were other sensations that she could neither understand nor utilize. One sense had to do with varying pressures on their skin as things passed near them. Another was a quivering, inner sensation she had no name for. As fish swam by, the quivering increased, as did the pressure on various parts of their bodies. All of the experiences were strange. But the most disturbing aspect, the one even worse than having to hold her breath, was losing connection with the Community as soon as her head was underwater. For some reason, the Community could not penetrate beneath the surface of the water. Hili had never before been without them. Had the Mermets not filled her thoughts, she would have been ALONE. No Pixet, and from what she saw from her brief connection with the Mermets, no Mermet either, had ever been ALONE. The idea was unimaginable. Unthinkable. Impossible. Unbearable.

Her imagining triggered a fear that became so great, she lifted her head out of the water again, gasping for air. The connection with the Mermets was immediately broken. The Community rushed blessedly back within her. Their presence soothed her spirit once again. They helped search her memories, but could not find the whereabouts of the Knife of Life.

For the third time, Hili had to hold her breath, submerge her head, and call to the Mermets underwater. The Community understood her fear of losing them but reassured her they would always be there for her when she lifted her head back into the air.

When she had dipped her head beneath the water the very first time, her wings had mercifully retracted by reflex. She could tell that the salt water splattering off the rocks would burn the thin film of her wings worse than it burned her eyes.

This time, in fact, Hili did not bother even opening her eyes. They still stung from her last dunking. The Mermets wondered what she wanted since she had appeared to them three times now. They could feel her need for something. Hili let her defenses down, and the Mermet Community took her more fully into their own Community mind. She saw infinite oceans and knew the Mermets numbered far more than all the Pixets that had ever lived. In a corner of her mind, she could even feel the Mermen. There were thousands more of them, too. That was all she could take. Her head was exploding with the scope of the ocean and its myriad inhabitants, and her lungs were aching, urgent for air. She straightened her back and lifted her sopping head again up into the world above the surface, She inhaled hoarsely and deeply while the Community absorbed her memories.

Still, the Knife of Life was not there. Hili's panting gradually slowed to pace the water lapping her toes on the other side of the rock she was lying upon. Realizing, too late, that the sea was now behind her as well as before her, a powerful swell reflected off the rocks behind her. It slapped her neatly off the slick green fronds of her perch. She slid headfirst into the waves. She had no chance to even take a breath, and she gulped salty water that clamped her throat shut. The next wave upended her, and she was thrown backwards. Her arms flailed in the bubbly surge. Another wave slammed her back against the rock. Her eyes were on fire as she tried to see which direction was up. Sand further assailed her eyes. She tried to grasp something but her hands gripped only more sand. Hili fought to control her panic. If there was sand in front of her, then the way up was behind her. She knew the water wasn't very deep, so she curled her knees beneath her, planted her feet as firmly as she could in the shifting, scratchy sand, and stood up. Her head was up just high enough to cough out a mouthful of water and croak in a stridulous breath.

Again, she was knocked her off her feet. An irresistible current like a watery hand pulled her through a gate of stone and out into the bay. This time the Community had time to steel her strength, and she inhaled just before going down. She knew it was for the last time. Her arms and legs were useless in the surf. Spreading them only managed to eliminate the little buoyancy she had, making her drop to the bottom like an acorn from a twig.

It was the Mermets that came to her aid. Through the watery ether, they told Hili to fly. It was her only hope. She knew it would injure her wings, maybe irreversibly. But she followed their advice. With the last of her lonely resolve, she strained to expand her wings. Searing pain came from both wings as they opened to their fullest. The salt water sucked out their scant liquid, and they became wrinkled, inefficient appendages that bent painfully with each stroke against the thick fluid. Still, she was moving.

Huge shadows passed in the murk. Kicking her legs helped. Even flapping her arms helped, now that her wings kept her from sinking. This time Hili bobbed to the surface, spitting and gasping with half her torso thrust up above the waves. It wasn't enough. Her ruined wings could not take her up out of the water that clutched at her hips and legs like honey. Back into the water she fell, inhaling just in time.

The waves again rolled her in different directions. In her mind, she could sense a Mermet coming toward her, riding a swift fish. As she sunk, straining to force her wings open again, she saw a stout, speckled, stern-mouthed fish rise up from the blackness of the depths. Suddenly she was in its mouth. She was being swallowed. All was black. To stop her descent into its gullet, she grabbed for any handhold she felt, a tongue, a tooth, or a gill. Her breath was bursting to get free, and she could not get to the air unless she forced her way out of its mouth. Even in the fish's mouth, Hili could perceive the Mermet's thoughts. Their name for the fish was a series of deep moans she translated as Big-Mouthed Swallower. Its mouth was so huge, all the fish needed to do was open it up quickly causing a sudden suction that drew her into it faster than she could think.

She felt she was going to die when, abruptly, she was looking at water again. A glinting hand lifted her through the water and up to the surface. Hili coughed and choked for a long time. Then Hili felt herself laying on her back, skimming across the water with her head bouncing on the waves. The Mermet sat on the fish and towed her from the bay back to the shore. By craning her neck backwards, she could see the Mermet and the goal of their travel. The monstrous fish swam so fast, it could keep the top of its back out of the water, allowing the Mermet to sit mostly above the churning waves. The Mermet held onto a thin gold chain which passed through the fish's mouth and behind its gills. He held Hili's hand tightly as she was dragged through the water.

The Community helped her to time and anticipate the waves With their help, she tried to gulp air just before she met a wave that washed over her. Sometimes the timing was right. Mostly, it failed. The Community was not used to swimming, or even floating in the sea.

At last, when Hili's meager reserves were nearly spent, they came within a few flutters of the crashing surf. The Mermet slid off the fish and slipped the gold chain from the fish's gill. Holding Hili ever so gently, he swam slowly and evenly, floating her back to a peaceful, protected pool.

In desperation to be rid of the sea and its treachery, Hili scrambled onto a flat rock slab quite a bit higher than the rock she had been washed from. The rock she had been on was already covered by the waves as the tide came in. The Mermet climbed nimbly up beside her, steadying her from slipping off again. His name she had learned when she was underwater. It was all whistles and peeps, part of the Mermet underwater language. Hili now understood the whistles and peeps enough to realize his name was Glimmerquick Master.

"Pixelle Hili, we can talk above the water. You needn't drown yourself anymore. I am Glimmerquick Master. The mount I rode is a Glimmerquick."

Hili looked at the scaled skin of the Mermet. It was silver and coruscating. The sun, the waves, and the rocks twisted and contorted on each mirror-like scale of the Mermet's body with his every movement. He could swim in a school of silvery-sided fish and blend right in.

Thankfully, the Community empowered her once more, but the connection with the Mermets had been lost. Somehow, they needed water to communicate mentally, just as the Community needed air. No wonder there had been no further communication between the two races in one hundred years.

From the Pixets' prison in Blaze, Elder Darrel encouraged her to get to the point. Hili said, "We thank you, Glimmerquick Master, for my life."

He nodded, acknowledging her gratitude.

"You sensed our need even before I was drowning in the Big-Mouthed Swallower. We need to find the Knife of Life and take it with us to fight the Demon." The Community had been confronted with too many thoughts and sensations with Hili's dunkings. They may have been able to sift through them over a day or two and come up with the location, but that would be too slow for the Brandmistress and Master Forthright.

"The Lord of the Sea will not give it up, Pixelle Hili." Glimmerquick Master's eyes were as cold as the water that licked her feet. The tone of his voice, though, was musical in the air. It sounded distant and gurgled, as if it originated from the bottom of the sea. It was beautiful, but daunting as the Mermet spoke the cruel words.

"Will you help us take it from him?"

"I will ask," he said, and immediately sliced into the water like a gleaming knife.

After five small waves had splashed Hili's rock and two huge ones had newly soaked her, almost throwing her into a watery crevice and making her clutch at the knobby surface of the rock to hang on, the Mermet reappeared. He hopped back onto the rock.

"I spoke with the Lord of the Sea. He found out that you wanted to steal the Knife of Life the moment you first entered his Kingdom. He has shielded it with Rings of Death to prevent anyone from coming near to it. He could not hide it without our knowing where it was, but there is no way you can achieve your aim. No one may take it away without risking a hundred deaths."

Anything that could help fight the Demon and preserve the spirit of the Community was worth the risk of a few lives. Hili looked the Mermet in the eyes, begging, "Please, you must help us against the will of the Lord of the Sea. We will pay any price you name."

He regarded her a moment. Then he stood and, with a neat hop, speared the pool beside them. His lithe form disappeared into the shifting clouds of silt. This time, he was down much longer.

Since the tide progressively encroached upon her slab, Hili climbed further up the slippery rocks to a slightly drier patch. After a good Thirty Favors above water, with the sun sinking but warming her from the clear western sky, Hili braved opening her wings. They had healed themselves and expanded to their filmy fullness, strong enough again to lift her up. The tide was still advancing. Scant moments before another particularly scary wave almost inundated her, Hili popped into the air and flew to a perfectly dry rock, one unencumbered by weeds and slippery sea life.

As the horizon reddened, five Mermets, two female and three male, waved her to fly back down to the water's edge. In response, she flew to them, landing beside the choppy pool, and prudently retracted her wings. There, four of the Mermets busied themselves dumping water out of a brown sea snail shell while Glimmerquick Master supervised them with hisses and guttural clicks. The shell was a conical spiral of spines, broadening to a smooth fluted opening large enough for a Mermet. Because it was so large, the four Mermets had trouble holding it above the surf to shake out the water. Twice they dropped it in the raucous surf. They had to retrieve it from beneath the waves to start the process over again.

Glimmerquick Master, whom Hili had begun to think of as her savior, stood by. He gave a few words of advice when needed. Then he turned to Hili. "Step into the water over here, Pixelle Hili. Do not touch the Finger Flowers." He waved a hand at a shallow part of the pool.

The pool was strewn with a variety of sea creatures - small snails, scuttling crabs, fish in nooks, and hundreds of green and red blossom-like things waving masses of fleshy fingers. As she stepped gingerly into the water, a frightened fish darted too close to one of the blossoms. The instant it blundered into the fingers, the fish stopped still, as if paralyzed by some power or poison exuded by them. The fish twitched once, pitiably, as the blossom fingers wrapped it up and inexorably drew it deep within their clenched fist. A flower that killed? This was no flower that Hili was familiar with by any means.

Walking in the moving water was difficult, and she feared being pushed against one of those deadly blossoms.

The Mermets seemed wary of the Finger Flowers too, but Glimmerquick Master lead her safely past, only to say, "Do not touch the Prickly Borers."

In the deepening water, she saw holes in the sides of the rocks filled with spiny black balls. She needed no demonstration this time to tell her that getting one of those thin, unwavering, black spines in her flesh would be excruciating.

The water was above her breasts. Since her wings were retracted, she was spared the discomfort associated with the rapid drying effect of the salty water.

The four Mermets holding the shell lifted it higher and brought it over her head. "Put your head inside," Glimmerquick Master said. "The Queen Crawler shell will hold air for you under water."

Hili lifted her head into the empty shell. As they lowered it over her head, all became dark above. There was merely a dim glow from the water below. The only sound was a constant deep whistling, until a splash signaled that a Mermet was joining her inside the shell.

The Mermet was Glimmerquick Master. He quickly said, "We must go deeper so the whole Queen Crawler shell is underwater."

Breathing the air inside the shell made Hili's time under water much easier. She was still buffeted by the waves, but now she could hold onto the lip of the shell, which was itself steadied by the Mermets, and found that she could walk in the soft sand. As she descended the shore's slope, the waves dampened to a gentle tugging to and fro. Standing in the soft sand unsupported, her legs wilted. Glimmerquick Master had to encircle her waist with his arm to hold her up. Otherwise, she would have fallen out of her Queen Crawler air chamber. With his help she was able to stand and walk again.

When the Queen Crawler shell was completely underwater, the thoughts of the Mermets were hers once more. This time, Hili saw the Knife of Life, a gleaming golden blade with a sparkling crystalline handle and scabbard, held by a statue of a god. The statue was encrusted with bright coral. What she saw was a memory of another time. The statue was in the bright noon light, not the reddening glow of the sunset sky above her. She could sense the Mermets were capable and willing to lead her to the statue. She sensed that they would do so only for a dear price.

While the image of the Knife of Life engaged her, the will of the Lord of the Sea appeared. It came rapidly, like the leading edge of a tidal wave that rose from the depths and grew to fill her mind to its farthest corners. The Lord of the Sea held all the oceans under his sway, and the oceans stretched much farther than the Hili could have imagined. His powers were vast. The Knife of Life was helpful, but insignificant in the scheme of the cycle of life of the denizens of the sea. Small fish were eaten by big fish which were consumed by even bigger ones. The Lord of the Sea had protected his treasure with rings of death. Jonathon Forthright with the Mermets could take it if they dared. As always in the sea, only the fittest would survive. She could not hide the shame of the Community, that the Demon could use them through Caene.

The Lord of the Sea reached into a recess of Hili's mind. He was unafraid of the Demon he witnessed there. He had the power to resist the Demon under the sea, but the Blue Dragons that Sverdphthik controlled, they could be a problem. Also, he knew what would await if Hell's Breach were unguarded and Hell were unleashed. The Demon Sverdphthik could only move on land, but there were others in Hell that might make the sea their home. Through Hili's thoughts, he saw that the Community and Jonathon were only unwilling tools used by the Demon. That gave some hope that the Demon would be defeated. Still, the Dragoncrown must never be used against the Lord of the Sea and his domain by humans again. He would speak to the Master Jeweler before he entered the sea.

The Lord of the Sea finally released Hili. She only had a few moments of air left to her inside the Queen Crawler shell, and she spent it communicating with the Mermets. The Mermets would take Jonathon and Hili to the vicinity of the Knife of Life and help them approach it. Jonathon would give them all the gold chains he still possessed from his shop, about six as Hili recalled, and the Community would be in debt to the Mermets until the Mermets decided the rest of their price. For all time no Pixet would ever forget the debt, and the Mermets could collect their recompense in any way they wished.

Before she agreed, Hili had the Mermets take her back to the shore. On land out of the Queen Crawler shell again, she was thankfully back in the bosom of the Community.

The Community did not like this arrangement any better than the one that had started all the destruction. But Hili had become the only ambassador for Isseltrent and the Community under the sea. She knew that the Knife of Life could aid them in the quest of the Brandmistress, and more importantly, allow the Community to take back the body of Caene. The Mermets had seen the Rod of Coercion in Hili's thoughts. The idea of owning it now possessed them. They could increase their influence in the Lord of the Sea's Kingdom with it. Perhaps they could give it to him as a foil against the power of the Dragoncrown, thus indebting the Lord to their own Community. With this new power, perhaps the Lord of the Sea would be able to withstand unknown future threats to his Kingdom.

The Mermets were ultimately caring beings, however, like their Pixet relatives. After that first heady moment of greed, they thought again. They saw through Hili what an abomination the Community thought the Rod of Coercion was. They saw how painful it had been and would be for the Pixets to see anyone keep the Unicorn Horn from its proper, sacred resting place in the nurturing soil. The Mermets reluctantly suppressed their covetous thoughts. Still, the Community recognized their obligation and resolved to attempt to honor it if the opportunity presented itself. The thought of perpetuating the abomination of the Rod of Coercion grated the soul of the Community. They could see no way to resolve the conflict. In the absence of a Unicorn to ask whether their race would permit the Mermets to use a Unicorn Horn in such a manner, the Pixets alone had to make the difficult decision in their stead. There would never be a Unicorn to ask. They had all been dead for centuries.

After Glimmerquick Master and the other Mermets disappeared back into the sea, Hili dried off slowly in the cool dusk as stars began appearing one by one, then thousands by thousands.

When she was fully dry, she sprouted her wings and flew back over the dark city to the Master Jeweler's cottage. Silently, she searched the cottage and the yard. The Master Jeweler was asleep, standing up, outside where he could smell herbs, and the Brandmistress slept nearby on the green grass. Hili's tiny wings were so quiet that she didn't wake even the Sinjery maiden. Hili chose to wait until dawn, when the Brandmistress always awoke, to tell them all of her successful arrangement with the Mermets. She found a comfortable tree branch and instantly fell asleep.

At midnight the Demon came.

Chapter 24

The Knife of Life

Jonathon awoke to a high, piercing scream that nearly split his skull. At first, he could not focus his thoughts enough to localize the scream. It was as hair-raising as the screech of a cat.

Trallalair leapt to her feet and cried, "Sinjer!". Her sword appeared in her hand. She knew immediately where the scream originated, the small oak off to the left. The darkness obscured the details of the tree, but she knew the screamer was Hili. With two leaps Trallalair was at the tree. There, in a moon shadow, she barely perceived Hili writhing on the ground, holding her head. Vailisk and Quintella were close behind her, searching the shadows about them for unseen enemies, bows ready and arrows notched.

Glad to have the back up to watch for the culprit, Trallalair picked Hili up carefully. Every tiny muscle in Hili's body was tight with agonizing pain. Trallalair took her out of the blackness beneath the tree and into the moon glow. She looked for wounds. There were none. "Pixelle Hili, who attacked you? Where are they now? How can I help?"

The jeweler joined them and looked as concerned as Trallalair felt. "Can you tell what is wrong, Brandmistress?"

"She seems in too much pain to answer."

Hili squeaked out, "The Demon knows of the Knife of Life. Run! Run to the harbor!" She screamed again, then gasped, "Take me with you."

At that Vailisk and Quintella spread out, still searching for the assailant. "I see and hear nothing, Trallalair," Vailisk said. "Quintella?"

"I hear no Dragonwings," her companion called back from the murk at the edge of a stand of bracken.

They were on edge, bewildered by Hili's cries of distress that cut through the darkness and grated their nerves. She seemed to be attacked by something they could not see.

"Pixelle Hili, where is the Demon now?"

Twisting as if trying to extricate herself from tight bindings, Hili croaked, "It is not here. It stabs our minds. Run. Run to the sea." She choked and gagged. Finally, still grimacing, she cried, "Soon it will be too late!"

Trallalair looked at the jeweler and said, "We must run, Jeweler. I believe I know why."

"Why?"

"The Demon has somehow infiltrated her mind and the minds of the Pixet Community. All our plans are known to him, including our quest to take the Knife of Life. And our intention to use it against him."

Jonathon never imagined that they could be betrayed so quickly. He thought that they would be discovered when they finally entered the Dead Lands, but not before they had even left Isseltrent. His pessimism was reinforced ten-fold. Shaking his head, gazing at the distant sea, he said, "I cannot run all the way to the harbor."

The Brandmistress rasped, "The Blue Dragons are now looking for the Knife of Life, too. If we don't get there to take the Knife of Life and leave before they find us, the Dragons will eat us."

Jonathon thought, *And if we take the Knife of Life and go to the Dead Lands, the Dragons will eat us there.* Pointless worries. They'd probably never make it to the Dead Lands, anyway. His only consolation from the loss of the Dragoncrown and the Dragons had been the comfort that he would never have to travel by a Black Dragon again. He had hoped he was done looking at the inside of a Dragon's mouth. If he ran fast enough, maybe he could avoid looking at the inside of a Blue Dragon's mouth. He snorted and wished he had hard hooves again instead of soft feet.

The Pixelle thrashed and struggled, but Trallalair held her safe, close to her bosom. She checked her pouch where she kept the vials containing the Liquor of Sustenance. "Vailisk, Quintella, you have aided me immensely here. I am leaving. I hope to be back before sunset." Turning to the jeweler, she said, "Jeweler, you may not be out of my sight." She pointed to the trail down the hill. "You need not run all the way, but you must go as fast as you can."

Some of the jeweler's's family were coming from the house to see what the commotion was, but Vailisk, the closest to the house, ushered them back inside, saying, "Brandmistress Trallalair must take the jeweler away. Go inside. Do not interfere."

With a groan, Jonathon waved to Heather and Patrick as they were pushed inside. Aiming himself at the dark patch of Farmer Gibbel's and the path beside it, he started off at a fast walk. When he saw the frayed silhouette of Gibbel's ill-kept farmhouse against the stars, he began to jog so he didn't have to listen to the foul old man in case he had been disturbed by Hili's cries. Thankfully, the farmer only peered between his dirty curtains, brown and tattered in the lamplight. Beyond Gibbel's on the path down the hill, Jonathon ran easier as the slope aided his weak legs. He only slowed to keep from flying off the path at the switchbacks.

Trallalair followed easily, nestling Hili, who continued to cry and flail but sounded weaker with fatigue. Trallalair held her speed to allow the fat jeweler to keep ahead of her. Together, they passed the unused Travel Plaza where the Black Dragon's treasure pile had been plundered. Only the few human bones were left. A few more charred skeletons had been added the previous fortnight.

Another half-Blessing passed before Jonathon saw the flat, business-district streets winding past empty, fire-blackened shops. Running was harder over the cobblestone than on the path downhill, and his legs began to ache. Through a dry, lathered mouth, he panted. He was pushing himself harder than ever before. He had never run so fast nor so far. That is, except when he had been a horse for a day. It was as if his soft muscles remembered their brief strength and strove to regain it. Still, he was slow, uncoordinated, running flat-footed where the Sinjery sped lightly, sprinting on her toes. Once, he slipped and tumbled. The Brandmistress used her free hand to drag him up by his collar, pushing him on ahead of her. The bump his head took as he fell reminded him that he had left his turban with the Charm of Luck at his house. He would have no luck under the sea that day. Down on his vest was the Charm of Dryness. At least he'd be dry while he drowned.

To his surprise, they had already run through Fiddler's Row and had entered Baker's Street. Of all the destroyed areas of the city, Baker's Street was the first to be salvaged. Although it was the middle of the night, lamps glimmered in the shops that had been partially rebuilt, and ovens were being fired to start the day's bread. In the dimness, Jonathon saw hand carts lining the streets, awaiting loaves to be baked in the early morning. Drowsy Knights leaned against walls, ostensibly to protect the bread from looters.

The Brandmistress let him lead, and he kept up the pace. Never in his life had he run so hard.

Long before he expected, they entered the Jungle. Hoof beats of ungulates hidden in the dark preceded them, and a lion's roar heralded their entry. They swept quickly into Choir's Strut and passed a heavy woman in the shadows leading a shuffling bear. At Molgannard Fey's wrecked tower, dogs, rats, and carrion fowl feasted on the remains of his once-powerful gang. Jonathon wondered how many of the animals were Skin-Splicers themselves who had taken free skins and gnawed on the bodies of the Skin-Splicer gang. The smell was worse than two days before, but the pile of skins was gone to the very last. As he slowed to gaze where the pile had been, wishing they had left just one horse skin, the Sinjery maiden pushed him again angrily. "Jeweler, to the wharf. Forget the skins."

Two pylons of carved stone, one broken, signified the entrance to the harbor. As they passed them, Hili cried, "Throw me into the sea!"

They slowed, approaching the wharves. Some piers were torn asunder. Others were only lonely wooden piles with the covering planks completely gone. One wharf slouched into the sea, bobbing with the waves. The Brandmistress walked to the end, bouncing slightly with each step as if testing its integrity. Jonathon followed, still concerned for the sanity of the Pixelle.

"Throw me in, please!" Hili begged.

Trallalair knew enough of Pixelles to remember they could not swim. She bent to the water, which was barely visible in the meager moonlight where it lapped over the edge of the unstable wharf. Still hesitant, she touched the Pixelle to the chill water. Hili, still shivering in distress, slid gently into the blackness. Immediately, the Pixelle disappeared from sight, and Trallalair lunged to retrieve her before she sank out of reach. She grasped the tiny body still struggling with alarm. Trallalair pulled her back up so Hili came sputtering into the air, only to cry out again, "Put me back!"

This time Trallalair lowered her to the water with both hands cradling her in the wavering tide. Hili plunged her head into the water but held onto Trallalair's hands for support. When the Pixelle's head came up, she grimaced in pain, took a breath, and dipped her head in again.

After a dozen such dunkings, Hili gasped and sobbed, "Take me up. I cannot fly or walk." She convulsed again in agony. "They will come. The Mermets will come."

Trallalair held Hili tenderly. Then she looked at Jonathon. "Now that the Demon has access to her mind, Jeweler, our every move is betrayed. Her presence with us will be a constant danger."

Jonathon's heart was still hammering, resolute as a stallion's. Far from exhausting him, the run had exhilarated him and took the edge off his pessimism. He was convinced that any surprise attack against the Demon would now be impossible because of Sverdphthik's ability to enter the mind of the Community. But, Jonathon thought, there might be a way to use the Demon's access to Hili's mind to their advantage. "You already thought I had betrayed us to the Demon. How is this any different? We need her and the Community, Brandmistress, in order to give us the best chance of taking back the Dragoncrown. Maybe we could feed the Demon false information through Hili."

The Brandmistress sneered at him. "Jeweler, are you just a fool, or are you still aiding him? He is listening to our every word through the Pixelle. He just heard what you said. So the Demon has now been informed of that ridiculous plan."

Jonathon grimaced and flushed. She was right. He had merely alerted Sverdphthik to another of his ideas. Despite what the Brandmistress thought, he was no conspirator. This situation would take a lot of careful planning, apparently more than he was capable of.

Trallalair felt a twinge of discomfort for the jeweler's obvious stupidity. Sighing, she said, "At least dawn is a while away. That's when the Blue Dragons will start looking in earnest for the Knife of Life." She knew that Blue Dragons needed light to see underwater. Unlike the Greens, the Blues spat blistering steam, not fire, so they could not light their way at night as they swam above the waves.

A strong night breeze whipped spray at them from the breakers, filling their heads with tangy freshness. Glimmers of whitecaps flashed faintly in the moonlight. The pounding of the waves surged through them as vibrations rising up through the wood of the floating wharf they huddled upon.

The surf would have been soothing to Trallalair, were it not for the tension she felt holding the mewling Pixelle. She did her best to quiet Hili. After she had dried Hili with her own tunic, she stroked the Pixelle's hair, so soft, like the finest down. Trallalair could barely feel it with her own battle-toughened hands. Despite Trallalair's gentle soothing, Hili's sobs shook her tiny limbs in irregular paroxysms.

Concentrating so intently on the Pixelle, Trallalair almost missed the approach of the Mermets. At the edge of her vision, she sensed miniscule green lights blinking in the rolling waves. First in one place, then another. As if in response to her awareness, the blinking lights converged on their wharf. They swirled in the water, barely out of reach, until the blinking lights all stopped in a wavy line like a string of sparkling diamonds undulating on a dancer's neck.

Four shadowy forms rose up, each one just behind the lights that blinked. Trallalair could see the light reflecting off tiny limbs astride a suggestion of a fish too black to be perceived. The lights seemed to come from just behind the eyes of the fish. All else was black. The sea was black, the fish black, the tiny figures black. Black as the night sky. The lights would blink for a moment, limning the Mermets in a greenish cast. The rise and fall of the waves, the blinking of the lights, it all fit together into a slow, hypnotizing rhythm.

A bubbly liquid voice barely audible, as if underwater, came from one tiny figure. "Brandmistress Trallalair, I am Glimmerquick Master." His outstretched arm appeared in a green blink as he motioned to the Mermelle beside him. "This is Mother of Eight. Beside her are Memory and Nipped. We fear for the life of Hili and the Community. The Demon uses them. Thankfully its power ebbs beneath the surface."

Hili croaked, still clenching every muscle, "You must go without me. The Community needs every mind to fight the Demon. I must stay here."

Trallalair saw that nothing would help the Pixelle in her internal battle. Better to find the Knife of Life and start out for the Dead Lands. Of course, the Demon would know they carried such a powerful weapon and he could simply climb on a Dragon and fly away whenever he wanted. But what other chance did they have?

385

Trallalair spoke to the Mermets. "Will you aid us?"

"Pixelle Hili promised that the jeweler would have chains of gold for us."

That was a surprise. Trallalair looked at the jeweler, who was still panting. He shrugged, "I didn't know about that. I have nothing with me. The chains are in the strongbox back at my house."

She looked at the sky to the east. It was still sable-black. "Jeweler, you must stay here with Pixelle Hili. Tell me where the strongbox is with the chains. I will bring it." She knew she could run to his house and back again to join them shortly before before Dawn Blessing. "Glimmerquick Master, can we swim to the location of the Knife of Life?"

"Yes, but the journey is long from here."

"How many Blessings?"

The Mermet turned to his companions, exchanging clicks and whistles with them. When the racket ceased, he turned back to her and said, "We know little of your measures of time, but my companions think your day is divided into seven of the divisions you call Blessings. We can provide mounts for you to ride to the Knife of Life. With mounts large enough for you to ride, the journey there and back will take about one of your Blessings."

Trallalair thought of the dawn and the prowling Blues that would come with it. If they rode above the waves until they were over the site of the Knife of Life and just went straight down to the sea floor where the Knife was hidden, they would have plenty of time. But with the first light of dawn, the Blues could see them a league away. To be as secretive as possible, they would have to ride there underwater.

"We have Liquor of Sustenance to allow us to breathe underwater, but only enough for one Blessing apiece." Speculating, looking at Hili completely disabled, she said as an afterthought, "With an extra vial we could split. Making somewhat more than a Blessing underwater to give us a little leeway."

Glimmerquick Master said, "If you can truly breathe the water as can we, your mounts can take you beneath the waves where they can travel much faster."

Trallalair offered Hili, who was still struggling, to the jeweler. He held her away cautiously at first, but in a moment, he drew her close to his chest, calming her like she was a whimpering baby. She sobbed on but relaxed slightly with his warmth. Trallalair noticed that he seemed much more comfortable with the crying Pixelle than she had felt. Comforting a small thing was not something she had been bred for. For the jeweler, it seemed all very natural, as if he had practiced cuddling wee ones as much as she had practiced slashing with her sword.

"Brandmistress," he said, "I will care for Hili. The strongbox is in my bedroom." As she adjusted her sword girdle to start running, the jeweler added, "And please bring my turban with the Dung Beetle charm. It will give us luck."

"We will need much more than your luck." With that, Trallalair sprang away into the shadows of the city.

Jonathon sat down to comfort Hili. He watched the half-setting moon sparkling the waves. The water. So silent. So deep. If he and Trallalair split the second vial of the Liquor of Sustenance, they would each have about one and a half Blessings to breathe underwater. Hili was certainly in no shape to take a plunge into the bay. Besides, she somehow had to help the Community in dealing with the awful presence of the Demon in their collective mind.

When Hili's eyes opened in terror, looking at him, Jonathon thought he could see the Demon's eyes looking at him again. All too clearly, he remembered the feeling of the Demonic presence from when he lost the Rod of Coercion. Perhaps Sverdphthik would be able to enter Jonathon's mind again and steal the Knife of Life as easily as he had stolen the Rod of Coercion. Jonathon never wanted to be possessed by the Demon again. Better to die.

There was no use worrying about it. Their course was clear unless they could devise a better plan. One thing at a time. First, he had to help Hili. He could not stand to see her suffer. He jiggled her gently and hummed a lullaby. Maybe a lullaby would drive the Demon away. At least his humming seemed to drive some of the chill away. Hopefully, the Blue Dragons would not get to them before the Brandmistress returned.

Three of the Mermets sank in the waves, and the blinking lights of the fish they rode receded into the harbor water. Glimmerquick Master came close to the wharf and released his fish. He floated so quietly, washing back and forth like a piece of flotsam moved by the waves beneath the wharf, that Jonathon imagined he dozed. Rocked asleep in the cradle of the sea.

In Jonathon's arms, Hili was quieter as well, her stuttering sobs coming only occasionally as she, too, slept, totally depleted. He suspected that the visitation by the Demon had passed during his hummed lullaby.

As the time passed, the stars began to fade and black of night grew into dawn. Looking behind him past the city and at the line of small hills in the Commonwealth of Dis, Jonathon saw the steel gray of high clouds slowly turn red with the hidden sun. Out to sea, beyond clear vision, shadows moved rapidly behind the mist. The shadows were too fast for sailing vessels. Besides, all the ships had been destroyed. The shadows had to be Blue Dragons. They were beginning their search for Jonathon and the Knife of Life.

The thumping of boots on the quay got his attention. Out of the corner of his eye, he saw Glimmerquick Master suddenly rouse and summersault under the surf.

The Brandmistress approached with the strongbox and his turban. "Here, Jeweler. I found it all. The gold chains, your pin for good luck, and the rest of our money." She presented them all to him. "I brought this for Pixelle Hili." She untied a soft woolen blanket she had around her shoulders and held it out to him.

"Thank you, Brandmistress." With a nod, he motioned at Hili, who he still held against his chest. "She's sleeping. The possession ended before dawn."

He took the proffered blanket and placed it on a dry part of the pier. Upon the soft blanket, still warm from the Brandmistress' body, he lay Hili, who was sleeping so soundly in her exhaustion that she did not even stir.

Once he had divested himself of the precious bundle, he jerked his head at the distant ocean horizon, saying, "I think I saw a Blue Dragon out in the fog. Maybe two."

The Brandmistress looked at Hili. "The Pixet seems at ease. Where are the Mermets?"

The sea at their feet moved with a morning laziness that concealed all the frenetic activity that Jonathon imagined lay beneath, out of sight.

As if in answer to the Brandmistress's question, two huge fish appeared. Each was as long as a bench with a tall curved fin on its back. They swam from the open ocean, their exposed, scimitar-like tail fins snaking toward them. When they neared the pier, Jonathon saw their flattened heads had rectangular side wings which ended in cold, roving eyes. Two Mermets sat on each fish, one on each of the head extensions around which they had looped gold chains to use as reins. The fish were apparently their mounts, and were each large enough for a human to ride.

Jonathon recognized Glimmerquick Master and hailed him. "We have the gold chains, Glimmerquick Master." From the strongbox he laid on the pier, Jonathon took the seven gold chains, all that was left from his shop. Reaching over the timid swells, he handed them to the Mermet.

Glimmerquick Master held them with both arms, then tipped forward into the sea. He came up, in turn, beside each Mermet and handed two chains to each of them. When he had remounted his steed, all the Mermets draped the chains diagonally over their shoulders and across their tiny, shiny torsos.

Jonathon said, "Wait. We need to leave someone with Hili. She is exposed and unprotected."

The Brandmistress said, "True, Jeweler," then turning to the sea again, she said, "Glimmerquick Master, can any of you stay to aid Hili?"

His response was assured. "Of course we will watch over her. Be not afraid of her safety."

Seeming mollified but anxious to find the Knife of Life, she said, "Shall we go now?"

"Soon. The Lord of the Sea approaches." Glimmerquick Master gestured to the ocean a few rods out into the harbor.

There, the waves were disrupted and the water boiled in commotion. Up from the depths, as if ascending a staircase, stepped a shimmering man. He was a Merman, as tall as a human, one of the beings the Mermets were tiny copies of. Clad in seaweed fronds, with a bright-red circlet crowning his head, the Lord of the Sea had skin exactly like the Mermets, reflective silver. Mirroring the sanguine sun from behind them, the swirling water below, and the azure, cloud-wisped sky above, he was all things at once but none of them and much, much more. After ascending from the depths, he walked over the surface of the water before them, confidently, as if he trod a solid path. Jonathon could see great, moving shadows beneath the water encircling the Lord of the Sea.

It was only when the Lord of the Sea came closer to the pier that Jonathon could see he walked, not on the water itself, but on the backs of a series of huge fish that swam in circles beneath him. One swam up and toward him so he could step on its back, his foot moving like he was walking in place. A second fish would come up for his other foot. They coordinated their passage beneath his feet to coincide with his every step, one diving to be replaced by another in precise rhythm. The Lord of the Sea walked on a living, moving road, constantly changing, like the waves surrounding them. Seemingly, every living thing in the sea obeyed his unspoken commands.

Jonathon knew the only exceptions were the Blue Dragons.

Even Hili woke from her stupor and watched in awe.

Smiling, looking haughtily self-possessed, with the knowledge that he was protected by his Ocean Kingdom and all the creatures within it, he stopped two rods away from them, walking in place. "Jonathon Forthright, I recognize you from the Pixet's memories. All of your deeds are known to me. Your Dragonlord's demise is my gain. For centuries, humans of Isseltrent have plundered my Kingdom. Your Dragonlord used his Dragons to extort vast quantities of fish from my Kingdom. Your fishermen take the biggest and healthiest of the fish, leaving only the stunted ones or mere scraps for my people.

"For a time now, the bounties of the sea are again mine to apportion. The Blue Dragons we learned to deal with long before the Dragoncrown existed, and we will deal with them again.

"Pixelle Hili, I know of your Community's chain to the Demon Sverdphthik. He has no power in the sea save that of the Blue Dragons, which he has let do as they wish. Now, spurred by your folly, his eye is upon us, and his Dragons search for Soul-Fetcher, as do you three.

"The Mermets have made a deal with the Pixelle and wish to help you find it. Soul-Fetcher is mine now, but I acknowledge humans originally made the knife, then cast it into the sea. I believe humans are frightened of it. I am not. I need not fight to hold it. The sea has power enough. Like all beneath the waves, the Law of the Sea will protect it. The weak will be devoured by the strong. So, too, will you be devoured if you try to take Soul-Fetcher. Rings of Death surround it. If you live to take it from the Rings of Death and you are not killed by the Blue Dragons, I will not further hamper your use of it. Having Soul-Fetcher out of my Kingdom may calm the present frenzy of the Blue Dragons.

"But... if you bring the Dragoncrown back, remember that I have not directly prevented your use of Soul-Fetcher. Jonathon Forthright, I could take your life if it pleased me, but you have in your bumbling way aided me. So I will only give you warnings that Soul-Fetcher is well protected."

Soul-Fetcher, that was what the Lord of the Sea called the Knife of Life. The name sounded odd but true. Jonathon was shivering with cold and fright at the power of the Lord of the Sea. "When we are finished with the Knife of Life, what you call Soul-Fetcher, we will bring it back to you if we are able. What's more, I vow to inform the Dragonlord of your complaints and your aid in our quest... if we live."

The self-assure smile of the Lord of the Sea did not change, but he nodded. Off-handedly, he said to Trallalair, "Brandmistress, your sword is useless in my Kingdom."

"We shall see," Trallalair said.

"That we shall." Still smiling, the Lord of the Sea sank beneath the waves.

Before they could blink, the sea returned to its slow rhythm of gentle peaks rolling toward them.

Trallalair rummaged in her pouch. She brought out the three vials of the Liquor of Sustenance and said, "Pixelle Hili, although you are no longer visited by the Demon, I agree you should stay here, away from danger. Even though you can communicate with the Mermets under the sea, you won't be able to communicate with us, so we cannot benefit. We are the ones who must take the Knife of Life. What is even more critical, if you are with us and are revisited by the Demon, we will all be at further risk."

Trallalair needed some assurance that they would not be attacked immediately by the Blue Dragons and the Rings of Death sounded daunting. She asked the Pixelle, "During your communication with the Mermets, did you at any time understand how to get to the Knife of Life?"

"No, Brandmistress. What was in the Mermets' mind was vague. We saw the location briefly, but we could not tell if the location was directly beneath Landprow Cliff, where the Knife had been thrown, or whether the Mermen had taken it leagues away."

No clue as how to proceed but some encouragement, nonetheless. "Good. There is some hope that the Demon also does not know where it is, and the Blue Dragons are still searching. Can we trust the Mermets?"

"Absolutely. They are related to Pixets." To the Community, that was reassurance enough.

Trallalair took out a Copper Order and touched her sword with it, feeling power surge into it. Useless under the sea? Not hardly. She doubted even the Lord of the Sea knew the power of the Sinjery when they wielded their swords.

At her side, the jeweler shifted from one foot to the other, anxious. This time he didn't have the Armlet of Tranquility to quell his anxiety. Just as well, she thought. When he had used the Armlet at Molgannard Fey's, he was calm but useless.

"Here, Jeweler, drink up," she said, handing him one of the vials of the Liquor of Sustenance.

Trembling, he took it and unstopped the vial, sniffing the contents and screwing up his face. With a great effort, he downed the blue elixir, gagging histrionically.

Placid and stolid, Trallalair drank her own elixir. It was bitter and tingling to the tongue, tasting slightly slimy and fishy, like distilled flotsam. Other than a smell like a fresh rain that filled her head, she had no other sensation to let her know if the Liquor of Sustenance was effective.

When the jeweler stopped gagging, she gave him the third vial. "Drink half, Jeweler." This time, he drank half. He only shuddered once. She noticed that he knew how to drink exactly half, watching the end of the elixir and stopping when it reached the top of the far end of the tube. She drank the rest and watched while the jeweler made his own preparations.

Jonathon touched coins to his Charm of Dryness and Charm of Luck and tied his turban to his head.

"Brandmistress, I am ready. Do you think the Liquor will work?"

She only shrugged. In the waves, several other Mermets had appeared, apparently there to watch over Hili until she recovered from her terror and exhaustion. "Let us go. Glimmerquick Master, bring our steeds."

Since both fish had drifted out from the pier, the Mermet acknowledged Trallalair with a wave and jerked the golden chain rein around his own fish's eye wing. Through a flurry of floating algal fronds, the fish dove, with the second fish close behind. In a moment, they both materialized out of the silty watery adjacent to the pier, close enough so Jonathon and Trallalair could mount them.

Trallalair hopped on hers, the one controlled by Glimmerquick Master and Memory. The fish settled down slightly into the water with her weight. The coolness of the sea invigorating her.

Jonathon put a tentative toe on his fish's back, asking, "What kind of fish are these?"

From the head, Mother of Eight said, "If we were to change the Mermet name for them into your words, they would be Rough-Scaled Fish-Rippers. I believe you call them sharks."

Jonathon had no idea what a shark was. The scales did not feel rough when he tested it with his shoe. He tried to slide onto the shark slowly, behind its tall fin, but he slipped off the bouncy pier and dropped abruptly on top of its back. He felt a distinct flash of pain in his testicles that made him groan. When he tried to adjust his position, he nearly slid off into the sea, barely catching himself by grabbing the tall fin in front of him. Holding the fin, he could feel that the roughness of the scales was like the sand-cloth he used for smoothing jewelry.

As the sharks began to swim ahead, Mother of Eight turned to him and said, "Whatever you do, don't fall off the Rough-Scaled Fish-Ripper."

"Why not?" Jonathon shouted.

"They eat humans."

With that frightening thought, his Rough-Scaled Fish-Ripper, and apparently human-ripper, submerged. Jonathon's cry of alarm turned into a bubbly gurgle. He wanted to jump off, but if he did, he'd be thrashing in deep water and eaten by the sharks. So he clutched to the fin, holding his breath as long as he could.

He could only hold his breath for mere moments until he had to gasp. his eyes popped out with fear. *Here I go*, Jonathon thought. *This may be my last breath.* When he inhaled, the water was sweet and pleasant. He panted for a while until he trusted the effect of the Liquor of Sustenance. Then he let his breathing slow to match the cadence of the shark tails as they moved through the darkening murk. He really *could* breathe underwater, at least until the power of the Liquor of Sustenance stopped working.

Only subtly-changing hues of the water indicated they were moving at all. No visual cues could be seen. In front of him, the first shark with Trallalair was an insubstantial wraith coursing through brown clouds of fine silt. Even closer, on the head of Jonathon's shark, the Mermets were invisible. Their mirror-like bodies reflected exactly the surrounding browns of the water behind them, above them, below them, and to all sides. All the water was the same, so what light reflected off their back could come from any angle, including from their front. The brown light he saw reflected from Mother of Eight's back seemed to pass straight through her like she was made of the brown water herself. Even their outlines were obscured by this effect. So most of the time, the Mermets blended in with the water around them. He felt like he was alone in the gloom.

All at once, the fog of silt surrounding them scattered, and Jonathon could see far into the green distance. They had left the silt-laden water of the shoreline and had moved into the featureless water of the deep bay. Clearly visible now, the gray sharks continued their methodic swim. The Mermets still looked as if they were made of water and virtually invisible. *What an amazing camouflage*, Jonathon pondered.

Even though Jonathon could see far into the ocean on all sides, there were no fixed points. All he saw was light green above, dark green around them, and indigo below. An occasional glitter of a silvery-sided anchovy caught his eye, but like the silvery-skinned Mermets, whole schools of fish were mere hints of movement in the uniformity of the greenness around them.

As they swam further, they moved through a cloud of upside-down gossamer bags that undulated constantly, trailing feathery tendrils. Some held stiff, ensnared fish. Jonathon ducked to avoid being conked by a sea turtle the size of a table. With flippers for wings, the turtle sailed slowly through the sea as it bit at the glassy bags.

Looking at the Sinjery Brandmistress, Jonathon saw her clothes, soaked of course, fluttering in the currents. His clothes were dry, thanks to his Charm of Dryness. Even his face felt dry. He thought that the Sinjery should be cold, but she looked comfortable.

Unusual smells swam through his head like the shark swam through the water. He recognized none of the smells except that of seaweed. Gradually, this smell grew stronger. Jonathon thought he was only noticing it more because all the other odors were so foreign to him. He realized that it was truly getting stronger when he felt a gradual descent of the shark steeds and saw a deepening of the shadows ahead. They were almost as dark as what lay below.

One by one, lines extending upward from the depths as far as Jonathon could see pinched off tiny patches of the darkness ahead. The lines were seaweed trees. They appeared as thin as his arm but were taller than the tallest of land trees. The trees swayed together in hypnotizing harmony. They entered the seaweed forest and moved through a vast cathedral of columns lost above and below in the green. Because of the seaweed, they could see only a short distance to either side. The sun above them, softened by fathoms of water, was further obscured by floating fronds like billowing clouds. Everywhere he looked, red- and brown-striped and speckled fish darted or hung snapping up smaller fish or nibbling tiny encrustations from the seaweed trees. Jonathon let go one hand to grasp a leaf as he passed. Pliable and slippery, the leaf eluded his grip as did several others he tried to pull off. Once he reached and snatched back his hand as a crab on a frond clipped his finger with a claw.

For many Favors, they swam and swayed with the seaweed forest until the darkness caused by the dense fronds brightened ahead. Suddenly, they were through and a new wonder lay before them. On the rising ocean floor, amid rocks that were covered with wisps of weed, spiral snails, and scuttling crabs, an ancient city lay. Perhaps it had once been above the water and had sunk over the centuries. Or maybe it was built by the Mermen to emulate mens' cities. Whatever the history, little was left but encrusted columns mostly broken. Scant small fish were there because a hundred sharks patrolled the wreckage, chasing fish into holes or shattering schools that blundered in. At the center of the circling sharks, a majestic, upside-down skull of some leviathan watched them approach with eye sockets that seemed to blink. Closer, Jonathon saw the boney holes held not eyes but green fish that cautiously looked out and quickly receded as patrolling sharks passed by. From the skull, stately ribs led like a colonnade to a statue fuzzy with coral.

Once, the statue could have been distinguished as man or woman, human or monster, but no longer. Its head sprouted tufts of green. Spikes of red and fleshy protuberances wriggled in a cloud that turned into tiny fish as Jonathon neared. One arm of the statue was held high, and there, a light flashed. From the battle with waves, kelp, and the depths of ocean, a lonely surviving ray of sunlight sparked a jeweled-glass handle of a sheathed dagger. The sheath itself gleamed golden, as if possessed of a brilliant soul that radiated living power. In contrast to the transmogrified statue, the sheath looked as virgin as the day it was made. Jonathon had no doubt that he looked upon the Knife of Life.

Upon seeing the circling sharks, Trallalair knew their goal was near. At the center of the sharks' cordon was a statue of a man holding a knife. The knife did not appear to be a sculpted part of the statue. Glowing, full of fire, it was surely the Knife of Life. That would make the sharks circling the statue one of the Rings of Death spoken of by the Lord of the Sea. In anticipation, as a test, Trallalair drew her sword and sliced through the sea, trying to cut a passing mackerel. As she predicted, the water slowed the blade so thoroughly, she only batted the mackerel without denting the flimsy armor of its scales.

She saw the jeweler gesture to the Mermets to proceed to the statue. With a few tugs on their golden bridles, the Mermets spurred on their shark toward the Knife of Life. Immediately, the patrolling sharks converged on the jeweler.

Before the sharks reached him, Trallalair held her sword braced against her side like a small lance and motioned to Glimmerquick Master in control to charge the shark closest to the jeweler. Behind her the crescent tail shook once, and they were catapulted toward the much smaller blue shark that cut away before they were within about a rod. Unknown to the jeweler, two other sharks followed him, gaining quickly. Trallalair showed them to Glimmerquick Master who moved the more massive predator they rode to intercept them. Again, the attackers split from each other and retreated before Trallalair was within striking distance. Apparently the smaller sharks feared the one she rode.

Another blue shark came quickly from her right, so Trallalair, without slowing, thrust the point of her sword through the fish's eye. Blood billowed as the hapless shark writhed until it yanked its head from her sword.

Passing through the sanguine cloud, Trallalair saw many of the patrolling sharks start toward their wounded comrade. They passed her by, intent on the disabled one. Within moments, the water was filled with bits of flesh as each shark, in turn, bit the wounded blue shark, and with a few violent shakes tore off a hunk of meat. With most of the sharks concentrating on ripping apart the victim, opportunistic smaller fish moved closer and gobbled the bits, risking death for an easy meal.

Trallalair noticed that the sharks seemed as likely to bite their living neighbor as the dead shark in their midst, so she had Glimmerquick Master move their steed away for their own protection. The Mermets had a hard time wrestling with the thin gold loops, almost losing their mount to the blood lust which captivated the other sharks. But since their bridles had probably been placed by experience at the most sensitive points on the shark's head, they finally succeeded in coaxing it away.

During all this, Jonathon felt rather than saw a flurry of activity behind him. Right then, nothing could take his eyes off the alluringly-beautiful Knife of Life. It was a magical object like none he had ever seen before. Without touching it, he felt power suffusing the surrounding sea. Life. Life from death. No miracle could match it. He knew if he held it in his hands, memorized the inscriptions, and perused its construction, he could reproduce it. What fool would not, given the chance. No one ever need die again.

He shook the fantasy from his head. Little time remained from the elixir. He must be efficient to gather the prize. The Mermets didn't hesitate, but Mother of Eight pointed to knobby rocks at the base of the statue. Like everything on the sea floor, the knobs were flabby and probably alive. Jonathon didn't think they looked particularly dangerous, but the Mermets stayed well above the statue as they circled it.

Determined to reach the Knife just out of reach below them, Jonathon twisted and stretched, holding onto the shark's fin with one hand and reaching downward. With amazing slowness in the buoyant water, his bulk overbalanced, and his tenuous grasp on the fin was pulled free. As he saw the knobby rocks approaching below him in his slow fall off the shark, he worried about dashing his bones to pieces on them. When he saw eyes on stalks sprouting from the lumps, all looking in his direction, he knew he had more to worry about.

With the suddenness of a thought, the knobs on the rocks disappeared, the pebbly maroon surface slickening to a smooth brown. Sinuous ropes like long boneless fingers snapped in his direction, encircling his waist and his throat. The ropes were living arms coming from one lump of stone that now rocked and quivered like fresh liver. More boneless arms wrapped around him. Each arm was slimy, muscular, and moved on its own like a snake. He was too startled to defend himself. His arms were quickly pinned to his sides as firmly as if he had been trussed like a pig for slaughter. Jonathon, kicking his feet feebly, was inexorably pulled toward the quivering lump. At arm's length away, the lump upended itself turning into a fleshy flower with rows of spots lining its petals. The undulating flower had a kind of symmetric beauty. For Jonathon, the flower lost a lot of its charm when he saw a beak, bigger than an eagle's, in the center of it. It opened wide to bite his face.

In the middle of his silent, underwater scream, just before the beak reached his right eye, everything went black. At first, he thought the beak had plucked out his eye and he was blind, but there was no pain. Instead, from his throat, arms and trunk, the tight ropes relaxed and slipped away, leaving dozens of coin-sized sore spots all over his body where the pliable arms had squeezed. He settled to the sea floor onto a hard lump of rock.

Beside him, something moved rhythmically in a black fog that had filled the ocean. Gradually, the fog cleared, revealing the rhythmic motion to be the Sinjery Brandmistress. She stood beside him at the base of the statue, jabbing each soft rock, one after the other. With every stab, another lump changed color from maroon to mottled white as it spewed forth another black cloud that again obscured their vision. After being stabbed, each one shot off, trailing its many ropey arms in a trail of smoke into the distance. Five or six were chased by sharks, making the creatures emit more black clouds, which in turn confused the predators who attacked the clouds instead of the creatures.

When Jonathon finally reoriented himself, he found himself in side a tapering row of paired, curved blades that led to the statue. It took him a moment to realize that he had fallen into the rib cage of the leviathan and the majestic ribs were an open cage. The rock he sat upon was its hard backbone.

Those ropey, slimy, boneless things were one of the Rings of Death, Jonathon thought. He hoped they were finished with death for now. Above them, the Mermets steered their own sharks in slow circles, waiting for them to take the Knife of Life. Their own sharks now seemed able to keep the other sharks guarding the Knife at bay. The hand of the statue grasping the Knife looked different up close. Brightly-striped conical snails foraged on the arm, and slender fish played about.

Jonathon was trying to stand up in the soft sea floor to grab the Knife, but he fell down repeatedly. Rings of Death echoed in his mind as the Brandmistress stepped easily past him. She climbed up onto the base of the coral covered rib closest to the statue and reached for the Knife of Life. Too late, Jonathon recognized a pattern. Around the statue's arm, the yellow and black conical snails formed a kind of bracelet, or more rightly, a ring! Jonathon struggled to grab the Brandmistress' arm or leg to alert her to the danger, but he could get no purchase with his feet. Before he could warn her, she pulled the Knife from the statue's hand.

Like an afterthought, she looked at her wrist where a small spot of blood bloomed into the water. She seemed to study her wrist, shaking her hand. She shook it harder and harder until she inexplicably let loose the Knife of Life.

Jonathon watched it drop into a nearby cluster of red sponges. He was about to reach for it when the Brandmistress, with a puzzled look in her eyes, turned to Jonathon and clutched her throat, opening her mouth wide trying to breathe. Jonathon thought her Elixir of Sustenance was exhausted and she was drowning, but that wasn't the problem. He was fine, and they had drunk the same amount at the same moment. He reached for her as she knelt to the sea floor. Even buoyed by the water, she was much too heavy for his arms to support. The Brandmistress slowly curled up, her eyes stopped moving, and her face became a vivid blue as she settled gently to the sea floor.

She was dead weight. Jonathon gave up trying to hold her. Instead, he grasped the Knife of Life, extracting it from the sponges. In horror, he looked from the Knife in his hand to the motionless Brandmistress at his feet. His Charm of Luck had worked for him. He had no doubt been very lucky. The Brandmistress had been in the right place at the right time to save him, first from the sharks, then from the fleshy soft creatures with their slimy ropey arms. Since he had slipped and fell before he could grab the Knife of Life, the Brandmistress had saved him one last time from what he now knew to be the poisonous sting of the bright shells. She had died so he would not. He held the Knife of Life, and his guard, the one who had promised to eventually execute him, was herself dead. He was obviously very lucky. So why did he feel so bad?

Jonathon did not want the Brandmistress dead, even though she had so fiercely hated him and wanted him dead. Jonathon did not want anyone dead. He needed the Brandmistress's help to get the Dragoncrown and to save his family. Without her, he was surely lost. There he was, at the bottom of the sea, with a hundred sharks stalking him, and much too far to get back to shore. Jonathon knew he couldn't do it alone. Trallalair had vowed to be his executioner, but in the last two days, she had saved his life half a dozen times. Over his heart, a shadow passed. Another person dead because of him.

Over his head a vaster shadow passed. With an upward glance, he saw the immense form of a Blue Dragon coursing through the waves. He begged The Three to avert the Dragon's eyes, but as if his prayer called to it, the Dragon dipped its head. Two orbs of cold silver looked directly into Jonathon's trembling gaze.

The Dragon saw Jonathon and it saw the Knife of Life in his hand. That was the key. It took a Dragon's gaze to remind him. The Brandmistress was dead, but he held the Knife of Life. Never in his life had he stabbed a human, dead or alive. There were only a few moments before the Dragon would be at the bottom and swallow Jonathon. He grasped the shimmering sheath of the dagger with his left hand and drew the golden blade free. The blade itself glowed with a blue arcane light. Sensing the waters dimness deepening as the approaching Dragon's shadow grew, Jonathon tore his eyes away from the beauty of the Knife of Life, and with a shudder, he drove the blade hilt deep into the Brandmistress's limp form.

Amidst a burst of scintillating bubbles like diamonds flying out from the Brandmistress's body, Jonathon pulled back the dagger and instinctively sheathed it. He was encased in a pulsating, trembling cloud made of sunbeams and jewels. Above him, barely perceived, the Blue Dragon veered off. Jonathon thought it was confused by the shimmering cloud. The current from its passing cast up more clouds, but these were only the detritus from the sea floor around him.

The Dragon would be back in moments. The coruscation surrounding the Brandmistress was waning, but she remained limp at the base of the statue. In the distant blur, the Dragon wheeled about and gave two strokes with his broad-finned tail. It was accelerating toward him alarmingly, so Jonathon dove for the only cover he could find, the row of huge ribs. At the impact of the Dragon, the rib next to Jonathon burst apart, and the entire skeleton rolled over, ending with the backbone above Jonathon. The bones could not have been all that old. The creatures of the sea had not eaten all the fibrous connections between the bones, so the entire skeleton moved as one piece. Jonathon realized that the leviathan must have died resting on its back.

The Blue Dragon's inertia took it into the underwater forest where the closely packed majestic seaweed wrapped itself about the beast. The Dragon thrashed, ripping up masses of fronds and entangling itself even more. It was a lucky break for Jonathon.

Jonathon looked for the Mermets and their sharks, but they had fled into the dimness, protecting themselves from the Dragon's bulk as it passed. They were holding back, as were the other sharks. None of them was willing to confront a raging Blue Dragon. The Dragon fought off the entwining weeds, but had to surface for a breath. That gave Jonathon a breather to focus his desperation. The Brandmistress was up but staggered drunkenly, the Dragon was diving again, and all he had was the Knife of Life.

And the bones of a dead leviathan.

The Mermets were too far away to help. Jonathon motioned to Trallalair to come to him. She fell through the rib cage and tripped over a rib trying to get near. Jonathon had no idea if the Knife of Life would affect something so huge as the bones of the leviathan, but the Dragon was approaching, and this time it didn't look like any cage of old bones would dissuade it from tearing them apart, and Jonathon with them.

Jonathon jabbed the nearest rib bone with the Knife of Life. He half-closed his eyes in fear. He felt the Brandmistress's hand on his arm as they were caught up in a swirling, sparkling whirlpool. He barely had time to slip the Knife in its sheath and shove the sheath beneath his belt when fleshy things enveloped them. They were thrown off their feet and pushed down against a soft, quivering floor. Jonathon started thinking that the boneless animals had him again. There was no light at all as they fell against each other, wrapped in an increasingly-enclosing leathery coffin.

If Jonathon could have spoken, he would have told Trallalair that he thought they had been swallowed by the Blue Dragon. They fell down, were slammed upward, and rolled around, tangling arms and legs together. Jonathon gripped the Knife of Life tightly. He could see nothing, but he heard a deep thrumming. It sounded like being in a horn the size of a mountain which was being blown by a sky-tall Giant. In a heartbeat, the sound became a rapid clicking, followed by a eerie high-pitched whine that rolled down the scale to the deep thrumming again. Weird whoops and groans mixed in.

Suddenly, Jonathon felt extremely light and nauseous, as if he had jumped from a cliff. The feeling left quickly and was replaced by their leathery tomb suddenly squeezing them together. They were allowed to fall apart for an instant, before they were pushed together again mercilessly. Again they separated, and with one final irresistible crush, they were hurtled together through a slimy tube into the sun above the water. They splashed down into the waves. Jonathon flailed his arms, trying to stay afloat, until Trallalair wrapped an arm around him to support him above the waves. As he relaxed in her firm grasp, he saw the dark gray flipper, big as a boat, sink in the waves.

"Why did you bring me back, Jeweler? You cheated me from the comfort of my Soulsister."

Jonathon realized that the Brandmistress was talking about his use of the Knife of Life on her. He expected Trallalair to be thankful that she had another chance at life, but he knew little of her thoughts or morals or beliefs. "Sorry. I need you to help me take back the Dragoncrown," he sputtered lamely.

She shook her head, as if frustrated to be alive and frustrated have to deal with traitors, Demons, and Dragons again. "I will fulfill my duty, but the next time I die, by Mother Earth, leave me to my rest."

"What is that creature I brought back?" he asked.

"It's a whale, Jeweler. We hunt them for food and oil in the winter. This is a Tusker. I think it just vomited us up. They eat the Monster Wrappers, much bigger than the Wrapper that had you down by the statue."

Jonathon thought back to the fleshy lump with the sinuous arms that almost sunk its beak into his eye. He imagined a Monster Wrapper, fleshy arms the size of trees and a beak big enough to bite him in half. He shivered, imagining that one could be looming up from the depths below him.

A few furlongs away, the Blue Dragon was swimming around and biting at the whale, but the Dragon clearly had an adversary worthy of him. The Brandmistress calmly swam toward shore, towing Jonathon with one arm around his chest, until the Mermets still astride the eye wings of the sharks surfaced again beside them and bade them remount for the ride back to Isseltrent harbor.

Jonathon had the Knife of Life safely clutched in his hand and tucked it under his belt. He thought it quite lucky that the Mermets even found them again. More luck for them, much more than they deserved.

Back on the shark, Jonathon looked toward the Brandmistress riding ahead of him astride her shark. She looked back to make sure he followed, but said nothing. He pointed up at the Charm of Luck and nodded his head, making her roll her eyes.

Even though Trallalair feigned disbelief, inwardly she felt luck had to be involved. How else could it happen that the whale had died and left its bones there, so conveniently, for their urgent use? She had felt her life drifting away, then her world blackened and she had felt light and free for a few brief moments, just like she had in the Dead Lands when she had her vision of the execution of the jeweler, Jonathon Forthright. For a brief moment, she had been hopeful she would find her Love again. The experience had gone no further before the Knife of Life called her back. Trallalair shook her head, puzzled. Why had she not flown up to the Sky Forests as she thought she had in the Dead Lands? In the Dead Lands, she had not truly died. Perhaps the boon of her vision from Mother Earth had been nothing but a delirium, a bad dream. Now that she breathed air again, all those questions would have to be answered with her final death. Death had not frightened her before. Even less did it frighten her now. She looked at the jeweler and thought again of her vision, killing him with an arrow. It was all so vague. Maybe she only thought it was the jeweler, but in reality it was someone similar. Maybe it was not a vision granted by Mother Earth after all. Trallalair had mixed feelings for the little man, and she didn't like mixed feelings. Most of the time, he just seemed outrageously gullible, sentimental, and often downright stupid. Other times, though, he seemed brilliant. Like when he used the horse's skin to help them out of the Giant's Lair. Like now. Using the whale to save them from the Dragon. She hated depending upon this silly, little man who repeatedly saved her from death.

They had the Knife of Life, the one weapon that might allow them to approach the Demon. They had even proved its worth, twice. Still, the Demon had the Dragoncrown, all the Dragons, all his minions, and the Rod of Coercion.

She looked back at the whale as it leaped from the water and landed with a splash that finally chased off the Blue Dragon. She wondered if the leviathan was sorry he had been brought back to life, too.

CHAPTER 25

THE GARDEN OF STONE STATUES

Trallalair worked on her sword at Jonathon's house. She didn't notice that it was a beautiful morning. She had other things on her mind. Her feelings about Jonathon continued to flip-flop like a fish out of water. Her feelings about the whole mission did the same. Was it just a few days before that Jonathon had been reviled by everyone in the Kingdom as the most evil human living? Was it just a few days ago, at Blaze with Seldric and all his cronies, that she had wanted to slit the traitor's neck? Yes. Only a few days before, Trallalair had been clear in her feelings toward Jonathon. Only a few nights had passed since the Dragonlord had given her, and her alone, the task of forcing the jeweler to go directly into the Dead Lands and take back the Dragoncrown. She, Trallalair, was to be in control, ordering Jonathon to do her bidding. As she sharpened her sword that morning, it seemed that, so far, it was the jeweler, with all his bungling ways, that had determined their road. But no. That was not exactly what was happening, either. Look at all the times that Jonathon had nearly failed, and she had

405

just barely rescued him. No, neither she nor the jeweler seemed in charge of their destiny and their choices. It was as if the control of their quest was out of their hands altogether. As if events were being influenced by yet another mind, using them for its purposes, like the Demon had done with the jeweler. The designs of Great Mother Earth, perhaps. If all this suited Her purpose, She had certainly sacrificed many of her beloved and devoted Sinjery Sisters to follow this path. For centuries, the Sinjery had sacrificed the lives and the dignity of a few for the good of the Sinjery race. Maybe this was just more of the same.

Trallalair had said nothing when the jeweler clung to the Knife of Life, studying it, for most of a whole night when they finally got to his home. She certainly wasn't worried that he'd use the knife on her. He'd already done that. If anything, she was grateful he held the Knife. The Lord of the Sea's name for the Knife, Soul-Fetcher, was most appropriate. She doubted that she could restrain herself from digging up all her dead friends from the battle in Blaze in an ill-advised attempt to fetch their souls from the Sky Forests. Her own soul had not been in the least pleased to be fetched back, and she doubted that anyone else would be. Any person pleased to come back to his body from the Afterlife was no doubt fetched from a place well-deserved, for sins too terrible to be pardoned. As Trallalair watched Jonathon memorizing the inscriptions on the Knife, she felt an urge to draw her sword and demand that he hand over the Knife so she could destroy it as an abomination. On the other hand, she was unsure that she could resist the temptation to use the Knife for the purpose it had been made, bringing back the dead. Namely, Saggethrie. Like the Dragonlord of old who had been brought back to wear the Dragoncrown once again for years more than his appointed time, even her beloved Saggethrie would probably curse her for her selfishness. That would be far worse for Trallalair than her lover's death.

The Knife of Life was now the most precious of all possessions. Many already knew of its existence here in the jeweler's care. The Pixets knew of it through Hili, and through their connection with the court, all of Seldric's advisors and more were now looking over the shoulders of Trallalair and her companions. Just to accomplish the mission of taking back the Dragoncrown, she would have to ensure that no one else stole the Knife of Life. Luckily, they had eliminated many of the thieves in Isseltrent when they fought Molgannard Fey. So far, none of the court had demanded she give them the Knife of Life. She and Jonathon could wait no longer, lest someone in Isseltrent be tempted. Even if a thief did not use the Knife to resurrect a loved one or an evil ally, it could be sold for half the Realm. They would take what supplies they had, use the Flying Carpet brought by the jeweler's son, and fly to the Dead Lands. They had planned to walk the whole way, all the way through the Commonwealth of Dis, the Forbidden Mountains, and on into the Dead Lands, before they were given the carpet. Despite all the delays finding the Knife of Life, they could still get there, ahead of schedule, if they flew.

Hili had rested through the rest of the day and night. To assuage her intense hunger, she had visited every flower on Jonathon's hill. In their prison in Blaze, the Community spent all their time reinforcing their psychic defense against incursions of the Demon into their minds. She was aiding them in their efforts by enjoying the brightness of the sunlight, smelling the fragrant garden air, and tasting the sweet nectar. Her freedom bolstered the rest of the Community. The only way she could help the Community further was to see the quest through to the bitter end. For her companions, she still was a dormant spy for the Demon, liable to awaken again as a real threat and reveal their actions and motives when their only strength was secrecy. Potentially, the Demon could anticipate their course and set traps for them. On the other hand, if the Community ever grew strong enough to resist the Demon, they would be the ones to share the Demon's plans and profit from them by diverting the Brandmistress and her companions from all his ambuscades.

Jonathon could barely keep his eyes open. He had stayed up all night studying the Knife of Life and the inscriptions on its blade and scabbard. Ingeniously, the poets that fashioned it centuries before had made a scabbard and a hilt of fused Glass Commands. He could just make out subtle variations in the texture of the clear glass scabbard where individual commands met. Forty-two separate Commands made up the body of the scabbard. Barely-perceptible inscriptions on the commands were still evident in the substance of the scabbard. The golden blade of the Knife was powered by sheathing the dagger and withdrawing it. Only forty-two such powerings remained, one for each Glass Command left. On the dagger, similar inscriptions told him that the Knife of Life could be used without being first placed in its scabbard. It could also be activated by a Glass Command. Jonathon was amazed that it could revive even huge animals, probably any animal that had ever lived.

Jonathon toyed with the idea of making dozens of Knives of Life and using them to bring back all the people killed by his tragic mistake. Of course, the danger remained that one of the Knives would get into the wrong hands and all manner of people would be brought back, including Molgannard Fey and all his ruffians. Theoretically, everyone who had died and left remains could be brought back. If too many were resurrected, they would return to a world filled with starvation, or perhaps filled with wars caused by the increased population all vying for the same land and food. His head reeled with the implications. It was even more complicated than Rhazburn's worries about the Demon Entrapment Gem. Better he leave decisions as to who to use the Knife of Life on to the Dragonlord and his court. Besides, to make dozens of Knives of Life, they would first need the Dragons.

There was another thing that Jonathon realized as he studied the Knife. By itself, it was incapable of destroying the Demon. If the Demon existed in the dead body of some person, that person would be brought back to life, but the Demon would still exist like some kind of untreatable tumor on the world. Hopefully, it would help protect them from the Sverdphthik's Zombies, like the ones that Rhazburn found. After their successes at Molgannard Fey's and under the sea, Jonathon had begun to think that, with the Brandmistress and the Community helping him, he had a chance of somehow stealing back the Dragoncrown and the Rod of Coercion. He now understood that, even if, by some miracle, they were successful, the Demon would still remain. It would remain, and become more and more powerful with each passing year. It was just as Rhazburn had told him. And if what Rhazburn claimed could become reality, eventually even the Dragoncrown would not be proof against an all powerful Sverdphthik.

If only the court had not thrown poor Rhazburn into Hell, they could have made the Demon-Entrapment Gem and rid the world of the Demon's presence forever. Jonathon couldn't worry much about all the other possible futures ahead of him. The reality of the present was complicated enough. He had his family to save, and Sverdphthik was only getting stronger. It was time to go to the Dead Lands.

Jonathon sauntered outside where the Brandmistress was already working with Patrick to pile supplies on the large Flying Carpet his son had brought. She said, "We'll need the rest of the Copper Orders your father left for you. Even combined with mine, it will only make a score or so."

Patrick agreed, saying he could earn or find more for the family, and ran to get them.

Jonathon's Keeper had been filled with crocks of hot baked beans and several loaves of fresh bread. These, too, along with a wheel of hard cheese, was placed on the Flying Carpet so the Brandmistress and Jonathon would have enough food for one fortnight. They would leave the replenishing pitcher with his family and the Sinjery Guards, but they would take ten bottles of wine with them. With the carpet, they could search for water. They had found a crock of honey and a few fresh fruits for Hili. Covering the foodstuffs were blankets and heavy clothes for all of them, including doll clothes from Jonathon's children for Hili. He had a pouch with all the coins he could scrape together - a few Copper Orders and plenty of Wooden Requests and Clay Suggestions. The Brandmistress had her pouch with eight Copper Orders left. Patrick supplied 15 more from the depleted stash.

The Flying Carpet was one of the best. The inscriptions were accompanied by embroidered golden snakes twined around vines and tropical flowers. Feral cats and cold eyed lizards glowered from the woven forest on the carpet. The greens, reds and oranges of the forest were fully as bright as the golden thread of the snakes. It was a traveling Flying Carpet, made for a family or for transporting goods from town to town. It was as big as Jonathon's living room, expansive enough to carry them all with all their supplies.

Patrick said, "Father, I know you are afraid to ride a carpet, but please, just try it."

Jonathon thought back to Molgannard Fey's where he had to fight all his fears to survive. In a strange way, the confidence that he had felt after using the Armlet of Tranquility to boldly, or maybe foolishly, walk the long green carpet spiraling up inside the Giant's tower, that confidence still affected him. It was as if some of it had never worn off. "I think I'll be all right. I don't think they scare me as much as they used to."

The Brandmistress arranged the supplies on the carpet, tying them together with a strong cord. Jonathon brought pillows from the house and a strong tarp to protect all the supplies from the rain. She took her Sinjery Sword and bow with more arrows borrowed from Vailisk and Quintella.

Hili took her tiny gem-engraving tools, so small that some were invisible to Jonathon's old eyes.

Jonathon, for his part, took all the gems he had left - a few small diamonds, two rubies, one nice green tourmaline the size of his fist, and a perfect, purple star sapphire he had been saving to make a Memoir Ring.

All their supplies were tied together in the center of the carpet and covered with the tarp. Before they left, Jonathon took the Charm of Dryness from his dresser and thought about it. Hili was much too small for it and Jonathon had a wool cloak that Arlen had woven that would keep him dry if it rained. He gave the Charm to the Sinjery maiden.

To his surprise, she refused it, saying, "I do not fear the rain. No Sinjery does. We thrive on rain as does Sinjer. I prefer to feel it on my skin."

Jonathon shrugged and pinned it on his own shirt. Why risk pneumonia? He was not as tough as a Sinjery maiden.

✸ ✸ ✸

Trallalair had to endure more crying and carrying on by the jeweler's family.

One little girl came up to her, stroked her hand, and said to her, "Goodbye, Mister."

Trallalair smiled and stroked the child's head. Trallalair knew that she still looked a fright, especially after all the injuries of the previous two days, but at least her voice was returning. She said, "Little girl, never let boys bully you. You can be as strong as they are." The child just smiled and danced away.

As his family finished their wishes of good luck and dry weather, Jonathon came up to Trallalair and asked, "Brandmistress?"

"Yes, Jeweler."

"If we come back with the Dragoncrown, will my family here be freed?"

She pondered a bit on what she had seen of his family. Normal men, women, and children who were as frightened of Dragons and Demons as anyone. None seemed the least bit criminal, and all were dedicated to restoring the Dragoncrown. "I think they may be freed now, if the Dragonlord consents. Quintella, go petition the Dragonlord to free the jeweler's family here. I feel that the jeweler's intention to restore his immediate family from seeds back to human life will be sufficient motivation to spur him to retrieve the Dragoncrown." It was a fair request, but one she doubted the Dragonlord would grant.

The jeweler waved to his family clustered in the yard as he, Trallalair and Hili boarded the carpet. Trallalair placed a Copper Order into a pocket set into the weave and commanded it, "Carpet, up slowly."

As the carpet lifted off the ground, the jeweler wobbled, shaking with visible fear, and sat down fast, holding onto the cord binding the supply pile. "Oh! I guess I still hate flying. Three save us!" Looking at the Trallalair, he said, "I can't even imagine riding a Dragon. That must really be frightening."

Trallalair said nothing. The jeweler had no concept of the wonder of Dragonflying and never would. Nobody would ever ride a Dragon again, thanks to his blunder.

As they rose into the clear summer air, the jeweler's family waved and watched. Vailisk and Quintella watched but did not wave. They knew of the tragedy of the Thousand Warriors. Now Trallalair was going back to the site where so many Sisters had died so horribly. None of them, including Trallalair, felt anything but woe at the prospect. When the carpet was well above the treetops, she said, "East" and they were off. The hill with the jeweler's house dwindled quickly behind them.

411

As with all Flying Carpets, there was little sense of movement. On the carpet, the wind was a gentle wafting of warm air. Jonathon scooted on his bottom near enough to the edge to stick his hand out beyond the fringes of the carpet. There, a chilly gust slapped his hand back, nearly dislocating his elbow. When he cried out in pain, the Brandmistress, standing comfortably with her arms crossed facing the East, scowled and asked, "Why in the world did you do that? Have you never ridden a Flying Carpet before?"

"Never, except at Molgannard Fey's."

"Oh, right. You said that at Molgannard Fey's. I had forgotten, it was so long ago." Only two days, Trallalair thought, but it seemed ages.

Faster than any bird and fully as fast as Hover they sped, passing the blackened hills and plains surrounding Isseltrent. Black stripes of burnt land, where flying Dragons had strafed farms as they flew, looked like pestilential scars. There would be no hiding from marauding Dragons in the blue skies in which they flew. Luckily, the Dragons had withdrawn for the time being. She feared the Demon was marshaling his forces for one final, all-out attack on Isseltrent destined to destroy every living creature and reduce it to cinders. She knew she had little left within her to prevent it.

Above the tattered landscape, they flew for most of the morning. The fields melded imperceptibly with those of the Commonwealth of Dis, the flat fields of which usually provided most of the sustenance for the Thuringland and the Tributary States. Since the loosing of the Dragons, the torn patchwork of the land stood as mute testament to a false economy. The land had been farmed for many years using the magic provided by the Dragons. With their release, it now withered and failed.

Far ahead of them, glazed with mist, the Forbidden Mountains yawned sleepily. It was a land of dreams, a land no one understood and no one had ever returned from. She silently prayed to Mother Earth that they would be allowed to just pass over the Forbidden Mountains safely as had the doomed host she had flown with on that fateful day.

After a few Blessings on the carpet, Trallalair and Hili both lay down under blankets and slept. The jeweler told them he couldn't sleep in the clouds. It just wasn't natural. What if he rolled off the Flying Carpet in his sleep?

Still somewhat irritated at his skin-splicing longings, Trallalair said, "Then just sleep standing up."

Jonathon actually considered it, but concluded that the danger of falling off standing upright would be even greater. He volunteered to watch their approach to the Forbidden Mountains, just beyond which lurked the Dead Lands. Constantly, he scanned the sky for Dragons and studied the horizon for any evidence of them, like smoke or fires. Once he woke the Brandmistress because he thought he saw smoke, but it was only a distant thunderhead. She snapped at him, peeved to be wakened for nothing. But like all warriors, pleased to rest when the opportunity availed, she fell deeply asleep as soon as she lay back down.

When they neared the mountains, Trallalair woke up, even without Jonathon touching her. Her Sinjery instincts woke her. Those instincts also told her to fly low through the mountains, so as not to be spotted by the Dragons in the Dead Lands before they even got there.

Forests abounded in the Forbidden Mountains. There were too many in hidden valleys for the Dragons to burn all of them. The rains and snows that drenched the western sides of the mountains extinguished most of the fires the Dragons had managed to start. Patches of desolation remained where denuded tree boles stood like ranked gibbets amidst clouds of ashen wraiths lifted by the winds.

The Sylvets were there somewhere, but Hili had no inkling of where they might be. From ancient memories of the Community, she knew that they could share her thoughts if they were near, but nothing came to her mind. Maybe they were all dead, killed during the holocaust. Somewhere in the back of her mind was a low thrumming, like the purring of cats the size of the Forbidden Mountains. She had no explanation for it, and neither did the Community.

In the mountains, the carpet had to bank around cliffs and peaks. At times, the clouds obliterated any sight of the mountains, and the Brandmistress had to tell the carpet to slow up so they didn't smack into a cliff face. She was animate, shouting instructions, standing at ease on the shifting stance as the carpet tipped to round unforgiving blocks of granite.

Hili held on tight to the cords around the supplies.

Jonathon lay rooted to the fabric as the peaks danced by, nauseating him.

Bitter coldness at these heights penetrated the calm atop the carpet. Despite his nausea, Jonathon made sure Hili was covered before he crawled over to where the Brandmistress stood and tossed her a blanket for her bare shoulders.

She donned it without breaking the cadence of her commands to the carpet. "Up six rods. Easy left. Hard left. Slow to half speed. Up to just below the clouds."

That sudden rise slammed Jonathon flat onto the weave and made him cry out in anguish. He kept his eyes closed. Seeing how high they were was tantamount to leaping over the edge of the carpet in his mind.

Their progress in the mountains was much slower than it had been across the Commonwealth of Dis. Thick, clinging clouds darkened and hampered their passage, and soon the sun would set. At times, when they burst out of a cloud, the light, coming from the setting sun behind them, split into rainbows that flew before them eluding them, taunting them like their goal of finding the Dragoncrown.

The Brandmistress told them that she decided to fly all the way to the Dead Lands before they stopped for the night. They would hide in the rocks while they slept, facing the challenges of the Dead Lands with the new day.

When they emerged from the last clouds and descended the dry eastern slopes of the Forbidden Mountains, the desert of the Dead Lands was a taut pall stretching ahead as far as they could see. Red as blood in the light of the setting sun, it glowed with vengeance.

An invisible line demarcated the Demon's lands at the foot of the Forbidden Mountains. As soon as they passed that line, horror and depression assailed them. No living thing, sucked dry of vitality by the Demon's power, survived for long in the Dead Lands. In Isseltrent, Sverdphthik had been stronger than any living being, but here at the stronghold of his mystical might, his power was incredible. The Demon was far away, a score of leagues or more. Even so, the stifling perversion of all creation emanated in waves from the center of the Dead Lands like an unholy wind vomited from Hell. Jonathon had felt none of that emanation of evil when the Demon was in his shop. Perhaps the Demon had suppressed it for the sake of its treachery. Sverdphthik could probably suppress that evil aura or augment it at its will. Or maybe the depressive feeling was a product of the evil inherent in the Demon's Hellpit, initiated by Sverdphthik but sustained by some other evil.

Jarringly, from behind Jonathon, Hili screeched and writhed like a trapped rodent. Jonathon turned, steadying himself, but the shock of hearing her distress added to his ongoing nausea and the shroud of gloom inundating them. She lay pinned to the carpet by a psychic needle, shaking her head violently against the weave, beating it with tiny futile fists. Jonathon was closest and lifted her frail tortured body before the Brandmistress could leap to her aid.

Trallalair spoke first. "The Demon possesses her again."

Through intense pain, Hili nodded, whimpering. "Fly. Fly away."

Trallalair knew that Hili understood the Demon's plan just as Sverdphthik knew theirs. She shouted to the carpet, "Turn back toward the mountains."

Cupping Hili in a gentle hand, Jonathon craned his head, searching the Demon's domain for Dragons. Within moments, winged beasts materialized by ones and twos from the shimmering incandescence of the desert.

"Brandmistress," Jonathon said.

"I see them," she replied. "We can make the cover of the mountains before they reach us."

Frighteningly fast, the Dragons grew in size. There were dozens - Reds, Greens, and a few ghostly White Dragons, all converging on their solitary, vulnerable carpet.

"We're not going to make it," Jonathon said.

The Sinjery Brandmistress only grunted. Hili whimpered in agony in Jonathon's gentle hand.

Suddenly, the oppression of the Dead Lands evaporated. Jonathon felt relieved but exhausted, as if he had been wrestling with the Demon himself. The Dragons were a good league distant but gaining fast, and the safety of the mountains seemed too far ahead.

Hili croaked, "We can see through the Dragon's eyes as if we wore the Dragoncrown."

This was a development none of them had expected.

The Brandmistress said, "Maybe you can manipulate the Dragoncrown through the Demon and turn the Dragons back."

"Oooh no. We do not have the power for that." Concentrating and quivering in pain, she cried out, her head thrown back like she had been slapped. After that, she lay deeply obtunded. At least she was still breathing.

The Brandmistress said, "I will not ask her to try that again. The Demon is too powerful."

To Jonathon's relief, their carpet was soon enveloped in the evening shadows of the Forbidden Mountains.

As she maneuvered them into the maze of connecting valleys between the peaks, their way was inadvertently lit by flashes of fire from the Dragons lighting their own way searching for the trio. She dropped the carpet into a valley and they rode along a rushing river. "Tonight, we can hide in the mountains, even if the Demon directs them," she stated confidently. "Tomorrow, they will find us."

Finally, they stopped and hid, huddled under a dripping overhang which the Brandmistress found during brief instants of light born of Dragonfire in the sky above.

With trepidation, Jonathon watched the shimmering, fiery Dragons racing and wheeling near and far, searching for their tiny carpet in the complex vastness of the Forbidden Mountains.

Many times, the Brandmistress quietly asked Hili, "Do the Dragons see us?"

At times, Hili would shake her head, indicating they were still safe. As she shivered in distress, the Pixelle kept her eyes tightly closed, presumably so the Demon could not see their hideout from her perspective.

At long last, the Dragons receded back to the Dead Lands, defeated by the darkness and the terrain. Even the Demon gave up and freed Hili. She collapsed into a troubled slumber. The Sinjery maiden had gone to sleep long before, but Jonathon stayed awake the whole night, cradling Hili. For the first time, they had turned the Demon's power over them to their own advantage and survived.

In the morning, glowing mists appeared. They looked warmly pink but felt frigid to their skin. Jonathon sneezed violently from the damp chill that penetrated his bones.

The Brandmistress tried to suppress his loud explosions with a stern look, but all he could do was hide under a blanket until he was done. She was busy cutting off small pieces of peach for Hili to eat. One peach would last many meals, but Pixets ate up to ten times a day.

Still weakened from sharing thoughts with the Demon the evening before, Hili devoured one small chunk and asked for more.

When she was finally finished, she said, "We do not understand why we are not in harmony with the thoughts of the Sylvets. For ages past, anytime one of the Community entered Sylvanward, the Sylvets were here with thoughts tough as oak leaves. But now, nothing." She withheld her wonder about the thrum coursing through her, like the murmuring of some ancient, gigantic beast. It made no sense, and the Community was equally puzzled. They had no name for the feeling, so she kept it to herself.

The Brandmistress volunteered, "Perhaps if we fly carefully to one of the forested areas, you will be able to sense them. Here there are only rocks. I doubt any Sylvets live around here. Maybe you just need to get closer."

"Maybe," Hili said. "If we could find the Sylvets, they might help us."

No human had returned from entering the Forbidden Mountains for the last several centuries. They were not looking for that kind of trouble. Searching out the Sylvets in the Forbidden Mountains did not appeal to Trallalair. But if the Sylvets could somehow hide them from the Dragons, finding them might be worthwhile. At the moment, the three of them seemed easy prey for the Demon and his Dragons.

"Then we had better find them before the Dragons find us," Trallalair said, not totally convinced that it was a viable plan.

They retied their supplies and settled themselves. Trallalair reenergized the carpet with a Copper Order and took them low through the valleys, past cliffs and boulders softened by the mist, until they came upon a pine forest still living, nestled around a cold, sapphire lake. Dew from the mist collecting in the pine needles pattered down as a soft rain beneath the trees. Outside the forest, the rocks were drier, protected by open sky from the dew rain. In the valley, she could hear no Dragonwings rushing above them, but she knew that they had started their search.

Hili concentrated on the deep thrum she felt throughout her body, trying to find the minds of the Sylvet Community. Any moment, she expected the Demon's brutal assault, but she tried to stay calm, receptive to the Sylvets. The Pixet Community was at a loss as to where the Sylvets might be. Surely they weren't all dead.

By the time shafts of sunlight warmed and thinned the morning fog, the jeweler began to wander off to look at the lake.

Trallalair stopped him, making him stay under the cover of the trees.

As he sat beneath the boughs, he admitted he coveted a rest at the flower-strewn stream bank because it reminded him of his garden. When he pointed out the smudge of smoke which dirtied the Eastern sky, clear evidence of the Dragons, he thanked her for pulling him back.

Trallalair could see the Dragons were systematically burning off the remaining forests and any cover they could have used in the Forbidden Mountains. Since their verdant dale was only a short distance from the eastern edge, very soon they would see the Dragons themselves, and their little haven would become a deadly inferno.

Patience was foreign to Trallalair, so after watching smoke plumes erupting from increasingly closer valleys, she began to ready the carpet to fly further into the mountain fastness.

She said to the jeweler, "If the Dragons follow us deeper and deeper into the mountains, we may be able to sneak past them and fly back to the Dead Lands, while they all search for us in the valleys. Without the Dragons, the odds will be a lot better for us against the Demon."

Jonathon shook his head. "The Demon can learn our plan whenever it wants."

"I just won't tell Hili our plan. Even if she believes we are continuing our search for the Sylvets, it will be no more dangerous for her than if she knew our every intention."

Jonathon sighed. Nothing they could do would make any difference. The Demon held them in his palm and could close his fist when ever he wished, crushing them like bugs.

Trallalair had no such fatalistic view. She planned to get farther into the safety of the mountains, biding her time until she could seize the opportunity and scurry right between the legs of the Dragons. She knew all the strengths and weaknesses of Dragons. She was confident that she could outsmart them.

Hili shook her head and said, "We cannot accept the concept that all the Sylvets are dead. Something is missing."

"I'm sure you are correct, Pixelle Hili. Let us move our camp deeper into the mountains and continue searching for the Sylvets."

They all positioned themselves on the carpet, and Trallalair flew them into the mountain wonderland, past veils of water falling from black cliffs, past ice fields like white tongues that spat rivulets scoring the meadows, on past jumbles of shattered rock tumbled from massive buttes split from their parent mountains.

It was far past noon before they found another hidden wood and settled the carpet deep inside. The pines of this wood were massive and old with green beards of moss hanging from every branch and protected by flocks of chattering birds that had claimed them for ages past. Older trees still littered the forest floor, huge fallen logs broken and dissolving with decay.

Trallalair stopped their carpet under one such fallen patriarch, supported on one end by a stump it had created when the great tree's crash split its neighbor into splinters. Beneath the bole, ground soft with moss was concealed from the sides by parallel walls of stately ferns. Since the stump on which the massive tree leaned was as tall as Jonathon's house, there was plenty of room underneath for them to settle the carpet.

After they stopped within the hidden grotto, they discovered that they could walk rods farther along the length of the trunk and remain hidden from Dragon eyes. There in the gloom, they sought the opposite end where the base of the tree was buried in the ground at the base of a granite cliff, six rods or more from where their carpet rested. As they proceeded into this wooden-capped cave, enclosed by glistening fern fronds, the space became progressively shorter until Trallalair and the jeweler had to stoop to avoid scraping their heads on the ancient bark. They stopped and sat beneath the the solid protection of the tree trunk, feeling safer and less exposed there in the cramped space. The ground was cool, so they covered themselves with blankets.

Hili's doll clothes were insufficient to exclude the chill from her tiny body, so she ate constantly to fuel the efficient furnace within her.

Beneath the downed tree, the thrumming felt much stronger. Hili knew that the feeling had something to do with the absent Sylvets, but exactly what was unclear. She and the Community searched for a sign of them in the surrounding forest, finding only silence.

When the evening sun set the snowy peaks above them aflame, the Dragons found them. A corner of their carpet was, no doubt, spotted from high above by the eagle-sharp eyes of a Green Dragon. A blast of fire consumed that piece of carpet and, as Dragonfire had a tendency to do, ate the rest of the carpet up rapidly, along with all their supplies. Hili boldly flew in the face of the advancing wall of fire to retrieve her precious gem-engraving tools. By the time she fled back to them, chased by the inferno, she had her tool bag safely tied to her waist. Even the Brandmistress was too far away to save anything but the bow and quiver she always carried, a pouch with a few coins tied to her girdle, and her Sinjery Sword. Jonathon had only the Knife of Life tucked in his belt and a pouch with the rest of their coins.

The ferns lining their sanctuary erupted in flame, turning the safety of the walls around them into a conflagration of fronds crackling and whistling as they writhed in the pyre. The heat and smoke seared and choked them, trying to cremate them in a pine coffin.

Trallalair, gasping, curled herself around Hili, irrationally trying to protect her when she knew nothing could withstand Dragonfire.

Jonathon tried to crawl further into the confined space beneath the end of the pine, jamming himself headfirst into the dwindling crack. Through tears of regret for all that he had done wrong, he prayed for a cave to crawl into.

He thought he was dead or dreaming as his prayer seemed to be answered. A balm of light bathed his face. He had broken through a thin flap of bark, revealing a garden of painted stone statues. Tiny, colorful figures of brown and green poised in a frozen dance were beneath realistic wooden sculptures of trees brilliant with shiny paper leaves. Although in a cave, the whole tableau was cast in an eerie light.

"There is something here!" he shouted to the others, turning around, uncertain if they heard him in the roar of the flames.

"The Sylvets. It is the Sylvets," Hili cried, flying right past Jonathon's head into the lit opening.

The Brandmistress did not hesitate either, but squirmed around Jonathon into the bright hole in front of him. The trunk of the tree was smoldering, and in moments, it too would burst into flame. After the others disappeared into the cave, Jonathon thrust his head through again. Once more, he saw the stone statues. One was a Pixelle who looked a lot like Hili. He knew his life depended on him squirming through. He looked to one side and saw Trallalair strangely prostrate on the unmoving grass. He was aided in his squirming through the opening by the hot foot provided by the Dragonfire behind him. He cried out in pain, jerking just enough to pop his ample hips through the opening.

Once he was fully inside, he was greeted by singing emanating from the glimmer, as if a celebration awaited them all. With Dragons above them and fire surrounding him, the incongruity was astonishing. The Brandmistress was standing beside him, surveying the cave, and Hili fluttered up beside them both. What he thought were statues suddenly came alive, tiny green and brown folk singing and dancing with happiness. He thought his fear at this unexpected haven must have somehow affected his mind, making it all appear like a garden of stone statues. There was no fire, no roaring overhead, not even smoke. All seemed strangely quiet and safe. They were in the forbidden land of the Sylvets.

CHAPTER 26

REPOSE

"Welcome to Repose," three Sylvets and two Sylvelles said in unison. They had taken time out from their pressing revelries to greet Jonathon, Trallalair, and Hili.

Jonathon had only seen paintings of the Sylvets in the past. They had all been wrong. Since no one had ever returned from the Forbidden Mountains, all images were conceived in the imagination of the artist. He had a premonition that they were about to find out why no one ever returned from the Forbidden Mountains.

The Sylvelles were as beautiful as Pixelles, just as diminutive but green of skin and without wings. They looked like new-grown willow wands with skin the color of budding leaves and withy fingers, long and graceful. Music sparkled in their eyes, and from their proximity, he inhaled a freshness like morning dew on garden mint. Fresh flower petals from daisies, roses, and forget-me-nots were strewn beneath their feet on moss soft and springy. The Sylvelles capered and twirled with a sensual allure that commanded the attention of their male counterparts, the Sylvets.

In stark contrast, the Sylvets, dark-brown, gnarled, and angular, looked like venerable oaken branches, small but tough, with bark for skin. They, too, had eyes that laughed with joy, patient and boundless. The Sylvets were dancing in a gangling fashion, tossing the petals beneath the feet of their lovely Sylvelles.

Songs and laughter pervaded the forest which was lit by myriad twinkling lights. Trallalair immediately recognized the twinkling as glimmerbugs, insects she remembered from the Sinjery swamp. In Sinjer, they were scattered through the reeds and trees but always unreachable, just at the edge of perception. In this land, they filled the air, giving a uniform radiance to all objects, as if everything and everybody glowed. From legends, she had heard how the Sylvets could control the plants and animals in their land. She surmised that the Sylvets promoted the presence of the glimmerbugs because ambient light from the sky was strangely inconstant, unreliable. The cloud-covered sky undulated with waves of brightness that coursed through the clouds like a glowing god riding a Dragon repeatedly across the sky, or like one of the large Ball Lightnings that the doomed Poets had produced during the ill-fated ride of the Isseltrent host against the Demon. If it had not been for the glimmerbugs, the light would vary from noonday brightness to black of night constantly like waves on a beach surging forward and sliding back.

Hili flew over their heads, dancing in flight rhythmically with the songs. To Jonathon's ears, the melodious tunes were sung in a language that he could almost understand. They were songs of love and wonder, that was clear, but the words, sung in the high-pitched, almost whistling, voices of the Sylvelles, were unrecognizable. Most of the songs came from the Sylvelles, the laughter from the Sylvets.

One of the Sylvelles, a lithe one with a wispy dress, light as dandelion fluff, danced up to them, hopping from one petal to the next. "My name is Sparrow Feather. There is food and drink under the elms and soft moss in the Rose Garden to lie upon if you are tired."

My name is Jonathon Forthright." He bowed and swept his hand toward his companions. "And this is Brandmistress Trallalair and Hili of the Pixet Community. Thank you for your invitation. We are famished and exhausted as you correctly perceive."

Sparrow Feather giggled like rain on bells, did a little spin, and with her tiny arms outstretched, she bowed gracefully back with a pleasing smile. Jonathon felt a glow of warmth within him as pleasant as the peaceful awe he felt when he first gazed upon one of his newborn children. Dragons spurting fire, Giants, and Demons seemed things from a legend, harmless, conjured to frighten a child to stay in bed.

Jonathon was ravenous. Their supplies were lost with the carpet. Why not have a meal and wait until the Dragons left, hopefully fooled into thinking they were all dead?

The Sinjery Brandmistress, clearly not as entranced as Jonathon was, said, "I'll go back out and scout around to see if the Dragons are still flying about."

Jonathon felt safe and was frightened such an action would bring the Dragons in after them destroying Repose, their land of sanctuary. "Brandmistress, please, wait until morning. I think we're safe here for the moment. We need to sleep anyway, and we have to walk back through the mountains. Our supplies have probably been destroyed, and once we leave, we may go hungry for days. Maybe we can beg for some supplies or at least have a meal here tonight."

Trallalair listened to the lilting melodies, gazed at the eerie sky, and sniffed the pungent aromas as if she had just noticed them all. "I don't like this place. Where are we?" She was the first to give voice to the alarming fact that they had crawled into a crack and come out into a huge forest which was unaffected by the Dragonfire and could not possibly fit into the small space they retreated into. Did neither the jeweler nor the Pixelle consider this bewildering turn of events?

Sparrow Feather said, "This is Repose."

"Where are the mountains?"

"The mountains are outside."

"Are we in a chamber, like a cave? How far away are the walls?" All the glimmerbugs and the brightness racing through the clouds suggested some vast forested cavern at the top of which was a Dragon or a Flying Carpet continuously flying over them carrying some huge source of light.

"There are no walls, Brandmistress. You may venture as far away as you like. If our singing annoys you, I will guide you far enough away so all will be quiet and you may rest. If you wish food and drink, you may join us at the Feast." She smiled broadly at that word, as if the Feast was full of pleasures.

The still-chubby jeweler seemed fixated on food. "I think we should at least eat before we leave. We don't know when we may have food again. All our provisions were burned."

Trallalair shook her head. Someone rational had to protect them from the seduction of this land. Luckily, she was still in charge. "One night, but only to eat, sleep and ask questions about how this place exists. Then we must leave and be on with our task."

Hili had stopped her dancing and flew close. "The Community is gone." She fluttered to Trallalair's wrist, shrinking her wings to nubbins. "When I sensed the Sylvets, they filled my thoughts and I thought the strength of their thoughts crowded out the Community."

She, too, looked above, as if, like Trallalair, she doubted the reality of Repose. "It is beautiful. Grievously, no thoughts penetrate this atmosphere. Outside, not ten flutters away, we knew not the Sylvets' mind. Here, a short flight from our hiding place, the Community's thoughts are shut out, but those of the Sylvets are everywhere. It is like being under the water again." She looked into Trallalair's eyes and nodded. "We must spend as little time as possible here."

The jeweler shrugged. "I feel protected here. We nearly died back there. These marvelous people saved us all just by their existence. Our quest would surely have foundered if we had not crawled through the hole that leads here. What distresses you? We have a new opportunity. The Dragons and probably the Demon consider us consumed by their flames. Maybe in here, Hili, you're likewise protected from another invasion of the Demon's mind, just as you're curtained from the Community's thoughts."

"Maybe so, Master Jeweler."

Hili was ill at ease and lonely. It was as if all her friends and family had suddenly died. The Sylvet thoughts flooded her mind, but they were foreign, unusual, not light and airy like those of the Pixets but earthy, full of lusts for sensual pleasures. They danced and sang, but it was not to mirror the beauty of the world and express their love of all nature. Their songs were of bodily pleasures, all suggestive of and leading up to coupling of Sylvets with Sylvelles. In her mind, the Sylvets were ugly and deformed, the Sylvelles lovely. The Sylvets constantly yearned for the charm and elegance of the Sylvelles and wanted to share it. The Sylvelles seemed fickle and capricious, teasing the stolid but unsightly Sylvets. Much ado was made in their songs and dances about homely Sylvets pursuing and finally catching beautiful Sylvelles, who surrendered to the love they saw in their monstrous suitors.

All the tension in their love games made Hili anxious. She longed for the peace of Pixet Community consciousness. No amount of probing of the Sylvets' minds told her much about the Land of Repose. All she could understand was that it was ancient beyond reckoning and cut off from the rest of the world as if it were a separate nation, unaffected by the changes and vicissitudes of the lands outside.

While Hili observed the Sylvets' society, she noticed that the Sylvet Community watched over a large number of other refugees like Jonathon, Trallalair, and herself. There were no Pixets, but through the Sylvets, she saw hundreds of humans, Dwarves, Rockskippers, even a few Giants. Not far from them, behind a fragrant hedge shadowed by a ring of stately elms, a few of the humans clustered, playing games on flat rocks. The Sylvets brought them thimble-sized wooden tumblers of spiced wine and leaves holding nuts, tiny sweet bits of fruit, and cakes not much bigger than crumbs for the humans. She recognized it as the Feast the Sylvets had mentioned. Apparently there was no end to the supply of food and wine, although in proportions more suited to Pixets or Sylvets than humans. Each leaf of food could fit in a Human's palm. No one seemed concerned with the meager portions, and all looked well fed and cheerful. The songs of love from the Sylvelles were not wasted on the humans as the only female there was in a passionate embrace with a dark-haired, muscular, sweating man.

"Master Jeweler." He looked up at her where she hovered beneath a poplar bough which swung slowly to and fro with the imperceptible movement of the air. "I know where the Feast is." The Master Jeweler's face brightened. "What's more, there are others there whom we could ask about this land."

The Brandmistress interjected, "Other people from Thuringland, not Sylvets?"

Hili fluttered up and said, "Yes, Brandmistress. Humans."

Trallalair was wary of anyone they would meet. She had heard of the Ghouls infesting caves beneath the Forbidden Mountains, but no humans were known to live in Sylvanward. As she remembered the mayhem following the Ghouls' attack on the host of Sinjery and Knights, she placed her hand on the pommel of her sword. If these were Ghouls feasting in this disconcerting habitation, she would gladly confront them and send them to Hell. "Yes, let us meet these people that live with the Sylvets. I thought the land of the Sylvets was forbidden to all others."

The jeweler frowned. "Brandmistress, I believe the title 'Forbidden Mountains' came not from the exclusion of people from the land. They were simply never seen again. The Sylvets never forbade anyone from entering. Only our fear of the unknown made the land forbidden to the people of the Realm. I believe people entered easily enough. I suspect people have been entering this Land of Repose for centuries. I wonder why no one has every returned to tell of this enchanting place. Maybe life here is so beautiful, no one ever wants to leave and go back to the outside world with all of its grief. I can kind of understand how that could happen. I have been thinking. We need to rest, but we must not stay here very long."

"I agree, Jeweler. That theory is in keeping with my concerns about this land. I, too, wonder why we have never heard of Repose before. I feel danger for us here, despite the veneer of hospitality. Maybe leaving Repose is not as easy as entering it."

Trallalair knew that beauty and repose could be tempting, even addicting for those of weak wills. It was so even for those of strong wills, like the Dragonlord and his obsession with the beauty of the Sinjery.

She was growing increasingly suspicious. This land was too close to the Dead Lands to be free of evil. All seemed pleasant and commodious, but something felt wrong. All the tales of wanderers heading for the Forbidden Mountains to discover a treasure that was only suspected but never proven and never coming back again were too consistent to be ignored. Centuries ago, the practice of sending search parties into the Forbidden Mountains had been abandoned because the search parties themselves never returned. Knights had flown over Sylvanward, but they were all cautioned not to land. Trallalair, the jeweler, and the Pixelle had landed in the Forbidden Mountains, and now, they were somewhere outside the forest, far from where they entered. She strengthened her resolve to spend as little time as possible there. So far she saw nothing to prevent their leaving, although she worried that if they wished to leave, only one small opening led back to the world they knew.

Once as a child, she and Saggethrie had taken torches and crept down a sinkhole on a hillside into a vast cavern. They giggled as they explored all the passages and twisting crawl-ways. One very tight hole led up through the floor of a large chamber. The ceiling had collapsed ages before, so the floor was a maze of fractured blocks. After they searched for other tunnels leading out of that chamber, their torches began to sputter, so they decided to go back outside. To their horror, the small hole they had crawled up through was completely hidden in the thousands of slabs. They had failed to clearly mark their way out. She remembered being chilled to the bone but sweating in fear as Saggethrie's torch fizzled out. With their last torch burning the last of its pitch, they found the hole and the way out by sheer luck.

Repose was a lot like a cave with one tiny entrance. Trallalair took pains to memorize the lay of the land, bushes and trees which were near their only way out. The entrance was the end of a large hollow log covered with moss. Two poplars, tall and rustling in a barely perceptible breeze, stood nearby as sentinels. She unsheathed her sword and, leaping up, swung it at one tree blazing it high above their heads.

When her sword struck the bark of the poplar, Sparrow Feather screamed as if Trallalair had instead struck her with the sword. Other cries echoed through the woods.

Shuddering, the Sylvelle walked shakily to Trallalair and lightly touched her leg, saying, "Please, Brandmistress, put away your sword. The trees are our friends and companions. They will do you no harm. We can feel their pain as if it were our own. We beg you, desist."

Trallalair thought of all the burning trees outside Repose. She pointed to the log from which they had emerged just a short time before. "And all the trees burnt by the Dragons just beyond the log opening, in the mountain forest. Do you feel their pain too?"

Sparrow Feather shook with the thought. "No, no, thankfully, no. Our land protects us from their trials. We would prevent it if we could, but against that power, we are helpless. Besides, the fire has already passed."

Trallalair looked at the Sylvelle, shaking her head, even more puzzled. Undoubtedly, the fires still burned. It had seemed much less than one Blessing of time, and there had been plenty of trees in the valley. Unless there were a heavy rain, the Dragonfire would without a doubt consume them all before dying out. Trallalair had seen Dragonfires in forests burn for days. Perhaps the Sylvelle meant that the Dragons had passed. The Brandmistress did not think it her duty to explain what a conflagration of Dragonfire was like to these isolated beings.

"I must blaze a trail so we will not be lost in your land."

"You cannot get lost in Repose. Every every hollow, stream, hill and copse is the most wonderful place to be in the world. Everyone finds what they want here."

"How about the way out?"

"The portals to your world are plentiful. Pixelle Hili can lead you to them easily."

Hili flew up to Trallalair. "It is true, Brandmistress, several near us are clear in their thoughts. We will have no trouble finding our way out when we want to leave."

Sparrow Feather offered, "If you wish to stay, you are welcome to remain here as long as you like."

Trallalair made it very clear. "We do not wish to stay for more than a day."

It was now the Sylvelle who looked puzzled. She seemed to think about what Trallalair said for a long time. "We hope you have a pleasant... day here." She emphasized 'day' as if she had no concept what the word meant, but simply repeated it by rote.

Trallalair addressed Hili. "We will trust you to lead us out, Pixelle Hili." She looked at the jeweler, "But we will not go beyond two hundred strides, and we will all stay together." Finally, terse and suspicious, she addressed Sparrow Feather. "Lead us to where we may eat and rest."

As they were all agreed, Sparrow Feather brightened. Dancing and capering to the songs in the air, she led them to the Feast.

CHAPTER 27

ISSELTRENT'S DEMISE

Listening to the love songs of the Sylvets mesmerized Jonathon. He ate and listened and dozed off. He thought a whole day could have passed in the idyllic land. It was easy to be lulled into complacency, especially when the Sylvets told them all they were safe in their land and should wait until the threat from the Dragons was long passed. Granted, the Sylvets had no inkling of the urgency of their mission, but Jonathon felt guilty. Even a day in Sylvanward was one more day in which his transformed family would grow, flower, and die. Jonathon's heart ached with the conviction that he was powerless to save them or alter their fate in any way. He knew that, soon, he had to face the peril of the Dragons or face his own inevitable death at the Demon's hand.

He had spoken with many of the humans inhabiting Repose and found them all pleasant and cheerful, but strangely unconcerned with the events of the last Moon. Apparently, none knew of the release of the Dragons. Isolated in this magical land for so long, they had forgotten much about the outside world, almost as if the tiny thimblefuls of wine the Sylvets served clouded their memories. He spoke to one man who was surprised that Seldric was the current Dragonlord. Seldric had held the title for forty years. The man looked much younger than Jonathon. Probably the wine again, he thought. Some magic was inherent in the Land of Repose, but how it worked, Jonathon could not fathom. That is, not until he met a woman as young as his daughter Heather who said she had run from Isseltrent with her lover when Sverdphthik appeared in the city at the beck and call of Nishbad. She claimed it had only been a few years before. Jonathon laughed and told her what a good story teller she was.

As he nodded off, the fragrance of roses filled his head. Thoughts of his conversations filled his head with disbelief that so many people could have such an unusual view of the passage of time. Still, he could sit and listen to the songs and drink the wine for many Favors and Blessings. It was easy to forget the time. Maybe it was as he suspected. Maybe the land of the Sylvets was so pleasant, and the cares of the outside world so far away, that people forgot to leave and go back to their normal lives. Maybe all the people still living there had things they'd rather forget or even flee. Jonathon and his companions certainly had a lot they would rather forget, but they did not have the luxury to flee their duty. He thought it was the right thing that they should leave the next morning rather than be seduced into wasting too much time in Repose.

Even without the sun and moon as clues, Trallalair was becoming convinced they had been in Sylvanward for days. The dancing and the meal seemed interminable. Their songs were alluring but, to her, they were depressing. All the talk of love, love she would never feel again, now that Saggethrie was dead. She would have to act, take them out of the enchanting land of the Sylvets, before too much of their precious time was wasted.

Hili sensed something far worse was happening in the Land of the Sylvets than the Master Jeweler or the Sinjery Brandmistress imagined. The Sylvets called the land Repose. Their references to the Land of

Repose bespoke a certain confidence that beauty, like love, was tied to something endless, eternal as the heavens. It was a haven for all time, a place untouchable and unassailable by the evil so close at hand in the Dead Lands. Their assurances to the group, that as long as the trio stayed in the Land of Repose they were safely hidden from all things evil, was uncomfortably ominous.

It was the shortly after Hili had this premonition that she began to have serious doubts. She was served a buttercup petal filled with the most delicious nectar by a healthy Sylvet named Olam who still had the pliable limbs and fuzzy bark skin which she recognized as youthful for a Sylvet. Searching her memory of the collective reminiscences of the Community and their history, she recalled another Sylvet named Olam that had spoken to her ancestors generations before. He had been young and infatuated with a nubile Pixelle named Morne that he had met while he accompanied a trading party visiting Isseltrent. No descendant, regardless of how pure the lineage from father to son, could be as exact a match to that memory as was this Olam. To have the same name as well, the chances of that were unbelievable. Olam grinned sheepishly when he handed her the buttercup leaf, just like a shy youth would. He had to be the same Olam of the Pixets' legends, but what was he doing here, centuries later?

Another aspect of their visit to Repose bothered Hili. Before they had entered the pine log that was the entrance to Repose, Hili could sense none of the Sylvets thoughts. It was as if their thoughts were excluded from the world she knew and as if the whole land was somehow outside reality, a mystical retreat. The strange lights in the sky, she thought, were illusions to delight them during their feast. But the supposed illusions were too bright and too regular, almost like a natural phenomenon, a visible golden wind in the heavens, or like the touted aurora that people in the Cajalathrium States claimed filled the night sky above the Northern High Plateau with marvelous lights at odd intervals.

Perhaps the fantastic appearance of the land and its weather explained their safety there. Perhaps they weren't detectable by the Demon and its minions because they weren't even in the world anymore.

Another memory plagued her. The constant thrum she felt in her mind when they first entered Sylvanward. A sense of something lower-pitched than the deep growling of a Black Dragon lying patiently in one place for years. When they passed the barrier of the pine into Repose, the thrum was replaced by a high-pitched whine, again not heard but of the mind. At the same instant, all the Pixets' thoughts were lost to her, just as they had been when her head was underwater in the Mermet's territory. After a while within Repose, the whining had stopped. She sensed the deep thrum and the high whine were linked, but how? Olam was her key to the puzzle, and she sensed the solution would be frightening. Nothing in his thoughts gave her a clue to the mystery.

"Olam," she said hesitantly. "How old are you?" He looked five years old, in the prime of his adulthood.

"I have danced the summer solstice moon a hundred times. But like everyone, I get busy and miss a lot of moons."

A hundred years old. That would be about right, if he was the same Olam of her memories. A hundred years was many times the length of a Pixet's life. Even for a human, to live so long without any signs of aging was impossible.

She had to resolve the paradox. "But how many years old are you, Olam?"

"Six."

By a reflex, Hili's wings shot out and she sprang into the air. "Six? Six? Six!" Horror hit Hili like the slap of a human hand. Olam lived six years but danced in the light of the summer solstice moon a hundred times. It was clear that more than a hundred years had passed while Olam was still only six. Somehow, time in the Land of Repose passed many times times slower than on the outside. The trio may have been in the land of the Sylvets for whole Moons instead of a just a night and a day. If Moons had passed outside Repose, everything had likely changed for the worse. For all they knew, Sverdphthik could be sitting on the throne of Isseltrent, and all the Demons of Hell may have been loosed on the world from an unguarded Hell's Breach. Not a hint of the secret of the Land of Repose intruded into the Sylvet's mind. The time paradox was as expected and accepted as the air itself. It was equally ignored.

In her distress, Hili forgot to thank Olam for the revelation. Without the least thought of courtesy, she raced to find the Brandmistress and the Master Jeweler. She looked through the ancient canopy of the trees, up at the trail of the monstrous comet streaking across the night sky, lighting it to the brightness of day. With a gasp, she realized that she saw, not a comet, but the sun itself flying as fast as a falling star. Three times it passed as she looked for the Brandmistress. Another three days.

Hili flew to Trallalair's side. "Brandmistress, we must leave at once."

"Yes, Pixelle Hili, I sense we have wasted days instead of Blessings here."

"It is much more than that. Many Moons, most likely."

"Moons? You're joking."

"Look at the sun." Hili pointed upward as the sun streaked above them as fast as a soaring hawk.

"The sun? Those constant blazes across the sky are the *sun?*"

"Another day has just passed." The streak was replaced by a few swirling dots of light barely seen through the mist above them. Hili pointed upward. "Stars. Or at least a few bright ones."

Trallalair was already in motion. She spoke with an urgent tone to the closest Sylvelle, Fallen Petal. "Jonathon Forthright, where is he?"

The Sylvelle said, "He looked so exhausted. We had hoped he would sleep."

"Never mind that. We must leave immediately. Where is he?"

"I last saw him in the Garden of Roses. The fragrance soothed his spirit."

"Please lead us there."

Shrugging at her impatience, the Sylvelle smiled and cavorted down a petal-strewn path, kicking up the petals gleefully as she danced. Hili flew above them, perceiving the path to the Garden of Roses from the Sylvet's thoughts. An image of the Master Jeweler lolling against a log, holding and admiring the natural elegance of a rose he held, was vivid in the Sylvelle's mind.

Rounding a copse, Hili saw the Master Jeweler readying himself, too. He looked up and said. "I'm glad you are here. I was about to look for you."

The Brandmistress interrupted him. "Jeweler, we are leaving now."

"Yes, Brandmistress, I'm as distressed as you. The time goes by quickly here. I sense some magic about that hoodwinks us and makes many Blessings seem like one."

Hili spoke up. "Master Forthright. We have been here not Blessings, but Moons."

He smiled and waggled his head. "Maybe a few days, Hili. I have napped some but not that much."

The Brandmistress said, "When we leave, you will see, Jeweler."

He puffed his cheeks and chuckled, as if they were joking with him.

Trallalair pushed the exasperating jeweler ahead. She was now gripped with a dogged determination to free them from this wondrous prison. She knew the way, remembering their path inward as clearly as would any Sister raised in the confusing maze of the Sinjery swamp.

Ahead of them both, Hili led, again anticipating their path to freedom with the memories of the Sylvets at her disposal. Ahead of them, the door beneath the fallen pine into their world glowed, inviting them to escape. Many Sylvets and Sylvelles raced along with them, marveling at their alarm when the world around them was so wonderful.

Hili flew through the opening first followed by the Master Jeweler who squeezed through shoved on the bottom by the Brandmistress who followed close behind. What awaited them made them all cry out simultaneously.

They came out through a piece of the pine log so small it was only a bare ring of wood. All the rest had been consumed by the Dragonfire. Where there should have been a burnt stubble of ferns surrounding the pine log, brown flowers had matured, died and were partially covered by snow. A bloody morning sun gave the snow a grisly, red cast.

Jonathon's voice was loudest. "What is this?" Turning to Hili, he cried, "Moons, you say? *Moons*? How?" He could say no more but fell to his knees, sputtering incoherently. Tears filled his eyes as he realized that the flowers he saw dead before him were annuals. Annuals like the seeds of his family. They had grown, withered, and died while he was feasting with the Sylvets. The same must have happened to his family. All his beautiful, happy children and his wife, gone forever. Weeping, he fell to the ground, his tears mixing with icy rivulets coursing from the snow banks.

Trallalair seethed in anger. Again, she had failed. If it had truly been Moons that had passed, the Demon had surely learned to control the power of the Dragoncrown to capture all the land. Even Sinjer had, no doubt, been destroyed by hungry Dragons. The denigrating tribute that her people had paid for centuries was all for naught. The Sinjery had sacrificed their pride and their morals and still, despite all their sacrifices, the Dragons had killed them all in the end.

Hili was the most distressed of them all. She flew about, scanning the sky and searching for a hint of a thought. All the Pixets' thoughts had been stilled. Not a thought came to her. But the deep thrum she had heard when she first came to the land filled her mind. Sonorous, slow voices. It could only be the thoughts of the Sylvets inside the Land of Repose slowed to near incomprehensibility. She knew that her entire Community of Pixets, Pixelles, and Pixies were gone. She searched and searched with her mind, and finally found the thoughts of a few Sylvets outside Repose that she would have disregarded in the past but who now stood out like beacons in a night. In their thoughts, she saw the embodiment of her worst fears. They all had the same memories. Flocks of passing birds had told them the news that Isseltrent was gone. All that was left of once-proud, once-powerful Isseltrent was an ashen ruin. Not a living thing remained.

Hili saw the Master Jeweler's and the Sinjery maiden's grief. Only more grief did she have to share with them. Of the three, she was the only one who knew the whole, awful truth. Isseltrent was gone. The Community was gone. Jonathon's family was gone. All the Sinjery sisters in Isseltrent were gone. The whole purpose of their fateful journey to the Dead Lands was for nothing, as even the Dragonlord was gone, and no one was left to wield the Dragoncrown.

BOOK III

THE SWORD OF BLISS

CHAPTER 28

HELL

For Rhazburn, screaming pierced his ears, darkness cloaked his vision, and deathly heat paralyzed his limbs. A nauseous smell of rotting flesh permeated his head, the taste of vomit filled his mouth, and despair bound his mind. Helpless and hopeless, he existed in terror for ages unknown. Each moment infinitely lengthened. Whole Moons flew past like a searing wind. It was all the same to him. Crushed under the heel of Kitilzgabwed, he was ground into a bed of broken glass. His poems were useless. None of his training could avail him. His fall into the depths of Hell would be eternal. There was no rest. No sleep. Nothing but suffering.

Nothing, that is, until he heard the tune. All the memories of his life were canceled by the terror, but one thin strain of a whistled song fought it all, caressing a tiny part of his mind. The screams tried to drown the tune, but it lived like a bird's song, chasing darkness away in the morning. The whistling became a refrain, repeated time and again, ever closer. If Rhazburn concentrated on the tune, the screams were mollified, and the paralytic heat lessened.

A gentle hand touched his arm lightly, reassuringly, and another cool hand stroked his hair, calming him further. All the time, the pleasant melody soothed him. From deep inside, where his memories quailed, Dollop, the gentle student Rhazburn had blown back to Hell, seemed to be beside him, still so gentle. Rhazburn realized that he no longer had a gag, nor was he trussed like a pig.

Fighting the stiff dryness of his tongue and mouth, he croaked, "Dollop."

The whistling stopped, but a voice equally soothing said, "Yes, Master?"

"I cannot see."

"Relax. Open your eyes."

Astonished, ignorant that he had shut his eyes tight trying to hide within himself, Rhazburn did as his student told him. He relaxed. His eyes fell open. There was Dollop's smile and his auburn hair.

"You're alive. I'm alive," Rhazburn stuttered.

"No, Master, we are not."

"But you are here and I hear your whistling."

"I don't understand it, but here our spirits feel substantial and seem to be living and breathing."

"But the smells and the tastes, the heat."

"All real for our spirits, but of no substance."

"I don't believe you."

"Then look at your body." Dollop waved Rhazburn's gaze a distance of a hundred wispy green clouds away. Rhazburn's inanimate flesh lay there, trussed as he had been when the guards threw him through the Musical Mystical Door. His body, gagged and tied that way, looked stiff and waxy, with his eyes staring in rigor mortis. "My body is lost then."

"Not completely lost. Just stolen."

"Stolen?"

"Any solid, living body that enters Hell is immediately stolen by a Demon. Mine was, and so was yours."

"Demons have no power to take a live body, Dollop. They first kill, then take the corpse."

"In our world they do, but here their power is much greater. They inhabit what they want, throwing out the soul within. All souls are in the power of Kitilzgabwed and his minions."

"So it was not you who tried to leave Hell, but a Demon as we thought."

"I wish that were true, Master. My mind was twisted. I made a deal with the Demon, helping it just so I could escape Hell myself. You understand. You have seen the terror Hell holds."

Rhazburn only nodded.

"But fighting against the Demonwards and, thank The Three, losing that fight released me from the hold of the Demon. It kept my body, but my soul was released. I have been looking for my wife and child."

"Looking for your wife and child? Do you still believe that ruse of the Demon we fought? Your wife and child are not here, Dollop. You know that."

"What else do I have to do? I don't belong here. The lost souls seem to leave me alone, even the Demons. I think my whistling frightens them." If Rhazburn were not in Hell, he would think that was funny.

"Where are all the lost souls? I'd think they'd be all crowded together, considering how much screaming there is." With that, the screaming swelled again. Holding his hands over his ears did little to suppress it. Again, Dollop's touch brought him back. "They sound like they are all in my head but just one touch from you and they recede."

"I can't explain it, but I feel like I can help and I do."

"It's like the inherent beauty of your spirit chases the evil away."

Dollop said, "The others, the lost souls and the Demons, are spread far apart. It's as if there is as much room as the Demons need to keep everyone isolated. The loneliness is as horrible as the tortures they carry on."

"I can believe that. When I was alone with the screaming, I was crazy with fear. How in the world, or, rather, how in Hell did you find me?"

"I don't exactly know. I was drawn to you. Or your cry. I could recognize your voice among all the others. I knew it was you. But, then, I wanted you to come looking for me."

"I wanted to come find you, Dollop, but I had something to do first. What I did went all wrong. The court threw me in here as punishment. I'm not supposed to leave... But I must."

Rhazburn needed to know more about how Hell worked. "So, where is your body, Dollop?"

"Just yonder." He pointed out a drifting husk. It looked a lot like Rhazburn's and was close, not a score of drifting clouds distant.

The heat gripped Rhazburn again, and the screaming built up. The sight of Dollop's body, as dead-looking as his own, fueled his fear like oil spilled on a fire. "There is no hope," Rhazburn said.

"There is hope!" Dollop shouted, as Rhazburn beginning to lapse into the eternal coma once more. He squeezed Rhazburn's spectral arm with his gentle soul. "Do not leave me, Master. I need you for my sanity."

Rhazburn tried to concentrate on Dollop's young face. His student's fresh cheer was a rope he clung to. Only by thinking of his friend's love of his family could Rhazburn suppress the power of the screaming that threatened to pull him back down into the depths of remorse.

"Can we get out of here, Dollop? With our bodies?"

"There is only one way. We must make a deal with a Demon."

"Deal with a Demon?"

"There is no other way."

"A deal they will not honor." Dollop of all people should know the improbity of Demons and the ploys they could use to pass through Hell's Breach.

"True. Plan to be double-crossed."

"I will have to double-cross the Demon before he has the chance to betray me."

"The timing must be impeccably precise."

"No doubt they will know what I am thinking, that I plan to renege on the deal."

"Assuredly."

Rhazburn tried to quell any thoughts of his plan. To do so, he had to constantly reiterate his intention to aid the Demon, thinking the words constantly, letting no hint of his true intentions surface. Meditating on that falsehood, he suppressed all his other thoughts. "Alright, show me the way."

They stood in a foul mist, yellow and noxious. It stank of death. Dollop led the way, past Rhazburn's body and toward Dollop's. Standing in the mist a few strides distant, Dollop shouted, "Demon, hear me. Behold, Rhazburn, the Loremaster, leader of the Demonwards that oppose you. With his knowledge and body, you can leave Hell. You can enter our world, where mortals will worship and serve you forever."

Rhazburn's thought flashed on how he could get out of Hell but avoid such a fate for the world. One Demon in the mortal world was enough to destroy it. Just as quickly, he left this thought and chanted in his mind his false plan to aid the Demon. It must have worked, because a clawed hand sprouted from Dollop's body, reached out for Rhazburn and pierced his head. A halo of spikes nailed him to the Demon's grasp. As the Demon emerged, Rhazburn recognized this Demon was same one he had fought on the day Jonathon had braved Hell's Breach. Its insubstantial body felt like a massive but twisted spider. Numerous articulated legs and tentacles scrabbled through the mist to Rhazburn's body. The bulk of the spider-Demon towed Rhazburn's spirit like an empty insect husk it had sucked dry. With a loud roar and a horrible stench, Dollop's Demon threw out the weaker Demon possessing Rhazburn's trussed body. That Demon, looking like a huge bat, flew immediately to Dollop's vacated body and disappeared within it. Dollop's spider-Demon superimposed his bulk onto Rhazburn's soulless vegetating body. Held in an agonizing, vise-like grip, Rhazburn, the spirit, trailed behind Rhazburn, the Demon-possessed body. The gag and the cords binding his body's limbs fell away, and his body straightened up and moved off. It ran at an alarming speed. Rhazburn followed. Dollop, left alone with all the terrors of damnation, was absorbed into the caustic mists behind them.

Rhazburn, facing backward, saw nothing until they stopped. When the spikes slid excruciatingly from his head, he turned and saw, surrounded by fumes, a tremendous, human-shaped Demon. It sprawled and faced them. It looked like a Black Dragon at a Travel Plaza waiting for travelers, but none of the complacency of a Black Dragon was there. The Demon was a trapped beast. Its red eyes searched anxiously, hopelessly, for an opportunity to escape. Its mouth was stretched wide open, and through the cavity, it screamed silently.

Within the frame of its peg-like teeth, Rhazburn saw the figure of Lethbud, a young Demonward well known to Rhazburn. He stood within the Demon's mouth and silently mouthed the word 'Forms', then turned his head over his shoulder toward the other Demonwards in the Chamber of Hell's Breach. Rhazburn realized that the Demon's mouth, itself, was Hell's Breach. Somehow, Nishbad had summoned and bound a Demon so its mouth formed the portal to Hell. For Rhazburn as for Dollop, the method to close Hell's Breach was obvious. The Musical Mystical Door had to be destroyed. By holding open the Demon's mouth, the door only strengthened the binding spell. The door merely had to be destroyed, and a counter spell developed. The procedure was much simpler than anyone had imagined. Rhazburn also realized that before the doorway to Hell was closed forever and the opportunity was lost, Sverdphthik had to be returned to Hell where he belonged. These thoughts passed through Rhazburn's mind, but he obliterated any idea of betraying the Demon.

A tentacle wrapped his neck in fire. The hundred eyes of the Demon bored into Rhazburn's soul. *Tell them to let me through.* His ruse had worked.

Rhazburn tried to free himself, but could not.

"Then, when I am free, your body will be yours again."

Rhazburn worked on suppressing the thought 'A dead body probably.' Instead, he applied his will to carefully think, '*Thank you, oh Mighty One*'. The Demon gave his neck an especially tight squeeze to reinforce the power he had over Rhazburn's soul. Then he released him with the same slicing pain as the claws slid out of his skull.

Rhazburn sidled off toward the side of Hell's Breach so as to approach the portal from an angle that Lethbud could not easily observe. The Demonward had retreated a few steps, and Rhazburn knew that they were readying the closing of the Musical Mystical Door.

Rhazburn's body in the control of its Demon acted as cocky as Rhazburn in real life. It strode right up to Hell's Breach. Rhazburn counted out in his mind the running steps of the Demonwards toward the Musical Mystical Door. He imagined Lethbud opening his coin pouch and pulling out a coin. At the precise instant when he imagined the coin flying through the air toward the door, Rhazburn grabbed the frame of the Musical Mystical Door and twisted around it with a single fluid motion into the real world. The sheet of energy erupted while he was still holding it, searing his hands. He was free, and the Demon was not. As he hoped, the Verse of Demon Recognition did not make his own ethereal substance visible. He was only a lost soul, a Ghost, and Ghosts were visible only in Hell but not in the real world. He was invisible to the Demonwards.

To his surprise, he found that he walked as slowly as if he were in a world made of honey. Every step was an effort. As a Ghost, he did not belong in the world on that side of Hell's Breach any more than did the Demons. Hell was his home now.

He recognized all the Poets manning their posts and watched their preparations to destroy Rhazburn the Demon. The Musical Mystical Door shimmered, a shield against the Demon, as the repaired instruments, the Silver Dulcimer and the Pipes of Power, strengthened the spell. In time past, Dollop had passed through the door, his corporeal body unaffected by the spell. Rhazburn's body might pass as easily. His younger brother Garrith led the Demonwards. Obviously, the court had ignored his relation to Jonathon and Rhazburn in their desperation to find veteran Poets to man Hell's Breach. Rhazburn walked toward his brother. Garrith turned and walked right through Rhazburn. As his brother passed through him, Rhazburn briefly shared his brother's thoughts.

Rhazburn learned that the Demonwards had readied the Epigram of Fiery Destruction to incinerate Rhazburn and the Demon within. They had correctly deduced that the Verse of Exclusion was only effective against Demons. No one knew if the verse would exclude the combination of a Demon in a human body. The safest thing was to destroy both at once with magical fire. Rhazburn certainly did not want the Demon to enter the world, but he wanted to save his own body. Hope still remained that he could get all of himself, body and soul, back out of Hell, especially with an ally like Dollop in the nether world. Besides, he still had to fulfill his vow and save Dollop from damnation. If he could get back in Hell again and get his body back, he could help Dollop as well. It was all a farfetched fantasy, but he would not give up on the notion until all was hopeless.

Garrith was his only hope. He grimaced and struggled to catch up with his brother. To Rhazburn's relief, the Verse of Exclusion seemed to be working on the Demon, holding it back, although the shimmering curtain was faltering. The Demonwards seemed to be preparing to open the Musical Mystical Door shortly so they could destroy Rhazburn completely. Garrith stopped and stood with his back to Rhazburn. As the two musicians stopped their playing, Garrith stepped backward right into Rhazburn's advance.

Garrith stopped cold, feeling the presence. *Garrith, it is I, Rhazburn. Fear not. I will help.*

Sharing all of Garrith's thoughts and sensations, Rhazburn felt his brother tremble and break out in a chilling sweat. "Rhazburn, go back!" Garrith said aloud. The Demon was advancing on the Musical Mystical

Door and all the Demonwards assumed he spoke to the Demon that wore Rhazburn's flesh.

I cannot, Garrith. I must rectify the trouble I have caused. Save my body. Use the Couplet of Wind.

Garrith hesitated, hardening his mind to Rhazburn.

Please, Brother, Rhazburn pleaded. *I can help get back the Dragoncrown. Our father needs me, I am certain.*

Garrith blinked once, hesitant. Rhazburn was within his mind, and he could reinforce his acceptance of the change in tactics. Garrith pulsed with a sudden resolve, his confidence promoted by Rhazburn's own willpower. He, too, wanted their father to survive all these troubles.

"Thanguil, the Dulcimer. I want to employ the Couplet of Wind used by Rhazburn against Dollop." Every Poet knew that story and had the couplet memorized. "We owe it to Rhazburn to preserve what is left of him."

None of the Poets argued. None had ever thought Rhazburn a traitor. The Door was reactivated, excluding the Demon, until the Couplet of Wind could be formed in pearl dust. As before, a Poem of Levitation would immobilize the Demon in the air, and the magical wind would carry him far away. Once before this combination had worked against this Demon. Rhazburn was confident that the two poems would be adequate again.

Garrith helped form the words. By willing Garrith's arms and legs to move, Rhazburn could augment any action his brother took, adding his own will power to Garrith's. The poems were formed quickly, and the Demon was released, strutting into the chamber, ready to give orders. It obviously thought that Rhazburn, fearing the loss of his body, had prepared the way. When the Poem of Levitation lifted him up, a piercing inhuman scream came forth from Rhazburn's body, unnerving the toughest of the Poets. No one doubted that a Demon possessed Rhazburn. The Couplet of Wind sent Rhazburn's body tumbling away just as it had done to Dollop when he tried to re-enter the Chamber of Hell's Breach. Rhazburn could just hear the Demon scream, "Poet, I will rend your useless body to pieces!" More lies from the Demon, Rhazburn hoped.

CHAPTER 29

THE DEMON RHAZBURN

Rhazburn was shocked. Through Garrith's mind, he learned that a whole Moon had passed while he was in Hell. His father had been commanded to go to the Dead Lands to take back the Dragoncrown shortly after Rhazburn was thrown into Hell. He had not been heard of since. His Mother and all the children who had still been at home were missing as well. Patrick, Herkimer, Laurel, Heather, and Will, along with Laurel's children, were all sequestered under guard at their father's house. All the grown children who had drifted away from home had grieved for a Moon or more. They felt sure that their father, mother, and all their young brothers and sisters were dead. Rhazburn felt the tears roll down Garrith's cheeks and sensed the trembling of his anger at the court. They had treated Jonathon's family so callously, as if they weren't in the least valuable, or even interesting enough to save. And all for one mistake. One mistake by their father, who had been fooled by a Demon. It was something that happened daily at Hell's Breach. How was it different? Yes, the mistakes had resulted in thousands of lives lost, rather than a few Poets. But the quality of the mistake was no different. Jonathon had acted in good faith.

Rhazburn had to ride within Garrith's body until the day Poets passed through the portal of the Chamber of Hell's Breach in the evening. A twilight fog clung to the ground, blurring the shadowy forms of the guards' double row. It seemed to Rhazburn like he and Garrith passed through a bristling corridor. Just beyond the guards, Priests of The Three thanked Tundudil for the safe return of the Poets from the threshold of Hell. Disturbingly, the lone Seer with them studied Garrith with a furrowed brow, as if she could see Rhazburn within. "Master Poet," she said as Garrith walked by.

Cool, without fear, Garrith turned and regarded the Seer. Rhazburn knew little of the skills the Seers possessed, but he realized that they had the ability to speak with the dead. As the Seer looked their way, Rhazburn was horrified to see a figure step out of the Seer's body and walk up to Garrith. The figure, an ethereal being walking in the mortal world, glowed distinctly in Rhazburn's sight. He was another disembodied soul, just like Rhazburn himself.

At that same moment, the layers of the world became visible to him like the layers of an onion. Dozens, no, hundreds of other souls, or more properly, Ghosts, walked about Isseltrent singly or in groups. They talked together as if a city of the Dead were just beneath everyone's perception, everyone but the Seers'. Obviously, the dead never transmigrated from the mortal world to Heaven or Hell. It looked, to Rhazburn's amazement, that they simply hung around Isseltrent, and all of Tundudil's Creation, for all eternity. But why? He had an urge to walk out of the protection Garrith's body and ask them why they were there, but the one standing before them, studying them, was disconcerting enough. He looked as if he was about to raise some sort of alarm of the Dead about Rhazburn's flight from Hell. As it was, the figure stared at Garrith for a few moments, cocking his spectral head this way and that. Finally, he gave up and turned with a backward, uncertain glance to slowly pass back into his host Seer. The Seer stood a moment, then let Garrith pass, apparently suspicious but unconvinced that Rhazburn rode within him. Rhazburn felt Garrith's amazement as he, too, saw all the spirits filling the unseen layer of Isseltrent. Since Rhazburn could see the spirits, and he shared Garrith's mind, so could

Garrith. Garrith thought that Rhazburn would know the meaning of it all, but Rhazburn had little to offer. It was all new to him and unexpected. A suspicion plagued Rhazburn that it was all related to the Demon and Hell's Breach.

The Dragons kept up their harassment of Isseltrent, but there were fewer flying about, and those that did attack did so half-heartedly. Apparently, they were no longer taking vengeance for centuries of enslavement. In fact, they were slaves again, this time the Demon's. They were, once again, the weapons of another. It was no wonder the ones in the sky looked tired. The others were probably off plundering the rest of Thuringland or the adjacent lands. Garrith clearly had no idea why they didn't just finish the job on Isseltrent. The Dragons were behaving very strangely. After killing a person, they would ever so gently swoop down and pick him up with talons or maw and fly away with the corpse. They acted as though they were venerating the body. As though they were planning to respectfully bury it. More likely, Rhazburn thought, the bodies were going to be used as food for the Ghouls or to produce more Zombies.

As Rhazburn took in more of his brother's memories, cognizance crashed over him like a breaker. The Demon had no use for a totally-destroyed Isseltrent. With the city still functioning, Sverdphthik had a constant supply of bodies, and perhaps all the souls tied to those lifeless vessels. The souls seemed unable to ascend to Heaven, so both bodies and souls would be slaves for him. Keeping them as they were would increase his power endlessly. Rhazburn understood that Sverdphthik was playing a balancing act. He could cull a few dozen souls every Moon, leaving enough people so that the population could continually renew itself. He would keep an eye on the balance, and kill sufficient numbers of the populace so Isseltrent would never again regain any power. The men, women, and children of Isseltrent would be tended like a herd of swine, forever. Just like Hell bled the world for an endless supply of souls for Kitilzgabwed, Sverdphthik's domain would drain the vitality of the people of Thuringland and the surrounding lands. Besides, if Sverdphthik could conquer more of the world, he could divert an ever-increasing number of bodies and souls to his own armies from other places in the world, even the Ocean Kingdom of the Lord of the Sea. Sverdphthik's forces would burgeon, while Hell's growth would eventually falter. Ultimately, the

Demon could have enough resources and minions to challenge the power of Kitilzgabwed himself. Perhaps he would bide his time in the world until he could crash through Hell's Breach and supplant its master as the Evil Lord of all existence.

Rhazburn returned his thinking to the mission his father's group had undertaken. What had happened to them? Garrith only knew that they were missing. Even the poor Pixelle Hili. And then there was Trallalair. She guarded both his father and Hili to aid them in an impossible, suicidal attempt to take back the Dragoncrown from the Demon locked in its stronghold. Rhazburn knew that if he was not available to help his father and protect him from the perils of the Dead Lands, there was no better person to protect his father. Rhazburn himself had failed in that role when he had the chance. Somehow, Rhazburn thought his father was still alive. He trusted the capabilities of Brandmistress Trallalair that much. It sickened him that Trallalair had been seriously injured. Then, to think that she was fallaciously convinced he and his father had plotted the downfall of the Dragonlord and the Realm. It was too much for him to bear.

Garrith felt sorrow along with Rhazburn for Trallalair's wounds. Still, she was part of the court who had condemned his father and the rest of his family. It was ironic that she now protected Jonathon. Of course, Jonathon was probably beyond needing protection. Garrith had heard nothing for more than a Moon. He felt sure they were lost. Then again, he had thought Rhazburn was lost.

The terror that the Pixet Community was going through, with their souls tied to the Demon, was common knowledge. It only added another justification for the Dragonlord to keep the harmless, fragile folk locked away from the sun and the flowers that sustained their short, tenuous lives. Rhazburn would tolerate none of it. He vowed in his mind to set them free as well. He felt the most efficient path to accomplish it all lay in helping his father, but he currently had no body to even move with, much less help anyone.

Time passed. Rhazburn spent his days nestled within Garrith's soul, instructing his brother on how best to protect Isseltrent from the travesty it was experiencing. But he longed for independence. Residing within his brother was uncomfortably intimate for Rhazburn. He shared all his thoughts, including his peculiar obsession for certain foods which Rhazburn hated. Luckily, little exotic food was available in Isseltrent, so Rhazburn was spared having to taste all those nauseating culinary treats that delighted Garrith. He felt all his brother's muscular aches and pains, like his bad knee that popped when he sat down and his daily headaches. Rhazburn tried to get his brother to get a potion for the pains, but Garrith thought the few healing and analgesic potions still produced in the city should be used for those more needy.

Odd thoughts, foreign to Rhazburn, surprised him as well. Since Rhazburn required no sleep as a free spirit, he was party to Garrith's dreams. Fighting Demons in his nightmares was much more realistic and frightening for Rhazburn, since the dream Demons had as much substance as he did and pain from dream injuries was as explicit as if he were living once more.

Cohabiting a body was surely more difficult than marriage. He could not see what had frightened him away from marriage for all his years living in the world. After experiencing every movement, itch, and belch of another as if they were his own, he'd now have no qualms about marriage. Not that he'd ever have the chance.

Rhazburn was well aware he was a Demon in Garrith's body, barely tolerated by his brother. Once, Garrith, who was a bachelor like Rhazburn, began having uncontrollable sexual urges. It seemed there was a sweet, pretty Choralist, Delinda, that Garrith was in the habit of visiting. He had little else to do with his money, and he treasured her company. Added to that, since the Dragons were freed, he constantly feared for her safety. Rhazburn was shocked how he shared the most intimate fantasies of Garrith's nubile courtesan. When Garrith could no longer tolerate the pressure of his youthful lust, he asked Rhazburn to leave him alone for a few Blessings.

Rhazburn had much to do. He felt it his duty to instruct Garrith in the verses and equipment he would need to protect Isseltrent. Laying with a courtesan seemed a waste of time. But Rhazburn was not prepared for the fervor of his brother's love toward Delinda. Garrith could not stand to be thwarted. He had to see her and touch her to reassure himself that she was safe and happy. She was fully as important to him as Rhazburn and his adoptive family. With an irresistible shake of his spirit and mind, Garrith threw Rhazburn from his body. Rhazburn tried to hang on like a flea, but Garrith's spirit, tied by life to his own body, swatted him away. Rhazburn was a naked soul again, alone in Garrith's meager room.

The next morning Garrith came through the door half-smiling, apparently contrite. "Rhazburn, Delinda is safe for the moment. I'm sorry. I had to make sure. If you can hear me, I'm ready for you. If I can protect Isseltrent, I can protect Delinda. Please forgive me, Rhazburn."

Out of Garrith's body, the world for Rhazburn was indistinct. He saw his brother as if through a mist. Even Garrith's voice sounded hollow. Rhazburn slowly approached his brother who stood in the center of the room squinting at his bed, passing his hand over a chair, trying to find what was left of Rhazburn. Garrith was shaking his head in exasperation as Rhazburn passed within him for the last time. He could not help himself as he thought to Garrith, *I told you so. Protecting Isseltrent is the first priority.* When Garrith bristled again with anger, Rhazburn quenched his criticism.

Sharing his body again and his thoughts, Rhazburn was easily aware that his brother's lusts were fulfilled. Rhazburn was welcomed back. Garrith forgot his anger and was, in truth, very apologetic for his inability to control his lusts, but after all, he was only human.

Rhazburn knew that being human was something he could no longer claim as an excuse for himself or anything he thought. Rhazburn noticed that the temptations of the flesh, never prominent in his life when he was alive, were quickly receding into a barely perceptible memory.

By High Day Blessing, Garrith had Rhazburn's plan to protect Isseltrent from further attacks by the Dragons. The time had come for them to part company. Rhazburn was more than glad to take his leave of his brother, body and soul. He felt unclean having access to Garrith's fantasies about Delinda. Having that kind of a relationship with a woman was something Rhazburn would never have again, not with his body in Hell. Still, while he had been within his brother's body, he experienced human emotions and senses once again. Rhazburn saw how tempting it would be for a Demon to have a human body. When it came down to it, however, Garrith had easily thrown him out. Rhazburn had been taught that a Demon could be thrown out of a human body eventually, but never before had he had such a clear demonstration of it. He could not say for certain if a human would be able to throw a real Demon out of his body as easily, but he suspected it was true. Certainly Poetic dogma claimed as much.

Rhazburn thought back to Sverdphthik in his father's shop. The Demon had used a corpse to approach them, not a living human. All of his efforts at Hell's Breach had been to stop Demons from entering the world, not only to protect people from being possessed by them, but to prevent all the other damage the Demons could do. The Demon Sverdphthik was not known to possess any human being except for the short time he had invaded his father's body in his shop the day he stole the Rod of Coercion. Still, he had caused much havoc in the world.

Rhazburn thought his good-byes and stepped forth, back into the world. After much cajoling, Garrith had promised to tell the rest of the family still around that Rhazburn was alive, more or less, and their big brother, the Loremaster, was personally going to deal with Sverdphthik.

Unfortunately, once Rhazburn left his Garrith's warm body, he found walking painfully slow. Parting from Garrith was like entering a world of freezing murk and mire. Every step was an effort, as if lead weights encumbered his limbs. The real world was again clouded and indistinct. Objects which had weight and texture wriggled like mirages glimpsed through rising currents of heat. Through Garrith's eyes, all substance had stood out solid and real. Alone as a hapless, incorporeal spirit, Rhazburn saw all material objects drained of their substance. Perhaps what he saw was the inner reality of things, the indistinct ideal that substance emulates. Despite all the disadvantages of cohabiting, Rhazburn felt increasingly tempted to slide back into Garrith and coexist with him forever, just as he imagined Demons he had fought at Hell's Breach yearned to enter his own body. Now he knew staying within a live human was only at their tolerance. He recalled that the spirit within the Seer who had inspected Garrith did not dare enter Garrith's body, although Rhazburn now believed he could have. No doubt that spirit, confidant and friend of the Seer, perhaps a dead relative, did not want to be thrown out of Garrith's body in disgust. Rhazburn agreed. He never wanted to enter another human against their will.

Rhazburn laid aside his longings. He realized that he had gained some powers as a free spirit as well as losing some. Indeed, he could pass through the very matter of any object or living being and feel nothing, save a thought or two if he passed through a living human. All his progress was slow, but it seemed no different whether he walked through air or through solid rock. Within rock or any substance devoid of light, his spectral eyes descried the same fuzzy details of the inside of objects, just as he saw fuzzy details outside. Gravel imbedded in plaster, veins of minerals in boulders, or the rings and sap of trees, they were all laid bare as he passed through them. While he had been in Garrith's body, he could bend his head down into Garrith's chest and see his brother's heart beating, his lungs expanding, and his blood coursing through pulsating vessels. He imagined a physician spirit being able to find internal disease as if doing a postmortem exam. Of course, in this case, it would be the doctor who was postmortem.

As a breathing human, Rhazburn could have walked from the Chamber of Hell's Breach to the outskirts of town in half a day. As a Ghost, it took him two days. The farther from Hell he ventured, the more exhausted his spirit became, as if he trudged up an increasingly steep slope. The pressure against which he struggled became intense. He felt as if he could, at any time, lose his footing and tumble backward toward Hell's Breach, propelled by some spiritual force like the Hand of Tundudil shoving him out of the world and back into Hell.

As Rhazburn had seen outside the Chamber of Hell's Breach, he was not alone. Many other spirits roamed the world. Again he wondered, why weren't they in Heaven or Hell? What were they doing wandering in the world? Perhaps each spirit had a purpose to fulfill before passing onto to their true Afterlife.

Rhazburn definitely had a purpose, to set the record straight and undo the damage his foolish actions had caused. His goal was to fight the Demon with whatever resources he had left in his paltry spirit. But even if he could accomplish his goal, what was beyond? Wander as a lonely spirit in the mortal world? Go back to Hell?

Maybe the spirits he saw were escapees like himself, needing help. As he wandered among them, he wanted to help them, too. If his father was dead, maybe he would find his spirit among them and help him in death more than he had in life.

Most other wandering Ghosts had respect for the space he occupied. Men, women, and children wandered separately. They spoke to each other occasionally but avoided each other. Every one of them was bright and distinct, as if his spectral eyes were more useful in the spiritual plane of existence. Speech, garbled from living humans, was loud and clear from the spirits of the dead. Rhazburn knew the opposite was true for the living. They clearly heard living beings, but Ghosts were silent or at best hollow-voiced, as if they were speaking from the bottom of a deep, dark well.

One of the stories of a wandering Ghost became clear to him as a spectral woman, watching over a gang of urchins, ran into him and seemed to feel his presence. She had been clearly visible to him, and when her spirit was superimposed upon his, her thoughts became transparent. She was watching her child, still residing in the real world, who had been adopted by the gang of urchins after he became an orphan. Had she not been so preoccupied with her task, she would have noticed Rhazburn and dodged around him. As her head moved through his, effrontery was her first response,. "Get away from me! Who are you?"

She was gone in an instant, having passed on through his brain, walking.

He turned around and tried speaking. "Madam, I am Rhazburn. A searching soul, like yourself." His voice seemed louder than he wanted, and the woman turned back to gaze upon him, this time in anger.

"You are the criminal Loremaster Rhazburn? He who has destroyed our world for his own benefit?"

"A horrible mistake, Madam, for which I have been justly punished, but I swear, I thought it was for the Dragonlord and the good of the Realm."

"Ask my son if killing his parents was for the good of the Realm. Go grovel to your master, the Demon, and leave my son alone. Leave him alone! Get away!" Her voice told him she would fight in whatever way she could to protect her son.

"There is no need to fear me, Madam. I shall leave you and your son. I will never approach you again."

This Ghost had a purpose, to protect her child. She was still tied to the mortal world by that purpose. Maybe that was better than Heaven for her.

Perhaps, he thought, that was the reason she lingered. Rhazburn backed off as quickly as he could. She glowered at him until he was far away.

Outside Blaze, a Green Dragon split the sky above him, turned its head, and toasted a party of archers following on a carpet before they could get off even one arrow. The archers and the carpet fell in a flaming, screaming clump that ricocheted off the western battlement of the Dragonlord's Palace and burst into a shower of blazing corpses. The corpses rained fire upon a cluster of dispirited lean-tos clustered against the castle wall. The flimsy hovels were promptly consumed in fire, flushing a covey of ragged refugees.

Rhazburn thought about the men who fell, burning, to their deaths. *More Ghosts to wander the streets?* Every moment he delayed, more tragedies occurred. Rhazburn felt that the Dragons, enslaved by the Dragoncrown and set upon their course by the Demon, wanted no more to attack the Knights than the Knights wanted to be attacked by them. All the Dragons wanted was to be free. Off on their own, flying the skies, hunting deer, elk, wild horses, or moose. If they had their choice, they would stay far away from humans and their weapons. Rhazburn's solution for the protection of Isseltrent would benefit them both, humans and Dragons alike. His solution could even drain some of the Demon's power, since a protected Isseltrent would eliminate a major source of Sverdphthik's supply of corpses and souls.

Ahead of him was another Ghost, again much clearer to him than the real humans running from the fire. Like a beacon, she stood out. She held aloft an insubstantial sword, threatening the Dragon if it came any nearer. "Come to me, people. Be not afraid. I will protect you." Golden armor identified her as having been a Guard in one of the Sinjery Rings. As fleeing people passed her, unheeding, unseeing, she brandished the sword with an impotent verve.

Pity gripped Rhazburn, forcing him to attempt to dissuade the Sinjery Ghost from wasting her efforts by lingering in the mortal world. He decided that her soul was tied to the mortal world because she had felt her life was somehow incomplete at the moment she died. Perhaps she felt that saving a few people or killing one Dragon for the good of the Realm was all she needed to free herself from her obligations to the living. Rhazburn thought that if he could ease her mind, she would let go and move on to her just reward.

"Ringmistress," he said, "I, Rhazburn, will help you."

Her response was nothing like he expected. "Rhazburn? Loremaster Rhazburn? Slave to the Demon? Freer of Dragons? Slaughterer of all humankind?"

"I am Rhazburn, but..."

"Then you shall die!" With that word, she sprang at him, cleaving him in two with her Ghost sword.

Pain ripped through his arms, chest and heart where the Sinjery Sword passed. He staggered backward, but his spirit did not fall apart as would a material torso. The pain lingered, nauseatingly, just as if he had been struck by a sword in life. He crumpled to the ground as the Sinjery maiden took another swipe, this one meant to decapitate him. He was already doubled over, clutching his chest, when the sword sliced his neck, making him choke and gurgle.

Crying out in rage, the woman thrust her sword again and again through Rhazburn's aching heart until spectral tears rolled down his cheeks, and he sobbed piteously.

"Die you monster, die! Why won't you die?! Is the Demon's power so great that I cannot kill one criminal?" She twisted the sword in his chest, withdrew it, and hacked at him until, he thought, her pity at his wailing rose to the point it matched her rage. Finally, succumbing to pity, she seemed no longer able to raise her sword arm in anger. Visibly frustrated at her inability to kill Rhazburn and, perhaps in empathy to his crying, she, too, fell sobbing to the ground next to him. "Why can't you just die?" she whimpered.

"I am dead, Ringmistress."

"Then why don't you leave us? I waste my strength on you when there are lives to save."

"You, too, are dead, Ringmistress."

Bridling and bristling, infused with new vigor, she turned and began hacking him with her sword once more. Again, they were crying together both in pain and misery.

At long last, exhausted, both spirits shuddered their final sobs. Pain still lingered in Rhazburn's soul, paralyzing him, but he said, "I came back from Hell to set things right."

A laugh erupted from the Ringmistress, "No one can set things right. All is lost, and the world is doomed."

"I have fought Demons all my life. I am the only one who can defeat Sverdphthik."

"You are the one who caused this, Loremaster, Demon friend."

"I was tricked by the Demon into believing I was aiding the Dragonlord."

"You lie."

Rhazburn shook his head, "Words are useless. Only my actions will prove my intentions. Let me go, Ringmistress, and I promise to use all my powers to set things right in the Realm and for Sinjer."

"I do not believe you can or want to help us." She looked at him, the spectral tears drying slowly like they were real. "I now understand why my actions have been useless. I am truly dead, as are you. That I believe. I can see there is nothing I can do to alter what will come in this world." With that, she released her sword. With great care, she then removed her golden armor, laying it all in a neat pile next to her sword. Dressed only in a glowing golden gown, she raised her arms to the sky. "Mother Earth, retrieve your loyal servant. Let me walk in your Sky Forests."

Nothing happened.

"Mother Earth, am I not worthy?"

Nothing happened.

"Mother Earth, what must I do to be worthy to walk in the Sky Forests?"

Nothing happened.

The Ringmistress dropped her arms and visibly deflated. With a hiss, she spun on Rhazburn again. "This is your doing. I now know I am truly dead, but for some reason I must walk this cursed world forever, deprived of the reward of everlasting life with my Sisters in the Sky Forests."

Rhazburn had no explanation. Who could know what lay before one after death? All beliefs were hopes and theories. Until the moment came, no one knew what was beyond the barrier of death. All the Poets believed in Heaven and Hell as described in *The Transmigrant*. They peered into

Hell every day. Still, none of them really knew if Heaven existed for the good souls. Maybe all the blessed stayed in the world and wandered forever. Maybe the Demon had somehow twisted the fate of everyone in the world, consigning all those who died to wander unfulfilled so as to be prey for his purposes.

He looked at all the other wandering Ghosts. "Not all these people died in the last few fortnights. There are too many. The souls have been prevented from entering Heaven for hundreds of years. Perhaps Tundudil and the Mother of Earth have closed off Heaven and the Sky Forests because they fear the Demon could enter from here. I take that as a sign that I must find the Demon and send it back to Hell."

She snorted a laugh. "As simple as that, is it?"

"I never said that it would be simple. Only that it must be done."

"I don't believe you care about the world. Even if you did care, I don't believe any power can defeat the Demon. If all the strength of my Sisters was not enough, you, too, will fail."

"If I succeed, I believe you will have your reward and see your Sisters. I vow to you to try. If you see your Sister Jiminic, ask her about me."

"I will, if I see her. I finally understand. All the bright souls I see are spirits of the dead as I am. The wandering souls all seem as distressed as I was. Like me, few even realize they are no longer living." Her anger had dissipated, but she was not finished. "If you fail or are lying, sometime in the eternity ahead, I will find you. I will torture you forever. I will make this world your personal Hell."

Rhazburn understood the threat. She would use her sword and keep him in pain forever if he failed. If he failed he might as well go back to Hell and be tortured. He doubted he could evade her forever. She bent and took back her spectral sword. The spectral armor had already disappeared, as if only her interest in it made it exist.

As Rhazburn left the Sinjery Ghost, he began to try and reason out a strategy to accomplish his monumental task.

During the time he was in Garrith, his brother was still in control of his body, not Rhazburn. He was convinced that even a Demon could only command a live body for a brief period until the human spirit took back control. At the time Sverdphthik entered Jonathon and forced his limbs to strike Rhazburn with the Rod of Coercion, it had full control over Jonathon. If the Demon had not left Jonathon so quickly, Jonathon's own spirit would have learned how to suppress the power of the Demon. In time, Jonathon would have thrown the Demon out, just as Garrith had done to Rhazburn.

No, living bodies were not that useful to the Demon. It was dead bodies that were the Demon's trusted steeds, just like the corpse Sverdphthik had animated,. No soul remained in a corpse to rebel against the will of the Demon. Rhazburn had a theory that the Zombies Sverdphthik ruled could not exist far from the Demon, but he had no proof. Perhaps the animated dead bodies were controlled by Ghosts like Rhazburn. All the skeletons and the Zombie Lord Rhazburn fought beneath Devil's Fang could have been animated by Ghosts controlled by Sverdphthik, just as the Dragonlord had controlled the Dragons by the psychic link provided by the Dragoncrown. They never ventured far from the Demon because it did not allow them to, but perhaps they could. Maybe any Ghost like himself could use the physical body of a dead human. Even a dead animal.

Rhazburn was not about to desecrate a human body and use it to walk the world, but a dead animal was a different matter. Rhazburn was moving so slowly on his own. He felt an urgency to find a dead animal and see if he could use its limbs to walk in the mortal world and make better time. To fight the Demon, he would have to become a Demon himself.

The first dead animal that Rhazburn came across was a mouse by a brick wall in a puddle. It was fairly fresh, as dead mice go, with a drop of blood at its mouth. Its eyes were newly crusted over. As good a vessel as any for his tired soul, though a little small, Rhazburn thought. Maybe he would not fit.

At his first attempt to commandeer the dead rodent and take its body for his own use, he stepped on it. He felt a funny flutter in his incorporeal foot, but nothing else. He reached down and tried to pick the mouse up, but of course, he could not with his Ghost hand. He could get no purchase on the furry handful, but as his fingers moved, the legs of the mouse shifted slightly.

Rhazburn was certain that no Ghost could move anything very far in the mortal world. Only material beings could could move material objects. However, somehow, he reasoned, the Ghosts in the control of the Demon could inhabit dead humans and skeletons. When his fingers were superimposed on the limbs of the mouse, the mouse's limbs moved in concert with his spectral fingers. Still, he could not pick it up. He could play little games with it, placing four of his fingers in the mouse's legs like the mouse was a glove. Walking his fingers along the ground, he could make the dead mouse shuffle along with him, but it was not much help to him. All he could do was frighten someone with the animated dead mouse. He needed to move himself.

Being a Ghost or a Demon could be very frustrating in the solid world. Rhazburn thought back to his encounter with Garrith. Only when Garrith's spectral head had been coincident in space with his, had Rhazburn shared his thoughts. The same held true for the Ghost mother watching over her child. Not until her spirit head was superimposed on his, did he perceive her mind.

Rhazburn theorized that having his Ghost head in the mouse's dead brain would help him to possess the mouse's body. To test his theory, Rhazburn sprawled on the ground and lay his head over the mouse. In a moment, his perspective changed. From the level of the dirt through a yellowish screen, he saw the world gigantic above him. Something obscured his vision, so he fluttered his paws over his face, scratching off rheumy crusts from his eyes. Once free of the exudative veils, his visual acuity was slightly sharper. It was all blacks and grays, since he saw through the eyes of the mouse. Still, features were dulled. Even in the mouse's body, substance was blurred. Sound, too, was muffled, but he could better distinguish the speech of humans around him. He could still think like a human, but he had a notion that the feel of his short limbs and the lack of colors in his vision would get more and more familiar. Perhaps the human side of his thinking would gradually shrink and the animal in him would swell. Already, he had the feeling that he could silently crawl under the crack of a door or hide in a corner. Something like what he heard happened to Skin-Splicers. He had a glimmer of the appeal, abandoning oneself to the feral instincts of an animal, forgetting the troubles of the world. But for a disembodied spirit like Rhazburn, it might become permanent.

When he stood up on his four legs, he felt a grinding in his back, as if the bones were broken apart, out of place, the shattered ends tearing and popping past each other. The mouse must have fallen from the roof and splintered its back. Despite the discomfort of his disrupted anatomy, he could stand on his four feet. To his delight, he could even walk. The mouse's broken back was only a concern for living flesh. For a Demon like Rhazburn, willpower could move joints and muscles which could never function in life.

He took off at a run, realizing that a mouse had no other speed except running as fast as it could, fleeing predators real or imagined. Nearly as fast as a real mouse, he darted along building walls, freezing instinctively when someone's boot shook the ground too close. Luckily for Rhazburn, in ruined Isseltrent, footfalls were few and far between.

Cats, however, were rampant, since vermin like rats and Rhazburn were multiplying exponentially. He saw one cat, sitting on a sill, fixing her cold stare on him. Rhazburn ran on, surprised that his eyes, which were on the sides of his head, could see the cat dropping lightly to the ground behind him as he ran. Though he saw the cat behind him, he forgot to fear it, enthralled by his amazing peripheral vision and thinking for the moment like a man rather than a mouse.

The cat made a few long leaps and lunged, pinning Rhazburn to the ground with ten claws thrust though his dead flesh. As with the Sinjery's spectral sword, Rhazburn felt pain like ten knives skewering him. Ten more knives, the cat's teeth, met in his brain. Rhazburn fled the dead mouse, growing once more into the size of a man-Ghost. On the way to his proper size, his head passed through the mind of the cat. Rhazburn felt glee at having found a meal in the mouse.

Becoming a mouse, attacked by a cat, sharing thoughts with a cat, it was like some nightmare. A nightmare from which there was no waking and which he could remember in detail, every sliding, fractured bone, every claw through his back.

Rhazburn stopped in an alley and watched as his next vessel was prepared for him. A small boy fired a rock from a sling, hitting a pigeon in the head. It fell into a pile of bricks, where the boy had to abandon it as a gang of toughs threatened him.

Rhazburn tried again to commandeer the dead pigeon by laying his head on the pigeon's. As the pigeon's head was deformed from the slung rock, Rhazburn's vision was double. Still, he could stand on his two legs. His wings were intact. After a few false starts, Rhazburn learned how to fly and fluttered up to a rooftop. He landed artlessly on his chest, sliding into a small group of live pigeons. A few flew away in surprise. When he stood up, the others, startled by the sight of his crushed head, bolted as quickly as if he were a fox landing in their midst.

From the rooftop, Rhazburn surveyed his path east. Since his vision was double, he had to concentrate to keep the two worlds from swimming before him. When he separated the two Isseltrents, he saw only a few rooftops obscuring his view of the fire-scarred plains which led, after two score further leagues, to the Forbidden Mountains. He counted the rooftops and divided by two to compensate for his double vision. It wasn't far. At least not far as the dead pigeon flies, or so he thought.

Rhazburn the pigeon took off again, this time with enough experience to stay aloft, but he had a hard time concentrating on flying and seeing with his diplopia. It was hard work avoiding chimneys and rooftops coming at him in pairs, so his path was circuitous and confused. He took many stops on rooftops to reconnoiter and reconsider his erratic flight path.

With no experience in the phenomenon of feathered flight, Rhazburn had to work hard just to keep aloft. At first, he thought that surely he could move faster walking as a Ghost through the mire of the material world. But when he saw the rooftops sliding beneath him, he realized that he was moving much faster than he had imagined.

Soon, he was free of the city. Often, another pigeon would approach as if to flock with him, only to stop, hover, and dart away in alarm after viewing his smashed head. As he flew, Rhazburn noticed that his feathers, no longer glued by regenerating living tissue, broke off frequently from his lifeless wings. With each feather lost, his loft degraded, and he had to pump his wings faster to fly. This frenetic activity dislodged more feathers. One thing he was grateful for, as a Demon in a dead body, he never tired. Only living birds tired in the material world.

Just beyond the city, he landed, or rather crashed, into the top of a fire-blackened tree. Righting himself on the burnt branch, he looked out toward the plains where he saw movement. With fewer roaming Dragons those days, the populace was bolder, and Rhazburn could barely make out one wagon scurrying to the relative safety of a distant village. It was that village that Rhazburn made his target as he stretched his unfamiliar wings and jumped from his perch into the sky.

Soon, the wagon was directly below him. It was driven furiously, obviously anxious to reach the village. Its driver must have started out before the Green Dragon that Rhazburn had seen in the city had appeared. He probably wanted to get as much distance as possible between his wagon and Isseltrent, hoping the Dragon would concentrate on the city and leave him alone. The supplies he carried must have be critical for the village. Or perhaps the supplies were exceedingly valuable, and the driver thought he would make a handsome profit. Otherwise, he could have waited for a better time, like nighttime when the Dragons slept.

As he watched the wagon below him, Rhazburn heard the sound of rumbling thunder and saw the driver look up in terror. Before Rhazburn could put the two together, he was enveloped in bright-orange, searing flames.

Burning, Rhazburn plummeted from the sky and hit the ground. He suffered with every ember that charred the dead flesh of the pigeon. It was too much agony. He broke out of the pigeon and looked up. His pain lessened immediately. One thing the pain taught him. Get out of a tortured dead body as quickly as possible in the future.

Peering at the sky, Rhazburn saw that it was the Green Dragon who had bathed him with fire and knocked him from the sky. It swooped down to snap up one of the burning horses that writhed in pain on the ground. When the Dragon rose into the sky from his swoop, the poor horse's legs protruded from the Dragon's mouth. The legs gave two short kicks and were still. The Green sailed up high into the air, tossed the limp horse up, opened his maw, and swallowed it whole. It made short work of the second burning horse. Then it went after the man. His smoldering corpse lay beside the wreckage of the wagon. Just like Garrith had intimated, the Dragon swooped again, plucking the man from the dirt with his forefoot, holding him gently. Taking one look east to where the Demon apparently called, it flew like a gale toward the Dead Lands.

Rhazburn was once again bodiless. He slogged through the density of concrete reality. Through the fire-blasted plains, he saw no more dead animals that he could use as vessels for his soul. Every possible candidate had been gobbled up by starving predators and humans. He didn't even see a dead bug. One thing he did see, in the distance, was distinct human figures, wandering Ghosts like himself. He wondered if they even knew they were dead. Like the dead mother and the dead Sinjery he had encountered, maybe they just wandered around, trying to do in death what they had tried to do in life.

Was this all there was after life? Pacing the land, unseen by the living, wandering in despair? Or was there a wonderful paradise as was described in *The Transmigrant*? And could it really be all that different, even if there was some other afterlife? Rhazburn certainly knew what Hell was like. Wandering in the world forever would, for most, be preferable to that. Rhazburn thought even oblivion would be preferable to that. Could it be that all the Ghosts wandering the world were destined for Heaven, or Hell, or the Sky Forests, as the Sinjery believed? Or maybe it would be oblivion and the return of one's substance back to the substance of the world, as he had heard the Pixets believed. Despite his uncertainty about an afterlife, he had a feeling things were not as they were meant to be. He still felt that whatever was wrong with the workings of the world and the disposition of the dead was somehow tied to the Demon Sverdphthik. Much more hinged on the defeat of the Demon than he or any human had considered before. Nothing in the world would be right until the Demon was back in Hell. But how to accomplish that, especially when he was a wandering Ghost himself, that was a question he did not have an answer for.

Rhazburn's immediate goal was the Forbidden Mountains, but no matter how hard he strove ahead, they seemed impossibly distant. Evening came, but he had no need to eat or drink, having no real stomach to fill. Night came, but he had no need for sleep, having no flesh to tire. As to a need for dreams, all his world was a dream. A dream or a nightmare. He had had his fill of dreams.

More nights of marching toward his distant goal passed over him. They were brief reminders of the darkness of Hell, but this darkness was lit by moon and stars. It was a time of rest and peace instead of terror. Never before, while he was alive, had Rhazburn simply enjoyed the quiet calm of night. Walking so slowly, he had nothing to occupy his mind but the peace surrounding him. All the fighting and dying of people and Dragons were left behind in Isseltrent. Once he entered the far-flung farming communities of the Commonwealth of Dis, he found the Dragon forays to be infrequent. He presumed that the Dragons were ordered by Sverdphthik to concentrate on Isseltrent as the main threat to the Demon.

Sinjer, with thousands of battle-tested, bellicose Sinjery maidens, would be his next biggest threat, Rhazburn thought. Perhaps the Demon had relegated a company of Dragons to patrol Sinjer, burning off the ancient jungles and swamps, rooting out the maidens. Since many of the retired Sinjery had been Brandmistresses, the Dragons would not have an easy time subduing them.

Between fields of burnt stubble, Rhazburn began meandering through vast verdant meadows untouched by fire, clear evidence that he neared the lands protected by the Sylvets in the Forbidden Mountains. The Dead Lands had always stopped at the foot of the Forbidden Mountains. Rhazburn was one of the few who realized how false this protection had become. The surface of the Sylvets' land may have been free of the power of death, but beneath the mountains, in caves and excavated tunnels, the Ghouls lived by the thousands, preying upon the people living on the borders of the Commonwealth of Dis. He wondered if the town of Paradise had been spared by Sverdphthik, so his enthralled Ghouls could sate themselves on the pitiful souls that died there. He would never know, since his path was two score leagues north of that pathetic town.

Above his path at the crest of a black lava rock wall, a jack rabbit trembled and suddenly leaped two rods to the rocks below. Moments later, the head of a panting fox appeared above the cliff at the same place the jackrabbit had leapt from. The rabbit died the instant it hit the rocks, but the fox, still worried he'd lose his prey, anxiously searched for foot holds that could take him down the side of the cliff. Rhazburn saw the fox make up his mind and take the first tentative step from the safety of the crest.

Rhazburn debated a moment whether to steal the rabbit's body and deprive the hunter. There were other predators that needed sustenance, he decided. Where one fox went hungry, another would find the rabbit's body and feed her young with it after Rhazburn had finished with it. While the fox picked his careful way down the cliff face, Rhazburn settled into the jackrabbit's body and felt a surge of strength. The rabbit, freshly killed, still had a vital energy that Rhazburn could feel. With a shudder as to what he was becoming, he tried to suppress the thought of how good a newly-dead body felt. Any Demon like himself would relish and long for that feeling. None of the Ghosts he had seen had any idea that they could use dead bodies and run faster than they had in life.

Rhazburn could justify his possession an animal's body for a time to bring about a greater good, but he also knew that was a trap for his soul. Even though he fashioned himself a spy for reality in the nether plane, how different was he really from the Ghouls in the Forbidden Mountains? He was not much different. Maybe they deserved his help as much as the people of Isseltrent. In a way, their perversion was just another manifestation of the possession of their souls by Sverdphthik.

As Rhazburn ran ahead, studying the tall grass ahead for obstacles, the jackrabbit's remarkable peripheral vision allowed him to clearly see activity almost directly behind him. He could watch the frustrated fox trying to clamber down the cliff behind him while he watched his footing ahead. Desperate, the fox tried to leap to an outcropping much too far away. It fell the last half rod. It got up very slowly from the rocks and tried to scramble over a boulder just to take another tumble. Now the fox, too far away from Rhazburn to give effective chase, turned and trotted away. He would look for easier prey.

Only as a pigeon flying had Rhazburn moved so quickly. The grass of the plains was a blur at his sides. Twice, small predators leaped after him, only to be left with a kick of dust in the face. Again, the days and nights passed without meals or sleep, and before long, he came to a river he recognized as the Goldflow.

Rhazburn realized that he could run along the bank and his path would eventually lead into the Forbidden Mountains. All the Goldflow's tributaries came from those mountains. He seemed to have slightly muddled thoughts, as if he were becoming more rabbit-like in his thinking. From what was left of his human mind, he remembered a map. He reasoned that he sought the Thistletumble, a tributary that led back up deep into the Forbidden Mountains.

Rhazburn's strength was inexhaustible, but the dead limbs of the rabbit were driven far beyond their capacity. Even in life, a rabbit's limbs were made for short bursts of speed to escape predators quickly and find a hiding place. After running for four days, his rabbit feet were becoming tattered by gravel and worn away by the constant pounding. Then he hit a stone with a forelimb, breaking it severely. Sharp fractured bones protruded though torn fur. His pace was slowed considerably. He limped on, but knew he could no longer evade predators. Purposefully, he stayed near the Goldflow to have a clear route into the canyons the river had gouged through the Forbidden Mountains.

It wasn't long before a hidden marten erupted from a bush and grabbed him with its clever claws. Rhazburn gave up the rabbit when he felt the squeeze of those little hands.

He turned toward the Goldflow, inhaling deeply before submerging himself in the swirling, silt-ridden current. As a Ghost, the deep breath was superfluous, but it came to him by instinct.

Completely submerged, walking against the current was no harder than walking on land through the plains. Full of silt, the water constantly surprised him by hurling branches or fish at him out of the murk. Once, a trout swam from behind him right through his stomach, oblivious to Rhazburn but intent on a higher, cooler pool buzzing with sweeter flies.

Rhazburn climbed slowly up the river through the foothills and into the Forbidden Mountains proper. At this point, he left the Goldflow taking a hard right turn into the Thistletumble which diminished considerably in width and depth but became faster. Clear bubbly water churned through gaps between boulders.

As he plodded up a particularly steep rapids, a ragged dead trout, staring with opaque eyes, rolled into him. Rhazburn immediately grasped the trout with his will and soon was in the fish's body. It was another amazing way to move, swimming upstream, floating through blue pools, jumping up cackling cataracts, and wiggling between slimy weeds. As a fish, he swam much faster than he could trudge through the rivers and streams as a Ghost. Eventually, he came to a waterfall far too high to leap. It was then he decided to leave the fish's body and move out again into the air and the world he knew better.

But there he was hindered. The cliff over which the Thistletumble fell was a wall blocking his way. It was much too steep to climb. Looking to either side, Rhazburn saw the cliff receding into obscure distance.

He stood and thought. He had walked through boulders and stone walls in Isseltrent. Why not a mountain? When he lifted his hand, his arm passed into the rock as easily as it passed through the air or the water.

Rising before him were the western ramparts of the mountains, covered with layered shale and lined with water trickles. But inside the rock, that was a mystery. There were leagues of unseeable, unknowable rock ahead. Would he get lost? Still, there was nothing else to be done.

Without a further thought, Rhazburn placed a foot into the rock and strode through the face of impenetrable cliff like it was an open door. This door, however, led to a world of his own. A world unshared by anyone. Even the other spirits had better sense than to wander in solid rock. As he walked, he could sense nothing alive, but, strangely, traces did remain of living beings from long ago. Empty shells and stone shadows of articulated sea creatures swam around him as he passed from shale to slate. He found the walking strangely calming. He walked on and on, on into the granite mountain core, peppered with crystals.

This gloomy world, too, seemed to be masked by a veil, though it should have been black and unseeable as the back of his own head. Instead, there was something like light, or maybe it was some other sensation of the spirit mind, that allowed him to distinguish texture, veins and crystals. It was as if he had taken a sledgehammer, long as the mightiest tree and cracked the mountain wide open, exposing all its secrets. His father had been a miner long before he became a jeweler. When Rhazburn was young, Jonathon had taught him all about the rocks and minerals that were the foundation of the world they stood upon. Jonathon would have loved to gaze at the rocks from within, as Rhazburn was now doing.

With his ghostly eyes, he could see it all, even if it were murky. The layers of rock were like pieces of a puzzle but crushed together with a massive pressure he could actually feel. The tension and stresses of the rock were transmitted to his spirit self as easily as the sensations in the limbs of the dead animals he had borrowed. To find his way, Rhazburn had a notion that he needed to feel and understand the structure of the rock, understand the way the seams led, the flow of the stress in the rock, and the order of the layers. Once he discovered what the pressures in the mountain meant, he would be able to discern whether to move through layers of rock against the grain or travel parallel to them, using them as a guide. He would be able to map out the best path to the Dead Lands.

All directions were a possibility, up and down included. With minimal effort of his incorporeal body, he could step upward or downward whenever he pleased. His movement was still slow in the mortal world, but not really any slower than when he walked on a road. There were, in truth, amazing powers and knowledge available to this spirit state of his.

Quickly, or so it seemed to Rhazburn, though time was nothing in the heart of rock where there were no clues as to the passage of days, he learned how to properly follow the veins of ore and joints of stress. He became increasingly assured that he knew the way to the Dead Lands. By constantly adjusting the direction of his travel, he tried to stay within the mountain substance and avoid the open air unless he became perplexed. If he found himself following a vein of feldspar when it should have been limestone and he was unsure as to the direction of his travel, he broke free from the rock and stepped out into a valley to get a feel for which direction he walked. More likely than not, he would step out of the mountain far above the valley floor. Even at those times, he could usually spy the deep dark valley of the Dead Lands in the distance, creeping ever closer as he proceeded.

The longer Rhazburn walked inside the rock, the more he gained confidence in the immutable solidity of the innards of the mountain. They were supremely unaffected by the troubles on the surface of the world. The rock was far older than the Demons that seemed eternal to humans. Encased in rock, he knew he could rest and forget everything. Here, in the center of the mountains, only peace and quiet existed. Alone as he was, that fantasy, that he could just stop and be at peace forever, was tempting.

He stopped for a few moments and enjoyed the absolute stillness. He was alone, but he still had his thoughts. Thoughts and memories. For his whole life, Rhazburn had been a loner. He had friends, a few, and a family who was important to him but whom he seldom visited. Not until he was dead did he understand the need for others in his life. Now, cleaved from his body, from the world and the people he knew, all he could think of was to spend every ounce of his strength healing the world for all those people he had ignored in his life. Peace and quiet was for another life. He had a good reason to move on.

For another reason, too, he forced himself to move onward. Something had been left undone, incomplete. Something in the world had bested Rhazburn. That could never be. Like battling the Demons at Hell's Breach, it had all started as a game to him, finding the Unicorn Horn, making the plans for the Rod of Coercion. Failing the purpose of that, his life ended justifiably. For a decade, "Loremaster Rhazburn" had been synonymous with "Champion of Good". His new name, "Demon's Friend", was intolerable. He would never take his eternal rest until he and what others called 'the traitor' Jonathon Forthright were vindicated.

For a moment, he entertained the idea that if he rose at the right spot on the surface of the mountains, he might be able to locate the Sylvets or get some news of his father and his travels. Garrith had told him before he left that their father had teamed up with Trallalair and Hili. He also said that their father and the Sinjery had ventured into the Jungle, and afterward, Molgannard Fey's power in the city was eliminated. The rumor that Jonathon and Trallalair had together cleansed the city of the blight of the Giant and his minions was too fantastic for Rhazburn to believe. Unquestionably, Trallalair could have handled herself in that den, but his father was not a fighter. He would have been killed in an instant. Still, Rhazburn suspected there was much to his father that could be surprising to his son and even to Jonathon himself. He had been willing to enter the Chamber of the Wishing Drop. Maybe he was just desperate enough to take on the Giant.

Rhazburn pondered the rest of his journey as he began walking again. Within the mountain, Rhazburn measured his progress by steps. With his ponderously slow movement in Isseltrent as a guide, Rhazburn calculated that he had fifty thousand steps, or nearly a fortnight of travel, before he would get to the eastern border of the Forbidden Mountains. With little else to occupy his mind, he began counting his steps and monitoring his progress. For days, he followed veins of lead, copper, silver, and gold deeper and deeper into the center of the range. Fossils and crystals whispered to him of eons past. They spoke of fiery volcanoes spitting red hot lava, of earthquakes rending mountains apart. Deep purple, bright red, sea blue and leaf green crystals, once plain rock, had been crushed by the pressure of mountains of rock over thousands of years into their vibrant forms. Those same pressures extruded mountains from the bowels of the world over thousands of millennia like putty squeezed from a closing fist.

He couldn't say exactly how he knew when he passed the midpoint. Maybe it was a sense that the majority of the cracks and layers tilted up before him like the eastern-facing slopes he sought. Maybe it was the changing sense of pressure he felt in the rock. It had been continuously building. Now, finally, it seemed to slowly lessen. He should have known exactly where he was because he had tried to count the steps he took. He had lost count, enthralled by the marvels he passed through. Maybe his calculating mind had subliminally counted for him, and he unconsciously knew he was more than half way.

No matter what the reason, he knew it was time to go up and see the sun once again. With no effort at all, he climbed in the rock as if a staircase had been placed beneath his feet. Willpower alone was all he needed to change his direction in the granite from horizontal to vertical. The climb was no faster or slower than walking anywhere in the material world. He felt a whole day passed before he reached a small outcropping of rock facing the rising sun.

As he emerged from his rocky womb, the forbidding desolation of the Dead Lands lay just beyond the fastness of the mountains. A strange desire came upon him as he gazed upon the Dead Lands. The desolation beckoned him, a lodestone of death to one who depended upon death. Deep within his soul, he perceived a gaping maw out ahead of him swallowing souls as it sucked life, breath, and spirit from the land. Even a score of leagues away, he felt that suction on his soul. Before, he was walking against a wind to get away from Hell. All the time, that ethereal wind was blowing him backward to where his soul belonged. Now, within sight of the Dead Lands, that wind had waned or, more properly, turned to push him toward Sverdphthik. If only he could ride those winds, he would confront the Demon much quicker. As a spirit, he was certainly light enough. Until the sun was high in the sky, he stood studying the misty mountains and snowy passes between him and his goal. Nothing lifted him up. He still had to find his own way.

Beside him, a small brown bird lit, pecking at seeds shed from a clump of grass. Rhazburn had an unholy urge to enter the bird's mind and cause it to smash itself against a boulder just so he could use its dead body. What was the death of one more animal in the world with thousands of deaths behind and thousands ahead? If Rhazburn didn't stop the Demon, what difference was one more death? If he were walking alive in the mountain passes and he were hungry, he would think nothing of killing the bird for food. But, somehow this was different. Taking possession of a living thing, while it looked on helplessly, seemed heinous to him. It was, Rhazburn remembered, just what had happened to Jonathon.

The seduction of his power constantly tugged at his principles. He could not allow the urgency of his quest tempt him to degenerate into a replica of the thing he fought against. Indirectly, he was responsible for thousands of deaths, but he refused to directly cause one more death, even that of a lowly beast, even if it could bring him closer to a worthy goal. He had already made the biggest mistake he could by helping his father make the Rod of Coercion. There was no need to compound it.

There were still ways Rhazburn could proceed. As a Ghost, he could walk straight down the precipitous slope in front of him without fear of falling. Without the human need for carefully following switch backs down the slopes, his path would be far shorter.

As if to reward him for his moral resolve, Rhazburn soon chanced upon a fallen vulture laying on a pinnacle. Its neck was broken, but its wings were relatively intact, with plenty of feathers to catch the wind. Rhazburn negotiated his way through rocky corridors and took the proffered body. At the top of the pinnacle, gazing to the valley floor far below him, he flapped his broad wings furiously. His feet barely rose. He tried again but just didn't have the technique right. Since he stood at the edge of a cliff custom made for a first flight, he hopped off and extended the wings. He imagined hands trying to grab hold of the air. It worked. His wings ballooned to their full extent, and he settled on an invisible plane of air. He glided quietly on between gauzy peaks softened by fog.

In a clearing of the clouds, a bright plateau gleamed in the sun. As he passed above it, a warm updraft pushed him upward, higher than the peaks. He was exhilarated by the perspective of mountains below wrapped in mist. With more experience, he found he could manage to stay aloft easily. Anytime his height was degraded by cool air weighing him down, he could recognize, by subtle signs of swirling mist, where to go and which way to tilt his wings to find the hot spots for updrafts to lift him higher. By the time the sun was setting behind him, Rhazburn had traveled to the eastern edge of the mountain range.

Sverdphthik's land lay ahead. The dry land was blackened by the long black fingers of the evening mountain shadows. He sensed that no rain fell on this desolate place. There with its strength increased by all the death it caused, the Demon seemed capable of altering the weather to suit its whims. Already, he could feel the tug of Sverdphthik's dark power inhaling all life.

As the sun set behind him and before he chanced an encounter with the strength of the Demon's soul-swallowing maelstrom, he lit on a dead tree. At the very least, he wanted to wait until morning to be able to see what lay ahead in the Demon's land. Life was in the lands behind him. He would see only death from there on. So he waited, a dead vulture sitting upon a dead branch, in the dead of night, before entering the Dead Lands.

CHAPTER 30

THE HELLPIT

Rhazburn slept not a wink. Of course, Demons, like him never slept. The pull of Sverdphthik's Hellpit felt like a siren song, urging him onward. He fell from the tree and grabbed air with his wings to ride the currents toward the middle of the Dead Lands. Soaring high in the sky, he gazed upon sterile rocks, gravel, sand, and dust, seeing no sign that any living thing existed in the world. A few stark boles with time-blasted branches clawed the sky, but nothing stirred except anemic dust devils, and even they died quickly. Sverdphthik's Demonic presence had even driven clouds from the sky. The Demon had cursed the land for a score of leagues around him. His thirst for power had sucked the land dry of life.

Flying for Rhazburn was much easier that day, as if he had a tailwind coaxing him right down the Demon's throat. Rhazburn had no confidence that his tenuous spirit could survive confronting Sverdphthik without some magical help. He had a feeling that Sverdphthik would eat what was left of him like some crumb it dropped.

His intent was to scout out and assess the Demon's weaknesses, if it had any, which was unlikely. He knew that if he got within range of the Rod of Coercion and the Demon used it on him, he would be lost, like all the others. Although he had no demonstration of it, he calculated that the Rod of Coercion could control the Ghosts inhabiting the world just as it controlled live humans.

In the back of his mind was a hope, albeit a tiny one, that he would find his father. Surely, after all this time, Jonathon, too, was lost. Rhazburn had taken at least a fortnight on his journey from Hell's Breach to the environs of Sverdphthik's Hellpit. If Trallalair was leading her father here with all the resources of the Dragonlord to aid her, she probably had a Flying Carpet to speed her journey. They had probably confronted the Demon long before, for good or ill. Since Rhazburn could literally feel the evil presence of the Demon off in the distance, he doubted that she and his father had had much success.

His father dead? Trallalair dead? He should be overcome with sadness, but there was nothing like grief within his ethereal body. His emotions had been dulled. He had felt pain and anguish when the Sinjery maiden had attacked him. He had felt some weird pain of the spirit when the dead animal bodies he used were attacked. He had certainly felt terror as a spirit in Hell. But at that moment, Rhazburn felt nothing. Perhaps his spirit could feel beyond the material plane and he could sense Jonathon and Trallalair were in existence as Ghosts in the ethereal plane of existence. And thus he felt no need to grieve. Or maybe his real human emotions were just wasting away with no living human body to support them. If his emotion wasted away, dribble by dribble, perhaps his motivation would peter out as well. Then his motivation for even thinking would disappear and he would just wink out of existence. That thought alone was enough to motivate him again. If his father and Trallalair were anywhere, dead or alive, he must help them.

Rhazburn knew he could have helped them if he had gone with his father on his almost hopeless mission. All of them together would have had a much better chance at defeating the Demon. With Hili along, with his father's ability to make gems, and with Rhazburn's knowledge of the verses engraved in the Jewel of Nishbad, they would have even had an opportunity to entrap the Demon and take him back to Hell's Breach, thus ridding the world of him forever. But Rhazburn was a Ghost alone in the material world and would have to come up with another plan.

Rhazburn continued to soar fluidly over the Dead Lands. Thermals abounded. With no vegetation to interfere with the unclouded rays of the sun baking the desert below, hot air constantly buoyed him up. In the distance ahead, he could already see movement and the object of his quest gleaming brighter than the desert in the High Day sun. Through the mists of his Ghost vision, he saw huge beasts flapping wings, circling an area that pulsated with spectral sparks swarming about a center that held them like flies lured by a foul smell to carrion.

Some of the tiny sparks trooped away in long lines like columns of ants leaving the anthill to return bearing sustenance for the Demon. Coasting on the thermals above the columns, Rhazburn saw that they were really Ghosts cloaked in dead bodies they had stolen. Zombies glowing perceptibly brighter than the sun to Rhazburn's spiritual sight. The spirits that motivated the Zombies were never quite covered by the foreign flesh they animated, so he saw spectral auras around all of them. There were free Ghosts as well, walking without the aid of tainted flesh. The ones leaving the Demon's Hellpit walked slowly, straining against the pull of the Demon's power. Those returning seemed to be dragging captured spirits that they had probably subdued for their ruler. The returnees walked rapidly, as if descending a slope instead of the perfectly flat plain they were on. Such was the attraction of enslaved souls to the Demon's Hellpit.

Above them all, dozens of live Dragons soared. Rhazburn knew that they were dying, like everything that entered the Dead Lands. Because of their bulk and the magic they generated, they were more resistant of the Demon's curse. Still, a score of Dragon corpses lay cast off from Sverdphthik's minions. None of them moved. Likely, they were much too large for a Ghost like Rhazburn to inhabit.

Thousands of Zombie birds flew toward the Hellpit. Thousands more flew outward. Together, they were mingling droplets in a cloud over the Hellpit. Rhazburn realized that he could fly in as if he was one of them. In actuality, he *was* one of them. All he lacked was enslavement to the Demon.

Rhazburn joined the congregation. Soaring inward within that cloud of Zombie birds became progressively easier as he got closer to the center of the Hellpit. It was like he was sliding down a slippery slope into a volcano spewing sulfurous death.

On closer examination, the birds returning to the Demon's fold became crazed. They seemed to be filled with a fury to blindly attack the Zombie birds leaving Sverdphthik's presence. Those leaving were weakened, while those approaching Sverdphthik became progressively stronger and more aggressive, lashing out at anything they met. Screams of pain began mounting like the howling of a gale. They were not mortal screams. If that were the case, they would have been muffled for Rhazburn, like all sounds from the mortal world. No, these were screaming spirits like the ones he had heard in Hell. The sounds pierced Rhazburn with knives of fear. They all screamed in pain or fury. The sight and the sound was horrible. Dead birds, already ragged with decay, were being ruthlessly ripped apart as their corroded feathers and bones sprinkled down onto the dusty plain.

Regardless of this violent display, Rhazburn felt himself inexplicably drawn to it. He could feel the Demon's power infesting him, darkening his soul. As he flew in the mob, he fought the urge to join the fray. Some repressed, angry part of him swelled uncontrollably like a bizarre obsession. If he didn't veer off immediately before the sadistic attraction became be too strong to resist, he, too, would be one of the lost, evil souls in their multitude.

Rhazburn would fly no closer. He wheeled away toward a tall peak that he could easily see because of his altitude. The peak stood out at the southern end of the Forbidden Mountains. It was Devil's Fang.

Before he could leave the chaotic area, a cluster of small birds spotted him and broke off from the mass toward him. With his spirit tainted by the Demon's subliminal summons, Rhazburn saw their approach as a challenge and an opportunity to vent his anger at the wickedness he saw. He started at them. A moment later, recognizing the sadistic pleasure he anticipated, he was horrified at own his thoughts. Rhazburn pulled up before he attacked the approaching birds. He tilted and soared to the south, barely resisting the gut-wrenching hatred that urged him to turn back and tear apart the smaller birds. After all, they were carrion, and he was a vulture, a carrion eater, he rationalized. His habitation of the vulture allowed him to experience instincts implanted in the carrion eater's brain, suppressing what still remained of his humanity. The instinct gripped him as did the sadism welling out of the Hellpit. At that moment, he knew that his soul had little power to resist the passions of animal instinct and anger augmented by the Demon's Hellpit. He flapped furiously, turning to evade those little birds. He saw the auras that were smeared on their wretched little bodies. He loathed them and longed to eat them, but his fear of becoming one of them was stronger still.

As he flew away, the small birds mobbed him, pecking and clawing away bits of his dead flesh. With each attack there was pain and mounting fear. The deranged spirits within the birds struck him at the command of the Demon. Rhazburn croaked at them through the vulture's withered larynx.

Rhazburn flew away southward raggedly. He was fighting a spiritual head wind, but he was getting far enough away from Sverdphthik's fountain of sadism to be able to reason again. His soul had nearly been lost like it had been in Hell, but his mind had saved him just in time.

His theory that his emotions were disappearing had been disproved by his proximity to the Demon. Apparently, there existed a distress of the spirit like that he felt in Hell. It was different but just as powerful as the emotions of the flesh. Once Rhazburn's reason suppressed his spectral passions, he outdistanced the mobbing birds. They did not seem to have the fortitude to fly too far away from the source of their strength. They were already lost souls and had no will left to fight against their sadistic anger or act on their own.

Rhazburn had again learned that no one could resist the awesome power of the Demon without magical help. At Jonathon's workshop, Sverdphthik's power had been sufficient to vanquish them, but he knew it was diminished, mostly contained in the corpse it animated. It was too far from its source of strength, its Hellpit, to twist their souls like it could in the Dead Lands. Here, at its epicenter, Sverdphthik's power was boundless. Clearly, its power increased with the suffering it caused here. Perhaps pain and terror were sustenance to Sverdphthik like food and water were to the living. With every scream, every sob, its power increased. Any soul brought to its loathsome Hellpit was lost as surely as if the soul had entered Hell itself. Only the Demon's complete elimination could end that pariah.

Rhazburn already had a plan to find magical help to defeat the Demon. His goal was a cavern beneath Devil's Fang, the one polluted by the Zombie Lord of the Clan of the Laughing Skull. Among the skeletons he fought with when he first liberated the Unicorn Horn, he would raise his own army. He had fled the cavern through a cave that exited into the Dead Lands. During his flight from the Zombie Lord, he wore the Cloak of Invisibility and had been ignored by all, even the spirits enslaved to the Zombie Lord. Somehow, the invisibility extended into the ethereal world as well as the practical world. He knew exactly where the cloak was buried, in a stand of scrub on the west side of Devil's Fang, far from any human habitation. No humans ever ventured onto Devil's Fang, especially now, and the Ghouls beneath seldom wandered outside except to collect the dead from towns like Paradise for their cannibalistic feasts.

Halfway to Devil's Fang, one of his corpse-wings broke off. Being a dozen rods off the ground when it happened, Rhazburn plummeted and hit the ground with such velocity that the vulture exploded on impact, bursting into feathers, bones, and rotten flesh. It was not a pleasant experience. He hit head first.

A few dozen Favors later, when his head stopped throbbing, he realized that he had to walk the rest of the way to the far side of Devil's Fang to find the Cloak of Invisibility. It was still a dozen leagues to the southern end of the Forbidden Mountains, and once again, he walked in mire against the pull of the Demon. The journey looked to him to take a fortnight if he did not come across a corpse. In the Dead Lands, he had little hope of that. All the corpses had been commandeered already by Sverdphthik's minions.

On the ground, he came across dozens of other Ghosts enthralled to the Demon. Some were dressed in Zombie rot, some were empty spirits, eyes glazed in apathetic stupor. Most of them let him be, but one, full of spite, challenged him. She rode within a crippled Unicorn's corpse. The dead Unicorn was a magnificent one, a half rod tall at the eyebrows, with a horn almost as long as he was tall. She was the Ghost of a Ghoul, warped from birth, who thought torture the proper way of life, so she considered herself an ally to the Demon rather than its slave.

The first indication Rhazburn had that the Ghost was behind him was a spear erupting painfully through his chest. It was the Unicorn's white spiral horn. Even as a Ghost, he felt the thrust of the Unicorn

Horn. Ethereality did not protect him from the power of Unicorn ivory. Rhazburn could see it shimmer with an arcane glow. He had felt the power of a Unicorn Horn when he fought the Ghosts animating the skeletons in the Zombie Lord's chamber, but at that time he was not on the receiving end. Back then, he used the Unicorn Horn he had stolen against other Ghosts inhabiting skeletons. Never did he imagine one would be used against him in the same way.

"I know you, Poet and traitor to my Master," said the female Ghost from inside the Unicorn. "Does the Great Master send you?" The voice was Screela's. Rhazburn was impaled on the horn, completely in her power. The Unicorn Horn was agonizing in his chest.

"I think you are running from him. This time you chose the wrong direction. You wanted a Unicorn Horn, Traitor. Now you have one. You think you are in pain now? Wait until my Master has his way with you."

The Unicorn began to run, limping but determined, and many times faster than Rhazburn could have walked. It was that clear Screela ran, not back toward the Demon's Hellpit but toward the domain of the Laughing Skull Clan. Little did Screela know she was assisting her sworn enemy in his only hope to battle the "Great Master". He'd have to revise his plans, this time without the aid of the Cloak of Invisibility. He made his new goal the lair of the Zombie Lord.

"For many days, I plotted how I would take revenge on you for stealing such power from my Master. I never thought I'd find you, disembodied, running from the Great One. It took me a long time to find this Unicorn. I had to fight to take it, but I won in the end. My Master is one of the Chosen, and soon, I will be, too. I already share his power. Soon the Waiting will worship me!"

Rhazburn assumed "the Waiting" comprised living humans, probably at least the Ghouls but maybe all living humans.

Every stride of the Unicorn was a shock to his chest, but Rhazburn endured it to ride along much quicker toward his goal. He was amazed that the horn did not simply slice through his nothingness. Instead, he remained impaled the whole distance. The pain in his chest made it hard for him to plan his escape, so he quit worrying about it, relying on his ability to ad lib at the last moment.

For two days and two nights the dust flew from the Unicorn's hooves. Had she not been limping, they would have made it in one. On the morning of the third day, the steep eastern face of the Forbidden Mountains rose above them. Wind-polished granite mirrored the awakening sanguine sun. With two days of agonizing pain in his chest, Rhazburn had degenerated into a twitching, tortured spirit. He had become oblivious to time and place. Nothing remained of his awareness but repeated shocks of pain radiating from his chest to every part of his soul.

When he realized that the Forbidden Mountains loomed near, cliffs he recognized from when he fled the Zombie Lord's chamber, he forced consciousness back upon himself. The horn was a spear through his chest, but just as the Unicorn Horn could impale his spirit, so, too, did he have the ability to grasp the horn. Unlike most other material objects, the Unicorn Horn existed in the ethereal plane as well as the material plane, hence its magical power.

He knew Screela saw his every move, but she could do little to stop him. With all the spectral strength he could muster, he grasped the Unicorn Horn as far forward as he could. Even though the result was a sensation of being ripped apart, he pulled on the horn sliding himself up toward the end. Screela stopped and reared up on her hind legs to make him slide down toward her head, but he hung on and stayed in place. It was not very difficult. As a spirit, he weighed nothing. When her front feet hit the ground again, Rhazburn repeated the process until he was only inches from the deadly tip of the Unicorn Horn. She reared again. Again, he resisted the pull of gravity, holding tight to the few inches protruding from his chest. As her front feet hit the ground a second time, Rhazburn reached for the horn behind him and with a final heave, pushed himself off the tip with the sensation that he left his heart still dangling from the horn. He fell to the ground and rolled, barely missed by the Unicorn Horn thrusting down into the ground where he had just fallen. Before Screela could extricate the horn from the dirt and recover to give chase, Rhazburn ran with his spectral, dreamlike slowness toward the cliffs of the Forbidden Mountains.

A black hole sank into the cliff directly before him. It was the exit from the cave of the Laughing Skull Clan and their Zombie Lord. The Unicorn was up, shaking her horn free of clay, galloping at him with her horn pointing at his back. He dodged to the side, but Screela hardly missed a step. Instead of turning to run after him, she ran to the cave opening and stood sentry, probably thinking the cave was the obvious place for Rhazburn to cower. She would be right, of course. The cave led to the Zombie Lord's cavern, and that was his new goal.

She stamped and snorted in anger as he turned off, approaching instead the granite of the cliff. He walked up to the cliff face and stepped inside. The movements of the Unicorn were lost to him once he was inside the rock, but he knew the Unicorn could not move through the substance of the rock like he could. Unfortunately, he had underestimated the power of the Unicorn Horn. It crashed through the granite like a knife through cheese, barely missing his head. Rhazburn delved deeper into the granite. He felt tremors as the Unicorn Horn thrust repeatedly into the rock, but it was by then too far away to skewer him. Rhazburn was deep within the granite. As long as Screela did not attempt to follow him into the granite of the tunnel wall, he was safe. He was wagering his soul that she would prefer to race down to the chamber of the Zombie Lord in order to intercept him. Within the rock, he had no clue as to whether he would even notice the approach of another spirit. Though uncertain of his safety, he chose to continue on, hoping his practiced knowledge of how to move through the rock mass was enough to leave Screela behind, even if she chose to enter the tunnel wall.

Rhazburn walked onward, feeling his direction to the cavern of the Zombie Lord as he had sensed his path through the Forbidden Mountains. Following the course of the tunnel was relatively simple. The tunnel had been roughly hewn over the centuries by Zombies and Ghouls. They had probably chipped away at it, using other rocks or sledgehammers. Since the tunnels through the hard granite had been bored by amateurs, there was no consideration for the natural lines of stress which Rhazburn could easily perceive. Thus, the mountain surrounding the tunnel had been weakened by their delving. Cracks fanned out from the tunnel like wounds, easily marking the way Rhazburn must travel. When he was uncertain of the path, Rhazburn stopped and caressed the buckling rock, sensing the direction of the stress. Thus, he navigated through the mountain by a refined sense of spectral touch.

Since he perceived no pursuit, he suspected that Screela had run to the Zombie Lord and his ghostly henchmen. Surely, they would be alerted to his approach. After his flight from the treasure chamber the last time, he hoped she would expect him to go anyplace but there. In actual fact, the very center of the Zombie Lord's domain was the only place in all the vast caverns that would serve Rhazburn's purposes. With any luck, the Zombie Lord had sent his slaves through the other tunnels to search for him, freeing up the chamber from much of the danger to Rhazburn. Still, he would have to be cagey, staying unobserved until the time was right.

Before long, Rhazburn noticed that the small cracks around the tunnel became distinct fissures, signaling a much more expansive section of the tunnel. It could only mean that he was nearing the treasure chamber of the Zombie Lord. With his memory of the layout of the Zombie's chamber, Rhazburn sidled around somewhere behind the great pile of treasure that had held the Unicorn Horn when he first confronted the Zombie Lord. He assumed that they could not see him inside the wall of rock unless they, too, entered. Even if the thralls of the Zombie Lord realized that they could pass through solid rock, the mountain was much too large to be searched from top to bottom for one soul. He thought that they would, at worst, cluster around their lord to protect him. Taking a chance on being seen, he stuck his head out of the wall.

His judgment, for once, had been flawless. His spectral head emerged on the opposite side of the treasure pile from the Zombie Lord's throne. He stared at coins, goblets, costly trinkets, and jewel-encrusted weapons before him. At his feet were scattered bones, some of which had probably lain there since his battle with the skeletons when he stole the Unicorn Horn.

Carefully, he searched the treasure pile, praying that what he sought was outside so he would not have to noisily extract it from the pile. After he moved his position halfway around, almost in view of the Zombie Lord, he spotted a gold-hilted sword with an untarnished blade. It had no doubt been stolen centuries before, but lying in there, it was protected from the elements by layers of rock. A diamond ring was nearby, as were dozens of other rings. He could hear the activity of Ghosts in the chamber. Above their noise was the unmistakable pleading of Screela. She beseeched the Zombie Lord to protect himself from a renegade spirit that meant to destroy his lovely perfection. Rhazburn thought it more like putrefaction than perfection.

He saw no need to confront the other inimical spirits until he was ready, so he faded back into the granite and stayed, biding his time until the initial alarm was over and the normal daily work of corrupting souls proceeded. Again, there was no measure of time for Rhazburn, so he planned his assault inside the wall for as long as he needed. He plotted his every move for the days to come, every action he must take to harass and bring down the Demon. The details swam in his mind until he was sure of his scheme. When that scheme was perfect, he peered out again into the chamber. All was quiet, but he sensed the presence of many spirits attending the Zombie Lord.

The sword and the diamond ring had not changed positions. From the broken bones on the chamber floor, he chose only a hand and lay his own hand upon it feeling the ability to move the fingers as he had moved the limbs of the dead animals he had possessed. Using the skeletal hand as his own, he could not lift it from the floor of the cave since he had no arm, no shoulder, no backbone. The hand would have to do by itself for a while. He walked it on fingertips to one of the diamond rings, grasping it between a boney thumb and forefinger. Much slower now, with only three fingers still available to walk his skeletal hand, he took the hand and the ring to the bright blade. It was a precious sword, probably worn by a duke or a king of another land.

With the diamond between his boney thumb and forefinger, he slowly scratched onto the steel of the blade, "Light sprinkled from Mother Moon caresses a hare's trembling whiskers." It was an experiment in spells on a weapon affecting the spirit. Experiments of the sort were easily conceived, though in the real world, the objects they empowered were absolutely useless. The concept had been bandied about among Demonwards, but it was not something anyone wanted to chance at Hell's Breach. The risk was too great. Of course, if it failed here, it would be a terminal mistake for Rhazburn and his plan. It was unlikely he would escape the Zombie Lord's enslaved Ghosts or ever have another chance to try a permutation of the spell. Still, if by some slim chance his sword worked as he planned, it would have great power in the Dead Lands over the lost souls walking in the ethereal plane who served the Demon.

In the treasure pile lay plenty of Glass Commands. With one of them, he touched the blade. Gratifyingly, the Command dissolved, activating the arcane power of the sword. Rhazburn was nothing if not determined. Some would call him rash. Still, Rhazburn chose to believe that it would work. He decided to call the blade the Sword of Bliss.

To use the Sword of Bliss properly, he needed an arm to wield it. To be precise, he needed a whole body. In his present situation, a whole skeleton would do. Well away from the center of activity, he searched through the bones around him, finding the bits and pieces of the skeleton he needed. First, he moved his hand to attach it to a wrist. He only needed to go slowly enough that the evil spirits he knew were standing guard on the other side of the treasure pile would not hear him. Reassured by the knowledge that physical sounds were at best muffled and indistinct to the spirits, he moved as slowly and as quietly as possible with each step in the process. As his skeletal hand moved into the correct anatomical position with the wrist, the two worked together as if they were attached. There must have been some psychic memory within the bones to keep all in alignment.

Next he slowly walked on fingers to what was left of a forearm. There was only one bone of two, but it would do for now. He rolled the arm over until it attached more or less with an upper arm loosely attached to a shoulder. The whole process seemed to take days, moving pieces of the skeleton close to each other, then attaching larger and larger pieces. He also had to place his spectral self into the skeleton as he grew it. Piece by brittle piece, he put himself together, until he stood up as a complete skeleton. He was still hidden from the center of the chamber. He hoped that the dead felt little need to patrol behind the huge mound of treasure. Still hidden, he tried out the skeleton, moving arms, bending boney knees, walking a few steps. Satisfied with his meager abilities, he donned a helmet of bronze, then picked up the Sword of Bliss. He was certainly an odd skeleton, thanks to pieces from a number of different individuals. Some had been tall some short, and his ribs and pelvis were askew, making him slouch to one side. Still, he could walk, hold the sword, and even swing it after a fashion. It would do.

With all his exercises, he was making a commotion much louder than he realized. A Ghost walked around the treasure heap. The Ghost had a feral, burning look in his eye. He said, "Who gave you permission to get dressed?"

Rhazburn said, "I did," and stepped right up, passing the Sword of Bliss through his questioner. The Ghost's eyes widened with initial fear and pain. Apparently, the Ghost could feel the Sword of Bliss, just as Rhazburn had felt the Unicorn Horn. After his initial surprise, the Ghost seemed to calm down and relax. Rhazburn could almost hear him sigh with relief. Rhazburn meant to save souls with this sword. He meant to cancel the Demon's evil domination over spirits such as this one. The Ghost looked at Rhazburn, not with suspicion but with pleasure. Almost bliss.

"I feel great! Who are you?"

"I am your friend," Rhazburn said.

"And I am yours," said the Ghost.

Two more Ghosts, one small and one huge, strutting, surly, came around the pile. "What are you two talking about?"

Rhazburn said nothing but immediately sliced through them both.

The small Ghost looked at Rhazburn and said, "Thanks, I needed that."

The huge one paused. He blinked again and again, like something still had a hold on his soul. Rhazburn cut what was left of the Demon's power out of him with another swing of the Sword of Bliss. The huge Ghost smiled broadly, looked up at the ceiling, and said, "This is a beautiful cave. I never noticed how marvelous it was before."

Howls of derision came from the other side of the treasure. Without waiting for others to appear, Rhazburn walked around the side. Dozens of Ghosts were before the Zombie Lord who stood out, a shadow of utter blackness. Even Screela was there without her Unicorn corpse.

Rhazburn waded into their midst, swinging the Sword of Bliss left and right. Shouts of scorn and anger from the attacking Ghosts were instantly stilled. They were left smiling or chuckling like beneficent Querites. Some even hugged each other.

Screela came at him, screaming with rage. She did not stop until she impaled herself on his sword. Now it was her turn to be astonished. She fell to the cave floor at his feet. But she did not smile. No chuckling. Not even a pleasant look. Curling herself up like a baby, she cried ghostly tears, the ones she had never shed for her baby that she killed. Perhaps not even the

Sword could erase the killing of pure innocence. Rhazburn had a sense that she had regretted the act of sacrificing her child at the time. He sensed that she had struggled, but, ultimately, had been too frightened of retribution from the Clan and too fearful of losing the only afterlife available to her, service to the Zombie Lord. He pitied her, as he did all the Ghouls. After all, despite Screela's evil ways, Rhazburn's own actions had inadvertently caused many more deaths than had hers.

With the change in Screela, only the blackness of the Zombie Lord was left to oppose him. He came on with a vengeance, bringing his dead and tattered body with him. He tried to wrest the sword from Rhazburn. Rhazburn ducked his head. It came off in the Zombie Lord's clutches. The Zombie Lord ripped off the helmet and dashed the skull to the cavern floor, stamping it into pieces. No matter, there were plenty of other heads he could use. While the Zombie Lord was preoccupied with Rhazburn's head, the Poet launched a two-handed downward swing and took off the Zombie's right arm.

The Zombie Lord howled in pain at the goodness instilled into his spirit. But being tougher and more sincerely evil than his followers, he was much more resistant to the effect of the Sword of Bliss. One slice through his ethereal substance was not enough to change him to a righteous spirit. With his left arm, he swung at Rhazburn striking his chest hard, scattering a few of the Poet's mismatched ribs. Rhazburn answered him with a backhanded slash that took off his assailant's remaining arm. Armless, the Zombie Lord ran at Rhazburn. He kicked him so hard between his legs that the Poet's spine broke apart and his pelvis flew skittering across the floor. The sword now lay on the floor, held in a skeletal hand that Rhazburn could not control. Rhazburn was a naked spirit. Even without his Zombie arms, the Zombie Lord still had black, smoldering spectral arms that clutched Rhazburn's neck. They squeezed his neck so tightly that Rhazburn's head felt like it would burst. The grip was so powerful that, had he been flesh and bone, Rhazburn's head would have popped off his shoulders as easily as the skull popped off his borrowed skeletal spine.

Rhazburn tried to peel away the hands, but the fierce evil infusing the ghastly spirit of the Zombie Lord had strengthened the spectral sinews to the strength of many men.

"Your sword is to me like spit on a fire, Poet. The Great One imbued me with his breath. No thing of metal can sap my strength. Now my Eternals will take you to the Pit of the Great One and you will feed him like all the others. Screela, come here! Mince, Snuffle."

Rhazburn saw all the Ghosts advance toward them, all except Screela. She remained on the floor weeping. One of the Eternals walked in a skeleton it had acquired while Rhazburn fought the Zombie Lord. Unseen by the Zombie Lord, that skeleton picked up Rhazburn's Sword of Bliss.

The Zombie Lord repeated, "Screela, Mince, Snuffle, take this renegade and restrain him."

Three Eternals came to the right of the Zombie Lord. Three came to the left. Altogether, the Eternals, three to a side, grabbed the Zombie Lord's spectral arms.

He cried out, "What are you doing? I'm losing my grip!"

The skeleton holding the Sword of Bliss stepped up behind the Zombie Lord and thrust the sword through his maimed body, holding it there. The sword was a proper one, made long enough for a noble to slash many enemies or for a king to knight a soldier. Its point stuck out from the Zombie Lord's stomach and entered Rhazburn. After a bright pain in his own stomach, Rhazburn felt new vitality surge into his limbs. Any residual anger the Demon's Hellpit had imbued him with was utterly dispelled. Coincidentally, the Zombie Lord's grip weakened apace.

The pitch black of the Zombie Lord's form lessened slowly as the Sword of Bliss converted evil to good. He turned dark gray. Shade by shade, he lightened further. Finally, when he was a light, light gray, he released Rhazburn's throat. The fierce snarl on the Zombie Lord's lips softened into a benign regard.

By the time the Zombie Lord's ethereal substance was white as snow, he smiled into Rhazburn's eyes. "Again I am bested by you, Poet." He craned his head. "That will do, Snuffle."

Snuffle slid the sword free.

The Zombie Lord stepped out of his body, which fell in an unsightly heap.

Regarding the maimed corpse, he said, "Men, we must bury all these poor people." He looked around and said, "Do any of these bones belong to anyone here?"

Snuffle said, "I think that thighbone is mine."

Another of the Eternals said, "I've been wearing my own skull most of the time, sir."

Snuffle addressed the Zombie Lord. "By the way, what is your name, Lord?"

"Please don't call me Lord any longer. Our savior has earned that title today. Centuries ago...," he paused, as if searching a memory filled with cobwebs, "... my name was Silver, Germidian Silver. I will tell you my story sometime, when I can remember it myself. I think we have much to repair before we will be acceptable in the eyes of The Three."

Rhazburn had finally recovered from his throttling. He addressed the smiling group. "Germidian Silver and friends. I need your bones and your help before you take your rest." Curious, they all turned to him. Even Screela looked up, stifling spectral sobs.

"I have proved this sword to have the ability to instill new hope in a wayward spirit." He passed his hand through the blade. The sensation of a sharp cut was followed by a feeling of justice that permeated every whisper of his soul.

"I need you as my Regiment of Righteousness." Then, pointing to the Sword of Bliss he added, "And we need fifty more of these."

CHAPTER 31

THE UNICORN

Jonathon searched his cupped hands for a reason to go on. Moments ago, or it could have been hours, Hili had told him that all of Isseltrent, along with all the city's inhabitants, was gone. Not a soul survived. He had been crushed back when he thought that his wife and young children were lost. Now, to think that every child he and Arlen had born and adopted was gone forever... it was too much for him to bear. Even though he could not quickly count up the several dozen children who had shared their lives with him, he remembered them all vividly, every difficulty they gave him and every joy. Now they were all gone.

A single snowflake wafted down, melting the instant it hit the warmth of his skin. More snowflakes followed. Tiny pinpricks of cold. Evanescent gems, like his family had been. Like all Isseltrent. Like all mankind. Like all living things. Never had winter defeated his spirit so thoroughly. The land had shed humans like leaves from a oak tree. Only ice and stillness remained.

Jonathon had been defeated long before he started out. The moment he took money from Molgannard Fey, he cut the thread holding together the string of priceless pearls that was his life. One after another, the pearls fell to the gravel, losing themselves among pebbles on the beach. The first priceless pearl that had fallen to the ground was his work as a jeweler, which he sacrificed to pay off the Giant. Next, he lost his uncompromising morals, substituting greedy self-preservation for love and simple responsibility. The loss of his morals precipitated the loss of admiration from his friends, the Pixets. By involving Rhazburn, he lost all his investment in steadfast virtue, a value he attempted to instill into his adopted son. Because of that, the Rod of Coercion was lost, and with it, the very fabric of the society he depended upon. Thousands more priceless pearls ran off the frayed end of the broken string in the form of the lives in Isseltrent lost to the Demon's ire. Rhazburn's life would be next. But it was not the worst. That was the loss of his entire family, and any chance he had of redeeming himself. All he had left was the Knife of Life. That, and for a while yet, his own miserable self.

Trallalair slid her sword from its sheath. She was ready to kill someone. The jeweler was the obvious choice. Her sword was cold, so cold that the falling flakes did not melt instantly. They stayed, little hexagons, crossing out random letters in the verses of power etched in the steel. It confused the meaning, as if negating the power of it. Just as their blunder into the Sylvet's land had negated the purpose of their quest. Only hot blood would restore the Sinjery Blade. Only the blood of the jeweler. He had a lot of debts to pay. There was no point in going on. Even if they regained the Dragoncrown, there was no Dragonlord to receive it. The last few dozen of the Sinjery Guard in Isseltrent had striven to save the Realm and had died with all the other pitiful people. Just as she had been saved by a fluke from dying with the host sent to recapture the Dragoncrown, now again, by chance, she was the only Sinjery spared in the destruction of Isseltrent. She would be shamed no more by this man's deeds.

The snow stung Hili with a pain new to her. Not that snowflakes were new, but the enervation they caused, unassuaged by the balm of the Community, was a new experience for her. Alone again. Hili felt ready to leave, too. The Natural Presence beckoned her. She was ready to become one with the goodness of the soil. After a while, as a bit of windblown dust, she would mingle with rain, nourish a plant, color a flower, or sweeten a drop of nectar somewhere in nature's bosom. As a mote of dust, she would not care where she was blown. It would be somewhere away from all of this tragedy.

Jonathon was about to bury his face in his hands.

Trallalair was about to send him to Hell to be with his traitorous son at the moment he covered his eyes.

Hili was about to lay down in the snow and quietly freeze. The Natural Presence would be her executioner.

Before the jeweler lowered his face into his hands, the sun cast a pitying glance on all three of them. Through a rift in the shivering clouds, a deliberate ray glanced off Trallalair's sword, accentuating the snowy dew on his hands. The bright promise of tiny morning suns seemed to shine in his hands. Instead of covering his face, he put his hands to his side. His right hand touched the Knife of Life. Trallalair hesitated just long enough so he had time to turn his head and look at Hili. She lay blue and still as ice.

Appearing truly concerned that his own distress had caused a fatal apathy in his tiny friend, Jonathon anxiously picked her up, cuddled her in his hands, and breathed warmth back into her frail body.

Trallalair's spite softened with his kindness to the Pixelle. He was still unaware of the sword poised to kill him. She sheathed it, watched, and listened.

"Hili," the jeweler pleaded. "Don't go. I can't bear to lose you, too. You're all I have left in the world." Slowly, he turned to Trallalair. "And you, Brandmistress..." He took a moment to exhale more warmth on the Pixelle. "You, too. I am proud to have you as a friend."

Trallalair had not thought of him as a friend. Maybe it was a trace of friendship that stayed her hand. She had certainly fought beside him, aided him and been aided by him, more times than she ever had with her friends. Even with Saggethrie. Having saved Trallalair from death under the sea, she supposed he deserved a stay of execution. Maybe that was friendship of a sort.

With the Dragoncrown in the possession of Sverdphthik, there were certainly no Brands left in the world. And she was no longer under the command of the Dragonlord, since the Dragonlord of Isseltrent was no more. Trallalair was not even sure she should be the leader of their little troop anymore. She had led little in the past several days. Instead, like Hili and the jeweler, she had been wafted by fate and circumstances. She said to both of them, "You need not call me Brandmistress anymore. That title is gone with the fire and the death. Call me Trallalair."

"Thank you, B... B... Trallalair," Jonathon said, "and I hope you will call me Jonathon."

She nodded.

★ ★ ★

Jonathon became resolute. "Even if my family is gone, all your Sisters, all the Community....

Hili sat up in his sheltering hands.

He smiled to her, then up to the Sinjery maiden. "... we still have each other. The three of us are unlike in many ways. Except what we mean to each other.

"I was ready to give up, but I'm going to press on for us. For you." He wanted to convince them. "Even if you two are the only ones left in the world, this quest is worth it. I don't want the Demon to hurt you anymore than I wanted it to hurt my family."

Hili shook her head. "No Community means no purpose in life."

"Even if we all die, if we can stop the Demon, Verdilon will have a chance again."

Hili replied, "There is no hope for us, but one abomination to the memory of the Community remains. The Demon has desecrated Caene and will not allow him to take his place in the essence of the Natural Presence. If what remains of him can be freed, let us try."

Trallalair was last to speak. "Sinjer and many of my Sisters may still exist. I will continue the quest for them. If we could steal the Crown from the Demon, it could still be taken to Sinjer and kept safe there, probably safer than it would ever have been in Isseltrent. There, safe in Sinjer, the Dragoncrown might still do some good."

Jonathon cared little what became of the Dragoncrown, as long as they could get it back from the Demon. "With the Knife of Life, we have a better chance than anybody will ever again. It is our duty to anyone remaining alive, even the ones we know little about far away in the world. I myself have a mother in the Cajalathrium states. If she still lives, I must do this for her, too. Her, and all the people who knew me as a youth. They still may live, even if Isseltrent is gone. There are many reasons to go on."

Hili nodded silently, extending her wings, fanning the chill out of her body with heat radiating from her wing muscles.

Trallalair agreed. "You are right, Jonathon. It is our duty."

Jonathon said, "We have no Flying Carpet, no food, and we are many leagues from the Dead Lands."

"I will lead us and supply us with food and shelter." Trallalair sounded so resourceful that Jonathon had little doubt she could provide for them. He was surprised when she said, "I have had to find my way through these mountains before on foot. That time I was a lot weaker... and, if possible, even sadder."

He had an inkling that she referred to the time when, burnt, injured, heart-stricken, shamed, and defeated by the forces of the Demon, she had hiked through the Forbidden Mountains on her way back to Isseltrent.

Hili offered, "There are a few Sylvets outside Repose. Their memories can help guide us through the mountains. Once we get to the Dead Lands, the Demon will not be hard to find."

Trallalair gave a perfunctory nod to that. For a moment, she looked around at the altered landscape. "That draw over there." She indicated the direction with a flick of her chin. Jonathon and Hili followed her gaze to a freshet. It sprang from a cleft in the rock. It looked slippery and cold.

"The thoughts of the Sylvets tell me that is indeed the way," Hili said, pointing to the cleft.

Trallalair started, "I thought as much. I will go first."

Jonathon began to shiver. All their warm clothes had been burned with their carpet. He certainly wasn't about to go ask the Sylvets for wraps. He didn't want to lose another Moon. It could have been six Moons they had been in Repose.

Trallalair threaded her way between obstinate boulders. She accepted the cramped footing of snowy cracks. It was better than being beguiled by deceptive ice on placid pools ready to freeze her feet.

Trying to keep up with her lead, Jonathon lost his balance and almost immediately plunged his leg up to the knee in the biting mountain stream. It didn't take long before his pants leg was stiff. Luckily, he couldn't feel it chafe his skin, since his entire leg was numb.

Miserable, he limped onward and upward, puffing with the exertion and the thin air of the high altitude. All the animal strength that the horse skin had granted him had evaporated. But just the idea that once he had been strong and fast heartened him. It was a good thing, since Trallalair refused to stop until they had climbed through that section of the mountain. When they reached the top of the pass, she made them descend far into the next valley. Only then would she let them look for kindling.

Out of her steel sword and a rock that Jonathon, with his practiced eye, selected, she conjured a small fire. Not until he had warmed the front half of himself and his pants were supple and steaming did he venture to ask, "Aren't you afraid we'll attract the Dragons again with this fire?"

She pursed her lips, shrugging. "Perhaps, but it was several Moons ago that they searched for us. They're concentrating on other victims now. The Demon thinks we're dead, I hope." She looked at Hili. The Pixelle was still a potential, unwilling vessel for the Demon's thoughts. "For a while, our only chance is secrecy."

Hili flew a loop, acknowledging the criticism. "You wish to separate."

Trallalair said nothing, so Jonathon interjected, "No, Hili, we'll need you if we have to fashion any magical jewels." Fully aware that the likelihood they would actually use Hili's services in that way was miniscule, he shot an exasperated glance at Trallalair. "We need each other now. What's to lose? The worst blow has been dealt to us. I say we stay together."

"I agree." Trallalair said. She would have to trust Hili and take the risks involved. "Hili, for once I hope the Demon makes the mistake of peering into your thoughts again. Maybe you can locate him for us so we can shove this Knife down his stinking throat." She thought of the Demon as male, like all other perfidious beings in the world. Although she did not say it aloud, she thought to herself, *And castrate him.*

Jonathon slept fitfully, frequently rolling to present the coldest half of his body to the small fire. Trallalair kept Hili warm in a pocket of her shirt. She herself stoically ignored the rigors of the weather.

The next day was much the same. And the next. Day after day, numbing weather shortened their slow progress through the mountains, forcing them to stop frequently and build fires from any wood available. Jonathon marveled at how Trallalair coaxed flames out of even the soggiest timber. They would have died days before from the cold had she not been so skilled. As it was, they were able to trek in small increments up slippery mountain passes, pick their way down treacherous cliffs, and trudge across shadowy valleys.

Trallalair provided sparse rations at irregular intervals by shooting small animals lurking on the snowy cliffs. She was careful to never waste an arrow. From the hides that she scraped clean, she fashioned a warm, fur-lined bed for Hili and mittens, caps, and socks for herself and Jonathon. She even found occasional nuts or dried fruit hanging on a tree. Because she realized that they would have no food in the Dead Lands, she saved the least perishable of these in her pockets. When storms threatened to cover them with snow, they sought rocky dens where they huddled like rats sharing warmth. Occasionally, she even formed rude shelters of branches. Once, to Jonathon's apparent amazement, she even made a shelter of packed snow. She had thought up the idea herself, reasoning that any shelter from the frigid wind would do in a pinch. The snow shelter turned out to be the warmest they had.

Cold and cheerless, they came close to death from exposure with every day they trudged through the frigid mountains. Only Trallalair's unfailing fires and scattered shelters saved them.

Many days had passed. Somehow, they survived each new day. On one sunny, bone-cold morning, she shot an Elk and made them all fur-lined jackets. Jonathon commented on how good it felt to only have only his legs frostbitten and not his whole body.

Trallalair searched the sky each day for Dragons. Each night, in her light sleep, she listened for wings and imminent death. Nothing came. It was as if the Demon had truly thought them dead. Or at least no longer a threat.

Hili continued to be spared the invasion of her mind by the Demon for the length of time they trudged through the Forbidden Mountains.

Apparently, in the long stretch when they were in the Land of Repose, the Demon had forgotten about them. He had even given up trying to look through the Pixelle's eyes. It gave Hili little comfort. He had already killed the whole Community trapped in Blaze when the Dragons destroyed it. Whenever she thought of all the Pixets trapped in their prison, burning and screaming, Hili froze in numbing grief. When she could not bear to move her limbs, much less fly, the Master Jeweler carried her in her warm little pouch in his pocket, or cuddled and warmed her as best he could with his breath.

On the twenty-fifth morning of their trek, they stood on the final slope of the Forbidden Mountains. Just looking upon the Dead Lands pierced their hearts. The Forbidden Mountains had provided the sparse rations of Winter to sustain them. In the bitter expanse ahead of them, they saw nothing that could possibly keep them alive. There was only wind across the plains that caught dust in towering spirals. The spirals looked like wraiths, and, indeed, they were probably made of innumerable bits of dead things which had been ground down by time and the elements. On the horizon far away, there was a blackness that sucked even the light out of the day and the moisture from the sky. Their souls shunned it as an abomination, vile and gluttonous, of no purpose, like a dusty cobweb still trapping gnats long after the spider was dead. This spider was dead but very much a threat to however many living beings were left in the world. There they stood, the three of them. The only hope for the world that remained. None of them felt they had any chance for success. Still, they were determined to move onward, onward toward that soul-sucking darkness.

The slope into the Dead Lands was by far the gentlest they had yet encountered in their journey, but every step downward was harder than the last. Stifling pangs of regret entered their souls, and their minds were obsessed with memories of lost loved ones. Food and water did not exist in the Dead Lands, but hopelessness would kill them faster than hunger or thirst. No one could abide the depression they felt.

Jonathon, especially, felt his doom approaching rapidly. But with nothing else to live for, he was strangely at peace with it.

Off in the distant heavy haze, Trallalair recognized a jumble of boulders as the grave of her Sisters lost in the battle with the walking dead. Surreptitiously, she glanced at the Knife of Life tucked in Jonathon's belt. Again she was tempted to demand he give her the knife so she could search for her Sisters and bring them all back to life. She would have an army again. This time, they would avoid their previous mistakes. She shuddered, thinking again about the way she had maimed her Soulsister at that desperate fight. If she resurrected Saggethrie, whose arms she had chopped from her body, would she come back alive without arms? The thought was too horrible to even consider. The Knife of Life was an evil artifact. Bringing back loved ones to a life more cruel than death was all that stayed her hand.

When they finally picked their way to the base of the slope, they encountered a skeletal forest, centuries dead, bleached stark and grotesque. It cluttered the first league into the Demon's demesne. Trallalair noticed a few rivulets from the Forbidden Mountains coursing between the dead trees. The streams had probably nourished the forest on the edge of Verdilon centuries before. Using this water coming from the mountains could save them from thirst for a short time.

Trallalair proposed that they make for the center of the Dead Lands. From the top of the slope, she had seen a small river made from those streams paralleling their path. Despite the water, no plants grew. Not a blade of grass. She could see no animals, either. Not even bugs crawled the ground or flew around them. Nothing to eat, then, except maybe some creatures long dead. She would rather die of starvation than eat such a vile repast. The little food she had saved could not sustain them, but it might keep them alive a couple of extra days. She estimated it would take six days of constant walking to get to the Demon's lair. It would be just barely enough time until they weakened of hunger.

Jonathon looked at Trallalair. "We're not going to make it, are we?" "No." Regardless, she led them through the withered trees.

Jonathon noted the trees remained standing after centuries of being dead. The Demon didn't have the decency to even let them rot. He wondered if the Knife of Life would bring a tree back to life. As he passed trees by the hundreds, he felt it unfair to the forests to deprive them of the benefits of the Knife of Life.

They rested leaning against trunks, denuded of bark, and shared a scant piece of dried fruit. Trallalair said, "I'll climb up as high as I can and locate that river. We can walk beside it most of the way, so at least we can have water to drink."

She scanned the trees, selecting the tallest. With three long striding leaps, she ran to the tree and kept running straight up the trunk. Three more strides, and she grabbed the thick bottom branch with both her hands. She hung there a moment, then swung her legs to gather momentum before she kicked up to a higher branch. She balanced herself perfectly, then launched off again. Up and up, among the tapering limbs, she bounded and swung until she met branches too weak to hold her. Few humans could climb as well as a Sinjery maiden. A half league to the east, the river, brown with silt, drew a wavering line in the naked sand, until near the horizon, it diverged from their intended route.

She was ready to call down that they had only a short walk to find a constant supply of water, but she was interrupted by the what sounded like the thundering approach of a horse. Right in front of her face, Hili popped up, pointing below. "Trallalair, we need your help. A Unicorn has been twisted into a lie. Its dead body is possessed and walks the land under the Demon's control."

Climbing down was much faster than climbing up, but she had not quite made it to the crotch where the two main limbs split apart when she heard Jonathon squawk. An instant later, the whole tree shook with a dull thud. She climbed down the trunk quickly sliding the last body-length, and landed close to the withered corpse of a Unicorn. It stood upright. Its horn was buried halfway into the tree trunk. The Unicorn bucked against its horn stuck fast in the trunk, trying to pull free, but the wasted muscles of its mummified neck were far too weak,.

Hili, down at their level again, was distraught. "Can't you do something? An evil force animates her. She should be settled, at peace, part of the land, not used by the Demon and thrown at us like some soulless dagger."

Remembering her tragic battle with Zombies, she took out her sword grasping the hilt with two hands to strengthen her blow so she could decapitate the Unicorn and render it harmless to them.

As she raised her sword, about to strike, Jonathon's hand stopped her.

She cast him an angry look. "Never stop my blow, Jeweler, unless you want to be the recipient."

"Trallalair, wait," he said. "The Knife of Life." He drew it from its gleaming sheath of fused glass. Stepping back, she lowered her sword but kept it out, ready.

She looked doubtfully at the knife. Even though she had been resurrected by the Knife of Life and had seen the whale that Jonathon brought back to life, she had never witnessed the knife in action. She still had a feeling that the power was too fantastic to be believed. Still, with the hampered Unicorn, they had an opportunity to safely test it, before attacking the Demon's Hellpit. "Proceed."

Jonathon looked at the knife. A tight worry creased his face. He adjusted his grip, placing both hands on the hilt and squeezing it so tightly that his knuckles whitened. Inexplicably, he said "Sorry" to the Zombie Unicorn. He gave a grunt to muster the strength he needed to thrust the knife into the Unicorn.

When Jonathon had used the Knife of Life on Trallalair and on the whale under the sea, he was beset by dangers and confused by murk. He had had no opportunity to marvel at the miracle created by the knife. Now, he was able to appreciate it. Where the knife met the dead flesh, fresh white hair sprouted in sparkles. The hair marched to the back and along the flanks, flaring as if death were being burned from the corpse. As the sparks reached the neck and started for the head, Jonathon yanked out the knife. The shimmering passed over the head of the Unicorn where a live eye looked forth in terror until it caught site of Hili, after which it relaxed.

Jonathon expected the effect to stop when the sparks finished transforming the Unicorn Horn. They all gasped when the magic of resurrection passed on into the tree, plating it with solid bark, making it burst with twigs replete with tiny buds. The energy suffused the ground beneath their feet and far beyond the tree. Jonathon felt movement under his feet and felt shoots of grass and flowers rise up out of the soil moistened by the streams, their vegetable souls retrieved as well from death. He hopped back but landed on more new growth which grew in moments what would normally take a fortnight. Soon, as far as they could see, there were live trees, some with blossoms and fruit, verdant grass, and fragrant, soft moss covering rocks in the shade of the trees. In the valley of the Dead Lands, beyond the mountains, the winter was milder and already waning. The greenery could have a chance. Its very presence seemed to warm the environs immensely. Jonathon looked up at the Unicorn Horn. It was more vibrant, glimmering with power, much more than the dead horn they had used for the Rod of Coercion.

They all stood away from the Unicorn, white as snow, as it twitched its flowing mane and waved its wispy white tail. It was clearly a mare, and more beautiful than any horse Jonathon could imagine. They could see and almost feel tension building up in the massive muscles of her neck as she strained to pull her horn from the renewed wood of the tree. Splinters flew forth from the wood as the Unicorn's magical horn sang free of the tree's grip, and the Unicorn sprang back with the burst of power released by her straining legs. Sweet sap smelling of maple immediately oozed from the hole in the tree.

Trallalair stood back, expecting the Unicorn to bolt.

Hili knew the Unicorn had nowhere to go. There was no living stallion for the Unicorn to run to, so she flew up to the Unicorn's ear. She sang to her an ancient song, remembered from when the Community sang together in reverence of the memory of their friends, the Unicorns. It was a song that had been used to soothe the Unicorns when a stallion was injured in a fight over a mate or when a mare was giving birth. This Unicorn was brought back abruptly, alone, to a world changed radically from the meadows and forests of old she had known. In giving her life, the Master Jeweler had thrust her into a stark and friendless desert just beyond their resurrected woods.

Hili worshiped the Unicorn as a symbol of the vitality of Verdilon at its most beautiful and prolific.

Trallalair recognized the Unicorn as a steed, magnificent and magical, with strength and speed to challenge a Dragon's.

Jonathon envied the dynamic energy in her barely-restrained, quivering muscles, and silently chided himself for coveting her horsely frame.

A new-grown carpet of grass and moss extended four rods from the tree in all directions. The effect of the Knife of Life had continued to include a good piece of the forest floor. The Unicorn whinnied. She stamped decades of dust from her hooves. She shook her head, slicing the air with her long spiral horn. Then she bent to nibble the only grazing she would find for many leagues. Jonathon felt more wholesome, just standing there on the grass beside her, in a new oasis wrested from the desert of the Dead Lands.

Trallalair wanted to ride the Unicorn, but the idea seemed profane. To use her for their purposes, after bringing the ancient magical beast back to life, was indecent. Every so often, as the Unicorn helped herself to the greenest moss, Hili flew to her and spoke. Sometimes when Hili spoke, the Unicorn would turn her head to gaze with her expressive huge brown eyes in their direction. Other times, she would nod, her horn flashing in the sun. Always, there was an intelligence about her, as if she understood every word Hili said. Hili too, seemed to understand the thoughts of the Unicorn.

As if obedient to instructions from the Unicorn, Hili flew up to Jonathon and Trallalair. "Her name is Whither, mare of Storm. We knew her well, as we did all of her race. We had a song about her loyalty to Storm and how they galloped through all the lands of the world in their joy together. I told her all about our mission." Hili made a little figure eight in the air for emphasis. "She wants to help us." Whither danced and snorted.

Trallalair suggested, "If we could ride her, we could cover the distance to the Demon in two days instead of six."

Hili spun around to the mare's head, talking to her again. On returning to them, she said, "Whither will only let the Sinjery maiden ride her. She will not abide the Master Jeweler. She says he smells of death."

The ominous pronouncement made Jonathon's skin crawl. He had never seen a Unicorn before, no one had, but after handling the Unicorn Horn and making a powerful tool out of it, he knew they were full of magic. He had no doubt that they could see into the dim mists of the future, or perhaps, the past, when he wore a dead horse's skin for a time.

Trallalair was not unnerved, but she still worried about wandering Dragons finding them. She asked Hili, "Can she lead us to a hiding place?"

Hili consulted Whither and came back. "There is a cave, formed of boulders rolled together from the mountains, in a depression not far from this woods."

It was Trallalair's turn to shudder. The same pile of boulders all her dead Sisters lay among. Trallalair quailed to go back there. "Can you lead Jonathon there if I ride Whither out scouting for a day?"

Hili nodded. "Yes, Trallalair. Whither told me your reasons for staying clear of those rocks. We will lead the Master Jeweler."

Trallalair had not heard Whither so much as grunt in reply to the Pixelle. She must communicate with Hili in mind and spirit. Hili looked much better, calm and self-assured, as if the very existence of the live

Unicorn sustained her. For the first time, they all felt a glimmer of hope that their goal could be achieved. In Whither, they had an ally capable of helping them beyond their wildest hopes.

Thankful to the Pixelle, Trallalair gave Jonathon the rest of their tiny supply of fruit and nuts still in her pockets. "Whither can bring me back to wherever you are when we return." Trallalair knew that splitting apart could be a big mistake, but the Unicorn's presence had changed their odds for the better. If she could see what they were up against and make a plan, there was now a slim chance of success. She would leave the Knife of Life with Jonathon. It would be his best defense in the Dead Lands if she was not there to protect him.

"Stay in the cave, Jonathon. Even if you starve to death waiting for me to return, with the Knife of Life, there will still be a chance. If you wander off so I cannot find you, all will be lost."

Jonathon hated to see her go, not only because he was losing his protector and strategist, but also because he had developed a fondness for her and he feared she would place herself in unnecessary danger. He was still too confused with the enormity of the events he had witnessed to think up an argument that would dissuade her, so he capitulated. Following Hili, he plodded back through the creepy woods to look for a creepy cave. At least he might get some sleep.

CHAPTER 32

SVERDPHTHIK

On Whither's back, Trallalair felt none of the depression and fear manifest in the atmosphere of the Dead Lands. Her heart was gay as she remembered herself a child in Sinjer, playing tag with her Sisters. They would dodge around tall trunks thickly entwined with vines that they climbed almost as quickly as they darted behind leaves big enough to hide behind. With the Unicorn so full of life, Trallalair felt that encountering the creatures of the Demon would be like those tag games of long ago. Whither was the fastest steed Trallalair had ever ridden on the ground. With tireless shoulders and thighs, she pounded the bare dirt. Her hooves drummed a rhythm that quickened Trallalair's own pulse, energizing her. The terrain raced past, and she could tell from the wind in her hair that Whither ran nearly as quickly as Hover had flown. They rode into the night, ceaselessly, and on into the morning light. She did not even feel the fatigue of missing a night's sleep. The vibrance of the Unicorn infused Trallalair with an intoxicating vigor.

She did not slow her pace when she came upon the first of the Zombies, though the exhilaration of the ride lessened when she saw the mindless stumbling thralls of the Demon. They came from all directions, carrying nothing but more of themselves. Dead humans carrying more dead humans, collecting them for Sverdphthik's foul use.

Thankfully, her speed prevented her from looking any of them in the face. Trallalair did not want to see her Sisters or her lover among them. Avoiding their dead eyes made her ride faster still to where the Zombies thronged. She had to get a measure of what lay before them. Whither had no problem negotiating the lines of converging Zombies. She leaped over solid ranks of them with the ease of hopping a stream.

She felt the Unicorn stood out like a beacon, but the Zombies seemed oblivious of her. Perhaps, she thought, she was obscure, unnoticed to the force that animated them.

At the top of a small rise, Whither stopped. They had come to the lip of the Demon's vast Hellpit, the opposite edge of which was so far distant that the masses of Zombies, milling about her nearby, diminished to nothing on the opposite wall. The din of the footsteps of thousands of Zombies mingled with chopping and digging sounds. Trallalair's mouth opened in surprise. Many of the Zombies lining the walls of the Hellpit were removing armloads of dirt, wresting rock from the hard clay, and scratching up gravel, using hands literally worn to the bone. The sight was disgusting. Worse, many of the best-preserved Zombies pounded, hacked or gouged others which groaned hideously through tongueless mouths.

Far off, in the middle of the Hellpit, was a white Tower which shifted and pulsated through the intense heat as if alive. Dozens of Dragons lounged about its base. Several flew near it, but their flight looked haphazard and purposeless.

At the top of the white Tower, a needle of spite emanated from a point of evil. Trallalair had no doubt that the Demon sat there. As she gazed in contempt at him, she realized her dreadful error. The Demon could see her and the Unicorn. Just as she felt his evil from leagues away, Sverdphthik probably felt the goodness of the Unicorn she rode.

Panic struck at her beneath her breasts. Her heart pounded anew, but this time it was not with exhilaration. It was with fear. She knew that he still held the scepter that allowed him to command them all. But she had thought that he was too far away to use it effectively. Fatal mistake. The blood drained from her as she felt, more than heard, a chilling scream of words. "Woman on the Unicorn, come to me. Bring me the Unicorn to eat!"

She knew she was lost. The magical scepter had forced her to stay her hand from protecting the Dragonlord, and once more, it was forcing her against her reason to sacrifice herself and the Unicorn. Trallalair had no will of her own left inside her scarred body with which to resist. Desperate to obey the Demon, she kicked Whither's flanks cruelly, repeatedly, trying to spur her onward. But the Unicorn would not budge. Trallalair would have to drag the beast into the Hellpit. She was compelled to follow the Demon's command even if she had to leap to her death down the precipice at her feet. Sensing the thousands of souls in the Hellpit, all of them enslaved by the Demon, even death, she thought, would not stop the compulsion.

But Whither stood, a goddess of the world, unaffected by the command. Instead, she craned her neck backwards, so her horn leaned against Trallalair's shoulder.

With this light touch of the vibrant Unicorn Horn, Trallalair was infused with an unshakable resolve to spurn the Demon's command. Apparently, no object made from a dead Unicorn's Horn could have influence over a living Unicorn or those she protected.

It was time to leave. Twenty Dragons were rousing themselves from the Demon's Hellpit. The Demon might no longer have control over Trallalair, but he had control over the Dragons. They rose out of the Hellpit, flying straight for her.

Whither knew what to do. Trallalair only had to ride. The Unicorn bolted for the open desert. She was as clever as she was beautiful. She ran in a direction away from their goal, the cave at the edge of the Dead Lands. The Dragons flew at them, spitting fire to destroy them, but to no avail. Trallalair had been right. Whither was a match even for the Dragons. The Unicorn cut. She leaped. At times, she bounded. She modulated her galloping, slowing abruptly to avoid a talon or accelerating rapidly to outdistance a dive.

As they ran, they threaded their way through the congregation of whirling, flapping, diving Dragons. The Dragons grasped at them with spear-sharp claws. They snapped at them with bone-crushing jaws. They spat fire at them with smoldering maws. Trallalair saw Cataclysm, the Dragonlord's personal Red, now ridden by Sverdphthik. He was followed by two more Reds. The Dragons crawled with Zombies crowded so close together that many fell off to smash apart on the hard clay below. She noticed that Cataclysm and his followers were not joining the fray, but flew west directly toward the secret cave where Jonathon and Hili hid.

Trallalair knew she had made another fatal mistake. In her overconfidence that she could, with the Unicorn's help, scout out the Demon's Hellpit, she had sorely underestimated the mind of the Demon. Of course, he recognized a live Unicorn. Of course, he knew that none could exist unless brought back by the Knife of Life, of which he was well aware thanks to his tie with Hili. And through that tie, Sverdphthik could easily find them in his domain, wherever they hid.

Trallalair sensed that the Demon was too fast for her to do any good. Still, she cried out, "To the cave, Whither, or all is lost! We must save our companions." Whither ran, raising a cloud of dust at her hooves, like a tornado chased them. She galloped as fast as the wind toward the edge of the Dead Lands, where Jonathon and Hili hid, unaware of their imminent danger.

Jonathon awoke to a shriek from Hili. The Pixelle was already outside their little rocky chamber, caroming off boulders in her distress. "The Demon finds us, Master Jeweler. He comes. Leave me, and do not tell me where you go. They will be here in less than a single Blessing. He means to destroy the Knife of Life."

Jonathon hated to leave Hili in her agony, but he realized that if the Demon was coming after him and the Knife of Life, Hili would be safer if he ran as far away from her as he could get. They had found the small cave in the center of the boulder pile. He had thrown up twice on the way, since the boulders were strewn with burnt bodies, many wearing the armor of Knights of the Realm or Sinjery Ringmistresses. He was glad that Trallalair had been spared the sight. He thought that the area was probably the battleground where all her friends had died. On the way out, his stomach was too empty for more vomiting. Besides, he was so frightened of meeting up with Sverdphthik again that he didn't even retch when he slipped and fell right on top of some poor corpse of a man, black and grisly.

He did not make very good time, barely getting free of the boulders, when a Dragon's roar turned him around. Even the roar wasn't loud enough to mask the Demon's screaming. "Through ears, hearts, minds I call, Obey my will, One and all. Jonathon Forthright, stand still." Of course he did as he was told, just as he had the day before the Dragonegg Festival. He was facing the right direction to see the Demon, riding the Dragonlord's Red, land heavily a couple of rods away. Two other Dragons, laden with animated dead human bodies that constantly fought among themselves, landed behind the Demon.

Sverdphthik, or rather the dead body that the Demon possessed, dismounted and lumbered up to Jonathon. Even for a Zombie, the dead body was disgraceful, one foot and half of an arm missing, flesh hanging in tatters. "I need a new body," the Demon said.

Without further ado, Sverdphthik turned the Rod of Coercion with the sharp point of the Unicorn Horn toward Jonathon. As effortlessly as if he were skewering a bug, the Demon thrust it through Jonathon's heart. Jonathon was surprised how little pain he felt, but the world swam and darkness enveloped him as his life drained away.

When he came to, he looked down at his body. It was cold, blue, with a grimace on its staring, dead face. Funny, he didn't remember that much pain.

The Demon's ethereal substance was clearly visible to him now. It was a feral beast hairy with gesticulating fingers that dug claws into the dead flesh he inhabited. One of the enslaved hands of that body removed the Knife of Life, sheath and all, from Jonathon's belt. Tossing the knife from one hand to the other as if it was painful to the touch, the Demon hurled the Knife of Life into the air where his Red Dragon snatched it in his jaws and swallowed it down. The Red blasted flame high into the air. The precious, irreplaceable Knife of Life was surely destroyed.

It was at that moment that Jonathon realized he was dead, but still standing nearby. His disembodied soul could see in a kind of misty way, and he could hear muffled sounds. Sverdphthik and the spirits of the dead that inhabited the Zombies riding the Dragons shimmered and glowed clearly in his sight. They were more real to him than his own body was now. When he was alive, he had never believed in Ghosts. Now he could see them clearly. In fact, looking down at his own substance, he shimmered and glowed himself. Why he didn't rise to Heaven like his belief in The Three had taught him he would, he wasn't sure. Maybe he was destined for Hell, but then, why did he just stand there? He should have been sucked into Hell.

Hili was, for the moment, freed from the Demon's possession. From a crack beneath a boulder, she cowered and watched. Just finding the Knife of Life had taken a tremendous toll on her, and now it was lost to them. Without Master Forthright, their quest was lost as well. Hili knew she had betrayed the Master Jeweler again, drawing the Demon to him and allowing him to be killed. Hiding in the small crevice, she was tiny, frightened, and alone. Even the strength of Trallalair was gone. There was little she could do. But she had to try. Hili was the last of her race. She sensed that Whither was far away but still alive. Trallalair would be fine, in the protection of Whither.

Hili had to act alone. Mercifully, the Master Jeweler had died quickly. She had never expected that she could prevent his death. Her concentration was on another matter, a tiny body in a sack at the waist of the Demon. Caene, the stolen soul of the Community, continued to be the channel through which the Demon pierced her thoughts and used them against her and anyone with her. For the moment, she was free of the Demon's attentions, but during the brief time it had possessed her, she discovered Sverdphthik's plans. She saw that it planned to kill the Master Jeweler and take his body. Briefly, while the Demon transmigrated from the corpse it inhabited and passed into Jonathon Forthright's body, the corpse with Caene's shriveled little husk at its waist would be empty. The Rod of Coercion and the Dragoncrown would be out of the Demon's control for a few moments.

Hili waited until she saw the old corpse collapse and the Master Jeweler, still dribbling blood from his chest, sit up and look around. Before she could think better about it, she flew straight at the pouch holding

Caene's pathetic body. The string around the top of the pouch lay loose. All she had to do was pull Caene free. She wrapped her arms around Caene's decayed corpse. Her tiny senses were assaulted by the terrible smell and nauseated by the unnatural, cold leathery feel of his dried flesh. As she grasped him, she heard Jonathon, the Demon, stand up only a human-stride away from her.

"What are you doing here?" she heard. Next would be a tight hand squeezing out her life. She didn't care about her life, but she wouldn't have Caene dishonored any longer in such a way. Suppressing the gorge rising in her throat, she tightened her embrace, feeling Caene's brittle bones crack with the pressure. She called on the strength of all the Pixets from all time. With one final effort, Hili pulled Caene free of the pouch. She could sense a hand behind her closing in. Fluttering her wings faster than she had ever in her life, she shot straight up, right through the Demon's clutching fingers.

Back to the forest and out of the Dead Lands toward the Land of Repose she flew. The strength of the lost Community and the presence of Whither in her mind sustained her flight. Despite being hampered by Caene's body, Hili was small enough and fast enough to elude the Dragons that Sverdphthik sent after her and find the Land of Repose in one day. Caene would nourish the soil there, and Hili would soon join him.

CHAPTER 33

TOWER OF BONES

Jonathon was dead, but he still had his emotions. When he saw the Knife of Life consumed by the Dragon's fiery maw, his ethereal heart sank to his ethereal knees. A moment later, he found he still had sensation also. A grip of steel grabbed his hair and pulled back his head. He cried out.

The Demon, encompassing his own dead body, was before him, laughing at his pain. Writhing hairs of the Demon's substance around Jonathon's grimacing, blue face looked like the worms that would soon feast upon him. His own dead face smiled in the Demon's power, and his body swelled as if gaining strength from something. The hand on his head twisted again. He cried out in misery once more. The Demon Jonathon laughed again, as if the pain Jonathon's spirit felt nourished the Demon's spirit. Fear and misery seemed like food to the Demon. His own eyes spoke of it. Jonathon's corpse was nice and fresh, unlike the crumbling one Sverdphthik had discarded. The Demon Jonathon now had the Dragoncrown on Jonathon's head, and he held the Rod of Coercion. "Jonathon Forthright, come with us," the Demon commanded.

"The traitor Jonathon Forthright is in my hands. I've waited a long time for this." A woman's voice spoke to him from behind. The hand, cruel as broken glass, dug again into his scalp, twisting his head for the enjoyment of the Demon. Jonathon said nothing. What was there to say? He could only scream as she gouged her fingers into his eyes.

"Men, huh! Selfish weaklings, all of you. Disgusting. What are you good for? Absolutely nothing." She waited while his agony tapered off, then she assaulted him again, ripping his ears. He howled again while his spiritual eyes quickly regenerated, staring dumbfounded at Sverdphthik's spectral form which swelled slightly in response to his misery.

The Demon Jonathon mounted its Red Dragon while the woman dragged Jonathon's miserable spirit back toward another of the waiting Reds. The borrowed, corrupt body of his tormentor was that of a slight male youth, cut down in his late teens, but Jonathon could tell the spirit within was that of a Sinjery war-maiden. She was clearly hateful of all men, especially of Jonathon Forthright.

As she dragged him over the gravel, Jonathon was surprised that he did not feel the ground scraping his ghostly flesh. Even a boulder, he passed through like a wraith. Actually, he reminded himself, he *was* a wraith, a Ghost, a lost soul. As he passed through the boulder, the inside of it was revealed as if he had cracked it with a sledge. There were veins of mica and crystalline quartz, quite enjoyable for an old prospector if it weren't for the torture that went with it.

The Sinjery didn't give up her rambling or her pummeling, even while they flew on the Red. His insubstantial form had a tendency to sink into the back of the Red unless the Ringmistress lifted him up. Apparently, her spirit clothed in the dead boy's flesh stayed put where she sat.

"The Demon will take all you have, Jeweler. This is your reward. Pain and suffering." She twisted his spectral arm up behind his back, all the way up to his ear. "My goal is to show you a little of the suffering you have wrought with your evil plot." Her knee met his groin as she spat in his face.

Amid the sharp flashes of pain, he glimpsed the Demon's Hellpit as they descended into it. Screaming and sobbing filled the air. It seemed that the human souls could animate dead bodies, human or animal. He thought back to his experience with the Skin-Splicers. All these dead, Zombie things were like the Skin-Splicers, but much worse.

Dead birds pecked at each other in a macabre frenzy. Torturers inside Zombie bodies or free Ghosts that he could easily see fought with each other, first one having sadistic dominance, then the other. Human flesh, dried, tattered and torn, was being ripped apart and thrown about. It littered the floor of the Hellpit. He could see limbs used by Ghosts crawling along the ground, looking for an opportunity to grab a Zombie's ankle and rend it. It was all a macabre dance of death.

In the middle of the Hellpit, he saw the Tower of Bones. He estimated it to be twelve rods tall. It was a hideous stack of skeletons which seemed to grow up out of the gloom at the bottom of the Hellpit.

At first, he could not understand how it could remain standing. Then he saw, to his horror, that the tower was inhabited by spirits fighting, screaming, and writhing with each other, all vying to crawl to the top. It was as if the tower was a living thing growing ever higher, but not one living thing remained within it. It was only a morbid pile of Ghosts, bones, and death, all in the power of the Demon's curse.

Jonathon grieved for them all. What a horrible fate. Hell could not be worse. He could not see anything of The Three here. He would pray to his gods, but he felt too undeserving of their attention. Jonathon knew that The Three had abandoned him and the Dead Lands to the Demon.

Again he wondered why all the spirits had not transmigrated to Heaven or had not been thrown into Hell itself. He knew Hell existed. He had seen it himself. But Heaven? Who could say? Only someone long dead brought back by the Knife of Life could give him the answer. Maybe the Demon had the power to keep the paths to Heaven and Hell blocked so it could collect all the spirits of the dead for its own satisfaction.

Despite all the pain of his spirit Jonathon was experiencing, he could not imagine blaming anyone for what they did to him. They were all caught up in a curse. The Demon was at fault, not the spirits it twisted. They all seemed evil, but he doubted it was that simple. To the Sinjery and even to Trallalair, he seemed evil, even though all that he had done had been out of love for his children. There, in the Hellpit where souls were being constantly tortured, Jonathon's pain and torture insured that one less soul had to suffer. His torturer would concentrate on him and not another. For that, he would endure the pain. Little choice remained for him, regardless.

The angry Sinjery warmaiden beat him, and ripped him, and gouged him, and scratched him. The days became constant punishment but strangely, they were not exhausting. His spirit renewed itself without sustenance of any kind. Every other tortured spirit he saw cried as loudly as he did, but they seemed in more anguish, probably because they thought the torture unjust. Jonathon knew he deserved to suffer. So his pain was tolerable. It was a paradox. He thought maybe he was becoming a Querite.

At the center of the Hellpit, high on the Tower of Bones, the Demon stood. It held Jonathon's arms outstretched, soaking up the cries and the clamor. Its form grew in size like a poisonous cloud surrounding Jonathon's body. Sverdphthik was the only one there that warranted Jonathon's hate. The only pain that made Jonathon truly suffer was the knowledge that he was helpless to stop the Demon.

Jonathon took heart in the fact he would not cease to exist. As he had imagined when he first witnessed the frenzied chaos in the Hellpit, his torture was like a dance with a rhythm. The Sinjery warmaiden slashed. He winced and cried. She twisted. He shouted. She hammered. He hollered.

The Sinjery maiden became more and more puzzled with his acceptance of his fate. "Don't you hate me, Jeweler?"

"No. You were a Sister and friend to Trallalair."

"Friend. Ha." She punched him in the stomach, making him croak. "Do not speak her name." She slapped his face, holding him by the neck. "I was her Soulsister."

Jonathon had an idea what that meant. The Sinjery maiden who tortured him was Saggethrie, Trallalair's lover, like her spouse. Trallalair had lost her mate as surely as Jonathon had lost Arlen. For the next few days, he was too preoccupied with her renewed jabs and scratches to respond.

Even the Sinjery war-maiden eventually had to take a break. During a brief respite, Jonathon said, "Trallalair came with me, here to the Dead Lands, to retrieve the Dragoncrown."

"With you? You are the one that gave it to the Demon," she snarled, tearing out handfuls of his spectral hair. "More lies. She was not with you when the Demon found you. Mother be praised. I saw her crawl away from that carnage that killed us all. I would know if she were dead. I know I would feel it. For an instant once, I thought she died, but I was wrong. The feeling passed as soon as it came. She lives yet. No thanks to you." This tirade was accompanied by a series of slaps that shut his mouth for the rest of the day. Jonathon thought she referred to the moment that Trallalair had died under the sea. The feeling that the Sinjery maiden torturer perceived had been fleeting because the Knife of Life had quickly brought Trallalair back from death.

The next day he offered, "She did die for a moment, but I brought her back with the Knife of Life." That stopped her for a thought, considering his claim.

"Liar!" The word preceded another series of attacks so savage that all he could do was howl in pain for days.

The time proceeded much the same, day after day. Whole fortnights passed. Sverdphthik seemed to no longer have any interest in Jonathon, nor in any of his victims in particular. Its power visibly grew with the cries of pain surrounding it as the numbers of victims brought by the Zombie hordes grew day by day. The spirit of every person who died in the world seemed at risk of capture by Sverdphthik's minions. What had happened to Heaven? Was it only a ruse of the faith of The Three to promote righteous behavior in those convinced they would be rewarded? He knew there was a clue somewhere.

Much later, at the end of a particularly long bout of torture, Jonathon blurted, "You must be Saggethrie."

That one word made her pause, as if she knew that Jonathon could not possibly know her name unless Trallalair had confided in him that she was her lover. After that, the Sinjery maiden began easing her torture a bit, so Jonathon could, in small snippets, tell Saggethrie much of the tale of the forming of the Rod of Coercion, the betrayal by Sverdphthik, and the quest he started with Trallalair. He told her the whole tale, right up to his death and capture by the Demon.

"Impossible," she said, slamming an elbow into his back. "You act as if you fought alongside my lovely Trallalair like one of the Sisters. She could never stomach your evil scheming or your weakness. She was self-sufficient. Seldric's favorite. Never would he saddle her with the likes of you." She gave him a few more slaps for emphasis.

"I just hope she and Hili are safe."

"I'm sure my lovely Trallalair still lives and is gone from the Dead Lands, if ever she were here. I trust that she has consigned you and your just punishment to me in her stead, while she rides to Sinjer to make a last stand against the Demon."

"Aren't you helping the De..." His last syllable was choked off by her wringing his neck.

"I perform the evil role here, accepting eternal punishment so some of my Sisters will be spared. Do you think I enjoy this?" As she said that, she took out her spectral Sinjery Sword, hacking at his limbs. He took a break from their conversation to scream in torment. "This is the first I have enjoyed my role as a torturer. Doing it to you!"

"Have you ever thought why you have not ascended to Heaven?"

She spread her fingers in a V and poked them in his eyes. Too preoccupied with the pain, he barely heard her reply. "Now you insult Mother Earth. By Her Grace, I was left here to see to your punishment."

Days later, he tried a different tactic. "The Dragons can still attack Sinjer. Don't you want to help your Sisters?"

"Sinjer and all the Realm will be destroyed, no matter what I do." For emphasis, she scratched his face.

He could believe her after what he had heard about Isseltrent. "I never meant any of this to happen."

"You are as stupid as you are evil." She kicked him in the head so many times, he lost count after a hundred.

The following day, between socks in the face, he ventured, "I will pray for your soul, Saggethrie. Anyone that Trallalair loved must be a wonderful person."

"Yes, pray for me and the thousands of others that wail because of you." He wailed as she disemboweled him with her sword.

His spectral bowels grew back, as did his resolve to try and take back the Dragoncrown. He never really saw the Knife of Life melt when the Dragonlord's Red swallowed it. Perhaps, he thought, the Knife still sat in the belly of the Red. "If we could find the Knife of Life, we could drive the Demon from the body it possesses."

She slapped him. "I thought you said it was the Knife of Life that was lost to Cataclysm." She was apparently referring to the name of the

Red Dragon. Like all the Sinjery Brandmistresses, she must know all the Dragons by name.

"The knife was swallowed by the Red Dragon. He may have ruined it with his fiery breath, but maybe it's still in his stomach, unharmed."

She stopped slapping him, earning her furtive glances from fellow tormentors, who were assiduous at their task.

"Cataclysm," she said, pensive for the first time he had ever seen.

He kept up his advantage. "I slipped right through the Dragon's flesh when we flew here. We could walk right inside him to look for the Knife of Life."

She hesitated in her striking him again. "Trallalair could surely use a weapon like that. Any of the Sisters could." Her eyes got a far-away look.

"I need the truth from you, Jeweler." She grabbed his throat, choking off even his cry of pain, and pulled him close. He flinched, preparing for the next torment. His head was dragged into the mummified skull of the body she used.

He felt nothing, but thoughts of forests and swamps, beautiful, unforgotten but unobtainable, crept into his mind. He was in her head, sharing her memories and stimulating his. He saw events from his own life through Saggethrie's spectral mind. Molgannard Fey raised his misshapen head. Jonathon saw his family and his son, Rhazburn. The Demon in disguise came forth. Jiminic played her role. He and Bob Thumblefoot made the Rod of Coercion, planning it only for the Dragonlord.

At that point, Saggethrie's own thoughts swelled again in his mind. He saw the lost love of woman for woman, not a shameful thing as he had been taught as a child, but beautiful, as all love was beautiful. He saw the Sinjery's own faith venerating Mother Earth, the Mother of All. In her mind he saw the sun, the moon and the twinkling stars bowing and doing homage to her greatness. Though in details different from his worship of The Three, at its core her faith was really the same, based on love. The Three believed in caring for human beings and spreading love in this way. The faith of the Sinjery believed in fighting fiercely to protect and love the natural world and those they gave their pledge to. He suspected that the hatred of men had evolved for the Sinjery only because some horrible degradation they had suffered as a race a millennium before, a time that was lost in the mists of legends. Whatever that degradation was, it was terrible enough for all the women of the land to revolt and flee until they had found the jungles and swamps of Sinjer. Once there, in a sanctuary they felt safe, they formed their curse on men on into the infinite future. The curse had been granted by Mother Earth, so went the legend, and since then, any male that stepped foot in Sinjer immediately fell sick with fever and pustules and died in great pain. No Sinjery maiden ever died in that way. It was as if in the land of Sinjer, there existed a plague on men alone.

Finally, Saggethrie perceived Trallalair's tragic tale remembered by Jonathon. Saggethrie herself added details in his mind of the battle in the Dead Lands when Saggethrie was killed. Countless spirits enthralled by the Demon had overpowered all the Sinjery and Knights as they were all killed. Sverdphthik's minions had stolen their bodies and, with them, attacked their own Sisters. Jonathon felt Saggethrie's anguish after her death. Six other spirits were needed to hold her spectral arms and legs. She tried so hard to go on protecting her Sisters. But the Demon won. He used her dead body as a mercenary to savagely attack Trallalair.

The suffering of the Sinjery women, their screams and their hopelessness, was all too familiar to him. It was just like the experience of the tortured souls in Sverdphthik's Hellpit. Jonathon was determined to stop their pain, somehow, sometime, even if it took him the rest of eternity.

Saggethrie saw in Jonathon's thoughts the tale of what happened after Trallalair, though grievously injured, came back to Isseltrent. He had no idea how Trallalair found her way through the Forbidden Mountains. But Jonathon had seen her ease at finding their way to the Dead Lands in the bitterness of the mountain winter. The shaky alliance of Trallalair and Jonathon, their journey to the point of his death, the rest of the details about their quest was laid bare for Saggethrie. She saw through Jonathon's memories Trallalair's bravery again and again, along with the scenarios of how Jonathon had saved her lover at Molgannard Fey's tower and under the sea. What was more revealing was how Jonathon felt about his dealings with the Demon. How he was tricked like anyone in his position would have been. How he had been striving with all his meager resources to bring back the Dragoncrown and help Trallalair. She could see how he respected both Saggethrie and Trallalair, even though both of them showed only hate for him when they first met him.

From her mind, he heard Saggethrie speaking to him. *Perhaps you were my Soulsister's friend. Though you still seem an enemy, you were twisted by the Demon.* She paused for a sober thought. *So was I. So were all these people. And most of them were here long before our part in all this.*

Slowly, she withdrew and lowered her hand. Like Trallalair, once Saggethrie was convinced of the truth, she decided on action quickly. "We will go together, Jeweler. Trallalair needs that Knife of Life."

Grabbing his arm, she pulled him roughly along the base of the Hellpit. Cataclysm lay exhausted, like all the Dragons, near the hub of the Hellpit where they periodically cooked the moving skeletons in the Tower of Bones at the direction of the Demon. They were a quarter league from the center, but since they, like all the dead, were pulled toward the Demon, they moved quickly. As expected, the other Ghosts struck out at them, trying to inflict any pain they could. Saggethrie used her spectral sword to fend off the assailants. By night when fears were multiplied by darkness, they came to Cataclysm. Few of the tormentors could have as easily identified the Dragon. All the Dragons looked much the same to Jonathon.

The magnificent beast was thin, and the bright redness of his scales now appeared dull and anemic. Saggethrie came out of her body, which fell to land most unnaturally with its head hyperextended behind its back. "We shall see if you will be my ally or my victim." She stepped through the wall of Dragonscales, pulling Jonathon with her, even though he needed no encouragement since searching for the Knife of Life had been his idea.

Not much was in Cataclysm's stomach, a couple of whole Zombies Cataclysm had probably sneaked while Sverdphthik was not thinking of him.

"See, it's gone, dissolved." She shook him.

"Wait. Try the bowels."

They turned toward the Dragon's tail and passed into the contortions of Cataclysm's intestines. There it was. Slowly moved along by the Dragon's ponderous peristalsis, the Knife of Life lay intact and unmelted. Jonathon realized that Sverdphthik had done him a favor by tossing the knife to Cataclysm. Forged of magical steel and glass fused by Dragonfire, one small burst of even Cataclysm's flame was inconsequential against its substance. Cataclysm had been a perfect, though huge, pouch as the Demon flew him back to the Hellpit. If Sverdphthik had merely tossed it down in the desert and kicked sand over it, they never would have found it in the vast expanse.

"Is this it, Jeweler?"

"It is, and it looks remarkably whole."

"Even if we take it, we have no coins to use it."

"The ancient Poets prepared for that, maybe just for us. The scabbard is made of fused Glass Commands. It grows thinner with each use, but no other coins are needed."

Saggethrie knew just how to take it. She went back into the Dragon's stomach. He followed.

"Jeweler, take that body."

"How?"

"Just lay on top of it and get your head in his head."

He did as he was told. The body was on fire as it was digested by the Dragon's acids. Searing pain was not new to him, though he was not sure how much of the constant burning he could stand. "Now what?"

"Wait here for me and grab the knife when you can. I will slice open those bowels." She disappeared through the side of the stomach.

Within one Favor, a real sword thrust into the stomach and quickly sliced up into the bowels. The Dragon lurched. Through the hole that Saggethrie made in the flank, Jonathon saw an intense flame. He heard Saggethrie scream and saw the flesh of the Zombie body melt away. Jonathon was jostled around in the stomach as Cataclysm bled copiously from the gaping wound in his side. Jonathon pushed his way into the intestine and fished around in the slimy contents. The flesh on his dead bones were dissolving as well. When he came up with the Knife of Life, he pushed his way out of the dying Red. But the flesh was dissolving quickly from his borrowed corpse limbs. Cataclysm kicked and flailed in his death throes, his tail striking Jonathon and shattering his body. Jonathon saw the Knife of Life fly off to bounce off a rock a single stride away as Cataclysm fell silent and inert, another dead thing in a pit filled with dead things.

He could see many Ghosts coming for him. Saggethrie, now a bare spirit with a spirit blade, stood in their way, swinging the sword as she held dozens of attacking spirits at bay. She shouted at him over her shoulder, "Take the knife and find Trallalair. What I saw in your thoughts and the way you accepted your torture have convinced me that you have the will to resist the Demon. You want a chance to redeem yourself? I have provided it." Hundreds more leering Ghosts and walking corpses surrounded her, ignoring the pain of her blade. They inundated her like a rising tide. Then they looked again toward Jonathon.

Jonathon could not grasp the Knife of Life, even though it was within an arm's length. His ghostly arm passed right through the knife. If only he could hold the Knife of Life, he could strike at the Zombies and bring them back to life to fight for him. He needed another body, fresher, more reliable, not one dissolving and falling apart. Rivers of blood poured past him from Cataclysm washing over crippled corpses.

Jonathon thought, *The head. When Saggethrie's head was coincident with mine, I could hear her thoughts. When the Demon was in my head, it controlled my limbs. Jonathon, you fool, get your head in the Dragon's.*

Leaving the Knife of Life where it was, confident that none of the inhabitants of the Hellpit would know its value, he ducked back through the gaping wound in the dead Dragon.

As he crawled his way up the Dragon's neck, hands clamped like vices around his ankles. He was about to be stopped. This was his last chance to save the few friends he had left in his world. He spun around and kicked the Ghost that held him savagely until the hands relaxed. Another spirit appeared within the Dragon's flesh. This one was huge. It was the Ghost of a powerful Knight. But Jonathon was in a frenzy. Spurred by his anger at the loss of all his family and his anger at the Demon for all it caused, he gained strength far beyond his size. He pounded the big man's face until the soul fell out of the Dragon's neck.

The will of Jonathon's spirit was on fire. He was stronger than that of any other Ghost in the Hellpit. Size meant nothing when it came to the power of a spirit. During his time in the Hellpit getting tortured, Jonathon had seen that Ghosts of men twice the size of himself had none of the power of their physique. The spectral muscles had no power after death. It was only the will power contained in the spirit that was important. That was why the Sinjery maiden could easily hold back dozens. Her spirit's rage strengthened her immeasurably.

Jonathon slapped his next few assailants out of his way like bothersome gnats. At Cataclysm's head, another Ghost was attempting to take over the

Dragon's body. Jonathon swatted him aside and thrust in his own head, peering down through the Dragon's gaping mouth.

When he turned his head, he was Cataclysm himself turning to regard masses of Zombies besieging Saggethrie. He stood upright to tower above the their masses, inhaled, and turned them all to ashes. Even the spirits felt the magical Dragonfire and many fled to torture easier prey. The newly-dead Dragon had plenty of fire within him still smoldering. At Cataclysm's feet, he spied the tiny knife. Unopposed, he picked it up between his still supple tongue and his front fangs. As he raised his head and opened his wings, he saw Saggethrie look his way to wave quickly before she waded back into the mass of Ghosts surrounding her.

No other Dragons even seemed to care about Cataclysm's movements. The Demon absorbing the misery about it, benefitted from the pain of the Cataclysm's death, but otherwise, it seemed to know nothing of what had just transpired. Dead Dragons apparently could not be affected by the Dragoncrown. A fortnight or so before, Sverdphthik had probably thought that the problem of the Knife of Life had been solved once and for all. The Demon, in its own arrogance, had brought together Jonathon and the Knife of Life once again.

Jonathon had never flown before, and he was still afraid of heights. Clumsy and unsure of himself, trailing entrails and dripping blood, Jonathon lumbered along the ground, crushing dozens of Zombies. Awkward when his wings caught the air, he fell twice before getting up enough speed to make it over the wall of the Hellpit. Zombie birds that failed to scatter before him, he blasted from the sky with Dragonfire. There seemed plenty left within the dead Red Dragon. After a few flocks were destroyed in such a way, the rest gave him a wide berth. How long the Dragonfire would last within a dead Dragon, he had no concept.

There was no lack of stars in the desert sky, so he used them to orient himself. Ever since leaving his home in the north, the Cajalathrium States, he looked in the night for the great ladle. Once he found that star cluster, he could find The Jewel in the Circlet of Tundudil, the north star hanging above his mother's home. Once Jonathon had identified The Jewel, he headed west. Nothing followed him. He was a Dragon. The largest Red there was. Nothing dared follow him. Apparently, the Demon did not care that one of his dead Dragons flew in the air. It just stirred up more chaos for the Demon to exploit.

Jonathon planned to fly to the only place he knew was safe for Hili and the Brandmistress, the Land of Repose. He doubted that the Brandmistress would go back there, but Hili may have taken refuge there, alone, severed from her precious Community. Once he was up in the air, he found flying as a Dragon very peaceful. There was nothing to fear after all. The height was irrelevant. What could happen if he fell? He was already dead.

By the light of a bright-pink sunrise, Jonathon the Dragon, losing entrails from his split gut, soared toward the eastern ramparts of the Forbidden Mountains.

Jonathon's eyes were those of a mature Dragon. Even in the warm, subdued light of morning, he could see distant objects with crystal clarity. As he flew, he searched the plains of the Dead Lands for Trallalair riding on Whither, but nothing stirred save the trudging lines of Zombies, those marching out at the Demon's behest to gather bodies and souls and those marching back with their captives. Jonathon shuddered to think how immense the tower of bodies and bones could become if nothing stopped them.

He gave up on finding Trallalair. He hoped that she had the sense to flee to Sinjer, where she had a chance. He wondered if the curse that prevented men from entering Sinjer would be effective against Ghosts and Zombies. If so, the Sinjery might succeed in surviving the Demon's attacks for years. Maybe they would eventually be able to raise an army powerful enough to rise against Sverdphthik.

Jonathon felt he needn't worry about Trallalair's safety, but he would need her assistance to steal back the Dragoncrown. After having fought off a few of the toughest looking Ghosts and befriending one, flying in the body of the largest of all the Red Dragons, he had new hopes they could prevail against the Demon. Jonathon Forthright was beginning to feel like he had the heart of a Dragon.

The entrance to the Land of Repose would be very hard to find. He had to search his memory for details of their journey to the Dead Lands and trace their trail backwards. The mountains were his first landmark. Soaring the updrafts that rushed up the precipitous cliffs along the eastern border of Sylvanward, he found the landmark he sought, the dead forest with several live trees surrounded by a patch of green, where they had resurrected Whither. The small dot of life was quite distinctive in the desert. Apparently, the Knife of Life had instilled the area with a vitality unquenchable by even the vilest of curses.

From the patch of moss and grass where they had split apart fatally, for Jonathon at least, finding subsequent landmarks was exceedingly difficult. Many times he started west, and as many times, he gave up and flew back to his starting point. It was so easy to get lost in the labyrinth of valleys in the Forbidden Mountains. To Jonathon's surprise, flying became easier with time because Cataclysm became progressively lighter as rotting chunks fell out of the his abdominal cavity. Constantly, he reminded himself of the precious Knife of Life held firmly in his mouth. He didn't want to lose his concentration and drop it with the other pieces of himself he kept losing down into the snows of the Forbidden Mountains. Luckily, the wings were the strongest feature of his host. The lighter he got, the faster he flew. Several days of this passed before he recognized the valley where they had found the pine log.

Jonathon had seen the valley in various states. He remembered its first appearance of lush greenery when he, Trallalair, and Hili ran from the Dragons. He recollected its second state as it smoldered, charred into ruin by the Dragonfire. He recalled its later appearance, snow-covered and deep in Winter's embrace. It remained a symbol of the death of his family, and its features were etched in his memory, every boulder and cliff of it. Even from the air high above, he knew it instantly. His Dragonsight and his memory had not failed him. He recognized not only the remains of the log but also the chilly cleft in the mountain through which he, Trallalair, and Hili had crept on their way into the Dead Lands.

Jonathon still had to land the Dragon's body. Even his Dragonsight would be insufficient to spy a thing as tiny as Hili. He hoped that Hili had fled inside Repose, but he worried that to wait outside would be interminable. He would have to somehow attract her attention or enter Repose himself. Clearly that would be impossible in his current form of a Red Dragon.

He tried to land gently by the last piece of the log, but he slammed the Dragon's carcass into the ground like a falling tree, smashing a few nearby trees asunder and rattling his head. That made him drop the Knife of Life from his mouth. When he regained his senses, he looked desperately for the opening into Repose, thinking he had destroyed his only point of entrance in his fall. Most of the log was gone, but a small piece at the end, merely a ring of wood, surrounded a bright doorway into Repose.

Even though Jonathon needed to get the knife to Hili and the Sylvets where it would be safe, he could not abide letting Cataclysm, who had died for his benefit, go unrewarded. Before he gave the knife of Life away, he would bring the Dragon back from death. He knew the Demon would see what was happening by virtue of the Dragoncrown, but he would take the chance and do the right thing by the Red Dragon.

In a part of the Dragon's guts which were still falling out was the second human body, the stolen Zombie there in Cataclysm's stomach. Its foot, caught in a fold of the huge stomach, had kept it from tumbling out when he flew. It was in an advanced state of decomposition. By twisting his neck downward, Jonathon could just see the macerated head of the corpse hanging through the rent in his side. Not a pretty sight.

He withdrew from the Dragon's head, making the entire huge beast crumple to the ground, still as a rock. Jonathon entered its belly once again and, laying himself down right on top of the human corpse, took it as his own body. The procedure was getting frighteningly familiar. As before, the digestive juices in Cataclysm's stomach felt to Jonathon like he had jumped into a vat of aqua regia, the only chemical strong enough to dissolve gold. The only thing that could abide those humors was glass forged by Dragonfire. Surely that was the reason the Knife of Life survived.

With his whole frame on acidic fire, Jonathon stumbled out into the snow-covered valley. He purposely fell down in the snow and flopped around, trying to dilute the digestive acids with melted snow. The cool bath relieved some of the sting of the juices, allowing him to concentrate better on the task at hand. With a hand reduced to little more than a few scraps of muscle on bone, he lifted up the Knife of Life, unsheathed it and, hesitating only a moment to imagine what Cataclysm would do to him once the Red was brought back to life, Jonathon plunged it into the dead Dragon.

As the familiar sparkling effect took place, he sheathed the knife and lurched toward the entrance to the Land of Repose. He figured that the

Sylvets would not appreciate one of the walking dead in their land, so he just tossed the Knife of Life through the entrance.

When Jonathon turned away from from the magical portal, a live and healthy Cataclysm regarded him with a sinister hatred. The few hairs still on the corpse's head stood on end as Cataclysm inhaled a deep breath. In the next moment, fire more excruciating than Jonathon could ever imagine burned him to a crisp. He only stayed in the body an instant before he fled, feeling for the first time the full power of Dragonfire. Even after fleeing the corpse, Jonathon felt the scalding would last for a long time. But he had learned to endure pain inflicted on his ghostly self from his teacher, Saggethrie.

Cataclysm flapped his wings a few beats, trying them out again to see if they were working properly before he gained confidence and rose into the air. Hovering in place for a bit, he blasted the area with Dragonfire one more time for good measure, making sure all his enemies were ashes. Then, with a bellow that made rocks clatter down the cliffs, he flew off through a cleft between two peaks gleaming with snow, back toward the Demon's Hellpit. He was probably being summoned again by the Dragoncrown.

Jonathon sat, his skin throbbing with the magical burn of his soul by Cataclysm's flame, waiting for something to happen. He was prepared to stay there a long time. Now that the Knife of Life was safe again, there was no hurry. He had time to imagine what he could do to fight his way back into the Demon's Hellpit and take the Dragoncrown. He knew he had been lucky that the Demon had not recognized the threat when he was stealing the Knife of Life. Surely the Demon was aware that Cataclysm came back to his consciousness suddenly and far from where he died. Jonathon was certain that Sverdphthik's Demon mind was clever enough to deduce that the only thing in the world that could have accomplished such a feat was the Knife of Life. He would be alert to any new threat, and if Jonathon tried to enter his Hellpit holding the Knife of Life, Sverdphthik still had the Rod of Coercion to stop him.

Days passed. Jonathon enjoyed the intermittent falling snow, the blustery winds, the dark nights. It was all seen with a blurriness he presumed was due to the fact he was not quite there. Indeed, he felt none of the dampness of the falling snow, none of the freshness of the wind, none of the bite of the cold. He could watch the sun and moon crawl overhead, the clouds muster, pelt him with snow, and scatter with the wind. It was all like a slow play for his benefit. He counted the days and calculated how many times of the rapid sun in the Land of Repose would pass over Hili's head before she found the Knife of Life lying there.

If Hili was elsewhere or dead, Jonathon would be sitting at the mouth of Repose for a long, long time. The Sylvets would have no concept of the purpose of the Knife of Life, nor would they care if they did know. But as a Ghost, Jonathon could sit there without food or sleep for all time. Eventually someone would come.

CHAPTER 34

THE FINAL CONFRONTATION

Jonathon counted twenty days before anything stirred at the entrance to Repose. Early on the twenty-first morning, he saw shadows slowly appear at the entrance, like the stone statues he had seen when he first saw the entrance to Repose. Morning had turned to noon before the shadows became solid beings. The first to appear was Hili and two Sylvets carrying the Knife of Life.

He had guessed right. The Pixelle had retreated into the safety of the Land of Repose. The group he saw appeared uncertain of what had transpired just beyond their door. Deep snow covered the evidence of Cataclysm's last inferno, but by virtue of the smoking corpse that Jonathon had borrowed, the snow had melted around the charred remains. The outline of a human was clearly evident.

More Sylvets ventured forth, taking the opportunity to sing and dance, skating gleefully on the ice, diving into snow banks, and bringing fresh fruit from within Repose to the hurried mice burrowing beneath the drifts. Their lively songs accompanied the food and drink, cheering the land and attracting a few wintering birds that sang with them. Predators too, coyotes and stoats, prowled nearby, watching for a chance to snatch a tidbit and avoid starvation for them and their young. Bedding, woven from grass fibers from the Land of Repose, was provided to keep Hili warm. Strangely, the Sylvets enjoyed the ice and snow as if their bark-like skin was immune to the cold. They sat on chunks of ice and even slept wrapped in snow for blankets.

Jonathon had no idea what was happening, why they were all waiting outside Repose. He was tempted to put his head on Hili's like Saggethrie did with him so he could share her thoughts and communicate with her, but he waited politely. After seeing the appalling effect of the Demon entering her mind, he did not want to frighten her like the Demon had.

Two more days of waiting passed before Jonathon heard thundering hooves from over a narrow pass. The afternoon sun was hidden behind gray clouds when he saw Whither galloping atop snow covered rocks, cantering and leaping from boulder to boulder. She threw up clouds of powder without slipping or missing a step as easily as if she ran on a paved road. On her back, Trallalair literally flew into the Sylvet's camp.

Healthy, all her burns healed, her black hair regrown almost down to her shoulders, Trallalair looked comfortable in the cold. She was covered with a rough fur cloak and slacks she had apparently fashioned from animals she must have had killed and eaten to remain in such good health.

She dismounted and began talking abruptly. "Pixelle Hili, Sylvan folk, well met. I thought you dead, Pixelle Hili, with the Jeweler. Whither came here on her own. You called her?"

"Yes, she was called."

"I have learned that Whither senses the best course through the mountains as if she knows my wishes. I never speak to her, and yet she anticipates my wishes and needs. When she headed here, I recognized the path and figured that you called her."

Her eyes widened as she recognized the Knife of Life lying beside Hili in the snow and exclaimed, "The Knife of Life! Where did you find it?"

"The Knife of Life simply appeared within the entrance to Repose. We think this poor person brought it and was, for his trouble, incinerated. A puzzle." Hili pointed to the ashes of the corpse Jonathon had used. Hili added, "Take the knife and keep it safe, Brandmistress."

Trallalair first took the precious Knife of Life and buried it underneath her rough fur cloak. Curious as to the identity of the incinerated corpse that lay nearby, she studied the form of the corpse but shook her head. "For a moment, I thought this might be Jonathon, but the body is much too tall and far too slim. Another person, I think."

Hili piped up, "Master Forthright's body was taken by the Demon. The Knife of Life was swallowed by a Dragon. It was all clear as Caene was pulled from his clutches. Now, we are finally free of the Demon."

"Then the Demon has no more hold over you?"

"Never again."

Trallalair nodded thoughtfully, musing on the implications of the Knife of Life Perhaps, at last, she and Hili would be able to have their plans stay secret. She noted how Hili had not given up speaking in the plural, as if the Community still survived.

Jonathon wondered if Trallalair would feel the same distress at being possessed. He remembered Sverdphthik entering his own mind when he stole the Rod of Coercion. Not an experience he wanted to repeat. He could see that even a friendly invasion of the mind was still an invasion. Few options were open to him as an insubstantial spirit. Despite his fear of the consequences to Trallalair's soul, she had to be the one. She was the strongest, or so it seemed. If the Community were around to support Hili, he may have chosen the Pixelle, but not while she groped for support from others to bolster her meager, lonely existence.

Trallalair sat beside Hili and the Sylvets in a stand of burnt trees not far from the entrance to Repose. Jonathon walked up and carefully bent to superimpose his head on Trallalair's.

Just as when Saggethrie entered his mind, he saw a solid core of the love of nature and respect for the creatures of the wild. Like Saggethrie,

Trallalair also had an irrational distrust of men. She stood up abruptly, breaking the connection. "I thought I heard Jonathon."

"We heard nothing," Hili said, speaking for herself and the Sylvets she shared thoughts with.

"Maybe it was his Ghost," Trallalair said, half-joking.

He tried again. For a moment, Jonathon saw the swamps of Sinjer. This time, she leapt away and shuddered, drawing her Sword, waving it before her as if to fend off an unseen assailant. "It *is* the jeweler. He is here and tries to steal my soul!"

Jonathon felt her recoil just as he had with the Demon in his mind. As long as she saw his attempts to speak to her as an attempt to possess her himself, all was lost.

"Do you think he means to harm us?" Hili cried as she flew up to the Sinjery maiden. "It must have been the Master Jeweler who brought the Knife of Life back. Who else would know its significance, or where to bring it?"

"I do not care what he has done. I cannot abide him attacking my mind." Trallalair searched the area with desperate eyes. "Stay away from me, Jeweler."

As long as there was the slightest chance they could, together, stop the Sverdphthik, Jonathon had to do as he saw fit. Once more he stepped up to enter her body. From within her, before she could react again, he gambled and thought, *Saggethrie helped me.*

That stopped her. *Yes Brandmistress, I am here and I brought the Knife of Life. I mean you no harm. I bring a message from Saggethrie. She wanted you to have the Knife of Life.*

Trallalair's face showed signs of relief, as if she needed only the name of her Soulsister to assuage her anger.

He imagined his story of the Hellpit and his torture by Saggethrie. He reviewed how, after they were able to fully share each other's lives, thoughts, and emotions, she helped him find and take back the Knife of Life. He finished his tale and was silent. He had not expected the strong Sinjery maiden to cry, but she did at the thought of the nobility and sacrifice of her Soulsister.

There was a perceptible shift in her emotions as she furiously wiped the tears from her eyes. She said to Hili and the Sylvets, "Jonathon's spirit or Ghost is within me talking to me, just as you said. He has told me of a grievous travesty of a marvelous woman."

Saggethrie, my faithful Saggethrie, how you have suffered, came the thought within her mind. But then he felt the emotions build up within her. They were as powerful as the anger he had felt in Saggethrie when she tortured him. They were angrier than he had ever seen Trallalair when she had been his unwilling guide. He felt anger at the injustice of the Sinjery maiden's treatment by the Dragonlord. Anger at Jonathon and his part in the death of so many of her Sisters. Anger at the futile attempt by the Isseltrent Host to regain the Dragoncrown, anger at her part in the fruitless attempt, and even anger at her foolish belief that they could help the Sinjery Sisters by aiding the Dragonlord when they all should have run away toward Sinjer. Finally, Jonathon felt Trallalair's anger at herself for maiming her Soulsister's beautiful body when she should have died right there so she could be with her in spirit as Jonathon had been. If she could be with her Soulsister in death, then she would race there as fast as she could.

Out loud she said, "I am taking Whither and going after the Demon. Jeweler, release me," and he was cast out like an unwanted thought.

"Trallalair." This time the Sylvets spoke. "We understand you are enemies of the Demon."

"You have no concept of my feelings." Trallalair barked.

"It may interest you that a band of skeletons approaches from the south," Hili said.

Trallalair said, "Thank you for the warning. I will take precautions."

Hili continued their thoughts. "No, these skeletons are not enemies but friends. The leader has communicated with the Sylvets to the south by writing in the snow. He asked them if they could find any allies to fight the Demon. They are raising an army of skeletons with souls freed from the Demon's hold by magical swords they made."

Jonathon thought that there was only one Poet that could accomplish that. Rhazburn. But Rhazburn was dead.

Trallalair paused, thinking, seeming to consider the possibilities. Who in Thuringland could possibly be that resourceful, take control of the minions of the Demon, and use them against him? Only a Demonward. Only the best of them.

"The Poet Rhazburn?" Trallalair said, coming to the logical conclusion. If her Soulsister existed as a spirit upon the world, as did Jonathon the jeweler, then why not Rhazburn?

Hili replied, "Yes."

Since Trallalair had ceased her agitation to leave, Jonathon entered her head again, this time without her even moving.

My son, thought Jonathon. *He knows how to make a Jewel of Nishbad. He was dead. Thrown into Hell,* came Trallalair's thought.

I am dead. Saggethrie was dead. And yet we can help you. Maybe he is no longer dead. Or maybe he is dead but a spirit like myself and Saggethrie who can still aid us. How can you doubt anything, after seeing the power of the Knife of Life?

She shook her head and shuddered miserably. The horror of spirits and Ghosts walking upon Mother Earth, enslaving the unfortunate bodies of humans and creatures, had caught up to her. *It is too much to bear, Jonathon. Get away from me!*

He did as she requested. He could feel the mounting distress within her, as if her capacity to cope with all the tragedy and the unreality of thousands of spirits walking the world was teetering on the edge, and she was about to break down. There was only so much even a Sinjery maiden could take.

Trallalair had to walk off, smell the sharp winter air, pass her hands through the snow to come back to the real world. The lives of the spirits and Demons did not appeal to her. Real, substantial plants and beings, even Dragons, she could understand. But this madness? No. For the rest of the evening, she wandered alone, looking at the mountains above, listening to the streams tumbling down cliffs.

She slowly calmed down some. The effects of nature were always soothing to her. She felt a need to be with Whither, grazing on brown grass that the Unicorn had uncovered by swishing her horn in the snow. As Trallalair stroked Whither's strong neck, she was renewed by the strength of the Unicorn. The animal was so full of life, as if Whither emanated the power of Life itself. Trallalair took another deep breath. She could now see all that had happened in better perspective.

The Knife of Life was back in their possession. Why not use Whither's knowledge of the Dead Lands, or more properly, her knowledge of Verdilon of old, to locate more Unicorns and resurrect them? Even if they could never defeat the Demon, the race of Unicorns could be brought back. Each one would be a powerful ally to fight the Demon and his followers in years to come. If each Unicorn had such a resplendence of Life that she felt in Whither, perhaps there was hope for the world and for her Sinjery Sisters still in Sinjer.

Standing with Whither, stroking her soft mane, Trallalair vowed that she would strive to renew the race of Unicorns. Whither looked straight at her. The unicorn understood the Sinjery love of the natural world just as the Pixet Community did. When they still lived, they had loved Verdilon and all the beauty it contained. The Pixets, save Hili, were all gone, but the Sinjery could help the Unicorns as the Pixets would have.

Perhaps the magical power in the Unicorns *could* counter that of the Demon. She already knew that Whither had saved her from the compulsion caused by the scepter the Demon wielded. Sinjer would need strong allies in the years ahead. If they had allies who could counteract the effect of that scepter, they would have a much better chance to oppose the Demon and his Dragons.

At ease with her decision, Trallalair would again allow the jeweler to possess her mind, this time willingly. She walked slowly toward the gathered Sylvets and Hili, where she assumed the Ghost of Jonathon Forthright still remained unseen.

"Jeweler, I am ready for you. I have decided to aid in whatever will stop the Demon and avenge my Sisters. Hili, I believe we can bring back more Unicorns to renew the race and oppose the Demon."

The Pixelle popped into the air and flew in twirls and spirals with the joy of the thought.

Jonathon took his cue and walked into the temple of her body. This time, she neither tensed nor forced him out. His thoughts melded with hers. She shared his memories of his life as a prospector, searching out jewels hidden in veins of rock under the ground, chipping away at the base rock to reveal sparkling gems. She shared his memories of work in his jewelry shop, skillfully cleaving gems to produce facets that caught the light, making them glow in the sun as if they were alive. These thoughts mixed with hers of rain and trees and wind flying through her hair as she rode Hover or Whither. Her thoughts also held a love for the softness and warmth of Saggethrie, just as Jonathon pined for the touch of his wife, Arlen. Strange how he shared the love of a woman with Trallalair.

Trallalair was finally in tune with him and said aloud, "This Jewel of Nishbad, could it help us?"

It has the power to entrap a Demon! he thought.

Too bad this Jewel of Nishbad is not available to us, she countered.

I believe we could fashion one. All we need is Rhazburn, he answered.

And you believe he is with the skeleton army? she thought.

I do. No one else in the world could accomplish what the Sylvets have seen, he thought.

Walking skeletons, not thralls of the Demon, but controlled by your son, Rhazburn, who has escaped from Hell?

If anyone could escape from Hell, the Loremaster is the one, Jonathon decided.

Yes, I believe you are right. I met him before his treachery, and I thought him capable of almost anything.

She shuddered at that thought, imagining her lover Saggethrie as one of the walking dead. The thought was disgusting. She could tell from her merging with the jeweler that he could hear her speak even if he was not in her brain. *Leave me, Jeweler. That is enough!*

He did as he was told. Even though he could no longer communicate to Trallalair and Hili, he still could hear them and watch. The Sylvets had summoned the skeletal army through a Sylvelle who was staying near to them, but many days would pass before they traveled the distance to them.

Trallalair said, "Riding Whither, I can cover the distance to the skeletal army in a day. Hili, if you go with me, we can talk to the Sylvets easier."

Hili flew up to her and stopped in the air.

In a few moments, the pounding of Whither's hooves could be heard as she galloped up from the farthest corner of the valley where she had been searching for grass under the snow. Apparently, she had already been called by Hili.

Hili said, "Whither already knows the way to the walking skeletons."

Trallalair hopped upon Whither, and Hili flew to one of the Sinjery's pockets to nestle beneath the insulation of her fur coat. Jonathon wanted to go with them, but he knew he could never keep up with Whither. Looking at the taut, strong muscles of the Unicorn's legs and torso without a trace of fat, Jonathon had a profane lust to have the Unicorn's body so he could race over snow and rocks and pound gravel to dust beneath his tireless feet. He suppressed it. His Skin-Splicer day as a horse had tainted his soul and made him forever long for that feeling of power.

The Brandmistress adjusted her cloak, checked on Hili's comfort, and cried out, "Away, Whither, to the skeletal army."

Inexplicably, Whither stood still as if she had not heard. Jonathon suspected that Unicorns did not take orders. They only cooperated of their own volition. He felt that no one could ride Whither unless she wanted it. Unicorns could be killed, but they could never be broken to the command of any other being. Even Hili's head peered out of Trallalair's jacket to see what was the matter.

To Jonathon's surprise, Whither turned her head slowly in his direction and gazed into his spectral eyes. He knew that Trallalair and Hili could not see him, but Whither? Who could tell?

Jonathon felt he was being invited along. The Unicorn's eyes drew him to her side. He walked up and stood politely next to her, close enough to stroke her neck. With a tentative touch, Jonathon laid his ghostly hand on her neck. The power that he recalled within the horse was there a thousand-fold in the Unicorn. Whither turned her head as if inviting more caresses, but her head passed into his and she stopped.

Suddenly, Jonathon's life and all his troubles shrank down to a grain of sand. His mind spanned ten thousand millennia, far beyond Dragoncrowns, humans, Pixets, or any other intelligent species he knew of. His mind sped far beyond the origins of religion, long before all the conflicting philosophies in the world existed. Only the world and the cosmos existing for millennia. The troubles of mankind would not appear for thousands of years. He saw all creatures content in their own existence and attempting to live in a constantly-changing world. Dragons flew then and had flown for much longer than the Unicorns had run on the plains.

He saw the balance in the world upset by men and their petty greed. The worst was the opening of Hell's Breach and the release of Sverdphthik. Even as the Unicorns died as a race, they knew that Jonathon Forthright would be born and come to battle the Demon. They had great expectations of Jonathon's ability to conquer their recent foe, the Demon. Within Whither's sage but innocent mind, Jonathon could almost believe it himself.

Another aspect of the curse of the Demon was clearly revealed. The Unicorns did have the power to see the spirits of the dead. Whither's memory of her life extended to years before Sverdphthik appeared. Never before that day had she seen the thousands of spirits roaming the world. The opening of Hell's Breach shut humanity off from the grace of the

Afterlife. It even excluded evil-doers from a just punishment in Hell. Every man, woman, or child who had died since Hell's Breach was opened was consigned to wander the surface of the world searching for meaning. That is unless they were gripped in the terrible clutches of the Demon. As time proceeded, more and more of the wanderers were forced into the Demon's Hellpit. Humans, in their infinite folly, had closed the doors of Heaven forever.

When Jonathon came to his senses, he was full of strength. His drumming hooves chewed up leagues as easily as he munched grass. The power of his equine limbs were unmatched in all the world. He could run on any surface that presented itself like it was flat ground beneath his hooves. Never had he felt such joy in the mere use of his muscles, running with Trallalair clinging to his back. Whither had accepted him within her, allowing him to experience all the power of her tireless limbs. Even a horse, strong as it was, seemed a mere shadow of this magnificent being.

Jonathon tried to thank Whither, but his thanks had been accepted long before Jonathon was even born. He sincerely apologized for using the horse skin back in Isseltrent, even if he had had good intentions when he put it on. Whither understood. Her previous distaste of his death-smell seemed to be gone. Maybe all the suffering he had been through since had cleansed him in some way. In any case, she had no discomfort, only an intense desire to run. They ran over boulders, leapt over fallen logs wide as a house was tall, wound between the pines of dense forests, and even left wide still frozen lakes behind them as quickly as if they were galloping over the plains. Through it all, every leap and turn was automatic as a heartbeat, every movement in harmony with the environment and the terrain. It seemed mere moments, but he knew from watching the setting sun, the stars, and then the dawn that they had been running through the Forbidden Mountains all night long. A new day was beginning as Jonathon saw fifty skeletons marching in the snow, holding swords and shields, with one skeleton holding a sword aloft as if it were a banner for the others to follow. Whither ran unhesitating up to the leader and stopped. Trallalair dismounted, and at Whither's behest, Jonathon, refreshed by the wondrous run, stepped back into his dull world. When he left Whither, he no longer craved the body of a horse. He had, for a brief time, been a god on the plains. He could covet nothing more.

Jonathon was again himself, a bare soul consigned to the task of wading through reality, lost to his final rest as long as the Demon possessed his body and Hell's Breach sullied the world. He could see his son, Rhazburn's spirit gleaming, handsome at the head of a company of gleaming spirits. All of them were loosely attached to the skeletons of creaking bones within them.

"Father, you have died, too. I came out of Hell to help you, but I am too late."

Jonathon went up and embraced his son, rattling bones and all. "I have much to tell you, as I am sure you have much to tell me."

He looked back toward Trallalair who stood beside Whither. She had her hand on her Sword and seemed puzzled as to what to do next.

He said to his son, "Scratch a message to Trallalair that we need to talk for a while to make plans."

After Rhazburn resolved the disappointment that he had not prevented his father's death, he felt great joy in seeing his father's spirit strong. Then he looked in embarrassment at Trallalair. All his charm and good looks were gone forever from her sight. He was now a horror to behold, moldy bones long due for a grave. He had participated in the worst debacle of the ages, causing the death of many of her Sisters. How she could even gaze upon him was miracle. Why she would accept his help was unfathomable. Still, he had to try and set out his plan. He had thought on it for many days.

They had to form a Jewel of Nishbad. No plan that did not include a Jewel of Nishbad to trap the Demon could possibly succeed against the odds they had all witnessed. Rhazburn, the skeletons' captain, mute with no voice box with which to speak, used a stick to write a message in the snow. He and his father had to confer for a while. The others must be patient.

Rhazburn and his father could sit and talk as spirits, just as if they both were living beings. Rhazburn told what he knew to his father and learned much in return. Jonathon had communicated with both Hili and

Trallalair. All together, the four of them had amassed considerable helpful information.

Hili knew their enemy's strength from sharing the Demon's thoughts when it possessed her mind. Jonathon had been in its Hellpit and witnessed all its power first hand. Trallalair had ridden Whither and had scouted it out as well. Rhazburn had flown there as a vulture. They had all seen the vastness of its Hellpit and the great numbers of its slaves. Both Trallalair and Rhazburn had retreated after seeing that horror, and both had been lucky to get away. Together, the four of them had all the resources they needed to fashion the Jewel of Nishbad. They had Jonathon's skill as prospector, miner, and jeweler to find a rough sapphire, and from it make a flawless gem. Rhazburn's knowledge as a Poet and his memory of the verses on the Jewel of Nishbad, along with Hili's skill at inscription with her tiny tools, was all they needed to complete the task.

Trallalair turned aside and found pine branches to weave a strong lean-to facing a boulder beside which she made a fire to keep herself and Hili warm while they waited. Then, from her cloak, she produced a piece of meat to cook for herself and a few walnuts to crack and crumble for the Pixelle. Whither ran off looking for edibles beneath the snow.

Rhazburn's army of skeletons, fifty strong were all armed with precious swords gleaned from the Zombie's hoard and converted into Swords of Bliss. They all stood, sat or lay directly in the drifts in a haphazard group spread in a stand of pines heavy with snow so the skeletons were hidden from view by marauding Dragons coming from the Demon's Hellpit.

Jonathon sat with his son, two Ghosts speaking together without Trallalair or Hili in the material world hearing their conversation.

Jonathon described every moment of his quest with Trallalair and Hili to find and return the Dragoncrown, including all that had gone wrong.

When he spoke of the destruction of Isseltrent and the loss of all their family, Rhazburn leapt to his feet.

"I haven't told you, Father. I am a fool. I never imagined that you would be alive to hear of the state of Isseltrent and fret about it."

"Who wouldn't fret? All Isseltrent has been destroyed and every soul killed. Is not Hell's Breach unmanned? Isn't that how you escaped?"

"No, no, Father. We must tell the others. Isseltrent is fine."

"Fine? Burnt to the ground, reduced to ashes, mingled with the dust according to the Sylvets. Hili hears nothing from the Pixets. They must all be dead, too."

Rhazburn was gesturing expansively with his spectral arms. "No. Isseltrent is no more burnt than before you left it. In fact, Isseltrent is probably in better shape since the city folk have had a respite to repair the damage. I told Garrith how to build a device to protect Isseltrent. But I left strict instructions that no one could learn that Isseltrent still exists, and no communication with anyone outside could be allowed."

"What are you talking about?" Jonathon was becoming depressed again, just thinking of all his dead children.

"Isseltrent is alive and well. It is all an illusion to deceive Sverdphthik. I don't know how long he can be deceived, but I imagine the Dragons flying above will see the same as did the Sylvets. The hardest part was containing the thoughts of the Pixet Community. Even Hili, outside the city, had to be excluded from the secret. We could tell no one outside, lest the information got back to the Demon. Believe me, stopping information from getting to Sverdphthik will be much easier to accomplish now that Molgannard Fey and his louts are gone. Garrith heard what you and Trallalair did to the Giant and was much impressed. I am too, Father."

"Then the city is still there? Patrick, Laurel, all the children, still alive?" He thought of the pot with the seeds in the Pixet's prison. "And the Pixet Community? Are they alive too?"

"Most assuredly. Of course, I left probably Moons ago, but it sounds like the illusion is still intact if the Sylvets were fooled."

Jonathon had to ask one more question to be sure such an illusion was possible, to make an entire city and all its inhabitants disappear. "You figured it out, wrote all the verses, and devised the fabrication of all the materials?" Only if Rhazburn had made the plan himself, did Jonathon feel it could succeed.

"Yes. The spell was not in place when I left, but I gave the instructions to Garrith, so I trust everything was done to my specifications. This is the first I have heard of its success. I have to admit, I'm pleased with Garrith. It must have taken a lot of effort to convince the court, but I think they are desperate. After all, they didn't put him in the dungeon right away, even though they knew he was my brother. They needed him. They know that if they don't use every one still available to guard Hell's Breach, things could get much worse very fast."

"And I am impressed by you, son," Jonathon said. "Only you would think of every detail to protect others while you were away."

Rhazburn, in turn, described his escape from Hell with the help of Dollop, his journey, and the forming of his own small army from the slaves of the Zombie Lord. He laid forth his plan to defeat Sverdphthik. The Demon still had the Rod of Coercion, the Dragoncrown, and all his minions. If they formed a Jewel of Nishbad, Trallalair, Rhazburn, Hili, and Jonathon would have a Demon-Entrapment gem, the Knife of Life, and the Swords of Bliss as a balance of power.

He was confident that his troops, armed with the Swords of Bliss, could fight off any attacking force of Ghosts and Zombies led by the Demon. It would not suffer the tragic fate of the army sent by the Dragonlord, which had become weaker with each death among them that then swelled the ranks of the enemy Zombies. No, Rhazburn's force, by using the Swords of Bliss, could free spirits from their tie to the Demon, increasing the strength of their own army at Sverdphthik's expense. The process would work just the opposite from what had happened when the Knights and Sinjery Ringmistresses were slaughtered.

Screela was one soul not among Rhazburn's troops. She had stayed behind at Devil's Fang, too despondent to be of use. She would have to go to her own punishment or reward, perhaps wander the world like so many other Ghosts Rhazburn had seen.

The plan was a good one and the only feasible one. But everything had to be in place simultaneously, and nothing could go wrong, since they would never again have all three critical magical objects assembled to oppose the Demon.

His father had already experienced that he could pass through solid objects easily and see details inside them where there was no light. Rhazburn reasoned that they could use that ability to pass into the layers of rock, as he had done on his trek through the Forbidden Mountains, and look for a star sapphire large enough to be made into a Jewel of Nishbad. Rhazburn said that only a star sapphire would be adequate to form the Demon-Entrapment gem. The original Jewel of Nishbad had been a star sapphire, and Rhazburn would not attempt to make another with anything less.

Once the plan was clear to them both, Rhazburn wrote more messages to Trallalair and Hili. As he had to his father, he explained the illusion that protected Isseltrent and made it seem gone from the face of the world, even screening out the thoughts of the Pixet Community.

Hili was ecstatic and not as skeptical as she would have been had not a similar loss of their thoughts happened underwater and in the Land of Repose.

Trallalair found it within herself to thank Rhazburn for saving the few dozen Sisters left in Isseltrent.

Jonathon told his son how to recognize the type of rock they might find in the Forbidden Mountains which could contain large star sapphires.

Hili was in constant communication with the Sylvets, so when she heard the description of the rock they must search for, she scanned the memories of the Sylvets which catalogued their entire land. She took only few moments to find a likely outcropping of rock, not too distant from where they rested.

Trallalair rode Whither to confirm that the vein existed, and the whole gathering hiked to the area in question where they set up their camp.

When Jonathon and Rhazburn arrived, Jonathon was pleased with the prospects that the exposed rock promised.

Rhazburn abandoned his bones to lead his father into the side of the mountain where they could pass through the solid rock and study the smatterings of crystals within. His bones he left at the base, where he could step back into them as he emerged from the rock.

Jonathon was amazed and entranced with what he could do as a ghostly prospector, and thought that maybe death was not as bad as everyone seemed to think.

They needed days, passing deep within the mountain substance, then walking in spirals from the center outward, to find a small cluster of large star sapphires. Luckily, the best were found not far inside a cliff face which was accessible by a narrow ledge high above their camp.

Rhazburn had plenty of experience with Unicorn Horns, wielding one with his hands and being impaled on one inhabited by Screela. He well remembered how her Unicorn Horn had passed through the stone walls of the caverns of the Zombie Lord like they were made of butter. Although a Unicorn Horn was not as hard as a diamond, they were tougher than the finest crowbar.

With no other mining tools available to them, Rhazburn wrote messages, asking Hili to suggest Whither use her horn to help them uncover the sapphire. Whither went to work with the same glee she approached any task. No miner could have been as efficient or as tireless as Whither. She balanced like a mountain goat on protuberances of rock from the cliff little larger than her hooves. Slicing through the rock, she caused it to shatter, crumble, and rain down upon their camp.

One of Rhazburn's skeletal troops was crushed in a subsequent small avalanche, after which the camp was moved out of harm's way. One morning, after days of constant toil, Whither reached the cluster of gems. Rhazburn used his skeletal hands and his Sword of Bliss to pry the blue star sapphire, the size of a pigeon egg, from the matrix. It was here that it had grown, squeezed and heated by the pressure of a mountain of rock above it, and was now being born into the world outside.

When all the clinging matrix had been chipped away, Jonathon gazed critically at the gem held between Rhazburn's brittle finger bones. The gleaming star within the deep blue gem would not be seen properly until it were cleaved and polished to pristine brilliance. He approved the choice. Hili could use her tiny diamond-tipped tools to polish the dome, but the star sapphire would have to be cleaved at least once.

Since he still had no tools to cleave the facet of the sapphire, he took the liberty to approach Whither again. Humbly, he walked up to the Unicorn, this time knowing the magical beast could, unlike other animals, see into the nether plane he inhabited. Again, Whither invited him within. Seeing through Whither's eyes the details of the sapphire, all the proper angles were clear. According to Rhazburn, the 'star' of the sapphire had to be as close to the center of the gem as possible for the desired effect.

Whither aided Jonathon as he held the sapphire with a hoof against a slab of granite. The tip of Whither's horn was remarkably sharp and Whither could place the tip with amazing precision against the large sapphire. With a twitch of her powerful neck, the gem was cleaved across a brilliant plane and the sunlight revealed the star within.

Jonathon politely exited Whither again, freeing her up for Trallalair to ride for an equally important task, looking for more dead Unicorns to resurrect.

Hili finished perfecting the surface of the gem. Then, under the tutelage of Rhazburn, she engraved all the proper verses.

While the fabrication of the Demon-Entrapment Gem was being completed, Trallalair rode Whither throughout the western Dead Lands all the way to Devil's Fang. Without hesitation, Whither galloped to a site where a second dead Unicorn lay.

Trallalair used the Knife of Life on that Unicorn and witnessed the fantastic resurrection of a Unicorn Stallion, even larger than Whither. The two Unicorns, together, galloped unerringly to many other sites as if they had never forgotten, even in death, where every individual of their race had died. A few of the Unicorn corpses, mummified by the atmosphere of the Dead Lands, were intact enough for the Knife of Life to be used to resurrect them. At the end, six Unicorns, two female and four male, raced together in a dazzling herd back to where the party hid.

Back at the excavation site, Hili completed the arcane verses which covered the flat facet of the gem, leaving the sparkling dome of the star sapphire as a clear door through which the Demon could be drawn and trapped.

Jonathon inspected every aspect of the gem held in Rhazburn's skeletal fingers.

The sapphire glowed brilliant blue, sparkling in the sun. Deep within, the star was seemingly distant, like it radiated its beams of light up through ocean depths, signifying some living creature, waiting, expectant. Only at the very center of the star could the Demon be trapped. The evil creature would be pierced and held by the scintillating rays radiating from it.

Rhazburn admitted that he did not know what would happen if a mere Ghost touched the gem once it had been activated with a coin. Possibly, he or Jonathon could be trapped as well inside the gem to stay with the Demon forever.

Jonathon shuddered at the thought.

Rhazburn knew that they had to use the prowess of Trallalair to deliver the final blow to the Demon. The Knife of Life had to be delivered to the Demon and stuck in the flesh of Jonathon's dead body which Sverdphthik was using. Since Sverdphthik would most likely be flying a Dragon, probably Cataclysm, no one would be able to just walk up and stab him. Jonathon had already tried that. Only Trallalair had the skill with bow and arrow to have a chance to get the blade of the Knife of Life in the Demon's flesh by firing at it from a distance. Only a Dragonflyer like Trallalair could anticipate the flight path of a Dragon and have a chance to hit the Demon riding on its back. There would be no second chance.

So, Rhazburn reasoned, Trallalair would be the object of Sverdphthik's revenge if the Knife of Life brought Jonathon's body back to life. Even though the skeletons could turn his Ghost slaves into beatified spirits, eager to help take the Dragoncrown from Sverdphthik, it would see them as little threat compared to the Sinjery maiden riding Whither. Therefore, she was the one that needed protection by the Jewel of Nishbad.

Rhazburn had Hili give her the Jewel, which Trallalair placed in her tunic close to her heart between her breasts. He was without a body to stimulate male instincts. He had no prospect of winning Trallalair's heart. Yet Rhazburn yearned to touch her warmth with real fingers. He knew that would never happen. Although a Ghost could not touch, he could be touched. Regret at his lost chance to approach Trallalair as a man, not as a fright, was more painful to him than any discomfort of the soul he had ever felt.

Trallalair fixed The Knife of Life to her best arrow. For a whole day she practiced shooting the strangely-balanced arrow at living trees until she could hit a twig at six rods or a branch thick as her arm at twelve. She always chose living trees as targets so as not to waste the power within the Knife of Life.

When all the preparations were finished, they assembled their force at the edge of the Dead Lands. There were fifty skeletons, all wielding Swords of Bliss, six Unicorns, one Sinjery carrying the Jewel of Nishbad, and the Knife of Life fixed to an arrow. Hili insisted on coming, despite Trallalair wanting her to return to the Land of Repose. This time, the Sylvets provided plenty of provisions for the living members of the group, food and water for Trallalair and Hili, as well as fodder for the Unicorns. All the magical items could be energized by plenty of Copper Orders Trallalair carried, brought from the Zombie Lord's hoard by Rhazburn's skeleton host.

Jonathon would be alone again. He could not possibly keep up with the assemblage, straining as he must against the mire of physical reality. He would be left behind with no knowledge of what would transpire. All could be lost without his knowledge. He wished he could travel within Whither as before, but it was too much to ask.

As if in answer to his wish, Whither trotted over to him and stood, nodding and whinnying, inviting. Jonathon hoped she was inviting him to re-enter her body and share her soul for a third time. He hesitated until she repeated her nod.

Love of Whither, like a reverence and devotion to Kris, the embodiment of Beauty, permeated every bit of his spirit. He bent to plant a kiss on the side of Whither's face. At that moment, he was within her again, full of fire, with eyes that could distinguish a leaf at the horizon or see the wanderings of troubled souls. He could hear Hili's thoughts just as he had heard those of Saggethrie or Rhazburn, but the Pixelle was apart, flitting about, watching the assemblage of their force.

Through Whither's eyes, Jonathon saw Trallalair bow slightly. Whither acknowledged her willingness to carry Trallalair by sidling up to her. The Brandmistress hopped up so fluidly that there was little impact on their back as she mounted them.

Jonathon felt safer within Whither than he had ever felt in his life. She could run fast enough and cleverly enough to elude Dragons. No Ghost could wrest him from within while her soul embraced and protected him.

He knew, without a doubt, that even the Rod of Coercion would have no hold over him. Besides, riding them was the most fearsome warrior to fight Demons and evil spirits that he could imagine, the diminutive Trallalair, armed with the Knife of Life and the Jewel of Nishbad. Ranged about them were all the Swords of Bliss, ready to beatify any spectral slaves of Sverdphthik who would dare approach them.

Early in the morning of the first day of spring, the allies set forth across the desert of the Dead Lands. After they left the foothills of the Forbidden Mountains, they encountered a sea of shifting sands with slippery, sloping dunes as monotonous as waves. Like they were jack rabbits hopping though a meadow, the Unicorns hurdled the dunes. The stumbling skeletons, however, had a hard time of it. Their fleshless heels acted more like stakes holding them back than feet propelling them.

The Unicorns had to carry them by threes over the sand dunes, leaving groups to wait on the far side while they leaped back for more. They had more than two score leagues to walk to reach Sverdphthik's Hellpit. Two days passed. Trallalair and Hili needed to stop and rest, at least at night. Three whole days total were spent in the sea of sand, but each morning brought them closer to the Demon.

In the boulder-strewn wastes beyond the sea of sand, the skeletons fared little better. They repeatedly broke their legs, so individuals had to stop and hop about for a few moments to retrieve lost appendages, then secure them back into place. All marching order was abandoned as each skeleton managed the best he could.

Within a few days' stumbling through the rocky wastes, Jonathon began to see masses of Ghosts, many clothed in dead bodies, trudging back and forth from the center of the Dead Lands. As was typical for the slaves of the Demon, they were constantly striking out at one another or rolling in fights to the accompaniment of screams and cries. He was glad that Trallalair, as a live human, was spared most of the commotion. Sverdphthik's Hellpit was still too far off to be easily seen, but it darkened the horizon before them.

When they reached the masses of Sverdphthik's marching minions, Rhazburn had his skeleton troops fan out on either side and in front of Trallalair to protect her and her precious tools.

The skeletons hacked at the Zombies with their Swords of Bliss and scythed through the streaming spirits, causing more commotion yet as the newly reformed spirits split apart into groups of their own and began chanting songs of love from the Faith of The Three. Many joined their cavalcade and, like children playing in a pleasing waterfall, ran up to be touched again by the Swords of Bliss as often as the wielders would tolerate.

To Jonathon, the entire rock-littered landscape around the procession was covered with a seething mass of spirits, good and bad, fighting and shouting or dancing with joy and raising their voices in adulation to the sky.

Trallalair only saw the skeletons waving their swords in the air around them, occasionally striking a Zombie which fell apart, instantly inert.

Rhazburn was watchful of the sky in the direction of the Hellpit. He knew that before long, the rumor of their passing would ripple through the crowds of Ghosts and reach Sverdphthik.

Before they were even half the distance to Sverdphthik's Hellpit, a mass of Dragons filled the sky. The skeletons alone would not have a chance against the Dragons. Hili, at the suggestion of Whither, had skeletons, three apiece, ride the Unicorns so a few had a chance to evade the Dragons. Rhazburn, the skeleton, mounted Whither and rode behind Trallalair.

In the face of the approach of the Demon, Hili needed to be very close to the one she loved, so she sat astride Whither's horn, hugging it for all the magic it could infuse into her tiny body.

Trallalair took her cue and took out a Glass Command given to her by one of Rhazburn's troops to activate the Jewel of Nishbad. The Knife of Life tied to the arrow in her quiver still had the sheath on it. She extracted the arrow with the knife and bared the magical metal. She took her bow, twanged the bowstring once to test it, and notched the arrow, holding it ready with both hands. With these actions, she lost the use of her hands to hold herself on Whither's back. But between her skill at riding and Whither's competence at keeping her rider safe, Trallalair could stay on her back, despite the rapid rushes, twists and swerves that would throw any less of a rider on any less of a steed.

As the Dragons approached, the enslaved Ghosts pressed their attack on the flanks of the allies. The skeletons on the ground fanned the air with their swords, beatifying spirit after spirit, swelling Rhazburn's troops, and eating away at Sverdphthik's ranks.

The Dragons, roaring together like rolling thunder in a storm, hit them. Fire blasted their ranks, but the Unicorns, even carrying the skeletons, seemed a step ahead of the attack and bolted in unison, scattering in six random directions. They never lost a skeleton but galloped between diving Dragons, cutting away from grasping talons, skirting, or leaping clear over bursts of flame. As the Unicorns passed through the ranks of Sverdphthik's hosts, the skeleton riders sliced through them, salvaging countless souls who helped restrain the further attacks of the Demon's host.

On the ground, Rhazburn's walking skeletons took a beating. They were doing well against the enslaved spirits, but were unprotected from the Dragons. The Dragons could fly just above their ranks and rake them with their talons, shattering them so they could no longer hold the Swords of Bliss. A dose of Dragonfire would finish them off, burning their bones to ashes and melting the Swords of Bliss. Within moments of the Dragons' attack, all the skeletons not riding Unicorns, along with their swords of Bliss, were destroyed.

Trallalair kept watch for Sverdphthik by twisting and turning as Whither scampered, evading the Dragons. She would know the Demon was approaching when she saw Cataclysm. She wanted to get off the shot before the Demon had time to use the Rod of Coercion. Although she had confidence that Whither would again aid her to counter the spell of the Rod of Coercion, she could lose the precious moments she needed for the single shot at the Demon. She thought that he might not be certain they had the Knife of Life. Their only advantage with the Knife of Life and the Jewel of Nishbad was surprise. If he knew they existed and were aimed at him, he only needed to keep away from them to foil their attack. He had done it before. He had avoided the Jewel of Nishbad for three hundred years.

Whither had just leapt through a cloud of smoke, and Trallalair had scanned the sky. Suddenly, there he was, Cataclysm rising high in the air, not fifty rods away. She shouted, "Whither, stand still!" Trallalair lurched forward a bit as Whither stopped like she had hit a wall.

Trallalair could discern what was left of Jonathon's body riding the Red Dragon. It was just beyond the farthest she could fire her arrow accurately. He raised the Rod of Coercion. She felt a chill as the words "Obey my will!" reached her in a scream. One chance was all she had before he commanded her to stop. The distance was irrelevant. Cataclysm's neck was in the way. Even though he was hovering conveniently in one place, the distance was too far to be accurate. Trallalair saw in her mind the arc needed to place the arrow behind the Dragon's neck and into the Demon's chest. Just at the instant Sverdphthik began the command, "No one...", she let the arrow fly and prayed to Mother Earth for guidance. "... Harm me or hinder me. All of you stop," came the completion of the command. Spurred by the command, she had a compulsion to reach out at the flying arrow to take it back, but it was too late. The Knife of Life was flying away.

All the combatants stopped perfectly still except the Unicorns, none of whom were affected by the command. The Dragons, still in control of the Demon, continued their attack on the Unicorns. Whither, by instinct, leaped away, despite Trallalair's paralysis, barely escaping a blast of fire.

Hili, touching the Unicorn Horn, was similarly unaffected by the command. At the moment the arrow flew, Hili, with her long experience of flight and flying things, could see how tenuous was the chance the arrow would hit its target. She spread her wings and flew with all her strength and anger at the Demon, following the flight of the arrow and the Knife of Life. Like Trallalair, she had not seen the Master Jeweler's body since the day he had been killed. As she approached the Demon, she saw the the change in him was astonishing.

Jonathon's previous gentle and pleasant features had been twisted and transformed into the hideous mask of a snarling, feral beast. Dried and brittle, the skin of his face cracked with each change in expression.

Cataclysm's hovering dipped ever so slightly, just enough so the Knife of Life hurtled over the Demon's head. Sverdphthik was looking at the scene below. Once the arrow passed, the Demon ignored Hili as an insignificant threat.

Hili flew past his ear and dived down at an angle to intercept the falling arrow. She reached it twenty flutters past Cataclysm and grasped the Knife by the hilt with both arms. Straining with all her strength, she fluttered her wings furiously to gain altitude. She knew she had little time before Cataclysm would be instructed to descend and join the attack on the Unicorns. She turned in the air and headed for the back of the heedless Demon.

With a little cry of fright, all alone again, without the Community or even Whither to aid her, Hili flew. Her furiously-beating wing muscles cried out in pain. Her meager arms were stretched to their limit. The weight of the knife tied to the arrow dragged her to the ground far below. Through it all, Hili flew.

She aimed her flight parallel to the row of spines along Cataclysm's tail and back, which led like a sinuous path to the Demon sitting at the base of Cataclysm's neck. She had to fight the buffeting wind of Cataclysm's wings as she darted along her path. Cataclysm's head was dipping as he started his dive to the ground, but Hili's cry was so loud that the Demon turned its head at the last moment, interrupting its concentration.

Even the dead eyes of the Master Jeweler became animate with fear as the Demon perceived its bane, the Knife of Life, a moment before Hili rammed the blade into the back of the dead Jonathon Forthright.

The Knife of Life exploded in a shower of sparks and light. It had expended all the rest of its potential energy against the Demon. Its power was done. The blast sent Hili catapulting far away. She recovered in time to steady herself in the air and witness the transformation of the Demon into a living Jonathon Forthright.

As Jonathon's form scintillated on Cataclysm's back, the Red Dragon seemed at a loss what to do. He hovered in place, abandoning his dive to the ground. The air around the Demon churned with streams of sparkling energy worming erratically around the glistening form of Jonathon Forthright. Like a howling baby being pulled from its womb, the Demon's form stretched and fought as life triumphed and pushed out death. The Demon was thrown out by the power of the Knife of Life, and the Knife of Life died in the process.

From within Whither, Jonathon could see it all.

Without any support in the air, the Demon fell toward the ground. Jonathon could sense a psychic scream from the Demon which he doubted Trallalair could hear. The Rod of Coercion and the Dragoncrown were lost to it. It had only one place it wanted to go, and it could alter its fall just enough to accomplish that. It tumbled and twisted to fall in the direction of the one who had fired the arrow, Trallalair. Jonathon felt his own soul being pulled out of his refuge within Whither as he sensed the Demon wanted to have its vengeance upon Trallalair. All was happening as Rhazburn had predicted.

Hili was thankfully out of his reach. She saw that her role was finished. Perhaps because she was still instilled with the power of Wither's horn, she could see the Demon's ethereal form.

Sverdphthik was heading toward the Jewel of Nishbad, but Hili had enough of Demons and death, enough of knives and crowns and swords. She could not even wait for the outcome. Either the Demon would be trapped or it would not. She had no need to see either. All she wanted was her Community, to hear, feel, taste and smell them, and to never be parted again. Flying straight up, she flew away from battles, away from dead things, away from loneliness, back to Isseltrent and the bosom of those she loved.

Trallalair had missed the final flight of her arrow and the Knife of Life, but she feared she had missed. When she heard the report of the Knife of Life's explosion, she looked up and saw a glimmering of the changes happening on Cataclysm's neck. She knew, from what she had seen of the power of the Knife of Life, that it was performing its miracle. It was changing a dead Jonathon Forthright back into a living Jonathon Forthright. A live jeweler with the Dragoncrown on his head. It was then that she remembered her vision, firing an arrow into Jonathon Forthright. At the time, she had thought she was executing the traitor, but it was his resurrection she was causing, not his death.

The Dragons, no longer in control of the Demon, broke off their attack. Still within Whither, Jonathon could see the transformation as she turned toward Cataclysm. Although he was still uncertain as to what was happening, Whither had no doubt that the Demon had been expelled from Jonathon's body. As he felt a tug from above, the call of his reforming body to his soul, Jonathon could see the frightening form of the Demon coming right toward them.

Trallalair was the target of the Demon's attack, and even though Whither had countered the spell of the Rod of Coercion by touching her again with her horn, Trallalair sat still, knowing she was the bait for their trap. She had heard that Demons were invisible to humans, but she could clearly see the rapacious form of Sverdphthik falling toward her. Perhaps, she thought, her lingering ability to see the ethereal was another benefit of her brief touch of the Unicorn's horn.

Jonathon, beckoned by his body, was yanked from the safety of Whither to fly like a thought to his reforming self.

Trallalair still held her ground as the Demon struck. He clutched at her throat with claws of ice. She was thrown from the Unicorn, backwards onto Rhazburn who burst apart into a useless pile of bones.

The Sword of Bliss lay useless on the ground, and Rhazburn dared not interfere, lest he be sucked within the Jewel of Nishbad along with the Demon.

When he touched Trallalair, Sverdphthik also touched the Jewel of Nishbad between her breasts. Before he seemed able to react, half of his insubstantial substance was sucked inside. Trallalair could do nothing but watch and feel. As the Demon touched her, she could still see his nether self. His face was like a putrid wolf with sharp, cold eyes that shoved icicles into her brain. The cold intensified as the Demon struggled to stop himself from being trapped in the Jewel of Nishbad.

The Jewel of Nishbad had been activated by a Glass Command, but that was not enough. Sverdphthik, holding himself out with his clawed hands braced against Trallalair, swelled with a scream that terrorized her. That terror he caused seemed to strengthen him enough so he could pull himself free of the Jewel of Nishbad. In a moment, cleft from his body but still apparently tied to the lure of the thousands of souls Trallalair knew were left in his Hellpit, the Demon took off, running fast. She imagined he was pulled away by his own awful might to his hideous sanctum.

On the Demon's way, his feral substance passed beneath Jonathon Forthright sitting astride the Red Dragon. Jonathon barely had time to realize that he was alive when a blow of hate hit him to rip his meager soul from his newly resurrected body. Just as long before, when the Demon had possessed his body and stolen the Rod of Coercion, the Demon gave him such a slashing of terror that Jonathon almost receded from contact with his own body again. But this time, Jonathon wore the Dragoncrown on his head. This time, Jonathon resisted easily, as if the Dragoncrown bolstered his naturally timid soul. Besides, Jonathon was the one who held the Rod of Coercion now, so he could do as he pleased. That brief contact, however, told Jonathon that the Demon could renew its power in its Hellpit. He heard, echoing in his mind, the Demon's vow that, by all that was unholy and vile in Hell, it would come back to Jonathon and devour his soul.

BOOK IV
THE DRAGONCROWN

CHAPTER 35

999 COMMANDS

The first thing Jonathon did when he was fully awake within his resurrected body high up on the Red Dragon's neck was freeze with fright. The memory of the Demon's last threat was fully enough to paralyze him. But besides that, the ground was much too far away. The Dragon could just shrug his shoulders and toss him off into the air like a bothersome flea. Jonathon would be dashed on the rocks, squashed by the other Dragons, burnt to a crisp, and his soul beat up again by Sverdphthik's minions. Cataclysm quivered, making Jonathon grab tightly with his free hand to the murderous-looking spine in front of him. Shifting about on the wavering muscles, he was still off-balance and clutched at the spine with his other hand, almost dropping the Rod of Coercion in the process.

He whimpered aloud, "Stop. Please don't throw me off."

Of course, Cataclysm obeyed, quelling his restlessness instantly. His neck became as stable and secure as a leaning column of stone. After all, Jonathon was now the Dragonlord.

He reached up and felt the Dragoncrown, shivering with the knowledge that he had such power. What if the Dragoncrown fell off? He shook his head to test if it was loose. It wasn't. Along with the function of the Dragoncrown came a conviction that it would never fall off unless he willed it. All these years, Jonathon had thought that the Dragoncrown could fall off the Dragonlord's head at any moment, releasing the Dragons, when, all along, the Crown was magically glued to the Dragonlord's head. Everything became clear.

Below him, all the Unicorns had stopped their dashing about, but stamped and shook their flowing manes, restless to be free and racing over the plains. The dead skeletons on their backs looked as still as... dead skeletons. At that moment, seeing the skeletons inanimate, he had the bizarre but accurate feeling that they should be moving along with the spirits within them. He never thought he would feel concern for the skeleton of a dead human. He thought back and realized that the Demon had commanded everyone to stop what they were doing. The command had not affected the Unicorns, but all the Zombies and skeletons around them, whether enemies of Jonathon or allies, were frozen. He looked down and saw the Rod of Coercion in his left hand. With a start, he realized that he, Jonathon Forthright, held the Rod of Coercion. Rhazburn had said that the Rod of Coercion would work only for one with extraordinary mental powers like the Dragonlord or, as they had seen, the Demon.

Since Jonathon was the Dragonlord now, maybe.... He raised the staff and shouted, "I release you all. Do what you want!" Nothing happened. The skeletons remained inert. He thought, *How presumptuous of me. I have no power.*

Frustration and disappointment enervated him until he recollected, behind his ingrained concept of his weakness, a memory... a memory of the verse needed to activate the rod's power.

Holding the Rod of Coercion high so none could mistake his authority, he shouted, "Through ears, hearts, minds I call. Obey my will, one and all. You are all released. Do as you please." With that, the skeletons began to move again. This time Jonathon shivered with disgust, just seeing them move. He was not one of the dead anymore.

Cataclysm waited, hovering in the air above the plain. Jonathon could see through his eyes whenever he wished. He could see through the eyes of any living Dragon, feel their bodies, their hunger and lusts. At the moment, he felt Cataclysm tiring, wanting to land and rest. Jonathon still felt giddy, as if he could fall off anytime. Having Cataclysm under his control did nothing to change the unreliability of Jonathon's own atrophied muscles as he tried to grip the Dragon's neck with weak legs. He wanted Cataclysm to land even more than the Red did. So with the grip on Cataclysm's mind by the Dragoncrown, Jonathon allowed it. More specifically, he was Cataclysm himself, part of the Dragon's thoughts and in tune with every aspect of his body. Jonathon, controlling the Dragon's body, simply flew down to the rocky plain. As opposed to the time when he had stolen Cataclysm's dead body, the movement was easy, instinctual. He landed, gracefully for a full grown Dragon, within one rod of Whither.

For a whole Blessing, Jonathon ignored the scene around him on the rocky wastes. He did nothing else but sit on Cataclysm's scaly neck as the Red Dragon sat still. Jonathon was absorbing and sorting out scores of thoughts.

He was alive, feeling his bottom on the prickly scales of the Dragon, rather uncomfortable but marvelous since he could feel through his skin once again. In his hand, the Rod of Coercion felt warm and filled with life, but Jonathon now knew that it was a mere shadow of the power in a living Unicorn Horn on a living Unicorn. It was completely clear to him that the Rod of Coercion he had put together was a cruel abomination, just as Hili and the Community had told him so long ago. As evil as the deed was, Jonathon had the courage to admit that he had known they were right at the time but chose to ignore the fact. He faced another realization. He, Jonathon Forthright, had to make amends somehow.

His mind was filled not only with these thoughts but simultaneously Dragonthought. Dragonthought, Dragonhunger, Dragonfeelings, Dragonhate for their enslavement - all of it mesmerized and dispirited him. At that very moment, all the world changed for him. Dragons had thoughts, plans, ideas, and fears just like all the supposedly-intelligent beings. Jonathon remembered Whither's complex mind. If Dragons and Unicorns were able to understand the world about them so well, then what about dogs, cats, birds, cows, sheep, fish... what about every living animal? Beauty and terror loomed before him in his heightened imagination, from the pleasures of a family of hawks to the terror of the squirrels they fed upon. All the complex relationships of all the animals throughout eternity dawned upon Jonathon. The needs of humans seemed an insignificant part of the whole. It was almost refreshing to know that other beings in the world mattered beyond those he had always considered intelligent. All creatures had an intelligence of their own and a place in the creation of The Three.

There was the paradox for the new Dragonlord. It was a cruel choice that Jonathon must make. He was the one who must decide how, and if, to keep the Dragons enslaved.

While he tried to sort out all these new concepts and accept them for the truth they represented, the Dragons sat, obedient, awaiting his orders. The binding force of the Dragoncrown was irresistible to them. But, just the same, the strength of the Dragoncrown ebbed. Even though it was made of black glass created by the very creatures it enslaved and its size gave it considerable longevity, it would not last forever. In less than two hundred years, its power would be gone. All Dragonlords knew this and hid it from the people. The power of the Dragoncrown had countered that of the Demon and held back Hell for hundreds of years, but all too soon, it would all be lost and Hell would be unleashed into the mortal realm.

No wonder the Dragonlord continually moped about. Everyone thought that his perpetual sadness was due to sharing the sad thoughts of the Dragons, but there was much more. The Dragonlord had to cope with the knowledge that all living things had a kind of spirit and could feel pain and grief just like humans. And with the knowledge that the world was doomed, no matter what any of them accomplished. It was far beyond anything a sane person could bear.

After Sverdphthik fled, all its wraiths and Zombies fled as well. Back to its Hellpit they streamed, drawn by its power, adding to its power. Their anguish was its strength. They would be tortured ten-fold to boost the Demon's fading substance.

All about Jonathon, the landscape had changed. Before, when he had been a Ghost, almost luminous Ghosts marched to the coercion of the Demon, and the substantial world was dull and foggy. Now, he saw the brightness of the sun carving out every detail of every miserable stone in the Dead Lands. The unrelenting depression of the Dead Lands persisted, weighing him down, even after their triumph. Sverdphthik still laughed at the world. Hell's Breach still stood like a chancre, spewing disease. Sverdphthik had proven that even Dragons were not safe from the malign influence of Demons. They, with the rest of the world, would suffer if Hell's Breach remained.

Jonathon realized that only one person had the power and experience to make a difference in the world. That person was Jonathon Forthright. Just taking back the Dragoncrown alone would doom the Realm as much as doing nothing. Jonathon had to go up against Sverdphthik, man to man, or rather, man to Demon. Twice, Sverdphthik had bested him, once in his shop and once at the edge of the Demon's domain. Jonathon had no choice but go after Sverdphthik in his seat of power, where the Demon could draw strength from all the tortured souls. That thought alone, of all those pathetic souls, tortured victims and resigned torturers, was all that Jonathon needed to spur him to use his weak muscles, now much weaker after being dead for fortnights, to challenge the Demon to a duel.

He would need the Jewel of Nishbad along with the Dragoncrown, the Rod of Coercion, and, for good measure, a Sword of Bliss. Trallalair, the skeletons, and a few Unicorns stood or ambled about, casting brief, expectant glimpses at him.

Well, at least Trallalair looked expectant.

The Unicorns looked ready to bolt if the Dragon attacked them.

The skeletons just looked dead, except when they moved. Then they looked silly. Gangly and uncoordinated, they bumped into each other, knocking off a collarbone or sometimes a skull that had to be retrieved. Not an army to foster confidence. Even though they had Swords of Bliss, there were only little more than a dozen left. Against the Demon's Hellpit, they would be overwhelmed by the vast numbers.

He suspected that Sverdphthik was collecting all its minions to increase its strength, regroup, and counterattack them all. The Demon had underestimated them once, but it would be wary and crafty the next time. Jonathon was not going to let that happen.

The only one missing was Hili. The Pixelle would be easy to miss in the expanse surrounding them with Unicorns carrying skeletons and weaving between retreating Zombies. She should come forth if she were not injured. There was no need for her to hide.

He shouted to the Sinjery warrior, "Trallalair, come closer." She slung her faithful bow and sauntered confidently right up to Cataclysm's tense forefoot. "Trallalair, I thank you for my body. Was this my execution? My ending that you had a vision of?"

"Yes, Jeweler, it was as I saw in my vision. But I had interpreted it wrongly. I was not executing you, but bringing you back. Never would I have thought that I would fire an arrow into you for your own good."

"I thank you again," he said.

Jonathon scanned the plains. He even looked through several Dragoneyes at his disposal. "I don't see Hili. Do you know where she is?"

Trallalair looked over the confusion of Dragons, Zombies, and Unicorns but could not make out the Pixelle. "I do not see her, Jeweler. I thought my arrow was bound to miss. The shot was hasty and at too far a distance to hit the Demon, I mean you, with certainty. I never saw it hit, but I knew the Knife of Life was in the Demon as the process of the change began. If the Pixelle is missing, I wonder if she had something to do with it all. Perhaps she flew up and redirected the arrow. We may owe her much more than we ever imagined."

She stopped, pensive. "You know, I have been arrogant. I thought I knew it all. But I did not know the Dragons. I did not know my strength and ability. I did not know my skill. I am not surprised that the smallest among us was the one who may have defeated the Demon. I did see the Knife shattered with a tremendous blast. I pray to Mother Earth that Pixelle Hili was not injured or killed when that happened."

"She may have fallen to the ground injured. We must search for her."

Trallalair bent and said in Whither's ear, "Whither, where is Hili?" Whither stood still but looked straight upward. Jonathon and Trallalair looked upward too, straining their eyes, but saw nothing.

Jonathon finally said, "Well, if she is in the sky, she will have to come back some time."

She never did return. He thought that maybe Whither looked to Heaven and Hili was really dead. If only he could enter the Unicorn's mind once more. No. He shuddered. Now that he was fully human again, the idea of possessing another's mind was absolutely repugnant to him. That he was in possession of dozens of Dragon's minds seemed just as repugnant now that he understood the ancient, inherent beauty of their thoughts. The slavery of the Dragons was just as wrong as the slavery of the minions of Sverdphthik, or, for that matter, the slavery of the Sinjery to the Dragonlord. Beyond the Dragon's hate of their slavery to him, he could sense that they agreed that the Demon must be stopped at all costs. From their awful experience in which so many of the Dragons died, many of whom were ancient beyond Jonathon's reckoning, they realized that the Demon's defeat would be impossible without their speed and strength. Even as his thralls, Jonathon asked them for their aid in defeating the Demon. He understood that they agreed.

Jonathon had to forget the fate of Hili for the moment and concentrate on the threat that the Demon still represented. He turned again to Trallalair. "I need the Jewel of Nishbad."

Trallalair shook her head to rid herself of her worry about the Pixelle, then regarded Jonathon. She knew nothing of his resolve to go after the Demon once and for all. She thought he only wanted the Jewel of Nishbad as protection so the Demon would not steal the Rod of Coercion and the Dragoncrown again.

She stepped on Cataclysm's foot and leaped up to the Dragon's elbow, just above the elbow spike. Her worn boots gripped his scales as easily as her bare feet had gripped the bark of a gnarled tree in Sinjer as she leaped to his shoulder. As her feet barely touched down she vaulted over his shoulder spike on up to his neck, just behind Jonathon.

As she extracted the disappointing Jewel of Nishbad from between her breasts, she said, "Under the sea, you brought me back to the world. Now I have done the same. I feel I have repaid the debt I owed you."

"I'm most appreciative, Trallalair, most appreciative, but I have work to do." He reached for the Jewel.

"Your work is done, Jeweler. You have taken back the Dragoncrown." She clutched the Jewel tightly, drawing it back.

"I must finish it. The Demon must be thrown back to Hell."

"You cannot go back to the Hellpit, Jeweler. All will be lost." She gripped his arm, seeing her duty again to save the Dragoncrown. "The Dragoncrown could be lost again. This time it will be forever since the Jewel of Nishbad was useless to trap the Demon and the Knife of Life is destroyed."

He looked into her steel eyes. He felt her steel grip. She could do what she wanted with him and the Jewel. She had twice his strength, despite her size. She placed the Jewel of Nishbad back into her bosom and reached for her Sword. Jonathon wished that he had a weapon.

Trallalair had her Sword out threatening, ready to behead him and take the Dragoncrown back to Seldric.

Jonathon realized that he did not need a weapon. He had the Rod of Coercion. He thought the verse, 'Through ears, hearts, minds I call, Obey my will one and all.' Then he said, "Trallalair, put away your Sword and let me go. I am the Dragonlord now. Give me the Jewel of Nishbad, and don't interfere with me."

Incredulous at what she was doing, Trallalair quickly put away her Sword, let go of his arm, plucked the Jewel from her bosom again, and handed it to him. She obeyed his every word within moments.

He chuckled. Not even an argument from the headstrong woman. Smiling to himself at the powers that he had suddenly been granted, he dismissed her with a casual wave of the Jewel of Nishbad before her face. "Now go back down."

She leaped to the ground, landing lightly. Jonathon checked the pouch at his hip, the one that had carried Caene's body. It was intact and had a string to close it. He slipped the Jewel of Nishbad inside.

One of the skeletons sheathed his Sword of Bliss through an opening in its pelvic bone and lurched to the Dragon. It began to climb, much more slowly than the Sinjery, slipping on scales because the boney feet had no traction. He left both kneecaps behind.

Wary of any hindrance, Jonathon spoke the verse for the Rod of Coercion and commanded the skeleton, "Do not interfere with me."

The skeleton kept coming, nodding, patting its breast bone at times, as if that had some hidden meaning.

Jonathon knew he needed Rhazburn. He couldn't tell the skeletons apart, but he took a chance that this one was Rhazburn and waited for it to climb the side of the Dragon. The skeleton came slipping and sliding doggedly up to Jonathon. His rattling bones, joints shamelessly misaligned, leaned forward. It motioned for Jonathon to do likewise.

At the moment that Jonathon's head bumped the bleached skull, he heard Rhazburn's voice in his mind. *Father, the Jewel of Nishbad will work. One Glass Command was not enough. I should have known. Sverdphthik is much too powerful. We need a lot more Glass Commands to fuel it, and I know where we can find them, the caves and tunnels in the Forbidden Mountains.*

Jonathon withdrew his head so he could look into the skull's eyes. He had hoped to find a trace of Rhazburn there. Nothing but air did he see inside that flimsy carapace. Yet he nodded to his invisible son.

The path to the caves in the Forbidden Mountains had been as clear in Rhazburn's thoughts as if he had laid a map between them. At the southern end of the range, Devil's Fang rose splendid and cruel. There beneath its impregnable bulk, serpentine tunnels had been tediously chipped by Ghouls and Zombies over the centuries. At the very center of the web of tunnels, like the precious eggs of a spider, a mound of treasure awaited them. All its prior protectors, who were intimately familiar with the contents of the treasure trove, stood in loose ranks as loyal Ghosts in Rhazburn's army.

Leaning forward again to touch skulls, Jonathon thought, *I will bring steeds for all of us. We will ride the Dragons. Stay here with me.*

Rhazburn broke contact, turned, and settled his rambunctious bones down upon the Dragon's back. Raising a hand, missing a couple digits, he signaled that he was ready.

Jonathon called out to the eight nearest Dragons, a White, five Greens, a Black, and a Red, to arrange themselves for his friends and allies. The one Black was nearby, and Jonathon knew that another one was within one league of Devil's Fang. Some of the skeletons would proceed there by Black Dragon travel, while the rest of them flew, riding atop the other Dragons.

With Jonathon giving mental orders to the Dragons, Trallalair and most of the skeletons arranged themselves on their scaly steeds. So all the others could hear his intention, Jonathon shouted to Cataclysm, "Fly south to Devil's Fang!" The other Dragons followed Cataclysm as he took to the air and flew.

When Jonathon was dead, he hadn't worried about heights. Alive again, rising up in the air with nothing but a Dragon slippery with scales beneath him, Jonathon felt a rush in his chest and a giddiness threatening to make him faint. Fainting would be disastrous, since everyone going to the caves depended on his control of the Dragons. He decided to use the Rod of Coercion on himself, shouting, "Through hearts, minds I call, obey my will, one and all! Jonathon Forthright, for Three's sake, do not faint!"

The Red Dragon started up at a steep angle, so Jonathon had to clutch the leather-wrapped spine protruding just in front of him from the Dragon's neck. He forgot all about fainting. Instead, he wildly clutched the flimsy spine as his legs were being jostled free from the security of Cataclysm's back. It wasn't until a skeletal hand tapped him on the shoulder and he turned to see Rhazburn with his legs flailing in the wind, pieces of toes flying off and a decrepit finger pointing at the Dragoncrown, that Jonathon remembered his total control over the Red's flight. He forgot that he only needed his thoughts to control Cataclysm and shouted at what he fantasized was the Dragon's ear, just beneath one of the twisted horns, "Cataclysm, don't fly so steep or so fast!" Cataclysm eased into a gentler climb and slowed enough so that Jonathon and Rhazburn could hold on easily by gripping with their legs alone. All the other Dragons climbing as steeply were dropping bones from the skeletons on their backs, higgledy-piggledy.

Jonathon shouted at them to go easy on their riders. Despite the fact that he was much too far for his words to carry, all the Dragons obeyed. Even Dragons a hundred leagues distant could respond to his thoughts, and he could see through their eyes. Controlling the Dragons was almost easier if he relaxed more and allowed his common sense to adjust what they were doing.

Mortal vision was marvelous after so long in the spirit world. All the mists that had clouded his view of living matter had disappeared. In the sky, much too high in the air, the details below were wanting, but who cared for details? The sun pained his eyes with precious radiance. If he wanted, the details became crystal clear as he allowed his vision to come from Cataclysm. Thinking so many thoughts simultaneously in contact with dozens of other beings must be similar to what the Pixets experienced constantly from the day they were born.

His fleet of Dragons glowed in the desert sun. They radiated a rainbow of feral insistence as they vied for positions in each others' wakes, snapping and slashing at each other with their jaws and claws. Knowledge granted him by the Dragoncrown told him that proximity to other Dragons was highly unnatural for them. A Dragon needed plenty of space. The area of an entire country was barely adequate to contain enough big game to sustain a single Dragon. Forced to be concentrated together, whether there in the sky or in Isseltrent, without the freedom to display their mastery over one another, they were afflicted by the very presence of their rivals. That only added a further stress to the humiliation of being controlled and abused by much less noble beings. Beings like humans and Demons.

For the moment, the ruminations of the Dragons were too painful for Jonathon to bear, so he suppressed them. Instead, he silently scolded the naughtiest bullies and broke up the arguments to keep peace until they all reached their destination.

He felt the Dragons' hunger too, an emptiness within them all, even in the Dragons a hundred leagues away. That unrelenting hunger had drained them of strength for several Moons. They all wanted was to fly or run away to hunt for food. Only outside the Dead Lands could they find live game. Jonathon worried they might become lost, just when he needed them as allies against the Demon and its Zombie hoards. So, he made them all fly with him in a neat V. He had the more distant Dragons sit still and await his pleasure. They all obeyed his command, hungry and despondent, just as they had done in Isseltrent under Seldric.

Wind vibrated Jonathon's ears, and the air echoed with flying sounds. From the booming of leathery wings stretched suddenly taut catching the air, to deep grunting of annoyance as the Dragons bullied each other, to the clattering of the skeletons riding on their backs, all the noise came together like a frightening but vivid dream. After leaving the vibrance of the real world for a time, he relished every sensation denied him as a Ghost. He now saw life, not as a right, but as a wonderful gift. A gift to be cherished or squandered. He would never fear death again, but he would always cherish life.

In the distance eastward, Jonathon saw a blot on the bright landscape. It grew before his eyes, and waves of hate and misery pulsated from it. Sverdphthik was garnering its forces, bleeding them with torture and fear, then bloating itself with all their misery. It was clearly fortifying its Hellpit and calculating its next attack.

A hundred leagues to a flying Dragon took only a couple of Blessings. Within that space of time, the fleet of Dragons had flown to Devil's Fang. They now approached a tiny black spot at the base of the eastern cliffs of Devil's Fang. The spot was the entrance into the labyrinth of tunnels and caves centering on the treasure chamber of the Clan of the Laughing Skull.

Beneath them, plodding to the cave, were a few skeletons, the ones Jonathon had sent by Black Dragon and who were hiking from the Black a league to the south.

Streaming from the entrance to the cave came a host of Ghouls. The entire Clan of the Laughing Skull trudged eastward. They looked confused, leaderless as their eyes sought the Demon's Hellpit and the evil emanations that beseeched them to come to his aid.

Jonathon could not bear to let them sacrifice themselves, no matter what vile acts they had committed. He took Cataclysm out of formation, spurring on the other Dragons to proceed to the cave entrance. Cataclysm banked in a tight curve and swooped over the Ghouls.

"Through ears, hearts, minds I call, obey my will one and all! Halt! Stay away from the Demon's Hellpit. Come back to the cave and do my bidding!"

Jonathon had Cataclysm pass over the Ghouls from west to east and north to south. He repeated the exhortaation unceasingly until he had collected all errant Ghouls and had them all in his power. With a word, they would do his bidding for a day. Changing their souls and their way of being would take much longer.

The Ghouls congregated by the mouth of the cave where the Dragons had deposited their charges. As Cataclysm descended among them, Jonathon noticed that the Ghouls looked expectantly toward the clustered skeletons as if somewhere among them was the Master they yearned for.

This time, Jonathon did not attempt to get off Cataclysm. He ordered the Red to reach up, pluck him from his scaly saddle, and set him gently down with the others. Two Dragonclaws encircled his chest, six inches short of impaling him. His heart pounded faster as the claws gripped tight. His own thought stopped them from crushing the life out of him. The grip was a little too tight, so he loosened it to suit him. The finesse with which he could modulate the grip of such an immense creature was astounding. It was as if the Dragon was an extension of his own mind and body, another limb in his complete control. He set himself gently down beside the skeletons.

Rhazburn did not wait for the Dragon but threw one leg across its back and slid down to the ground, breaking off both legs which he quickly realigned. Before he moved on, he flexed the replaced limbs, testing their integrity. When he was satisfied, he lurched over to Jonathon and touched skulls.

Father, I'll handle my people. You're in charge of the Ghouls. If they find out we're changed, they won't obey me anyway. Let them think they are working for the Demon. Maybe they can be convinced to stay here after the spell of the Rod wears off.

Jonathon agreed. It seemed easier to fool them into thinking their obedience would aid the Demon. Some of the Ghouls had begun mingling with the skeletons, obviously expecting to be contacted by the Ghosts within. It seemed that was their typical style of communicating with the revered dead.

He turned and called out to them, "My friends of the Laughing Skull Clan! Follow the skeletons to the treasure and bring back all the coins you find."

Although he named them 'friends', the power of the Rod of Coercion still held sway, so they would do as ordered, regardless of their inclination.

"Trallalair, stay with me," he said, becoming accustomed to ordering everyone about. As a second thought, he realized how rude he was being and added, "If you like."

She stayed, standing as sentinel the rest of the day and all the night while the coins were extracted from the pile and brought to his feet.

Like her, Jonathon did not sleep.

By the time the eastern sky blushed with dawn, enough coins had been brought from the treasure pile. Jonathon was amazed at how many there were. Of course, the Ghouls never used the coins, and they had been accumulated over three hundred years.

Since they had completed the task, the Ghouls and skeletons reclined against the cliff, the people chattering, the skeletons nodding and clapping their jaws, talking together in the spiritual world.

Jonathon needed one more service from them, so he roused the Ghouls and had them separate from the other coins, then carefully count out all the Glass Commands. He had them stop when they got to one thousand.

With his skull against Jonathon, Rhazburn thought, *That should be enough.*

If all those Commands did not empower the Jewel of Nishbad with enough magical strength to trap the Demon, then all avenues were blind. Jonathon was the only hope for all the mortal world.

"Now or never," Jonathon said, fingers trembling as he opened the pouch at his waist and removed the Jewel of Nishbad. The red light of dawn glinted off the surface of the blue star sapphire. The illusory star within it seemed to draw things, like Demons Jonathon hoped, into its optical center.

He took one Command and slipped it into the slot beneath the Amethyst of Kingly Power on the Rod of Coercion. A little hesitant as to the reaction he would elicit, he bent down and touched the Jewel of Nishbad to the mound of Glass Commands. When the first few disappeared, transferring their magic to the Jewel of Nishbad, he began to sweep the sapphire through them in broad circles. The Commands dissolved scores at a time, the sapphire greedily imbibing all their magical power. Blue puissance radiated from his hand, but the gem stayed cold. It looked like it could freeze any soul, no matter how powerful, into a small chunk of ice that would never melt. All of the nine hundred ninety nine

Glass Commands were thus taken up. Jonathon gazed at the glowing gem and wished he had a proper chain to hang it around his neck. He hated to entrust its preciousness to the thin pouch at his side, but if he flew on the Dragon and held it in his hand, he could drop it and lose it, one rock among an infinite ocean of rocks on the vast plains of the Dead Lands.

Rhazburn drew his Sword of Bliss from his crotch and thrust it into the pile of other coins, thousands of Clay Suggestions, Wooden Requests, and Copper Orders. They, too, dissolved, extending the magic of that weapon for days. He began to climb Cataclysm, obviously expecting to accompany Jonathon as he confronted the Demon.

Jonathon knew that his son had done his part. This duel was between Jonathon and Sverdphthik. If he, Jonathon Forthright, perished attacking the Demon, Rhazburn and Trallalair had to survive to carry on in whatever way they could. With Rhazburn existing, even as a Ghost, to aid them, they had a chance to make another Jewel of Nishbad. Even if Hili was lost, other Pixets existed in Isseltrent.

"Through hearts, minds I call, obey my will one and all." Rhazburn turned his skull to look at his father. Jonathon didn't need to see eyes and lips to recognize puzzlement. "Rhazburn, stay here. Give me the Sword of Bliss." Rhazburn clambered back down and presented the Sword to Jonathon. With only two hands but three magical objects to hold, the Jewel of Nishbad was relegated to the pouch again.

One last time, perhaps the last ever in this world, he raised his hands in salute to his friends and allies. Using Cataclysm's forefoot to raise himself up, he positioned himself on the Dragon's neck and clutched with his legs.

Without further pomp, Cataclysm lifted off in a whirl of dust and headed straight toward the disgusting smudge to the east. As Jonathon watched the smudge grow, his trepidation grew with it. The smudge became a thundercloud churning with arcane evil. It looked from a distance like a great rotting beast rippling with worms. The worms grew further into black whips and striking snakes bigger than Dragons.

The Demon had grown with its sadistic torture of the enslaved spirits until it was the size of a mountain squatting on its Hellpit. It was like a black cloud of acrid smoke billowing out of a volcano, but with a power to form its substance into whips to flail and tendrils to ensnare enemies of the Demon. Never had Jonathon been more unsure of himself. At the same time, he had never felt more determined to shove the Jewel of Nishbad right down Sverdphthik's throat.

It had come down to Dragonpower, the essence of his world, against Demon power, the essence of the nether world. The Dragons supplied the worldly magic of the Dragoncrown, the Rod of Coercion, the Sword of Bliss, and the Jewel of Nishbad. Sverdphthik had at his command all the evils of Hell, Ghosts, Zombies, the drug of depression that spewed from his Hellpit, and the allure of sadistic pleasure at another's pain.

All the Dragons close enough for Jonathon to summon converged upon the maelstrom of dark magic that Sverdphthik had become. The clouds which made up the Demon's material substance seemed to be made from thousands of dead birds and bats animated by the tortured spirits controlled by Sverdphthik. Their constant circling raised a towering dust devil,whirling around and centering on the Tower of Bones still hideously holding up the Demon's throne.

Even before Cataclysm flew the distance, Jonathon was in the minds of the other Dragons, fueling their anger. Flying Zombie birds attacking them from the cloud around the Demon were burned from the sky. Many dead Dragons rose to challenge the living Dragons, but the Ghosts possessing them were inept in draconian ways and were quickly ripped apart. Dragonfire penetrated the walls of the immaterial curtain between the worlds that was Sverdphthik's skin, so every spirit within the Hellpit tasting the Dragonfire cried with anguish.

Still, every pang of the spirits' anguish was absorbed by Sverdphthik, bolstering it anew until it was able to absorb the very sunlight, turning the three league wide Hellpit into a bottomless well of starless black. Noisome whips scourged every enthralled spirit for a league beyond the Hellpit. The air thickened with their screams. Finally, the strength of dread was so profound that even the Dragons caught in the blackness were lost, snuffed out like bright candles. Jonathon had those Dragons still living flee far away before they were all killed.

Jonathon placed both the Rod of Coercion and the Sword of Bliss in his left hand and reached in the pouch at his belt for the Jewel of Nishbad. The arrangement was ungainly, but he wanted the Jewel out where he could feel it, hold its security before him. He did not want the least chance that it could be dislodged from the pouch and lost. Indigo emanations from the Jewel suffused the flesh of his hand.

Jonathon flew directly at the blackest of the blackness, where pure death awaited him. For a moment, he wondered if the Demon's power had become so intensified that he was able to open another breach into Hell. When the black tendrils rose, transforming into livid vipers that struck at him, Jonathon slowed them with Dragonfire, but he knew he needed to use the Sword of Bliss. Swinging it together with the Rod of Coercion in the same hand was impossible, he needed his right hand free.

Since he no longer trusted the pouch to hold the Jewel of Nishbad, he quickly slipped it in one container he knew would stay with him, his mouth. Muffled cries of terror still came from him as the tendrils snaked out at him. The desperation of his fear invigorated his wild swings with the Sword of Bliss as he sliced off their heads. Trallalair would have done much better, but this was his battle, his Dragoncrown, his nemesis, his world to save.

There were so many of the tendrils accosting him, he had to whirl the Sword around his head. Each tendril touched recoiled back into the shadowy depths, unable to abide against beauty with which the Sword of Bliss was imbued.

He wanted to use the Rod of Coercion, but his mouth was so full with the Jewel, he could not speak even if he could think the empowering words. Besides, he figured the Demon was much too strong for the Rod of Coercion to influence. The blackness of the Hellpit was directly beneath him, seeming to extend to both horizons, covering the entire world. With the Jewel of Nishbad held firmly between his tongue and his teeth, with a muffled scream of anger and fear, Jonathon Forthright dove into the center of the Demon's Hellpit.

Cataclysm's head struck first jolting Jonathon's mind the Dragon's spirit trying to flee, leaving him riding a dead falling beast, but Jonathon refused to let the Red die. He buttressed the Dragon's will to survive until his own face hit the ebon evil of Sverdphthik.

The Demon wanted to kill Jonathon with sheer terror, but Sverdphthik touched the Jewel of Nishbad in the jeweler's outthrust mouth just as the Demon touched Jonathon's mind.

Sheer horror tore at Jonathon's soul, but Jonathon's spirit was a hundred times stronger than it had been when he had first been invaded by the Demon in his jewelery shop. This time Jonathon had the Dragoncrown and the Sword of Bliss. He had the strength from holding the Unicorn Horn, bolstered by traces of the fullness of life granted him by the living Unicorn. He even had his righteous anger from the dealings of the Demon and its treatment of the thousands of souls tortured in his Hellpit. All this made him far too strong for even Sverdphthik to control.

Jonathon's mouth vibrated with an ethereal wind that threatened to shake his brains loose. He heard the Demon's howl, fighting against the power of nine hundred ninety-nine Glass Commands. By instinct, Jonathon pulled up before Cataclysm hit the floor of the Hellpit. Jonathon's eyes nearly popped with disbelief, watching the entire mountain of black shadow rush into his mouth. When the last of Sverdphthik howled into his mouth, Jonathon gasped and there was an abrupt slap, shoving the Jewel of Nishbad deep into his throat, far from where his tongue could get at it. He gagged and choked on the glowing gem, finally swallowing it down by reflex. The Demon was certainly the biggest thing Jonathon had ever eaten.

Chapter 36

The Flight of the Dragons

Jonathon couldn't believe he swallowed the whole thing. The Jewel of Nishbad, Sverdphthik, and all that evil were there in his stomach. It was enough to make him sick.

When he opened his shirt and looked, his abdomen glowed with a pulsating green light. The beautiful blue glow of the Jewel had been transmogrified into a vile green. He felt like he was going to vomit, but that would surely bring up the Demon. Even though Jonathon was astride a four rod long Red Dragon above the pit, he was too fastidious to vomit on himself. By reflex, he'd lean over the side to retch the Demon onto the rocks far below, probably shattering the gem, releasing Sverdphthik again. That had not been part of the plan - a weak stomach starting up the whole mess again.

Breathing deep and fast suppressed his nausea and forestalled vomiting, but it made him dizzy, more likely to fall right off Cataclysm's back onto those same rocks. Then he'd be dead again, but his body would cushion the fall of the gem, so at least the Demon wouldn't be released.

This made the third time that Sverdphthik was within his body. Thankfully, Jonathon was in charge this time. Having the Jewel of Nishbad in his stomach made it a lot harder to set the Demon down and forget where he put it. At least until nature called.

With Sverdphthik imprisoned, all the emanations of evil harnessing and torturing the spirits surrounding him for leagues around disappeared. Most of the Zombies that lined the amphitheater around the Tower of Bones began falling down in masses, turning back into dead bodies. Since Jonathon could no longer see into the spirit world, he could not tell what was exactly happening to the enslaved spirits. Were they finally passing from the world and flying to their rewards in Heaven or their punishment in Hell? Or were they still walking the material plane, free from the curse of Sverdphthik dominating them? Maybe they would be able to ascend to Heaven once Sverdphthik was thrown back into Hell, but he had an idea that they were doomed to wander until Hell's Breach was closed.

After facing Sverdphthik, closing Hell's Breach didn't seem such a big deal to Jonathon. Hopefully, Tundudil would go easy on the ones Sverdphthik forced to commit such horrible acts. Jonathon didn't think that they deserved eternal pain in Hell just because they gouged a few eyes trying to avoid eternal pain. With the Sword of Bliss that he still held in his right hand, he could possibly save their souls, like the Final Oath to The Three. That would only work, of course, if he could see them. Now that he was fully human again, they were all lost to his sight.

Both his hands were painfully cramped because he still gripped the Rod of Coercion and the Sword of Bliss as tightly as he could, still unconsciously fearing something would snatch them from him. He stowed the Sword in his belt, stretching the fingers of his right hand in ecstatic relief. The Rod of Coercion was too big to stick in his belt. It would split his flimsy belt, fall out and be lost. He would have to hold it until he landed. At least he could alternate hands.

Cataclysm was soaring through the sky, joyful that the pall covering the Dead Lands was gone. He felt little empathy for any other animal, including other Dragons, but the expanse of his love for the natural world was astounding. He could see far and clearly. Every miserable rock was a pearl. Cataclysm was glad to be alive, and he was very hungry.

The Dragons had been on strict rations during their incarceration in the Dead Lands. Since all dead things were useful to Sverdphthik, the Dragons had little to eat. A few Zombies, too broken to stand, or an occasional arm or leg that had fallen off and not been missed, was all they had had for nourishment. For Moons, the Dragons had been the only living things in the Dead Lands, and many of them had died of starvation. Grief had played its lethal hand, too.

Jonathon perceived the thoughts of Cataclysm more readily than all the other Dragons, since he was the closest. All the Dragons were there in his thoughts. Their mental chorus was a rabble. They were definitely glad to be free of the Demon, but all were famished.

Plenty of food lay about. Jonathon looked at all the dead bodies cast off by abandoning spirits. The Dragons were restrained from eating them by the force of the Dragoncrown, but Jonathon thought, why let all that food go to waste? Burying them all was impossible, and he'd rather have the Dragons gorge on long-dead humans than go after live ones. If they didn't eliminate the great numbers of dead bodies, he worried that they would putrefy, sending a reek that would reach Isseltrent a hundred leagues away. He just made sure the hungry Dragons spared Rhazburn and his skeletal army. The Dragons were fine with that, since the skeletons were pretty poor fare anyway.

Cataclysm plummeted and banked around the inner surface of Sverdphthik's pit. It could no longer be called a Hellpit. Now it was just a Deathpit, and the Dragon snatched dead bodies and swallowed them with great relish. Jonathon could experience every thought and sensation, though the taste of half-year-old, rotten flesh did not help his nausea much. Suppressing most of the Dragons' thoughts and sensations was essential, otherwise he would be overwhelmed by the rush. Even as Jonathon strained to ignore them, myriad pictures still swam in his vision. A school of fish sliced by a Blue Dragon. Two Green Dragons posturing in dispute over some huge beast one had killed. A Black Dragon in the plains of Dis, still as a monolith, ready to wait days until a buck wandered near enough to kill. An overheated White Dragon soaring above the plateau crowning the cliffs of the Cajalathrium States, on his way to guzzle a glacial stream. All of these scenarios and many more, Jonathon saw and felt. And underneath every thought was a tremendous sadness, a bitter resistance to the binding of the Dragoncrown. One Green Dragon swooped toward a knot of Ghouls that wandered aimlessly, probably in search of the their lost Master. They probably wanted to die without their Master to worship, and after all that they had done, they surely deserved to die. Still, Jonathon could not sanction it. No matter how many people they had killed and eaten under the evil spell of the Demon, they were still human. They deserved a chance to redeem themselves. He stopped the diving Dragon with a thought and told her to search for some nice, tasty, rotten meat, like all the other Dragons in the Dead Lands were doing.

Jonathon could see that it was a full time job reigning in the Dragons, very tiring. They could be like rebellious teenagers. With the Crown, he could simply substitute his thoughts for theirs to instantly change their behavior, if he could catch it in time. They still knew they were being manipulated, suffering a loss of freedom that demeaned the whole concept of their ancient place in the world. Wildness tugged at them constantly. Jonathon was controlling their bodies just as Sverdphthik had controlled him in his shop so long before, and doubtless they appreciated the loss of their control no less than did Jonathon at that time.

Jonathon thought back to those days. Never, before wearing the Dragoncrown, had he seen the Dragons as anything but a danger restrained, a resource to be used by humans, like forests to be cut down to make houses or the water of the rivers to drink. Now, inside their brains, he saw things from their perspective. Why *should* Dragons be enslaved so humans could be free? Jonathon had his fill of slavery in the Demon's Hellpit. Everyone thought all human life would end if the Dragons were free, but the last few Moons had proved that wrong. Many people had died, but humans had held their own against the Dragons. If Dragons were free but unorganized, fighting even each other, humans could persevere. Jonathon, of all the people, had the best reason to keep Dragons enslaved. If Isseltrent still existed, so did the Pixet Community. If anyone could extend the life of annual plants like his family, they could, and he might again see his family, Arlen and all his young children. As long as there was a chance that his family survived, he could not let them down. He would just have to suppress any thoughts of the Dragons' pain until his family was safe.

High in the sky again, Jonathon flew, gazing down upon the six Unicorns resurrected by the Knife of Life as they raced together across the plains of the Dead Lands. Nothing could stand in their way. Not even a flying Dragon with breath of fire could catch them. Far beyond the eastern borders of the Dead Lands began the vast Sea of Grass where the legendary Wind People roamed. The Unicorns would find good grazing there.

Above the Forbidden Mountains in the west, dark clouds gathered. To his eye, they were as dark as the cloud of evil had been over Sverdphthik's Hellpit, but he felt only goodness emanating from them. These clouds looked like a promise of rain for the first time in hundreds of years coming to the Dead Lands. In a few years, maybe less if the Pixets could return, Verdilon would flourish again, and the Unicorns would return. Before Jonathon divested himself of the power he carried, the Pixets had to be released to nurture their ancestral home. With their Community mind and racial memories, they would know just where to start and how to proceed to make Verdilon sweet with the fragrance of a million wildflowers. They would know how to make it verdant again, just like its name implied.

As far as he knew, Hili was still missing. Had she been killed? Lost? Had she fled? Only a break in the magical barrier surrounding Isseltrent that Rhazburn had devised and Garrith had instituted could restore the Pixet Community's link to Hili. Only then would they know what happened to their stalwart companion. It saddened Jonathon and took something away from his triumph to think Hili may have been killed during the battle with Sverdphthik's army. He knew he owed her his life. They all did.

Once the Sylvets recognized that Sverdphthik was gone, they would venture forth from their timeless Land of Repose. The Forbidden Mountains would become the Hospitable Mountains as they had been centuries before.

First order of business, Sverdphthik had to be thrown back into Hell. Jonathon sincerely hoped that the Demon would be out of his innards by the time he got to Hell's Breach. Otherwise, instead of going for a visit to Hell like he intended to get Rhazburn and Dollop out, he'd have to take up residence there. *Well,* he thought, *at least land would be cheap, and Rhazburn would be a seasoned guide in Hell.*

Once Cataclysm had had his fill of the nauseating dinner available, Jonathon tightened his legs and ordered the Red back to the caves of the Devil's Fang where all his friends and allies had been left. It was twenty leagues through cloudless skies with wind beating at him, but he hung on, slowing the Red when the wind threatened to rip him from the Dragon's back. The land was still dead but in a benign way now, like any normal desert ready to bloom with a good rain to awaken the sleeping seeds in the dust. If he were to be Dragonlord, he imagined himself ordering Sinjery Dragonflyers to sow the clouds with Raindust. The thought of it stopped him, however. He shied away from ordering anyone or anything to do something, no matter how minor, against their will. He was thankful that he would only have the Dragoncrown for a brief stewardship and could give it back to Seldric, someone who was comfortable with commanding others to do his will.

Within one Blessing, Cataclysm was hovering above the skeletal army of Rhazburn and Trallalair. It was a little past High Day. Jonathon had been wide awake ever since his soul had re-entered his body and he had been resurrected. When he was dead, his disembodied spirit never needed to sleep, but now that he was again alive, he tired like everyone else.

The dark clouds in the west had proceeded over the western extent of the Dead Lands, and a fine drizzle had indeed begun to fall. He noticed that many of the skeletons in Rhazburn's troop had also begun to fall. Mud was something none of the skeletons had any experience with. Bare bones didn't seem to afford them much in the way of traction on the slippery ground.

Jonathon had the Dragon land and crouch down so he could slide off. He twisted to the side, scooting toward Cataclysm's shoulder. Holding onto the elbow horn, he slid feet first on his belly until he was only a body length from the ground. With a yelp, he let go, almost spraining his ankle when his weak legs hit the ground. If he hadn't slipped on the muddy surface himself and landed splat in a puddle, he probably would have. He could tell that being dead for a couple of fortnights was bad for the muscles.

The skeleton, Rhazburn, with Trallalair close behind, came up to him quickly, eager for news.

Rhazburn seemed only slightly more adept at staying upright on the slippery mud.

When Jonathon stood up in the puddle and turned, the green glow coming from his abdomen made Trallalair gasp.

Rhazburn lurched up, carefully raising Jonathon's tattered, sopping shirt. He touched his skull to Jonathon's head, *Sverdphthik?*

Jonathon nodded.

Well, no one can steal him from you, Father.

He makes me sick.

I'm not surprised. He made a lot of people sick. He held out a pouch full of Glass Commands to give to Jonathon.

With all that potential magical energy, Jonathon felt all the more powerful since he wore the Dragoncrown, carried the Rod of Coercion, and had the Sword of Bliss tucked in his belt.

Having learned his lesson the hard way about getting on and off his gigantic mount, Jonathon turned to Cataclysm and had the Red with a couple of claws lift him up and place him astride his neck.

"Rhazburn?" he called, instructing Cataclysm to open his forefoot, sole upward, so Rhazburn could get a ride up, as well, to the Dragon's neck. He didn't want Rhazburn to lose more pieces climbing up the slippery scales.

Riding up, carried by the Dragon's forefoot would be insulting to the Sinjery warmaiden. "Trallalair, there is nothing more for us here. Hop up, and let's go to Isseltrent."

Trallalair was thankful that he had not used the power of the Rod of Coercion. Outwardly, she beamed, glad to ride a Dragon once more. She leaped from forefoot to shoulder hurling herself through the misted air, twisting adroitly to straddle the back just behind Rhazburn.

"Our Lord will need Dragonflyers again. I will happy to volunteer," she said.

Inwardly she thought, *Of course I will volunteer. It is my passion.* Her heart swelled with the thought of it, to have a Dragon once more as a friend, to minister to it and ride it in the skies. Only an honorable death in battle could be more glorious, and since the Demon was imprisoned, the chance of another war in her time of service was miniscule.

After so many Sisters had died in battle over the last several Moons, she prayed to Mother Earth that no more wars or battles would plague them. Since she knew that the Dragonlord was still alive, she still had one duty, to bring the Dragoncrown back to the Dragonlord. She fully recognized that the Demon in the Jewel in the jeweler had to be thrown back to Hell first. The longer they delayed in that task, the more likely it was that the Demon would escape and infect the world again.

Trallalair grew more uncomfortable the longer she thought. If the Demon could somehow emerge from the Jewel of Nishbad, he would be right where he was before they defeated him, inside the jeweler wearing the Dragoncrown, in control of the Dragons again, and holding the Rod of Coercion to control the rest of them. This time there would be no Knife of Life and no Jewel of Nishbad. With those thoughts and all their implications, an idea began to erode her loyalty to the bearer of the Dragoncrown.

She had a profane urge to slice the jeweler in two with her Sword, take the Jewel from his split bowels, and keep it safe along with the Dragoncrown. An unspoken vow she had made to herself reinforced her idea. Never again would she let any man or Demon order her about with the Rod of Coercion. If the jeweler tried to command her again with the Rod, she would strike viper-quick, slash off the offending arm holding that hideous rod, and take it herself. Or maybe dash it to pieces. At least, by riding behind Jonathon as she was, she would be in a position to take the initiative if pressed.

"How will you throw the Demon back into Hell?" she asked cautiously.

Jonathon looked sheepish. "I'll have to get him out some way," he said, laughing nervously.

Cataclysm took off like a tornado toward the mountains. The rain thickened and lashed at them. Trallalair whooped for joy at the feel of it.

Jonathon was wet and tired. He knew he should be hungry, somewhere inside all his nausea. He hadn't eaten in at least two fortnights. Maybe some food would coat his stomach and protect it from the weird Demon-glow that made him ill. He knew Trallalair needed food as well. For the moment, they had to leave all the skeletons and Ghouls to their own devices and find food. Spring was beginning even in Sylvanward, and he hoped Trallalair could find them some game. "Trallalair, we must fly back to Isseltrent, but first, you and I need to eat. Rhazburn can rest his bones while we find some food."

"Thank you, Jonathon. I feel weak as a mouse. I need sleep and food as I'm sure do you. Fly Cataclysm to the Forbidden Mountains. Take him low over the woods. Even in the rain, he'll flush deer. I'll take one for us. He can have the rest." Of course, Trallalair was also thinking of their mount and his needs. She always considered her steed.

She had a premonition. The jeweler was planning to enter Hell through Hell's Breach in a vain attempt to find his son's body, somehow bind the soul to the body again, and bring him back out against the command of the Dragonlord. After using the Knife of Life, such ridiculousness could seem almost possible. She certainly could see that what was previously a rabbit of a man had become foolishly dauntless. What was worse, he planned to take everything with him into Hell, just as he had done when he flew to the Demon's Hellpit. Why shouldn't he? The Rod of Coercion and the Sword of Bliss would aid him and were the source of his courage. He had taken them to the Hellpit and achieved his goal there, but Hell was a different matter. All the Demons of Hell and the Devil himself would be there to oppose him. All would be unleashed on the world, a thousand Sverdphthiks instead of one. Someone had to prevent it.

Trallalair sat closely behind Rhazburn, finally inured to the presence of dead things in this land. Sick of death, she longed to immerse herself again in the vibrant life of the swamps and forests of Sinjer. She wanted to smell the blooms, feel the warm mud between her toes, and hear the singing of the birds. She longed to see the trees festooned with vines and orchids, and taste the sweet flesh of the fruit ripening on trees all year long. Two years of the five committed to the Dragonlord still remained. Two more years of defilement by Seldric's lust.

All the lives of Sinjery maidens spent in servitude to the Dragonlord, all the debauchment, the illegitimate progeny they bore over the years, all of it was meant to be insurance for Sinjer to be protected from Dragonfire and death. All that had become meaningless with the Rod of Coercion.

Their servitude had not protected them from being decimated with all the others. They should be free of it all.

There was more to see here, though. The portents were clear. The jeweler, like the true Dragonlord, restrained the Dragons easily. If he could control the Dragons, why could she not do the same? All these centuries, everyone had thought that the Dragonlords were special, gifted by their blood lineage in the strength of their minds. No one suspected that it was merely the Dragoncrown itself that was the power. The rulers were as weak as any other men. Jonathon Forthright had proven that it was the Dragons' courage that infused the Dragonlord, whether he was from a pure line of spectacular men or was a bumbling jeweler suddenly granted power by finding the Dragoncrown on his head. For all these centuries, Sinjery Sisters had fiercely protected the Dragonlord when they should have killed him at once and taken the Dragoncrown for Sinjer. Trallalair was certain that the spurned daughters of Seldric, the few still left in the Inner Ring, would agree with her. Certainly, all the Ringmistresses defiled by him would agree. It was the Sinjery who deserved to control the Dragons. Many were daughters of Seldric with his blood in their veins. The Sinjery were the pinnacle of womanhood. They should be the rulers of the world, not Seldric. Who said that the Dragoncrown belonged to a Dragonlord? Why not a Dragonlady? Why not Trallalair, Dragonlady?

There in the rain on Cataclysm's back, sitting behind a mess of bones and a timid man who was now much more powerful than he deserved to be, Trallalair plotted to take the Dragoncrown for her Sisters. She and her Sisters had paid all debts. They owed men nothing. They would retire to their home, Sinjer, protected by the millennium-old curse, the curse that allowed women to live in Sinjer but killed any man who dared enter.

Rhazburn, the skeleton, riding just in front of the Sinjery, had never made time for a woman in his life. At first, he had been too busy proving himself to all the other Royal Bastards by learning the arcane Science of Poetry. Then his work took precedence, battling Demons for the good of all. With death just a few steps away every day at Hell's Breach, involving a woman in his life would have been cruel. He had virtually lost his natural father and mother before he was five. He knew what loss was like. Why would he subject a woman he loved to that? Besides, the only women he felt strong enough to be worth his while was one of the Sinjery, the very one riding behind them. He understood their hate of men, with their subjugation and misuse by the Dragonlord. So what if they had been his prize guards, Dragonflyers, and soldiers? That did not prevent Seldric from maltreating them.

Rhazburn was fully aware that he would not even be there, would not have been born, were it not for that maltreatment. He owed the Sinjery a debt for that and for the deaths of so many Sinjery maidens due to his actions. Trallalair could not possibly forgive him or ever think of him with love. Regardless, there was nothing of him for her to see, nothing to love, a disembodied spirit dead to this world. All she or anyone saw of him was a clattering horror of mismatched bones which deserved to rest in a grave, not walking in the world or riding with a living, strong, beautiful woman. If only she could see him, she might recognize the love within him.

Even that love at the moment was more like respect and admiration, unencumbered as he was with a physical self or real human emotions. He was more like a thought than a person. He needed his body. His father knew that and Rhazburn felt that Jonathon was going to do his utmost to take back his body and get him out of Hell. As when Jonathon went to the Hellpit of Sverdphthik and confronted the Demon in its Sanctum of Hate, Jonathon was his best chance for success, especially with Rhazburn at his side. First they had to free Dollop before he would try to take back his own body. Even if Rhazburn could find his body, regain it with his spirit inside, and had the chance to actually escape from Hell alive again, he would go nowhere without Dollop.

It was only since he had been separated from his body, barely able to see material things, hearing only muffled words, feeling nothing but an occasional pain, that he had learned to value little pleasures like a shared sunset or a touch of warmth from someone with whom he could be content to sit for several Blessings. His father cared what happened to him, that he knew. He knew that his father genuinely felt the love he professed for all his family. Rhazburn saw it in his every deed. In fact, Jonathon Forthright felt love for everyone he met.

Rhazburn had been as dry as the desert below and, in reality, just as dead, even when he was clothed in living flesh instead of a bunch of dry bones. He had thought that only by confronting his fears and using logic to battle terror could he feel alive. Logic conquered all. He had been dead wrong. Death showed him that logic was empty. Only love and life mattered. He saw a slim chance that he could get himself, body and soul, out of Hell. If he accomplished it, he would savor the world like no one ever had before.

Behind him sat the one woman he admired most in the world. Her stability alone through all the troubles they had faced together was laudable. She had proven her worth many-fold by accompanying his father, finding the Knife of Life, and going on into the Forbidden Mountains. All Sinjery displayed consummate skill with steel and bow, but she had, with an awkward arrow, proved her worth with the shot that helped restore his father's life. She had ridden the Unicorn like a dream, lightly holding a wisp of mane, balancing perfectly through the Unicorn's leaps, cuts and bounds. Trallalair's intensely honest eyes spoke to him the most, even through the mists separating his world from hers. Wisdom and resolve shone through the weariness that lined her face. Were he still alive, he'd yearn for her companionship. But insubstantial as he was, nothing could ever come of it.

She was real. He was not. Her darkly-tanned thighs on either side of him tightened in rhythm with each turn of the Dragon's neck. At times, she would lean forward, unknowingly nudging his spirit with her breasts. She felt nothing of his ethereal form, but he knew when the spirit within her flesh overlapped his. He tried to deny it as the allure of a Demon for a living body, but he knew it to be spurred by his need for meaningful companionship. Besides, the Sinjery loved only their Sisters.

On his way back to the loneliest place in existence, Hell, he was just brash enough to enter her body, merge with her spirit, and declare his love for her. What was the worst that could happen? She'd be offended by the invasion of the privacy of her thoughts. No matter, a little embarrassment did not account for much where he was headed. Still, he waited. The time was not right. But sometime before they parted and he was headed to Hell's Breach, he was determined to enter her body and have a look at her thoughts and how she saw him. He had to know the truth before he possibly left the world forever.

Jonathon flew from the Dead Lands into the eastern ramparts of the Forbidden Mountains. Soon the rain cleared for a while, and through Cataclysm's sharp vision, he watched for a valley that could provide them with food. Few unscathed valleys remained. Half way through the range, Jonathon found a deep cleft misted in rainbows from ten scant waterfalls that were just emerging after the rainfall. Melting snow from the peaks added to the waterfalls. Green forests carpeted the valley, and birds flushed from trees filled the air as Cataclysm passed above the canopy. On landing, they found the leaf litter emerging from the snow crust dotted with walnuts too numerous for the fattened squirrels to bury and a herd of scrawny elk overgrazing what little new growth was appearing on the valley floor. The herd needed culling of sickly oldsters.

Trallalair obliged them with a perfectly placed arrow at the base of a lame buck's skull. As she approached the dead elk, the Sinjery maiden loudly thanked Mother Earth for the bounty.

Cataclysm did not move. Jonathon could tell that he was, for the moment, sated on Zombies.

It took only a few wild sprigs of withered herbs that Jonathon found to make a feast like none they had eaten since they left Repose. The rest of the elk meat was wrapped in its own skin which had been quickly scraped with Trallalair's Sword and tanned by the barest whiff of Dragonfire.

To Jonathon, the Red Dragon now felt like an old friend, full of shared experiences. So what if Cataclysm had tried to roast him alive once or twice? Sometimes the best friends were those one had the strongest disagreements with.

The Dragon obeyed Jonathon's every wish. He had no choice, of course, but he was like a faithful dog. In many ways, a dog was no different, constrained not by the magic of the Dragoncrown but by the magic of training. Training was really nothing more than the expectation of eventual rewards of food and shelter in exchange for obedience. Unlike a dog, happy with its place in the human world, the Dragon was fretfully out of place, a wild, wanton beast requiring great plains filled with herds of fresh game to prey upon. Laying in a paddock, being groomed by ones he thought of as food and being doled out precise portions of fat flesh from an animal too stupid to run away, these things debased him no end.

Now that the exigency of the moment had passed, Jonathon could again feel all the pain of the Dragons. Silently, they begged him to let them be. The world was out of balance. The Demon had destroyed Verdilon and made the Dead Lands, but humans had themselves destroyed the plains of the Commonwealth of Dis, plowing under the wild flowers, ground squirrels, and quail coveys to plant wheat and flax. They protected herds of stupid cattle that grazed and trampled the land to dust. The dust blew away and clogged the streams. In longing for their freedom, the Dragons longed for the return of proper balance in the natural world. Seldric had to realize this as well as Jonathon did. Yet Seldric was beholden to the people of Isseltrent among whom none in his right mind would dare give up the benefits of the Dragoncrown to society.

That evening, Trallalair fashioned lean-tos for them to sleep in. Jonathon realized that sleep would relinquish the power of the Dragoncrown, during which time he would have no control over Cataclysm. What would stop the Dragon from blasting them with fire and eating him and Trallalair? He was puzzled. Why did not this happen every night that the Dragonlord slept in Isseltrent? All the Dragons should have been loosed to destroy the city and scatter to the winds. Certainly his dreams did not stop them.

Trallalair would know, having been as close to the Dragonlord as anyone could have been. Sharing the mind of Saggethrie had shown him the degradation Trallalair had been through.

"Trallalair?" he said. She was sitting for the first time that evening, relaxed, leaning against the bole of a massive pine. The pine needles beneath the tree were a soft cushion for them both. She looked up. For the first time, Jonathon noticed some undisclosed determination in her eyes. She said nothing.

"What does the Dragonlord do with the Dragons at night when he sleeps?"

She laughed like he was obviously a fool. "What kind of a Dragoncrown would it be if the Dragons were free to do as they wished every night?"

That wasn't much help. "But what do I do? I'm worried that we'll die, you'll die if I do the wrong thing."

Her look shifted to a thoughtful one. "Seldric never told me the secret, but he shared little of the use of the Dragoncrown with any of us Sinjery."

"Hmmm. Let's see," she continued. "We could take turns staying awake. You could take the first watch, and when you are tired and can barely hold your eyes open, I could wear the Crown and ensure our safety for the rest of the night until the morning."

Handing over the Dragoncrown to Trallalair was not what Jonathon had in mind. Not that she and the Sinjery Sisters did not deserve owning the Dragoncrown after what they had been through. But he still had to fulfill his quest and bring the Dragoncrown back to the Dragonlord if he was going to have the smallest chance of restoring his family.

He could tell that the Dragoncrown could not be taken from him unless he willingly gave it up. If he slept and still had control over Cataclysm in his sleep, she could simply kill him and steal the Crown, assuming that she got it on her head quickly enough to stop Cataclysm, who would definitely be freed once Jonathon was dead. If she could not transfer it fast enough, she would not be able to stop Cataclysm from killing her as well.

Maybe she would prefer death to allowing Seldric to regain the Dragoncrown and, with it, the power over herself and her Sinjery Sisters. He still had the Rod of Coercion and could use one of the Glass Commands in his pouch to order her to refrain from hurting him or taking the Dragoncrown. He had done it before, and even though it went against his moral principles, the lives of his family were involved. Jonathon had a feeling, probably supplied by the power of the Dragoncrown, that all he really had to do was to command Cataclysm and all the Dragons to obey his wishes, sleep or hunt for themselves, but harm no human throughout the night and even after he awakened. The more he thought of it, the greater his conviction was. He was certain, too, that the Dragoncrown would not allow the Dragons to be freed from his will unless they were far away, out of its range, far beyond Verdilon to the East, beyond Sinjer to the South, beyond the Cajalathrium States to the North, and far out into the sea and the Kingdom of the Lord of the Sea. Beyond the control of the Dragoncrown they could never go unless he willed it.

So Cataclysm was not the problem, only the Sinjery warmaiden. He looked at her and said, "Yes, I can feel it in the Dragoncrown, almost as if it speaks to me. All the Dragons and especially Cataclysm, so near by, can do nothing I do not command or agree to, as long as I wear the Crown and am alive." He let the word alive linger on his lips with emphasis. "I believe I will sleep."

And he knew he would sleep well, having had a rather full day commanding Dragons and defeating Demons.

But Trallalair could not sleep again that night, despite what she had said earlier. With the jeweler lying there sleeping, she was torn between her new-found loyalty to Jonathon Forthright, because of all he had done, and her need to better the plight of her Sisters. She did not really want to kill the jeweler. She owed him a lot. She only hoped that he would understand her reasons for taking the Dragoncrown from him and agree to it. She had a new sense that the jeweler was kind and just at heart. He would see that to bring the Crown back to Seldric would enslave her Sisters again. She must act, but there was time yet until they entered the city itself.

The next morning as Jonathon awoke, he saw Trallalair sitting a small distance from him. She was again deep in thought. He was thankful to still be alive. He had trusted her, as he had for these many Moons on their perilous journey. He still was troubled by what effect bringing the Dragoncrown back to the Dragonlord would have on her and her Sisters. Any words he had for her were far from adequate. "I'm sure we can fly nearly to Isseltrent tonight. That will give us another day to plan before we enter the city."

If Trallalair had been unchanged from the time they met he would have expected her to say to him, "You will do as you are told and take the Dragoncrown and the Rod of Coercion to the Dragoncrown," but now he saw doubt in her eyes and felt the fear she had for her Sisters. His senses and empathy seemed enhanced by the Dragoncrown. Maybe it was his realization of the disheartening enslavement of the powerful Dragons that he felt every moment he breathed. No being should suffer enslavement and degradation like that.

He solemnly admitted to her, "I dislike the idea of anyone having power over another. This Dragoncrown," he nearly spat the word like he wanted it away from him, "this was made for another time when the Demon roamed free and the might of the Dragoncrown was all that stood in the way of Sverdphthik conquering the entire world. But now... I don't know. Somehow, feeling all this power does not seem right."

Trallalair thought the jeweler to be more considerate that she had thought possible. She almost felt that he might come up with a solution for them, just by the words he spoke and what he had seen of his behavior in the past. Still, she knew that the coming night would be her last opportunity to save the Dragoncrown from slipping through the hands of the Sinjery. Her first duty was to them. Encouraging his decision to think about the implications of what he would do when he entered Isseltrent would give her time as well, time to bolster her resolve.

She agreed with him. "Like yourself, Jeweler, I believe we should sleep and plan before entering the city."

Jonathon regarded the enigmatic look in her eyes. "Trallalair, am I still a traitor to Isseltrent, and my son with me?" He waved a hand toward the skeleton standing beside them.

She hedged, "Until the Dragoncrown is brought to its proper place, yes, Jeweler." In her mind, the proper place was in Sinjer and on her head.

Jonathon noted her words and the fact that she no longer addressed him as 'Jonathon' but was addressing him as 'Jeweler' again. At least, that was better than 'Traitor'.

Until the Dinner Blessing and on toward Dusk, they flew over the western half of the Forbidden Mountains into the marred plains of the Commonwealth of Dis. The people of the plains ran from Cataclysm into their homes, as if they feared the Dragons were upon them once again.

Jonathon wanted to reassure them but knew better than to land Cataclysm by their homes lest the people die of fright. A hint of spring green softened the harsh scars of the plains. In the distance, Jonathon saw with the clarity of Cataclysm's sight a group of people plowing the land. They were attempting to plant their crops again despite their fear that the Dragons were still loose. Jonathon was in no hurry and let Cataclysm soar as high as he wanted in the sky, piercing clouds or banking around the swirling mists. He had a lot to consider.

In the evening, they came upon the illusory burnt-out rubble that was the site of Isseltrent. From above, the city did not exist. The myriad lights that should have been there were absent. Even though he knew it was only an illusion, having the city where he raised his family seemingly obliterated was still depressing for Jonathon. He had Cataclysm drop down a league out of town in the lee of a small copse of elm. A family of deer bolted away from the proximity of the Red, as if running from a healthy Dragon meant they could be safe.

After they were all back on solid ground, Jonathon looked in the direction of the deer and said to Trallalair, "Cataclysm is hungry again. I'm going to let him hunt."

Trallalair did not question the decision, being well familiar with the appetite of Dragons.

Before he let Cataclysm leave, Jonathon gathered a large pile of wood with Trallalair's help. Rhazburn's skeleton arms had a tendency to break off if he tried to lift anything too heavy, so he was delegated to collecting kindling. Jonathon had Cataclysm light the bonfire. Then he let the Dragon take off and fly away.

Jonathon intended lighting the fire to be the last service he would ask of Cataclysm. He didn't want to see the proud and magnificent beast ever again.

Jonathon and Trallalair roasted some of the elk meat and ate it greedily.

Rhazburn was not interested in watching a meal he could not enjoy, so he settled his bones away from them, watching the hazy sunset, maybe the last he would ever see.

After dinner, the jeweler, full and sleepy, sat down beside a tree and lay down the Rod of Coercion.

Trallalair gathered a pile of leaves and soft brush to lay upon, discreetly taking note where Rhazburn chose to rest his bones, pleased to see he faced toward Isseltrent but away from the jeweler, her intended victim. In a moment, the skeleton was still as death.

Jonathon seemed unaware of her intentions and said pleasantly, "Goodnight, Trallalair. Goodnight, Rhazburn."

The trunk of the tree was a hard uneven pillow, but it was part of Jonathon's world, not the Demon's, so he enjoyed every rough poke it gave him. Tiny bugs crawled from the bark into his hair. In ages past - and it seemed like ages since his life had a semblance of normalcy - he would have swatted them just because they irritated him. But this close to home and alive again, they were part of the real world. He now considered them all to be little friends. Chirping crickets accompanied the thoughts of Dragons filling his mind.

After dying, being tortured by the Demon, and being wrenched back to life, Jonathon finally realized the place of humans in the world. Humans needed to be custodians of the beauty, like the Pixets in Verdilon, the Sylvets in Repose, the Mermets under the sea, and the Sinjery in their jungles. The role of humans should be the same, to nurture the world, not fight it and drain off all the resources they could master. Dragonpower only gave humans free license to rape nature and enslave others. As tribute to the power of the Dragonlord, the Sinjery maidens fought for the Realm and were part of it. But Jonathon knew, as did everyone in Isseltrent, that the Sisterhood of Sinjery maidens hated their enslavement. Even Rhazburn's confided memories of his birth mother told Jonathon that the Sinjery mothers fled Isseltrent in ignominy as soon as their five years service was paid. Everyone else in Isseltrent and all of Thuringland depended on the Glass Commands to make their lives pleasant, but even the Isseltrenters were virtually enslaved to the system themselves, dependent on the constant flow of coins and magic. Only since the Dragons were released had the people learned again that they could exist without them or their magical coins.

Only Jonathon, like the Dragonlords, knew the unwarranted grief of the Dragons.

Before he walked into Isseltrent and gave the Dragoncrown away, Jonathon Forthright Dragonlord had to decide in his own mind if enslaving Dragons, with everything else that implied, was right. If he let the Dragons go, there would never again be the slightest chance he could save his family. For him, the main purpose of his quest had been to save them. Maybe they were already dead, or maybe he still had a chance save them. It was yet uncertain. One thing was certain, though. If he took the Dragoncrown and the Rod of Coercion back to Seldric, the Dragons and the Sinjery would be still be in the control of the Dragonlord. Even the Lord of the Sea and all his subjects would be subjugated by the use of the Rod of Coercion and would be at the beck and call of a dictator outside their undersea territory, namely the Dragonlord. Was it right for anyone in the world to have all that power? The possibility of saving his beloved family was on one hand. All the others' lives and freedom were on the other hand.

Selfishness told him to think only of his family, but it was selfishness that had started all of the mess and caused all of the deaths, even the deaths of his wife and children. Even when he forced the Dragons to help him battle the Demon, a lofty purpose in itself, some of them had died. Generals and kings were calloused to ordering others to do their will, inured to the the fact those they ordered around might be killed in their service, like all the Knights and Sinjery that had died in the fight to take back the Dragoncrown. Jonathon was neither ruler nor leader. For a soul like his, it hurt to be responsible for the death of trusting servants, even for a good cause. If he took back the Dragoncrown and all the Dragons with it, their continued enslavement and hopelessness would be his doing. The degradation of the Sinjery would be his doing, and the subjugation of all the peoples of the land and sea would be his doing.

Jonathon had never made a more difficult choice. His family was probably already lost, but the Dragons depended on him alone. As he debated with himself, he already felt his binding of the Dragons weakening. A few flying at the outer limits of his control slipped quietly away. He could have stopped them, but he didn't. Cataclysm was flying south toward Sinjer. If he soared past the Sinjery swamps, he would be beyond the range of the Dragoncrown. Jonathon encouraged him. A few Blue Dragons in the Kingdom of the Lord of the Sea could easily swim beyond the range of the Dragoncrown. Jonathon ignored their absconding. White Dragons over the Cajalathrium States were close enough to bother his elderly mother gazing out her cliff window. He bade them to fly past and out of his knowledge northward into the land of the Giants beyond the North Wall. All the Dragons in what was the Dead Lands and was now becoming Verdilon again, all those Dragons sleeping after a long overdue feast, he woke them all up and flew them east until he could no longer see from their eyes or feel the movement of their wings. Each Dragon's mind he sought out, forcing each to leave the area controlled by the Dragoncrown, imprinting on their minds that this was their one chance for freedom from Thuringland and the Tributary States. If they came again within the sway of the Dragoncrown, they would be slaves forever.

Jonathon had toiled all through Dusk Blessing and well into the night. In the darkest part of the night, the last Dragon flew beyond the range of the Dragoncrown. Jonathon Forthright, Dragonless Dragonlord, with little bugs nestled in his hair, fell into a deep, pleasant sleep.

Trallalair surreptitiously watched the jeweler as he tossed and turned during that entire time, knowing that he was awake, thinking to herself that he was listening for movement from her. She fought against her own long-needed sleep that entire time, until finally the jeweler's snores drowned out the crickets, an owl on silent wings passed overhead, and wind rattled a few twigs of the bare elm.

Silently, Trallalair thanked Mother Earth that the moon was only a light smear behind leaden clouds and the plains were wrapped in darkness deep enough to hide a deliberate thief. No one could stalk prey more quietly than a Sinjery maiden. The skeleton of Rhazburn had not changed position since it had laid down. The Loremaster, she hoped, was asleep like his father. She snuck to the jeweler's side, listening to his snores for signs of his awakening. Over her shoulder, she watched the misaligned dirty white bones of Rhazburn, barely visible but unmoving in the shadows.

After all her plotting, Trallalair did not want to kill the jeweler to take the Dragoncrown. The Dragoncrown itself could not be removed without startling the jeweler from sleep, of that she was certain. Beside the jeweler lay the Rod of Coercion. It was loosely held. She could purloin it without a rustle. She had seen it used and heard the activating chant enough times that she knew she could use it against the jeweler and even the Loremaster. Taking out her Sword and killing the jeweler would have been easier and certainly final, but after all she had done for the jeweler, it seemed a waste of all her efforts. Besides, after fighting at his side, experiencing the jeweler's loyalty to her and seeing his steadfastness in their quest, she no longer had the heart to kill him. If she had felt the same as she had when she first laid her blistered eyes on the pudgy, whimpering traitor in Honor Gashgrieve's chamber, her Sinjery blade would already be in his heart.

Slowly, Trallalair lifted the Rod of Coercion. By reflex, Jonathon's hand clamped shut. Gently, she pushed away his fingers without rousing him and again lifted the rod. A few coins still jingled in her own pouch. She took out the last Glass Command she had saved, and by feel, she slid it into the slot beneath the amethyst on the head of the Rod of Coercion. The lustrous purple of the amethyst was a thing of black in the night, black as her thoughts about how her people had been treated.

"Through ears, hearts, minds I call, obey my will one and all." That was one verse that Trallalair would never forget. The jeweler didn't hear her, remaining fast asleep. She kicked his foot, making him startle and grunt. He shook the sleep out of his mind, sitting forward from the tree that propped him up. Now *she* had his power. She repeated the verse to be sure he heard it, then said, "Jeweler, give me the Dragoncrown."

Jonathon felt no compunction to do as she said, since without the Dragoncrown, her mind was not adequate to use the Rod of Coercion. However, he could think of no reason not to give her the Dragoncrown, since all the Dragons were safely away. He figured that she was only doing her duty to the Dragonlord. Seldric was welcome to the useless bauble. He doubted that Isseltrent would need it. The Dragons knew better than to come back within its range. With a smile, he removed the Dragoncrown and handed it to her. "My pleasure, Trallalair."

Rhazburn was not asleep. Ghosts do not need to sleep. He was watching Trallalair creeping up to his father's side. At first, he thought that she was only going to rouse him to ask some question. He never imagined she should want to steal the Dragoncrown, but he should have. He had become complacent, thinking Trallalair was a friend to his father after they had weathered so much together. Rhazburn had foolishly thought that, for one night, his father could sleep in peace. He had watched Jonathon wrestle himself to sleep, and long after the Dusk Blessing, his father finally seemed at peace. He had thought Trallalair was only being considerate, walking so quietly. When she carefully took the Rod of Coercion from his father's grasp, he knew that something was amiss. He left the bones he had become accustomed to and once again waded through the thickness of reality. By the time he got to Trallalair, she had already wakened Jonathon and commanded him to give her the Dragoncrown.

As Trallalair placed the Dragoncrown on her head, she felt a bizarre heat within her and broke out in a sweat. Hundreds of new thoughts flooded her mind, but not those of Dragons. She saw Demons in battle with Poets, heard music of flutes and pipes, and imagined memorized poems and verses, rhyming, and meter. She felt an inexplicable but confusing sense of love directed toward herself, mixed with loyalty toward the jeweler. It was much more intimate than speech. Foreign thoughts came to her again, as when the jeweler, as a Ghost, first invaded her mind outside Repose. Beneath it all, she heard Rhazburn's voice in her mind.

Trallalair, give back the Crown.

This time the invader was Rhazburn, and she knew from his thoughts that he meant to prevent her from taking the Dragoncrown. There was anger, but it was tempered by something she was shocked to feel, love for her. The thoughts were too intimate, love from a man to a woman. They were something she thought she knew nothing about. Even though his feelings for her were not wholly unpleasant, she felt like she was being raped.

Rhazburn was equally surprised when he entered her mind. All the love for her Sisters and the natural world was there, but his own thoughts of her in his disembodied state now had the power of the emotions of her body. They augmented his love a hundred-fold.

She had to expel him. It was too much, too intimate, these sexual feelings for a man. She had always denied them when she was with the Dragonlord. She had always considered them unnatural. Using the Unicorn Horn in her hand was the only action she could think of, but she was uncertain if the Rod of Coercion could even work on a Demon within her.

"Rhazburn...," she started.

Before she could finish the simple sentence, Rhazburn took control of her hand holding the Rod of Coercion and, to her amazement, spread apart her own fingers so she dropped the Rod of Coercion.

"Mother of..." she exclaimed, unprepared for her limbs to do anything but her own bidding. She stooped to pick it up, concentrating on her hand to fight Rhazburn's control. Trallalair found herself in the maddening position of being privy to his thoughts as he quickly planned ways to thwart her.

Rhazburn moved her leg, snapping the foot back smartly. She could not even stop from kicking herself in the seat of her pants.

She toppled forward, but on her way to sprawl in the dirt, she was fast enough to grab the Rod of Coercion. This time she tightened her grip on it and concentrated to frustrate Rhazburn's ability to make her drop it again.

Still lying on the ground she shouted, "Rhazburn..."

Again, he stopped her, but with a different ploy, by cleaving her tongue to the roof of her mouth.

With a cry, she forced her tongue to obey her mind and shouted, "Rhazburn..."

This time he used her free hand that she had not been concentrating on to flick a handful of red dirt into her eyes and mouth, making her cough and spit before she could command him.

During this charade, Jonathon stood stunned at the Sinjery's antics, fighting with herself. "Trallalair, can I help you?"

Finally, she clasped both hands to the Rod of Coercion and concentrated just on getting out a terse command. "Rhazburn, stop!"

He stopped. Stopped opposing her, stopped even thinking. She thought that he was gone, looking around her and at the cast away bones. Rhazburn rode within her but remained quiet.

Jonathon stepped up, extending a helping hand to Trallalair. She shook it off and leaped to her feet. She still considered the jeweler a menace. He stepped away politely.

The Dragoncrown on her head was a dead thing. Silence met her. She interpreted the silence to mean that she had no control over the Dragoncrown after all.

"Jeweler, how do you use this?"

"Just put it on your head."

She took it off and rearranged it. Still nothing.

"It doesn't work. What have you done to it?"

She took it off and tried to look at it, but the early morning dimness prevented her. "Did you break it deliberately?"

"It's not broken."

"It doesn't work!" she repeated more emphatically.

"I assure you it is quite intact," he replied calmly.

She shook the Rod of Coercion with her left hand as if that would make its effect stronger. "Then show me. Bring Cataclysm back." She gave him back the Dragoncrown which he donned.

Jonathon did as he was told, since the Rod worked while she wore the Dragoncrown. He searched the land for Cataclysm in an attempt to retrieve the Red Dragon, but the Red had done as he was told. In the night, he had flown beyond the reach of the Dragoncrown.

"I cannot," Jonathon admitted.

"Then call another Dragon."

This time she did not wear the Dragoncrown, so he was unaffected. He answered regardless. "I cannot."

"Why not, Jeweler?" She was seething.

"I released the Dragons and let them all fly to where they were safe from the Dragoncrown. I warned them never to come back."

Trallalair looked from him to the Dragoncrown, then to the Rod of Coercion. She did not know whether the rod was useless in her hand as well, but she knew it mattered little.

Even though her grand plan to make her Sisters the new masters of the world was sabotaged before she had even started, she could already envision more freedom for her Sisters with Jonathon's actions. With the Dragoncrown useless and the Dragons' aversion to coming anywhere near Sinjer by their fear of the Dragoncrown, it really was the best solution. Her Sisters would not wield the power she coveted over all others, but neither would they grow greedy and calloused to others suffering like the Dragonlord and his court had.

She had no need for the Rod of Coercion anymore. "Here, Jeweler, take this, too."

Jonathon thought of all he had yet to do in Isseltrent. He'd still need his son. First he thought the poem to control the Rod of Coercion, then he said, "Rhazburn, wake up. Raise your arm if you hear me."

Trallalair raised her arm. Jonathon regarded Trallalair with her arm raised, gazed at the unmoving skeletal pile, and pieced things together.

"Rhazburn, speak to me if you can through Trallalair. If the Rod of Coercion has affected you, you are released to do as you wish."

Trallalair said, "Hello, Father."

As before, unusual thoughts, like someone else's dream, insinuated themselves into Trallalair's mind. She shut her mouth tight, refusing to speak while Rhazburn took liberties with her body. Rhyming and songs flitted through her, mostly pleasing to the ear. Underneath was a core of loyalty to the people of the Realm, despite the fact that Rhazburn had felt, as much as the Sinjery, the inequalities of Seldric's court. He had a vast knowledge of his art which he shared freely. When he helped form the Rod of Coercion, he had truly thought only to protect the land and his family. No one else in the Realm had the knowledge or the courage to accomplish that.

Rhazburn tried to protect Trallalair from his worst memories, so she only had a glimpse of the terror of Hell. She also saw that he was determined, despite his terror of it, to go back into Hell, not only to recover his own body but out of loyalty to his friend, Dollop. As she probed deeper, she saw how Rhazburn had fully expected to sacrifice his life for Jiminic when he gave her his shrinking suit in the Chamber of the Drop. She saw how he had waited in the Chamber until Jiminic and Jonathon had freed all the other prisoners, despite the fact that those men had tried to steal the shrinking suit from him only the day before. It was to these acts of kindness that her Sister Jiminic had alluded when she said, "Let none of the Sinjery forget Rhazburn and Jonathon Forthright." Jiminic had wanted to praise and remember them for their efforts in saving her from the Chamber of the Drop. Jiminic had known nothing of their involvement with the Demon.

Trallalair saw the memories of the little crippled boy in Paradise that Rhazburn had risked his own life to save. She saw Rhazburn's attempt to save the repulsive, traitorous Ghoul, Screela. Everyone who had attempted to harm Rhazburn, the Loremaster had saved in one way or another. Even the Zombie Lord and his minions who had tried to kill Rhazburn under Devil's Fang, Rhazburn had saved their souls with the Sword of Bliss. Rhazburn would sacrifice himself anytime to help a friend or even to help an enemy in need. Rhazburn was truly magnanimous and altruistic.

Then Trallalair perceived the deep, abiding respect that Rhazburn had for Jonathon and Arlen Forthright. She saw the way they had worked their utmost and stretched their finances for so many children, many of them the children of her Sinjery Sisters. The demonstration of their love to the orphaned children of Isseltrent made her respect Jonathon even more than she had from his sacrifices in saving her time and again.

Above all this was a deep, glowing love that Rhazburn had for Trallalair herself. It was a respect for her strength and intelligence, and a strange intimate pleasure in sharing her body. Even in the heights of her feelings for Saggethrie, she had never felt closer to any human being. Nor had she ever felt such awe for the character of any man in the world. When Jonathon's spirit had been within her, he had been all business and apologies, but Rhazburn was different. He burned with passion for her and passion for all his principles. She could find nothing of the vision she had held of him as a plotting traitor to the Dragonlord. Part of his love was an anger at the injustice to her race. It was an understanding that she had never expected from any man.

Trallalair joined her thoughts with his, not even needing to form words but just understanding. Here was one male she could respect. Maybe Jonathon too. Certainly, no Dragonlord in the history of the Realm would have had the courage to free the Dragons, especially after going through so much to save his family, only to sacrifice them in the end. Jonathon Forthright was truly noble.

With that thought, Trallalair felt warmth and pleasure from her Demon lover Rhazburn. She could speak for the Poet, sharing his thoughts. "Rhazburn must go with you to Hell, Master Jeweler."

Jonathon nodded. "First, we have to find the city."

Trallalair was relieved that Rhazburn was astute enough to know he should leave her to herself for a while. He withdrew his magnificent spirit from her and passed into his father. But when he did so, Trallalair felt a strange emptiness, even worse than when she had realized Saggethrie was truly dead. She shuddered silently, feeling disloyal to Saggethrie, her friend and lover for most of her life. She knew many Sisters who had lost lovers and found others to fill that gap in their lives. Never before had she felt the lack so strongly. It was like falling off Hover from high in the sky and falling through the air. If only she had Hover to save her from it now.

Rhazburn had to enter again into his father's mind to lead him into Isseltrent.

Rhazburn? Jonathon was now almost used to the thoughts of others coming and going.

Rhazburn quickly learned of Jonathon's freeing of the Dragons, but it took some time for him to be at ease with the decision. At Hell's Breach, he knew what the power of the Coins could accomplish against the Demons. Even though he felt they had a chance to close Hell's Breach, the loss of the Dragons and the magical coins meant that they had to succeed or the world was doomed. Rhazburn would have waited until their mission succeeded.

As Rhazburn thought all this, Jonathon made him realize that the enslavement of the Dragons made Jonathon no better than the Demons he wished to exclude from the world.

His son's thoughts, though, were in turmoil, with conflicting ideas of duty to his father and Thuringland. On top of all the rest was an ardent love for Trallalair colored by an unreasonable and impossible lust, considering that he no longer sported a body. Rhazburn still had a deep resignation that he was no longer part of her world. Jonathon wondered what his son would do when he had to part from Trallalair forever.

Rhazburn's thoughts explained his method for hiding Isseltrent so Jonathon knew how to approach the city. Then Rhazburn asked permission of his father to remain within him so they could make better time. He left his tired bones behind and Jonathon noted where they were so they could be buried later.

Dawn found them all with a clear understanding of what needed to be done. They skipped breakfast and walked to the Isseltrent ruins.

The ruins of Isseltrent stayed before their eyes until Rhazburn, within Jonathon, led them to a corner marked by a jade boulder. When they passed it, all of Isseltrent with the sounds and smells came back into being.

Jonathon saw above them a thin golden wire. Like the thread of spider silk, it stretched from a golden pole near the boulder all the way to a hub atop the central dome of Blaze. Where the dome itself had been golden when Jonathon left Isseltrent, now it was only dull stone. The gold of the dome had been torn off and used to make thousands of gold threads passing over the city in all directions, anchored at the perimeter by gilt staves. The mechanism needed a dozen Glass Commands to activate it every day. Rhazburn knew from his calculations before he left that they defeated the Demon just in time. The court only had enough coins for a few more days before the coffers of the Dragonlord would be completely exhausted. The court would be very anxious. No one yet knew of their victory.

Jonathon and Rhazburn had to proceed to Hell's Breach to deposit the Demon in Hell, but Trallalair had nothing to do there. Her place was with the few Sisters left in Isseltrent.

Uncertain of the reaction he would get from his son, Jonathon addressed her. "Trallalair, you must go tell your people about what I have done with the Dragons, but do not inform the Dragonlord, please." He silently chided himself for forgetting that he was commanding her to do his requests by holding the Rod of Coercion in his hand.

Trallalair gave him a rare smile. "Jonathon Forthright, because of what you have done, I believe the Sinjery Sisters' obligation to the Dragonlord has ended. We will all leave Isseltrent and return to Sinjer as soon as we can gather all the Sisters and the girl children together. No longer will this land shame us. We will be independent again. We will not betray your secret."

She thought a moment, then said, "After I leave, I will never see you again." She hesitated to collect her thoughts. "I have had a long time to think on this. When we met, I hated you for what you had done. My Soulsister was lost with the others. Now I understand that you and the Loremaster were not responsible for all the loss. Only the Demon is to blame. It took a sacrifice of thousands to free my people. For us, it was a battle for our freedom. Without you two, all our struggles would have been for naught. You were the ones who persevered when all was lost. You both came out of death to aid us all. You two are the bravest men I have ever known. Really too brave to be men. After all that has happened, I can truly thank you, Jonathon Forthright. I hope you find those of your family that are still left. I know what it is to lose one you loved."

She peered deeply into Jonathon's eyes, but talked to Rhazburn. "Loremaster, I forgive you for assaulting me like you did. When I first met you, even while I was fuming on my way to Seldric's chamber, I sensed your spirit was noble. Now I know it is. Go with your Three, if that is what you believe in."

She turned to go but stopped, still turned away. Ashamed to look back, she kept her head drooped. Her words were quiet. "I never thought it possible to love anyone but one of the Sisters." She lifted her head and strode away.

Jonathon felt a jolt pass though his son. His arm snapped up as Rhazburn reached for her, but then his eyes saw his own hand, not Rhazburn's, and Rhazburn was reminded that he no longer existed as a human that Trallalair could see or feel. Tears came to his eyes as his son began to cry. Rhazburn's emotions were getting all tangled up with Jonathon's. Jonathon, too, cried for the loss of his sweet family. He felt his son curling up, disconsolate within him, receding like a mere transient thought that could be lost in a moment.

Rhazburn, don't go away, I need you with me in Hell, he thought, addressing what was left of his son's receding spirit.

I am here, Father. Now you know. I always loved Trallalair, ever since I met her. To be with her was impossible then. Now there is only a slim chance, but I must try. I need my body, Father. Let's go find Dollop.

Jonathon thought, that was more like it. Rhazburn crying? Not for long.

CHAPTER 37

THE ONLY WAY TO GO TO HELL

Jonathon could have had an easier walk through Isseltrent on his way to the Chamber of Hell's Breach. Many people still wanted to kill him. They had all suffered because of him. If they knew that Rhazburn was within him, they would have been doubly intent upon it. They were unaware of the binding of the Demon inside the Jewel of Nishbad inside Jonathon. He felt no obligation to explain it to every person he met. Besides, just because he had defeated the Demon, freed all the Ghost thralls, cleansed Verdilon, and allowed the Sinjery to be free again, what would it matter to them? Isseltrent was still a mess.

The sight of the Sword of Bliss in his right hand, the Dragoncrown on his head, and the Rod of Coercion in his left hand was enough to dissuade anyone from confronting him face to face. But a few, consumed by hatred, picked up rocks to pelt him from a distance.

Jonathon had fueled the Rod of Coercion with a Glass Command before he had entered the city. All the way to the Chamber of Hell's Breach, he used it to command his assailants to leave him alone. He had a few important jobs to do and, despite his belief that forcing others to do his bidding was wrong, he had little time left. He needed to be efficient. He did not want to argue with anyone about what he knew must be done.

For a brief moment, Jonathon had been the Dragonlord. After all he had been through, he was more than ready to be ruler of Isseltrent, if need be, to keep peace until he fulfilled all his obligations to the Demonwards, Rhazburn, and the Pixets. Throwing the Demon back into Hell took precedence over anything else. The vengeance of the people upon Jonathon Forthright would just have to wait. Jonathon felt that he and Rhazburn had paid the price, anyway. After all, each of them had journeyed through Hell, Rhazburn beyond Hell's Breach and Jonathon in the Demon's Hellpit. Having died once, death held little more terror for either of them. He had plenty of Glass Commands in his belt pouch, and was ready to use them to ease his passage to Hell's Breach.

Jonathon expected resistance to his entering the Chamber of Hell's Breach. No one in Isseltrent, including the Poets at Hell's Breach, yet knew of their success in the Dead Lands. Likewise, no one expected that he had the help of Rhazburn or that he had used a Jewel of Nishbad to entrap the Demon. Accordingly, he was not surprised to see Wesfallen and ten Poets standing in front of the Chamber of Hell's Breach. A double rank of guards with their wicked halberds at the ready stood behind them as backup. A few Priests and Priestesses stood by, useless, but present as witnesses.

The news of his entry into Isseltrent had apparently traveled fast. A Seer stood to one side with a smirk on her face, blindfolded as always by her long hair tied over her eyes. Now Jonathon knew how she could see to walk or eat. A Ghost inhabited her and saw with its ghostly vision the blurry material world. Presumably the Seer had warned Wesfallen of their coming, and the news had been relayed by the hundreds of unseen spirits milling about Isseltrent.

His suspicions were corroborated by Rhazburn within him. Jonathon now fully understood how the Seers obtained their information. They melded with spirits of the dead who acted as their informants, willing or unwilling. He was well aware how the spirits could gather information, as they were unseen, able to walk through walls and listen to muffled conversations. The knowledge of dead relatives that the Seers claimed to have was actually gathered from the dead relatives themselves that the Seers could contact freely. The reason why the dead chose not to communicate with their own relatives was undoubtedly because they did not want to frighten or sadden their loved ones. Seers had years of secret training to allow them access to the spirit world. Too much contact was likely to drive anyone untrained in the art completely mad. How many times had friends or colleagues told him they had spoken with their long-departed relatives? Jonathon himself had passed them off as foolishly whimsical or even crazy. If others continually thought you were crazy, sooner or later, you believed it yourself. Never again would he doubt their veracity.

"Salutations, Honor Wesfallen. I am ecstatic that you still live after all this turmoil, and I am truly honored that you have come to greet me." He bowed expansively, showing what respect he could for Wesfallen's new title as Court Poet to Seldric. None deserved the position and all its influence more than Wesfallen, Rhazburn's close associate and trusted ally for years.

Jonathon felt his son's spirit warm to his comrade, but underneath that feeling was a caution at seeing such an array of strength between them and their goal. Surrounding the lot of them on the cobblestone walk leading up to the Chamber of Hell's Breach were arcs of inscriptions in various gem dusts. They looked like the layers of a rainbow laid on the ground. The poems to Jonathon meant nothing, but Rhazburn read them upside down to his perspective.

Jonathon quietly digested Rhazburn's thoughts. *The first is a Verse of Silence, probably to stop you from using the Rod of Coercion. The second a wall of fire. I don't think they'll use that for fear of damaging the Dragoncrown. With the third, they mean to blind you to make you helpless. The others will cripple you and cause you to forget everything you know.*

"Master Forthright," Wesfallen said, brows furrowed, "you have fulfilled your mission and returned the Dragoncrown, and I see the perfidious staff you fashioned. I will be happy to present both to the Dragonlord."

"Honor Wesfallen, thank you for your kind offer, but I have a much greater burden."

Rhazburn saw, as did Jonathon, that Wesfallen recognized something new in Jonathon. The Court Poet was calculating all the risks of confronting one wielding the Rod of Coercion. He was considering whether he confronted not the man Jonathon but the Demon Sverdphthik within the jeweler, controlling him. He raised his hand with a finger up to make a point, but Rhazburn looked away from the obvious and saw his other hand slipping into a pouch of some kind of jewel dust. Rhazburn held the Rod of Coercion along with Jonathon, so before Wesfallen could complete his surreptitious slight of hand, Rhazburn thought the activating phrase, *Through ears, hearts, minds I call, obey my will one and all.*

"Everyone around me, stop," Rhazburn said with his Father's voice.

Jonathon shuddered, but then realized that his son did the right thing. Jonathon himself was unaffected since he was coincident with Rhazburn's spirit and not *around* him.

"Do as I say!" Jonathon said with his own voice, finishing Rhazburn's thought.

Jonathon was privy to all Rhazburn's thoughts and plans. He wondered whether he was losing his free will by having his son's spirit within him. It was a fine line, and if he was possessed by his son for long enough, he did not know if Rhazburn would take over his mind in the end or if Rhazburn's spirit would simply fade like a dream. Neither alternative was acceptable to him. It was time for action.

"Rhazburn is here within me. We have a Jewel of Nishbad with us. The Demon Sverdphthik is trapped inside and harmless. We have come far and suffered much for this. The Demon's power is obliterated in the Dead Lands. Now, for the safety of the entire world, we must throw the Demon back into Hell. You will assist us and do as we say."

Wesfallen, when commanded to stop, froze in position. Jonathon remembered himself being frozen for the first time in his jewelry shop. He also remembered the agonizing pain of holding one position for half a day. He wanted none of that for the people around him.

"You may all move and talk, but you will still do nothing to prevent me from performing what I must, and you will assist me to your utmost."

Wesfallen came out of his trance and made a few inchoate sounds, shaking his head in disbelief. Obviously, he was not expecting that turn of events. Finally, he got hold of himself and said, "Fine, but take the Dragoncrown back to the Dragonlord first."

Well, Jonathon did allow them to speak, but he had no time for debate. "You will not argue with me. I am the Dragonlord at this time."

"Close your pouch, Wesfallen," Rhazburn said, using Jonathon's speech. Wesfallen obeyed him again as he would have Jonathon.

"All you poets, scatter the dust in those verses."

They all came forth, bent down and, with their hands and feet, erased all the work they had so tediously prepared to stop Jonathon.

Jonathon expected that Wesfallen still believed the Dragoncrown would bring society back to where it was before the Demon stole the Dragons. Everyone in Isseltrent still hoped for a return of their affluent, prolific, ways, all fueled by the power of the Dragons. No one but Jonathon, Rhazburn, and Trallalair knew that the Dragons had all been freed. Wesfallen did not know that the Dragoncrown would from then on act only as a deterrent against the return of the Dragons. As long as they stayed out of the Dragoncrown's sway, they could never be enslaved again.

Smiling to his would-be captors - after all, he saw no reason to be unpleasant just because they had wanted him dead or thought him a Demon to destroy - Jonathon said, "Wesfallen, Poets, Seer, guards, and you members of the Holy Few, stand aside and let me pass. Open the door to the Chamber of Hell's Breach."

As they obeyed his will, he thought the words needed for the Rod of Coercion to take control of the Demonwards within the chamber. At the same time, he felt a need to re-emphasize his commands to those without, and stated again, "Do nothing to stop me. Do not in any way harm me." They all obeyed the Rod of Coercion, parting before him as the obsequious courtiers in Blaze had bowed and backed away before Seldric. The two guards nearest the door had looks of astonishment on their faces as to what their limbs were doing against their wills when they opened the door to the Chamber of Hell's Breach. As the door swung open, the Poets inside looked similarly shocked. They had all been similarly affected by the words they heard.

Turning back toward the Poets and guards outside as he entered the door, Jonathon commanded them, "Leave the door open and guard that no one else enters." The guards lined up in their usual double column, and the Poets with Wesfallen spread out to watch the flanks. The Poets began tracing verses on the cobblestones again, this time to protect Jonathon rather than restrain him. The command through the Rod of Coercion was good for an entire day and night, plenty of time to save Rhazburn and divest himself of his own Demons, Rhazburn and Sverdphthik.

Garrith was the head Poet of the Demonwards that day. "Father, Father," he ran to embrace him. "I thought you were dead. We all did until the Pixets told us how you defeated Sverdphthik with the Knife of Life. I heard all the stories. How you fought Molgannard Fey and his murderers, how you dealt with the Lord of the Sea and recovered the Knife of Life, how you passed out of all knowledge, and how the Demon was captured by a Jewel of Nishbad around the Brandmistress Trallalair's neck."

Jonathon thought to himself and Rhazburn, *Garrith acts like he has only part of the story.*

Rhazburn reasoned, *Hili has to be alive and either in Isseltrent or close enough that she could share her thoughts and experiences with the community. The details of Garrith's story ends when she disappeared, right after you were resurrected. Hili must have thought that Trallalair had been successful the first time we confronted Sverdphthik. She, of course, knew nothing of your final, even more harrowing confrontation with Sverdphthik and his spectral horde.*

Jonathon thought, *I'm glad to know Hili is safe.*

Garrith's countenance darkened and he stepped back from his father. "I only wish Mother and the children were here to see it."

"Me too, son. At least Rhazburn is here."

"Where?"

"In me."

Recognition spread across Garrith's face. "I see."

Jonathon had all Rhazburn's memories of the time he spent inside his brother Garrith.

"And the Jewel of Nishbad?"

"Also in me, I'm afraid."

"H... h... huh?" Garrith stuttered, apparently flabbergasted.

"Don't ask," Jonathon said, dead serious, not wanting to recount how he ended up with the Demon in his belly.

"How do you propose to get it out and throw the Demon back to Hell?"

No one was prepared for Jonathon's answer. "I'll take it in myself. With Rhazburn."

Rhazburn thought that Garrith knew better than to question Rhazburn's judgement. After all, Garrith had used Rhazburn's plan to save Isseltrent from the marauding Dragons.

Garrith turned on his heel and shouted, "Thanguil, go to the dulcimer and wait. Grunion, watch the Vortex. Meerdrum, get ready to slam the door if anything tries to break loose."

Garrith, by instinct, grabbed Jonathon's arm. "No, Father. You, the Dragoncrown and the Rod of Coercion? I can't allow it." He apparently had not heard the command not to argue with him. Jonathon smiled benignly, thinking to himself the verse for the Rod of Coercion. He hated to command his son against his will, but he would apparently have no choice.

"I'll need them both. I'm not leaving Rhazburn like this. Rhazburn's been there and knows what to expect. Besides, we have to save Dollop."

Garrith desisted. Not only was the rod commanding him, but after all, Jonathon thought, he was his father and he had never before taken an order from Garrith.

His eyes held Jonathon's long enough to communicate his fear.

Jonathon's confidence won the staring contest.

Garrith shook his head but released him as ordered, perhaps resigned to the fact that he was about to lose his father and brother again so soon after having them return against all odds.

Jonathon sighed in relief. He truly despised the exigency forcing him to use the very power the Demon had abused.

Garrith said finally, "I'll stay here every shift until you return. If the Demons get the Rod of Coercion and the Dragoncrown again, we'll all die, Father."

Rhazburn thought to Jonathon, *Tell him we can close Hell's Breach.* Jonathon saw a picture in his mind of a huge Demon with his mouth pried open. He had no idea what it meant.

"Rhazburn is with me. He has been in Hell and knows a way to close Hell's Breach."

Looking at Jonathon but speaking to Rhazburn, Garrith said, "Why didn't you tell me this long ago, Rhazburn?" The revelations were all coming too fast for Garrith to register and organize in his own thoughts.

Jonathon let Rhazburn form his words. "Closing Hell's Breach before throwing the Demon back would only have ensured that Sverdphthik would be here torturing the world and all its inhabitants forever."

Garrith could clearly see the logic in that. If Hell's Breach was to be closed, Sverdphthik must be thrown back first.

Rhazburn spoke through Jonathon again. "If the Dragoncrown is lost, the world is no worse off than before. But if we close Hell's Breach, you'll only have Dragons to fight, not Demons, too."

He was, once again, logically correct. Poets were great ones for logic. Romance, emotions and fantasy were for people with little important to do, not for Poets.

Garrith thought a bit, looking from one musing Poet to another. "Irrefutable logic, Father. Poets, stand aside. Jonathon Forthright will pass through the Musical Mystical Door."

The other poets all saw the danger and protested, but Garrith held up his hand. "I know. He is my father and that influences my judgment." Then he addressed Meerdrum, the most experienced Poet there beside himself, discounting Wesfallen who had stayed outside the chamber in deference to the Poets manning Hell's Breach. And, of course, not including Rhazburn. "What say you, Meerdrum?"

"It all makes sense. If Rhazburn's spirit truly resides within the Master Jeweler, like a Demon, but a good Demon," he qualified, "his judgment must be taken into account. Let us all study the Rod of Coercion and all its verses and the Sword he carries. Then two of us will leave and record the verses in case they are both lost. In that way, we will have a chance of making something to counter Demons if some disaster befalls us all. The information will be safe."

Every Poet knew the verses on the Dragoncrown and the story of how it was made. Another rival Dragoncrown had never been made only because Dragonfire was needed to fuse the glass in its production. Since the first Dragoncrown controlled all the Dragons, no rival to the Dragonlord could have ever forced one of the Dragons to help make another.

As Jonathon listened to Meerdrum, he began to realize the further implications that freeing the Dragons would have on the Realm. That would all have to wait. The Demon was first priority.

Garrith deferred to Jonathon.

Jonathon said, "Fair enough. The Sword of Bliss that I carry was made by Rhazburn to alter the ties binding Ghosts to the Demon. It instills a sense of beauty and love in anyone it touches. That is its only purpose. We believe that it will have power against the Demons." He held it out for them all to study before taking a chance with the Rod of Coercion. For a dozen Favors, the Poets murmured over the verses like they were praying. When they were finished committing the verses to memory and gave back the Sword of Bliss, they all looked to the Rod of Coercion.

Rhazburn broke into his thoughts. *Father, don't let them memorize the inscriptions on the Rod of Coercion, it is too dangerous.*

Nonsense. You said yourself that none but the Dragonlord could use it. I will let them do as they please. Rhazburn relinquished his protest.

Before he held the Rod out for them to study, Jonathon used its power to command them again, just to be safe. *Through ears, hearts, minds I call, obey my will one and all,* he thought to himself.

"None of you will attempt to take the Rod of Coercion, the Sword of Bliss, or the Dragoncrown from me. You will do nothing to hinder me from proceeding through Hell's Breach." Once he was satisfied that he and the magical objects he carried were safe, he let them memorize the inscriptions on the Rod of Coercion.

At Garrith's order, Meerdrum and Thanguil left the chamber to save the vital information in case the disaster they feared came about and the Demons of Hell were released with the power to command them all. Meerdrum protested, feeling that his experience was needed at the Musical Mystical Door, but Garrith pointed out that it was that very experience which made him the best choice to protect the vital information. Jonathon suspected that they would also report his actions to the Dragonlord. After all, his command had been to not stop him from proceeding through Hell's Breach. He did not have the time to figure out the perfect wording for further commands. Jonathon felt that there would be a lot more trouble to deal with, if and when he re-emerged from Hell.

After the Poets were satisfied, Jonathon thought, *Rhazburn, are you ready?*

I am, Father, came to his his mind. *As soon as you enter Hell, Demons will attack you and try to take your body, just like Sverdphthik did in your shop.*

This time I am prepared. Stay with me until we find your body. I think you can help me, but I'm not sure how. I think if you keep chanting the phrase regularly and help me fend off anything trying to possess us and if I keep watch to fend them off with the Rod and the Sword, we'll make it.

Neither of them was sure how they would find Rhazburn and Dollop in the infinity of Hell. With Glass Commands he reactivated the Rod of Coercion and the Sword of Bliss. He carried the rod in his left hand, and the Sword in his right. He wore the Dragoncrown on his head, the Jewel of Nishbad in his gut, and his son Rhazburn in his soul, mind, and body. No one was readier than Jonathon Forthright to take on all the forces of Hell. But it didn't make him any less clumsy. As he stepped over the threshold of the Musical Mystical Door and into Hell, he tripped on the edge and fell a long, long way.

"Through ears, hearts, minds I call, obey my will one and all," he remembered to yell in his desperation.

From the door, he fell straight down into a heat so intense that sweat rolled off every part of his body and ran into his eyes, making him blink. By the time he cleared his eyes of the sweat and looked up, his exit had receded so far that it was nothing but a glimmer disappearing in the mingling mists. He never even saw the Demon that formed Hell's Breach with its open mouth. The noxious fumes of Hell bit his nostrils and nauseated him. They did not kill him outright, but he could tell that if he loitered there too long, he would surely wither and die.

Even before a Demon approached him, and here in Hell they were visible to his mortal eyes, he began shouting, "Demons, stay away from me."

Rhazburn kept repeating the verse of power while Jonathon ordered them all away. There were hundreds approaching from all directions, as if every unnatural thing in Hell sensed the presence of one more live being. And they all wanted his body.

Many of them stopped short, held back by the Rod's power, but more came on through the masses, heedless of the shouts they had not heard.

So he shouted again, "Ahh! Stay away from me."

One came ahead regardless, initially too far away to be affected by the command. Jonathon was much too slow to notice him or be able to respond. It was up to Rhazburn to see him coming. Using Jonathon's muscles like his own, he raised the Sword of Bliss just in time. The Demon, all fire and sparks, was neatly impaled upon it. He swelled up like lava welling from the caldera of a volcano, filling up with beauty far beyond his capacity to contain it. Like a blossom-laden tree in spring that Jonathon had disturbed, the Demon exploded into a shower of butterflies that flew about chasing Demons who howled in fear at their loveliness.

Before Jonathon could utter another command, a second Demon shaped like a spiked club hurtled their way. Rhazburn parried it with the Sword, changing it into a rose bud which floated harmlessly but which filled the area with a sweet fragrance, causing the closest Demons to smile. The smiles split their heads in two with the strain.

For the moment, the hundreds of Demons had shrunk to only a few dozen.

Jonathon reiterated the verse and his command, "Demons, stay away."

Back into the noxious mists, one particularly massive blue Demon began to move off.

Jonathon decided that he and Rhazburn had spent quite enough time fending off the attacks of the Demons. "You, blue Demon, stop."

It froze like a sculpture made of ice.

Jonathon took the chance that the Demons in Hell had learned of the other live humans within the nether world. "Take us to Rhazburn's body, but do us no harm."

A blue arm clutched them like a frosty blanket. With alarming alacrity, they accelerated away. Moments later, they floated near Rhazburn's body.

Jonathon and Rhazburn had to keep up a constant stream of commands to all the other Demons swirling about them to hold them away. This was easier than they had anticipated since Rhazburn was free to turn his spectral head completely around within Jonathon and watch behind them. Jonathon now literally had eyes in the back of his head. The Rod of Coercion seemed unable to distinguish between Rhazburn and Jonathon together in one body and worked for commands from either.

A warmth of relief filled Jonathon when they approached Rhazburn's body floating face up, still intact. He thanked the Demon and passed the Sword of Bliss through him, turning him into a bluebird that whistled. The sweet tune in turn made nearby Demons clutch at their heads, whether or not they had ears, and run away.

"Bluebird keep singing," Jonathon said. There in Hell, anything beautiful seemed to have a devastating effect upon the evil creatures, apparently unable to deal with anything filled with beauty instead of fear. The power of the beauty in the bluebird's song, just like Dollop's whistling, seemed enough to keep away most of the Demons while Jonathon took care of business. Jonathon took a moment to think, *Beauty, one of the aspects of The Three, had power here just as it had in the real world.* Rhazburn was too busy watching for trouble from behind to respond. Jonathon wondered if the effect of the Sword of Bliss would wear off as did every other Poetic effect he knew of.

I made the Sword of Bliss, and yet I am not sure if the effect is lasting like making water with a Replenishing Pitcher. Perhaps the goodness will last, came Rhazburn's thought.

That would be an interesting discussion if they were not soon to be besieged by countless Demons. *Rhazburn, keep watch.*

The Sword whirled through the space around them. It hit any Demons that got past the song of the bluebird. Such a cheerfulness in the immediate vicinity kept most of the evil at bay.

Jonathon was able to concentrate on Rhazburn's body.

"Demon within Rhazburn, do not harm him and leave this instant. Stay nearby." He said the commands carefully, trying to cover all eventualities. From within Rhazburn, a multi-limbed, feral Demon emerged. It was the very one that had promised to rend Rhazburn's body when the Poet had betrayed him to the Demonwards. The one who had lured Dollop into Hell. It immediately howled at the bluebird's song and retreated a respectful distance. There it remained, watching but constrained by the Rod of Coercion.

"No other Demon may enter Rhazburn!" Jonathon shouted.

From within Jonathon, Rhazburn's soul leaped, being sucked by mutual attraction back into his own body. Once his body and soul clung together, he screamed in pain. Then he shuddered. Then he vomited. Even though the Demon was gone, a body previously inhabited by a Demon was a miserable thing. Demons took a lot from a life. Rhazburn felt like he had the world's worst hangover. Also like he had been trampled by a mob. His eyes swam, his ears rang, his mouth tasted bilious, he was naked, smelled of skunks, and every muscle and bone felt burnt and ached. It was a most glorious feeling. He was alive again.

"Rhazburn, take the Sword." Jonathon didn't want to lose their advantage. He handed it to the Poet. From all the clouds surrounding them, more Demons ran and flew close, attracted by the living bodies. Jonathon ordered them to freeze and leave them be. With the Sword of Bliss, Rhazburn turned the twisted and scurrilous ethereal beings into bees which fed on wildflowers, songs of love that wafted through the area, sparkling rain, or jewels that shimmered and shone. All the beauty that was produced forced dozens of Demons away from the area, far from the goodness and cheer.

Jonathon wanted to command a Demon to take them to Dollop. "Son, which Demon should we use to take us back to Hell's Breach?"

Rhazburn chose for his father the same multi-limbed evil thing that had stolen Dollop's body the day he was lost and had inhabited Rhazburn's body for so long. It had been awaiting Jonathon's pleasure off to the right in a small whirlpool of black gas. Jonathon felt that there was a certain justice in using the Demon that had duped the youth into entering Hell in the first place. It was about to help them release Dollop from the clutches of the nether world.

As opposed to the trip Rhazburn had made with the Demon to escape Hell, when Rhazburn's brain had been gripped with its claws, on this trip he and Jonathon were cradled carefully in a bed of tentacles. The trip took longer than they expected, but at length, Dollop's body appeared, rotating slowly in a jealous green mist. Unlike Rhazburn's body, Dollop's had on the clothes he wore when he leapt through Hell's Breach. Dollop's soul was there too, crooning to his body as if to soothe it. Rhazburn had the sense that Dollop expected them.

"Dollop, you're here," Rhazburn said as soon as they stopped.

"All Hell is affected by your coming," Dollop replied. "The effects of goodness you have wrought here attracted me like a new dawn."

"My father has the power to command much. He is able to command Demons with the rod in his hand, Dragons with the Dragoncrown on his head, and he has a Jewel of Nishbad with Sverdphthik trapped within his stomach." Then held up the Sword of Bliss. "And with this Sword, I can change the nature of Demons from evil to goodness."

"Forever?"

"Probably not, but long enough so we can accomplish what we came for."

Dollop said, "A Jewel of Nishbad *and* the Dragoncrown? Sverdphthik picked the wrong enemy in you, Loremaster."

As he thought again of all the deaths and destruction caused by making the Rod of Coercion, Rhazburn had little to say. Certainly there was little he felt suitable to brag about. At least he could restore Dollop and, hopefully, after Sverdphthik was dealt with, get them all back to the real world. He would do his best to fulfill the promise he made to himself immediately after Dollop's possessed body was thrown back into Hell by the Demonwards.

Jonathon ordered the Demon to stand off but to be ready for more orders. Like a trained dog, the Demon stayed a few noxious clouds away. Rhazburn warned Dollop to be ready to jump immediately into his Demon-less body. Jonathon commanded the Demon inside Dollop to come out. Rhazburn, using the Sword of Bliss, turned the smoking, black, snarling thing into a cute puppy. Since it was a puppy spirit, it gamboled about as if it was on solid ground. There were still plenty of Demons around, but the puppy frightened them all away by running up and trying to lick them. The Demons seemed to have power over humans full of fear, but against innocent love, they were helpless. Like Rhazburn before him, Dollop was sucked instantly back into his body. He yelled, shook, snorted and rejoiced as did his mentor.

Jonathon commanded Rhazburn's Demon, "Take us all back to Hell's Breach. Be gentle and do not attempt to steal any of our bodies."

A cool cloud of limbs enveloped them and whisked them back up an impossible distance. There Jonathon saw, for the first time, the massive Demon of Hell's Breach, its mouth pried open by the golden Musical Mystical Door. Jonathon knew of the Demon forming Hell's Breach through the shared thoughts with Rhazburn. But the memory of the massive monster, as huge as the largest Dragon, did not prepare Jonathon for what he saw.

"Well, that is certainly big enough. But that's all it is? Hell's Breach? A Demon held by a spell? All I have to do is command it to close its mouth and begone?"

"That's all, Father. All these centuries, no one but Nishbad knew the truth. He kept no record of his method, and he died with the knowledge. We could have come up with poems to close it long ago, if only the truth had been known."

Again Jonathon commanded their traveling-companion Demon, "Make a platform that we may stand upon to approach Hell's Breach," and it was done. A blue carpet of mist, insubstantial in appearance but with the feeling of thick, springy grass flowed out, formed by the Demon's appendages.

Jonathon looked to his companions. "Let's go back through. I'll close it with the Rod of Coercion."

★ ★ ★

Rhazburn said, "I believe the Musical Mystical Door strengthens and retains the power of the spell."

"Then it must be destroyed. Demon, place us at the threshold to Hell." They were all lifted up right to the Door. "Come on. You first, Dollop."

Dollop looked longingly into the world outside the Demon's throat, then he looked back at the noxious cacophony of Hell. Resignation replaced the longing. "I cannot. I must stay here."

Rhazburn said, "Stay? Why? There is nothing for you here. Your family is elsewhere, not in Hell. This is for lost souls."

"Like you were lost, Rhazburn."

Rhazburn wanted to think that he was different, that Dollop saving him so he could fight Sverdphthik was a special case. After all, he had been thrown into Hell due to a single mistake. Then again, maybe most of the lost souls were the same. Maybe they all landed there through some stupid mistake that was ultimately evil, though not intentionally so.

"I must stay as long as there is a chance that some of the lost souls can be saved and released from Hell."

"You'll lose your body to the Demons again, and you'll never see your wife and child."

"That's as it should be. Until I prove myself."

"You have nothing to prove to anyone, Dollop."

"Except to myself."

"You'll starve."

"I don't think hunger and thirst have any meaning here. Time hasn't. Starving takes time. I can't explain it, but I think that's the least of my worries. I guess I'll find out."

Rhazburn could see that, foolish as the idea was, Dollop's mind was made up. He seemed to feel he belonged among the lost, like a Querite ministering to sinners regardless of danger to himself. Except for being clothed, he certainly looked the part, with his tranquil smile softening his already pleasant face. Rhazburn knew he was wrong, if only he would listen. Dollop, however, had learned more in his time in Hell than Rhazburn had ever taught him. He was totally selfless, intent on trying to help those beyond help.

Rhazburn sighed deeply, "If you are resolved..."

"I am."

"... then take the Sword of Bliss. The Sword has no power against living beings. We will have no need of it once Hell's Breach is closed." He bowed to his student and handed him the Sword, hilt first.

Jonathon took a big handful of Glass Commands from his pouch. "And, here, you'll need these. Do as much good as you can with them."

"Thank you, my friends." Dollop took the Glass Commands and stuffed them in his pocket. "Now go," he said, brandishing the Sword. "I will protect the world until Hell's Breach is closed."

Shaking his head at the loss of his best pupil and his closest friend, Rhazburn said quietly, "Go with The Three." Beauty, love and caring for those one loved, the teachings of The Three seemed to be what had sustained them during all their labors in the last several Moons.

Just as Jonathon was about to cross the threshold of the Musical Mystical Door, Rhazburn held him back with a restraining hand. "Father, the Jewel of Nishbad."

A chill went up Jonathon's spine. His hair stood on end. "Tundudil! I was so caught up in telling Demons what to do, I almost brought the worst one back into the world and closed Hell's Breach behind me." He had gotten so used to the Demon within him that he had completely forgotten it was there in his stomach in the Jewel of Nishbad.

Rhazburn said, "You need a cathartic."

Jonathon screwed up his face. Sitting on a chamber pot for half a day in Hell did not appeal to him.

There beside him was the nasty, smelly Demon all aquiver with undulating arms and tentacles. There was nothing to do but use what resources he had at his command. He asked Rhazburn, "Is the Jewel still able to entrap a Demon?"

"It is full of Sverdphthik. I believe it may be touched by another. Besides, the entrapment effect needs the power of a coin to activate it."

"But you're not sure."

"It's never been tried. We did use a lot of coins to activate it."

He'd have to chance it. Jonathon decided the Jewel would probably be no bigger with two Demons inside than one. He just hoped it wouldn't start flopping around inside his belly because the Demons were fighting each other.

He took a breath and said to their Demon guide, "Demon, harm me not, but reach down my throat and take out the Jewel of Nishbad in my gut." He pinched his nose shut to the hideous smell.

It made no difference. The writhing tentacle that slithered down his throat tasted like vomit. His insides vibrated as the slippery appendage twisted and turned through his intestines. Somewhere just past his navel it stopped like it hit a wall. He waited for this second Demon to be sucked into the gem.

The Demon vibrated violently as if in contact with something noxious, painful.

Jonathon was stuck. He could not speak with the Demon's tentacle down his throat. He began to choke and gag, retching violently. He retched repeatedly until he could feel the tentacle sliding up through his throat. After interminable heaving, worse than any bout of the flu, he vomited up the tentacle, bit by slimy bit, until the entire disgusting thing had been retched up.

Sverdphthik, bitter green in the Jewel of Nishbad, was stuck on a sucker.

After he coughed up a little more Demon filth, Jonathon, with eyes watering, said, "Give me the Jewel," and pried the gem from the sucker.

He handed the sapphire, glowing unnaturally green, to Dollop. "Dollop, can you dispose of Sverdphthik for us?"

The youth was taken aback. "Sverdphthik? Is this a Jewel of Nishbad? With Sverdphthik inside? The Jewel has been vilified. Disgusting."

"It is the Demon, Dollop. Rest assured."

Trembling with excitement, Dollop took the Jewel. "I have always dreamed of destroying Sverdphthik."

"What Demonward hasn't?" Rhazburn said. "Just lose him somewhere. Do not break the Jewel and try to fight him."

"I'll just cast him adrift far away."

"All Hell looks the same. How can you tell one place from another?" Jonathon asked.

"There are subtle differences. The acoustics vary. I can tell when I'm whistling."

"You cannot even stand in the mist."

"I believe I will be able to walk, perhaps even fly if I want. I think we souls with or without our bodies are much more capable here than the Demons would like us to believe."

"Come out with us, Dollop." Jonathon implored again.

"No, sir. I have work to do here."

"You will die," Rhazburn said.

"I'm already dead."

"Only by definition. I don't believe in definitions."

"There is nothing for me in the world. Here, I have a chance of finding my Love and my Little One." A tear rolled down his cheek.

Rhazburn knew it was time to stop arguing. Even if he won the argument and convinced Dollop to flee Hell with them, Rhazburn knew that Dollop would end up disconsolate and mourn a lost opportunity to find his loved ones.

After a silent touch of his friend's shoulder, he turned to Jonathon and said, "Come, Father. Dollop is resolved to stay. He is no longer of our world."

He pointed through the threshold of the Musical Mystical Door at the Demonwards lined up, fascinated at what they were seeing. For the last time ever, he spoke to his student. "Dollop, you are the bravest man I have ever met. I have no doubt that your dream will be fulfilled at some time. You have eternity to succeed."

"Peace to you, Dollop," Jonathon said. "I hope you find your family quickly so you can spend eternity with them instead of in the company of all these Demons and lost souls."

Dollop only nodded with a childlike smile on his boyish face, expectant, clearly optimistic of what he could accomplish. "Thank you, Loremaster. Thank you, Master Jeweler." One last time, he held up the Jewel of Nishbad in his left hand and the Sword of Bliss in his right. "You have fulfilled my dreams and those of all Thuringland."

To Jonathon, the compliment was fantastic. All the lives lost in the process. Was it worth it? He could not stop to mull over all that he had done wrong and right. There was yet much to be achieved. Quickly, saying no more, he led the way through Hell's Breach with Rhazburn behind.

Cheers rang out from the Poets waiting for them. Only Garrith seemed to notice that Rhazburn was naked and took off his shirt so Rhazburn could tie it around his waist. Jonathon held up the Rod of Coercion, not to intimidate them, but rather to lead them. "We must close Hell's Breach."

Garrith and Tindal said in unison, "It is not possible."

They had been taught their lessons well. For centuries, various methods had been tried. All failed, sometimes with frightful consequences, killing many Poets in backlashes that taught them all to be wary of any attempt to alter the rift in the fabric of reality that allowed free egress of Demons from Hell. Fatalistically, they all believed that the task was impossible and eventually they would all be overwhelmed by armies of Demons that could not be denied.

Jonathon proceeded to the entrance of the chamber. He called all the sentries, Wesfallen, and the other Poets inside. To the sentries, he said, "Take your halberds and smash the Musical Mystical Door. The door itself prevents the closure of Hell's Breach."

The Demonwards looked horrified. Still, under the spell of the Rod of Coercion, they could neither say nor do anything to prevent them.

For an entire Blessing, the sentries hacked at the gold frame with their steel axes. Sweat soaked their tunics with the hard work. They needed to work in shifts, some resting while others banged away at the metal. They could see Dollop on the other side, still held up by the Demon obedient to the effects of the Rod of Coercion. Every so often, a Demon would be attracted by the noise and coalesce out of the mists making for Dollop first. Every time, he stopped them with the Sword of Bliss.

Rhazburn took the time they had waiting for the tough metal of the Musical Mystical door to be fractured to talk with the other Poets. He gave them all the details of his escape from Hell as a Ghost, his journey to the Dead Lands using the bodies of dead animals, his view of the Demon's Hellpit, his fashioning of the first Sword of Bliss, his part in the trapping of Sverdphthik, and their trip back. The only thing he left out was the intimate details of his merging with Trallalair's spirit.

The steel halberds were harder than the soft gold. Slowly, they beat a dent in the side of the Musical Mystical Door. Long before any progress was evident, nearly all the sentries lay panting, barely able to lift their heavy weapons. They were not used to such hard physical work. The Poets were next, hefting the steel and giving blow after blow, making the frame shake and ring like a gong. When all the Poets were exhausted as well, including Rhazburn, who had done his share, Jonathon walked up and inspected the golden frame with his critical jeweler's gaze.

He pointed to a tiny crack in the metal. "Here, right here. You," he said indicating one sentry still standing, "bring me your halberd." The halberd was brought. Jonathon set down the Rod of Coercion and took the Halberd, placing the tip of the spear point atop the complex blade right into the tiny crack. He held the sturdy wood shaft of the halberd straight out and shouted, "Rhazburn, pound this into that crack."

Rhazburn took another halberd and aiming with the flat of the weapon's blade, struck the end of the shaft Jonathon held. The point of the spear was driven deep into the softened metal, expanding the crack considerably.

"Again," Jonathon shouted.

Again the flat of the ax whistled through the air and clanged against the makeshift chisel. When the spear point sank deep and the crack split further, Rhazburn's strength came back to him, fueled by success. He pounded it deeper, the crack widening and penetrating through the side until the spear point burst through the outer casement of the door and the entire side collapsed outward. Once half of the support was broken, the weight of the gold in the top of the Musical Mystical Door was sufficient to tear the rest down into a jangling, gleaming pile in front of Hell's Breach.

Dollop stood just beyond with the Sword of Bliss in hand, himself buoyed by the still-obedient Demon.

Jonathon picked up the Rod of Coercion. He raised it, thinking the verse of activation. In a clear loud voice, he intoned, "Demon of Hell's Breach, close your mouth." To the astonishment of the Demonwards present, Hell's Breach slammed shut, leaving in its place a frightening double row of huge peg-like teeth.

Wesfallen fell back, bewildered. "A Demon. Hell's Breach is a Demon?"

"What else could it be?" said Rhazburn.

Before anyone could say another word, they saw the blade of the Sword of Bliss pierce the Demon's mouth, slicing it from one side to the other. A rainbow of light filled the chamber. When their dazzled eyes adjusted to the relative darkness left in the chamber, Hell's Breach was gone, forever.

They all looked, rapt in awe, at the far end of the chamber which had always before been partially hidden. All they saw was a blank wall lit by sunlight coming from the door behind them and the dancing, multi-colored glimmerings of the ball lightnings surrounding them.

CHAPTER 38

SEEDS OF TRUST

"You may all go back to your homes, if you like." This time, Jonathon had no need of the power of the Rod of Coercion when he talked to the sentries, the Seer, and all the Poets. Hell's Breach was gone. Nothing remained for them to guard. It was not a command, just a suggestion.

Out of all the people present, only one appeared to be in distress. The Seer. She was wailing, stumbling around until one of the nearby Priestesses restrained her. In his grasp, she crumpled to the ground, whimpering, "Where are you? My love, come back to me." She sobbed pitiably.

Jonathon realized that she had lost the departed soul that she had lived with ever since she had become a Seer. All the souls, lost in the mortal world for centuries, had probably fled to Heaven or Hell. The Three had apparently prohibited any soul from ascending to Heaven after the opening of Hell's Breach, perhaps because Sverdphthik or some other Demon coming through Hell's Breach could have infested Heaven. Nishbad had released a Demon from the prison of Hell and The Three had taken no chances, erecting a barrier to all evil spirits, Demons and even the blessed.

'My Love?' she had cried. Jonathon wondered if the soul that had co-inhabited her own body had been a lover who had died. Perhaps she became a Seer to find him and indeed found him wandering near her. Then she melded with him, her lover, and cherished his presence as a spirit when she could no longer cherish him in the flesh. Now she had lost him forever to his final reward. Finally, she was truly mourning the death of her beloved.

Jonathon gave the Rod of Coercion to Rhazburn, knowing that none of the others realized Rhazburn could not wield its power and would do nothing untoward as long as he held it. Then, he went to the Seer and said as gently as he could, "Madame Seer, please, untie your hair. Look on the sun again. You have no need to see wholly through another's eyes. Use your own. Your beloved has ascended to Heaven, a better place."

Indeed, the sun was bright in the sky and birds flew over the rooftops. For the first time in many Moons, Isseltrent was truly at peace. The Dragons were free. The Sinjery were free. Even the miserable souls who had been tied to the world but unable to partake in its beauty were free. Verdilon had also been freed, so once the wildflowers were in full bloom again, the Pixets could abandon Isseltrent and fly free again in fields of beauty.

Jonathon had had no idea what was destined for him to accomplish that fateful day when Molgannard Fey had accosted him at his home. But that decision to fashion the Rod of Coercion, fueled by his need for cash, suggested by the Demon Sverdphthik itself the spawn of Hell in the world, that one turn of events had lead to all of this. So was it Molgannard Fey and Sverdphthik who had inadvertently brought this all about? But then, he thought, his and Arlen's decision to adopt and shelter as many of the orphans of Isseltrent as they could decades before was the cause of Jonathon's financial plight. He and his wife had only been following the teachings of *The Transmigrant*. They had seen the Beauty in the children and, of course recognizing the Beauty, felt Love for them. Caring for them led to adopting them. So he reasoned, it was ultimately not he that had caused all the troubles and resolutions of late. It was, rather, the teachings of *The Transmigrant*. The plan of The Three.

In other words, it was Tundudil who had been in charge the whole time. Who else could so subtly direct the course of events from afar?

Certainly not a bumbling little jeweler. Yes, Jonathon was convinced that other powers, as always, were at work in this. He had only been a pawn. That at least would let him feel better about all the mayhem caused by his actions. In the end, he still could not exonerate himself, but he was left with a glimmer that he might not end up in Hell the next time he died. That is, if he was careful for a few more years.

The Seer had not made any attempt to do as Jonathon had suggested. "Madame Seer, your loved one has left to his reward far beyond what any of us can imagine. I am sorry it is so painful for you. I believe closing Hell's Breach has brought the world back into balance. All the spirits have been released and have transmigrated to a better place." He left out the part that some doomed souls were destined for the Hell which he just closed off from the mortal world. Perhaps some of them would be saved by Dollop. Who could know?

"Please, undo your hair."

She shuddered as if frightened, still refusing to take the logical step. Certainly she knew that the connection with the dead had been lost.

Jonathon stepped around her. "Here. Let me help you." He touched her hair and she did not move. He took that for a good sign and tried to undo the knot of her hair tied behind her head, but it was so tightly knotted that he could not budge it.

"It cannot be undone once we tie it," she stated, as if everyone in the world knew that fact. With a feral grimace as if in emotional pain at what she was about to do, she drew a curved dagger from her robe, grabbed the knot behind her head with one hand, reached back with the knife, and slashed off the knot. What was left of her ravaged hair fell away from her eyes and hung like a scarf around her neck. She let the hair stay there and released the knife to clatter onto the cobbles.

When she finally opened her eyes, she cried out at the light. "Aiee, it burns!" she wailed again, clutching at her tearing eyes.

Jonathon said, "Your eyes have forgotten the light, but they will remember in time."

Still blind, but now because of the relative brightness of the light, she was led away by the Priestess.

Jonathon noticed that no one else had moved. The Guards and the Poets still watched him. They were constrained by the Rod of Coercion not to interfere with him or harm him, but they had not been ordered to leave the area. Jonathon went back to Rhazburn and accepted back the Rod of Coercion. His son gladly handed it to him. Again, he reiterated his request. "Please, be my guest to go back to your homes and rest." He didn't think that he had phrased that as a command.

Two Blessings before, the captain of the guard had been forced by the Rod of Coercion to disobey the order of the Dragonlord and let Jonathon and Rhazburn into the Chamber of Hell's Breach. He was the very same captain of the guard who, so long before, took the authority upon himself to let Jonathon into the chamber of Hell's Breach. His action allowed the jeweler to talk with Rhazburn, starting the avalanche that destroyed the world that had nurtured them all.

"Master Jeweler?" the captain of the guard said, hesitant. Jonathon noticed he did not address him as "Traitor".

"Yes, Captain?"

"Begging your pardon, sir. Shouldn't we take you back to the proper Dragonlord?" He was not precisely interfering with Jonathon, merely inquiring, so the Rod of Coercion allowed the polite question.

"Captain, your loyalty to the Dragonlord is unquestioned. I vow that I will return the Dragoncrown to him myself and give myself up to his mercy or his punishment. Rest assured, you and your men have done your part. Hell's Breach is gone forever. All the time it was open, you and yours have protected all Isseltrent, all the world from the Demons."

The burly captain smiled at the thought. "It were the Demonwards who protected us, sir. Things have certainly changed since I let you in here, many long Moons ago. Not all for the worse, I'll wager."

In place of the old world the captain knew, a world in which the old tenet of protection of the people at all costs existed, a new world had sprung up, one in which freedom, freedom for all people and things was the prime tenet. The captain appeared to be debating with himself whether to attempt to battle the power of the Rod and try to arrest Jonathon and Rhazburn. It was clear that he recognized the futility of guarding the empty chamber. After a few tense moments, quivering with tension, he capitulated and yelled, "Pikes up, column of fours!" At his order, the tired guards lifted their halberds, scrambled into formation, and cheerfully marched toward their barracks.

At the entrance, all the Poets who had been ensconced in the chamber for all of Dawn, Breakfast, and Work Blessing shaded their eyes from the brightness of the Highday sun. They were not blinded, like the Seer had been, but their eyes hurt a bit. Normally, they would not exit the chamber before Dusk Blessing, when the night shift came on duty.

Garrith shook his father's hand one more time. "I'll gather the family and meet you at home. There's a lot we all need to hear about."

Jonathon said, "Our entire family?" He looked at Rhazburn, who gave him an enigmatic, exhausted smile. "As many as you can find, Garrith."

Garrith gave a curt nod. "Rhazburn, I did everything as you said."

"You saved the city."

"I never told anyone but the Poets that the verses were yours. No one else would have understood, and every Poet would have figured it out, anyway."

Rhazburn smiled at the recognition. Soon, Poetry would be only an art with no power to release magical properties. How strange. "I didn't want you to tell the others. They never would have cooperated if they thought the ideas were mine."

Jonathon turned to Rhazburn. He looked up at Blaze and regarded the Rod of Coercion in his left hand. "Someone must have reported to the Dragonlord by now what we have done. The Dragonlord deserves his Crown back, but first, I'm going to free the Pixets."

Rhazburn looked puzzled. "I thought you said they would be freed once you brought the Dragoncrown back."

"I know. I trust the Dragonlord, but I don't trust Rulupunerswan."

"Don't trust the Dragonlord."

Jonathon had certainly changed in the preceding Moons. Maybe it was death that changed him. Maybe it was the return of life, in him and in the world around him. But a lot of his anxiety was gone. In its place, he had a certainty about all he yet needed to do. His emotions were a glassy-smooth lake in the morning, cold and dark. He felt that he must accomplish as much as he could while he still had the Rod of Coercion. He no longer feared anything that Rulupunerswan could do. Nor did he fear the retribution of the Dragonlord, even what he would do after he discovered that Jonathon had freed the Dragons. But Jonathon imagined that he might be given another quest to bring back the Dragons before the Pixets could be freed.

"No," he spoke to himself, dreamily, "I will go to the Pixets first. Finally they have their land to go back to. Once they are freed, they will flee the human world and fly their fastest to Verdilon. They need to see the Unicorns again. They need the strength the Unicorns can give to them, as of times long past."

Rhazburn thought that Jonathon was speaking to him. He said, "I agree, Father. The Pixets have been held down long enough. I will assist you."

"Son," he said to Rhazburn, "I trust you have a lot to tell your colleagues."

"I should come with you, Father. We work better together."

"You cannot help me now." He tried not to give Rhazburn commands as he spoke with him. "I must do this alone. My mistake is between me and the Pixets. You had no part in it."

"I stole the Unicorn Horn and devised the verses," Rhazburn asserted.

"No, son. It was all my doing from the beginning. You were forced by circumstances, just like the Pixets. I was the instigator in all of this. Reparation and atonement are mine alone. You could, if you like, relax, rest, do what you want." He still held the Rod of Coercion and could command his son to leave him, but he did not want to interfere with his free will. "You paid your debt when you were thrown into Hell. I still owe the Dragonlord recompense."

"He deserves no more from you, Father." Rhazburn could see his chance of dissuading his father was nil. He knew that Jonathon could simply order him to go rest, but he hadn't. He had said, "Do what you want," leaving the choice to Rhazburn.

Immediately, Rhazburn thought of Trallalair and her Sinjery Sisters. He was human again, but without a profession. Closing Hell's Breach and releasing the Dragons had taken the necessity out of being a Poet. He could play the flute and the lute and he could compose songs and poems. Even though the poems would have no power, maybe he could sell them. But none of it would hold much meaning for him if he was still alone. From sharing her marvelous soul, Rhazburn knew that Trallalair accepted his feelings for her, even enjoyed them. He could have no rest until he found her and spoke with her. She was on her way to Sinjer. The only thing in his way was the deadly curse of the Sinjery to any man who tried to enter.

One memory nagged at him from his vision at the Hall of Mirrors. Thinking back to that time, he recalled the reflections of himself first disappearing, then fading off into the distance. At the time, he could not fathom how his body had disappeared so soon, then appeared as a wild progression of animals, then skeletons. Now it all made sense. He disappeared from the world when he was thrown into Hell, and he became animals and skeletons on his journey through the Dead Lands as an ethereal spirit. The only reflection that he had not fulfilled so far was the tattooed savage that marched off far into the future. Like a man living in a jungle. Like the jungles of Sinjer.

Rhazburn followed his father for a while, deep in thought. Jonathon replenished the Rod of Coercion's power with one of the many Glass Commands he still carried in his pouch. Striding through the city, his only evident purpose to get as quickly as possible to the Pixets' prison, he used the verse of activation constantly and barked at guards and people he met to leave him alone and clear his path. Knights, courtiers, and Poets scattered before him like chickens from a fox.

At the base of the gloomy tower stairs which led to the Pixets' prison, Rhazburn said, "Father, I am leaving and going to find Trallalair."

Surprised, Jonathon said, "She has gone to Sinjer with her Sisters. I don't believe you can find her. You will only die there if you try."

"Father, you brought me back to the world and I don't think it was only to assist you in restoring everything in Isseltrent to what it was before we made the Rod of Coercion. You and I both know that you no longer need my help. You are fully capable of doing whatever you wish.

"On the contrary, I am now poorly equipped to accomplish my task. My only hope for love lives in Sinjer, and there must I go. After what I experienced of Trallalair's soul, I will wither and die if she does not love me as I love her. Better to die in the attempt than do nothing and die of loneliness. Besides I have seen my future in the Hall of Mirrors and I saw something that hints of success. What good can I do here? Poetry serves no purpose now."

Jonathon saw that his son was set in his path, but he did not think it a wise one. "There are still thousands of coins left in the world. True, most of them may be with the Ghouls, but they might be persuaded to trade for something of value to them. Poetry still has a place in the world."

"You mean the Ghouls could barter with us for something like fresh corpses?"

"No, no. They will change their ways now that the emanations of evil and hatred have been quenched in Verdilon. Have faith in human nature."

"You may be right, but I have a feeling that if I don't go to Sinjer soon, I'll lose Trallalair."

"Are you so certain she loves you?"

"No, I think she doesn't yet, but if I could only talk with her..." Rhazburn could not even finish the idea, since he had no inkling of what he could say to make her love him like he loved her. Just finding her would a start, though, and hopefully, before whatever feeling she had for his spirit faded, he could see her again in the flesh.

Jonathon shook his head, capitulating. "Fine. Go with The Three. But, here." he reached in his pouch to give Rhazburn some of the dwindling Glass Commands. "Goodbye, Son. You have made us all proud."

"No, Father." Rhazburn held up his hand. "The age of Dragonpower and Poetry is coming to a close. I must learn how to live without it."

"All right then. Tundudil protect you." Jonathon shook Rhazburn's hand, clasped it warmly, then embraced him one last time.

Rhazburn hesitated. He had a hunch that Poetry could still be helpful in his journey in some way. "Maybe a couple of Commands if you can spare them."

Jonathon laughed. "Here, Son. If anyone can counter the Curse of Sinjer, you can. Maybe these will help." He handed him two.

"And buy some clothes." Rhazburn looked down at the borrowed shirt around his waist, realizing he had a body again and needed to cover it. "Oh … right."

Jonathon watched Rhazburn hurry away. *He's changed. Some of his brashness had gone. Probably it had been left in Hell. Probably for the better.* Jonathon turned his thoughts to his next task, the freeing of the Community of Pixets. Since he was at the base of the tower which contained their depressing and unhealthy prison, he began climbing the stairs.

For once, he noticed how peaceful it was to have only his own thoughts in his mind, not the Demon's, Trallalair's, Saggethrie's, the Unicorn's, Rhazburn's, or the Dragons'. Peaceful and lonely, that is. Jonathon felt that he would never again have Arlen and the children to disturb him and cheer him. He would sacrifice that peace of mind anytime to rid himself of his loneliness.

The climb went quickly, much faster than when he had made it with Jiminic. At the top, two Knights drew their swords. The Sinjery Guards had already heard about the defeat of Sverdphthik from Trallalair and had vacated their posts. Knights had taken their places.

After thinking the verse of empowerment, he said, "Free the Pixets, then leave us alone and go to your homes."

He saw them struggle inwardly with the command, trying simultaneously to obey the previous, weaker command of Seldric. After a few moments of agitated paralysis, they relented and opened the door where another Knight who had heard Jonathon's command had already kicked out the screen that covered the only window in the prison. All three Knights crisply saluted Jonathon, slapping their sword hilts at their waists, then they turned and marched down the stairs.

Jonathon, standing by the open door, was immediately greeted by the one Pixelle he hoped to find. There she was. Hili hovered in the air with a smile on her tiny face. "We knew you would come to free us, Master Jeweler."

"Hili! Well met indeed. Nothing could please me more than seeing you alive and well. Until I spoke with Garrith at the Musical Mystical door, I thought you were dead. I know what role you played in resurrecting me. I can never repay you. The world can never repay you. Even those blessed souls in Heaven owe you everything, Hili."

"We all do what we must. The memories of the Demon's invasion into the Community still taints us. Even in our release from its threat, the soul of the Community was vilified into using a knife to strike another living being. That it was a knife to restore life rather than take it has little merit for us. Were it not to save Verdilon and the Unicorns, we would have sooner nourished the land with our essence. Like a rock dropped in a pond, the ripples of this act are yet to be felt."

Jonathon had no words of reassurance for her. He still had no idea what the loss of the Dragons meant for Isseltrent. It was true, nothing good comes without a price. Already, the price of freedom had been high for all those freed by his acts.

Although he was pleased to see Hili with the Community, he was amazed that she had flown to Isseltrent faster than did Cataclysm, even with the day's delay to capture Sverdphthik with the Jewel of Nishbad. "How did you get here so quickly? I never knew that Pixelles could outdistance Dragons."

Hili said, "High in the sky, higher than birds soar, higher than clouds drift, the Winds of Haste fly faster than Dragons. Never again will we be separated," she said.

Jonathon had to think about what she was referring to. No Pixelle could fly fast enough to cover the many leagues from Verdilon to Isseltrent in two days. Yet Hili was there, talking to him. Hili had to have had some help. Apparently some rapid winds existed high above the clouds, winds she rode to match speeds with Cataclysm who brought the rest of them to Isseltrent in little more than two days.

"Hili, words cannot express my thankfulness for the sacrifice you and the Community made for me." Jonathon understood how the last few Moons had scarred the Community forever. If at all possible, he was determined to make it up to them, somehow.

The Community stood behind her, gathered together, apparently thinking in accord as usual, waiting patiently for Jonathon to speak to them. "My faithful Pixets," Jonathon whispered to Hili, and through her, to the others, "You are free."

He expected them all to fly out the broken screen to Verdilon immediately. Instead, a venerable Pixelle extended her wings and rose before him gesturing to a row of flower pots with withered plants. They had replaced his one large pot with several, one for each seed. All the plants were brown. Jonathon saw not plants, but his beautiful wife and children dried up and silent.

"They are dead!" he wailed, turning away from the pathetic, crisp-brown plants. "Leave... if you wish. You should leave, before you die, too." He was careful not to phrase his thoughts as commands but make them only choices they could pick from. The Rod of Coercion was still activated.

"No, Master Jeweler, they are not dead. The seeds of these plants are the same as the ones they grew from. We have been very careful. See, they have many seeds. Take one of each." She flew to each plant in turn and reverently picked one perfect seed from each. She flew back to Jonathon, one seed at a time, placing them in his hand.

He looked up, bewildered. "I know something of plants, gardens, and flowers. Seeds that come from a flower are like children, a mixture of two plants." He held the seeds with reverence, but was forlorn, tears filling his eyes. He saw no hope for happiness in his life.

Hili spoke again. "Master Jeweler, we know plants as well. Many hundreds of years we have nurtured flowers. Each flower has some control over its destiny, just as those of us allowed to move in the world. They are not as powerless as they would seem from their vulnerability. They all can produce seeds at need that are exact replicas of those which they grew from. We explained to them your need and they agreed."

Jonathon merely stood still, blinking repeatedly, dumfounded, as he slowly processed what she had said. *Explained it to the plants?* Just one more crazy thing in a progression of crazy things he had witnessed over the last year.

"So you are saying these seeds I hold are truly my family."

"We so believe," she replied.

So close, he thought. His family perhaps safe in his hand despite his tardiness, but with the Dragons freed by his will, there was still nothing that could ever restore his family back into real humans. He could only plant them and watch them grow and die again the next Summer. Oh, how he had prayed for the return of his family to him, completely whole and living again in his home.

Even as he was ready to give them up to their tragic fate, he felt a subtle warmth in his mind, like a tentative answer to his prayers. Something warm and clever to bolster his wailing heart. Something blind and deaf without the hint of feeling on its skin. But warm, warm inside, another mind which insinuated itself into his own. But from where? It was asleep, comfortable, waiting for someone.

With a start, Jonathon realized that it was waiting for him or more likely, waiting for the Dragoncrown. A sleeping Dragon. Restrained, curled up and quiet, nearby. One Dragon was all he would need, if he could find it. He had the seeds, the Rod of Coercion, plenty of Glass Commands, and now, a Dragon, somewhere. Through the Dragoncrown, he could almost pinpoint it. It was lying close by, as if in the main courtyard of Blaze.

"Do you think there is a chance?" he asked, speaking more to himself than to the Pixets. Any possible chance that he could have his family back after he had been mourning their loss for at least a Moon was much more than he could have imagined, much more than he could have hoped for.

All the seeds fit in his right hand. Clasping them gently so as to safely enclose them in his warm, loving palm, he turned back to Hili and the venerable Pixelle. "My dear Pixets, even after my foolishness cost you your freedom and put you through the terror of the Demon's mind, you have proved yourselves again to be people of boundless love and wonderment to all of us. You have made me happy beyond anything in my life."

He knew that he had forgotten to command the Knights not to send others to recapture the Pixets. That must be attended to first. Once he knew that the Pixets were safe, he could seek out the sleeping Dragon he sensed through the Dragoncrown. With the Dragon to do his bidding, he would command Rulupunerswan to restore his family. Afterwards, he must come back and give the Unicorn Horn to the Pixets before they all left for Verdilon.

Hili and the old Pixelle bowed in unison with all the Pixets. Together, the wings of the Community sprouted.

"Wait," Jonathon said, forgetting the Rod of Coercion he had in his hand still held them in its grip.

All their filmy wings retracted and they regarded him expectantly.

He had to reverse the command. "You may now do as you please. You need not follow any of my requests." He had no idea if couching things in those terms would alter the function of the Rod of Coercion, but he intended that they should be able to disobey him if they wished. Although the Rod of Coercion had been indispensable to Jonathon, he knew it was rude, if not evil, to force one's friends into servitude.

He tried again. "If you want, some of you could stay here until I return. I need to use the Unicorn Horn once more to try and restore my family. After that, I will bring it back and give it to you, to use as you wish for the good of Verdilon. Or you may remove the stones and inscriptions and restore it to its previous untouched beauty, if you like. I don't know if the Rod of Coercion will work its power if it is wielded by anyone without the Dragoncrown on their head. I doubt it will."

Hili spoke up again for the Community. "It can never be restored to its original beauty. We would wish the Unicorn Horn could never be used to force a person to obey the will of another. However, to destroy the Demon and remove its accursed spirit from our Community, we made a promise to the Mermets. We will keep the Unicorn Horn inviolate as it is and ask the permission of our friends the Unicorns to give it to the Mermets. We hope that it will never again be used for evil purposes."

Jonathon fully realized that included in the Pixets' list of evil purposes could be his intention to force Rulupunerswan to change his family back into living humans, but he chose to ignore their implication. Even he, Jonathon Forthright, who had once felt himself above anything self-serving and had been proved blatantly wrong in that conviction, felt his soul tugged in the wrong direction by the temptation of that awful power he could wield over others with the Rod of Coercion. His present purpose, he felt convinced, was just and good. With a Dragon available and Dragonfire to complete the requirements for changing the seeds in his hand back into his living, breathing family, he had no intention to give up the opportunity to ensure his success. After that, they could have the the Unicorn Horn and be free of dealing with fickle humans, forever. He felt that no one should retain this power, even the Lord of the Sea wanting to protect his own Ocean Kingdom.

That is to say, no one should have the power after Jonathon Forthright used it just one more time. He could see how easily a Dragonlord could slip into a mode of enslaving a race of Dragons or Sinjery. How easily anyone with power over others could abuse the opportunity for their own benefit. To live with his conscience, Jonathon had to give up all of his objects of power, but not quite yet.

Jonathon asked the Pixets, "May I have your permission to use the Unicorn Horn to save the lives of my family?"

Hili said, "We have watched over them for long Moons and feel their plight is unfair. You may use the Unicorn Horn by our permission, in the absence of the Unicorn to whom it belongs."

"Thank you all. I will return as fast as I can."

Without speaking, the Pixets organized themselves. Some huddled together again in the room, while the majority flew out through the window, gleefully back into the open air. Soon, a cloud of Pixets merged high above with the other clouds in the sky. There were only about twenty Pixets and Pixelles left in the room, just enough to carry the Unicorn Horn when Jonathon returned. Hili was one of them.

Jonathon heard some quiet footfalls outside the door. He figured that the Knights had sent others to recapture the Pixets. The verse of activation was in his mind as instinctively as a horse's ears pricking up at the smell of a wolf. Without waiting for them to burst through the door, he shouted. "No one shall hinder me or the Pixets. Knights, stay here and protect the Pixets until I return. Then leave for your barracks."

Slowly, he opened the door and peeked around it. Ten Knights, many more than he expected, stood at attention. "Get out of my way and place yourselves in positions to protect the Pixets." Like obedient children, they did as they were told.

Just before Jonathon descended the stairs, he realized that he had no idea how to get to Rulupunerswan's chamber. When he went there with Jiminic, he wasn't watching to memorize the path. Turning to the brawniest Knight, he said, "I am Jonathon Forthright. Sir, what is your name?"

"Quint."

"Sir Quint," he commanded, "lead me to the main courtyard, but stay with me. I will need you to show me to the chamber of Honor Rulupunerswan."

Immediately, Sir Quint, a head taller than Jonathon and solid as a tree, trotted past him and down the stairs, the sounds of jangling mail reverberating off the close walls. Jonathon had a hard time keeping up with him, but not nearly as hard as he would have had in his previous life. Jonathon's big belly was gone, and his muscles were tougher, more like a healthy horse's and less like a mud-wallowing pig's.

With Sir Quint leading through the halls of Blaze, everyone let them pass. Artisans and engineers were bustling about, continuing the long process of repairing all the damage done to Blaze in the past Moons. At least employment would not be a problem for Isseltrent. Courtiers stood idly by or gave orders to the artisans. All of them stepped away from the burly Knight. They took a second look at Jonathon. The courtiers recognized the Dragoncrown and gawked at the unlikely bearer, Jonathon Forthright, one that they had for years ignored and, more recently, hated with a vengeance. As he passed them, they muttered snide comments to each other.

Wearing the Dragoncrown, Jonathon's senses were honed to a sharpness totally new to him. As they brushed past one clump of courtiers, he clearly made out their murmuring. They were discussing seditious thoughts of allying themselves with the new Dragonlord, Jonathon Forthright. They did not care who controlled the strength of the Dragons, as long as they could partake of the benefits. *Too bad,* Jonathon thought, *the courtiers know nothing of the loss of all that power, the very Dragons themselves. Me, the new Dragonlord? They had a lot to learn.*

At a trot, Jonathon and Sir Quint exited a door into the main courtyard of the Blaze. Once they entered the courtyard, the Dragoncrown led Jonathon to the very center. There was a pit of sand circled by more Knights, whom Jonathon quickly ordered away so they would not interfere with his plans. In the exact center of the pit of sand, unmoved for all the Moons of the chaos, lay the Dragonegg, just as it had lain on the eve of the Dragonegg Festival. Glittering gold, as big as a table, it lay in the early afternoon sun, obvious to every eye. During the long Moons of battles in the courtyard, no Dragonfire, Dragonclaw, or Dragonfang had disturbed it. By instinct, all the Dragons had stayed clear of it. Jonathon now knew Dragons, and he knew that they had shied away from destroying the egg.

There was no doubt that the emanations of quiet warmth Jonathon felt came from the Dragonegg. Without the deep rumblings of its mother Dragon encouraging it to break free or the influence of the Dragoncrown forcing it to break open its shell, the Dragon inside had slept. Everyone knew that Dragoneggs could stay unbroken for years, maybe decades, if the time wasn't right for emergence. Some had changed to solid rocks, the baby Dragon inside slowly losing its magic, returning to the elements from which it came.

The Dragonegg lay in front of Jonathon. The inhabitant was exceedingly quiet. Its heart was beating very slowly, barely alive. Jonathon was worried that he had come too late and the magic he needed to restore his family lost forever.

"Break free of your dreams, awaken, and come into the world." Jonathon spoke aloud, even though a thought was all that was needed.

In his mind, Jonathon felt the Dragon stir. It opened an eye to darkness surrounding it inside its tough shell. As the infant Dragon shook off its torpor, the egg wobbled and rolled a bit. At first, there were two tentative taps. Then there was a pause that frightened Jonathon. The baby Dragon was frightened to come out of his shell. Jonathon was not a bit surprised. The egg and its baby had for many fortnights been the center of a whirlwind of diving Dragons, rushing Knights, crashing walls, and raging fires. Enough to scare off an adult Dragon, much less a baby. He encouraged the timorous spirit to take its place in the world, come forth and show itself, see the sun and ride the winds of the sky. The young Dragonmind took heart, as though it was called by its mother. Pressure built up inside the shell, which quivered with the tension. With a report like a breaking branch, a crimson claw burst through the golden shell, casting pieces of the shell about like rough coins thrown on the sand. Four more claws punctured the shell, and the forefoot grasped the shell between its claws. A second forefoot pushed its way through, and together they ripped a hole big enough for the Dragon within to drag itself out, slimy and tremulous, flopping onto the sand.

It was a Red Dragon, and a male. Even without a Dragoncrown, anyone could tell it was a male from the forward direction in which its eyebrow horns projected. He looked up at Jonathon with that perpetual smiling shape of a Dragon's mouth. He knew Jonathon had called him forth and saved him from languishing in the shell, dying and turning to stone as he would have done had he not broken free. He felt strangely related to the soft creature standing above him. He tried to stand but flopped down again, shoving his head into the sand. Finally, after shaking sand out of his eyes, he struggled to his feet and stumbled to Jonathon to curl his neck around Jonathon's chest.

"What a sweet little thing you are," Jonathon said, thinking only pleasant thoughts which he projected to the Dragon. With the heat radiating from the fires within the small Red, Jonathon began to get very warm. At Jonathon's unspoken command, the baby Dragon uncurled himself and backed away.

Even though the Dragon was still very young, Jonathon felt he had plenty of the ancestral flames within him, but he had to be sure. He had the baby Dragon waddle back a couple of steps, extend his neck and blow fire into the air. At first, it was only a disappointing puff of smoke, but the second breath came out in a burst that reflected off the walls, making everyone in Blaze take heed.

A score of Knights poured from the entrance to the Dragonlord's throne room. Many had crossbows they lifted to aim at the baby Dragon.

With the horrible thought that he might lose this baby Dragon and his last chance to save his family, Jonathon cried out the poem of activation so fast he thought the Knights might not understand it. When he shouted, "Stop. Do not harm this Dragon," he held the Rod of Coercion high for emphasis. The Knights stopped but still held arrows notched and aimed at the Dragon's head.

"Put away your weapons. I wear the Dragoncrown. This Dragon is restrained."

Much too slowly for Jonathon's comfort, the Knights shouldered their bows.

Jonathon sighed in relief. "All of you, go to your homes. Have a nice rest."

They all disappeared through the many doors in the courtyard walls.

Even Sir Quint began to walk away.

"No, no, Sir Quint. Not you. You must show me the way to Rulupunerswan's."

Sir Quint stopped and gestured toward another of the many towers in the castle.

By himself, Jonathon would have taken all day to find the tower of the Alchemist. He was glad for his enthralled guide. Again, he saw the temptation to use the Rod of Coercion. He would certainly not trust Seldric with it. Rhazburn was right. No one deserved such omnipotence.

Jonathon looked at the baby Dragon, who sat obediently in the dirt. "Come with me, you sweet thing."

At first, he did not mean it to be a name. Of course, since Jonathon wore the Dragoncrown, the baby Dragon got up and scampered up beside him. He nuzzled Jonathon with his lethal snout. The name was so true, Jonathon decided to let it stick. From then on, the Red Dragon would be "Sweet Thing".

Like a puppy, Sweet Thing tried to keep up with Jonathon and Sir Quint, but there was so much to explore. He ended up taking a lot of small misadventures, splashing into puddles then boiling them away, or leaping up to snap at horseflies, only to fall, summersaulting, in the dust when his feeble wings didn't hold him up. Jonathon could have restrained him better, but he indulged him a little freedom as long as he caught up with them.

Through an empty courtyard, Sir Quint led them to a dark tower and inward to a stairway twisting slowly and upward to the chamber of Rulupunerswan. There was no railing, and all that was on his left was an open space that fell away to the bottom of the tower. Jonathon felt vulnerable to discovery by the treacherous Alchemist. Just as if he was climbing the spiral carpet in Molgannard Fey's tower, Jonathon's old fear of heights returned. He still couldn't fly, despite the magical items he carried. The Rod of Coercion wouldn't save him from breaking his neck if the Alchemist had a way to toss him off the stairs.

Anxious that he would be attacked, he shouted out the activating verse of the Rod of Coercion and yelled, "Rulupunerswan, I'm coming to talk with you. Stay where you are and do nothing to stop me!"

He heard nothing in reply. Maybe the Alchemist had flown.

At the top of the stairs once again, Jonathon faced the oily curtain that was the entrance to Rulupunerswan's chamber. When he had first come to the Alchemist's chamber, moons before with Jiminic, he had thought that Rulupunerswan, being protected by deadly potions and mists, disparaged doors as weak. Now Jonathon realized that the Alchemist was just frightened. He was frightened of imprisonment. The bitter old man was far from his birth and, although very old, no nearer to his death, thanks to all the elixirs protecting him. Despite all his precautions, fear of death was not something the elixirs held back. For him, a shut door was a lid on his coffin.

Sir Quint swept away the curtain, revealing the Alchemist waiting with his arms crossed. "If it isn't the traitor, Jonathon Forthright."

Jonathon ignored his prattle. Obviously, the Rod of Coercion had done its job. He turned his back on Rulupunerswan and, after running through the words of activation for the Rod of Coercion again for good measure, he spoke to the Sir Quint. "Thank you for your help, Sir Quint. Now go to the Dragonlord and tell him I will bring him the Dragoncrown soon. After that, go to your home and rest."

The Knight turned and started down the twisting stairs.

Behind his back, Jonathon felt Rulupunerswan moving. With the Alchemist's propensity for causing trouble, Jonathon was not about to take any chance that would jeopardize his family. "Stop!" he commanded. He turned to see Rulupunerswan paralyzed between strides with his left arm outstretched. "You will do nothing to hinder my purpose or make any attempt to have me stopped."

He waited until his command had taken effect and longer still, until beads of sweat on the Alchemist's brow told him he was in pain from keeping his arm outstretched for too long. When he was satisfied he had punished the Alchemist enough, he said, "You may move again and speak."

The Alchemist relaxed but shied away from Sweet Thing who waddled toward him sinuously. Rulupunerswan stuck out a foot to ward off the little Dragon. Not taking his eyes off the beast, he said, "You are too late, Traitor. I called the guard as you began walking up the stairs."

The Dragoncrown enhanced Jonathon's perception, so he could almost feel the Knights stealing up the stairs.

"Stay here, Alchemist." He wasn't taking a chance the Alchemist would run away. *Don't let him leave,* he ordered Sweet Thing silently through the Dragoncrown.

Jonathon stepped back to the landing and shouted down the dim stairwell the activation verse, then the command, "No one shall harm me or my family or prevent us from doing as we please! Guard the entrance and protect me and my family!"

Within a few moments, he felt the danger in the stairwell recede. He expected that the Knights had fanned out in the courtyard, crossbows ready to protect the entrance.

When he reentered the Alchemist's laboratory, Rulupunerswan was trying, under the watchful eye of Sweet Thing, to mix ingredients to some purpose of which Jonathon had no idea. He suspected that Rulupunerswan was trying to counter the spell of the Rod of Coercion or make a poison to kill Sweet Thing. "Stop that, Rulupunerswan."

Sweet Thing added emphasis by flaming the Alchemist's feet, making him jump and yelp. He dropped a vial of blue crystals that burst into a green cloud which expanded and contracted like it was breathing. Even Sweet Thing recoiled at the appearance of the cloud and flamed it too, making it disappear with a loud pop.

Jonathon would never use Rulupunerswan's title "Honor" again. He believed that the Alchemist little deserved the title, considering all the evil that he had caused. Jonathon was finished playing games with the Alchemist. "Rulupunerswan, restore my family to their normal selves at once."

The Alchemist was being forced against his will and he could see Jonathon had Dragonfire at his command. Despite that, Rulupunerswan's spared none of his acrimonious tone as he sneered, "I require eight Glass Commands, one for each seed."

Jonathon dug in his pouch and pulled out a dozen Glass commands, selected eight and lay them on the workbench.

He looked the Alchemist in the eye and said, "You will do nothing to us that could be harmful. You will restore my family to their human selves and never do anything to threaten them for as long as you live. If you do anything to harm me or any of my family, the power of this rod will slay you outright."

Jonathon knew that the command enforced by the Rod of Coercion would only last a day, but maybe Rulupunerswan didn't know that. He hoped that he valued his seamy life enough to stop him from even taking a chance that the words might come true.

Rulupunerswan carped, "Of course, your liege."

Jonathon was tired of his sarcasm and about ready to command him to be civil, but he decided not to waste his breath.

From gallons of a green liquid that smelled of alcohol, a whole bottle of gold-flecked elixir the consistency of honey, two large yellow crystals, and a black powder which floated up to the ceiling and had to be coaxed with a ladle back down into the mixture, the Alchemist prepared a cauldron full of nasty gray syrup which filled the chamber with a ponderous reek. Holding out a wrinkled hand that looked like a shriveled spider, Rulupunerswan said, "The first seed."

Jonathon carefully picked the Blue-Eyed Kaitlin seed from his sheltering hand. It was the one that was supposed to be Arlen. He trembled with the fear that these seeds, copies of the originals, might not contain the essence of his family. Even if they did produce his family, maybe they would be only duplicates, not the original people. Either way, to drop anything he valued into that evil claw was terrifying.

"You will not harm my family," he emphasized, just to reassure himself that he had taken all necessary precautions.

Rulupunerswan took the seed and tossed it rudely into the cauldron. The Alchemist was still afraid of Sweet Thing and danced around, trying to keep the cauldron between him and the active Dragon.

He hesitated but finally said, "Have your beast blow fire on the top of the mixture."

With a thought from Jonathon, Sweet Thing seared the surface of the mixture which boiled and popped making Rulupunerswan step back to avoid the spattering liquid.

"Again!" Rulupunerswan shouted. Again Sweet Thing blasted the surface with fire.

Jonathon saw movement within the cauldron like the head of a baby about to be born into the world.

"More fire!" Rulupunerswan shouted at Sweet Thing.

The Dragon inhaled deeply this time and blew fire in a smaller concentrated stream that gently bathed a gray amorphous blob as it emerged from the cauldron. He stopped several times for breaths but resumed blowing repeatedly, sculpting rough facial features, arms and legs. With more breaths Sweet Thing breathed more life into the creature. Although the fire came from Sweet Thing, Jonathon, through the Dragoncrown, was really doing much of the molding of the emergent being.

Fingers appeared, moving uncertainly. Hair grew from sparks that burst from its scalp. When the creature's eyes opened and peered through cloaking steam, Rulupunerswan yelled, "Stop."

At Jonathon's sharp thought, Sweet Thing recoiled and whimpered like a kicked puppy.

The gray fluids encasing the figure steamed away, slowly revealing Arlen, naked and moist like a newborn, standing before them. She looked around her, just like a baby seeing the world for the first time. Jonathon was afraid to speak.

"Goo!" she said.

For a frantic moment Jonathon thought she really had the untrained mind of a baby again, and he would have to teach her how to talk and think.

She threw out her hands, beseeching, "*What* am I doing in this pot of *goo?*"

It was Arlen, all right. No one else would greet him with such obstreperousness.

Before she could rail at him for standing and gawking with a foolish look on his face, he ran to her and lifted her quickly out of the cauldron. She seemed light as a child.

"Jonathon?" she said, squeezing his unusually-muscular shoulders with her hands. "Is that you?" She was thinner and lighter herself.

"You never could lift me before!"

As he nodded, unsure what to say first, he removed his shirt to cover her up.

Studying his head, she said, "Is that the Dragoncrown on your head?"

"It's a long story, Dumpling. First, the children."

"The children? Where are they?"

He held out his hand and opened his fist.

She looked at the seeds and gazed at him uncomprehending, shaking her long hair "I don't understand."

"You will. Just have patience and watch."

She folded her arms over her ample chest and glared at him suspiciously, more proof that the woman from the vat was truly his wife. Patience was not one of her traits.

Jonathon chose the Foxglove seed next, expecting it to be Theodore. After the procedure was repeated - Sweet Thing had already become quite confident in sculpting humans with his knives of flame - the emerging person became Judith, not Theodore.

With his naked nubile daughter in the room, Jonathon ordered Rulupunerswan to turn his head and find clothes for all his family. The clothing the Alchemist came up with was old, threadbare, and dirty, but good enough to cover them for the journey home.

What was left of the afternoon was spent restoring the rest of his family. Rulupunerswan had to light more candles to light the darkening chamber between Sweet Thing's fire sculpting. While he was performing his duties, the Dragonfire lit the chamber to near daylight.

Arlen cried out with joy at the appearance of each child, and Jonathon gave each one a big hug as he took them from the cauldron. The little ones cried with fright and had to be soothed by Arlen for a long time before they quieted down. Jonathon was glad that he had a squad of Knights protecting the only entrance to the tower. Baby Nathaniel was last. By that time, all the other children were there to hover over the baby and keep him warm and safe. He didn't cry at all, recognizing his mother and his father despite their changes. He only looked at their eyes and listened to their cooing.

After the children and Arlen were all back to their normal selves, clothed and soothed, Jonathon saw that the children still cringed in fear of Sweet Thing. Jonathon knew that Sweet Thing had a special interest in the children's welfare since the Dragon himself brought them back to life. The Dragon thought of them as his children too, even Arlen. He would never harm them, even if the Dragoncrown did not restrain him, and he would protect them like he would his own family. Dragons were usually independent loners that cared little what happened to their offspring, but Sweet Thing was different. He had been the object of the love of Jonathon Forthright from the moment he broke out of his egg, and love was imprinted on his intelligent mind forever.

"Don't worry, children. He's harmless."

Jonathon released his hold on the baby Dragon, letting it romp about. It capered for the children's delight, stumbling or trying to fly, just to crash into workbenches. It infuriated Rulupunerswan. The children laughed at the Alchemist's distress, thinking it was all a playful skit for their benefit. Jonathon allowed it all, keeping the Alchemist still and enjoying a little revenge for Rulupunerswan's treatment of his wife, children, and Rhazburn.

After Arlen heard the story of what the Alchemist had done to her and the children, she stepped up to the leering Alchemist. Jonathon, taking his cue, told Rulupunerswan to stand very still. Arlen wound up a tight fist and slugged him so hard he spun completely around, making the children clap with glee, again like it was all a show.

Once vengeance had been served, Jonathon told Rulupunerswan to go wait with Seldric until Jonathon, the Dragonlord, came to them. As he and his family walked into the evening air at the foot of the tower stairs, he held the Rod of Coercion high. Dozens of Knights and many of the courtiers, including Gashgrieve, were there in the courtyard awaiting them. One line of Knights stood with their backs to the door, their crossbows leveled at the mob. They were the ones who had tried to sneak up the stairs to take him prisoner and whom Jonathon had conscripted to keep them safe. Wesfallen was there, but Rhazburn had gone off on his hopeless quest.

After the requisite verse, Jonathon said, "Now everyone will let us pass and will do nothing to hinder us. Ten Knights will escort my family to my house. After that, those Knights will go back to their own homes."

The captain of the Knights delegated ten to do as ordered.

Arlen clung to Jonathon's arm. "Aren't you coming with us?"

"I will be home soon, Dumpling. I will tell you everything when I return." Holding out the Rod of Coercion, he explained, "I need to give this back to the Pixets."

"And this," he said, pointing to the Dragoncrown, "to the Dragonlord."

Arlen didn't question a thing, having witnessed how Jonathon controlled Sweet Thing and how he ordered the Court Alchemist around. Jonathon radiated power and confidence, so she remained silent.

To Sweet Thing, she said, "I wish you didn't have to be enslaved to make Glass Commands." To Jonathon she said, "He's really sweet. I hate to just leave him to the whims of the Court. Can't we do something?"

"I thought he was sweet, too. In fact, I named him Sweet Thing." Again he pointed at the Dragoncrown. "I know he likes the name. As to his fate, soon the real Dragonlord will decide, but I have a feeling that we'll see a lot of Sweet Thing. There's something different about him. Different from all the other Dragons."

Arlen was awestruck. "All the other Dragons? You know all the other Dragons? You really are the Dragonlord now." She thought a bit, as if knowing how quickly things could change. "What will happen to us once you give that and the Unicorn Horn back?"

"I'm not sure." The secret knowledge that he had freed all the other Dragons passed through his thoughts. "It's not over yet. But you and the children will be safe for now."

When they were all safely escorted away, Jonathon ordered everyone in the courtyard to go home. He ordered Gashgrieve and Wesfallen to report what had happened to the Dragonlord.

After the courtyard was cleared, he hurried back to the tower where the remaining Pixets awaited his return. At the landing before the chamber, the Knights he had commanded to protect the Pixets were standing, heedful of any intrusion. Jonathon waved them aside and said, "For your loyalty and care in protecting the Pixets, you may now all go home." With looks of concern on their faces, struggling within themselves to disobey, they left as expeditiously as possible.

Within the chamber, the Pixets were in the air fluttering, anxious to leave that awful place with its depressing aura of incarceration and fright.

Jonathon stepped up to the stone casement of the window. He raised the Rod of Coercion high above his head to dash it against the stone and shatter the head piece. He knew that was what the Pixets wanted, despite their promise to the Mermets. He would do it and they would be blameless.

"Shall I destroy its power?"

With horrified looks on their tiny faces, the Pixets sped to grasp his arm, straining, beating the air with their wings to slow his blow. Jonathon stopped, saying, "All right, I'll stop. But why? I thought that the Community saw this use of the Unicorn Horn as a travesty and wanted it torn apart."

The gray, venerable Pixelle bowed in the air. All the others flew to the Unicorn Horn and relieved Jonathon of the burden. He gave it up gladly.

"We must keep the Rod of Coercion inviolate. One more covenant must be honored. The Mermets aided us in finding the Knife of Life that brought back the Unicorns from their corruption. We know that the Mermets want the Rod of Coercion to secure their place in the oceans by negotiating with the Lord of the Sea. When the Unicorns return to Verdilon, we will ask their permission to fulfill our part of the covenant and give this to the Mermets. The Lord of the Sea will soon hold the Rod of Coercion."

Jonathon mused that the Lord of the Sea was probably the one being on the world that could successfully wield the Rod of Coercion without using the Dragoncrown, but he still needed the activating poem and coins to power it. "When you take it to the Mermets, let me know so I can instruct them in its use."

"We will remember."

One last time, the old Pixet bowed in the air. As he motioned with a wave at all the Pixets who bowed as well, he said, "Master Jeweler, we rescind all previous proscriptions of dealing with you. All has been made whole again. We see that you desecrated the Unicorn Horn in distress, confused as to what you were doing. But we now feel that you had been chosen by the Natural Presence to fulfill an ancient prophesy. It was this - that only by allying the Unicorns with human greed and ambition could Verdilon be restored. For that reason, centuries ago, we made our home in the center of human greed, Isseltrent. It was for that reason that we became artisans engulfed in the manufacture of trinkets and baubles to be sold by the greedy to the greedy. Only now, after all the terror we have sustained in this dreary prison, do we see the meaning of these events. Without intention, you have been the salvation of Verdilon and the Community. You have fulfilled the ancient prophesy. The Unicorns live again."

Through the stone window they went, carrying the Rod of Coercion, adorned with Pixet-engraved jewels, the last that ever would be made. On they flew, on into the sky and back into the sight of the Natural Presence. As one, they all shouted, "Goodbye, Master Forthright, Savior of Verdilon."

"Goodbye," Jonathon said, waving to them, tears running down his cheeks. At long, long last, he could feel proud again. He let himself cry in relief. All was accomplished. He was ready to face the anger of the Dragonlord.

CHAPTER 39

JONATHON FORTHRIGHT, BANE OF DEMONS, FRIEND OF DRAGONS AND SAVIOR OF VERDILON

Twilight was falling on Isseltrent. A few muttering men lit torches, apparently irritated that they could no longer depend upon the simpler, glowing magical sconces they had used when the Dragons were in Seldric's power.

Since all of Jonathon's important obligations were complete, he could finally take the Dragoncrown back to the Dragonlord. As he walked through the corridors of Blaze, all the courtiers and Knights shrank back against the walls, remembering how he commanded them when he held the Rod of Coercion just a couple of Blessings before. Besides, everyone recognized the Dragoncrown, and they all knew the power of the Red Dragon following Jonathon's determined stride, even a Dragon only two strides long with stubby, ineffectual wings.

Jonathon had commanded Sweet Thing to leave the area before he gave the Dragoncrown back to the Dragonlord. But the baby Dragon was so overwhelmed with fear of leaving Jonathon that he allowed Sweet Thing to stay close by. Sweet Thing was the only Dragon within the sway of the Dragoncrown, the only one that he could not save from servitude.

Jonathon could sense Sweet Thing's prankish thoughts, and he quickly learned how to suppress the baby Dragon's tendency to give everyone that they passed a hot foot. He only needed to suggest it to him by a thought, and Sweet Thing turned his head away and swallowed the fire. Still, he knew that Sweet Thing was hungry. Even the Dragoncrown could not suppress the furious hunger of a Dragon. Because of the fires they produced, Dragons ate prodigious amounts and Jonathon sensed that Sweet Thing would need a few dozen rats that day. He planned to walk through the alleys on the way home to give him a chance to practice his hunting skills. Somehow Jonathon suspected that even after he gave up the Dragoncrown to the Dragonlord, Sweet Thing would go home with him unless restrained.

He knew the Dragonlord would be awaiting the Dragoncrown in Dragonthrone Hall. It was easy to find. All corridors in Blaze eventually led there. He merely followed the ever widening pathway which led, circuitously but inexorably, up to the Great Doors guarding Dragonthrone Hall. At the entrance, he merely waved to the two Knights who immediately pulled open the ornate gilt doors. It was the authority of the Dragoncrown on his head that silently commanded them. Raised eyebrows was their only reaction to Sweet Thing as he waddled behind his master.

Inside Dragonthrone Hall, two more guards holding halberds fell in beside him as he strode confidently up the simulated Dragontail on the floor leading to the Dragonthrone. From the carved Dragon heads atop the ranked pillars, red light shone through their glass eyes steeping the already red tiles in a bloody sheen. Jonathon couldn't help glancing at Sweet Thing, noticing his reaction to the statues. They might be the closest he would ever come to his kin.

At the end of Dragontail Walkway sat the Dragonlord upon the Dragonthrone. His head was bare. His hand was loosely clenched. The flared jaws of the tall Dragonhead behind the dais belched flames again, just as it had during Jonathon's last visit there as a condemned prisoner.

At that time, he had been spurred up the walkway by angry Sinjery warmaidens. This time, not one Sinjery maiden was in sight.

Beside the Dragonlord to the right, Wesfallen stood, smiling benevolently. Since Hell's Breach was no more, the cares of a decade had melted from his face. No longer was he responsible for manning the Musical Mystical Door, leading the Poets, deciding whom to sacrifice if necessary to stop Demons from invading the world. Next to him was Pavnoreth, quite a bit thinner but with a haughty look, as if he felt the prayers of his Holy Few had been answered by The Three and Hell's Breach had been closed by Tundudil's grace alone. To the left of the Dragonthrone, Rulupunerswan, watching Jonathon from the corners of his wary eyes, leaned toward Seldric but stopped, still constrained from whispering venom against Jonathon into the Dragonlord's ear by the lasting effect of the Rod of Coercion that same day. Off to the side, holding the royal scepter, Gashgrieve started lauding the titles and accomplishments of Seldric. He was cut off in mid-sentence with a curt gesture by the Dragonlord, who seemed to prefer to brood in silence as he awaited the return of the unruly and disquieting thoughts of scores of Dragons which it was his job to quell and force into painful service.

He looked smaller to Jonathon and much older than he had seemed half a year before. Where Jonathon had felt intense fear then, pity was all he could muster for the old ruler now. Even though they would all soon find out that Jonathon had freed the Dragons, surely a capital offense, there was no fear left within him. He had used all the fear his meager body had ever contained long before in the Demon's Hellpit. He would miss his family when he died. Even if he was destined for Hell, he had already been there once, so he knew what to expect. Maybe he'd run into Dollop again and help the brave lad. At that moment, he saw opportunities in everything, even death. He'd be just fine.

When Jonathon stopped two strides before the Dragonthrone, he stood straight and looked Seldric in the eyes, waiting for the ruler to speak first. Since he had divested himself of the Jewel of Nishbad, the Sword of Bliss, and the Rod of Coercion before he entered Dragonthrone Hall, the Dragoncrown was the only item of power left to him, and it counted for little now.

Even without the Dragoncrown on his head, Seldric was careworn, restive, and imperious. "Humph! So you own the Dragoncrown now, do you, Jeweler? And you presume to command us in Isseltrent as if you were the Demon's spawn. I am surprised that you did not ride a Dragon back to frighten us with your power." He reached up to run his fingers over a ropey scar on his forehead where the Rod of Coercion wielded by the Demon had struck him down.

"Why have you not brought that perfidious wand you brandished about so, doing as you pleased in my court? Do you have it hidden to bring forth someday just torment all of us again?"

Jonathon felt waves of anger radiating out from Seldric as palpably as the evil had been radiating from the Demon in its Hellpit. "The Rod of Coercion passed onto the Pixets, to do with as they please. I am ashamed that I caused them so much pain when I turned it into that vile thing."

"Not so vile that it didn't come in useful for your own purposes. You've been very busy today taking what you will, lording it over all of us. Now you come back to gloat, do you?"

"I return at your bidding, Your Highness, to bring back the Dragoncrown as you commanded."

"I don't recall commanding you to free the Sinjery from their age-old pledge, nor did I command you to force my guards willy-nilly to abandon their posts. I also never commanded you to let the treacherous Pixets flee from justice. What say you to this, Lord Traitor Supreme?"

"I went to the Dead Lands on your command, but I was forced to save my family while there was still a chance. The Pixets never meant you any harm and never will. I thought that my only chance to ensure their freedom was to was to accomplish the task prior to your donning the Dragoncrown."

"Now you question our word? What presumption!"

Jonathon reached up without saying another word to take off the Dragoncrown.

Two guards turned their halberds on Jonathon, the sharp tips pricking the sides of his neck. They misunderstood him, thinking he wanted to keep the Dragoncrown. Nothing was further from his mind. Jonathon reached up slowly so as not to alarm the guards. With the halberd points touching his jugulars, he didn't want them to even twitch. Slowly, he took off the Dragoncrown and held it out before him to show all present that it was undamaged. Black unbroken glass with pearl eyes stared down at the Dragonlord.

As soon as Seldric saw him grasp the Dragoncrown to remove it, he reached out and waved his hand impatiently as if to say, "Get on with it".

Solemn as an embalmer, knowing what the Dragonlord was about to discover, and resigned to the fate awaiting him, Jonathon handed him the Dragoncrown.

Seldric snatched it away, snarling in contempt, and tossed it on his head, where the Crown settled into a well-formed groove. After the Dragoncrown was back on his head, Seldric waved the guards' halberds away from Jonathon, but they grasped Jonathon's arms as if they feared he would reach out and pluck the Dragoncrown back off Seldric's head. Jonathon stood obediently still, surprisingly calm, satisfied that he had accomplished all he was capable of before this perilous moment. He doubted that many moments remained in his life once Seldric discovered what he had done with the Dragons. At first, Seldric seemed to take no notice of the lack of Dragons.

"If the Pixets mean us no harm, then why have they not brought us that perfidious wand to use for the benefit of our Realm?"

"I believe you heard from the Pixets about the bargain they made with the Mermets for their help in finding the Knife of Life."

"I never sanctioned such a bargain. Now the Sea King will use that wand and come take what he pleases from us. What is to stop him from taking the Dragoncrown just like the Demon did?"

"Perhaps peace, harmony, and mutual respect between the your realm and the Kingdom of the Lord of the Sea? I believe that would stay his hand."

"What do you know of the Sea King?"

"I have met him and talked to him. I believe he wishes only for peace in his Kingdom."

Seldric seemed not to hear Jonathon. He was listening to something within. Or nothing within, Jonathon speculated. In a way uncharacteristic for the Dragonlord, Seldric hesitated with his next statement. "I... I don't think the Sea King will be able to turn aside my Blue Dragons with that perfidious wand."

Oblivious to what was going on inside the Dragonlord's mind, Wesfallen stood, patiently smiling. Pavnoreth tried to make his expression beatific, as if he expected Seldric to summon all the Dragons back, rebuilding the society according to the teachings of *The Transmigrant*, enforced by the power of the Dragons. Rulupunerswan sneered. He obviously wanted Jonathon executed, no matter what happened with the Dragons, and the Dragonlord seemed to share his views. Jonathon stood calmly, a serene look on his face.

Seldric wrinkled his brow. He looked this way and that as if listening, searching. He looked at Sweet Thing who, apparently in response to a command, twirled in a neat circle, then stopped and gazed, awaiting further instructions. The Dragonlord stood and stepped down, passing Jonathon and the guards with his eyes playing over the columns supporting the magnificent ceiling as if he expected to sense thoughts from the stone Dragons. Down the tile Dragontail he walked, drawing along everyone with looks of concern on their faces. He passed out through the gilt doors. He looked up at the sky, crying, "What treachery is this? All my Dragons, where are they? Dead? All of them?"

No one spoke while the Dragonlord turned around slowly, reaching for the open sky. "It cannot be. They are all silent, but one." He twirled and looked at Sweet Thing who cowered. Sweet Thing knew who was in command.

Seldric acted like Jonathon was the culprit. He whirled upon the jeweler. "What have you done to the Dragoncrown, you and your son?" He took it off and inspected every surface and jewel of it anxiously. "I see nothing different." After nearly forty years living with the Dragoncrown, he knew every gem and inscription on it. "What could you have done to it?" He looked up. "Speak, Jeweler."

The grip of the guards increased tenfold, but since his time in the Demon's Hellpit, Jonathon disregarded any pain less than that of dismemberment or being flayed alive. Jonathon stood tall and said simply, "Your Highness, the Dragons are gone."

"Gone? What do you mean, gone?"

"Your Highness, I freed them."

Seldric shouted, "Freed them? Freed them! You mean to destroy us yet again? Rend out the heart of Isseltrent once more?"

Jonathon saw the other Knights step forward to take him into custody again. Not much could save him this time. He was all alone and without power. Even Sweet thing was now in Seldric's control. But what did his life matter? The suffering of the Dragons, of the Sinjery, of the Pixets, and even of the people of the sea had been wrong. Now it was at an end. "It was the better of two wrongs. The suffering was too great for them to bear. I believe you knew how intolerable it was. Like Hell for them... And I know what Hell is like, as does my son."

Seldric barked, "What about the suffering of the people of Thuringland and all the surrounding lands? What of that?" Then Seldric stepped up to Jonathon, towering over him, threatening. "What gives you the right to judge what is right and what is wrong?"

Jonathon said. "Your Highness, with all respect, I have seen more evil than even you can imagine. I have died and come back from the dead. I have been in Hell and shared thoughts with Ghosts, Dragons, and the Demon, itself. I know what evil is. It is enslaving others for your own benefit. Like the Demon did with me and many others. That is the pinnacle of evil. Even The Three consign that horror to Hell alone. Why would we want to be like Demons? Indeed, to the Dragons, we *are* Demons when we control them with the Dragoncrown."

"Why would we want to control the minds of the Dragons?" Seldric said sarcastically. "To protect the Realm and our people, of course. Just as we have for centuries."

"But the Demon is gone with all its Zombie armies. Hell's Breach is closed. The Dragons are beyond our borders and will not return, lest they be enslaved again. Why not promulgate peace with your neighbors? While we have the opportunity."

"Peace? The Demon may be gone, but what of the Mermen who oppose us at our very shore? Molgannard Fey may be gone, but beyond the Cajalathrium States, the armies of Giants have been held back only by the Dragons. Likewise the Wind People to the east and the Gibbering Flippers to the south. Peace is a pretty weak word in the face of the onslaught we face from them all."

"I spoke with the Lord of the Sea. The Mermen want only the freedom of their seas. The North Wall protects us from the Giants as it always has. Verdilon, repopulated with Unicorns, will protect us from the Wind

People. And if your Lordship befriends Sinjer, the Sinjery will guard us against the Gibbering Flippers. Thuringland and the humans within it existed long before the Dragoncrown."

"Yes, but now that the Dragoncrown exists and you have sent the Dragons to those other lands, what if those other peoples decide they have had enough of Dragons? The pressure will be great to flee their lands and come to ours where we are safe from the Dragons. Or maybe they will send thieves and assassins to steal the Dragoncrown to protect themselves."

Jonathon had not thought out all the potential ramifications of losing the Dragons and sending them elsewhere. Still, he thought it the better of two evils.

"I should give it back to you. Let you be the target of the assassins."

Rulupunerswan raised a sepulchral finger and blurted, "Your Highness exec... c... c...." He choked on the words, gagging on his own tongue as the effect of the Rod of Coercion stopped his suggestion to execute Jonathon in mid-sentence.

Seldric skewered him with an angry gaze. "Alchemist, comport yourself and leave us."

Rulupunerswan did as he was commanded.

Jonathon was not in the least sorry to see him skulk away.

Turning back to Jonathon, Seldric said, "So, Jeweler. I sent you to the Dead Lands to take back the Dragoncrown, expecting you to die in the attempt. You died as I foresaw. I did not foresee that you would come back to life and render the Dragoncrown and all that this court stands for utterly useless." He shook his head in disgust. "You expect us to thank you for destroying the one thing which united all Thuringland and the Tributary States, the solidarity that we all felt in league against the Demon and its hordes. The Dragoncrown kept the Realm safe from the Demon and everyone else surrounding us. Now, you have hamstrung our unassailable defense and reduced Isseltrent to the level of every other savage kingdom in the world." He let that sink in. Then he added, "We don't even have the loyalty of the Sinjery maidens to help defend us against invasion. What's more, even if we could use this one pathetic Dragon to fire the Dragonkilns, what good would it do without the services of the Pixets to inscribe the Glass Commands?"

"We can still trade for their services and those of the Sinjery, just as other lands do. The resources of Thuringland are undiminished," Jonathon said.

"Trade, you say? Who in the court knows of trade?" He eyed Wesfallen who shrugged. His gaze fell next upon Pavnoreth who held up his hands unsullied by earthly concerns. Finally, he spotted Gashgrieve, who nodded to himself in a cagey manner, as if mulling over just how to exploit this new need of his ruler.

"Well, we may be able to adapt," Seldric, said more to himself than to the others present. Then he pointed a cogent finger at Jonathon. "I will have my Dragons back. You shall pay for this treachery. You may have forcibly freed your family, but I am still Dragonlord. Your family belongs to me. All of your brood shall answer to the court for the rest of their lives. They are all to serve the court."

Jonathon was not expecting that.

"As for you, Jeweler. You will produce a new system of coinage to pay for all the goods with the kingdoms surrounding us. That is, until you can begin to produce Glass Commands with your little friend here. You, alone, shall be the one to negotiate with the Pixets for their services to inscribe the Glass Commands. I believe they owe you a considerable amount. I expect the Pixet Community to be properly appreciative. See to it!"

Jonathon thought to himself, *You're letting me live?*

With a dismissive wave, the Dragonlord released Jonathon for the moment. "Guards, he may leave my presence, but he may not leave Isseltrent unless we assign him a task outside the city."

"Your Highness, if I come to the court every day, may I rebuild my shop and my house?"

"If you come to the court and if you make progress, I suppose you may. At your own expense." He added, with a hard look, "I haven't given up on the notion of sending you to fetch a few Dragons for us. I have to think on it. We may have to make another Dragoncrown." His eyes looked off into the future. "Two Dragoncrowns... I don't know. Dealing with one is bad enough."

Jonathon hoped that he would see reason and forget a second Dragoncrown. If they made another, it might end up on the head of Rulupunerswan. Wouldn't that be nice.

Seldric looked again at Sweet Thing and shook his head. One tiny Red Dragon could not produce many Glass Commands, and Dragons took thirty years to mature. "Jeweler, why didn't you free this one?"

Jonathon, too, looked at the baby Dragon. "I tried, but he refused to go. I believe he thinks I'm his mother."

Seldric's stern face nearly softened at that. "You may be his trainer, Jeweler. All the Sinjery Brandmistresses have left and most of the Knight Brandmasters are all dead. Besides, through him I can watch you. If I see any more treachery or contempt for this court, your family will be in easy reach of my wrath through your little friend."

He turned to his advisors and said, "Release the gold wires. Isseltrent must rise again out of its ashes."

CHAPTER 40

SINJER

After twenty days hiking south through the coastal hills, Rhazburn was fatigued, footsore, and famished. All he had brought with him to eat was a wheel of cheese from his sister Heather and a flask of wine, which had been long since exhausted and filled with water from rills. Despite the fact that spring had officially just begun in Isseltrent, the air far to the south was already muggy and thick with flies. Every exposed piece of Rhazburn's skin was covered in welts, and he was so hot that he had to expose more skin and take off his tunic, so his sweat had somewhere better to go than downhill into his boots.

As he feared, the small band of surviving Sinjery had outdistanced him by days. At every farmstead where he stopped to trade a tune for a piece of bread and a bed in a shed, the farmers told him that the Sinjery maidens were many days ahead. Each successive farmer told him an increased number of days by which they preceded him. None of them had seen the Sinjery move so fast, two days worth of travel for each one of his. One of the farmer's wives had anxiously asked the Sinjery if there was some new danger that they were fleeing. After the terror of Dragons descending upon them, snapping up their cattle and razing their fields only a few Moons before, the farm folk were disturbed at the thought of any new threat.

Rhazburn tried to reassure the uninformed, anxious farmers. They could rest assured. Dragons and Demons were a thing of the past. They could get on with their lives and pursue their livelihood.

As the well-tended farms became scarce further south, they were replaced by hunting shacks haunted by surly hermits jealously guarding their stacks of hides. They seemed especially angry at the Dragonlord and his court. Rhazburn sensed that they were angry because the Skin-Splicer trade had been interrupted when Jonathon and Trallalair cleansed Isseltrent of Molgannard Fey and his lot.

He spoke little to them, only enough to trade a tune for some meat or glean the direction in which the Sinjery maidens had passed. The hermits had little use for the Sinjery either, but they told him where they had gone, probably hoping Rhazburn meant them ill as well. No man traveled to Sinjer in friendship.

Always he was pointed in the direction of the wide valley into which the Green Choke River ran. As Rhazburn descended deeper into the valley, the rapidly-flowing Green Choke slowed, as did the heavy, hot air above it. Tended fields had long since given way to thorny scrub that tore at his clothes. Raucous flocks of colorful birds boiled out of scattered trees dense with leaves, passing from one tree to the next, stripping each of insects and fruit. Early one morning, after many more days of picking and crashing his way through bushes full of spiders that overhung the meager trail beside the river, his rations of food and water dwindled to nothing. The trail he followed ended at the side of the Green Choke which had widened into a lake teeming with ripples.

Rhazburn stopped and brushed dozens of clinging spiders from his clothes and hair. Squinting past the sky shimmering on the surface of the water, he could see movement just beneath the surface. Here, fish swam, searching for insects to suck from the surface. The fish in turn were prey of others. Waterfowl lunged and dove through the trembling mirror, coming up most of the time with their beaks full of flapping fish. Higher up the chain of life, huge floating reptiles took their due, snapping up birds that blundered too close to their fanged jaws. Rhazburn could see that trying to swim across the Green Choke among the floating lizards would be suicidal. Some were fully large enough to take off his leg. Or his head.

The only establishment on the bank of the lake was a hovel. Near it were twenty stakes pounded into the bank to which long flat bottomed boats were tied. As Rhazburn approached, a limping man in soiled leather clothes walked warily out of the shack.

The limping man started out emphatically, "Come to gloat, are yeh? Well, be off! Les' yeh want the women's pox. Ah'll not have yeh stinkin' up me cottage."

Rhazburn regarded him curiously. He figured that the man was referring to the accursed disease that killed only the men in Sinjer. He only wondered why the man thought Rhazburn was there to gloat. "I'm sorry?"

"Me cottage may not look a'much, but Ah like the way she smells."

"No, not that, you asked me if I were here to gloat."

"The women. Me main source of income. Gone for good. One of 'm towed 'm all back and paid me for hern. Said they'd never be back. At leas' the women pay me! Might'swell sell me boats for firewood, now. Leas' people still need to eat!" He spat off to the side for emphasis. "Now be off!"

"I want to hire a boat."

The man peered heavenward and swore. "Ilsa's breeches! Ah don't rent to men. Have yeh no brains?" Canting his head to the side, he squinted into Rhazburn's eyes, apparently looking to see if there were any brains inside Rhazburn's skull.

"I'll bring it back."

"No, yeh won't. Les' yeh can come out'n yer grave, or from Hell." He laughed at his cleverness, unaware of how close he stood to the truth of it. "Ah'll sell yeh a boat. Ah don't 'spec to see it again. Kris p'tect me from seeing it again. With yeh full a' boils, running pus all over me boat? Ah'll thank yeh to p'litely stay away an' die in a bush. Or hop in the Choke an' feed the crocs. Had t' burn the last boat that was brought back here by a fool of a man. Saw that feller's eye, big and fulla' pus, then the eye jus' burst, all the pus jus' flyin' out. Good thing Ah can still jump. The festerin' a'most hit me. Liked to puke!"

Rhazburn was convinced that his chances of ever seeing Trallalair were slim. After escaping Hell, he'd hoped to put death behind him for a while. He had acquired a new impetus, an obsession to see Trallalair as a man, not a Ghost. He kept hearing in his mind Trallalair's last words as she left Jonathon with Rhazburn inside, "I never thought it possible to love anyone but one of the Sisters". Since that day, he had resolved to find her before he died again. He did not need the boatman to confirm his belief that he would never see her again outside Sinjer. It would have taken him many days to devise a counter to the curse that hung over Sinjer, and without the Pixets to engrave jewels for it, he could never make it. Poetry was no longer a tool he could depend upon. Yet he was driven to find Trallalair. He had shared her soul and found it passionate and sublime, the only soul worthy of his love. He would gladly die to touch her hair or even glimpse her again. Then he could rest. Go to his fate. He did not care what that fate would be.

"I'll buy a boat, and I won't be back."

"If yeh go in there, Ah pray to The Three Ah never spy yeh face again. Ye fellas'r sure strange. What's so whistlin' important yeh want outa the women? Revenge? Most'uv em want revenge. Some 'spect they can make money stealin' from women. They don't know these women." He shook his head in frustration at fools. "Yeh won't find 'em, yeh know. No one does. All of them tha' try? They all die."

The surly man sighed and led the way to the shore. "My scummers fetch ten Orders apiece."

"Scummers?"

"Y'know, skimmers. But Ah call em scummers 'cause they push around the scum on the Choke." He leered a grin with hardly a tooth to be seen.

Rhazburn gave him a Glass Command. "I'll take a scummer."

The man gawked, took the Command, examined it for authenticity, and pronounced, "Ah haven't nearly the change for this, fella. What do yeh take me fer? A flamin' Duke?"

"Keep it. I won't be needing the change."

The man gawked again. "Take the lot, if yeh want. Take the shack. Ah'll be leavin' this stinkin', wretched and mudsuckin' river, thank yeh. Buy me a fishing fleet on the sea! Rent to the Dragonlord, Ah will."

Rhazburn just raised his hand and flicked him a wave in response.

The scummer, or skimmer, was a long flat-bottomed boat. It drew only a couple inches of water and was propelled by an long oar that could be used as a paddle or turned over to pole through the swamps while the boat skimmed over the surface of the water.

Rhazburn easily pushed the skimmer off into the placid lake. He sat on a thwart at the rear and paddled out into the steaming water. At first, due to his naivety at paddling a boat, he was not so much moving as simply spinning around. After a few ineffectual twirls, he figured how to dig the blade in the water and twist it at the last moment to keep the boat moving in approximately one direction.

One of the massive reptiles began following him, apparently having learned that any man paddling into Sinjer would soon be food. The reptile started out far astern. Rhazburn's skimmer left the broad lake and entered the swamp where the slow river, stagnant and stinking, stopped completely. The lurking creature, ridged scales leaving tiny wakes, became bolder and swam closer, almost bumping the stern. The reptile was twice the length of the skimmer but graceful as a snake in the water.

Rhazburn lifted the paddle out of the water and rapped the reptile sharply on the snout.

With a commotion of waves that wobbled Rhazburn's craft, almost flipping it over, the creature dove beneath and was lost in the brown murk of the swampy river.

Rhazburn felt that the creature was still there but hidden, watching him from under the muddy haze. He had the ominous premonition that the reptile could flip his skimmer over whenever it judged Rhazburn to be too weak to fight it.

Tiny plants the size of beans, each no more than a single leaf, covered the water on Rhazburn's right side all the way to a quaking bog. A field of rushes clogged the left of the rapidly contracting river. Every dozen paddles or so, the river divided, shrinking the stream even further and puzzling Rhazburn as to which direction to take. After many such forks in the river and a good deal of time, the sky darkened and a warm torrent fell upon Rhazburn, pooling in his boat. If the torrent did not abate the rising water inside could eventually top the gunwales and sink him. He had no way to empty it. If he stayed in the middle of the stagnant stream, he would have no way to stop from sinking there.

The bottom of the stream was somewhere beneath the massed, green plants covering its surface. But how deep, it was impossible to tell. Even if he could see past the massed tiny plants, the murky brown water hid it from him. There in the encroaching swamp, the water felt thicker, like he paddled watery mud instead of muddy water. So he gave up on paddling altogether. Rhazburn turned the paddle over to use it as a pole, pushing as best he could against the soft mud on the stream bed. With frequent slips of the pole deep into the mud that soaked his arm in green slime, he slowly poled over to the rushes. Once among the rushes, he pushed the boat into them. Now, as it filled with water, it was at least supported by the floating rafts of rush roots. He still imagined the huge reptile lurking nearby, eager to clamp his jaws on his leg, so Rhazburn dared not step into the uncertain depths of the mud.

After the rain stopped, the mosquitoes which had been released by the torrent swarmed up, covering him. The skimmer was now full of water to the brim, much too heavy and unstable to pole. Only the mats of rush roots just beneath the surface of the water kept the boat from sinking. Onto the quivering mats he stepped, careful not to slip off into the quagmire around it. Standing upon the shifting mats, he lifted one side of the skimmer up to dump out the water. The effort took all his strength and balance. It was strange, because the boat had not seemed nearly so heavy earlier in the day. He thought that he was much more tired than he should have been from simply pushing the boat through water and mud for one or two Blessings.

Twice more that day, Rhazburn had to lift the boat and empty the water, and each time, his muscles seemed weaker than the last. That night, although the fen was filled with buzzing and biting insects, meaning the night was warm, Rhazburn shook, chilled to the bone. For the first time since he had his body back, he yearned to be nothing but a Ghost again, invisible to insects and incapable of getting bitten or ill.

In the morning after a sleepless night, he saw that his skin was peppered with red spots. He was still chilled, even in the heat of the day. He knew he was febrile. One day was all he had searched before the curse of the Sinjery had affected him. He had hoped to at least glimpse Trallalair before he died, but apparently, fate was dealing him a different hand. He wondered what he had seen in the Hall of Mirrors. Maybe what he saw was not the truth but a hallucination caused by his fever just before he died.

A drizzle had begun sometime in the night, too light to awaken him in his febrile stupor and, to his relief, too light to fill up the skimmer. In his state, Rhazburn could never have lifted the boat to pour out the water again. If it filled up this time, he would sink with it into the cloudy water to be eaten by the huge reptiles.

Too weary to stand, he fell against the boat to push it back into the stream. The only thing that kept him upright long enough to take up his paddle and tumble into the boat was a vision of Trallalair in his mind. Rhazburn imagined her amongst the trees, beautiful and pensive. As if he were still a Demon in her body, he called to her with a thought. Love, just love was all he felt and all he wanted to express to her. One final time. As he collapsed, he hoped that he would just die and disappear in the jungle, mingling with the elements like the Pixets believed. He wanted to cause her no more grief, even the grief of seeing him dead.

Three leagues away, squatting beneath huge fern fronds to shelter her briefly from the incessant rain, Trallalair suddenly stood up. She had an uneasy feeling of impending doom. Someone dear to her was in trouble. She left her fern shelter and strode over the sopping leaf litter into the Sinjery village. The thatched huts shed water even better than the fern, but many of the Sisters, like her, ignored the downfall and went about their business. All were dressed like her in the traditional embroidered loincloth, naked above but for pendants made by their lovers. With no men around and free of the social conventions of Isseltrent, they were free to dress according to their comfort. Some of the youngest girls didn't even bother with the loincloth. By Mother Earth, it was glorious to be free of the greed and lusts of men. The Sinjery Swords were not needed in Sinjer. They were all piled in one hut along with dozens of Copper Orders and Wooden Requests they had used in Isseltrent. The Swords were kept there only as memoirs of their servitude. They would never wear them again as long as they stayed in Sinjer.

Trallalair only wished that she had taken the time to see if the jeweler's crazy plan to retrieve Rhazburn's body from Hell had succeeded. Rhazburn was a man she could have enjoyed as a friend. At times during the previous few days, she even fantasized what he would have been like as a lover. Gentler but more passionate than the Dragonlord, she was sure.

After sharing his soul, she knew exactly what he would be like under all circumstances. It was almost like he had left a part of him with her. It was much different from the connection she still felt for Saggethrie. Despite their closeness, Saggethrie would still surprise her. Her memories of Rhazburn were more like he was now part of her. Each time she dreamed of him, she chided herself for her weakness and was glad she had the company of the Sisters to help her reform. None of them could replace Saggethrie. After loving her, Trallalair doubted that any of her Sisters would be as warm and loving for her. As for Rhazburn... No. It would be wrong. He could never come to Sinjer, even if he were alive.

Trallalair thought again. She knew him better than that. He would come for her, even if he knew he would die. With that thought, she suddenly prickled with fear. The sense of doom she had felt. Was it possible?

Something was amiss somewhere with someone she loved. That was clear to her. She looked around her. The Sisters seemed calm, doing chores, bringing back game or roots, or preparing for forays for food. Young girls helped their older Sisters, learning the ways of the forest as they helped. Three of the youngest played tag, climbing vines hanging from Mother Cypress. Even their carefree games trained their limbs to live in the forest. Sinjery life was very simple compared to life in Isseltrent. Food, shelter, love, and devotion to Mother Earth was all that mattered here.

No, none of the Sisters, young or old, were the source of her feeling of doom. The dread welled up from her soul like a tainted spring. It came from someone very close to her. Someone she had shared her most intimate thoughts with. Rhazburn had come out of Hell and was calling to her with all of his soul and his love.

Tears burst from her eyes. She had lost Hover, then Saggethrie. It was wrong to love a man, but there she was, loving him. How could she not, his indomitable spirit, his steadfastness, his intelligence. She would not let Rhazburn's plea go unheeded. Her soul ached. But what if she could save Rhazburn, a man in Sinjer? What would it mean for all her Sisters? Would the curse be abandoned for Rhazburn? She sought the only one who could help her with her disquiet, the Sister Protector. Trallalair ran to her.

Three Sisters attended Ruminique, the Sister Protector. The elderly woman, skin like leather, lay on her pallet. Joaquel massaged her feet eliciting sighs of relief from Ruminique. Baneling cleared out bowls of food barely touched. Wisferia poured her tea. Smells of soothing, fresh herbs hanging from the ceiling calmed Trallalair's agitation almost as much as Ruminique's pleasant smile. No matter how infirm the old woman was, her joy in life never ceased, and she made everyone who came to her tranquil and content.

"Trallalair, Child." She called everyone child and had done so for the last ten years, since the last of her generation died. "You are agitated. Sit down beside me. Have some tea." Wisferia produced another tea bowl and filled it. The herb tea had been steeped in the sun and was warm but not hot, a pleasing drink with aromas that relaxed the tightness in her jaw and scalp. With a nod from Ruminique, Joaquel transferred her therapy to Trallalair's shoulders, who accepted the added pleasure thankfully. Ruminique waited politely for Trallalair to initiate the conversation.

"My Sister, I have a confession and a fear."

"You needn't worry, Child. First the fear."

"You are a balm to my spirit. I fear that someone I love is dying, and there is nothing I can do to stop it." They had all heard the story of the battle against the Demon's forces in the Dead Lands. All knew Saggethrie had died horribly there.

"You, of all of us, have seen the most tragedy. You see yet more tragedy? Even here where we are all safe? That bodes poorly. What could harm one of us? Do you think it could be one of the children?"

"You are selfless as always, caring only for the rest of us, but the one in trouble is not one of the Sisters."

Joaquel's light massage suddenly stopped. Wisferia, on her way out the door, stopped and turned. In Sinjer, few things existed that could be inimical to the Sinjery. Their prowess in forest matters was much greater than their prowess in arms had been as Guards for the Dragonlord. If someone other than one of the Sisters was in danger in Sinjer, it usually meant the one in trouble was a man. All men were in trouble in Sinjer.

The Sister Protector shook her head, dismissing Trallalair's apprehension. "You love a man? Is that your confession, Child?"

"You can feel my shame, but I know he needs me. I cannot let him down. He came here for me, disregarding the risk to himself. He is dying. I must find him and speak to him before he passes from this world again."

"You say he has passed from this world before?"

"You already know his name. The man is Rhazburn."

Trallalair had shared her experiences of Rhazburn with Ruminique and any Sinjery maiden who was interested. None of them had even seen men as anything but predators on women, salacious and cruel. Any experience different from what they all expected was unique and fascinating for them.

Ruminique made an effort to sit up and reach for Trallalair, but her frailty defeated her, so Joaquel lifted her up. The Sister Protector hugged Trallalair warmly. She held herself up by clasping her delicate hands behind Trallalair's neck. "You realize, Child, that none of us understand what has happened to you, least of all me. You tell us you died when Saggethrie was killed, then you died again beneath the sea. You killed the Demon and brought a man back from the dead. You even wore the Dragoncrown, the only woman ever to do so. Now you love a man because you have shared his inscrutable mind. My times were much simpler. Everything is changing. I feel our hidden world will be revealed. Alliances must be made with the world of men.

"Because of you, we are able to guard our own people, not Isseltrent's. You already seem to have a Soulbrother among them. When I die, you must carry on in my place and be a link and shield between our world and theirs."

Many times before, the Sister Protector had named Trallalair as her heir. Trallalair knew that Ruminique saw her death to be close at hand, and she was wise enough to prepare for it. Trallalair would never insult the Sister Protector by arguing with her about the old woman's death. Ruminique welcomed it with open arms. No Sinjery steeped in the love of her Sisters and devoted to Mother Earth feared death.

Trallalair felt the old woman go limp, tired from the strain. She let her down on her pallet gently. Joaquel went to sit beside the Sister Protector and hold her hand.

"When you find him, you must accept him as your Soulbrother, Child. Do not go just to watch him die again. He will be a worthy ally for Sinjer, if he is worthy of you. When you take my place, Sinjer will need all the allies we can find."

Trallalair kissed her hand. "No one can replace you, my Sister."

"Nonsense," was all the sister Protector had the strength to say.

Trallalair left her to rest and hurried outside. The rain had stopped. Water dripped pleasingly from the trees and the air smelled fresh. For the moment, the sun had chased away the rain clouds. Birds were singing to each other while they had a chance. In Sinjer, another torrent of rain was never far off. She could feel Rhazburn close, less than a half-day's walk. At a run, she could make the distance in a third of the time. Quintella was standing nearby and seemed curious as to what Trallalair had spoken to Ruminique about.

"Quintella, you are ever faithful and strong. My friend needs help. Will you come with me?"

"Do we need bows?"

Trallalair shook her head. The hunting knives in embroidered sheaths hanging from their loincloths would be all they would need. She did not want to be hampered in the least. They would have to move quickly through the forest.

After smelling the breeze and looking to the sky, listening for a sound of him, Trallalair took off to the east. She didn't hear his moans but felt them within her. She could close her eyes and picture the scene. He was adrift in a skimmer, his paddle lost when he collapsed with weakness.

They bounded down well-trodden paths, passing trees that were old friends, named and blessed by Mother Earth. There was Wellspring, with a clear freshet gurgling from beneath her root. There they passed the Tigress, with thorns thick as hair on her trunk, crawling with biting ants that protected her from any climbers after her tasty fruit. There was the Eye of the Moon, with two curved limbs a frame that caught the full moon only once a year and signaled the Moondance Festival for all the Sinjery villages. Many other trees had stories the Sinjery told about their spirits, how they guarded the forest from intruders. All of them they ran past, Trallalair wondering if even Rhazburn could understand what the trees meant to the Sisters. He would know, she decided. If he had a chance, he would memorize all the stories and tell them to the children endlessly, then he would carve Poems of his own on fallen logs around the villages to add his own protection to that of the trees. Of this she was as certain as if it were her own thought. If only he would have a chance. If only he would live. By the Mother of all the Earth, she wanted him to live.

A league from their village, the trails were less traveled and more overgrown. She slashed at vines with her knife to quickly clear a path and hasten her journey. Normally, she walked silently, her bare toes sliding between the leaves of the littered forest carpet, so nothing living could hear her approach. Normally, she was a part of the forest that bred her, but right then the wild growth was in her way. Trallalair felt increasingly desperate as she felt Rhazburn's breath becoming ragged and coarse.

The last part of the journey was the slowest, swimming through muck too deep for her to stand. Reeking, slimy mud matted her hair, but her nakedness allowed her to slide through almost as quickly as a croc would. Only her loincloth hung up on the thick ropey stuff. If she wasn't certain that the knife on her loincloth would come in handy, she would have slipped it off as well.

When she finally swam into the relatively mud-free stream channel, Quintella was not far behind her, even though she was not spurred onward by the fear of Rhazburn's death as was Trallalair. They saw a frightening sight. A huge croc was nudging Rhazburn's boat out into the open water where it could easily capsize it for a meal of human flesh.

She struggled to the middle of the stream just as the croc began to position itself for the task. It backed up, giving itself enough room to shake its flattened tail back and forth in acceleration. Then, it would launch its massive body into the air and onto the boat to capsize it. Almost close enough to stab the croc, Trallalair drew her knife and screamed at it like one of the black leopards that frequently fed upon smaller crocs.

This one seemed surprised to be disturbed from its meal preparations. But it was large enough to eat anything in the forest, including any Sinjer maiden foolish enough to enter its territory. After it turned away from the boat and fixed its tiny eyes upon her, Trallalair knew it reassessed her as its new quarry. Without the least disappointment that its meal would be a woman, it slashed at her with its fangs a handspan from her eyes. That attack was only meant to bully her into backing off so it could dive beneath her in the murky water to come up underneath where she was defenseless.

It worked. She had to dodge the fangs and missed the croc when she swung her knife at its eyes. She knew she was no match for a croc that big, but it was too late to back off.

Water moved by her feet where the croc searched with its powerful jaws to crush her leg. She waited only a heartbeat. From the commotion beneath her, she felt the croc's huge bulk rising up.

Before its had a chance to clamp onto her leg, she pulled both of them up, slipping them through its closing jaws. She turned and dove straight down with her knife held firmly in both hands before her. The knife plunged straight into the croc's snout. Between the strength of the croc's upward rise and the downward thrust of her dive, the knife was driven through the croc's upper jaw, striking the soft tongue within.

The croc shook its head, ripping the knife from her hand, but the knife stayed imbedded in the upper jaw.

Quintella, swimming close behind Trallalair, stabbed it in the tail for good measure.

A swipe of its tail almost tore that knife away and brushed Quintella aside like she was a floating leaf, then it thrashed its head about trying unsuccessfully to dislodge the knife from its jaw.

Neither Trallalair nor Quintella was seriously injured, but Trallalair had lost her knife and Quintella clutched painful ribs. They were grateful to Mother Earth that the croc was more wary of two bellicose assailants than one unresisting, weakened victim it had intended on eating, especially two with such sharp teeth. It retreated far down the stream.

Trallalair waited to see what the croc would do. When she saw him swim away, she swarmed up into the boat with Quintella steadying the opposite side. Once Trallalair was in the boat, Quintella began towing it to the closest shore they could use to pull it up out of the stream.

Trallalair settled down into the bottom of the boat and lifted Rhazburn's head and shoulders up onto her lap. He was as cool and limp as death. She recognized the signs of fever, but he was cool to the touch. Death was very close.

Most of the muck of the quagmire they had swum through had been washed off of her skin in the open stream, but some mud and rootlets tangled her hair which drooped onto Rhazburn's still face as Trallalair gazed at him for signs of life.

The skin over Rhazburn's body was blistered extensively. Even his face, once handsome and confident, was blistered and slack with the ravages of disease. The curse of the Sinjery was upon him, and he was quickly dying in her arms. Only his lips were spared. She knew that he had sacrificed his life just to see her.

"Rhazburn, I am here," she whispered, hesitant, still unsure if she felt love or just pity. No response. He was too far gone.

She knew she had to make up her mind before he died.

Love. Yes, love it was. Trallalair kissed his cold lips. There was but a tiny spark left in him, but she could feel it within her soul. She stayed connected to him, kissing his still lips, wishing in her mind that the Sinjery Curse on men never existed.

She felt him exhale against her cheek. It was not a final sigh, releasing his soul to the Sky Forests. It was a breath of hope. She intensified the kiss, shedding tears that sprinkled his ravaged skin. Her tears reminded her of the healing elixir brewed from cones of the Mother Cypress that the Sinjery sprinkled on minor cuts and bruises.

In response to the sincerity of her love, Rhazburn's lips warmed and moistened, quivering slightly.

As if Trallalair were possessed by his soul again, her passion mounted as she called him away from death. All she saw in him was a craving to love her. She accepted it as did Saggethrie, who was locked forever in her memory. In Rhazburn, there was hope for her, for all Sinjer. In this Poet was a confirmation, not a repudiation, of their freedom.

As he stirred in her arms, she broke off the kiss and peered into his fluttering eyes.

When his bloodshot eyes fixed on her, Rhazburn shook with a great effort as he raised his head ever so slightly. "Trallalair?" he said, then collapsed again with weakness. Smiling with his eyes closed, he said, "My Love."

During all this, Quintella had been swimming, towing the skimmer to the only serviceable shore nearby, the scoured-out slide that the huge swamp reptile used to crawl up onto shore when it was resting. Digging her toes into the compacted mud of the slide, she pushed the boat up a good length to where she could haul herself up by nearby bushes. She turned and stood guard over the two, holding her knife loosely at her side.

"He will die, you know," she said to Trallalair who still cradled Trallalair in the boat. "All men die here."

Trallalair thought back to her instruction in the history of the Sisters and the Sinjery Curse that doomed the men who entered their land.

She jogged Quintella's memory. "Quintella, what are the exact words of the curse?"

"You know them as well as I. 'Mother Earth, hear our plea, let all men, defilers of women, forever die if they dare enter our land.'"

"As you said, 'Defilers of women'. I know Rhazburn as well as I know myself. He is no defiler of women. I don't think the curse applies to him."

"But you can see the illness of the curse takes him."

"You see he was sick, near death. But he will recover." She looked hard into her Sister's eyes. "With our help."

Quintella stood still for only a moment, then said, "If you choose of your own free will to help this man, I will do all I can for him as well."

"You have heard that I am tied to him by a bond in my soul. If he dies, part of me will die with him. I believe it will be the last part I have to lose." She would die to save Sinjer, but Rhazburn was no threat to their land or to the Sisters. He would never do anything to harm Sinjer or any of them. Perhaps he was the only man so in tune with her Sisters. Maybe he wasn't the only one. Just maybe, if one existed, others could be found. It would be hard to continue hating all men when she loved one man.

Quintella would do as she said. She began moving with a renewed vigor, taking charge and pushing the boat further up the bank, helping Trallalair unload Rhazburn. She left Trallalair to guard and comfort Rhazburn, who still lay helpless. Quintella cut long poles and fashioned a woven litter that they rolled Rhazburn onto to carry him deeper into the jungle, away from the croc's slide. Together, they made a lean-to and a sheltered fire. Quintella climbed a tall Colobo Palm to harvest the head-sized, rock-hard "nuts". They cracked them with her knife and ate the white meat. Using the shells as bowls, they gave the sweet, milky liquid within to Rhazburn. They found a honey tree, battling the myriad biting ants guarding it, and tapped it for the sweet sap. More nourishment for their patient. Herbs were gathered for medicinal teas and moist leaf poultices to heal his blistered skin. These were treatments the Sinjery used every day for bites and skin problems their Sisters had.

With this care, Rhazburn recovered over the days, gaining strength enough to sit up and speak with them. The first words he uttered were,

"Thank you. Both of you. I never wanted this. I only wanted to see you before I died, Trallalair."

Trallalair was secure in her belief that he would survive. "Well, Rhazburn, you're not going to die." Titles 'Brandmistress' and 'Loremaster' were a thing of the past. They were too close for that. "So now what are you going to do?"

"I'd like to stay here... with you, if I may." He said it in a way that told Trallalair he would die, heartbroken, if he could not stay in Sinjer by her side.

"We will talk with the Sister Protector. She is the one who decides what is best for the Sisters. If she decides you cannot stay, I will go wherever you want." She shrugged, smiling. "I don't want to have to do this again." He looked up from his rude bed. She wiggled her head seriously. "But I would."

He chuckled, something he hadn't done in many Moons. "Now that I've found you, I'll be much more careful with my life. Never has living been so precious to me."

"I believe the Sister Protector will allow you to stay." Oddly, she was certain of it.

Rhazburn stood up. He was clothed only in a loincloth they had fashioned out of his worn trousers. He teetered a bit with the weakness. With still trembling hands, he brushed off the poultices that had healed most of his sores. He embraced her, pleased by the feel of her naked breasts against his naked chest. He kissed her for the second time in his renewed life. This time his kiss was as passionate as hers had been. They lingered in the kiss and the embrace, sharing their souls and their bodies at the same time. After a long while, they parted and looked into each other's eyes. The union was marvelous for both of them, to share thoughts of love for each other while they shared a kiss. They wanted much more, but demurred out of politeness to Quintella. Rhazburn and Trallalair knew each other's thoughts. They smiled in each other's eyes in shared anticipation of all their future lovemaking. They knew there would be no end to their love.

CHAPTER 41

THINGS CHANGE

The morning came much more quickly than it had a year before. This morning, the Dragon's Lament did not awaken Jonathon. It was more like a whimper.

Sweet thing was just outside his window, sprawled in the garden. His broad wings flapped, raising little clouds of dust. Alas, dust was all he could raise up. Himself, he could not. No matter how frantically he flapped his growing wings, he still could not take off from the flat of the yard. Jonathon had encouraged him to climb the elm behind the cottage a few days before to see if he could soar, but the resounding crash that resulted from Sweet Thing's plummet into the bushes started Farmer Gibbel's chickens squawking and brought such a fusillade of curses from the nasty old man that Jonathon vowed to let the little Dragon learn to fly in his own way.

The garden was a marvel to behold. Beds of Blue-Eyed Kaitlins sat in front of rows of pansies. Daisies were nestled up against tall Foxglove and Sweet Peas. Behind them all were bushes of Baby's Breath. Intermixed and left to thrive were scattered Dandelions. The array was so vibrant that Jonathon was dazzled every time he gazed upon them. His herb garden, previously the pride of the yard, was pretty but now seemed an afterthought. Arlen and the children spent much of the day tending their flowers all very familiar to them since they had each been one of the flowers themselves.

Arlen was already out in the yard. During the night, a soft rain had soaked the soil of the garden. She stood in her bare feet, gripping the mud and giggling as it squeezed out between her toes. She faced the morning sun with her arms wide in rapt pleasure, drinking in the sunbeams. Arlen and all the children took the same great pleasure in being outside in the sun as in the rain. Sometimes they would stand outside, smiling, for so long that Jonathon thought they would grow roots again. They all preferred sweet rainwater they collected in barrels to any other drink available.

Jonathon wished that he could spend the day in the garden, too, but this was another work day for him. He slid out of bed and got ready for a new day in his new Hell.

After a rather long walk down the hill of his house and into the city, he still had to walk all the way to the center of town. If his muscles hadn't remembered his time as a horse and seemed much more capable these days of long walks, he would have wished for a Travel Dragon to shorten his journey. Since a Black Dragon would probably love a meal of horse flesh, Jonathon was glad that he never had to depend on them again.

Jonathon stopped, facing the double row of dour guards lining the last three rods up to the iron door to the Chamber of Hell's Breach. Each guard held his halberd with two hands, all the better to slice off the head of a wayward jeweler. As he walked down that formidable defile, each guard tensed and slapped his thigh, coming to attention. Jonathon nodded to each in turn as he passed. Once he got to the iron door, the captain of the guard, the same one who had let him into the chamber Moons before when he came to talk with Rhazburn, barked an order to the two guards at the door, who muscled the iron doors open to let him in. He was glad for their presence. Only once had he tried to open the iron doors by himself. They had not budged and he had about given himself a hernia with the effort.

"Sean, Thomas, my feeble body expresses heartfelt appreciation for your politeness and the power of your arms." They nodded and he turned, as he did every day, and said to the captain of the guard, "Please, extend my gratitude and that of my colleagues to all your steadfast soldiers for protecting the Dragonlord's coinage establishment."

The captain, as always, snapped to attention and said, "Honor Forthright, the will of His Highness the Dragonlord shall be done."

Jonathon nodded in reply, turned, and entered the Chamber of Hell's Breach. The blast of heat hit him as soon as he walked through the iron door. He squinted at the fires of Hell before him.

That day the fires were in the furnaces he was in charge of, not the real Hell. It might as well have been Hell, though. He was consigned to spend endless days there, toiling for the Dragonlord. Of course, Bob Thumblefoot was already there, and probably had been since Dawn Blessing. Jonathon knew that he also stayed up until late at night at their rebuilt jewelry shop, turning out his exquisite pieces. Jonathon was hard pressed to keep up with the quality of the boy's gems and settings. Even though they never made magical jewelry anymore, customers fawned over Bob and his creations. His followers insisted they still held supernatural powers..

Bob bowed. "Master, the first pour of the day is ready."

As usual, Bob had the gold set to pour into the mold for the Dragonlord's coins.

"Bob, suffer yourself to call me Jonathon, if you please. Ever since you've been my partner, I've felt particularly uncomfortable with the title Master. I have yearned to eliminate masters from the world." He knew the world would turn many, many times before that would happen, but he could always hope.

"My apologies, M... M... J... Jonathon. Uh, how about if I call you Honor Forthright?"

"Jonathon will do quite nicely, my dear Bob." The boy looked haggard, as no doubt did Jonathon. The responsibility to keep the Dragonlord flush with coins for his resurrected Realm kept both of them busy most of each day. His shop had to take second place in their priorities. It was only because his whole family had contributed money and all their skills that Jonathon was able to afford to rebuild his shop. They only opened it in the evenings, but loyal customers still came to buy the most beautiful jewelry in all Isseltrent.

Inside the Chamber of Hell's Breach, the air was thick and warm. It was not quite as hot as he remembered Hell, thanks to several vents which had been bored through the tough obsidian of the Chamber. No one had bothered to rename the massive structure. Jonathon privately called it the Spewer of Gold.

Gleaming, molten gold poured from a rolling crucible onto a steel plate molded on the back with twenty-five carefully cut faces of the Dragonlord inside small circles. The coins called Gold Dragons were recognized by small renditions of the Dragonlord in profile on one side, fashioned by Jonathon, and a flying Dragon on the other side, fashioned by Bob. Never mind that there was only one Dragon left in the land and that one was immature, unable to fly, and in Jonathon's charge.

The steel plate was secured to a press which was the base on which the top plate of cut steel was laid. After the pour, the entire assemblage was compressed with a steel screw that vented excess gold into a trough to be reused. The Spewer of Gold could, with twenty laborers and Jonathon and Bob to oversee, turn out four presses of Gold Dragons a day. Less precious coins of silver were also minted there. The silver coins had the face of Cithoney, Seldric's queen, on one side and the Dragoncrown on the other. They were named Silver Crowns. They were making about five times as many Crowns as Dragons, all of the precious metals coming from the North Wall mines in the Cajalathrium States, Jonathon's birthplace.

The court accountants, all former gossip Dwarves, felt that the best rate of exchange was thirty-three Crowns for one Dragon. Jonathon felt that the smaller coins were needed for proper trade to work in Isseltrent. Without the magic of Transmuting Boxes, the Crowns could not be subdivided, and they would be too precious for many minor transactions. They needed smaller coins, but wooden coins like the old Wooden Requests or clay coins like the Clay Suggestions would be far too tedious to make and would not last like metal could. Of the precious metals, platinum was too rare to even consider. Gold was a fine and rare metal, and it should be used for the most precious coins. No one would make counterfeit gold coins, since the fake ones would be as expensive to make as the real ones. The same held for the Silver Crowns. For the minor coins, worth less than a loaf of bread, they needed a metal that was distinctive and easy to melt.

Copper had come to Jonathon's mind. Copper was easily mined and much more plentiful than gold or silver. Even though Copper Orders had been the second most precious of the magical coins, they would have to be the least valuable in the new era. They would be Copper Knights, with a Knight brandishing a halberd on one side and the Dragonlord's palace of Blaze on the other. The idea was that the Knight guarded Blaze. Once the Spewer of Gold was finished with a Moon of making Gold Dragons and Silver Crowns, they would convert the molds to make Copper Knights. He estimated that three Moons minting Copper Knights would make enough for the Dragonlord to begin distribution of the coins.

When the first batch of the day cooled sufficiently to be handled, Jonathon and Bob personally inspected every one of the gold coins. The imperfect ones were tossed in a bin to be recycled. Jonathon did not feel that the gold as impressive as the glass of a Glass Command, but they were only expected to be recognized as something of value, not used to power spells. They produced fewer Gold Dragons per day than the number of Glass Commands produced by the Dragon Kilns. But the Glass Commands had been constantly used up, whereas the Gold Dragons would stay around, circulating in their use for trade forever. Jonathon hoped that the supply of Gold Dragons would eventually be sufficient, so he would be able to cut back on his time at the Spewer of Gold and spend more time in his own shop doing what he loved the most, making beautiful jewelry. It all hung on the Dragonlord's greed and the supply of gold from the Cajalathrium States.

That was another aspect of the coinage process for which he was responsible, obtaining the materials for the coins of Thuringland. He was the one person in Isseltrent with the best contacts in the mining community of the Cajalathrium States, where his mother still lived.

One fine evening a few Moons later, Jonathon sent Bob home early from their shop. The boy worked much too hard. Jonathon wanted him to have some time outside to be with his family, or even meet some girls his age. He was already taller than Jonathon and his voice was changing. Soon he would be a man with responsibilities for his own family.

As Jonathon bent over his work, filing away a bit of gold on an amethyst pendant, he felt just a hint of a pleasant breeze wafting through the window beside his workbench. The Daisies and Pansies with which Arlen filled his workspace fluttered slightly in a sigh of wind. He looked up. There, hovering and curtseying in the air above his workbench, was Hili. With her was a Pixie no bigger than Hili's own leg.

Jonathon straightened his tired back muscles and smiled with surprise. "Hili! How marvelous to see you again. This beautiful little one is your bud, I presume?" Jonathon remembered that the Pixets called their children buds.

"Greetings, Master Jeweler. Yes. This is Dreem. My bud."

Jonathon looked askance at Hili. She had said 'my bud'. Something had changed in the Pixelle. Acknowledging a Pixie of her own was very brazen for a Pixelle. All the Pixies were shared equally by the Community. No distinction was made between Pixies born of one of the Pixelles or another. All of Hili's trials away from the solace of the Community seemed to have colored her perspective. Maybe she was a rebel, trying to change her Community so they could deal with the future better than they had dealt with the past. He set out two velvet ring cushions on his bench for them to rest upon.

"We are tired and hungry. A long flight. Our last stop for refreshment was at Highday." Hili fluffed one of the cushions for the Pixie who, after curtseying in the air to Jonathon, deposited herself a little clumsily on the pillow. She looked no more than six Moons old. Pixets needed to eat many times a day to fuel their rapid metabolism, so a single Blessing without food would be like a whole day to a human.

Jonathon accepted the change in Hili like he had accepted all the other recent changes in his world. He turned his head toward the back of his shop and gently, so as not to hurt the Pixets' ears, called out, "Sweetheart, Hili is here!"

Arlen spent much more time in his shop in the evening these days. She wanted to spend what little time she could with her husband. She also wanted to keep an eye on him. Since his fiasco with Molgannard Fey, she had told him that she little confidence in his judgment in dealing with trouble. Theodore and Judith were responsible enough to take care of the younger children while she chaperoned Jonathon.

While she bustled about in the back room for a few moments before her entrance, Jonathon noticed a bee buzzing around the pansies. He knew how dangerous bee stings could be for Pixets and warned Hili, "Careful of that busy bee."

Hili looked up and said. "We never fear bees or any other thing with more than four limbs." She tipped her head to Dreem. The tiny Pixie simply looked at the bee and it buzzed right at her. Jonathon feared for her life, but she seemed perfectly content to let the bee alight on the cushion beside her.

Jonathon saw a fast spider scrambling across the table toward Dreem and, by reflex, raised his hand to whack it.

"Wait, Master Jeweler," Hili said.

His tensed hand quivered with the restraint, but he let the spider live.

The spider scrambled to the pansies and up to a stem where it quickly spun a web.

Jonathon watched in awe as the spider wove a complex pattern. To his utter amazement, the spider wove the image of a tiny Unicorn in its web.

Dreem flew up to the pansy pot and detached the web picture while the spider stood dutifully by. She gave her mother the picture which looked like a tiny embroidered lace doily. Hili smiled and accepted it, then attached the sticky picture to her dress like an apron.

Arlen came through the doorway into the showroom carrying a pot of shooting stars. "Pleased to see you, Hili." Then she saw the Pixie. "And your precious little bud. Here you go, the sweetest nectar in the shop."

Hili and Dreem smiled and curtseyed, then flew to nourish themselves with the nectar. Hili explained to Jonathon between dips and sips, "Dreem is unique. In the distant past, Pixelles and Pixets lived who could communicate with our insect and spider friends as easily as we do with the Unicorns. The Community has recognized that skill in Dreem and encourages it. We are not certain that the time is proper for the Community to practice the art of Bug Friendship, but we will need every strength we have to protect Verdilon from the onslaught we face from all quarters. Sharing thoughts with other beings takes a toll on the Community. If we constantly shared bugs' thoughts, every time an insect died we'd feel pain. A lot of insects die constantly. Dreem is like the root of a flower that takes only what it needs from the soil. She can screen us from all their pain but allow us to be their intimate friends."

The Pixie looked up at Hili and smiled broadly.

"We have always cherished our friends the spiders and ants, but Dreem has broadened our friendship to all the little ones. Already, the Windriders approach our land, hoping to graze their herds once the meadows we care for are green again. Dragons still fly over Verdilon, but until the deer and elk return, they have little to attract them. The Unicorns they can never touch. There will be much to guard against in the coming years."

Arlen said, "I wonder if Dreem could ask the bees on our hill to spend more time in our garden. I'd love a lot of seeds this year to plant in the spring. Sample our nectar while you are there."

"Thank you for the offer. We would be happy to return to your home, now that all is safe and calm. We'll have a chat with the bees. We'll talk with the flowers as well."

"We have the sweetest nectar in any garden in Isseltrent," Arlen said.

"Arlen should know. She's the world expert on flowers," Jonathon said.

"We thank you for your hospitality. Now, we have a proposal for you, Master Jeweler."

"Hili, the Community is welcome to anything I have."

"We request your services as Master Jeweler to fashion Gems of Power for us, and perhaps another object we have been speaking to someone about."

Jonathon was confused. How could Gems of Power benefit the Pixets or anyone? The sources of their power, coins derived from Glass Commands, were dwindling quickly. Jonathon had saved five Glass Commands as a memoir in a small frame above his fireplace. He felt no need to ever use them. *Speaking to someone? To whom and about what?*, he wondered.

"I don't understand, Hili. How can Gems of Power be of use to you? Coins are getting scarce." He would be more than happy to give them his five Commands.

As an answer to his question, four Pixets holding the leather thongs of a small pouch flew through the window and dropped the pouch in Jonathon's lap. He poured the contents onto a white plate made to view gems. The pouch contained twenty-five uncut stones, mostly garnets, tourmaline, and topaz, along with a few emeralds, sapphires, and rubies.

Also in the pouch were four Clay Suggestions, two Wooden Requests, two Copper Orders, and one Glass Command.

"Where did you find these?"

"Verdilon, Repose, and Sinjer are allies now. The Ghouls either killed themselves to join their so-called Eternal Order or mended their ways. Those spirits they named the Eternal Ones are all gone from the Natural Presence, along with all the other wandering souls in Verdilon. No evil remains in Verdilon or Sylvanward. Those people who were formerly Ghouls now call themselves Seekers, probably because they now seek treasure within the mountain caverns. We and the Sylvets supply the Seekers with food from the lands. They supply us with gemstones mined from their tunnels, coins, and already-cut gems harvested from all their Clan treasure troves. There is quite a lot under Sylvanward. The Loremaster has supplied us with the verses for our Gems of Power and all the wards that now protect Verdilon. We are further protected by the warmaidens from Sinjer. All the kingdoms to the east of Verdilon and to the south of Sinjer respect our alliance and bid for our gems, as well as for the services of the warmaidens. We are even speaking with the Rockskippers in the Cajalathrium States and, through the Mermets, with the Lord of the Sea. We have hope they, too, will join our alliance. As stewards of Verdilon, we now realize that it is not enough just to nurture the meadows. We must insure that they are protected from invaders as well."

She waited politely while Jonathon's flabbergasted expression turned into one full of visions of future business. The Ghouls, now Seekers, and their treasure hoards from clans previously led by the Zombie Lord all the way up the Range of the Forbidden Mountains. If they were as huge as the one Rhazburn had told him about in the treasure of the Laughing Skull, then there was also silver and gold objects that he could trade for to be used at the Spewer of Gold. And, of course, Rhazburn was involved with Hili's enigmatic *other object.* It was probably some powerful tool that his son had dreamed up. But what could that be? For the moment, he put those thoughts aside. He answered Hili, "You want me to fashion the gems?".

"You will have the exclusive contract. Members of the Community will rotate through your shop, one Moon at a time, to engrave the gems. Your profit will be some of the Gems of Power that you can use for your jewelry and the coins to go with them. We could also supply you with jewelry and metal from weapons traded from the Seekers' treasure troves."

She was thinking Jonathon's very thoughts. Maybe she could now share his thoughts as she shared the Community's. No, he could not exclude logic in this. Business logic was burgeoning in the land, now that people other than the Dragonlord were making plans.

Jonathon nodded, considering the boon to his business, but he was bothered by the implications for others in Isseltrent. If his was the only shop in Isseltrent producing magical jewelry, he could name his price. But no, that would be unfair to the Jewelers' Guild and the people of Isseltrent. He refused to form a monopoly. Instead, he would share the bounty with all of Isseltrent. Now that others had followed his and Arlen's example in adopting the lost and orphaned children in the city, his needs were modest.

Conversely, the Pixets and the Sinjery had a perfect right to make some profit in their dealings with Isseltrent, considering all they had given the city. But it was unusual for the Pixets to be so businesslike. Normally he saw them as dreamers, always with the mind of the Community on the restoration of Verdilon. Now that Verdilon was restored, it seemed that their priorities had changed. They had become much more practical. To have all their minds working together on planning for the safety and financial health of Verdilon was formidable. He had no doubt that they were capable of forming an empire of financial deals and alliances.

As Chief Metallurgist and Jeweler of the Court of the Dragonlord, Jonathon had to say, "You know, Seldric will want to hire the Community to engrave Glass Commands again."

"We do not feel that would be in our best interest right at the moment."

"Good for you. I don't blame you after what you were put through. Sweet Thing will be glad to hear that he won't be chained to the Dragonkilns." Jonathon still had little feeling of loyalty to the Dragonlord. He would do his job for the Realm, but he planned to keep his business up as well. No one had to convince him of the instability and uncertainty of governments or their leaders.

"All right, Hili, tell the Community, the Sylvets, the Sinjery, and the Seekers. I will be your liaison with the Guilds of Isseltrent. Maybe even with the Dragonlord, if you want."

Hili and Dreem flew a dance of patterns in the air that expressed their joy and the joy of the Community with such vigor that Arlen and Jonathon laughed with cheer as well.

When Hili and Dreem came to rest and curtseyed in the air, Arlen spoke up. She was anxious to hear about her son. "Tell Rhazburn for me that it is high time for a visit to his family. And I don't want any 'It's too far' excuses from him."

Hili said, "He is on his way, with a delegation from Sinjer at this very moment."

Arlen's pretty face lit up with renewed happiness. "Thank you, Hili. That's like a warm clean rain on a spring day. Here, eat. Freshen yourselves up." She produced another pot, this one overflowing with sprays of Fragrant Jasmine.

When they had had their fill, Hili and Dreem left the four Pixets in Jonathon's shop to begin the commission. As Hili and Dreem rose to fly away, Hili said, "We will be back in a few Moons. I will be your contact with the Community from now on." She smiled broadly and curtseyed again in the air. "We have one more word for you. Whither has told us that we are to let you and Trallalair know that if either of you ever need anything from the race of Unicorns, you need but ask us. Whither and all the Unicorns will know of it. They will do anything within their power for you and all your descendants, forever. They owe their very existence to you and Trallalair."

With that, she and Dreem flew out the window and off into the sky, leaving Jonathon pleasantly stunned.

Days later, Jonathon wakened early one morning from one such pleasant dream in which he was talking to the herbs and flowers in their garden like they were old friends or, more likely, family. Talking with the herbs in his dream had none of the attendant anxiety of trying to talk with his family when they were seeds. Instead, it was as if his herbs were cherished friends and children whom he nursed through childhood, adulthood and into old age, seeing to their every need. He understood not a word they said, but he still felt confident they were content with his nurturing.

The dream was interrupted by a thumping and commotion out back of the house. Arlen slept at his side with a little smile on her face, probably talking with the same herbs and flowers. Unlike Jonathon, she could probably understand what the flowers said. She did not wake up at the sounds, nor did the children. All of them seemed as calm as the flowers they planted these days. Jonathon was aroused and concerned, much as when the tree outside his window was uprooted by Molgannard Fey, oh so many Moons before.

Anxious but strangely unafraid, Jonathon stole quietly from bed and tiptoed through the house toward the back door. On his way, he looked out one of the small back windows and saw the old downed oak, which had been rudely tossed in the back by Molgannard Fey, lift up again into the air. Without any Giant to toss it, the huge dead oak flew on its own a whole rod distance and slowly settled down to the ground in a bare patch that Jonathon had tilled, snapping off big branches beneath it with the sound of a dozen thunderclaps.

Sweet Thing was lying on the opposite corner of the yard in his special place, snuggling in a thistle patch (he loved the smell and ignored the thorns). The growing Dragon, red as a rose, big as a wagon, tough as boulder but sweet as a puppy, opened an eye, but didn't seem to care much about flying trees and went back to sleep.

By the time Jonathon opened his back door to peer out through his rose bushes into the morning mists, the tree began breaking apart on its own into small logs. First the branches split on their own into small chunks that would just fit into his hearth, then the massive trunk simply burst into sections which further subdivided themselves. All of this was amidst a din of chopping and a hail of flying chips, as if the oak were being assailed by a gang of ghostly arborists. Of course he knew better, having had plenty of experience as a Ghost. Ghosts could touch the tree in a way, feel it from without and from within, but they could never move it or chop it with spectral axes. Besides, after he had taken Sverdphthik back to Hell, Jonathon had hoped that most of the wandering spirits in the world had gone to their peace in Heaven. There was only one living person who could accomplish the feat he saw.

"Rhazburn! I know you're here."

At his words, the tree stopped its subdividing and a dozen beautiful female laughs tinkled in the leaves around him. Two dozen Sinjery maidens appeared from nothing in his yard, standing around the old oak. They all held Sinjery Swords which they hefted like axes in the act of chopping up Jonathon's downed oak. They were dressed in embroidered loincloths and wore nothing from their waists up except their bows and complex tattoos of writing. The tattoos were mostly on their arms and legs, but some had them on their backs or breasts. One of the women was Trallalair, similarly garbed and smiling with a chuckle Jonathon had never before seen on her pretty lips. He had never thought her capable of mirth before.

"You would never be fooled, Rhazburn told us," she said. "You woke before we could do you this service. Perhaps it was the commotion. Our apologies, Master Jeweler."

"Trallalair, where did you come from?"

"As you see... thin air. Thanks to these tattoos Rhazburn wrote on our skin, each Sister can be strong as a hundred, have skin like steel, fly in the sky, and become invisible at will."

Jonathon noticed a pouch at her waist bulging with coins, no doubt from the former Zombie treasures under the Forbidden Mountains. They had since been renamed the Guardian Range, since the mountains now guarded Thuringland from dangers beyond Verdilon and especially protected Verdilon from humans. The legends of people wandering into the mountains and never coming out again still held back most of those from points west who would exploit Verdilon. Jonathon had said nothing to anyone except his family about the reality of the Land of Repose. He was content to let the legend protect the peace of Sylvanward and Verdilon. Jonathon never knew that Verses of Power could be written in tattoos on human skin, but leave it to Rhazburn to figure out a way.

Trallalair continued, "No one will subjugate Sinjer ever again. Our warmaidens can name their price as guards for monarchs near and far from Sinjer. Those in the lands plagued by Dragons are particularly anxious to have our help, since we are more familiar with the ways of Dragons than anyone else.

"We came back here to bring protectors for the Sinjery Bough which has been under the tutelage of Cithoney since we left. The Sinjery boys will from now on have protection equal to that of kings and queens. While we are here, we may let Seldric bid for our services. If he wants the protection of the Sinjery now, he will have to bid for it like all the other monarchs we are now protecting."

Jonathon had never seen the Sinjery in their traditional dress before. Even though all the beautiful, young, nearly naked women would fire lust in any man not made of stone, no one would dare try to take advantage of them or even make a rude comment, now that they were independent of the Dragonlord's restraint and much more powerful than they had ever been before. Insult or leer at a woman who could become invisible, fly, and could, with her hands, crush you or some important part of you? He doubted any man would dare.

"Father?" Rhazburn, true to his mischievous character, suddenly appeared at Jonathon's side, making him startle. Jonathon laughed at himself and said, "Rhazburn, Rhazburn, what a joy!"

With tears in his eyes, he gave his son a tremendous hug, noting that Rhazburn's strong muscles were even more powerful than when he was the Loremaster. Then he stood back and looked at Rhazburn with an eye to his raiment. His son had always been clean shaven. He now had a brilliant red beard. He was dressed in only a loincloth, like the Sinjery maidens, but his was plain and briefer, not as extravagant as those worn by the women. He was tattooed as well. Jonathon read the verses of flying and invisibility on his legs and chest.

"I have no need for the verses of strength and invulnerability that I tattooed on the Sisters. My services are only needed in Sinjer." Then he winked, "And I have plenty of protection there."

With questions brimming over in his mind, Jonathon asked, "How did you survive the Curse? And how in the world did the Sinjery accept you among them? I would have thought that they had their fill of men when they left Isseltrent."

Rhazburn smiled an impish smile. "I don't think I did survive. At least, the old Rhazburn, I'd say, is pretty dead. Independence and self reliance, I decided, aren't worth much in Sinjer. Interdependence, cooperation and love are what sustain the Sinjery. As to their acceptance of me, I am very close to their Sister Protector." He bowed to Trallalair, beaming with admiration and love.

Trallalair again chuckled pleasantly. Very pleasantly, Jonathon thought. In her scant garb, artfully tattooed, Trallalair was alluring in a healthy way. The attraction between Rhazburn and Trallalair was something that Jonathon could almost touch and smell. "Our Sister Protector died the day I found Rhazburn floating in a boat on the Green Choke," Trallalair said.

"The day you and Quintella risked your lives to save mine," he corrected.

"You proved that only love could break the Curse of Sinjer. We are all in Rhazburn's debt for that alone."

"And I in yours." By the looks between Rhazburn and Trallalair, Jonathon could see that they wanted to embrace, but forewent the pleasure out of courtesy to the Sisters and Jonathon.

"So you are the new Sister Protector, Trallalair?"

"You are correct, Master Jeweler, now Honor Forthright, I believe. I notice that you no longer call me Brandmistress. Thanks to you, there are no more Brandmistresses or Ringmistresses or Seldric's mistresses."

Soberly, stuttering, suppressing a sob at the memory, Jonathon said, "I only wish that so many lives hadn't been lost in the process."

"Your words are true." A brief cloud passed over her face. "But those that died have now passed from Mother Earth and are in a better place. All the world will remember you for that. For three hundred years, none of our Sisters who died flew to the Sky Forests. Only after you and Rhazburn closed Hell's Breach was the balance intended by Mother Earth restored. Even my sweet Saggethrie is at rest at last." She looked again to Rhazburn, who had a look of empathy on his face. Jonathon had never before seen that in him.

Trallalair finished. "One day we will be with my sweet Saggethrie, together."

Jonathon had no doubt that she spoke the truth. He knew Saggethrie from sharing her spirit for a brief moment, and knew that she would accept Rhazburn or anyone that Trallalair truly loved. He smiled with admiration for the Sister Protector and a certain pride in the final consequences of their accomplishments over the last year. "Thank you, Sister Protector. And thank you for my life and my family. I believe we all had a part in this. Hili and the Community of Pixets as well."

"We still thank the Community for all they have given and continue to give the world, and we have become steadfast allies of Verdilon."

Then from Rhazburn, "Let's go wake up Mother and the family."

Rhazburn stayed outside with the Sinjery maidens, while Jonathon went back to their bedroom. "Sweetheart," Jonathon said, bending and kissing his wife's soft cheek. "Come out back with me. I have something to show you."

Arlen opened her eyes, initially puzzled, then stretched and smiled, saying, "All Right, Dear." She donned her robe and followed him to the back door. Jonathon swung open the door to reveal the two dozen Sinjery maidens with their bows and swords, dressed in only their loincloths and their tattoos, all of them looking toward the door.

Arlen rolled her eyes and said, "Not again, Jonathon. Now what have you done?"

CHAPTER 42

THE WRATH OF
MOLGANNARD FEY

Jonathon's herb garden, like Arlen's flower garden, flourished once more. On a day early in the summer, a rare day off from his work, his wife and all the children had gone to the market. He was alone in his beloved garden, nurturing the cornucopia around him. As he inhaled the fragrance of a few leaves of mint he had just crushed, he felt a tremor in the ground beneath his feet. An angry growl accompanying and reinforcing the tremor approached from the path. Looking up, Jonathon spied the last person he ever expected to see.

Molgannard Fey, growling with rage, a black patch covering his right eye and a livid scar pinching his face into a permanent scowl, limped toward him.

Jonathon couldn't believe that the Giant still lived. His fall to the bottom of his tower and through the floor would have killed a Dragon. Either the Giant was made of iron, or his anger and vengeance had been so intense that the fire of it had shielded him from serious injury and knit his limbs back together. He must have been hiding out all those Moons, just waiting for revenge.

As he lurched up the path, he howled, "Now, you little rat, I've waited until you became a complacent toad squatting under a leaf waiting for bugs. Destroy my power, will you? Well wimp, now you are gonna die!"

This time, the Giant's lumbering hulk bearing down upon Jonathon spurred no fear in him, just pity for the miserable fool.

It was only when Molgannard Fey's smelly foot squashed Jonathon's apple sage that Jonathon became truly enraged. The Giant had ruined his garden once before, but now Jonathon saw all the plants in a new light, like family. Only a few Moons before, one of those cherished herbs could have been his daughter.

He stood his ground, shouting, "Do not take one more step, Molgannard Fey. I've died and come back. I've ruled Dragons and Demons, and I'm not about to be frightened by the likes of you. I've killed you once before, and I'm mad enough to do it again."

The Giant hesitated, as if uncertain what to make of the angry pip-squeak in front of him. Then he shrugged it off and stomped right through Jonathon's prized perennials.

Getting more angry with each leaf that Molgannard Fey stomped, Jonathon waited until the Giant was within a few Giant strides from him, then he said, "That's about enough!"

Turning away abruptly, making the Giant laugh as if he thought his quarry was about to run, Jonathon picked up his whole bag of Raindust lying undisturbed for many Moons, dormant but with much latent power. Mad enough to jump up and throttle the Giant with his bare hands, he ripped open the knot at the top of the bag, held it open, and threw all of the Raindust up and into the Giant's ludicrous face.

Molgannard Fey howled, stumbling backward, clutching his good eye, blinded and stung by the the Raindust. Above the Giant's head, unbeknownst to him, the Raindust coalesced and transformed into a black cloud rumbling ominously and shimmering with tiny flashes. Jonathon ran into his house and grabbed his Replenishing Pitcher, then from the frame above his fireplace he took one glass Command and ran back to the front of his cottage.

The Giant was cursing, still blinded, flailing his arms around in his attempt to find the jeweler.

Jonathon could see the lightning building up in the miniature thundercloud above the Giant's head.

Once Theodore had experimented by putting a Wooden Request in their Replenishing Pitcher and water had welled up like a fountain pouring over their carpet and out the door. Jonathon had imagined what a Glass Command in the pitcher would do. Molgannard Fey was in perfect position. He had turned about in his blind rage until he faced away from Jonathon's cottage and toward Farmer Gibbel's. To Jonathon's delight, he bent over, pawing the ground, feeling for Jonathon, presenting his huge bottom as a target that Jonathon could not miss. Jonathon held the pitcher tightly against his hip and aimed the opening at Molgannard Fey's posterior. Into the opening of the pitcher, he tossed the Glass Command.

The blast of water from the Pitcher was much stronger than Jonathon had expected. The recoil from the blast threw Jonathon back against the door jamb so hard that the wind was knocked out of him. All he could do was watch in amazement and amusement at the burlesque before him.

The solid stream of water hit Molgannard Fey directly on his bottom with such force that it straightened him upright, yowling with pain. Still blinded, Molgannard Fey was unaware that standing upright brought the top of his head very close to the little thundercloud, churning and crackling above him. Since he was the tallest object around, and lightning always favors the tallest, a small bolt of lightning slammed into the top of his head hard enough to make his feet bounce off the ground and his hair disappear in a shower of sparks and smoke. Molgannard Fey, still squinting away Raindust, ducked to avoid more blows on his head, which he seemed to believe the intrepid jeweler was raining upon him. Of course, ducking down only presented an alternate target for the angry cloud and another lightning bolt kicked him in the behind. More bolts snapped the hapless Giant, leaving smoldering patches on his shirt and breeches. By the time he was smoking from twenty such blistering holes, he hopped and ran in place, holding his bottom and crying, "Lord Singabya on a Mountain! Enough, Jeweler! I'll leave!"

As he started off at a sprint, Sweet Thing, having grown to almost four strides in length, flew from the back, having been woken by the commotion. The Dragon looked questioningly at Jonathon, who nodded cogently toward the Giant. Sweet Thing took his cue and flew right behind the Giant to where he had a direct shot at the Giant's beleaguered bottom. He inhaled and spat fire, raising more clouds of steam from the Giants pants. Molgannard Fey howled even louder and raced into Farmer Gibbel's yard where he collided with the miser's best chicken coop, scattering shattered boards and squawking fowl.

Jonathon saw a rake ready to strike held high above the chaos. The last Jonathon ever heard of Molgannard Fey was Farmer Gibbel shouting, "You big lug, get away from MY CHICKENS!"

Some things never change.

Edwards Brothers Malloy
Thorofare, NJ USA
May 20, 2016